ISBN 978-1-5283-7229-9
PIBN 10092425

Devereux

BY.

THE RIGHT HON. LORD LYTTON

[4.]

LONDON
GEORGE ROUTLEDGE AND SONS
BROADWAY, LUDGATE HILL
GLASGOW AND NEW YORK

—

1888

THE POCKET VOLUME EDITION

OF

LORD LYTTON'S NOVELS

ISSUED IN MONTHLY VOLUMES

Styles of Binding.

A Paper Cover, Cut Edges.
B   ,,   ,,   Uncut Edges.
C Cloth Cover, Cut Edges.
D   ,,   ,,   Uncut Edges.
E Half-bound   Gilt Tops.   Cut Edges.
F   ,,   ,,   ,,   Uncut Edges.

————◇————

London.

My dear Auldjo,

Permit me, as a memento of the pleasant hours we passed together, and the intimacy we formed, by the winding shores and the rosy seas of the old Parthenope, to dedicate to you this romance. —It was written in, perhaps, the happiest period of my literary life —when success began to brighten upon my labours, and it seemed to me a fine thing to make a name. Reputation, like all possessions, fairer in the hope than the reality, shone before me, in the gloss of novelty—and I had neither felt the envy it excites, the weariness it occasions, nor (worse than all) that coarse and painful notoriety, that something between the gossip and the slander, which attends every man whose writings become known—surrendering the grateful privacies of life to

The gaudy, babbling, and remorseless day.

In short—yet almost a boy—(for, in years at least, I was little more, when "Pelham" and "The Disowned" were conceived and composed,) and full of the sanguine arrogance of hope, I pictured to myself far greater triumphs than it will ever be mine to achieve : and never did architect of dreams build his pyramid upon (alas !) a narrower base, or a more crumbling soil ! . . . . . Time cures us effectually of these self-conceits, and brings us, somewhat harshly, from the gay extravagance of confounding the much that we design with the little that we can accomplish.

"The Disowned" and "Devereux" were both completed in retirement—and in the midst of metaphysical studies and investigations, varied and miscellaneous enough, if not very deeply conned.—At that time I was indeed engaged in preparing for the press a Philosophical Work, which I had afterwards the good sense to postpone to a riper age and a more sobered mind. But the effect of these studies is somewhat prejudicially visible in both the romances I have referred to ; and the external and dramatic colourings which belong to fiction are too often forsaken for the inward and subtle analysis of motives, characters, and actions.—The workman was not sufficiently master of his art to forbear the vanity of parading the wheels of the mechanism, and was too fond of calling attention to the minute and tedious operations by which the movements were to be performed, and the result obtained. I believe that an author is generally pleased with his work, less in proportion as it is good, than in proportion as it fulfils the idea with which he commenced it. He is rarely, perhaps, an accurate judge how far the execution is in itself faulty or meritorious—but he judges with tolerable success how far it accomplishes the end and objects of the conception.—He is pleased with his work, in short, according as he can say, "This has expressed what I meant it to convey."—But the reader, who is not in the secret of the author's original design, usually views the work through a different medium—and is perhaps, in this, the wiser critic of the two ; for the Book that wanders the most from the idea which originated it, may often be better than that which is rigidly limited to the unfolding and *dénouement* of a single conception. If we accept this solution, we may be enabled to understand why an author not unfrequently makes favourites of some of his productions most condemned by the public. For my own part, I remember that "Devereux" pleased me better than "Pelham" or "The Disowned," because the execution more exactly corresponded with the design. It expressed with tolerable fidelity what I meant it to express. That was a happy age, my dear Auldjo, when, on finishing a work, we could feel contented with our labour, and fancy we had done our best ! Now, alas ! I have learned enough of the wonders of the Art to recognize all the deficiencies of the Disciple ; and to know that no author, worth the reading—can ever in one single work do half of which he is capable.

What man ever wrote anything really good, who did not feel that he had the ability to write something better ?—Writing, after all, is a cold and a coarse interpreter of thought.—How much of the imagination—how much of the intellect, evaporates and is lost while we seek to embody it in words !—Man made language, and God the genius. Nothing short of an eternity could enable men who imagine, think, and feel, to express *all* they have imagined, thought, and felt. Immortality, the spiritual desire, is the intellectual *necessity*.

In "Devereux," I wished to portray a man flourishing in the last century, with the train of mind and sentiment peculiar to the present ;—describing a life, and not its dramatic epitome, the historical characters introduced are not closely woven with the main plot, like those in the fictions of Sir Walter Scott—but are rather, like the narrative romances of an earlier school, designed to relieve the predominant interest, and give a greater air of truth and actuality to the supposed memoir. It is a fiction which deals less with the Picturesque than the Real.—Of the principal character thus introduced (the celebrated and graceful, but charlatanic, Bolingbroke) I still think that my sketch, upon the whole, is substantially just. We must not judge of the politicians of one age by the lights of another. Happily we now demand in a statesman a desire for other aims than his own advancement ; but, at that period, ambition was almost universally selfish—the Statesman was yet a Courtier—a man whose very destiny it was to intrigue, to plot, to glitter, to deceive. It is in proportion as politics have ceased to be a secret science—in proportion as courts are less to be flattered, and tools to be managed, that politicians have become useful and honest men : and the statesman now directs a people, where once he outwitted an antichamber. Compare Bolingbroke—not with the men and by the rules of this day—but with the men and by the rules of the last. He will lose nothing in comparison with a Walpole, with a Marlborough, on the one side—with an Oxford or a Swift, upon the other.

And now, my dear Auldjo—you have had enough of my egotisms.

As our works grow up—like old parents, we grow garrulous, and love to recur to the happier days of their childhood ;—we talk over the pleasant pain they cost us in their rearing—and memory renews the season of dreams and hopes ; we speak of their faults as of things past—of their merits as of things enduring :—we are proud to see them still living, and, after many a harsh ordeal and rude assault, keeping a certain station in the world ;—we hoped perhaps something better for them in their cradle—but, as it is, we have good cause to be contented. You, a fellow-author, and one whose spirited and charming sketches embody so much of personal adventure, and therefore so much connect themselves with associations of real life as well as of the studious closet ; *you* know, and must feel, with me, that these our books are a part of us, bone of our bone, and flesh of our flesh ! They treasure up the thoughts which stirred us—the affections which warmed us, years ago—they are the mirrors of how much of what we were ! To the world, they are but as a certain number of pages—good or bad—tedious or diverting ; but to ourselves, the authors, they are as marks in the wild maze of life by which we can retrace our steps—and be with our youth again. What would I not give to feel as I felt—to hope as I hoped—to believe as I believed—when this work was first launched upon the world ! But time gives, while it takes away—and, amongst its recompenses for many losses, are the memories I referred to in commencing this letter, and gratefully revert to at its close.—From the land of cloud and the life of toil, I turn to that golden clime and the happy indolence that so well accords with it—and hope once more, ere I die, with a companion whose knowledge can recall the past, and whose gaiety can enliven the present, to visit the Disburied City of Pompeii—and see the moonlight sparkle over the waves of Naples. Adieu, my dear Auldjo,

And believe me,

Your obliged and attached friend,

E. B. LYTTON.

AUTOBIOGRAPHER'S INTRODUCTION.

My life has been one of frequent adventure and constant excitement. It has been passed, to this present day, in a stirring age, and not without acquaintance of the most eminent and active spirits of the time. Men of all grades, and of every character, have been familiar to me. War—love—ambition—the scroll of sages—the festivals of wit—the intrigues of states—all that agitate mankind, the hope and the fear, the labour and the pleasure—the great drama of vanities, with the little interludes of wisdom ; these have been the occupations of my manhood ;—these will furnish forth the materials of that history which is now open to your survey. Whatever be the faults of the historian, he has no motive to palliate what he has committed, nor to conceal what he has felt.

Children of an after century—the very time in which these pages will greet you destroys enough of the connection between you and myself, to render me indifferent alike to your censure and your applause. Exactly one hundred years from the day this record is completed will the seal I shall place on it be broken, and the secrets it contains be disclosed. I claim that congeniality with you which I have found not among my own coevals. *Their* thoughts, their feelings, their views, have nothing kindred to my own. I speak their language, but it is not as a native—*they* know not a syllable of *mine!* With a future age my heart may have more in common—to a future age my thoughts may be less unfamiliar, and my sentiments less strange ; I trust these confessions to the trial !

Children of an after century, between you and the being who has traced the pages ye behold—that busy, versatile, restless being—there is but one step—but that step is a century ! His *now* is separated from your *now*, by an interval of three generations ! While He writes, he is exulting in the vigour of health and manhood—while ye read, the very worms are starving upon his dust. This commune between the living and the dead—this intercourse between that which breathes and moves, and *is*—and that which life animates not, nor mortality knows—annihilates falsehood, and chills even self-delusion into awe. Come, then, and look upon the picture of a past day, and of a gone being, without apprehension of deceit—and as the shadows and lights of a chequered and wild existence flit before you—watch if, in your own hearts, there be aught which mirrors the reflection.

MORTON DEVEREUX.

NOTE TO THE PRESENT EDITION,
1852.

IF this work possess any merit of a Narrative order, it will perhaps be found in its fidelity to the characteristics of an Autobiography. The reader must, indeed, comply with the condition exacted from his imagination and faith—that is to say, he must take the hero of the story upon the terms for which Morton Devereux himself stipulates ; and regard the supposed Count as one who lived and wrote in the last century, but who (dimly conscious that the tone of his mind harmonized less with his own age than with that which was to come) left his biography as a legacy to the present. This assumption (which is not an unfair one) liberally conceded, and allowed to account for occasional anachronisms in sentiment, Morton Devereux will be found to write, as a man who is not constructing a romance, but narrating a life. He gives to Love, its joy and its sorrow, its due share in an eventful and passionate existence : but it is the share of biography, not of fiction. He selects from the crowd of personages with whom he is brought into contact, not only those who directly influence his personal destinies, but those of whom a sketch or an anecdote would appear to a biographer likely to have interest for posterity. Louis XIV., the Regent Orleans, Peter the Great, Lord Bolingbroke, and others less eminent, but still of mark in their own day, if growing obscure to ours, are introduced not for the purposes and agencies of fiction, but as an autobiographer's natural illustrations of the men and manners of his time.

And here be it pardoned if I add that so minute an attention has been paid to accuracy, that even in petty details, and in relation to historical characters but slightly known to the ordinary reader, a critic deeply acquainted with the memoirs of the age will allow that the novelist is always merged in the narrator.

Unless the Author has failed more in his design, than, on revising the work of his early youth with the comparatively impartial eye of maturer judgment, he is disposed to concede—Morton Devereux will also be found with that marked individuality of character which distinguishes the man who has lived and laboured, from the hero of romance.   He admits into his life but few passions—those are tenacious and intense ; conscious that none who are around him will sympathize with his deeper feelings he veils them under the sneer of an irony which is often affected and never mirthful.   Where-ever we find him, after surviving the brief episode of love, we feel—though he does not tell us so—that he is alone in the world.   He is represented as a keen observer and a successful actor in the busy theatre of mankind, precisely in proportion as no cloud from the heart obscures the cold clearness of the mind.   In the scenes of pleasure there is no joy in his smile ; in the contests of ambition there is no quicker beat of the pulse.   Attaining in the prime of manhood such position and honour as would first content and then sate a man of this mould, he has nothing left but to discover the vanities of this world, and to ponder on the hopes of the next ; and, his last passion dying out in the retribution that falls on his foe, he finally sits down in retirement to rebuild the ruined home of his youth,—unconscious that to that solitude the Destinies have led him to repair the waste and ravages of his own melancholy soul.

But while outward Dramatic harmonies between cause and effect, and the proportionate agencies which characters introduced in the Drama bring to bear upon event and catastrophe, are carefully shunned—as real life does for the most part shun them—yet there is a latent coherence in all that, by influencing the mind, do, though indirectly, shape out the fate and guide the actions.   ,

Dialogue and adventures which, considered dramatically, would be episodical,—considered biographically, will be found essential to the formation, change, and development of the narrator's character.

The grave conversations with Bolingbroke and Richard Cromwell, the light scenes in London and at Paris, the favour obtained with the Czar of Russia, are all essential to the creation of that mixture of wearied satiety and mournful thought which conducts the Probationer to the lonely spot in which he is destined to learn at once the mystery of his past life, and to clear his reason from the doubts that had obscured the future world.

Viewing the work in this more subtle and contemplative light, the reader will find not only the true test by which to judge of its design and nature, but he may also recognize sources of interest in the story which might otherwise have been lost to him ; and, if so, the Author will not be without excuse for this criticism upon the scope and intention of his own work. For it is not only the privilege of an artist, but it is also sometimes his duty to the principles of Art, to place the spectator in that point of view wherein the light best falls upon the canvas. "Do not place yourself there," says the painter : "To judge of my composition you must stand where I place you."

DEVEREUX.

BOOK I.

CHAPTER I.

OF THE HERO'S BIRTH AND PARENTAGE.—NOTHING CAN DIFFER
MORE FROM THE END OF THINGS THAN THEIR BEGINNING.

MY grandfather, Sir Arthur Devereux, (peace be with his ashes!) was a noble old knight and cavalier, possessed of a property sufficiently large to have maintained in full dignity half a dozen peers—such as peers have been since the days of the First James. Nevertheless, my grandfather loved the equestrian order better than the patrician, rejected all offers of advancement, and left his posterity no titles but those to his estate.

Sir Arthur had two children by wedlock—both sons; at his death, my father, the younger, bade adieu to the old hall and his only brother, prayed to the grim portraits of his ancestors to inspire him, and set out—to join as a volunteer the armies of that *Louis*, afterwards surnamed *le grand*. Of him I shall say but little; the life of a soldier has only two events worth recording, his first campaign and his last. My uncle did as his ancestors had done before him, and, cheap as the dignity had grown, went up to court to be knighted by Charles II. He was so delighted with what he saw of the metropolis that he forswore all intention of leaving it, took to Sedley and champagne, flirted with Nell Gwynne, lost double the value of his brother's portion at one sitting to the chivalrous Grammont, wrote a comedy corrected by Etherege, and took a wife recommended by Rochester. The wife brought him a child six months after marriage, and the infant was born on the same day the comedy was acted. Luckily for the honour of the house, my uncle shared the fate of Plemneus, king of Sicyon, and all the

B

offspring he ever had (that is to say, the child and the play) "died as soon as they were born." My uncle was now only at a loss what to do with his wife—that remaining treasure, whose readiness to oblige him had been so miraculously evinced. She saved him the trouble of long cogitation—an exercise of intellect to which he was never too ardently inclined. There was a gentleman of the court, celebrated for his sedateness and solemnity; my aunt was piqued into emulating Orpheus, and, six weeks after her confinement, she put this rock into motion—they eloped. Poor gentleman!—it must have been a severe trial of patience to a man never known before to transgress the very slowest of all possible walks—to have had two events of the most rapid nature happen to him in the same week: scarcely had he recovered the shock of being run away with by my aunt, before, terminating for ever his vagrancies, he was run through by my uncle. The wits made an epigram upon the event, and my uncle, who was as bold as a lion at the point of a sword, was, to speak frankly, terribly disconcerted by the point of a jest. He retired to the country in a fit of disgust and gout. Here his natural goodness soon recovered the effects of the artificial atmosphere to which it had been exposed, and he solaced himself by righteously governing domains worthy of a prince, for the mortifications he had experienced in the dishonourable career of a courtier.

Hitherto I have spoken somewhat slightingly of my uncle, and in his dissipation he deserved it, for he was both too honest and too simple to shine in that galaxy of prostituted genius of which Charles II. was the centre. But in retirement he was no longer the same person; and I do not think that the elements of human nature could have furnished forth a more amiable character than Sir William Devereux presiding at Christmas over the merriment of his great hall.

Good old man! his very defects were what we loved best in him —vanity was so mingled with good nature that it became graceful, and we reverenced one the most, while we most smiled at the other.

One peculiarity had he, which the age he had lived in and his domestic history, rendered natural enough, viz.,an exceeding distaste to the matrimonial state: early marriages were misery, imprudent marriages idiotism, and marriage, at the best, he was wont to say, with a kindling eye, and a heightened colour, marriage at the best —was the devil! Yet it must not be supposed that Sir William Devereux was an ungallant man. On the contrary, never did the *beau sexe* have a humbler or more devoted servant. As nothing in his estimation was less becoming to a wise man than matrimony, so nothing was more ornamental than flirtation.

He had the old man's weakness, garrulity; and he told the wittiest stories in the world, without omitting anything in them but the point. This omission did not arise from the want either of memory or of humour; but solely from a deficiency in the malice natural to all jesters. He could not persuade his lips to repeat a sarcasm hurting even the dead or the ungrateful; and when he came to the drop of gall which should have given zest to the story, the milk of human kindness broke its barrier, despite of himself,— and washed it away. He was a fine wreck, a little prematurely broken by dissipation, but not perhaps the less interesting on that account; tall, and somewhat of the jovial old English girth, with a face where good nature and good living mingled their smiles and glow. He wore the garb of twenty years back, and was curiously particular in the choice of his silk stockings. Between you and me, he was not a little vain of his leg, and a compliment on that score was always sure of a gracious reception.

The solitude of my uncle's household was broken by an invasion of three boys—none of the quietest; and their mother, who, the gentlest and saddest of womankind, seemed to follow them, the emblem of that primeval Silence from which all noise was born. These three boys were my two brothers and myself. My father, who had conceived a strong personal attachment for *Louis Quatorze*, never quitted his service, and the great King repaid him by orders and favours without number; he died of wounds received in battle— a Count and a Marshal, full of renown, and destitute of money. He had married twice : his first wife, who died without issue, was a daughter of the noble house of La Tremouille—his second, our mother, was of a younger branch of the English race of Howard. Brought up in her native country, and influenced by a primitive and retired education, she never loved that gay land which her husband had adopted as his own. Upon his death, she hastened her return to England, and refusing, with somewhat of honourable pride, the magnificent pension which Louis wished to settle upon the widow of his favourite, came to throw herself and her children upon those affections which she knew they were entitled to claim.

My uncle was unaffectedly rejoiced to receive us.—To say nothing of his love for my father, and his pride at the honours the latter had won to their ancient house—the good gentleman was very well pleased with the idea of obtaining four new listeners, out of whom he might select an heir, and he soon grew as fond of us as we were of him. At the time of our new settlement, I had attained the age of twelve; my second brother (we were twins) was born an hour after me; my third was about fifteen months younger. I had never been the favourite of the three. In the first place, my brothers (my youngest especially) were uncommonly handsome, and, at most, I was but tolerably good-looking; in the second place, my mind was considered as much inferior to theirs as my body—I was idle and dull, sullen and haughty—the only wit I ever displayed was in sneering at my friends, and the only spirit, in quarrelling with my twin brother; so said or so thought all who saw us in our childhood; and it follows, therefore, that I was either very unamiable or very much misunderstood.

But, to the astonishment of myself and my relations, my fate was now to be reversed, and I was no sooner settled at Devereux Court, than I became evidently the object of Sir William's pre-eminent attachment. The fact was, that I really liked both the knight and his stories better than my brothers did; and the very first time I had seen my uncle, I had commented on the beauty of his stocking, and envied the constitution of his leg; from such trifles spring affection! In truth, our attachment to each other so increased that we grew to be constantly together; and while my childish anticipations of the world made me love to listen to stories of courts and courtiers, my uncle returned the compliment, by declaring of my wit, as the angler declared of the River Lea, that one would find enough in it, if one would but angle sufficiently long.

Nor was this all; my uncle and myself were exceedingly like the waters of Alpheus and Arethusa—nothing was thrown into the one without being seen very shortly afterwards floating upon the other. Every witticism or legend Sir William imparted to me (and some, to say truth, were a little tinged with the licentiousness of the times he had lived in), I took the first opportunity of retailing, whatever might be the audience; and few boys, at the age of thirteen, can boast of having so often as myself excited the laughter of the men and the blushes of the women. This circumstance, while it aggravated my own vanity, delighted my uncle's; and as I was always getting into scrapes on his account, so he was perpetually bound, by duty, to defend me from the charges of which he was the cause. No man defends another long without loving him the better for it; and perhaps Sir William Devereux and his eldest nephew were the only allies in the world who had no jealousy of each other.

CHAPTER II.

A FAMILY CONSULTATION.—A PRIEST, AND AN ÆRA IN LIFE.

"YOU are ruining the children, my dear Sir William," said my gentle mother, one day, when I had been particularly witty, "and the Abbé Montreuil declares it absolutely necessary that they should go to school."

"To school!" said my uncle, who was caressing his right leg, as it lay over his left knee—"to school, Madam! you are joking. What for, pray?"

"Instruction, my dear Sir William," replied my mother.

"Ah, ah; I forgot that; true, true!" said my uncle, despondingly, and there was a pause. My mother counted her rosary; my uncle sank into a reverie; my twin brother pinched my leg under the table, to which I replied by a silent kick: and my youngest fixed his large, dark, speaking eyes upon a picture of the Holy Family, which hung opposite to him.

My uncle broke silence; he did it with a start.

"Od's fish, Madam,"—(my uncle dressed his oaths, like himself, a little after the example of Charles II.)—"od's fish, Madam, I have thought of a better plan than that; they shall have instruction without going to school for it."

"And how, Sir William?"

"I will instruct them myself, Madam," and Sir William slapped the calf of the leg he was caressing.

My mother smiled.

"Ay, Madam, you may smile; but I and my Lord Dorset were the best scholars of the age; you shall read my play."

"Do, mother," said I, "read the play. Shall I tell her some of the jests in it, uncle?"

My mother shook her head in anticipative horror, and raised her finger reprovingly. My uncle said nothing, but winked at me; I understood the signal, and was about to begin, when the door opened, and the Abbé Montreuil entered. My uncle released his right leg, and my jest was cut off. Nobody ever inspired a more dim, religious awe than the Abbé Montreuil. The priest entered with a smile. My mother hailed the entrance of an ally.

"Father," said she, rising, "I have just represented to my good brother the necessity of sending my sons to school; he has proposed an alternative which I will leave you to discuss with him."

"And what is it?" said Montreuil, sliding into a chair, and patting Gerald's head with a benignant air.

"To educate them himself," answered my mother, with a sort of satirical gravity. My uncle moved uneasily in his seat, as if, for the first time, he saw something ridiculous in the proposal.

The smile, immediately fading from the thin lips of the priest, gave way to an expression of respectful approbation. "An admirable plan," said he, slowly, "but liable to some little exceptions, which Sir William will allow me to point out."

My mother called to us, and we left the room with her. The next time we saw my uncle, the priest's reasonings had prevailed. The following week we all three went to school. My father had been a Catholic, my mother was of the same creed, and consequently we were brought up in that unpopular faith. But my uncle, whose religion had been sadly undermined at court, was a terrible caviller at the holy mysteries of Catholicism ; and while his friends termed him a Protestant, his enemies hinted, falsely enough, that he was a sceptic. When Montreuil first followed us to Devereux Court, many and bitter were the little jests my worthy uncle had provided for his reception ; and he would shake his head with a notable archness whenever he heard our reverential description of the expected guest. But, somehow or other, no sooner had he seen the priest, than all his purposed railleries deserted him. Not a single witticism came to his assistance, and the calm, smooth face of the ecclesiastic seemed to operate upon the fierce resolves of the facetious knight in the same manner as the human eye is supposed to awe into impotence the malignant intentions of the ignobler animals. Yet nothing could be blander than the demeanour of the Abbé Montreuil—nothing more worldly, in their urbanity, than his manner and address. His garb was as little clerical as possible, his conversation rather familiar than formal, and he invariably listened to every syllable the good knight uttered, with a countenance and mien of the most attentive respect.

What then was the charm by which this singular man never failed to obtain an ascendancy, in some measure allied with fear, over all in whose company he was thrown? That was a secret my uncle never could solve, and which, only in later life, I myself was able to discover. It was partly by the magic of an extraordinary and powerful mind, partly by an expression of manner, if I may use such a phrase, that seemed to sneer most, when most it affected to respect ; and partly by an air like that of a man never exactly at his ease ; not that he was shy, or ungraceful, or even taciturn—no ! it was an indescribable embarrassment, resembling that of one playing a part, familiar to him, indeed, but somewhat distasteful. This embarrassment, however, was sufficient to be contagious, and to confuse that dignity in others which, strangely enough, never forsook himself.

He was of low origin, but his address and appearance did not betray his birth. Pride suited his mien better than familiarity—and his countenance, rigid, thoughtful, and cold, even through smiles, in expression was strikingly commanding. In person, he was slightly above the middle standard; and had not the texture of his frame been remarkably hard, wiry, and muscular, the total absence of all superfluous flesh would have given the lean gauntness of his figure an appearance of almost spectral emaciation. In reality, his age did not exceed twenty-eight years; but his high, broad forehead was already so marked with line and furrow, his air was so staid and quiet, his figure so destitute of the roundness and elasticity of youth, that his appearance always impressed the beholder with the involuntary idea of a man considerably more advanced in life. Abstemious to habitual penance, and regular to mechanical exactness in his frequent and severe devotions, he was as little inwardly addicted to the pleasures and pursuits of youth, as he was externally possessed of its freshness and its bloom.

Nor was gravity with him that unmeaning veil to imbecility, which Rochefoucauld has so happily called "the mystery of the body." The variety and depth of his learning fully sustained the respect which his demeanour insensibly created. To say nothing of his lore in the dead tongues, he possessed a knowledge of the principal European languages besides his own, viz., English, Italian, German, and Spanish, not less accurate and little less fluent than that of a native; and he had not only gained the key to these various coffers of intellectual wealth, but he had also possessed himself of their treasures. He had been educated at St. Omer; and, young as he was, he had already acquired no inconsiderable reputation among his brethren of that illustrious and celebrated Order of Jesus which has produced some of the worst and some of the best men that the Christian world has ever known—which has, in its successful zeal for knowledge, and the circulation of mental light, bequeathed a vast debt of gratitude to posterity; but which, unhappily encouraging certain scholastic doctrines, that by a mind at once subtle and vicious can be easily perverted into the sanction of the most dangerous and systematized immorality, has already drawn upon its professors an almost universal odium.

So highly established was the good name of Montreuil that when, three years prior to the time of which I now speak, he had been elected to the office he held in our family, it was scarcely deemed a less fortunate occurrence for us, to gain so learned and so pious a preceptor, than it was for him to acquire a situation of such trust and confidence in the household of a Marshal of France, and the especial favourite of Louis XIV.

It was pleasant enough to mark the gradual ascendancy he gained over my uncle; and the timorous dislike which the good knight entertained for him, yet struggled to conceal. Perhaps that was the only time in his life in which Sir William Devereux was a hypocrite.

Enough of the priest at present—I return to his charge. To school we went—our parting with our uncle was quite pathetic—mine in especial. "Harkye, Sir Count," whispered he (I bore my father's title), "harkye, don't mind what the old priest tells you; your real man of wit never wants the musty lessons of schools in order to make a figure in the world. Don't cramp your genius, my boy; read over my play, and honest George Etherege's 'Man of Mode;' they'll keep your spirits alive, after dozing over those old pages which Homer (good soul!) dozed over before. God bless you, my child—write to me—no one, not even your mother, shall see your letters—and—and be sure, my fine fellow, that you don't fag too hard. The glass of life is the best book—and one's natural wit the only diamond that can write legibly on it."

Such were my uncle's parting admonitions; it must be confessed that, coupled with the dramatic gifts alluded to, they were likely to be of infinite service to the *débutant* for academical honours. In fact, Sir William Devereux was deeply impregnated with the notion of his time, that ability and inspiration were the same thing, and that, unless you were thoroughly idle, you could not be thoroughly a genius. I verily believe that he thought wisdom got its gems, as Abu Zeid al Hassan [1] declares some Chinese philosophers thought oysters got their pearls—viz.—*by gaping!*

---

[1] In his Commentary on the account of China by two Travellers.

CHAPTER III.

A CHANGE IN CONDUCT AND IN CHARACTER — OUR EVIL
PASSIONS WILL SOMETIMES PRODUCE GOOD EFFECTS; AND
ON THE CONTRARY, AN ALTERATION FOR THE BETTER IN
MANNERS WILL, NOT UNFREQUENTLY, HAVE AMONGST ITS
CAUSES A LITTLE CORRUPTION OF MIND; FOR THE FEELINGS
ARE SO BLENDED, THAT IN SUPPRESSING THOSE DISAGREEABLE
TO OTHERS, WE OFTEN SUPPRESS THOSE WHICH ARE AMIABLE
IN THEMSELVES.

Y twin brother, Gerald, was a tall, strong, handsome boy,
blessed with a great love for the orthodox academical
studies, and extraordinary quickness of ability. Nevertheless, he was indolent by nature, in things which were
contrary to his taste—fond of pleasure—and, amidst all his personal
courage, ran a certain vein of irresolution, which rendered it easy
for a cool and determined mind to awe or to persuade him. I
cannot help thinking, too, that, clever as he was, there was something commonplace in the cleverness; and that his talent was of
that mechanical, yet quick, nature, which makes wonderful boys,
but *médiocre* men. In any other family he would have been considered the beauty—in ours he was thought the genius.

My youngest brother, Aubrey, was of a very different disposition
of mind and frame of body; thoughtful, gentle, susceptible, acute;
with an uncertain bravery, like a woman's, and a taste for reading,
that varied with the caprice of every hour. He was the beauty of
the three, and my mother's favourite. Never, indeed, have I seen
the countenance of man so perfect, so glowingly, yet delicately
handsome, as that of Aubrey Devereux. Locks, soft, glossy, and
twining into ringlets, fell in dark profusion over a brow whiter than
marble; his eyes were black and tender, as a Georgian girl's; his
lips, his teeth, the contour of his face, were all cast in the same
feminine and faultless mould; his hands would have shamed those
of Madame de la Tisseur, whose lover offered six thousand marks to
any European who could wear her glove; and his figure would
have made Titania give up her Henchman, and the King of the
Fairies be anything but pleased with the exchange.

Such were my two brothers; or, rather (so far as the internal
qualities are concerned), such they seemed to me; for it is a singular
fact that we never judge of our near kindred so well as we judge of

B 2

others ; and I appeal to any one, whether, of all people by whom he has been mistaken, he has not been most often mistaken by those with whom he was brought up !

I had always loved Aubrey, but they had not suffered him to love *me ;* and we had been so little together that we had in common none of those childish remembrances which serve, more powerfully than all else in later life, to cement and soften affection. In fact, I was the scapegoat of the family. What I must have been in early childhood, I cannot tell—but, before I was ten years old, I was the object of all the despondency and evil forebodings of my relations. My father said I laughed at *la gloire et le grand monarque,* the very first time he attempted to explain to me the value of the one and the greatness of the other. The countess said I had neither my father's eye, nor her own smile—that I was slow at my letters, and quick with my tongue ; and, throughout the whole house, nothing was so favourite a topic as the extent of my rudeness, and the venom of my repartee. Montreuil, on his entrance into our family, not only fell in with, but favoured and fostered, the reigning humour against me ; whether from that *divide et impera* system, which was so grateful to his temper, or from the mere love of meddling and intrigue, which in him, as in Alberoni, attached itself equally to petty as to large circles, was not then clearly apparent ; it was only certain that he fomented the dissensions and widened the breach between my brothers and myself.—Alas ! after all, I believe my sole crime was my candour. I had a spirit of frankness which no fear could tame, and my vengeance for any infantine punishment was in speaking veraciously of my punishers. Never tell me of the pang of false-hood to the slandered : nothing is so agonizing to the fine skin of vanity as the application of a rough truth !

As I grew older, I saw my power, and indulged it ; and, being scolded for sarcasm, I was flattered into believing I had wit ; so I punned and jested, lampooned and satirized, till I was as much a torment to others as I was tormented myself. The secret of all this was that I was unhappy. Nobody loved me—I felt it to my heart of hearts. I was conscious of injustice, and the sense of it made me bitter. Our feelings, especially in youth, resemble that leaf which, in some old traveller, is described as expanding itself to warmth, but when chilled, not only shrinking and closing, but presenting to the spectator thorns, which had lain concealed upon the opposite side of it before.

With my brother Gerald, I had a deadly and irreconcileable feud. He was much stouter, taller, and stronger than myself ; and, far from conceding to me that respect which I imagined my priority of birth entitled me to claim, he took every opportunity to deride my pretensions, and to vindicate the cause of the superior strength and vigour which constituted his own. It would have done your heart good to have seen us cuff one another, we did it with such zeal. There is nothing in human passion like a good brotherly hatred! my mother said, with the most feeling earnestness, that she used to feel us fighting even before our birth : we certainly lost no time directly after it. Both my parents were secretly vexed that I had come into the world an hour sooner than my brother ; and Gerald himself looked upon it as a sort of juggle—a kind of jockeyship by which he had lost the prerogative of birthright. This very early rankled in his heart, and he was so much a greater favourite than myself that, instead of rooting out so unfortunate a feeling on his part, my good parents made no scruple of openly lamenting my seniority. I believe the real cause of our being taken from the domestic instructions of the Abbé (who was an admirable teacher) and sent to school, was solely to prevent my uncle deciding everything in my favour. Montreuil, however, accompanied us to our academy, and remained with us during the three years in which we were perfecting ourselves in the blessings of education.

At the end of the second year, a prize was instituted for the best proficient at a very severe examination ; two months before it took place we went home for a few days. After dinner my uncle asked me to walk with him in the park. I did so : we strolled along to the margin of a rivulet, which ornamented the grounds. There my uncle, for the first time, broke silence.

"Morton," said he, looking down at his left leg, "Morton—let me see—thou art now of a reasonable age—fourteen at the least."

"Fifteen, if it please you, sir," said I, elevating my stature as much as I was able.

"Humph! my boy ; and a pretty time of life it is, too. Your brother Gerald is taller than you by two inches."

"But I can beat him, for all that, uncle," said I, colouring, and clenching my fist.

My uncle pulled down his right ruffle. "'Gad so, Morton, you're a brave fellow," said he ; "but I wish you were less of a hero and more of a scholar. I wish you could beat him in Greek, as well as in boxing. I will tell you what Old Rowley said," and my uncle occupied the next quarter of an hour with a story. The story opened the good old gentleman's heart—my laughter opened it still more. "Hark ye, sirrah!" said he, pausing abruptly, and grasping my hand with a vigorous effort of love and muscle, "hark ye, sirrah—I love you—'Sdeath, I do. I love you better than both your brothers, and that crab of a priest into the bargain ; but I am grieved to the heart to hear what I do of you. They tell me you are the idlest boy in the school—that you are always beating your brother Gerald, and making a scurrilous jest of your mother or myself."

"Who says so? who dares say so?" said I, with an emphasis that would have startled a less hearty man than Sir William Devereux. "They lie, uncle, by my soul they do. Idle I am—quarrelsome with my brother I confess myself; but jesting at you or my mother —never—never. No, no ; *you*, too, who have been so kind to me— the only one who ever was ! No, no ; do not think I could be such a wretch," and as I said this the tears gushed from my eyes.

My good uncle was exceedingly affected. "Look ye, child," said he, "I do not believe them. 'Sdeath, not a word—I would repeat to you a good jest now of Sedley's, 'Gad, I would, but I am really too much moved just at present. I tell you what, my boy, I tell you what you shall do : there is a trial coming on at school— eh ?—well, the Abbé tells me, Gerald is certain of being first, and you of being last. Now, Morton, you shall beat your brother, and shame the jesuit. There—my mind's spoken—dry your tears, my boy, and I'll tell you the jest Sedley made : it was in the Mulberry Garden one day——" And the knight told his story.

I dried my tears—pressed my uncle's hand—escaped from him as soon as I was able—hastened to my room, and surrendered myself to reflection.

When my uncle so good-naturedly proposed that I should conquer Gerald at the examination, nothing appeared to him more easy; he was pleased to think I had more talent than my brother, and talent, according to his creed, was the only master-key to unlock every science. A problem in Euclid, or a phrase in Pindar, a secret in astronomy, or a knotty passage in the fathers, were all riddles, with the solution of which, application had nothing to do. One's mother-wit was a precious sort of necromancy, which could pierce every mystery at first sight ; and all the gifts of knowledge, in his opinion, like reading and writing in that of the sage Dogberry, "came by nature." Alas ! I was not under the same pleasurable delusion ; I rather exaggerated than diminished the difficulty of my task, and thought, at the first glance, that nothing short of a miracle would enable me to excel my brother.—Gerald, a boy of natural talent, and as I said before, of great assiduity in the orthodox studies— especially favoured too by the instruction of Montreuil—had long been esteemed the first scholar of our little world ; and though I knew that with some branches of learning I was more conversant than himself, yet, as my emulation had been hitherto solely directed to bodily contention, I had never thought of contesting with him a reputation for which I cared little, and on a point in which I had been early taught that I could never hope to enter into any advantageous comparison with the " genius " of the Devereuxs.

A new spirit now passed into me—I examined myself with jealous and impartial scrutiny—I weighed my acquisitions against those of my brother—I called forth, from their secret recesses, the unexercised and almost unknown stores I had from time to time laid up in my mental armoury to moulder and to rust. I surveyed them with a feeling that they might yet be polished into use : and, excited alike by the stimulus of affection on one side, and hatred on the other, my mind worked itself from despondency into doubt, and from doubt into the sanguineness of hope. I told none of my design, —I exacted from my uncle a promise not to betray it—I shut myself in my room—I gave out that I was ill—I saw no one, not even the Abbé—I rejected his instructions, for I looked upon him as an enemy ; and, for the two months, before my trial, I spent night and day in an unrelaxing application, of which, till then, I had not imagined myself capable.

Though inattentive to the school exercises, I had never been wholly idle. I was a lover of abstruser researches than the hackneyed subjects of the school, and we had really received such extensive and judicious instructions from the Abbé during our early years that it would have been scarcely possible for any of us to have fallen into a thorough distaste for intellectual pursuits. In the examination, I foresaw that much which I had previously acquired might be profitably displayed—much secret and recondite knowledge of the customs and manners of the ancients, as well as their literature, which curiosity had led me to obtain, and which I knew had never entered into the heads of those who, contented with their reputation in the customary academical routine, had rarely dreamed of wandering into less beaten paths of learning. Fortunately too for me, Gerald was so certain of success that latterly he omitted all precaution to obtain it ; and as none of our school-fellows had the vanity to think of contesting with him, even the Abbé seemed to imagine him justified in his supineness.

The day arrived. Sir William, my mother, the whole aristocracy of the neighbourhood, were present at the trial. The Abbé came to my room a few hours before it commenced ; he found the door locked.

"Ungracious boy," said he, "admit me—I come at the earnest request of your brother, Aubrey, to give you some hints preparatory to the examination."

"He has indeed come at my wish," said the soft and silver voice of Aubrey, in a supplicating tone : "do admit him, dear Morton, for my sake!"

"Go," said I, bitterly, from within, "go—ye are both my foes and slanderers—you come to insult my disgrace beforehand ; but perhaps you will yet be disappointed."

"You will not open the door?" said the priest.

"I will not—begone."

"He will indeed disgrace his family," said Montreuil, moving away.

"He will disgrace himself," said Aubrey, dejectedly.

I laughed scornfully. If ever the consciousness of strength is pleasant, it is when we are thought most weak.

The greater part of our examination consisted in the answering of certain questions in writing, given to us in the three days immediately previous to the grand and final one ; for this last day was reserved the paper of composition (as it was termed) in verse and prose, and the personal examination in a few showy, but generally understood, subjects. When Gerald gave in his paper, and answered the verbal questions, a buzz of admiration and anxiety went round the room. His person was so handsome, his address so graceful, his voice so assured and clear, that a strong and universal sympathy was excited in his favour. The head-master publicly complimented him. He regretted only the deficiency of his pupil in certain minor but important matters.

I came next, for I stood next to Gerald in our class. As I walked up the hall, I raised my eyes to the gallery in which my uncle and his party sat. I saw that my mother was listening to the Abbé, whose eye, severe, cold, and contemptuous, was bent upon me. But my uncle leant over the railing of the gallery, with his plumed hat in his hand, which, when he caught my look, he waved gently— as if in token of encouragement, and with an air so kind and cheering, that I felt my step grow prouder as I approached the conclave of the masters.

"Morton Devereux," said the president of the school in a calm, loud, austere voice, that filled the whole hall, "we have looked over your papers on the three previous days, and they have given us no less surprise than pleasure. Take heed and time how you answer us now."

At this speech a loud murmur was heard in my uncle's party, which gradually spread round the hall. I again looked up—my mother's face was averted: that of the Abbé was impenetrable, but I saw my uncle wiping his eyes, and felt a strange emotion creeping into my own. I turned hastily away, and presented my paper—the head-master received it, and, putting it aside, proceeded to the verbal examination.

Conscious of the parts in which Gerald was likely to fail, I had paid especial attention to the minutiæ of scholarship, and my fore-thought stood me in good stead at the present moment. My trial ceased—my last paper was read. I bowed, and retired to the other end of the hall. I was not so popular as Gerald—a crowd was assembled round him, but I stood alone. As I leant against a column, with folded arms, and a countenance which I felt betrayed little of my internal emotions, my eye caught Gerald's. He was very pale, and I could see that his hand trembled. Despite of our enmity, I felt for him. The worst passions are softened by triumph, and I foresaw that mine was at hand.

The whole examination was over. Every boy had passed it. The masters retired for a moment—they re-appeared and re-seated themselves. The first sound I heard was that of my own name. I was the victor of the day—I was more—I was one hundred marks before my brother. My head swam round—my breath forsook me. Since then I have been placed in many trials of life, and had many triumphs; but never was I so overcome as at that moment. I left the hall—I scarcely listened to the applauses with which it rang. I hurried to my own chamber, and threw myself on the bed in a delirium of intoxicated feeling, which had in it more of rapture than anything but the gratification of first-love, or first vanity can bestow.

Ah! it would be worth stimulating our passions if it were only for the pleasure of remembering their effect; and all violent excitement should be indulged less for present joy than for future retrospection.

My uncle's step was the first thing which intruded on my solitude. "Od's fish, my boy," said he, crying like a child, "this is fine work—'Gad, so it is. I almost wish I were a boy myself to have a match with you—faith I do—see what it is to learn a little of life. If you had never read my play, do you think you would have done half so well?—no, my boy, I sharpened your wits for you. Honest George Etherege and I—we were the making of you; and when you come to be a great man, and are asked what made you so, you shall say—'My uncle's play'—'Gad, you shall. Faith, boy—never smile!—Od's fish—I'll tell you a story as *à propos* to the present occasion as if it had been made on purpose. Rochester, and I, and Sedley, were walking one day,—and *entre nous*—awaiting certain appointments—hem!—for my part I was a little melancholy or so, thinking of my catastrophe—that is, of my play's catastrophe ; and so, said Sedley, winking at Rochester, 'our friend is sorrowful.' 'Truly,' said I, seeing they were about to banter me —for you know they were arch fellows—'truly, little Sid,' (we called Sedley Sid), 'you are greatly mistaken ;'—you see, Morton, I was thus sharp upon him, because, when you go to Court, you will discover that it does not do to take without giving. And then Rochester said, looking roguishly towards me, the wittiest thing against Sedley that ever I heard—it was the most celebrated *bon mot* at Court for three weeks—he said—No, boy, od's fish, it was so stinging I can't tell it thee ; faith, I can't. Poor Sid ; he was a good fellow, though malicious—and he's dead now.—I'm sorry I said a word about it. Nay, never look so disappointed, boy. You have all the cream of the story as it is. And now put on your hat, and come with me. I've got leave for you to take a walk with your old uncle."

That night, as I was undressing, I heard a gentle rap at the door, and Aubrey entered. He approached me timidly, and then, throwing his arms round my neck, kissed me in silence. I had not for years experienced such tenderness from him ; and I sat now mute and surprised. At last I said, with the sneer which I must confess I usually assumed towards those persons whom I imagined I had a right to think ill of :

"Pardon me, my gentle brother, there is something portentous in this sudden change. Look well round the room, and tell me at your earliest leisure what treasure it is that you are desirous should pass from my possession into your own."

"Your love, Morton," said Aubrey, drawing back, but apparently in pride, not anger ; "your love—I ask nothing more."

"Of a surety, kind Aubrey," said I, "the favour seems some-what slight to have caused your modesty such delay in requesting it. I think you have been now some years nerving your mind to the exertion."

"Listen to me, Morton," said Aubrey, suppressing his emotion ; "you have always been my favourite brother. From our first childhood my heart yearned to you. Do you remember the time when an enraged bull pursued me, and you, then only ten years old, placed yourself before it and defended me at the risk of your own life ? Do you think I could ever forget that—child as I was ? —never, Morton, never ! "

Before I could answer, the door was thrown open, and the Abbé entered. "Children," said he, and the single light of the room shone full upon his unmoved, rigid, commanding features—"children, be as Heaven intended you—friends and brothers. Morton, I have wronged you, I own it—here is my hand ; Aubrey, let all but early love, and the present promise of excellence which your brother displays, be forgotten."

With these words, the priest joined our hands. I looked on my brother, and my heart melted. I flung myself into his arms and wept.

"This is well," said Montreuil, surveying us with a kind of grim complacency, and, taking my brother's arm, he blest us both, and led Aubrey away.

That day was a new era in my boyish life. I grew henceforth both better and worse. Application and I, having once shaken hands, became very good acquaintance. I had hitherto valued myself upon supplying the frailties of a delicate frame, by an uncommon agility in all bodily exercises. I now strove rather to improve the deficiencies of my mind, and became orderly, industrious, and devoted to study. So far so well—but as I grew wiser, I grew also more wary. Candour no longer seemed to me the finest of virtues. I thought before I spoke ; and second thought sometimes quite changed the nature of the intended speech ; in short, gentlemen of the next century, to tell you the exact truth, the little Count Devereux became somewhat of a hypocrite !

CHAPTER IV.

A CONTEST OF ART, AND A LEAGUE OF FRIENDSHIP—TWO CHA-
RACTERS IN MUTUAL IGNORANCE OF EACH OTHER, AND
THE READER NO WISER THAN EITHER OF THEM.

THE Abbé was now particularly courteous to me. He made Gerald and myself breakfast with him, and told us nothing was so amiable as friendship among brothers. We agreed to the sentiment, and, like all philosophers, did not agree a bit the better for acknowledging the same first principles. Perhaps, notwithstanding his fine speeches, the Abbé was the real cause of our continued want of cordiality. However, we did not fight any more—we avoided each other, and at last became as civil and as distant as those mathematical lines, which appear to be taking all possible pains to approach one another, and never get a jot the nearer for it. Oh ! your civility is the prettiest invention possible for dislike ! Aubrey and I were inseparable, and we both gained by the intercourse. I grew more gentle, and he more masculine ;

and, for my part, the kindness of his temper so softened the satire of mine that I learned at last to smile full as often as to sneer.

The Abbé had obtained a wonderful hold over Aubrey; he had made the poor boy think so much of the next world, that he had lost all relish for this. He lived in a perpetual fear of offence—he was like a chemist of conscience, and weighed minutiæ by scruples. To play, to ride, to run, to laugh at a jest, or to banquet on a melon, were all sins to be atoned for; and I have found (as a penance for eating twenty-three cherries instead of eighteen) the penitent of fourteen standing, barefooted, in the coldest nights of winter, upon the hearth-stones, almost utterly naked, and shivering like a leaf, beneath the mingled effect of frost and devotion. At first I attempted to wrestle with this exceeding holiness, but finding my admonitions received with great distaste and some horror, I suffered my brother to be happy in his own way. I only looked with a very evil and jealous eye upon the good Abbé, and examined, while I encouraged them, the motives of his advances to myself. What doubled my suspicions of the purity of the priest was my perceiving that he appeared to hold out different inducements for trusting him, to each of us, according to his notions of our respective characters. My brother Gerald he alternately awed and persuaded, by the sole effect of superior intellect. With Aubrey he used the mechanism of superstition. To me, he, on the one hand, never spoke of religion, nor, on the other, ever used threats or persuasion, to induce me to follow any plan suggested to my adoption; everything seemed to be left to my reason and my ambition. He would converse with me for hours upon the world and its affairs, speak of courts and kings, in an easy and unpedantic strain; point out the advantage of intellect in acquiring power and controlling one's species; and, whenever I was disposed to be sarcastic upon the human nature I had read of, he supported my sarcasm by illustrations of the human nature he had seen. We were both, I think (for myself I can answer), endeavouring to pierce the real nature of the other; and perhaps the talent of diplomacy for which, years afterwards, I obtained some applause, was first learnt in my skirmishing warfare with the Abbé Montreuil.

At last, the evening before we quitted school for good arrived. Aubrey had just left me for solitary prayers, and I was sitting alone by my fire when Montreuil entered gently. He sat himself down by me, and, after giving me the salutation of the evening, sunk into a silence which I was the first to break.

"Pray, Abbé," said I, "have one's years anything to do with one's age?"

The priest was accustomed to the peculiar tone of my sagacious remarks, and answered dryly—

"Mankind in general imagine that they have."

"Faith then," said I, "mankind know very little about the matter. To-day I am at school, and a boy, to-morrow I leave school—if I hasten to town I am presented at court—and lo! I am a man; and this change within half-a-dozen changes of the sun!—therefore, most reverend father, I humbly opine that age is measured by events—not years."

"And are you not happy at the idea of passing the age of thraldom, and seeing arrayed before you the numberless and dazzling pomps and pleasures of the great world?" said Montreuil, abruptly, fixing his dark and keen eye upon me.

"I have not yet fully made up my mind, whether to be happy or not," said I, carelessly.

"It is a strange answer," said the priest; "but" (after a pause) "you are a strange youth—a character that resembles a riddle, is at your age uncommon, and, pardon me, unamiable. Age, naturally repulsive, requires a mask; and in every wrinkle you may behold the ambush of a scheme; but the heart of youth should be open as its countenance! However, I will not weary you with homilies—let us change the topic. Tell me, Morton, do you repent having turned your attention of late to those graver and more systematic studies which can alone hereafter obtain you distinction?"

"No, father," said I, with a courtly bow, "for the change has gained me your good opinion."

A smile, of peculiar and undefinable expression, crossed the thin lips of the priest; he rose, walked to the door, and saw that it was carefully closed. I expected some important communication, but in vain; pacing the small room to and fro, as if in a musing mood, the Abbé remained silent, till, pausing opposite some fencing foils, which, among various matters, (books, papers, quoits, &c.) were thrown idly in one corner of the room, he said—

"They tell me that you are the best fencer in the school—is it so?"

"I hope not, for fencing is an accomplishment in which Gerald is very nearly my equal," I replied.

"You run, ride, leap, too, better than any one else, according to the votes of your comrades?"

"It is a noble reputation," said I, "in which I believe I am only excelled by our huntsman's eldest son."

"You are a strange youth," repeated the priest; "no pursuit seems to give you pleasure, and no success to gratify your vanity. Can you not think of *any* triumph which would elate you?"

I was silent.

"Yes," cried Montreuil, approaching me—"yes," cried he, "I read your heart, and I respect it;—these are petty competitions and worthless honours. You require a nobler goal, and a more glorious reward. He who feels in his soul that Fate has reserved for him a great and exalted part in this world's drama, may reasonably look with indifference on these paltry rehearsals of common characters."

I raised my eye, and as it met that of the priest, I was irresistibly struck with the proud and luminous expression which Montreuil's look had assumed. Perhaps something kindred to its nature was perceptible in my own; for, after surveying me with an air of more approbation than he had ever honoured me with before, he grasped my arm firmly, and said, "Morton, you know me not—for many years I have not known you—that time is past. No sooner did your talents develop themselves than I was the first to do homage to their power—let us henceforth be more to each other than we have been—let us not be pupil and teacher—let us be friends. Do not think that I invite you to an unequal exchange of good offices--you may be the heir to wealth, and a distinguished name—I may seem to you but an unknown and undignified priest—but the authority of the Almighty can raise up, from the sheepfold and the cottar's shed, a power, which, as the organ of His own, can trample upon sceptres, and dictate to the supremacy of kings. And *I—I—*" the priest abruptly paused, checked the warmth of his manner, as if he thought it about to encroach on indiscretion, and, sinking into a calmer tone, continued, "Yes, I, Morton, insignificant as I appear to you, can, in *every* path through this intricate labyrinth of life, be more useful to your desires than you can ever be to mine. I offer to you in my friendship, a fervour of zeal and energy of power, which in none of your equals, in age and station, you can hope to find. Do you accept my offer?"

"Can you doubt," said I, with eagerness, "that I would avail myself of the services of any man, however displeasing to me, and worthless in himself? How, then, can I avoid embracing the friendship of one so extraordinary in knowledge and intellect as yourself? I do embrace it, and with rapture."

The priest pressed my hand. "But," continued he, fixing his eyes upon mine, "all alliances have their conditions—I require implicit confidence; and, for some years, till time gives you experience, regard for your interests induces me also to require obedience.

Name any wish you may form for worldly advancement, opulence, honour, the smile of kings, the gifts of states, and—I—I will pledge myself to carry that wish into effect. Never had eastern prince so faithful a servant among the Dives and Genii as Morton Devereux shall find in me ; but question me not of the sources of my power— be satisfied when their channel wafts you the success you covet. And, more, when I in my turn (and this shall be but rarely) request a favour of you, ask me not for what end, nor hesitate to adopt the means I shall propose. You seem startled ;—are you content at this understanding between us, or will you retract the bond ? "

" My father," said I, " there is enough to startle me in your proposal ; it greatly resembles that made by the Old Man of the Mountains to his vassals, and it would not exactly suit my inclinations to be called upon some morning to act the part of a private executioner."

The priest smiled. "My young friend," said he, "those days have passed ; neither religion nor friendship requires of her votaries sacrifices of blood. But make yourself easy ; whenever I ask of you what offends your conscience, even in a punctilio, refuse my request. With this exception, what say you ? "

" That I think I will agree to the bond ; but, father, I am an irresolute person—I must have time to consider."

" Be it so. To-morrow, having surrendered my charge to your uncle, I depart for France."

" For France !" said I ; "and how ?—Surely the war will prevent your passage."

The priest smiled. Nothing ever displeased me more than that priest's smile. " The ecclesiastics," said he, "are the ambassadors of heaven, and have nothing to do with the wars of earth. I shall find no difficulty in crossing the Channel. I shall not return for several months, perhaps not till the expiration of a year : I leave you, till then, to decide upon the terms I have proposed to you. Meanwhile, gratify my vanity, by employing my power ; name some commission in France which you wish me to execute."

" I can think of none—yet, stay,—" and I felt some curiosity to try the power of which he boasted—"I have read that kings are blest with a most accommodating memory, and perfectly forget their favourites, when they can be no longer useful. You will see, perhaps, if my father's name has become a gothic and unknown sound at the court of the Great King. I confess myself curious to learn this, though I can have no personal interest in it."

"Enough, the commission shall be done. And now, my child, Heaven bless you ! and send you many such friends as the humble

priest, who, whatever be his failings, has, at least, the merit of
wishing to serve those whom he loves."

So saying, the priest closed the door. · Sinking into a reverie, as
his footsteps died upon my ear, I muttered to myself :—"Well,
well, my sage ecclesiastic, the game is not over yet ; let us see if,
at sixteen, we cannot shuffle cards, and play tricks with the gamester
of thirty.   Yet, he may be in earnest, and faith I believe he is ; but
I must look well before I leap, or consign my actions into such
spiritual keeping.   However, if the worst come to the worst, if I
do make this compact, and am deceived—if, above all, I am ever
seduced, or led blindfold into one of those snares which priestcraft
sometimes lays to the cost of honour—why I shall have a sword,
which I shall never be at a loss to use, and it can find its way
through a priest's gown as well as a soldier's corslet."

Confess, that a youth, who could think so promptly of his sword,
was well fitted to wear one!

CHAPTER V.

RURAL HOSPITALITY—AN EXTRAORDINARY GUEST.   A FINE
GENTLEMAN IS NOT NECESSARILY A FOOL.

WE were all three (my brothers and myself) precocious
geniuses.   Our early instructions, under a man, like the
Abbé, at once learned and worldly, and the Society into
which we had been initiated from our childhood, made
us premature adepts in the manners of the world ; and I, in especial,
flattered myself that a quick habit of observation rendered me no
despicable profiter by my experience.   Our academy, too, had been
more like a college than a school ; and we had enjoyed a license
that seemed, to the superficial, more likely to benefit our manners
than to strengthen our morals.   I do not think, however, that the·
latter suffered by our freedom from restraint.   On the contrary, we
the earlier learnt that vice, but for the piquancy of its unlawfulness,
would never be so captivating a goddess ; and our errors and crimes,
in after life, had certainly not their origin in our wanderings out of
academical bounds.

It is right that I should mention our prematurity of intellect,
because, otherwise, much of my language and reflections, as detailed
in the first book of this history, might seem ill suited to the tender
age at which they occurred.   However, they approach, as nearly as

possible, to my state of mind at that period ; and I have, indeed, often mortified my vanity, in later life, by thinking how little the march of time has ripened my abilities, and how petty would have been the intellectual acquisitions of manhood—if they had not brought me something like content!

My uncle had always, during his retirement, seen as many people as he could assemble out of the "mob of gentlemen who *live at ease.*" But, on our quitting school, and becoming men, he resolved to set no bounds to his hospitality. His doors were literally thrown open ; and as he was by far the greatest person in the district—to say nothing of his wines, and his French cook—many of the good people of London did not think it too great an honour to confer upon the wealthy representative of the Devereuxs the distinction of their company and compliments. Heavens! what notable samples of court breeding and furbelows, did the crane-neck coaches, which made our own family vehicle look like a gilt tortoise, pour forth by couples and leashes into the great hall—while my gallant uncle, in new periwig, and a pair of silver-clocked stockings (a present from a *ci-devant* fine lady), stood at the far end of the picture gallery, to receive his visitors, with all the graces of the last age.

My mother, who had preserved her beauty wonderfully, sat in a chair of green velvet, and astonished the courtiers by the fashion of a dress only just imported. The worthy Countess (she had dropped in England the loftier distinction of *Madame la Maréchale*) was however quite innocent of any intentional affectation of the mode : for the new stomacher, so admired in London, had been the last alteration in female garniture at Paris, a month before my father died. Is not this "Fashion" a noble divinity to possess such zealous adherents !—a pitiful, lackey-like creature, which struts through one country with the cast-off finery of another !

As for Aubrey and Gerald, they produced quite an effect—and I should most certainly have been thrown irrevocably into the back-ground, had I not been born to the good fortune of an eldest son. This was far more than sufficient to atone for the comparative plainness of my person ; and when it was discovered that I was also Sir William's favourite, it is quite astonishing what a beauty I became! Aubrey was declared too effeminate ; Gerald too tall. And the Duchess of Lackland one day, when she had placed a lean, sallow, ghost of a daughter on either side of me, whispered my uncle in a voice, like the *aside* of a player, intended for none but the whole audience, that the young Count had the most imposing air and the finest eyes she had ever seen. All this inspired me with courage, as well as contempt ; and not liking to be beholden

solely to my priority of birth for my priority of distinction, I resolved
to become as agreeable as possible. If I had not in the vanity of
my heart resolved also to be "myself alone," Fate would have
furnished me at the happiest age for successful imitation with an
admirable model.

Time rolled on—two years have flown since I had left school,
and Montreuil was not yet returned. I had passed the age of
eighteen, when the whole house, which, as it was summer, when
none but cats and physicians were supposed gifted by Providence
with the power to exist in town, was uncommonly full—the whole
house, I say, was thrown into a positive fever of expectation. The
visit of a guest, if not of greater consequence, at least of greater
interest, than any who had hitherto honoured my uncle, was
announced. Even the young Count, with the most imposing air
in the world, and the finest eyes, was forgotten by everybody but
the Duchess of Lackland and her daughters, who had just returned
to Devereux Court, to observe how amazingly the Count had
grown! Oh! what a prodigy wisdom would be, if it were but
blest with a memory as keen and constant as that of interest!

Struck with the universal excitement, I went to my uncle to
inquire the name of the expected guest. My uncle was occupied
in fanning the Lady Hasselton, a daughter of one of King Charles's
Beauties. He had only time to answer me literally, and without
comment; the guest's name was Mr. St. John.

I had never conned the "Flying Post," and I knew nothing
about politics. "Who is Mr. St. John?" said I; my uncle had
renewed the office of a zephyr. The daughter of the Beauty heard
and answered, "The most charming person in England." I bowed
and turned away. "How vastly explanatory!" said I. I met
a furious politician. "Who is Mr. St. John?" I asked.

"The cleverest man in England," answered the politician, hurrying
off with a pamphlet in his hand.

"Nothing can be more satisfactory," thought I. Stopping a
coxcomb of the first water. "Who is Mr. St. John?" I asked.

"The finest gentleman in England," answered the coxcomb,
settling his cravat.

"Perfectly intelligible!" was my reflection on this reply; and I
forthwith arrested a Whig parson—"Who is Mr. St. John?" said I.

"The greatest reprobate in England!" answered the Whig
parson, and I was too stunned to inquire more.

Five minutes afterwards the sound of carriage wheels was heard
in the court-yard, then a slight bustle in the hall, and the door of
the ante-room being thrown open, Mr. St. John entered.

He was in the very prime of life, about the middle height, and of a mien and air so strikingly noble that it was some time before you recovered the general effect of his person sufficiently to examine its peculiar claims to admiration. However, he lost nothing by a farther survey: he possessed not only an eminently handsome, but a very extraordinary countenance. Through an air of non-chalanee, and even something of lassitude, through an ease of manners sometimes sinking into effeminate softness, sometimes bordering upon licentious effrontery, his eye thoughtful, yet wandering, seemed to announce that the mind partook but little of the whim of the moment, or of those levities of ordinary life over which the grace of his manner threw so peculiar a charm. His brow was, perhaps, rather too large and prominent, for the exactness of perfect symmetry; but it had an expression of great mental power and determination. His features were high, yet delicate, and his mouth, which, when closed, assumed a firm and rather severe expression, softened, when speaking, into a smile of almost magical enchantment. Richly, but not extravagantly dressed, he appeared to cultivate, rather than disdain, the ornaments of outward appearance; and whatever can fascinate or attract was so inherent in this singular man that all which in others would have been most artificial was in him most natural: so that it is no exaggeration to add that to be well dressed seemed to the elegance of his person not so much the result of art as of a property innate and peculiar to himself.

Such was the outward appearance of Henry St. John; one well suited to the qualities of a mind at once more vigorous and more accomplished than that of any other person with whom the vicissitudes of my life have ever brought me into contact.

I kept my eye on the new guest throughout the whole day; I observed the mingled liveliness and softness which pervaded his attentions to women, the intellectual, yet unpedantic superiority he possessed in his conversations with men; his respectful de-meanour to age: his careless, yet not over familiar, ease with the young; and, what interested me more than all, the occasional cloud which passed over his countenance at moments when he seemed sunk into a reverie that had for its objects nothing in common with those around him.

Just before dinner, St. John was talking to a little group, among whom curiosity seemed to have drawn the Whig parson whom I have before mentioned. He stood at a little distance, shy and uneasy; one of the company took advantage of so favourable a butt for jests, and alluded to the bystander in a witticism which drew laughter from all but St. John, who, turning suddenly towards the parson, addressed an observation to him in the most respectful tone. Nor did he cease talking with him (fatiguing as the conference must have been, for never was there a duller ecclesiastic than the gentleman conversed with) until we descended to dinner. Then, for the first time, I learned that nothing can constitute good breeding that has not good nature for its foundation :—and then, too, as I was leading Lady Barbara Lackland to the great hall, by the tip of her forefinger, I made another observation. Passing the priest, I heard him say to a fellow-clerk,

"Certainly, he is the greatest man in England ;" and I mentally remarked, "there is no policy like politeness ; and a good manner is the best thing in the world, either to get one a good name or to supply the want of it."

CHAPTER VI.

A DIALOGUE, WHICH MIGHT BE DULL IF IT WERE LONGER.

THREE days after the arrival of St. John, I escaped from the crowd of impertinents, seized a volume of Cowley, and, in a fit of mingled poetry and melancholy, strolled idly into the park. I came to the margin of the stream, and to the very spot on which I had stood with my uncle on the evening when he had first excited my emulation to scholastic rather than manual contention with my brother.—I seated myself by the water-side, and, feeling indisposed to read, leant my cheek upon my hand, and surrendered my thoughts as prisoners to the reflections which I could not resist.

I continued, I know not how long, in my meditation, till I was roused by a gentle touch upon my shoulder : I looked up, and saw St. John.

"Pardon me, Count," said he, smiling, "I should not have disturbed your reflections had not your neglect of an old friend emboldened me to address you upon his behalf."—And St. John pointed to the volume of Cowley which he had taken up without my perceiving it.

"Well," added he, seating himself on the turf beside me, "in my younger days, poetry and I were better friends than we are now. And if I had had Cowley as a companion, I should not have parted with him as you have done, even for my own reflections."

"You admire him, then ? " said I.

"Why, that is too general a question. I admire what is fine in him, as in every one else, but I do not love him the better for his points and his conceits. He reminds me of what Cardinal Pallavicino said of Seneca, that he 'perfumes his conceits with civet and amber-gris.' However, Count, I have opened upon a beautiful motto for you:

> Here let me, careless and unthoughtful lying,
> Hear the soft winds above me flying,
> With all their wanton bows dispute,
> And the more tuneful birds to both replying;
> Nor be myself too mute.

What say you to that wish? If you have a germ of poetry in you, such verse ought to bring it into flower."

"Ay," answered I, though not exactly in accordance with the truth; "but I have not the germ. I destroyed it four years ago. Reading the dedications of poets cured me of the love for poetry. What a pity that the Divine Inspiration should have for its oracles such mean souls!"

"Yes, and how industrious the good gentlemen are in debasing themselves. Their ingenuity is never half so much shown in a simile as in a compliment; I know nothing in nature more melancholy than the discovery of any meanness in a great man. There is so little to redeem the dry mass of follies and errors from which the materials of this life are composed, that anything to love or to reverence becomes, as it were, the sabbath for the mind. It is bitter to feel, as we grow older, how the respite is abridged, and how the few objects left to our admiration are abased. What a foe not only to life, but to all that dignifies and ennobles it, is Time! Our affections and our pleasures resemble those fabulous trees described by St. Oderic—the fruits which they bring forth are no sooner ripened into maturity than they are transformed into birds, and fly away. But these reflections cannot yet be familiar to you. Let us return to Cowley. Do you feel any sympathy with his prose writings? For some minds they have a great attraction."

"They have for mine," answered I: "but then I am naturally a dreamer; and a contemplative egotist is always to me a mirror in which I behold myself."

"The world," answered St. John, with a melancholy smile, "will soon dissolve, or for ever confirm, your humour for dreaming; in either case, Cowley will not be less a favourite. But you must, like me, have long toiled in the heat and travail of business, or of pleasure, which is more wearisome still, in order fully to sympathize with those beautiful panegyrics upon solitude which make, perhaps, the finest passages in Cowley. I have often thought that he whom God hath gifted with a love of retirement possesses, as it were, an extra sense. And among what our poet so eloquently calls 'the vast and noble scenes of nature,' we find the balm for the wounds we have sustained among the 'pitiful shifts of policy ;'—for the attachment to solitude is the surest preservative from the ills of life : and I know not if the Romans ever instilled, under allegory, a sublimer truth than when they inculcated the belief that those inspired by Fcronia, the goddess of woods and forests could walk barefoot and uninjured over burning coals."

At this part of our conference, the bell swinging hoarsely through the long avenues, and over the silent water, summoned us to the grand occupation of civilized life ; we rose and walked slowly towards the house.

"Does not," said I, "this regular routine of petty occurrences— this periodical solemnity of trifles, weary and disgust you ? For my part, I almost long for the old days of knight-errantry, and would rather be knocked on the head by a giant, or carried through the air by a flying griffin, than live in this circle of dull regularities —the brute at the mill."

"You may live even in these days," answered St. John, "without too tame a regularity. Women and politics furnish ample food for adventure, and you must not judge of all life by country life."

"Nor of all conversation," said I, with a look which implied a compliment, "by the insipid idlers who fill our saloons. Behold them now, gathered by the oriel window, yonder; precious distillers of talk — sentinels of society with certain set phrases as watchwords, which they never exceed ; sages, who follow Face's advice to Dapper—
Hum thrice, and buzz as often."

CHAPTER VII.

A CHANGE OF PROSPECTS—A NEW INSIGHT INTO THE CHARACTER OF THE HERO—A CONFERENCE BETWEEN TWO BROTHERS.

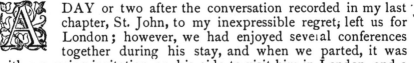 DAY or two after the conversation recorded in my last chapter, St. John, to my inexpressible regret; left us for London ; however, we had enjoyed several conferences together during his stay, and when we parted, it was with a pressing invitation on his side to visit him in London, and a most faithful promise on mine, to avail myself of the request.

No sooner was he fairly gone than I went to seek my uncle; I found him reading one of Farquhar's comedies. Despite my sorrow at interrupting him in so venerable a study, I was too full of my new plot to heed breaking off that in the comedy. In very few words I made the good knight understand that his descriptions had infected me, and that I was dying to ascertain their truth; in a word, that his hopeful nephew was fully bent on going to town. My uncle first stared, then swore, then paused, then looked at his leg, drew up his stocking, frowned, whistled, and told me at last to talk to him about it another time. Now, for my part, I think there are only two classes of people in the world, authorized to put one off to "another time,"—prime ministers and creditors; accordingly, I would not take my uncle's dismissal. I had not read plays, studied philosophy, and laid snares for the Abbé Montreuil, without deriving some little wisdom from my experience; so I took to teasing, and a notable plan it is too! Whoever has pursued it may guess the result! My uncle yielded, and that day fortnight was fixed for my departure.

Oh! with what transport did I look forward to the completion of my wishes, the goal of my ambition. I hastened forth—I hurried into the woods—I sang out in the gladness of my heart, like a bird released—I drank in the air with a rapturous sympathy in its freedom; my step scarcely touched the earth, and my whole frame seemed ethereal—elated—exalted—by the vivifying inspiration of my hopes. I paused by a little streamlet, which, brawling over stones and through unpenetrated thicknesses of wood, seemed, like confined ambition, not the less restless for its obscurity.

"Wild brooklet," I cried, as my thoughts rushed into words, "fret on, our lot is no longer the same; your wanderings and your murmurs are wasted in solitude and shade; your voice dies and re-awakes, but without an echo; your waves spread around their path neither fertility nor terror; their anger is idle, and their freshness is lavished on a sterile soil; the sun shines in vain for you, through these unvarying wastes of silence and gloom; Fortune freights not your channel with her hoarded stores, and Pleasure ventures not her silken sails upon your tide; not even the solitary idler roves beside you, to consecrate with human fellowship your melancholy course; no shape of beauty bends over your turbid waters, or mirrors in your breast the loveliness that hallows earth. Lonely and sullen, through storm or sunshine, you repine along your desolate way and only catch, through the matted boughs that darken over you, the beams of the wan stars, which, like human hopes, tremble upon your breast, and are broken, even before they

fade, by the very turbulence of the surface on which they fall.
Rove—repine—murmur on! Such was my fate, but the resemblance
is no more. I shall no longer be a lonely and regretful being; my
affections will no longer waste themselves upon barrenness and
stone. I go among the living and warm world of mortal energies
and desires; my existence shall glide alternately through crested
cities, and bowers in which Poetry worships Love; and the clear
depths of my heart shall reflect whatever its young dreams have
shadowed forth—the visioned form—the gentle and fairy spirit—
the Eve of my soul's imagined and foreboded paradise."

Venting, in this incoherent strain, the exultation which filled my
thoughts, I wandered on, throughout the whole day, till my spirits
had exhausted themselves by indulgence; and, wearied alike by
mental excitement and bodily exertion, I turned, with slow steps,
towards the house. As I ascended the gentle acclivity on which it
stood, I saw a figure approaching towards me; the increasing
shades of the evening did not allow me to recognize the shape until
it was almost by my side—it was Aubrey.

Of late I had seen very little of him. His devotional studies and
habits seemed to draw him from the idle pursuits of myself and my
uncle's guests; and Aubrey was one peculiarly susceptible of neglect,
and sore, to morbidity, at the semblance of unkindness; so that he
required to be sought, and rarely troubled others with advances:
that night, however, his greeting was unusually warm.

"I was uneasy about you, Morton," said he, drawing my arm in
his; "you have not been seen since morning; and, oh! Morton,
my uncle told me, with tears in his eyes, that you were going to
leave us. Is it so?"

"Had he tears in his eyes? Kind old man! And you, Aubrey,
shall you, too, grieve for my departure?"

"Can you ask it, Morton? But why will you leave us? Are we
not all happy here, now? *Now* that there is no longer any barrier
or difference between us—*now* that I may look upon you, and listen
to you, and love you, and *own* that I love you? Why will you
leave us now? And"—(continued Aubrey, as if fearful of giving me
time to answer)—"and every one praises you so here; and my uncle
and all of us are so proud of you. Why should you desert our
affections merely because they are not new? Why plunge into that
hollow and cold world which all who have tried it picture in such
fearful hues? Can you find anything there to repay you for the love
you leave behind?"

"My brother," said I, mournfully, and in a tone which startled
him, it was so different from that which I usually assumed,—"my

brother, hear, before you reproach me. Let us sit down upon this bank, and I will suffer you to see more of my restless and secret heart than any hitherto have beheld."

We sat down upon a little mound—how well I remember the spot! I can see the tree which shadows it, from my window at this moment. How many seasons have the sweet herb and the emerald grass been withered there and renewed! Ah, what is this revival of all things fresh and youthful in external nature, but a mockery of the wintry spot which lies perished and *irrenewable* within!

We drew near to each other, and as my arm wound around him, I said, "Aubrey, your love has been to me a more precious gift than any who have not, like me, thirsted and longed even for the love of a dog, can conceive. Never let me loose that affection! And do not think of me hereafter as of one whose heart echoed all that his lip uttered. Do not believe that irony, and sarcasm, and bitterness of tongue, flowed from a malignant or evil source. That disposition which seems to you alternately so light and gloomy had, perhaps, its origin in a mind too intense in its affections, and too exacting in having them returned. Till you sought my friendship, three short years ago, none but my uncle, with whom I could have nothing in common but attachment, seemed to care for my very existence. I blame them not; they were deceived in my nature; but blame *me* not too severely if my temper suffered from their mistake. Your friendship came to me, not too late to save me from a premature misanthropy, but too late to eradicate every morbidity of mind. Something of sternness on the one hand, and of satire on the other, has mingled so long with my better feelings that the taint and the stream have become inseparable. Do not sigh, Aubrey. To be unamiable is not to be ungrateful; and I shall not love you the less if I have but a few objects to love. You ask me my inducement to leave you. 'The World' will be sufficient answer. I cannot share your contempt of it, nor your fear. I am and have been of late, consumed with a thirst—eager, and burning, and unquenchable—it is ambition!"

"Oh, Morton!" said Aubrey, with a second sigh, longer and deeper than the first—"that evil passion! the passion which lost an angel Heaven."

"Let us not now dispute, my brother, whether it be sinful in itself, or whether, if its object be virtuous, it is not a virtue. In baring my soul before you, I only speak of my motives; and seek not to excuse them. Perhaps on this earth there is no good without a little evil. When my mind was once turned to the acquisition of mental superiority every petty acquisition I made increased my desire to attain more, and partial emulation soon widened into universal ambition. We three, Gerald and ourselves, are the keepers of a treasure more valuable than gold—the treasure of a not ignoble nor sullied name. For my part, I confess that I am impatient to increase the store of honour which our father bequeathed to us. Nor is this all: despite our birth, we are poor in the gifts of fortune. We are all dependents on my uncle's favour; and, however we may deserve it, there would be something better in earning an independence for ourselves."

"That," said Aubrey, "may be an argument for mine and Gerald's exertions; but not for yours. You are the eldest, and my uncle's favourite. Nature and affection both point to you as his heir."

"If so, Aubrey, may many years pass before that inheritance be mine. Why should those years, that might produce so much, lie fallow? But though I would not affect an unreal delicacy, and disown my chance of future fortune, yet you must remember that it is a matter possible, not certain. My birthright gives me no claim over my uncle, whose estates are in his own gift; and favour, even in the good, is a wind which varies without power on our side to calculate the season or the cause. However this be,—and I love the person on whom fortune depends so much that I cannot, without pain, speak of the mere chance of its passing from his possession into mine,—you will own at least that I shall not hereafter deserve wealth the less for the advantages of experience."

"Alas!" said Aubrey, raising his eyes, "the worship of our Father in Heaven finds us ample cause for occupation, even in retirement; and the more we mix with His creatures, the more, I fear, we may forget the Creator. But, if it must be so, I will pray for you, Morton; and you will remember that the powerless and poor Aubrey can still lift up his voice in your behalf."

As Aubrey thus spoke, I looked with mingled envy and admiration upon the countenance beside me, which the beauty of a spirit seemed at once to soften and to exalt.

Since our conference had begun, the dusk of twilight had melted away; and the moon had called into lustre—living, indeed, but unlike the common and unhallowing life of day—the wood and herbage, and silent variations of hill and valley, which slept around us; and, as the still and shadowy light fell over the upward face of my brother, it gave to his features an additional, and not wholly earth-born, solemnity of expression. There was indeed in his face and air that from which the painter of a seraph might not have disdained to copy; something resembling the vision of an angel in the dark eyes that swam with tears, in which emotion had so little of mortal dross—in the youthful and soft cheeks, which the earnestness of divine thought had refined by a pale but transparent hue—in the high and unclouded forehead, over which the hair, parted in the centre, fell in long and wavelike curls—and in the lips, silent, yet moving with internal prayer, which seemed the more fervent, because unheard.

I did not interrupt him in the prayer, which my soul felt, though my ear caught it not, was for me. But when he had ceased, and turned towards me, I clasped him to my breast. "My brother," I said, "we shall part, it is true, but not till our hearts have annihilated the space that was between them ; not till we have felt that the love of brotherhood can pass the love of woman. Whatever await you, your devoted and holy mind will be, if not your shield from affliction, at least your balm for its wounds. Remain here. The quiet which breathes around you well becomes your tranquillity within ; and sometimes bless me in your devotions, as you have done now. For me, I shall nòt regret those harder and harsher qualities which you blame in me ; if hereafter their very sternness can afford me an opportunity of protecting your gentleness from evil, or redressing the wrongs from which your nature may be too innocent to preserve you. And now let us return home, in the conviction that we have in our friendship one treasure beyond the reach of fate."

Aubrey did not answer ; but he kissed my forehead, and I felt his tears upon my cheek. We rose, and with arms still embracing each other as we walked, bent our steps to the house.

Ah, earth ! what hast thou more beautiful than the love of those whose ties are knit by nature, and whose union seems ordained to begin from the very moment of their birth ?

CHAPTER VIII.

FIRST LOVE.

WE are under very changeful influences in this world ! The night on which occurred the interview with Aubrey, that I have just narrated, I was burning to leave Devereux Court. Within one little week from that time my eagerness was wonderfully abated. The sagacious reader will readily discover the cause of this alteration. About eight miles from my uncle's house was a seaport town ; there were many and varied

C

rides leading to it, and the town was a favourite place of visitation with all the family. Within a few hundred yards of the town was a small cottage, prettily situated in the midst of a garden, kept with singular neatness, and ornamented with several rare shrubs and exotics. I had more than once observed in the garden of this house a female in the very first blush of youth, and beautiful enough to excite within me a strong curiosity to learn the owner of the cottage. I inquired, and ascertained that its tenant was a Spaniard of high birth, and one who had acquired a melancholy celebrity by his conduct and misfortunes in the part he had taken in a certain feeble but gallant insurrection in his native country. He had only escaped with life and a very small sum of money, and now lived in the obscure seaport of ——, a refugee and a recluse. He was a widower, and had only one child—a daughter ; and I was therefore at no loss to discover who was the beautiful female I had noted and admired.

On the day after my conversation with Aubrey, detailed in the last chapter, in riding past this cottage alone, I perceived a crowd assembled round the entrance ; I paused to inquire the cause.

"Why, your honour," quoth a senior of the village, "I believe the tipstaves be come to take the foreigner for not paying his rent ; and he does not understand our English liberty like, and has drawn his sword, and swears, in his outlandish lingo, he will not be made prisoner alive."

I required no further inducement to make me enter the house. The crowd gave way when they saw me dismount, and suffered me to penetrate into the first apartment. There I found the gallant old Spaniard with his sword drawn, keeping at bay a couple of sturdy-looking men, who appeared to be only prevented from using violence by respect for the person, or the safety, of a young woman, who clung to her father's knees, and implored him not to resist, where resistance was so unavailing. Let me cut short this scene—I dismissed the bailiffs, and paid the debt. I then endeavoured to explain to the Spaniard, in French, for he scarcely understood three words of our language, the cause of a rudeness towards him which he persisted in calling a great insult and inhospitality manifested to a stranger and an exile. I succeeded at length in pacifying him. I remained for more than an hour at the cottage, and I left it with a heart beating at the certain persuasion that I had established therein the claim of acquaintance and visitation.

Will the reader pardon me for having curtailed this scene ? It is connected with a subject on which I shall better endure to dwell as my narrative proceeds. From that time I paid frequent visits to the cottage ; the Spaniard soon grew intimate with me, and I thought the daughter began to blush when I entered, and to sigh when I departed.

One evening I was conversing with Don Diego D'Alvarez (such was the Spaniard's name), as he sat without his threshold, inhaling the gentle air, that stole freshness from the rippling sea that spread before us, and fragrance from the earth, over which the summer now reigned in its most mellow glory. Isora (the daughter) sat at a little distance.

"How comes it," said Don Diego, "that you have never met our friend Señor Bar—Bar—these English names are always escaping my memory. How is he called, Isora?"

"Mr.—Mr. Barnard," said Isora (who, brought early to England, spoke its language like a native), but with evident confusion, and looking down as she spoke—"Mr. Barnard, I believe, you mean."

"Right, my love," rejoined the Spaniard, who was smoking a long pipe with great gravity, and did not notice his daughter's embarrassment—"a fine youth, but somewhat shy and over-modest in manner."

"Youth!" thought I, and I darted a piercing look towards Isora. "How comes it, indeed," I said aloud, "that I have not met him? Is he a friend of long standing?"

"Nay, not very—perhaps of some six weeks earlier date than you, Señor Don Devereux. I pressed him, when he called this morning, to tarry your coming ; but, poor youth, he is diffident, and not yet accustomed to mix freely with strangers, especially those of rank ; our own presence a little overawes him"—and from Don Diego's gray mustachios issued a yet fuller cloud than was ordinarily wont to emerge thence.

My eyes were still fixed on Isora ; she looked up, met them, blushed deeply, rose, and disappeared within the house. I was already susceptible of jealousy. My lip trembled, as I resumed : "And will Don Diego pardon me for inquiring how commenced his knowledge of this ingenuous youth?"

The question was a little beyond the pale of good breeding ; perhaps the Spaniard, who was tolerably punctilious, in such matters, thought so, for he did not reply. I was sensible of my error, and apologizing for it, insinuated, nevertheless, the question in a more respectful and covert shape. Still Don Diego, inhaling the fragrant weed with renewed vehemence, only—like Pion's tomb, recorded by Pausanias—replied to the request of his petitioner *by smoke.* I did not venture to renew my interrogatories, and there was a long silence. My eyes fixed their gaze on the door by which Isora had disappeared. In vain; she returned not—and as the chill of the increasing evening began now to make itself felt by the frame of one accustomed to warmer skies, the Spaniard soon rose to re-enter his house, and I took my farewell for the night.

There were many ways (as I before said) by which I could return home, all nearly equal in picturesque beauty; for the county in which my uncle's estates were placed was one where stream roved and woodland flourished even to the very strand, or cliff of the sea. The shortest *route*, though one the least frequented by any except foot-passengers, was along the coast, and it was by this path that I rode slowly homeward. On winding a curve in the road about one mile from Devereux Court, the old building broke slowly, tower by tower, upon me. I have never yet described the house, and perhaps it will not be uninteresting to the reader if I do so now.

It had anciently belonged to Ralph de Bigod. From his possession it had passed into that of the then noblest branch of the stem of Devereux, whence, without break or flaw in the direct line of heritage, it had ultimately descended to the present owner. It was a pile of vast extent, built around three quadrangular courts, the farthest of which spread to the very verge of the gray, tall cliffs that overhung the sea: in this court was a rude tower, which, according to tradition, had contained the apartments ordinarily inhabited by our ill-fated namesake and distant kinsman, Robert Devereux, the favourite and the victim of Elizabeth, whenever he had honoured the mansion with a visit. There was nothing, it is true, in the old tower calculated to flatter the tradition, for it contained only two habitable rooms, communicating with each other, and by no means remarkable for size or splendour; and every one of our household, save myself, was wont to discredit the idle rumour which would assign to so distinguished a guest so unseemly a lodgment. But, as I looked from the narrow lattices of the chambers, over the wide expanse of ocean and of land which they commanded—as I noted, too, that the tower was utterly separated from the rest of the house, and that the convenience of its site enabled one, on quitting it, to escape at once, and privately, either to the solitary beach, or to the glades and groves of the wide park which stretched behind—I could not help indulging the belief that the unceremonious, and not unromantic noble, had himself selected his place of retirement, and that, in so doing, the gallant of a stately court was not, perhaps, undesirous of securing at well-chosen moments a brief relaxation from the heavy honours of country homage—or that the patron and poetic admirer of the dreaming Spenser might have preferred, to all more gorgeous accommodation, the quiet and unseen egress to that sea and shore, which, if we may believe the accomplished Roman,[1] are so fertile in the powers of inspiration.

However this be, I had cheated myself into the belief that my conjecture was true, and I had petitioned my uncle, when, on leaving school, he assigned to each of us our several apartments, to grant me the exclusive right to this dilapidated tower. I gained my boon easily enough; and—so strangely is our future fate compounded from past trifles,—I verily believe that the strong desire which thenceforth seized me to visit courts, and mix with statesmen—which afterwards hurried me into intrigue, war, the plots of London, the dissipations of Paris, the perilous schemes of Petersburg, nay, the very hardships of a Cossack tent—was first formed by the imaginary honour of inhabiting the same chamber as the glittering but ill-fated courtier of my own name. Thus youth imitates, where it should avoid; and thus that which should have been to me a warning became an example.

In the oaken floor to the outer chamber of this tower was situated a trap-door, the entrance into a lower room or rather cell, fitted up as a bath; and here a wooden door opened into a long subterranean passage that led out into a cavern by the sea-shore. This cave, partly by nature, partly by art, was hollowed into a beautiful Gothic form : and here, on moonlight evenings, when the sea crept gently over the yellow and smooth sands, and the summer tempered the air from too keen a freshness, my uncle had often in his younger days, ere gout and rheum had grown familiar images, assembled his guests. It was a place which the echoes peculiarly adapted for music; and the scene was certainly not calculated to diminish the effect of "sweet sounds." Even now, though my uncle rarely joined us, we were often wont to hold our evening revels in this spot; and the high cliffs, circling either side in the form of a bay, tolerably well concealed our meetings from the gaze of the vulgar. It is true (for these cliffs were perforated with numerous excavations), that some roving peasant, mariner, or perchance smuggler, would now and then, at low water, intrude upon us. But our London Nereids and courtly Tritons were always well pleased with the interest of what they graciously termed "an adventure :" and our assemblies were too numerous to think an unbroken secrecy indispensable. Hence, therefore, the cavern was almost considered a part of the house itself; and though there was an iron door at the entrance which it

[1] "O mare, O litus, verum secretumque Μουσειον, quam multa dictatis—quam multa invenitis !"—PLINIUS.
"O sea, O shore, true and secret sanctuary of the Muses, how many things ye dictate, how many things ye discover."

gave to the passage leading to my apartments, yet so great was our confidence in our neighbours or ourselves that it was rarely secured, save as a defence against the high tides of winter.

The stars were shining quietly over the old gray castle (for castle it really was), as I now came within view of it. To the left, and in the rear of the house, the trees of the park, grouped by distance, seemed blent into one thick mass of wood; to the right, as I now (descending the cliff by a gradual path) entered on the level sands, and at about the distance of a league from the main shore, a small islet, notorious as the resort and shelter of contraband adventurers, scarcely relieved the wide and glassy azure of the waves. The tide was out; and passing through one of the arches worn in the bay, I came somewhat suddenly by the cavern. Seated there on a crag of stone I found Aubrey.

My acquaintance with Isora and her father had so immediately succeeded the friendly meeting with Aubrey which I last recorded, and had so utterly engrossed my time and thoughts, that I had not taken of that interview all the brotherly advantage which I might have done. My heart now smote me for my involuntary negligence. I dismounted, and fastening my horse to one of a long line of posts that ran into the sea, approached Aubrey and accosted him.

"Alone, Aubrey? and at an hour when my uncle always makes the old walls ring with revel! Hark, can you not hear the music even now? it comes from the ball-room, I think, does it not?"

"Yes," said Aubrey, briefly, and looking down upon a devotional book, which (as was his wont) he had made his companion.

"And we are the only truants!—Well, Gerald will supply our places with a lighter step, and, perhaps, a merrier heart."

Aubrey sighed. I bent over him affectionately (I loved that boy with something of a father's as well as a brother's love), and as I did bend over him, I saw that his eyelids were red with weeping.

"My brother—my own dear brother," said I, "what grieves you?—are we not friends, and more than friends?—what can grieve you that grieves not me?"

Suddenly raising his head, Aubrey gazed at me with a long, searching intentness of eye; his lips moved, but he did not answer.

"Speak to me, Aubrey," said I, passing my arm over his shoulder; "has any one, any thing, hurt you? See, now, if I cannot remedy the evil."

"Morton," said Aubrey, speaking very slowly, "do you believe that Heaven pre-orders as well as foresees our destiny?"

"It is the schoolman's question," said I, smiling, "but I know how these idle subtleties vex the mind—and you, my brother, are ever too occupied with considerations of the future. If Heaven *does* pre-order our destiny, we know that Heaven is merciful, and we should be fearless, as we arm ourselves in that knowledge."

"Morton Devereux," said Aubrey, again repeating my name, and with an evident inward effort that left his lip colourless, and yet lit his dark dilating eye with a strange and unwonted fire—"Morton Devereux, I feel that I am predestined to the power of the Evil One!"

I drew back, inexpressibly shocked. "Good Heavens!" I exclaimed, "what can induce you to cherish so terrible a phantasy? what can induce you to wrong so fearfully the goodness and mercy of our Creator?"

Aubrey shrunk from my arm, which had still been round him, and covered his face with his hands. I took up the book he had been reading: it was a Latin treatise on predestination, and seemed fraught with the most gloomy and bewildering subtleties. I sat down beside him, and pointed out the various incoherencies and contradictions of the work, and the doctrine it espoused—so long and so earnestly did I speak that at length Aubrey looked up, seemingly cheered and relieved.

"I wish," said he, timidly, "I wish that you loved me, and that you loved *me only*:—but you love pleasure, and power, and show, and wit, and revelry; and you know not what it is to feel for me, as I ee at times for you—nay, perhaps you really dislike or despise me."

Aubrey's voice grew bitter in its tone as he concluded these words, and I was instantly impressed with the belief that some one had insinuated distrust of my affection for him.

"Why should you think thus?" I said: "has any cause occurred of late to make you deem my affection for you weaker than it was? Has any one hinted a surmise that I do not repay your brotherly regard?"

Aubrey did not answer.

"Has Gerald," I continued, "jealous of our mutual attachment, uttered aught tending to diminish it? Yes, I see that he has."

Aubrey remained motionless, sullenly gazing downward and still silent.

"Speak," said I, "in justice to both of us—speak! You know, Aubrey, how I *have* loved and love you: put your arms round me, and say that thing on earth which you wish me to do, and it shall be done!"

Aubrey looked up ; he met my eyes, and he threw himself upon my neck, and burst into a violent paroxysm of tears.

I was greatly affected. "I see my fault," said I, soothing him ; "you are angry, and with justice, that I have neglected you of late ; and, perhaps, while I ask your confidence, you suspect that there is some subject on which I should have granted you mine. You are right, and, at a fitter moment, I will. Now let us turn homeward : our uncle is never merry when we are absent ; and when my mother misses your dark locks and fair cheek, I fancy that she sees little beauty in the ball. And yet, Aubrey," I added, as he now rose from my embrace, and dried his tears, "I will own to you that I love this scene better than any, however gay, within ; " and I turned to the sea, starlit as it was, and murmuring with a silver voice, and I became suddenly silent.

There was a long pause. I believe we both felt the influence of the scene around us, softening and tranquillizing our hearts ; for, at length, Aubrey put his hand in mine, and said, "You were always more generous and kind than I, Morton, though there are times when you seem different from what you are ; and I know you have already forgiven me."

I drew him affectionately towards me, and we went home.

But although I meant, from that night, to devote myself more to Aubrey than I had done of late, my hourly increasing love for Isora interfered greatly with my resolution. In order, however, to excuse any future neglect, I, the very next morning, bestowed upon him my confidence. Aubrey did not much encourage my passion : he represented to me Isora's situation—my own youth—my own worldly ambition—and, more than all (reminding me of my uncle's aversion even to the most prosperous and well-suited marriage), he insisted upon the certainty that Sir William would never yield consent to the lawful consummation of so unequal a love. I was not too well pleased with this reception of my tale, and I did not much trouble my adviser with any farther communication and confidence on the subject. Day after day I renewed my visits to the Spaniard's cottage ; and yet time passed on, and I had not told Isora a syllable of my love. I was inexpressibly jealous of this Barnard, whom her father often eulogized, and whom I never met. There appeared to be some mystery in his acquaintance with Don Diego, which that personage carefully concealed ; and once, when I was expressing my surprise to have so often missed seeing his friend, the Spaniard shook his head gravely, and said that he had now learnt the real reason for it : there were circumstances of state which made men fearful of new acquaintances, even in their own country. He drew back, as if he had said too much, and left me to conjecture that Barnard was connected with him in some intrigue, more delightful in itself than agreeable to the government. This belief was strengthened by my noting that Alvarez was frequently absent from home, and this, too, in the evening, when he was generally wont to shun the bleakness of the English air—an atmosphere, by the by, which I once heard a Frenchman wittily compare to Augustus placed between Horace and Virgil; viz., in the *bon mot* of the emperor himself—*between sighs and tears.*

But Isora herself never heard the name of this Barnard mentioned without a visible confusion, which galled me to the heart; and at length, unable to endure any longer my suspense upon the subject, I resolved to seek from her own lips its termination. I long tarried my opportunity; it was one evening, that, coming rather unexpectedly to the cottage, I was informed by the single servant that Don Diego had gone to the neighbouring town, but that Isora was in the garden. Small as it was, this garden had been cultivated with some care, and was not devoid of variety. A high and very thick fence of living box-wood, closely interlaced with the honeysuckle and the common rose, screened a few plots of rarer flowers, a small circular fountain, and a rustic arbour, both from the sea breezes and the eyes of any passer by, to which the open and unsheltered portion of the garden was exposed. When I passed through the opening cut in the fence, I was somewhat surprised at not immediately seeing Isora. Perhaps she was in the arbour. I approached the arbour tremblingly. What was my astonishment and my terror when I beheld her stretched lifeless on the ground!

I uttered a loud cry, and sprang forwards. I raised her from the earth, and supported her in my arms; her complexion—through whose pure and transparent white the wandering blood was wont so gently, yet so glowingly, to blush, undulating while it blushed, as youngest rose-leaves which the air just stirs into trembling—was blanched into the hues of death. My kisses tinged it with a momentary colour not its own; and yet as I pressed her to my heart, methought hers, which seemed still before, began, as if by an involuntary sympathy, palpably and suddenly to throb against my own. My alarm melted away as I held her thus—nay, I would not, if I could, have recalled her *yet* to life—I was forgetful—I was unheeding—I was unconscious of all things else—a few broken and passionate words escaped my lips, but even they ceased when I felt her breath just stirring and mingling with my own. It seemed to me as if all living kind but ourselves had, by a spell, departed from the earth, and we were left alone with the breathless and

C 2

inaudible Nature from which spring the love and the life of all things.

Isora slowly recovered ; her eyes, in opening, dwelt upon mine— her blood rushed at once to her cheek, and as suddenly left it hueless as before. She rose from my embrace, but I still extended my arms towards her ; and words over which I had no control, and of which now I have no remembrance, rushed from my lips. Still pale, and leaning against the side of the arbour, Isora heard me, as—confused, incoherent, impetuous, but still intelligible to her —my released heart poured itself forth. And when I had ceased, she turned her face towards me, and my blood seemed at once frozen in its channel. Anguish, deep ineffable anguish, was depicted upon every feature ; and when she strove at last to speak, her lips quivered so violently that, after a vain effort, she ceased abruptly. I again approached — I seized her hand, which I covered with my kisses.

"Will you not answer me, Isora?" said I, tremblingly. "*Be* silent, then ; but give me one look, one glance of hope, of pardon, from those dear eyes, and I ask no more."

Isora's whole frame seemed sinking beneath her emotions ; she raised her head, and looked hurriedly and fearfully round ; my eye followed hers, and I then saw upon the damp ground the recent print of a man's footstep, not my own ; and close to the spot where I had found Isora, lay a man's glove. A pang shot through me—I felt my eyes flash fire, and my brow darken, as I turned to Isora, and said, " I see it—I see all,—I have a rival, who has but just left you —you love me not—your affections are for him !" Isora sobbed violently, but made no reply. " You love him," said I, but in a milder and more mournful tone—"you love him—it is enough—I will persecute you no more ; and yet—" I paused a moment, for the remembrance of many a sign, which my heart had interpreted flatter-ingly, flashed upon me, and my voice faltered. " Well, I have no right to murmur—only, Isora—only tell me with your lips that you love another, and I will depart in peace"

Very slowly Isora turned her eyes to me, and even through her tears they dwelt upon me with a tender and a soft reproach.

" You love another?" said I—and from her lips, which scarcely parted, came a single word which thrilled to my heart like fire,— " *No!* "

" No ! " I repeated, " No ?—say that again, and again ;—yet who then is this that has dared so to agitate and overpower you ? Who is he whom you have met, and whom, even now while I speak, you tremble to hear me recur to ? Answer me one word—is it this

mysterious stranger whom your father honours with his friendship?
—is it Barnard?"

Alarm and fear again wholly engrossed the expression of Isora's
countenance.

"Barnard!" she said, "yes—yes—it is Barnard!"

"Who is he?" I cried vehemently—"who or what is he?—and
of what nature is his influence upon you? Confide in me"—and I
poured forth a long tide of inquiry and solicitation.

By the time I had ended, Isora seemed to have recovered herself.
With her softness, was mingled something of spirit and of self-
control, which was rare alike in her country and her sex.

"Listen to me!" said she, and her voice, which faltered a little
at first, grew calm and firm as she proceeded. "You profess to
love me—I am not worthy your love ; and if Count Devereux, I do
not reject nor disclaim it—for I am a woman and a weak and fond
one—I will not at least wrong you by encouraging hopes which I
may not and I dare not fulfil. I cannot—" here she spoke with
a fearful distinctness,—" I cannot, I can never, be yours ; and when
you ask me to be so, you know not what you ask nor what perils
you incur.—Enough—I am grateful to you. The poor exiled girl
is grateful for your esteem—and—and your affection. She will
never forget them,—never ! But be this our last meeting—our very
last—God bless you, Morton !" and, as she read my heart, pierced
and agonized as it was, in my countenance, Isora bent over me, for
I knelt beside her, and I felt her tears upon my cheek,—"God bless
you—and farewell."

"You insult, you wound me," said I bitterly, "by this cold and
taunting kindness ; tell me, tell me only, who it is that you love
better than me."

Isora had turned to leave me, for I was too proud to detain her ;
but when I said this, she came back, after a moment's pause, and
laid her hand upon my arm.

"If it make you happy to know *my* unhappiness," she said, and
the tone of her voice made me look full in her face, which was one
deep blush, "know that I am not insensible—"

I heard no more—my lips pressed themselves involuntarily to
hers—a long, long kiss—burning—intense—concentrating emotion,
heart, soul, all the rays of life's light into a single focus ;—and she
tore herself from me—and I was alone.

CHAPTER IX.

A DISCOVERY, AND A DEPARTURE.

HASTENED home after my eventful interview with Isora, and gave myself up to tumultuous and wild conjecture. Aubrey sought me the next morning—I narrated to him all that had occurred—he said little, but that little enraged me, for it was contrary to the dictates of my own wishes. The character of Morose in the "Silent Woman," is by no means an uncommon one. Many men—certainly many lovers—would say with equal truth, always provided they had equal candour—"All discourses but my own afflict me; they seem harsh, impertinent, and irksome." Certainly I felt that amiable sentiment most sincerely, with regard to Aubrey. I left him abruptly—a resolution possessed me—"I will see," said I, "this Barnard; I will lie in wait for him; I will demand and obtain, though it be by force, the secret which evidently subsists between him and this exiled family."

Full of this idea, I drew my cloak round me, and repaired on foot to the neighbourhood of the Spaniard's cottage. There was no place near it very commodious for accommodation both of vigil and concealment. However, I made a little hill, in a field opposite the house, my warder's station, and, lying at full length on the ground, wrapt in my cloak, I trusted to escape notice. The day passsed—no visitor appeared. The next morning I went from my own rooms, through the subterranean passage, into the Castle Cave, as the excavation I have before described was generally termed. On the shore I saw Gerald, by one of the small fishing-boats usually kept there. I passed him with a sneer at his amusements, which were always those of conflicts against fish or fowl. He answered me in the same strain, as he threw his nets into the boat, and pushed out to sea. "How is it that you go alone?" said I; "is there so much glory in the capture of mackarel and dogfish that you will allow no one to share it?"

"There are other sports besides those for men," answered Gerald, colouring indignantly; "my taste is confined to amusements in which he is but a fool who seeks companionship; and if you could read character better, my wise brother, you would know that the bold rover is ever less idle and more fortunate than the speculative dreamer!"

As Gerald said this, which he did with a significant emphasis, he rowed vigorously across the water, and the little boat was soon half way to the opposite islet. My eyes followed it musingly as it glided over the waves, and my thoughts painfully revolved the words which Gerald had uttered. "What can he mean?" said I, half aloud, "yet what matters it?—perhaps some low amour, some village conquest, inspires him with that becoming fulness of pride and vain glory—joy be with so bold a rover!" and I strode away, along the beach, towards my place of watch; once only I turned to look at Gerald—he had then just touched the islet, which was celebrated as much for the fishing it afforded as the smuggling it protected.

I arrived, at last, at the hillock, and resumed my station. Time passed on, till, at the dusk of evening, the Spaniard came out. He walked slowly towards the town; I followed him at a distance. Just before he reached the town, he turned off by a path which led to the beach. As the evening was unusually fresh and chill, I felt convinced that some cause, not wholly trivial, drew the Spaniard forth to brave it. My pride a little revolted at the idea of following him; but I persuaded myself that Isora's happiness, and perhaps her father's safety, depended on my obtaining some knowledge of the character and designs of this Barnard, who appeared to possess so dangerous an influence over both daughter and sire—nor did I doubt but that the old man was now gone forth to meet him. The times were those of mystery and of intrigue—the emissaries of the House of Stuart were restlessly at work, among all classes—many of them, obscure and mean individuals, made their way, the more dangerously from their apparent insignificance. My uncle, a moderate tory, was opposed, though quietly, and without vehemence, to the claims of the banished House. Like Sedley, who became so staunch a revolutionist, he had seen the Court of Charles IL, and the character of that King's brother, too closely to feel much respect for either; but he thought it indecorous to express opposition loudly, against a party among whom were many of his early friends; and the good old knight was too much attached to private ties to be very much alive to public feeling. However, at his well-filled board, conversation, generally, though displeasingly to himself, turned upon politics, and I had there often listened, of late, to dark hints of the danger to which we were exposed, and of the restless machinations of the Jacobites. I did not, therefore, scruple to suspect this Barnard of some plot against the existing state; and I did it the more from observing that the Spaniard often spoke bitterly of the English Court, which had rejected some claims he had imagined himself entitled to make upon it; and that he was naturally of a temper vehemently opposed to quiet, and alive to enterprise. With this impression, I deemed it fair to seize any opportunity of seeing, at least, even if I could not question, the man whom the Spaniard himself confessed to have state reasons for concealment ; and my anxiety to behold one whose very name could agitate Isora, and whose presence could occasion the state in which I had found her, sharpened this desire into the keenness of a passion.

While Alvarez descended to the beach, I kept the upper path, which wound along the cliff. There was a spot where the rocks were rude and broken into crags, and afforded me a place where, unseen, I could behold what passed below. The first thing I beheld was a boat, approaching rapidly towards the shore ; one man was seated in it ; he reached the shore, and I recognized Gerald. That was a dreadful moment. Alvarez now slowly joined him ; they remained together for nearly an hour. I saw Gerald give the Spaniard a letter, which appeared to make the chief subject of their conversation. At length they parted, with the signs rather of respect than familiarity. Don Diego returned homeward, and Gerald re-entered the boat. I watched its progress over the waves with feelings of a dark and almost unutterable nature. " My enemy ! my rival ! ruiner of my hopes !—*my brother !—my twin brother !*" I muttered bitterly between my ground teeth.

The boat did not make to the open sea—it skulked along the shore, till distance and shadow scarcely allowed me to trace the outline of Gerald's figure. It then touched the beach, and I could just descry the dim shape of another man enter ; and Gerald, instead of returning homewards, pushed out towards the islet. I spent the greater part of the night in the open air. Wearied and exhausted, by the furious indulgence of my passions, I gained my room, at length. There, however, as elsewhere, thought succeeded to thought, and scheme to scheme. Should I speak to Gerald ? Should I confide in Alvarez ? Should I renew my suit to Isora ? If the first, what could I hope to learn from mine enemy ? If the second, what could I gain from the father, while the daughter remained averse to me ? If the third—there my heart pointed, and the third scheme I resolved to adopt.

But was I sure that Gerald was this Barnard ? Might there not be some hope that he was not ? No, I could perceive none. Alvarez had never spoken to me of acquaintance with any other Englishman than Barnard ; I had no reason to believe that he ever held converse with any other. Would it not have been natural too, unless some powerful cause, such as love to Isora, induced silence—would it not have been natural that Gerald should have mentioned his acquaintance with the Spaniard?—Unless some dark scheme, such as that which Barnard appeared to have in common with Don Diego, commanded obscurity, would it have been likely that Gerald should have met Alvarez alone—at night—on an unfrequented spot ? What that scheme *was*, I guessed not—I cared not. All my interest in the identity of Barnard with Gerald Devereux, was that derived from the power he seemed to possess over Isora. Here, too, at once, was explained the pretended Barnard's desire of concealment, and the vigilance with which it had been effected. It was so certain that Gerald, if my rival, would seek to avoid me—it was so easy for him, who could watch all my motions, to secure the power of doing so. Then I remembered Gerald's character through the country, as a gallant and a general lover—and I closed my eyes as if to shut out the vision when I recalled the beauty of his form, contrasted with the comparative plainness of my own.

-- "There is no hope," I repeated—and an insensibility, rather than sleep, crept over me. Dreadful and fierce dreams peopled my slumbers ; and, when I started from them at a late hour the next day, I was unable to rise from my bed—my agitation and my wanderings had terminated in a burning fever. In four days, however, I recovered sufficiently to mount my horse—I rode to the Spaniard's house, I found there only the woman who had been Don Diego's solitary domestic. The morning before, Alvarez and his daughter had departed, none knew for certain whither ; but it was supposed their destination was London. The woman gave me a note—it was from Isora—it contained only these lines :

"Forget me—we are now parted for ever. As you value my peace of mind—of happiness I do not speak—seek not to discover our next retreat. I implore you to think no more of what has been ; you are young, very young. Life has a thousand paths for you ; any one of them will lead you from remembrance of me. Farewell, again and again !

"ISORA D'ALVAREZ."

With this note was another, in French, from Don Diego ; it was colder and more formal than I could have expected—it thanked me for my attentions towards him—it regretted that he could not take leave of me in person, and it enclosed the sum by the loan of which our acquaintance had commenced.

"It is well !" said I, calmly, to myself, "it is well ; I will forget her :" and I rode instantly home. "But," I resumed in my soliloquy, "I will yet strive to obtain confirmation to what perhaps needs it not. I will yet strive to see if Gerald can deny the depth of his injuries towards me—there will be at least some comfort in witnessing either his defiance or his confusion."

Agreeably to this thought, I hastened to seek Gerald. I found him in his apartment—I shut the door, and seating myself, with a smile, thus addressed him :

"Dear Gerald, I have a favour to ask of you."

"What is it?"

"How long have you known a certain Mr. Barnard?" Gerald changed colour—his voice faltered as he repeated the name "Barnard!"

"Yes," said I, with affected composure, "Barnard! a great friend of Don Diego D'Alvarez."

"I perceive," said Gerald, collecting himself, "that you are in some measure acquainted with my secret—how far it is known to you I cannot guess; but I tell you, very fairly, that from me you will not increase the sum of your knowledge."

When one is in a good sound rage, it is astonishing how calm one can be ! I was certainly somewhat amazed by Gerald's hardihood and assurance, but I continued, with a smile—

"And Donna Isora, how long, if not very intrusive on your confidence, have you known her?"

"I tell you," answered Gerald doggedly, "that I will answer no questions."

"You remember the old story," returned I, "of the two brothers, Eteocles and Polynices, whose very ashes refused to mingle—faith, Gerald, our love seems much of the same sort. I know not if our ashes will exhibit so laudable an antipathy; but I think our hearts and hands will do so while a spark of life animates them; yes, though our blood" (I added, in a voice quivering with furious emotion) "prevents our contest by the sword, it prevents not the hatred and the curses of the heart."

Gerald turned pale. "I do not understand you," he faltered out —"I know you abhor me; but why, why this excess of malice?"

I cast on him a look of bitter scorn, and turned from the room.

It is not pleasing to place before the reader these dark passages of fraternal hatred; but in the record of all passions there is a moral; and it is wise to see how vast a sum the units of childish animosity swell, when they are once brought into a heap, by some violent event, and told over by the nice accuracy of Revenge.

But I long to pass from these scenes, and my history is about to glide along others of more glittering and smiling aspect. Thank Heaven, I write a tale, not only of love, but of a life; and that which I cannot avoid I can at least condense.

CHAPTER X.

A VERY SHORT CHAPTER—CONTAINING A VALET.

MY uncle for several weeks had flattered himself that I had quite forgotten or foregone the desire of leaving Devereux Court for London. Good easy man! he was not a little distressed when I renewed the subject with redoubled firmness, and demanded an early period for that event. He managed, however, still to protract the evil day. At one time it was impossible to part with me, because the house was so full; at another time it was cruel to leave him, when the house was so empty. Meanwhile, a new change came over me. As the first shock of Isora's departure passed away, I began to suspect the purity of her feelings towards me. Might not Gerald, the beautiful, the stately, the glittering Gerald, have been a successful wooer under that disguised name of Barnard, and *hence* Isora's confusion when that name was mentioned, and hence the power which its possessor exercised over her?

This idea, once admitted, soon gained ground. It is true that Isora had testified something of favourable feelings towards me; but this might spring from coquetry or compassion. My love had been a boy's love, founded upon beauty and coloured by romance. I had not investigated the character of the object; and I had judged of the mind solely by the face. I might easily have been deceived—I persuaded myself that I was! Perhaps Gerald had provided their present retreat for sire and daughter—perhaps they at this moment laughed over my rivalry and my folly. Methought Gerald's lip wore a contemptuous curve when we met. "It shall have no cause," I said, stung to the soul; "I will indeed forget this woman, and yet, though in other ways, eclipse this rival. Pleasure—ambition —the brilliancy of a Court—the resources of wealth invite me to a thousand joys. I will not be deaf to the call. Meanwhile I will not betray to Gerald—to any one—the scar of the wound I have received; and I will mortify Gerald, by showing him that, handsome as he is, he shall be forgotten in my presence?"

Agreeably to this exquisite resolution, I paid incessant court to the numerous dames by whom my uncle's mansion was thronged; and I resolved to prepare, among them, the reputation for gallantry and for wit which I proposed to establish in town.

"You are greatly altered since your love?" said Aubrey, one day to me, "but not by your love. Own that I did right in dissuading you from its indulgence!"

"Tell me!" said I, sinking my voice to a whisper, "do you think Gerald was my rival?" and I recounted the causes of my suspicion.

Aubrey's countenance testified astonishment as he listened—"It is strange—very strange," said he; "and the evidence of the boat is almost conclusive; still I do not think it quite sufficient to leave no loop-hole of doubt. But what matters it?—you have conquered your love now."

"Ay," I said, with a laugh, "I have conquered it, and I am now about to find some other empress of the heart. What think you of the Lady Hasselton?—a fair dame and a sprightly. I want nothing but her love to be the most enviable of men, and a French *valet-de-chambre* to be the most irresistible."

"The former is easier to obtain than the latter I fear," returned Aubrey; "all places produce light dames, but the war makes a scarcity of French valets."

"True," said I, "but I never thought of instituting a comparison between their relative value. The Lady Hasselton, no disparagement to her merits, is but one woman—but a French valet who knows his *métier*, arms one for conquest over a thousand"—and I turned to the saloon.

Fate, which had destined to me the valuable affections of the Lady Hasselton, granted me also, at a yet earlier period, the greater boon of a French valet. About two or three weeks after this sapient communication with Aubrey, the most charming person in the world presented himself a candidate *pour le suprême bonheur de soigner Monsieur le Comte.* Intelligence beamed in his eye; a modest assurance reigned upon his brow; respect made his step vigilant as a zephyr's; and his ruffles were the envy of the world!

I took him at a glance; and I presented to the admiring inmates of the house a greater coxcomb than the Count Devereux in the ethereal person of Jean Desmarais.

CHAPTER XI.

THE HERO ACQUITS HIMSELF HONOURABLY AS A COXCOMB—A
FINE LADY OF THE EIGHTEENTH CENTURY, AND A FASHION-
ABLE DIALOGUE—THE SUBSTANCE OF FASHIONABLE DIALOGUE
BEING IN ALL CENTURIES THE SAME.

AM thinking, Morton," said my uncle, "that if you are to go to town, you should go in a style suitable to your rank. What say you to flying along the road in my green and gold chariot? 'Sdeath I'll make you a present of it. Nay—no thanks—and you may have four of my black Flanders mares to draw you."

"Now, my dear Sir William," cried Lady Hasselton, who, it may be remembered, was the daughter of one of King Charles's beauties, and who alone shared the breakfast room with my uncle and myself—"now, my dear Sir William, I think it would be a better plan to suffer the Count to accompany us to town. We go next week. He shall have a seat in our coach—help Lovell to pay our post-horses—protect us at inns—scold at the drawers in the pretty oaths of the fashion, which are so innocent that I will teach them to his Countship myself, and unless I am much more frightful than my honoured mother, whose beauties you so gallantly laud, I think you will own, Sir William, that this is better for your nephew than doing solitary penance in your chariot of green and gold, with a handkerchief tied over his head to keep away cold, and with no more fanciful occupation than composing sonnets to the four Flanders mares."

"'Sdeath, madam, you inherit your mother's wit as well as beauty," cried my uncle, with an impassioned air.

"And his Countship," said I, "will accept your invitation without asking his uncle's leave."

"Come, that is bold for a gentleman of—let me see, thirteen—are you not?"

"Really," answered I, "one learns to forget time so terribly in the presence of Lady Hasselton, that I do not remember even how long it has existed for me."

"Bravo," cried the knight, with a moistening eye: "you see, madam, the boy has not lived with his old uncle for nothing."

"I am lost in astonishment," said the lady, glancing toward the glass; "why you will eclipse all our beaux at your first appearance

—but—but—Sir William—how green those glasses have become?
bless me, there is something so contagious in the effects of the
country, that the very mirrors grow verdant. But—Count—Count—
where are you, Count? (I was exactly opposite to the fair speaker.)
Oh, there you are—pray—do you carry a little pocket-glass of the
true quality about you? But, of course you do; lend it me."

"I have not the glass you want, but I carry with me a mirror
that reflects your features much more faithfully."

"How! I protest I do not understand you!"

"The mirror is here!" said I, laying my hand to my heart.

"'Gad I must kiss the boy!" cried my uncle, starting up.

"I have sworn," said I, fixing my eyes upon the lady—"I have
sworn never to be kissed even by women. You must pardon me,
uncle."

"I declare," cried the Lady Hasselton, flirting her fan, which
was somewhat smaller than the screen that one puts into a great hall,
in order to take off the discomfort of too large a room—"I declare,
Count, there is a vast deal of originality about you. But tell me,
Sir William, where did your nephew acquire, at so early an age—
(eleven you say he is)—such a fund of agreeable assurance?"

"Nay, madam, let the boy answer for himself."

"*Imprimis*, then," said I, playing with the ribbon of my cane—
"*imprimis*, early study of the best authors—Congreve and Farquhar,
Etherege and Rochester. Secondly, the constant intercourse of
company which gives one the spleen so over-poweringly that despair
inspires one with boldness—to get rid of them. Thirdly, the
personal example of Sir William Devereux; and, fourthly, the
inspiration of hope."

"Hope, sir!" said the Lady Hasselton, covering her face with
her fan, so as only to leave me a glimpse of the farthest patch upon
her left cheek—"hope, sir?"

"Yes—the hope of being pleasing to you. Suffer me to add that
the hope has now become certainty."

"Upon my word, Count—"

"Nay, you cannot deny it—if one can once succeed in impudence,
one is irresistible."

"Sir William," cried Lady Hasselton, "you may give the
Count your chariot of green and gold, and your four Flanders mares,
and send his mother's maid with him. He shall not go with me."

"Cruel! and why?" said I.

"You are too"—the lady paused, and looked at me over her fan.
She was really very handsome—"you are too *old*, Count. You
must be more than nine."

"Pardon mé," said I, "I *am* nine—a very mystical number nine is too, and represents the muses, who, you know, were always attendant upon Venus—or you, which is the same. thing ; so you can no more dispense with my company than you can with that of the Graces."

"Good morning, Sir William!" cried the Lady Hasselton, rising.

I offered to hand her to the door—with great difficulty, for her hoop was of the very newest enormity of circumference, I effected this object. "Well, Count?" said she, "I am glad to see you have brought so much learning from school ; make the best use of it, while it lasts, for your memory will not furnish you with a single simile out of the mythology by the end of next winter."

"That would be a pity !" said I, "for I intend having as many goddesses as the Heathens had, and I should like to worship them in a classical fashion."

"Oh! the young reprobate!" said the beauty, tapping me with her fan. "And pray what other deities besides Venus do I resemble?"

"All!" said I—"at least all the celestial ones!"

Though half way through the door, the beauty extricated her hoop, and drew back ; "Bless me, the gods as well as the goddesses?"

"Certainly."

"You jest—tell me how."

"Nothing can be easier ; you resemble Mercury, because of your thefts."

"Thefts!"

"Ay ; stolen hearts, and" (added I, in a whisper) "glances—Jupiter, partly because of your lightning, which you lock up in the said glances—principally because all things are subservient to you—Neptune, because you are as changeable as the seas—Vulcan, because you live among the flames you excite—and Mars, because—"

"You are so destructive," cried my uncle.

"Exactly so ; and because," added I—as I shut the door upon the beauty—"because, thanks to your hoop, you cover nine acres of ground."

"Od'sfish, Morton," said my uncle, "you surprise me at times—one while you are so reserved, at another so assured ; to-day so brisk, to-morrow so gloomy. Why now, Lady Hasselton (she is very comely, eh! faith, but not comparable to her mother) told me, a week ago, that she gave you up in despair, that you were dull, past hoping for ; and now, 'Gad, you had a life in you that Sid him-self could not have surpassed. How comes it, sir, eh?"

"Why, uncle, you have explained the reason; it was exactly because she said I was dull that I was resolved to convict her in an untruth."

"Well, now, there is some sense in that, boy; always contradict ill report, by personal merit. But what think you of her ladyship? 'Gad, you know what old Bellair said of Emilia. 'Make much of her—she's one of the best of your acquaintance. I like her countenance and behaviour. Well, she has a modesty not i' this age, a-dad she has.' Applicable enough—eh, boy?"

"'I know her value, sir, and esteem her accordingly,'" answered I, out of the same play, which by dint of long study I had got by heart. "But, to confess the truth," added I, "I think you might have left out the passage about her modesty."

"There, now—you young chaps are so censorious—why 'sdeath, sir, you don't think the worse of her virtue, because of her wit?"

"Humph!"

"Ah, boy—when you are my age, you'll know that your demure cats are not the best; and that reminds me of a little story—shall I tell it you, child?"

"If it so please you, sir."

"Zauns—where's my snuff-box?—oh, here it is. Well, sir, you shall have the whole thing, from beginning to end. Sedley and I were one day conversing together about women. Sid was a very deep fellow in that game—no passion you know—no love on his own side—nothing of the sort—all done by rule and compass—knew women as well as dice, and calculated the exact moment when his snares would catch them, according to the principles of geometry. D—d clever fellow, faith—but a confounded rascal:—but let it go no farther—mum's the word!—must not slander the dead—and 'tis only my suspicion, you know, after all. Poor fellow—I don't think he was such a rascal; he gave a beggar an angel once,—well, boy, have a pinch?—Well, so I said to Sir Charles, 'I think you will lose the widow, after all—'Gad I do.' 'Upon what principle of science, Sir William?' said he. 'Why, faith, man, she is so modest, you see, and has such a pretty way of blushing.' 'Harkye, friend Devereux,' said Sir Charles, smoothing his collar and mincing his words musically, as he was wont to do—'Harkye, friend Devereux, I will give you the whole experience of my life in one maxim—I can answer for its being new, and I think it is profound— and that maxim is—' No faith, Morton—no, I can't tell it thee— it is villainous, and then it's so desperately against all the sex."

"My dear uncle, don't tantalize me so—pray tell it me—it shall be a secret."

"No, boy, no—it will corrupt thee—besides, it will do poor Sid's memory no good. But 'sdeath, it was a most wonderfully shrewd saying—i'faith, it was. But zounds—Morton—I forgot to tell you that I have had a letter from the Abbé to-day."

"Ha! and when does he return?"

"To-morrow, God willing!" said the knight, with a sigh.

"So soon, or rather after so long an absence! Well, I am glad of it. I wish much to see him before I leave you."

"Indeed!" quoth my uncle—"you have an advantage over me, then! But, od'sfish, Morton, how is it that you grew so friendly with the priest before his departure? He used to speak very suspiciously of thee formerly; and, when I last saw him, he lauded thee to the skies."

"Why, the clergy of his faith have a habit of defending the strong, and crushing the weak, I believe—that's all. He once thought I was dull enough to damn my fortune, and then he had some strange doubts for my soul—now he thinks me wise enough to become prosperous, and it is astonishing what a respect he has conceived for my principles."

"Ha! ha! ha!—you have a spice of your uncle's humour in you—and, 'Gad, you have no small knowledge of the world, considering you have seen so little of it."

A hit at the Popish clergy was, in my good uncle's eyes, the exact acme of wit and wisdom. We are always clever with those who imagine we think as they do. To be shallow you must differ with people—to be profound you must agree with them. "Why, sir," answered the sage nephew, "you forget that I have seen more of the world than many of twice my age. Your house has been full of company ever since I have been in it, and you set me to making observations on what I saw before I was thirteen. And then, too, if one is reading books about real life, at the very time one is mixing in it, it is astonishing how naturally one remarks, and how well one remembers."

"Especially if one has a genius for it,—eh, boy! And then, too, you have read my play—turned Horace's Satires into a lampoon upon the boys at school—been regularly to assizes during the vacation—attended the county balls, and been a most premature male coquette with the ladies. Od'sfish, boy! it is quite curious to see how the young sparks of the present day get on with their love-making."

"Especially if one has a genius for it—eh, sir?" said I.

"Besides, too," said my uncle, ironically, "you have had the Abbé's instructions."

"Ay, and if the priests would communicate to their pupils their experience in frailty, as well as in virtue, how wise they would make us!"

"Od'sfish! Morton, you are quite oracular. How got you that fancy of priests?—by observation in life already?"

"No, uncle—by observation in plays, which you tell me are the mirrors of life—you remember what Lee says—

> 'Tis thought
> That earth is more obliged to priests for bodies
> Than Heaven for souls.'"

And my uncle laughed, and called me a smart fellow.

CHAPTER XII.

THE ABBÉ'S RETURN—A SWORD, AND A SOLILOQUY.

THE next evening, when I was sitting alone in my room, the Abbé Montreuil suddenly entered. "Ah, is it you? welcome!"—cried I. The priest held out his arms, and embraced me in the most paternal manner.

"It *is* your friend," said he, "returned at last to bless and con-gratulate you. Behold my success in your service," and the Abbé produced a long leather case, richly inlaid with gold.

"Faith, Abbé," said I, "am I to understand that this is a present for your eldest pupil?"

"You are," said Montreuil, opening the case, and producing a sword; the light fell upon the hilt, and I drew back, dazzled with its lustre; it was covered with stones, apparently of the most costly value. Attached to the hilt was a label of purple velvet, on which, in letters of gold, was inscribed, "To the son of Marshal Devereux, the soldier of France, and the friend of Louis XIV."

Before I recovered my surprise at this sight, the Abbé said—"It was from the King's own hand that I received this sword, and I have authority to inform you, that if ever you wield it in the service of France, it will be accompanied by a post worthy of your name."

"The service of France!" I repeated; "why at present that is the service of an enemy."

"An enemy only to a *part* of England!" said the Abbé, em-phatically; "perhaps I have overtures to you from other monarchs, and the friendship of the court of France may be synonymous with the friendship of the true sovereign of England."

There was no mistaking the purport of this speech, and even in the midst of my gratified vanity I drew back alarmed. The Abbé noted the changed expression of my countenance, and artfully turned the subject to comments on the sword, on which I still gazed with a lover's ardour. Thence he veered to a description of the grace and greatness of the royal donor—he dwelt at length upon the flattering terms in which Louis had spoken of my father, and had inquired concerning myself; he enumerated all the hopes that the illustrious house, into which my father had first married, expressed for a speedy introduction to his son; he lingered with an eloquence more savouring of the court than of the cloister, on the dazzling circle which surrounded the French throne; and when my vanity, my curiosity, my love of pleasure, my ambition, all that are most susceptible in young minds, were fully aroused, he suddenly ceased, and wished me a good night.

"Stay," said I; and looking at him more attentively than I had hitherto done, I perceived a change in his external appearance, which somewhat startled and surprised me. Montreuil had always hitherto been remarkably plain in his dress; but he was now richly attired, and by his side hung a rapier, which had never adorned it before. Something in his aspect seemed to suit the alteration in his garb: and whether it was that long absence had effaced enough of the familiarity of his features, to allow me to be more alive than formerly to the real impression they were calculated to produce, or whether a commune with kings and nobles had of late dignified their old expression, as power was said to have clothed the soldier-mien of Cromwell with a monarch's bearing—I do not affect to decide; but I thought that, in his high brow and Roman features, the compression of his lip, and his calm but haughty air, there was a nobleness, which I acknowledged for the first time. "Stay, my father," said I, surveying him, "and tell me, if there be no irreverence in the question, whether brocade and a sword are compatible with the laws of the Order of Jesus?"

"Policy, Morton," answered Montreuil, "often dispenses with custom; and the declarations of the Institute provide, with their usual wisdom, for worldly and temporary occasions. Even while the constitution ordains us to discard habits repugnant to our professions of poverty, the following exception is made: 'Si in occurrenti aliquâ occasione, vel necessitate, quis vestibus melioribus, honestis tamen, indueretur.'" [1]

"There is now, then, some occasion for a more glittering display than ordinary?" said I.

[1] "But should there chance any occasion or necessity, one may wear better, though still decorous garments."

"There is, my pupil," answered Montreuil; "and whenever you embrace the offer of my friendship made to you more than two years ago,—whenever, too, your ambition points to a lofty and sublime career,—whenever, to make and unmake kings,—and, in the noblest sphere to execute the will of God,—indemnifies you for a sacrifice of petty wishes and momentary passions, I will confide to you schemes worthy of your ancestors and yourself."

With this the priest departed. Left to myself, I revolved his hints, and marvelled at the power he seemed to possess. "Closeted with kings," said I, soliloquizing,—"bearing their presents through armed men and military espionage,—speaking of empires and their overthrow, as of ordinary objects of ambition—and he himself a low-born and undignified priest, of a poor though a wise order—well, there is more in this than I can fathom; but I will hesitate before I embark in his dangerous and concealed intrigues—above all, I will look well ere I hazard my safe heritage of these broad lands in the service of that House which is reported to be ungrateful, and which is certainly exiled."

After this prudent and notable resolution, I took up the sword, re-examined it, kissed the hilt once and the blade twice—put it under my pillow—sent for my valet—undrest—went to bed—fell asleep—and dreamt that I was teaching the Maréchal de Villars the thrust *en seconde.*

But Fate, that arch-gossip, who, like her prototypes on earth, settles all our affairs for us without our knowledge of the matter, had decreed that my friendship with the Abbé Montreuil should be of very short continuance, and that my adventures on earth should flow through a different channel than, in all probability, they would have done under his spiritual direction.

CHAPTER XIII.

A MYSTERIOUS LETTER—A DUEL—THE DEPARTURE OF ONE OF THE FAMILY.

THE next morning I communicated to the Abbé my intention of proceeding to London. He received it with favour. "I myself," said he, "shall soon meet you there;—my office in your family has expired, and your mother, after so long an absence, will perhaps readily dispense with my spiritual advice to her. But time presses—since you depart so soon, give me an audience to-night in your apartment. Perhaps our conversation may be of moment."

I agreed—the hour was fixed, and I left the Abbé to join my uncle and his guests. While I was employing, among them, my time and genius with equal dignity and profit, one of the servants informed me that a man at the gate wished to see me— and alone.

Somewhat surprised, I followed the servant out of the room into the great hall, and desired him to bid the stranger attend me there. In a few minutes, a small, dark man, dressed between gentility and meanness, made his appearance. He greeted me with great respect, and presented a letter, which, he said, he was charged to deliver into my own hands, "with," he added in a low tone, "a special desire that none should, till I had carefully read it, be made acquainted with its contents." I was not a little startled by this request ; and, withdrawing to one of the windows, broke the seal. A letter, enclosed in the envelope, in the Abbé's own handwriting, was the first thing that met my eyes. At that instant the Abbé himself rushed into the hall. He cast one hasty look at the messenger, whose countenance evinced something of surprise and consternation at beholding him ; and, hastening up to me, grasped my hand vehemently, and, while his eye dwelt upon the letter I held, cried, "Do not read it—not a word—not a word, there is poison in it !" And so saying, he snatched desperately at the letter. I detained it from him with one hand, and pushing him aside with the other, said—

"Pardon me, Father—directly I have read it you shall have that pleasure—not till then !" and, as I said this, my eye falling upon the letter, discovered my own name written in two places—my suspicions were aroused. I raised my eyes to the spot where the messenger had stood, with the view of addressing some question to him respecting his employer, when, to my surprise, I perceived he was already gone ; I had no time, however, to follow him.

"Boy," said the Abbé, gasping for breath, and still seizing me with his lean bony hand,—"boy, give me that letter instantly. I charge you not to disobey me."

"You forget yourself, sir," said I, endeavouring to shake him off, "you forget yourself : there is no longer between us the distinction of pupil and teacher ; and if you have not yet learnt the respect due to my station, suffer me to tell you that it is time you should."

"Give me the letter, I beseech you," said Montreuil, changing his voice from anger to supplication ; "I ask your pardon for my violence ; the letter does not concern you, but me ; there is a secret in those lines which you see are in my handwriting, that implicates my personal safety. Give it me, my dear, dear son—your own honour, if not your affection for me, demands that you should."

I was staggered. His violence had confirmed my suspicions, but his gentleness weakened them. "Besides," thought I, "the hand-writing *is his*, and even if my life depended upon reading the letter of another, I do not think my honour would suffer me to do so against his consent." A thought struck me—

"Will you swear," said I, "that this letter does not concern me ?"

"Solemnly," answered the Abbé, raising his eyes.

"Will you swear that I am not even mentioned in it ?"

"Upon peril of my soul, I will."

"Liar—traitor—perjured blasphemer !" cried I, in an inex-pressible rage, "look here, and here !" and I pointed out to the priest various lines in which my name legibly and frequently occurred. A change came over Montreuil's face; he released my arm and staggered back against the wainscot ; but recovering his composure instantaneously, he said, "I forgot, my son—I forgot—your name is mentioned, it is true, but with honourable eulogy, that is all."

"Bravo, honest Father !" cried I, losing my fury in admiring surprise at his address—"bravo ! However, if that be all, you can have no objection to allow me to read the lines in which my name occurs ; your benevolence cannot refuse me such a gratification as the sight of your written panegyric !"

"Count Devereux," said the Abbé, sternly, while his dark face worked with suppressed passion, "this is trifling with me, and I warn you not to push my patience too far. I *will* have that letter, or—" he ceased abruptly, and touched the hilt of his sword.

"Dare you threaten me ?" I said, and the natural fierceness of my own disposition, deepened by vague and strong suspicions of some treachery designed against me, spoke in the tones of my voice.

"Dare I ?" repeated Montreuil, sinking and sharpening his voice into a sort of inward screech. "Dare I !—ay, were your whole tribe arrayed against me. Give me the letter, or you will find me now and for ever your most deadly foe ; deadly—ay—deadly, deadly !" and he shook his clenched hand at me, with an expression of countenance so malignant and menacing that I drew back in-voluntarily, and laid my hand on my sword.

The action seemed to give Montreuil a signal for which he had hitherto waited. "Draw then," he said through his teeth, and unsheathed his rapier.

Though surprised at his determination, I was not backward in meeting it. Thrusting the letter in my bosom, I drew my sword in time to parry a rapid and fierce thrust. I had expected easily to master Montreuil, for I had some skill at my weapon;—I was deceived—I found him far more adroit than myself in the art of offence; and perhaps it would have fared ill for the hero of this narrative had Montreuil deemed it wise to direct against my life all the science he possessed. But the moment our swords crossed, the constitutional coolness of the man, which rage or fear had for a brief time banished, returned at once, and he probably saw that it would be as dangerous to him to take away the life of his pupil, as to forfeit the paper for which he fought. He, therefore, appeared to bend all his efforts towards disarming me. Whether or not he would have effected this it is hard to say, for my blood was up, and any neglect of my antagonist, in attaining an object very dangerous, when engaged with a skilful and quick swordsman, might have sent him to the place from which the prayers of his brethren have (we are bound to believe) released so many thousands of souls. But, meanwhile, the servants, who at first thought the clashing of swords was the wanton sport of some young gallants as yet new to the honour of wearing them, grew alarmed by the continuance of the sound, and flocked hurriedly to the place of contest. At their intrusion, we mutually drew back. Recovering my presence of mind (it was a possession I very easily lost at that time), I saw the unseemliness of fighting with my preceptor, and a priest. I therefore burst, though awkwardly enough, into a laugh, and, affecting to treat the affair as a friendly trial of skill between the Abbé and myself, resheathed my sword and dismissed the intruders, who, evidently disbelieving my version of the story, retreated slowly, and exchanging looks. Montreuil who had scarcely seconded my attempt to gloss over our *rencontre*, now approached me.

"Count," he said, with a collected and cool voice, "suffer me to request you to exchange three words with me, in a spot less liable than this to interruption."

"Follow me then!" said I—and I led the way to a part of the grounds which lay remote and sequestered from intrusion. I then turned round, and perceived that the Abbé had left his sword behind. "How is this?" I said, pointing to his unarmed side— "have you not come hither to renew our engagement?"

"No!" answered Montreuil, "I repent me of my sudden haste, and I have resolved to deny myself all further possibility of unseemly warfare. That letter, young man, I still demand from you; I demand it from your own sense of honour and of right—it was

written by me—it was not intended for your eye—it contains secrets
implicating the lives of others besides myself;—now—read it if you
will."

"You are right, sir," said I, after a short pause; "there is the
letter; never shall it be said of Morton Devereux that he hazarded
his honour to secure his safety.—But the tie between us is broken
now and for ever!"

So saying, I flung down the debated epistle, and strode away.
I re-entered the great hall. I saw by one of the windows a sheet
of paper—I picked it up, and perceived that it was the envelope
in which the letter had been enclosed. It contained only these
lines, addressed to me in French:

"A friend of the late Marshal Devereux encloses to his son a
letter, the contents of which it is essential for his safety that he
should know.

                                              "C. D. B."

"Umph!" said I—"a very satisfactory intimation, considering
that the son of the late Marshal Devereux is so very well assured
that he shall not know one line of the contents of the said letter.
But let me see after this messenger!" and I immediately hastened
to institute inquiry respecting him. I found that he was already
gone; on leaving the hall he had remounted his horse, and taken
his departure. One servant, however, had seen him, as he passed
the front court, address a few words to my valet, Desmarais, who
happened to be loitering there. I summoned Desmarais and
questioned him.

"The dirty fellow," said the Frenchman, pointing to his spattered
stockings with a lachrymose air, "splashed me, by a prance of his
horse, from head to foot, and while I was screaming for very
anguish, he stopped and said, 'Tell the Count Devereux that I
was unable to tarry, but that the letter requires no answer.'"

I consoled Desmarais for his misfortune, and hastened to my
uncle with a determination to reveal to him all that had occurred.
Sir William was in his dressing-room, and his gentleman was very
busy in adorning his wig. I entreated him to dismiss the *coiffeur*,
and then, without much preliminary detail, acquainted him with
all that had passed between the Abbé and myself.

The knight seemed startled when I came to the story of the
sword. "'Gad, Sir Count, what have you been doing?" said he;
"know you not that this may be a very ticklish matter? The king
of France is a very great man, to be sure—a very great man—and

a very fine gentleman ; but you will please to remember that we are at war with his Majesty, and I cannot guess how far the accepting such presents may be held treasonable."

And Sir William shook his head with a mournful significance. "Ah," cried he, at last (when I had concluded my whole story), with a complacent look, "I have not lived at court, and studied human nature, for nothing : and I will wager my best full-bottom to a night-cap, that the crafty old fox is as much a jacobite as he is a rogue ! The letter would have proved it, sir—it would have proved it ! "

"But what shall be done now !" said I ; "will you suffer him to remain any longer in the house ?"

"Why," replied the knight, suddenly recollecting his reverence to the fair sex, "he is your mother's guest, not mine ; we must refer the matter to her. But zauns, sir, with all deference to her ladyship, we cannot suffer our house to be a conspiracy-hatch as well as a popish chapel ;—and to attempt your life too—the devil ! Od's-fish, boy, I will go to the countess myself, if you will just let Nicholls finish my wig—never attend the ladies *en déshabille*—always, with them, take care of your person most, when you most want to display your mind ;" and my uncle ringing a little silver bell on his dressing-table, the sound immediately brought Nicholls to his toilet.

Trusting the cause to the zeal of my uncle, whose hatred to the ecclesiastic would, I knew, be an efficacious adjunct to his diplomatic address, and not unwilling to avoid being myself the person to acquaint my mother with the suspected delinquency of her favourite, I hastened from the knight's apartment in search of Aubrey. He was not in the house. His attendants (for my uncle, with old-fashioned grandeur of respect, suitable to his great wealth and aristocratic temper, allotted to each of us a separate suite of servants as well as of apartments) believed he was in the park. Thither I repaired, and found him, at length, seated by an old tree, with a large book of a religious cast before him, on which his eyes were intently bent.

"I rejoice to have found thee, my gentle brother," said I, throwing myself on the green turf by his side : "in truth you have chosen a fitting and fair place for study."

"I have chosen," said Aubrey, "a place meet for the peculiar study I am engrossed in ; for where can we better read of the power and benevolence of God than among the living testimonies of both. Beautiful !—how very beautiful—is this happy world ; but I fear," added Aubrey, and the glow of his countenance died away,—"I fear that we enjoy it too much."

"We hold different interpretations of our creed then," said I,
"for I esteem enjoyment the best proof of gratitude ; nor do I think
we can pay a more acceptable duty to the Father of all Goodness.
than by showing ourselves sensible of the favours he bestows upon
us."

Aubrey shook his head gently, but replied not.

"Yes," resumed I, after a pause—"yes, it is indeed a glorious
and fair world which we have for our inheritance. Look, how the
sunlight sleeps yonder upon fields covered with golden corn, and
seems, like the divine benevolence of which you spoke, to smile
upon the luxuriance which its power created. This carpet at our
feet, covered with flowers that breathe, sweet as good deeds, to
Heaven—the stream that breaks through that distant copse, laughing in the light of noon, and sending its voice through the hill and
woodland, like a messenger of glad tidings,—the green boughs over
our head, vocal with a thousand songs, all inspirations of a joy too
exquisite for silence,—the very leaves, which seem to dance and
quiver with delight,—think you, Aubrey, that these are so sullen
as not to return thanks for the happiness they imbibe with being ;—
what are those thanks but the incense of their joy? The flowers
send it up to heaven in fragrance—the air and the wave in music.
Shall the heart of man be the only part of His creation that shall
dishonour His worship with lamentation and gloom? When the
inspired writers call upon us to praise our Creator, do they not say
to us,—'Be *joyful* in your God?'"

"How can we be joyful with the Judgment-Day ever before us?"
said Aubrey—"how can we be joyful" (and here a dark shade
crossed his countenance, and his lip trembled with emotion), while
the deadly passions of this world plead and rankle at the heart?
Oh, none but they who have known the full blessedness of a commune
with heaven can dream of the whole anguish and agony of the conscience, when it feels itself sullied by the mire and crushed by the
load of earth!" Aubrey paused, and his words—his tone—his look
—made upon me a powerful impression. I was about to answer,
when, interrupting me, he said, "Let us talk not of these matters,—
speak to me on more worldly topics."

"I sought you," said I, "that I might do so!" and I proceeded
to detail to Aubrey as much of my private intercourse with the Abbé
as I deemed necessary in order to warn him from too close a confidence in the wily ecclesiastic. Aubrey listened to me with earnest
attention :—the affair of the letter—the gross falsehood of the priest
in denying the mention of my name, in his epistle, evidently dis-
mayed him. "But," said he, after a long silence—"but it is not

for us, Morton—weak, ignorant, inexperienced as we are—to judge prematurely of our spiritual pastors. To them also is given a far greater license of conduct than to us—and ways enveloped in what to our eyes are mystery and shade ; nay, I know not whether it be much less impious to question the paths of God's chosen, than to scrutinize those of the Deity himself."

" Aubrey, Aubrey, this is childish ! " said I, somewhat moved to anger. " Mystery is always the trick of imposture : God's chosen should be distinguished from their flock only by superior virtue, and not by a superior privilege in deceit."

" But," said Aubrey, pointing to a passage in the book before him, " see what a preacher of the word has said ! "—and Aubrey recited one of the most dangerous maxims in priestcraft, as reverently as if he were quoting from the Scripture itself. " ' The nakedness of truth should never be too openly exposed to the eyes of the vulgar. It was wisely feigned, by the ancients, that Truth did he concealed in a well ! ' "

" Yes," said I, with enthusiasm, " but that well is like the holy stream at Dodona, which has the gift of enlightening those who seek it, and the power of illumining every torch which touches the surface of its water ! "

Whatever answer Aubrey might have made was interrupted by my uncle, who appeared approaching towards us with unusual satisfaction depicted on his comely countenance.

" Well, boys, well," said he, when he came within hearing—"a holyday for you ! Od'sfish,—and a holier day than my old house has known since its former proprietor, Sir Hugo, of valorous memory, demolished the nunnery, of which some remains yet stand on yonder eminence. Morton, my man of might, the thing is done—the court is purified—the wicked one is departed. Look here, and be as happy as I am at our release ; " and he threw me a note in Montreuil's writing—

To Sir William Devereux, Kt.

" My Honoured Friend,

" In consequence of a dispute between your eldest nephew, Count Morton Devereux, and myself, in which he desired me to remember, not only that our former relationship of tutor and pupil was at an end, but that friendship for his person was incompatible with the respect due to his superior station, I can neither so far degrade the dignity of letters, nor, above all, so meanly debase the sanctity of my divine profession, as any longer to remain beneath your hospitable roof,—a guest not only unwelcome to, but insulted by, your relation

D

and apparent heir.   Suffer me to offer you my gratitude for the
favours you have hitherto bestowed on me, and to bid you farewell
for ever.

  "I have the honour to be,
   "With the most profound respect, &c.   .
     "JULIAN MONTREUIL."

"Well, sir, what say you!" cried my uncle, stamping his cane
firmly on the ground, when I had finished reading the letter, and
had transmitted it to Aubrey.

"That the good Abbé has displayed his usual skill in composition.   And my mother?   Is she imbued with our opinion of his
priestship?"

"Not exactly, I fear.   However, Heaven bless her, she is too
soft to say ' nay.'   But those Jesuits are so smooth-tongued to women.
'Gad, they threaten damnation with such an irresistible air, that they
are as much like William the Conqueror as Edward the Confessor.
Ha! master Aubrey, have you become amorous of the old jacobite,
that you sigh over his crabbed writing, as if it were a *billet-doux?*"

"There seems a great deal of feeling in what he says, sir," said
Aubrey, returning the letter to my uncle.

"Feeling!" cried the knight; "ay, the reverend gentry always
have a marvellously tender feeling for their own interest—eh,
Morton?"

"Right, dear sir," said I, wishing to change a subject which I
knew might hurt Aubrey; "but should we not join yon party of
dames and damsels?   I see they are about to make a water
excursion."

"'Sdeath, sir, with all my heart," cried the good-natured knight;
"I love to see the dear creatures amuse themselves; for, to tell you
the truth, Morton," said he, sinking his voice into a knowing whisper,
"the best thing to keep them from playing the devil is to encourage
them in playing the fool!" and, laughing heartily at the jest he had
purloined from one of his favourite writers, Sir William led the way
to the water-party.

CHAPTER XIV.

BEING A CHAPTER OF TRIFLES.

THE Abbé disappeared! It is astonishing how well every-body bore his departure. My mother scarcely spoke on the subject : but, along the irrefragable smoothness of her temperament, all things glided without resistance to their course, or trace where they had been. Gerald, who, occupied solely in rural sports or rustic loves, seldom mingled in the festivities of the house, was equally silent on the subject. Audley looked grieved for a day or two ; but his countenance soon settled into its customary and grave softness ; and, in less than a week, so little was the Abbé spoken of or missed that you would scarcely have imagined Julian Montreuil had ever passed the threshold of our gate. The oblivion of one buried is nothing to the oblivion of one disgraced.

Meanwhile, I pressed for my departure ; and, at length, the day was finally fixed. Ever since that conversation with Lady Hasselton, which has been set before the reader, that lady had lingered and lingered—though the house was growing empty, and London, in all seasons, was, according to her, better than the country in any—until the Count Devereux, with that amiable modesty which so especially characterized him, began to suspect that the Lady Hasselton lingered on his account. This emboldened that bashful personage to press in earnest for the fourth seat in the beauty's carriage, which we have seen in the conversation before mentioned, had been previously offered to him in jest. After a great affectation of horror at the pro-posal, the Lady Hasselton yielded. She had always, she said, been dotingly fond of children, and it was certainly very shocking to send such a chit as the little Count to London by himself.

My uncle was charmed with the arrangement. The beauty was a peculiar favourite of his, and, in fact, he was sometimes pleased to hint that he had private reasons for love towards her mother's daughter. Of the truth of this insinuation I am, however, more than somewhat suspicious, and believe it was only a little *ruse* of the good knight, in order to excuse the vent of those kindly affections with which (while the heartless tone of the company his youth had fre-quented made him ashamed to own it) his breast overflowed. There was in Lady Hasselton's familiarity—her ease of manner—a certain good-nature mingled with her affectation, and a gaiety of spirit, which never flagged—something greatly calculated to win favour with a man of my uncle's temper.

An old gentleman who filled in her family the office of "the *chevalier*" in a French one; viz., who told stories, not too long, and did not challenge you for interrupting them—who had a good air, and unexceptionable pedigree—a turn for wit, literature, note-writing, and the management of lap-dogs—who could attend *Madame* to auctions, plays, court, and the puppet-show—who had a right to the best company, but would, on a signal, give up his seat to any one of the pretty *capricieuse* whom he served might select from the worst— in short a very useful, charming personage, "vastly" liked by all, and "prodigiously" respected by none;—this gentleman, I say, by name Mr. Lovell, had attended her ladyship in her excursion to Devereux Court. Besides him there came also a widow lady, a distant relation, with one eye and a sharp tongue—the Lady Needle- ham, whom the beauty carried about with her as a sort of *gouvernante* or duenna. These excellent persons made my *compagnons de voyage*, and filled the remaining complements of the coach. To say truth, and to say nothing of my *tendresse* for the Lady Hasselton, I was very anxious to escape the ridicule of crawling up to town like a green beetle, in my uncle's verdant chariot, with the four Flanders mares trained not to exceed two miles an hour. And my Lady Hasselton's *private* railleries—for she was really well bred, and made no jest of my uncle's antiquities of taste, in his presence, at least— had considerably heightened my intuitive dislike to that mode of transporting myself to the metropolis. The day before my departure, Gerald, for the first time, spoke of it.

Glancing towards the mirror, which gave in full contrast the mag- nificent beauty of his person, and the smaller proportions and plainer features of my own, he said, with a sneer, "Your appearance must create a wonderful sensation in town."

"No doubt of it," said I, taking his words literally, and arraying my laced cravat with the air of a *petit-maître*.

"What a wit the Count has!" whispered the Duchess of Lackland —who had not yet given up all hope of the elder brother.

"Wit," said the Lady Hasselton; "poor child, he is a perfect simpleton!"

CHAPTER XV.

THE MOTHER AND SON—VIRTUE SHOULD BE THE SOVEREIGN OF THE FEELINGS, NOT THEIR DESTROYER.

 TOOK the first opportunity to escape from the good company who were so divided in opinion as to my mental accomplishments, and repaired to my mother; for whom, despite of her evenness of disposition, verging towards insensibility, I felt a powerful and ineffaceable affection. Indeed, if purity of life, rectitude of intentions, and fervour of piety, can win love, none ever deserved it more than she. It was a pity that, with such admirable qualities, she had not more diligently cultivated her affections. The seed was not wanting; but it had been neglected. Originally intended for the veil, she had been taught, early in life, that much feeling was synonymous with much sin; and she had so long and so carefully repressed in her heart every attempt of the forbidden fruit to put forth a single blossom, that the soil seemed at last to have become incapable of bearing it. If, in one corner of this barren, but sacred spot, some green and tender verdure of affection did exist, it was, with a partial and petty reserve for my twin-brother, kept exclusive, and consecrated to Aubrey. His congenial habits of pious silence and rigid devotion—his softness of temper—his utter freedom from all boyish excesses, joined to his almost angelic beauty —a quality which, in no female heart, is ever without its value—were exactly calculated to attract her sympathy, and work themselves into her love. Gerald was also regular in his habits, attentive to devotion, and had, from an early period, been high in the favour of her spiritual director. Gerald, too, if he had not the delicate and dreamlike beauty of Aubrey, possessed attractions of more masculine and decided order; and for Gerald, therefore, the Countess gave the little of love that she could spare from Aubrey. To me she manifested the most utter indifference. My difficult and fastidious temper—my sarcastic turn of mind—my violent and headstrong passions—my daring, reckless, and, when roused, almost ferocious nature—all, especially, revolted the even and polished and quiescent character of my maternal parent. The little extravagances of my childhood seemed to her pure and inexperienced mind, the crimes of a heart naturally distorted and evil; my jesting vein, which, though it never, even in the wantonness of youth, attacked the substances of good, seldom respected its semblances and its forms, she considered as the effusions of malignity;

and even the bursts of love, kindness, and benevolence, which were
by no means unfrequent in my wild and motley character, were so
foreign to her stillness of temperament that they only revolted her
by their violence, instead of affecting her by their warmth.

Nor did she like me the better for the mutual understanding
between my uncle and myself. On the contrary, shocked by the
idle and gay turn of the knight's conversation, the frivolities of his
mind, and his heretical disregard for the forms of the religious sect
which she so zealously espoused, she was utterly insensible to the
points which redeemed and ennobled his sterling and generous
character—utterly obtuse to his warmth of heart—his overflowing
kindness of disposition—his charity—his high honour—his justice of
principle, that nothing save benevolence could warp—and the shrewd,
penetrating sense, which, though often clouded by foibles and
humorous eccentricity, still made the stratum of his intellectual
composition. Nevertheless, despite her prepossessions against us
both, there was in her temper something so gentle, meek, and un-
upbraiding, that even the sense of injustice lost its sting, and one
could not help loving the softness of her character, while one was
most chilled by its frigidity. Anger, hope, fear, the faintest breath
or sign of passion, never seemed to stir the breezeless languor of her
feelings ; and quiet was so inseparable from her image that I have
almost thought, like that people described by Herodotus, her very
sleep could never be disturbed by dreams.

Yes ! how fondly, how tenderly I loved her ! What tears—secret,
but deep—bitter, but un-reproaching—have I retired to shed, when
I caught her cold and unaffectionate glance. How (unnoticed and
uncared for) have I watched, and prayed, and wept, without her
door, when a transitory sickness or suffering detained her within ;
and how, when stretched myself upon the feverish bed, to which my
early weakness of frame often condemned me, how have I counted
the moments to her punctilious and brief visit, and started as I
caught her footstep, and felt my heart leap within me as she
approached ; and then, as I heard her cold tone, and looked upon
her unmoved face, how bitterly have I turned away with all that
repressed and crushed affection which was construed into sullenness
or disrespect. O mighty and enduring force of early associations,
that almost seems, in its unconquerable strength, to partake of an
innate prepossession, that binds the son to the mother, who concealed him in her womb, and purchased life for him with the travail
of death !—fountain of filial love, which coldness cannot freeze, nor
injustice embitter, nor pride divert into fresh channels, nor time, and
the hot suns of our toiling manhood, exhaust—even at this moment,

how livingly do you gush upon my heart, and water with your divine waves the memories that yet flourish amidst the sterility of years!

I approached the apartments appropriated to my mother — I knocked at her door; one of her women admitted me, the Countess was sitting on a high-backed chair, curiously adorned with tapestry. Her feet, which were remarkable for their beauty, were upon a velvet cushion; three handmaids stood round her, and she herself was busily employed in a piece of delicate embroidery, an art in which she eminently excelled.

"The Count—madam!" said the woman who had admitted me, placing a chair beside my mother, and then retiring to join her sister maidens.

"Good day to you, my son," said the Countess, lifting her eyes for a moment, and then dropping them again upon her work.

"I have come to seek you, dearest mother, as I know not, if, among the crowd of guests and amusements which surround us, I shall enjoy another opportunity of having a private conversation with you—will it please you to dismiss your women!"

My mother again lifted up her eyes—"And why, my son?—surely there *can* be nothing between us which requires their absence; what is your reason?"

"I leave you to-morrow, madam; is it strange that a son should wish to see his mother alone before his departure?"

"By no means, Morton; but your absence will not be very long, will it?"

"Forgive my importunity, dear mother—but *will* you dismiss your attendants?"

"If you wish it, certainly; but I dislike feeling alone, especially in these large rooms; nor did I think our being unattended quite consistent with our rank; however, I never contradict you, my son," and the Countess directed her women to wait in the anteroom.

"Well, Morton, what is your wish?"

"Only to bid you farewell, and to ask if London contains nothing which you will commission me to obtain for you?"

The Countess again raised her eyes from her work.—"I am greatly obliged to you, my dear son; this is a very delicate attention on your part. I am informed that stomachers are worn a thought less pointed than they were. I care not, you well know, for such vanities; but respect for the memory of your illustrious father renders me desirous to retain a seemly appearance to the world, and my women shall give you written instructions thereon to Madame Tourville—she lives in St. James's Street, and is the only person to be employed in these matters. She is a woman who has

known misfortune, and appreciates the sorrowful and subdued tastes
of those whom an exalted station has not preserved from like afflictions.—So, you go to-morrow—will you get me the scissors, they are
on the ivory table, yonder.—When do you return?"

"Perhaps never!" said I, abruptly.

"Never, Morton; how singular—why?"

"I may join the army—and be killed."

"I hope not.—Dear, how cold it is—will you shut the window?
—pray forgive my troubling you, but you *would* send away the
women.—Join the army, you say?—it is a very dangerous profession
—your poor father might be alive now but for having embraced it ;
nevertheless, in a righteous cause, under the Lord of Hosts, there is
great glory to be obtained beneath its banners. Alas, however, for
its private evils! alas, for the orphan and the widow!—You will be
sure, my dear son, to give the note to Madame Tourville herself?
her assistants have not her knowledge of my misfortunes, nor
indeed of my exact proportions ; and at my age, and in my desolate
state, I would fain be decorous in these things—and that reminds
me of dinner. Have you aught else to say, Morton?"

"Yes!" said I, suppressing my emotions—"yes, mother! do
bestow on me one warm wish, one kind word, before we part—see—
I kneel for your blessing—will you not give it me?"

"Bless you, my child—bless you! look you now—I have dropped
my needle!"

I rose hastily—bowed profoundly — (my mother returned the
courtesy with the grace peculiar to herself)—and withdrew. I hurried
into the great drawing-room—found Lady Needleham alone—rushed
out in despair—encountered the Lady Hasselton, and coquetted
with her the rest of the evening. Vain hope! to forget one's real
feelings by pretending those one never felt!

The next morning, then, after suitable adieux to all (Gerald
excepted) whom I left behind—after some tears too from my uncle,
which, had it not been for the presence of the Lady Hasselton, I
could have returned with interest—and after a long caress to his dog
Ponto, which now, in parting with that dear old man, seemed to me
as dog never seemed before, I hurried into the Beauty's carriage,
bade farewell for ever to the Rubicon of Life, and commenced my
career of manhood and citizenship by learning under the tuition of
the prettiest coquette of her time, the dignified duties of a Court
Gallant, and a Town Beau.

BOOK II.

CHAPTER I.

THE HERO IN LONDON—PLEASURE IS OFTEN THE SHORTEST, AS IT IS THE EARLIEST ROAD TO WISDOM, AND WE MAY SAY OF THE WORLD WHAT ZEAL-OF-THE-LAND-BUSY SAYS OF THE PIG-BOOTH, "WE ESCAPE SO MUCH OF THE OTHER VANITIES BY OUR EARLY ENTERING."

T had, when I first went to town, just become the fashion for young men of fortune to keep house, and to give their bachelor establishments the importance hitherto reserved for the household of a Benedict. Let the reader figure to himself a suite of apartments magnificently furnished, in the vicinity of the court. An anteroom is crowded with divers persons, all messengers in the various negotiations of pleasure. There, a French valet—that inestimable valet, Jean Desmarais—sitting over a small fire, was watching the operations of a coffee-pot, and conversing, in a mutilated attempt at the language of our nation, though with the eviable fluency of his own, with the various loiterers who were beguiling the hours they were obliged to wait for an audience of the master himself, by laughing at the master's Gallic representative. There stood a tailor with his books of patterns just imported from Paris — that modern Prometheus, who makes man what he is! Next to him a tall, gaunt fellow, in a coat covered with tarnished lace, a night-cap wig, and a large whip in his hand, comes to vouch for the pedigree and excellence of the three horses he intends to dispose of, out of pure love and amity for the buyer. By the window stood a thin starveling poet, who, like the grammarian of Cos, might have put lead in his pockets to prevent being blown away, had he not, with a more paternal precaution, put so much in his works that he had left none to spare. Excellent trick of the times, when ten guineas can purchase every virtue under the sun, and when an author thinks to vindicate the sins of his book by proving the admirable qualities of the paragon to whom it is dedicated.[1] There, with an air of

---

[1] Thank Heaven, for the honour of literature, *nous avons changé tous cela!*
—ED.

supercilious contempt, upon his smooth cheeks, a page, in purple and silver, sat upon the table, swinging his legs to and fro, and big with all the reflected importance of a *billet-doux*. There stood the pert haberdasher, with his box of silver-fringed gloves, and lace which Diana might have worn. At that time there was indeed no enemy to female chastity like the former article of man-millinery—the delicate whiteness of the glove, the starry splendour of the fringe, were irresistible, and the fair Adorna, in poor Lee's tragedy of Cæsar Borgia, is far from the only lady who has been killed by a pair of gloves.

Next to the haberdasher, dingy and dull of aspect, a book-hunter bent beneath the load of old works gathered from stall and shed, and about to be re-sold according to the price exacted from all literary gallants, who affect to unite the fine gentleman with the profound scholar. A little girl, whose brazen face and voluble tongue betrayed the growth of her intellectual faculties, leant against the wainscot, and repeated, in the anteroom, the tart repartees which her mistress (the most celebrated actress of the day) uttered on the stage; while a stout, sturdy, bull-headed gentleman, in a gray surtout and a black wig, mingled with the various voices of the motley group the gentle phrases of Hockley in the Hole, from which place of polite merriment he came charged with a message of invitation. While such were the inmates of the anteroom, what picture shall we draw of the *salon* and its occupant?

A table was covered with books, a couple of fencing foils, a woman's mask, and a profusion of letters; a scarlet cloak, richly laced, hung over, trailing on the ground. Upon a slab of marble lay a hat, looped with diamonds, a sword, and a lady's lute. Extended upon a sofa, loosely robed in a dressing-gown of black velvet, his shirt collar unbuttoned, his stockings ungartered, his own hair (undressed and released for a brief interval from the false locks universally worn) waving from his forehead in short yet dishevelled curls, his whole appearance stamped with the morning negligence which usually follows midnight dissipation, lay a young man of about nineteen years. His features were neither handsome nor ill-favoured, and his stature was small, slight, and somewhat insignificant, but not, perhaps, ill-formed either for active enterprise or for muscular effort. Such, reader, is the picture of the young prodigal who occupied the apartments I have described, and such (though somewhat flattered by partiality) is a portrait of Morton Devereux, six months after his arrival in town.

The door was suddenly thrown open with that unhesitating rudeness by which our friends think it necessary to signify the extent of their familiarity; and a young man of about eight-and-twenty, richly dressed, and of a countenance in which a dissipated nonchalance and an aristocratic hauteur seemed to struggle for mastery, abruptly entered.

"What! ho, my noble royster," cried he, flinging himself upon a chair—"still suffering from St. John's Burgundy! Fie, fie, upon your apprenticeship!—why, before I had served half your time, I could take my three bottles as easily as the sea took the good ship 'Revolution,'—swallow them down with a gulp, and never show the least sign of them the next morning!"

"I really believe you, most magnanimous Tarleton. Providence gives to each of its creatures different favours—to one wit—to the other a capacity for drinking. A thousand pities that they are never united!"

"So bitter, Count!—ah, what will ever cure you of sarcasm?"

"A wise man by conversion, or fools by satiety."

"Well, I dare say that is witty enough, but I never admire fine things of a morning. I like letting my faculties live till night in a *déshabille*—let us talk easily and sillily of the affairs of the day. *Imprimis*, will you stroll to the New Exchange?—there is a black eye there that measures out ribbons, and my green ones long to flirt with it."

'With all my heart—and in return you shall accompany me to Master Powell's puppet-show."

"You speak as wisely as Solomon himself in the puppet-show. I own that I love that sight; 'tis a pleasure to the littleness of human nature to see great things abased by mimicry—kings moved by bobbins, and the pomps of the earth personated by Punch."

"But how do you like sharing the mirth of the groundlings, the filthy plebeians, and letting them see how petty are those distinctions which you value so highly, by showing them how heartily you can laugh at such distinctions yourself. Allow, my superb Coriolanus, that one purchases pride by the loss of consistency."

"Ah, Devereux, you poison my enjoyment by the mere word 'plebeian!' Oh, what a beastly thing is a common person!—a shape of the trodden clay without any alloy—a compound of dirty clothes —bacon breaths, villainous smells, beggarly cowardice, and cattish ferocity.—Pah, Devereux! rub civet on the very thought!"

"Yet they will laugh to-day at the same things you will, and consequently there would be a most flattering congeniality between you. Emotion, whether of ridicule, anger, or sorrow—whether raised at a puppet-show, a funeral, or a battle—is your grandest of levellers. The man who would be always superior should be always apathetic."

"Oracular, as usual, Count,—but, hark!—the clock gives tongue. One, by the Lord!—will you not dress?"

And I rose and dressed. We passed through the anteroom, my attendant assistants in the art of wasting money, drew up in a row.

"Pardon me, gentlemen," said I, ('Gentlemen, indeed!' cried Tarleton,) "for keeping you so long, Mr. Snivelship, your waist-coats are exquisite—favour me by conversing with my valet on the width of the lace for my liveries—he has my instructions. Mr. Jockelton, your horses shall be tried to-morrow at one. Ay, Mr. Rymer, I beg you a thousand pardons—I beseech you to forgive the ignorance of my rascals in suffering a gentleman of your merit to remain for a moment unattended to. I have read your ode—it is splendid—the ease of Horace, with the fire of Pindar—your Pegasus never touches the earth, and yet in his wildest excesses you curb him with equal grace and facility—I object, sir, only to your dedication —it is too flattering."

"By no means, my Lord Count, it fits you to a hair."

"Pardon me," interrupted I, "and allow me to transfer the honour to Lord Halifax—he loves men of merit—he loves also their dedications. I will mention it to him to-morrow—everything you say of me will suit him exactly. You will oblige me with a copy of your poem directly it is printed, and suffer me to pay your bookseller for it now, and through your friendly mediation; adieu!"

"Oh, Count, this is too generous."

"A letter for me, my pretty page. Ah! tell her ladyship I shall wait upon her commands at Powell's—time will move with a tortoise speed till I kiss her hands. Mr. Fribbleden, your gloves would fit the giants at Guildhall—my valet will furnish you with my exact size—you will see to the legitimate breadth of the fringe. My little beauty, you are from Mrs. Bracegirdle—the play *shall* succeed—I have taken seven boxes—Mr. St. John promises his influence. Say, therefore, my Hebe, that the thing is certain, and let me kiss thee,—thou hast dew on thy lip already. Mr. Thumpem, you are a fine fellow, and deserve to be encouraged; I will see that the next time your head is broken it shall be broken fairly;—but I will not patronize the bear—consider that peremptory. What, Mr. Bookworm, again! I hope you have succeeded better this time— the old songs had an autumn fit upon them, and had lost the best part of their *leaves*—and Plato had mortgaged one half his republic, to pay, I suppose, the exorbitant sum you thought proper to set upon the other. As for Diogenes Laertius, and his philosophers—"

"Pish!" interrupted Tarleton; "are you going, by your theo-retical treatises on philosophy, to make me learn the practical part of it, and prate upon learning while I am supporting myself with patience?"

"Pardon me! Mr. Bookworm—you will deposit your load and visit me to-morrow at an earlier hour. And now, Tarleton, I am at your service."

CHAPTER II.

GAY SCENES AND CONVERSATIONS :—THE NEW EXCHANGE AND THE PUPPET SHOW :—THE ACTOR, THE SEXTON, AND THE BEAUTY.

"WELL, Tarleton," said I, looking round that mart of millinery and love-making, which, so celebrated in the reign of Charles II., still preserved the shadow of its old renown in that of Anne—"well, here we are upon the classical ground so often commemorated in the comedies which our chaste grandmothers thronged to see. Here we can make appointments, while we profess to buy gloves, and should our mistress tarry too long, beguile our impatience by a flirtation with her milliner. Is there not a breathing air of gaiety about the place?—does it not still smack of the Ethereges and Sedleys?"

"Right," said Tarleton, leaning over a counter and amorously eyeing the pretty coquette to whom it belonged—while, with the coxcombry then in fashion, he sprinkled the long curls that touched his shoulders with a fragrant shower from a bottle of jessamine water upon the counter—"right ; saw you ever such an eye? Have you snuff of the true scent, my beauty—foh !—this is for the nostril of a Welsh parson—choleric and hot, my beauty—pulverized horse-radish—why, it would make a nose of the coldest constitution imaginable sneeze like a washed schoolboy on a Saturday night.—Ah, this is better, my princess—there is some courtesy in this snuff—it flatters the brain like a poet's dedication. Right, Devereux, right, there *is* something infectious in the atmosphere ; one catches good humour, as easily as if it were cold. Shall we stroll on?—*my* Clelia is on the other side of the Exchange.—You were speaking of the playwriters—what a pity that our Ethereges and Wycherleys should be so frank in their gallantry, that the prudish public already begins to look shy on them.—They have a world of wit !"

"Ay," said I ; "and, as my good uncle would say, a world of knowledge of human nature, viz., of the worst part of it. But they are worse than merely licentious—they are positively villainous—pregnant with the most redemptionless *scoundrelism*,—cheating, lying, thieving, and fraud ; their humour debauches the whole moral system—they are like the Sardinian herb—they make you laugh, it is true—but they poison you in the act. But who comes here!"

"Oh, honest Coll!—Ah, Cibber, how goes it with you?"

The person thus addressed was a man of about the middle age—very grotesquely attired—and with a periwig preposterously long. His countenance (which, in its features, was rather comely) was stamped with an odd mixture of liveliness, impudence, and a coarse, yet not unjoyous spirit of reckless debauchery. He approached us with a saunter, and saluted Tarleton with an air servile enough, in spite of an affected familiarity.

"What think you," resumed my companion, "we were conversing upon?"

"Why, indeed, Mr. Tarleton," answered Cibber, bowing very low, "unless it were the exquisite fashion of your waistcoat, or your success with my Lady Duchess, I know not what to guess."

"Pooh, man," said Tarleton, haughtily, "none of your compliments;" and then added, in a milder tone, "No, Colley, we were abusing the immoralities that existed on the stage, until thou, by the light of thy virtuous example, didst undertake to reform it."

"Why," rejoined Cibber, with an air of mock sanctity, "Heaven be praised, I have pulled out some of the weeds from our theatrical parterre——"   .

"Hear you that, Count? Does he not look a pretty fellow for a censor?"

"Surely," said Cibber, "ever since Dicky Steele has set up for a saint, and assumed the methodistical twang, some hopes of conversion may be left even for such reprobates as myself. Where, may I ask, will Mr. Tarleton drink to-night?"

"Not with thee, Coll. The Saturnalia don't happen every day. Rid us now of thy company; but stop, I will do thee a pleasure—know you this gentleman?"

"I have not that extreme honour."

"Know a Count, then! Count Devereux, demean yourself by sometimes acknowledging Colley Cibber, a rare fellow at a song, a bottle, and a message to an actress; a lively rascal enough, but without the goodness to be loved, or the independence to be respected."

"Mr. Cibber," said I, rather hurt at Tarleton's speech, though the object of it seemed to hear this description with the most unruffled composure—"Mr. Cibber, I am happy, and proud of an introduction to the author of the 'Careless Husband.' Here is my address; oblige me with a visit at your leisure."

"How could you be so galling to the poor devil?" said I, when Cibber, with a profusion of bows and compliments, had left us to ourselves.

"Ah, hang him—a low fellow, who pins all his happiness to the skirts of the quality, is proud of being despised, and that which would excruciate the vanity of others only flatters *his*. And now for my Clelia——."

After my companion had amused himself with a brief flirtation with a young lady, who affected a most edifying demureness, we left the Exchange, and repaired to the Puppet-show.

On entering the Piazza, in which, as I am writing for the next century, it may be necessary to say that Punch held his court, we saw a tall, thin fellow, loitering under the columns, and exhibiting a countenance of the most ludicrous discontent. There was an insolent arrogance about Tarleton's good-nature which always led him to consult the whim of the moment at the expense of every other consideration, especially if the whim referred to a member of the canaille whom my aristocratic friend esteemed as a base part of the exclusive and despotic property of gentlemen.

"Egad, Devereux," said he, "do you see that fellow? he has the audacity to affect spleen. Faith, I thought melancholy was the distinguishing patent of nobility—we will smoke him." And, advancing towards the man of gloom, Tarleton touched him with the end of his cane. The man started and turned round. "Pray, sirrah," said Tarleton coldly, "pray who the devil are you, that you presume to look discontented?"

"Why, sir," said the man, good humouredly enough, "I have some right to be angry."

"I doubt it, my friend," said Tarleton. "What is your complaint? a rise in the price of tripe, or a drinking wife? those, I take it, are the sole misfortunes incidental to your condition."

"If that be the case," said I, observing a cloud on our new friend's brow, "shall we heal thy sufferings? Tell us thy complaints, and we will prescribe thee a silver specific; there is a sample of our skill."

"Thank you, humbly, gentlemen," said the man, pocketing the money, and clearing his countenance; "and, seriously, mine is an uncommonly hard case. I was, till within the last few weeks, the under-sexton of St Paul's, Covent Garden, and my duty was that of ringing the bells for daily prayers: but a man of Belial came hitherwards, set up a puppet-show, and, timing the hours of his exhibition with a wicked sagacity, made the bell I rang for church serve as a summons to Punch,—so, gentlemen, that whenever your humble servant began to pull for the Lord, his perverted congregation began to flock to the devil; and, instead of being an instrument for saving souls, I was made the innocent means of destroying them. Oh, gentlemen, it was a shocking thing to tug away at the rope till the sweat ran down one, for four shillings a week; and to see all the time that one was thinning one's own congregation, and emptying one's own pockets!"

"It was indeed a lamentable dilemma; and what did you, Mr. Sexton?"

"Do, sir, why, I could not stifle my conscience, and I left my place. Ever since then, sir, I have stationed myself in the Piazza, to warn my poor, deluded fellow-creatures of their error, and to assure them that when the bell of St. Paul's rings, it rings for prayers, and not for puppet-shows—and, Lord help us, there it goes at this very moment; and look, look, gentlemen, how the wigs and hoods are crowding to the motion [1] instead of the minster."

"Ha! ha! ha!" cried Tarleton, "Mr. Powell is not the first ·man who has wrested things holy to serve a carnal purpose, and made use of church bells in order to ring money to the wide pouch of the church's enemies. Harkye, my friend, follow my advice, and turn preacher yourself; mount a cart opposite to the motion, and I'll wager a trifle that the crowd forsake the theatrical mountebank in favour of the religious one; for the more sacred the thing played upon, the more certain is the game."

"Body of me, gentlemen," cried the ex-sexton, "I'll follow your advice."

"Do so, man, and never presume to look doleful again; leave dulness to your superiors." [2]

And with this advice, and an additional compensation for his confidence, we left the innocent assistant of Mr. Powell, and marched into the puppet-show, by the sound of the very bells the perversion of which the good sexton had so pathetically lamented.

The first person I saw at the show, and indeed the express person I came to see, was the Lady Hasselton. Tarleton and myself separated for the present, and I repaired to the coquette: "Angels of grace!" said I, approaching; "and, by the by, before I proceed another word, observe, Lady Hasselton, how appropriate the exclamation is to *you*! Angels of *grace!* why you have moved all your patches!—one—two—three—six—eight—as I am a gentleman, from the left side of your cheek to the right! What is the reason of so sudden an emigration?"

"I have changed my politics,[3] Count, that is all, and have

[1] An antiquated word in use for puppet-shows.
[2] See Spectator, No. 14, for a letter from this unfortunate under-sexton.
[3] Whig ladies patched on one side of the cheek, tories on the other.

resolved to lose no time in proclaiming the change. But is it true that you are going to be married?"

"Married! Heaven forbid! which of my enemies spread so cruel a report?"

"Oh, the report is universal!" and the Lady Hasselton flirted her fan with a most flattering violence.

"It is false, nevertheless; I cannot afford to buy a wife at present, for, thanks to jointures, and pin-money, these things are all matter of commerce; and (see how closely civilized life resembles the savage!) the English, like the Tartar gentleman, obtains his wife only by purchase! But who is the bride?"

"The Duke of Newcastle's rich daughter, Lady Henrietta Pelham."

"What, Harley's object of ambition![1] Faith, Madam, the report is not so cruel as I thought for!"

"Oh, you fop!—but is it not true?"

"By my honour, I fear not; my rivals are too numerous and too powerful. Look now, yonder! how they already flock around the illustrious heiress,—note those smiles and simpers. Is it not pretty to see those very fine gentlemen imitating bumpkins at a fair, and grinning their best *for a gold ring!* But you need not fear me, Lady Hasselton, my love cannot wander, if it would. In the quaint thought of Sidney,[2] love having once flown to my heart, burnt its wings there, and cannot fly away."

"La, you now!" said the beauty; "I do not comprehend you exactly—your master of the graces does not teach you your compliments properly."

"Yes, he does, but in your presence I forget them; and now," I added, lowering my voice into the lowest of whispers, "now that you are assured of my fidelity, will you not learn at last to discredit rumours and trust to me?"

"I love you too well!" answered the Lady Hasselton in the same tone, and that answer gives an admirable idea of the affection of every coquette!—love and confidence with them are qualities that have a natural antipathy, and can never be united! Our *tête-à-tête* was at an end, the people round us became social, and conversation general.

"Betterton acts to-morrow night," cried the Lady Pratterly, "we must go!"

"We must go," cried the Lady Hasselton.

[1] Lord Bolingbroke tells us that it was the main end of Harley's administration to marry his son to this lady. Thus is the fate of nations a bundle made up of a thousand little private schemes.

[2] In the Arcadia, that museum of oddities and beauties.

"We must go!" cried all.

And so passed the time till the puppet-show was over, and my attendance dispensed with.

It is a charming thing to be the lover of a lady of the mode! One so honoured does with his hours as a miser with his guineas, —viz., nothing but count them!

CHAPTER III.

MORE LIONS.

THE next night, after the theatre, Tarleton and I strolled into Wills's. Half-a-dozen wits were assembled. Heavens! how they talked! actors, actresses, poets, statesmen, philosophers, critics, divines, were all pulled to pieces with the most gratifying malice imaginable. We sat ourselves down, and while Tarleton amused himself with a dish of coffee and the "Flying Post," I listened very attentively to the conversation. Certainly if we would take every opportunity of getting a grain or two of knowledge, we should soon have a chest full;—a man earned an excellent subsistence by asking every one who came out of a tobacconist's shop for a pinch of snuff, and retailing the mixture as soon as he had filled his box.[1]

While I was listening to a tall lusty gentleman, who was abusing Dogget, the actor, a well-dressed man entered, and immediately attracted the general observation. He was of a very flat, ill-favoured countenance, but of a quick eye, and a genteel air; there was, however, something constrained and artificial in his address, and he appeared to be endeavouring to clothe a natural good humour with a certain primness which could never be made to fit it.

"Ha, Steele!" cried a gentleman in an orange-coloured coat, who seemed, by a fashionable swagger of importance, desirous of giving the tone to the company—"Ha, Steele! whence come you? from the chapel or the tavern?" and the speaker winked round the room as if he wished us to participate in the pleasure of a good thing.

Mr. Steele drew up, seemingly a little affronted; but his good-nature conquering the affectation of personal sanctity, which, at the time I refer to, that excellent writer was pleased to assume, he contented himself with nodding to the speaker, and saying:—

---

[1] Tatler.

"All the world knows, Colonel Cleland, that you are a wit, and therefore we take your fine sayings, as we take change from an honest tradesman,—rest perfectly satisfied with the coin we get, without paying any attention to it."

"Zounds, Cleland, you got the worst of it there," cried a gentleman in a flaxen wig. And Steele slid into a seat near my own.

Tarleton, who was sufficiently well educated to pretend to the character of a man of letters, hereupon thought it necessary to lay aside the "Flying Post," and to introduce me to my literary neighbour.

"Pray," said Colonel Cleland, taking snuff and swinging himself to and fro with an air of fashionable grace, "has any one seen the new paper?"

"What!" cried the gentleman in the flaxen wig, "what! the Tatler's successor,—the 'Spectator?'"

"The same," quoth the colonel.

"To be sure—who has not?" returned he of the flaxen ornament. "People say Congreve writes it."

"They are very much mistaken, then," cried a little square man with spectacles; "to my certain knowledge Swift is the author."

"Pooh!" said Cleland imperiously—"pooh! it is neither one nor the other; I, gentlemen, am in the secret—but—you take me, eh? One must not speak well of oneself—mum is the word."

"Then," asked Steele, quietly, "we are to suppose that you, Colonel, are the writer?"

"I never said so, Dicky; but the women will have it that I am," and the colonel smoothed down his cravat.

"Pray, Mr. Addison, what say you?" cried the gentleman in the flaxen wig, "are you for Congreve, Swift, or Colonel Cleland?" This was addressed to a gentleman of a grave, but rather prepossessing mien; who, with eyes fixed upon the ground, was very quietly, and to all appearance very inattentively, solacing himself with a pipe; without lifting his eyes, this personage, then eminent, afterwards rendered immortal, replied—

"Colonel Cleland must produce other witnesses to prove his claim to the authorship of the 'Spectator'; the women, we well know, are prejudiced in his favour."

"That's true enough, old friend," cried the colonel, looking askant at his orange-coloured coat, "but faith, Addison, I wish you would set up a paper of the same sort, d'ye see; you're a nice judge of merit, and your sketches of character would do justice to your friends."

"If ever I do, colonel, I, or my coadjutors, will study at least to do justice to you."[1]

"Prithee, Steele," cried the stranger in spectacles, "prithee tell us thy thoughts on the subject : dost thou know the author of this droll periodical?"

"I saw him this morning," replied Steele, carelessly.

"Aha! and what said you to him?"

"I asked him his name."

"And what did he answer?" cried he of the flaxen wig, while all of us crowded round the speaker, with the curiosity every one felt in the authorship of a work then exciting the most universal and eager interest.

"He answered me solemnly," said Steele, "in the following words,

'Græci carent ablativo—Itali dativo—Ego nominativo.'"[2]

"Famous—capital!" cried the gentleman in spectacles; and then, touching Colonel Cleland, added, "what does it exactly mean?"

"Ignoramus!" said Cleland, disdainfully, "every *schoolboy knows Virgil!*"

"Devereux," said Tarleton, yawning, "what a d—d delightful thing it is to hear so much wit—pity that the atmosphere is so fine that no lungs unaccustomed to it can endure it long. Let us recover ourselves by a walk."

"Willingly," said I; and we sauntered forth into the streets.

"Wills's is not what it was," said Tarleton; "'tis a pitiful ghost of its former self, and if they had not introduced cards, one would die of the vapours there."

"I know nothing so insipid," said I, "as that mock literary air which it is so much the fashion to assume. 'Tis but a wearisome relief to conversation to have interludes of songs about Strephon and Sylvia, recited with a lisp by a gentleman with fringed gloves and a languishing look."

"Fie on it," cried Tarleton, "let us seek for a fresher topic. Are you asked to Abigail Masham's to-night, or will you come to Dame de la Riviere Manley's?"

"Dame de la what?—in the name of long words who is she?"

"Oh! Learning made libidinous : one who reads Catullus and profits by it."

"Bah, no, we will not leave the gentle Abigail for her. I have promised to meet St. John, too, at the Mashams."

[1] This seems to corroborate the suspicion entertained of the identity of Colonel Cleland with the Will Honeycomb of the Spectator.
[2] "The Greeks want an ablative—the Italians a dative—I a nominative."

"As you like. We shall get some wine at Abigail's, which we should never do at the house of her cousin of Marlborough."

And, comforting himself with this belief, Tarleton peaceably accompanied me to that celebrated woman, who did the Tories such notable service, at the expense of being termed by the Whigs, one great want divided into two parts, viz.—a great want of every shilling belonging to other people, and a great want of every virtue that should have belonged to herself. As we mounted the staircase, a door to the left (a private apartment) was opened, and I saw the favourite dismiss, with the most flattering air of respect, my old preceptor, the Abbé Montreuil. He received her attentions as his due, and, descending the stairs, came full upon me. He drew back —changed neither hue nor muscle—bowed civilly enough, and disappeared. I had not much opportunity to muse over this circumstance, for St. John and Mr. Domville—excellent companions both —joined us ; and the party being small, we had the unwonted felicity of talking, as well as bowing, to each other. It was impossible to think of any one else when St. John chose to exert himself; and so even the Abbé Montreuil glided out of my brain as St. John's wit glided into it. We were all of the same way of thinking on politics, and therefore were witty without being quarrelsome—a rare thing. The trusty Abigail told us stories of the good Queen, and we added *bons-mots* by way of corollary. Wine, too, wine that even Tarleton approved, lit up our intellects, and we spent altogether an evening such as gentlemen and Tories very seldom have the sense to enjoy.

O Apollo ! I wonder whether Tories of the next century will be such clever, charming, well-informed fellows as we were !

CHAPTER IV.

AN INTELLECTUAL ADVENTURE.

 LITTLE affected by the vinous potations which had been so much an object of anticipation with my companion, Tarleton and I were strolling homeward when we perceived a remarkably tall man engaged in a contest with a couple of watchmen. Watchmen were in all cases the especial and natural enemies of the gallants in my young days ; and no sooner did we see the unequal contest than, drawing our swords with that true English valour which makes all the quarrels of other people its own, we hastened to the relief of the weaker party.

"Gentlemen," said the elder watchman, drawing back, "this is no common brawl ; we have been shamefully beaten by this here madman, and for no earthly cause."

"Who ever did beat a watchman for any earthly cause, you rascal?" cried the accused party, swinging his walking-cane over the complainant's head with a menacing air.

"Very true," cried Tarleton coolly. "Seigneurs of the watch, you are both made and paid to be beaten ; ergo—you have no right to complain. Release this worthy cavalier, and depart elsewhere to make night hideous with your voices."

"Come, come," quoth the younger Dogberry, who perceived a reinforcement approaching, "move on, good people, and let us do our duty."

"Which," interrupted the elder watchman, "consists in taking this hulking swaggerer to the watchhouse."

"Thou speakest wisely, man of peace," said Tarleton ; "defend thyself ; " and without adding another word, he ran the watchman through—not the body, but the coat ; avoiding, with great dexterity, the corporeal substance of the attacked party, and yet approaching it so closely, as to give the guardian of the streets very reasonable ground for apprehension. No sooner did the watchman find the hilt strike against his breast, than he uttered a dismal cry, and fell upon the pavement as if he had been shot.

"Now for thee, varlet," cried Tarleton, brandishing his rapier before the eyes of the other watchman, "tremble at the sword of Gideon."

"O Lord, O Lord!" ejaculated the terrified comrade of the fallen man, dropping on his knees, "for heaven's sake, sir, have a care."

"What argument canst thou allege, thou screech owl! of the metropolis, that thou shouldst not share the same fate as thy brother owl?"

"Oh, sir!" cried the craven night-bird (a bit of a humourist in its way), "because I have a nest and seven little owlets at home, and t'other owl is only a bachelor."

"Thou art an impudent thing to jest at us," said Tarleton ; "but thy wit has saved thee ; rise."

At this moment two other watchmen came up.

"Gentlemen," said the tall stranger whom we had rescued, "we had better fly."

Tarleton cast at him a contemptuous look, and placed himself in a posture of offence.

"Hark ye," said I, "let us effect an honourable peace. Messieurs the watch, be it lawful for you to carry off the slain, and for us to claim the prisoners."

But our new foes understood not a jest, and advanced upon us with a ferocity which might really have terminated in a serious engagement, had not the taller stranger thrust his bulky form in front of the approaching battalion, and cried out with a loud voice, "Zounds, my good fellows, what's all this for? If you take us up you will get broken heads to-night, and a few shillings perhaps to-morrow. If you leave us alone, you will have whole heads, and a guinea between you. Now, what say you?"

Well spoke Phædra against the dangers of eloquence (καλοὶ λιάν λογοι). The watchmen looked at each other. "Why really, sir," said one, "what you say alters the case very much; and if Dick here is not much hurt, I don't know what we may say to the offer."

So saying, they raised the fallen watchman, who, after three or four grunts, began slowly to recover himself.

"Are you dead, Dick?" said the owl with seven owlets.

"I think I am," answered the other, groaning.

"Are you able to drink a pot of ale, Dick?" cried the tall stranger.

"I think I am," reiterated the dead man, very lackadaisically. And this answer satisfying his comrades, the articles of peace were subscribed to.

Now, then, the tall stranger began searching his pockets with a most consequential air.

"Gad, so!" said he at last; "not in my breeches' pocket!—well, it must be in my waistcoat. No. Well, 'tis a strange thing—demme it is! Gentlemen, I have had the misfortune to leave my purse behind me, add to your other favours by lending me where-withal to satisfy these honest men."

And Tarleton lent him the guinea. The watchmen now retired, and we were left alone with our portly ally.

Placing his hand to his heart, he made us half-a-dozen profound bows, returned us thanks for our assistance in some very courtly phrases, and requested us to allow him to make our acquaintance. We exchanged cards, and departed on our several ways.

"I have met that gentleman before," said Tarleton. "Let us see what name he pretends to. 'Fielding—Fielding;' ah, by the Lord, it is no less a person! It is the great Fielding himself."

"Is Mr. Fielding, then, as elevated in fame as in stature?"

"What, is it possible that you have not yet heard of Beau Fielding, who bared his bosom at the theatre in order to attract the admiring compassion of the female part of the audience?"

"What!" I cried, "the Duchess of Cleveland's Fielding?"

"The same; the best looking fellow of his day! A sketch of his history is in the 'Tatler,' under the name of 'Orlando the Fair.'

He is terribly fallen as to fortune since the day when he drove about
in a car like a sea-shell, with a dozen tall fellows, in the Austrian
livery, black and yellow, running before and behind him. You
know he claims relationship to the house of Hapsburg.   As for the
present, he writes poems, makes love, is still good-natured, humorous, and odd ; is rather unhappily addicted to wine and borrowing,
and rigidly keeps that oath of the Carthusians which never suffers
them to carry any money about them."

" An acquaintance more likely to yield amusement than profit."

" Exactly so.   He will favour you with a visit—to-morrow,
perhaps, and you will remember his propensities."

" Ah ! who ever forgets a warning that relates to his purse ! "

" True !" said Tarleton, sighing.   " Alas ! my guinea, thou and
I have parted company for ever ; *vale, vale, inquit Iolas !* "

CHAPTER V.

THE BEAU IN HIS DEN, AND A PHILOSOPHER DISCOVERED.

MR. FIELDING having twice favoured me with visits,
which found me from home, I thought it right to pay my
respects to him ; accordingly one morning I repaired to
his abode.   It was situated in a street which had been
excessively the mode some thirty years back ; and the house still
exhibited a stately and somewhat ostentatious exterior.   I observed
a considerable cluster of infantine ragamuffins collected round the
door, and no sooner did the portal open to my summons, than they
pressed forward in a manner infinitely more zealous than respectful.
A servant in the Austrian livery, with a broad belt round his
middle, officiated as porter.   " Look, look ! " cried one of the
youthful gazers, " look at the Beau's *keeper !* "   This imputation on
his own respectability, and that of his master, the domestic seemed
by no means to relish, for, muttering some maledictory menace,
which I at first took to be German, but which I afterwards found to
be Irish, he banged the door on the faces of the intrusive impertinents, and said, in an accent which suited very ill with his continental
attire,

" And is it my master you're wanting, sir ? "

" It is."

" And you would be after seeing him immadiately ? "

" Rightly conjectured, my sagacious friend."

"Fait then, your honour, my master's in bed with a terrible fit of the megrims."

"Then you will favour me by giving this card to your master, and expressing my sorrow at his indisposition."

Upon this the orange-coloured lacquey, very quietly reading the address on the card, and spelling letter by letter in an audible mutter, rejoined—

"C—o—u (cou) n—t (unt) Count, D—e—v. Och, by my shoul, and it's Count Devereux after all? I'm thinking?"

"You think, with equal profundity and truth."

"You may well say that, your honour. Stip in a bit—I'll tell my master—it is himself that will see you in a twinkling!"

"But you forget that your master is ill?" said I.

"Sorrow a bit for the matter o' that—my master is never ill to a jontleman."

And with this assurance "the Beau's keeper" ushered me up a splendid staircase into a large, dreary, faded apartment, and left me to amuse myself with the curiosities within, while he went to perform a cure upon his master's "megrims." The chamber, suiting with the house and the owner, looked like a place in the other world, set apart for the reception of the ghosts of departed furniture. The hangings were wan and colourless, the chairs and sofas were most spiritually unsubstantial,—the mirrors reflected all things in a sepulchral sea-green; even a huge picture of Mr. Fielding himself, placed over the chimney-piece, seemed like the apparition of a portrait, so dim, watery, and indistinct had it been rendered by neglect and damp. On a huge tomb-like table in the middle of the room, lay two pencilled profiles of Mr. Fielding, a pawnbroker's ticket, a pair of ruffles, a very little muff, an immense broadsword, a Wycherly comb, a jackboot, and an old plumed hat;—to these were added a cracked pomatum-pot, containing ink, and a scrap of paper, ornamented with sundry paintings of hearts and torches, on which were scrawled several lines in a hand so large and round that I could not avoid seeing the first verse, though I turned away my eyes as quickly as possible—that verse, to the best of my memory, ran thus: "Say, lovely Lesbia, when thy swain." Upon the ground lay a box of patches, a periwig, and two or three well-thumbed books of songs. Such was the reception-room of Beau Fielding, one indifferently well calculated to exhibit the propensities of a man, half bully, half fribble; a poet, a fop, a fighter, a beauty, a walking museum of all odd humours, and a living shadow of a past renown. "There are changes in wit as in fashion," said Sir William Temple, and he proceeds to instance a nobleman, who was the greatest wit of the court of Charles I., and the greatest dullard

in that of Charles II.[1]   But Heavens how awful are the revolutions
of coxcombry! what a change from Beau Fielding the Beauty, to
Beau Fielding the Oddity!

After I had remained in this apartment about ten minutes, the
great man made his appearance.   He was attired in a dressing-
gown of the most gorgeous material and colour, but so old that it
was difficult to conceive any period of past time which it might not
have been supposed to have witnessed; a little velvet cap, with a
tarnished gold tassel, surmounted his head, and his nether limbs
were sheathed in a pair of military boots.   In person he still
retained the trace of that extraordinary symmetry he had once
possessed, and his features were yet handsome, though the complexion had grown coarse and florid, and the expression had settled
into a broad, hardy, farcical mixture of effrontery, humour, and
conceit.

But how different his costume from that of old?   Where was the
long wig with its myriad curls? the coat stiff with golden lace?
the diamond buttons—"the pomp, pride, and circumstance of
glorious war?" the glorious war Beau Fielding had carried on
throughout the female world—finding in every saloon a Blenheim—
in every play-house a Ramilies?   Alas! to what abyss of fate will
not the love of notoriety bring men!   To what but the lust of
show do we owe the misanthropy of Timon, or the ruin of Beau
Fielding!

"By the Lord!" cried Mr. Fielding, approaching, and shaking
me familiarly by the hand, "by the Lord, I am delighted to see
thee!   As I am a soldier, I thought thou wert a spirit, invisible and
incorporeal—and as long as I was in that belief I trembled for thy
salvation, for I knew at least that thou wert not a spirit of Heaven;
since thy door is the very reverse of the doors above, which we are
assured shall be opened unto our knocking.   But thou art early,
Count; like the ghost, in Hamlet, thou snuffest the morning air.—
Wilt thou not keep out the rank atmosphere by a pint of wine and
a toast?"

"Many thanks to you, Mr. Fielding; but I have at least one
property of a ghost, and don't drink after daybreak,"

"Nay, now, 'tis a bad rule! a villainous bad-rule, fit *only for*
ghosts and graybeards.   We youngsters, Count, should have a more
generous policy.   Come now, where didst thou drink last night?
has the bottle bequeathed thee a qualm or a headache, which
preaches repentance and abstinence this morning?"

"No, but I visit my mistress this morning; would you have me
smell of strong potations, and seem a worshipper of the '*Glass* of

1 The Earl of Norwich.

Fashion,' rather than of 'the Mould of Form?' Confess, Mr. Fielding, that the women love not an early tippler, and that they expect sober and sweet kisses from a pair of 'youngsters' like us."

"By the Lord," cried Mr. Fielding, stroking down his comely stomach, "there is a great show of reason in thy excuses, but only the show, not substance, my noble Count. You know me, you know *my* experience with the women—I would not boast, as I'm a soldier —but 'tis something! nine hundred and fifty locks of hair have I got in my strong box, under padlock and key; fifty within the last week—true—on my soul—so that I may pretend to know a little of the dear creatures; well, I give thee my honour, Count, that they like a royster; they love a fellow who can carry his six bottles under a silken doublet; there's vigour and manhood in it—and, then, too, what a power of toasts can a six-bottle man drink to his mistress! Oh, 'tis your only chivalry now—your modern substitute for tilt and tournament; true, Count, as I'm a soldier!"

"I fear my Dulcinea differs from the herd, then; for she quarrelled with me for supping with St. John three nights ago, and—"

"St. John," interrupted Fielding, cutting me off in the beginning of a witticism, "St. John, famous fellow, is he not? By the Lord, we will drink to his administration, you in chocolate, I in Madeira. O'Carroll, you dog—O'Carroll—rogue—rascal—ass—dolt!"

"The same, your honour," said the orange-coloured lacquey, thrusting in his lean visage.

"Ay, the same indeed—thou anatomized son of St. Patrick; why dost thou not get fat? thou shamest my good living, and thy belly is a rascally minister to thee, devouring all things for itself, without fattening a single member of the body corporate. Look at *me*, you dog, am *I* thin? Go and get fat, or I will discharge thee—by the Lord, I will! the sun shines through thee like an empty wine glass."

"And is it upon your honour's lavings you would have me get fat?" rejoined Mr. O'Carroll, with an air of deferential inquiry.

"Now, as I live, thou art the impudentest varlet!" cried Mr. Fielding, stamping his foot on the floor, with an angry frown.

"And is it for talking of your honour's lavings? an' sure that's *nothing* at all, at all," said the valet, twirling his thumbs with expostulating innocence.

"Begone, rascal!" said Mr. Fielding, "begone; go to the Salop, and bring us a pint of Madeira, a toast, and a dish of chocolate."

"Yes, your honour, in a twinkling," said the valet, disappearing.

"A sorry fellow," said Mr. Fielding, "but honest and faithful, and loves me as well as a saint loves gold; 'tis his love makes him familiar."

Here the door was again opened, and the sharp face of Mr. O'Carroll again intruded.

"How now, sirrah!" exclaimed his master.

Mr. O'Carroll, without answering by voice, gave a grotesque sort of signal between a wink and a beckon. Mr. Fielding rose, muttering an oath, and underwent a whisper. "By the Lord," cried he, seemingly in a furious passion, "and thou hast not got the bill cashed yet, though I told thee twice to have it done last evening! Have I not my debts of honour to discharge, and did I not give the last guinea I had about me for a walking-cane yesterday? Go down to the city immediately, sirrah, and bring me the change."

The valet again whispered.

"Ah," resumed Fielding, "ah—so far, you say, 'tis true; 'tis a great way, and perhaps the Count can't wait till you return. Prithee (turning to me), prithee now, is it not vexatious—no change about me, and my fool has not cashed a trifling bill I have for a thousand or so, on Messrs. Child! and the cursed Salop puts not its *trust* even in princes—'tis its way—'Gad now—you have not a guinea about you?"

What could I say? my guinea joined Tarleton's, in a visit to that bourne whence no *such* traveller e'er returned.

Mr. O'Carroll now vanished in earnest, the wine and the chocolate soon appeared. Mr. Fielding brightened up, recited his poetry, blessed his good fortune, promised to call on me in a day or two; and assured me, with a round oath, that the next time he had the honour of seeing me, he would treat me with another pint of Madeira, exactly of the same sort.

I remember well that it was the evening of the same day, in which I had paid this visit to the redoubted Mr. Fielding, that, on returning from a drum at Lady Hasselton's, I entered my anteroom with so silent a step, that I did not arouse even the keen senses of Monsieur Desmarais. He was seated by the fire, with his head supported by his hands, and intently poring over a huge folio. I had often observed that he possessed a literary turn, and all the hours in which he was unemployed by me, he was wont to occupy with books. I felt now, as I stood still and contemplated his absorbed attention in the contents of the book before him, a strong curiosity to know the nature of his studies; and so little did my taste second the routine of trifles in which I had been lately engaged, that in looking upon the earnest features of the man, on which the solitary light streamed calm and full; and impressed with the deep quiet and solitude of the chamber, together with the undisturbed sanctity of comfort presiding over the small, bright hearth, and contrasting what I saw with the brilliant scene—brilliant with gaudy, wearing, wearisome frivolities—which I had just quitted, a sensation of envy, at the enjoyments of my dependent, entered my breast, accompanied with a sentiment resembling humiliation at the nature of my own pursuits. I am generally thought a proud man; but I am never proud to my inferiors; nor can I imagine pride where ₊there is no competition. I approached Desmarais, and said, in French,

"How is this? why did you not, like your fellows, take advantage of my absence, to pursue your own amusements? They must be dull, indeed, if they do not hold out to you more tempting inducements than that colossal offspring of the press."

"Pardon me, sir," said Desmarais, very respectfully, and closing the book, "pardon me, I was not aware of your return. Will Monsieur doff his cloak?"

"No; shut the door—wheel round that chair, and favour me with a sight of your book."

"Monsieur will be angry, I fear," said the valet (obeying the first two orders, but hesitating about the third), "with my course of reading: I confess it is not very compatible with my station."

"Ah, some long romance, the *Clelia*—I suppose—nay, bring it hither—that is to say, if it be movable by the strength of a single man."

Thus urged, Desmarais modestly brought me the book. Judge of my surprise when I found it was a volume of Leibnitz—a philosopher, then very much the rage—because one might talk of him very safely, without having read him.[1] Despite of my surprise, I could not help smiling when my eye turned from the book to the student. It is impossible to conceive an appearance less like a philosopher's than that of Jean Desmarais. His wig was of a nicety that would not have brooked the irregularity of a single hair; his dress was not preposterous, for I do not remember, among gentles or valets, a more really exquisite taste than that of Desmarais; but it evinced, in every particular, the arts of the toilet. A perpetual smile sat upon his lips—sometimes it deepened into a sneer—but that was the only change it ever experienced; an irresistible air of self-conceit gave piquancy to his long, marked features, small glittering eye, and withered cheeks, on which a delicate and soft bloom excited suspicion of artificial embellishment. A very fit frame of body this for a valet; but I humbly opine, a very unseemly one for a student of Leibnitz.

"And what," said I, after a short pause, "is your opinion of this philosopher; I understand that he has just written a work,[2] above all praise and all comprehension."

[1] Which is possibly the reason why there are so many disciples of Kant at the present moment.—ED. [2] The Theodicœa.

"It is true, Monsieur, that it is above his own understanding. He knows not what sly conclusions may be drawn from his premises; but I beg Monsieur's pardon, I shall be tedious and intrusive."

"Not a whit; speak out, and at length. So you conceive that Leibnitz makes ropes, which *others* will make into ladders?"

"Exactly so," said Desmarais; "all his arguments go to swell the sails of the great philosophical truth—'Necessity!' We are the things and toys of Fate, and its everlasting chain compels even the Power that creates, as well as the things created."

"Ha!" said I, who, though little versed at that time in these metaphysical subtleties, had heard St. John often speak of the strange doctrine to which Desmarais referred, "you are, then, a believer in the fatalism of Spinosa?"

"No, Monsieur," said Desmarais, with a complacent smile, "my system is my own—it is composed of the thoughts of others—but my thoughts are the cords which bind the various sticks into a faggot."

"Well," said I, smiling at the man's conceited air, "and what is your main dogma?"

"Our utter impotence."

"Pleasing! Mean you that we have no free will?"

"None."

"Why, then, you take away the very existence of vice and virtue; and, according to you, we sin or act well, not from our own accord, but because we are compelled and preordained to it."

Desmarais' smile withered into the grim sneer with which, as I have said, it was sometimes varied.

"Monsieur's penetration is extreme—but shall I not prepare his nightly draught?"

"No; answer me at length; and tell me the difference between good and ill, if we are compelled by Necessity to either."

Desmarais hemmed, and began. Despite of his caution, the cox-comb loved to hear himself talk, and he talked, therefore, to the following purpose:—

"Liberty is a thing impossible! Can you *will* a single action, however simple, independent of your organization—independent of the organization of others—independent of the order of things past—independent of the order of things to come? You cannot. But if not independent, you are dependent; if dependent, where is your liberty? where your freedom of will? Education disposes our characters—can you control your own education, begun at the hour of birth? You cannot. Our character, joined to the conduct of others, disposes of our happiness, our sorrow, our crime, our virtue. Can you control your character? We have already seen that you cannot. Can you control the conduct of others—others perhaps whom you have never seen, but who may ruin you at a word—a despot, for instance, or a warrior? You cannot. What remains? that if we cannot choose our characters, nor our fates, we cannot be accountable for either. If you are a good man, you are a lucky man; but you are not to be praised for what you could not help. If you are a bad man, you are an unfortunate one; but you are not to be execrated for what you could not prevent." [1]

"Then, most wise Desmarais, if you steal this diamond loop from my hat, you are only an unlucky man, not a guilty one, and worthy of my sympathy, not anger?"

"Exactly so—but you must hang me for it. You cannot control events, but you can modify man. Education, law, adversity, prosperity, correction, praise, modify him—without his choice, and sometimes without his perception. But once acknowledge Necessity, and evil passions cease; you may punish, you may destroy others, if for the safety and good of the commonwealth; but motives for doing so cease to be private: you can have no personal hatred to men for committing actions which they were irresistibly compelled to commit."

I felt, that however I might listen to and dislike these sentiments, it would not do for the master to argue with the domestic, especially when there was a chance that he might have the worst of it. And so I was suddenly seized with a fit of sleepiness, which broke off our conversation. Meanwhile I inly resolved, in my own mind, to take the first opportunity of discharging a valet who saw no difference between good and evil, but that of luck; and who, by the irresistible compulsion of Necessity, might some day or other have the involuntary misfortune to cut the throat of his master!

I did not, however, carry this unphilosophical resolution into effect. Indeed, the rogue doubting, perhaps, the nature of the impression he had made on me, redoubled so zealously his efforts to please me in the science of his profession, that I could not determine upon relinquishing such a treasure for a speculative opinion, and I was too much accustomed to laugh at my Sosia, to believe there could be any reason to fear him.

[1] Whatever pretensions Monsieur Desmarais may have had to originality, this tissue of opinions is as old as philosophy itself.—ED.

CHAPTER VI.

AN UNIVERSAL GENIUS—PERICLES TURNED BARBER—NAMES OF
BEAUTIES IN 171— —THE TOASTS OF THE KIT-CAT CLUB.

S I was riding with Tarleton towards Chelsea, one day, he asked me if I had ever seen the celebrated Mr. Salter. "No," said I,, "but I heard Steele talk of him the other night at Wills's. He is an antiquarian and a barber, is he not?"

"Yes, a shaving virtuoso; really a comical and strange character, and has oddities enough to compensate one for the debasement of talking with a man in his rank."

"Let us go to him forthwith," said I, spurring my horse into a canter.

"*Quod petis hic est*," cried Tarleton, "there is his house." And my companion pointed to a coffee-house.

"What," said I, "does he draw wine as well as teeth?"

"To be sure: Don Saltero is an universal genius. Let us dismount."

Consigning our horses to the care of our grooms, we marched into the strangest looking place I ever had the good fortune to behold. A long narrow coffee-room was furnished with all manner of things that, belonging neither to heaven, earth, nor the water under the earth, the redoubted Saltero might well worship without incurring the crime of idolatry. The first thing that greeted my eyes was a bull's head, with a most ferocious pair of vulture's wings on its neck. While I was surveying this, I felt something touch my hat, I looked up and discovered an immense alligator swinging from the ceiling, and fixing a monstrous pair of glass eyes upon me. A thing which seemed to me like an immense shoe, upon a nearer approach, expanded itself into an Indian canoe, and a most hideous spectre with mummy skin, and glittering teeth, that made my blood run cold, was labelled, "Beautiful Specimen of a Calmuc Tartar."

While lost in wonder, I stood in the middle of the apartment, up walks a little man as lean as a miser, and says to me, rubbing his hands—

"Wonderful, sir, is it not?"

"Wonderful, indeed, Don!" said Tarleton; "you look like a Chinese Adam, surrounded by a Japanese creation."

"He, he, he, sir, you have so pleasant a vein," said the little Don, in a sharp shrill voice. "But it has been all done, sir, by one man ; all of it collected by me, simple as I stand."

"Simple, indeed," quoth Tarleton ; "and how gets on the fiddle?"

"Bravely, sir, bravely ; shall I play you a tune?"

"No, no, my good Don ; another time."

"Nay, sir, nay," cried the antiquarian, "suffer me to welcome your arrival properly."

And, forthwith disappearing, he returned in an instant with a marvellously ill-favoured old fiddle. Throwing a penseroso air into his thin cheeks, our Don then began a few preliminary thrummings, which set my teeth on edge, and made Tarleton put both hands to his ears. Three sober-looking citizens, who had just sat themselves down to pipes and the journal, started to their feet like so many pieces of clockwork ; but no sooner had Don Saltero, with a *dégagé* air of graceful melancholy, actually launched into what he was pleased to term a tune, than an universal irritation of nerves seized the whole company. At the first overture, the three citizens swore and cursed, at the second division of the tune, they seized their hats, at the third they vanished. As for me, I found all my limbs twitching as if they were dancing to St. Vitus's music ; the very drawers disappeared ; the alligator itself twirled round, as if revivified by so harsh an experiment on the nervous system ; and I verily believe the whole museum, bull, wings, Indian canoe, and Calmuc Tartar, would have been set into motion by this new Orpheus, had not Tarleton, in a paroxysm of rage, seized him by the tail of the coat, and whirled him round, fiddle and all, with such velocity that the poor musician lost his equilibrium, and falling against a row of Chinese monsters, brought the whole set to the ground, where he lay covered by the wrecks that accompanied his overthrow, screaming and struggling, and grasping his fiddle, which every now and then, touched involuntarily by his fingers, uttered a dismal squeak, as if sympathizing in the disaster it had caused, until the drawer ran in, and raising the unhappy antiquarian, placed him on a great chair.

"O Lord!" groaned Don Saltero, "O Lord—my monsters—my monsters—the pagoda—the Mandarin, and the idol—where are they?—broken—ruined—annihilated!"

"No, sir—all safe, sir," said the drawer, a smart, small, smug, pert man ; "put 'em down in the bill, nevertheless, sir. Is it Alderman Atkins, sir, or Mr. Higgins?"

"Pooh," said Tarleton, "bring me some lemonade—send the pagoda to the bricklayer—the mandarin to the surgeon—and the

E

idol to the Papist over the way! There's a guinea to pay for their carriage. How are you, Don?"

"Oh, Mr. Tarleton, Mr. Tarleton! how could you be so cruel?"

"The nature of things demanded it, my good Don. Did I not call you a Chinese Adam? and how could you bear that name without undergoing the fall?"

"Oh, sir, this is no jesting matter—broke the railing of my pagoda—bruised my arm—cracked my fiddle—and cut me off in the middle of that beautiful air!—no jesting matter."

"Come, Mr. Salter," said I, "'tis very true! but cheer up. 'The gods,' says Seneca, 'look with pleasure on a great man falling with the statesmen, the temples, and the divinities of his country;' all of which, Mandarin, pagoda, and idol, accompanied *your* fall. Let us have a bottle of your best wine, and the honour of your company to drink it."

"No, Count, no," said Tarleton, haughtily; "we can drink not with the Don; but we'll have the wine, and *he* shall drink it. Meanwhile, Don, tell us what possible combination of circumstances made thee fiddler, barber, anatomist and virtuoso!"

Don Saltero loved fiddling better than anything in the world, but next to fiddling he loved talking. So being satisfied that he should be reimbursed for his pagoda, and fortifying himself with a glass or two of his own wine, he yielded to Tarleton's desire, and told us his history. I believe it was very entertaining to the good barber, but Tarleton and I saw nothing extraordinary in it;—and long before it was over, we wished him an excellent good day, and a new race of Chinese monsters.

That evening we were engaged at the Kit-Cat Club, for though I was opposed to the politics of its members, they admitted me on account of my literary pretensions. Halifax was there, and I commended the poet to his protection. We were very gay and Halifax favoured us with three new toasts by himself. O Venus! what beauties we made, and what characters we murdered! Never was there so important a synod to the female world, as the gods of the Kit-Cat Club. Alas! I am writing for the children of an after age, to whom the very names of those who made the blood of their ancestors leap within their veins will be unknown. What cheek will colour at the name of Carlisle? What hand will tremble as it touches the paper inscribed by that of Brudenel! The graceful Godolphin, the sparkling enchantment of Harper, the divine voice of Claverine, the gentle and bashful Bridgewater, the damask cheek and ruby lips of the Hebe Manchester—what will these be to the race for whom alone these pages are penned! This history is a union of strange contrasts! like the tree of the Sun, described by Marco Polo, which was green when approached on one side, but white when perceived on the other—to me it is clothed in the verdure and spring of the existing time; to the reader it comes covered with the hoariness and wanness of the Past!

CHAPTER VII.

A DIALOGUE OF SENTIMENT SUCCEEDED BY THE SKETCH OF A CHARACTER, IN WHOSE EYES SENTIMENT WAS TO WISE MEN WHAT RELIGION IS TO FOOLS, VIZ.—A SUBJECT OF RIDICULE.

ST. JOHN was now in power, and in the full flush of his many ambitious and restless schemes. I saw as much of him as the high rank he held in the state, and the couse- quent business with which he was oppressed, would suffer me—me who was prevented by religion from actively embracing any political party, and who, therefore, though inclined to Toryism, associated pretty equally with all. St. John and myself formed a great friendship for each other, a friendship which no after change or chance could efface, but which exists, strengthened and mellowed by time, at the very hour in which I now write.

One evening he sent to tell me he should be alone, if I would sup with him; accordingly I repaired to his house. He was walking up and down the room with uneven and rapid steps, and his countenance was flushed with an expression of joy and triumph, very rare to the thoughtful and earnest calm which it usually wore. "Congratulate me, Devereux," said he, seizing me eagerly by the hand, "congratulate me!"

"For what?"

"Ay, true—you are not yet a politician—you cannot yet tell how dear—how inexpressibly dear to a politician is, is a momentary and petty victory—but—if I were Prime Minister of this country, what would you say?"

"That you could bear the duty better than any man living—but remember, Harley is in the way."

"Ah, there's the rub," said St. John, slowly, and the expression of his face again changed from triumph to thoughtfulness; "but this is a subject not to your taste—let us choose another." And flinging himself into a chair, this singular man, who prided himself on suiting his conversation to every one, began conversing with me upon the lighter topics of the day ; these we soon exhausted, and at last we settled upon that of love and women.

"I own," said I, "that in this respect, pleasure has disappointed as well as wearied me. I have longed for some better object of worship than the trifler of fashion, or the yet more ignoble minion of the senses. I ask a vent for enthusiasm—for devotion—for romance —for a thousand subtle and secret streams of unuttered and unutterable feeling. I often think that I bear within me the desire and the sentiment of poetry, though I enjoy not its faculty of expression ; and that that desire and that sentiment, denied legitimate egress, centre and shrink into one absorbing passion—which is the want of love. Where am I to satisfy this want ? I look round these great circles of gaiety which we term the world—I send forth my heart as a wanderer over their regions and recesses, and it returns sated, and pallid, and languid, to myself again."

"You express a common want in every less worldly or more morbid nature," said St. John, "a want which I myself have experienced, and if I had never felt it, I should never, perhaps, have turned to ambition, to console or to engross me. But do not flatter yourself that the want will ever be fulfilled. Nature places us alone in this inhospitable world, and no heart is cast in a similar mould to that which we bear within us. We pine for sympathy ; we make to ourselves a creation of ideal beauties, in which we expect to find it— but the creation has no reality—it is the mind's phantasma which the mind adores—and it is because the phantasma can have no actual being that the mind despairs. Throughout life, from the cradle to the grave, it is no real or living thing which we demand ; it is the realization of the idea we have formed within us, and which, as we are not gods, we can never call into existence. We are enamoured of the statue ourselves have graven ; but, unlike the statue of the Cyprian, it kindles not to our homage, nor melts to our embraces.".

"I believe you," said I ; "but it is hard to undeceive ourselves. The heart is the most credulous of all fanatics, and its ruling passion the most enduring of all superstitions. Oh ! what can tear from us, to the last, the hope, the desire, the yearning for some bosom which, while it mirrors our own, parts not with the reflection. I have read that, in the very hour and instant of our birth, one exactly similar to ourselves, in spirit and form, is born also, and that a secret and unintelligible sympathy preserves that likeness, even through the vicissitudes of fortune and circumstance, until, in the same point of time, the two beings are resolved once more into the elements of earth—confess that there is something welcome, though unfounded, in the fancy, and that there are few of the substances of worldly honour which one would not renounce, to possess, in the closest and fondest of all relations, this shadow of ourselves ! "

" Alas ! " said St. John, " the possession, like all earthly blessings, carries within it its own principle of corruption. The deadliest foe to love is not change, nor misfortune, nor jealousy, nor wrath, nor anything that flows from passion, or emanates from fortune ; the deadliest foe to it is *custom !* With custom die away the delusions and the mysteries which encircle it ; leaf after leaf, in the green poetry on which its beauty depends, droops and withers, till nothing but the bare and rude trunk is left. With all passion the soul demands something unexpressed, some vague recess to explore or to marvel upon—some veil upon the mental as well as the corporeal deity, Custom leaves nothing to romance, and often but little to respect. The whole character is bared before us like a plain, and the heart's eye grows wearied with the sameness of the survey. And to weariness succeeds distaste, and to distaste, one of the myriad shapes of the Proteus Aversion—so that the passion we would make the rarest of treasures fritters down to a very instance of the commonest of proverbs —and out of familiarity cometh indeed contempt ! "

" And are we, then, " said I, " for ever to forego the most delicious of our dreams ? Are we to consider love as an entire delusion, and to reconcile ourselves to an eternal solitude of heart ? What, then, shall fill the crying and unappeasable void of our souls ? What shall become of those mighty sources of tenderness which, refused all channel in the rocky soil of the world, must have an outlet elsewhere, or stagnate into torpor ? "

" Our passions, " said St. John, " are restless, and will make each experiment in their power, though vanity be the result of all. Disappointed in love, they yearn towards ambition ; *and the object of ambition, unlike that of love, never being wholly possessed, ambition is the more durable passion of the two.* But sooner or later even that, and all passions are sated at last ; and when wearied of too wide a flight, we limit our excursions, and looking round us, discover the narrow bounds of our proper end, we grow satisfied with the loss of rapture, if we can partake of enjoyment : and the experience which seemed at first so bitterly to betray us becomes our most real benefactor, and ultimately leads us to content. For it is the excess and not the nature of our passions which is perishable. Like the trees which grew by the tomb of Protesilaus, the passions flourish till they reach a certain height, but no sooner is that height attained than they wither away."

Before I could reply, our conversation received an abrupt and complete interruption for the night. The door was thrown open, and a man, pushing aside a servant with a rude and yet a dignified air, entered the room unannounced, and with the most perfect disregard to ceremony—

"How d'ye do, Mr. St. John," said he—"how d'ye do?—Pretty sort of a day we've had.—Lucky to find you at home—that is to say if you will give me some broiled oysters and champagne for supper."

"With all my heart, doctor," said St. John, changing his manner at once from the pensive to an easy and somewhat brusque familiarity —"with all my heart ; but I am glad to hear you are a convert to champagne : you spent a whole evening last week in endeavouring to dissuade me from the sparkling sin."

"Pish ! I had suffered the day before from it, so like a true Old Bailey penitent, I preached up conversion to others, not from a desire of their welfare, but a plaguy sore feeling for my own misfortune. Where did you dine to-day ? At home ! Oh ! the devil ! I starved on three courses at the Duke of Ormond's."

"Aha ! Honest Matt was there ?"

"Yes, to my cost. He borrowed a shilling of me for a chair. Hang this weather, it costs me seven shillings a day for coach-fare, besides my paying the fares of all my poor brother parsons, who come over from Ireland to solicit my patronage for a bishopric, and end by borrowing half-a-crown in the meanwhile. But Matt Prior will pay me again, I suppose, out of the public money?"

"To be sure, if Chloe does not ruin him first."

"Hang the slut : don't talk of her. How Prior rails against his place.[1] He says the exercise spoils his wit, and that the only rhymes he ever dreams of now-a-days are ' docket and cocket.' "

"Ha, ha ! we must do something better for Matt—make him a bishop or an ambassador. But pardon me, Count, I have not yet made known to you the most courted, authoritative, impertinent, clever, independent, haughty, delightful, troublesome parson of the age : do homage to Dr. Swift. Doctor, be merciful to my particular friend, Count Devereux."

Drawing himself up, with a manner which contrasted his previous one strongly enough, Dr. Swift saluted me with a dignity which might even be called polished, and which certainly showed that however he might prefer, as his usual demeanour, an air of negligence and semi-rudeness, he had profited sufficiently by his acquaintance with the great to equal them in the external graces, supposed to be peculiar to their order, whenever it suited his inclination. In person Swift is much above the middle height, strongly built, and with a remarkably fine outline of throat and chest ; his front face is

---

[1] In the Customs.

certainly displeasing, though far from uncomely ; but the clear chiselling of the nose, the curved upper lip, the full, round Roman chin, the hanging brow, and the resolute decision, stamped upon the whole expression of the large forehead, and the clear blue eye, make his profile one of the most striking I ever saw. He honoured me, to my great surprise, with a fine speech and a compliment ; and then, with a look, which menaced to St. John the retort that ensued, he added : "And I shall always be glad to think that I owe your acquaintance to Mr. Secretary St. John, who, if he talked less about operas and singers—thought less about Alcibiades and Pericles—if he never complained of the load of business not being suited to his temper, at the very moment he had been working, like Gumdragon, to get the said load upon his shoulders ; and if he persuaded one of his sincerity being as great as his genius,—would appear to all time, as adorned with the choicest gifts that Heaven has yet thought fit to bestow on the children of men. Prithee now, Mr. Sec., when shall we have the oysters ! Will you be merry to-night, Count ?"

"Certainly ; if one may find absolution for the champagne.'

"I'll absolve you, with a vengeance, on condition that you'll walk home with me, and protect the poor parson from the Mohawks. Faith, they ran young Davenant's chair through with a sword, t'other night. I hear they have sworn to make daylight through my Tory cassock—all Whigs you know, Count Devereux, nasty, dangerous animals, how I hate them ; they cost me five-and-sixpence a week in chairs to avoid them."

"Never mind, Doctor, I'll send my servants home with you," said St. John.

"Ay, a nice way of mending the matter—that's curing the itch by scratching the skin off. I could not give your tall fellows less than a crown a-piece, and I could buy off the bloodiest Mohawk in the kingdom, if he's a Whig, for half that sum. But, thank Heaven, the supper is ready."

And to supper we went. The oysters and champagne seemed to exhilarate, if it did not refine, the Doctor's wit. St. John was unusually brilliant. I myself caught the infection of their humour, and contributed my quota to the common stock of jest and repartee ; and that evening, spent with the two most extraordinary men of the age, had in it more of broad and familiar mirth than any I have ever wasted in the company of the youngest and noisiest disciples of the bowl and its concomitants. Even amidst all the coarse ore of Swift's conversation, the diamond perpetually broke out ; his vulgarity was never that of a vulgar mind. Pity that, while he condemned St. John's over affectation of the grace of life, he never perceived that his own affectation of coarseness and brutality was to the full as unworthy of the simplicity of intellect;[1] and that the aversion to cant, which was the strongest characteristic of his mind, led him into the very faults he despised, only through a more displeasing and offensive road. That same aversion to cant is, by the way, the greatest and most prevalent enemy to the reputation of high and of strong minds; and in judging Swift's character in especial, we should always bear it in recollection. This aversion—the very antipodes to hypocrisy—leads men not only to disclaim the virtues they have, but to pretend to the vices they have not. Foolish trick of disguised vanity! the world, alas, readily believes them!—Like Justice Overdo—in the garb of poor Arthur of Bradley, they may deem it a virtue to have assumed the disguise; but they must not wonder if the sham Arthur is taken for the real, beaten as a vagabond and set in the stocks as a rogue!

CHAPTER VIII.

LIGHTLY WON—LIGHTLY LOST.—A DIALOGUE OF EQUAL INSTRUC-
TION AND AMUSEMENT.—A VISIT TO SIR GODFREY KNELLER.

NE morning Tarleton breakfasted with me. "I don't see the little page," said he, "who was always in attendance in your anteroom, what the deuce has become of him?"

"You must ask his mistress; she has quarrelled with me, and withdrawn both her favour and her messenger."

---

[1] It has been said that Swift was only coarse in his later years, and, with a curious ignorance both of fact and of character, that Pope was the cause of the Dean's grossness of taste. There is no doubt that he grew coarser with age; but there is also no doubt that, graceful and dignified as that great genius could be when he pleased, he affected at a period earlier than the one in which he is now introduced, to be coarse both in speech and manner. I seize upon this opportunity, *mal à propos* as it is, to observe that Swift's preference of Harley to St. John is by no means so certain as writers have been pleased generally to assert. Warton has already noted a passage in one of Swift's letters to Bolingbroke, to which I will beg to call the reader's attention.

"It is *you were* my hero, but the other (Lord Oxford) *never was;* yet if he were, it was your own fault, who taught me to love him, and often vindicated him, in the beginning of your ministry, from my accusations. But I granted he had the greatest inequalities of any man alive; and his whole scene was fifty times more a what-dye-call it than yours; for I declare yours was *unite*, and I wish you would so order it that the world may be as wise as I upon that article."

I have to apologize for introducing this quotation, which I have done because (and I entreat the reader to remember this) I observe that Count Devereux always speaks of Lord Bolingbroke as he was spoken of by the eminent men of that day —not as he is now rated by the judgment of posterity.—ED.

"What, the Lady Hasselton quarrelled with you! *Diable!* Wherefore?"

"Because I am not enough of the 'pretty fellow;' am tired of carrying hood and scarf, and sitting behind her chair through five long acts of a dull play; because I disappointed her in not searching for her at every drum and quadrille party; because I admired not her monkey; and because I broke a tea-pot with a toad for a cover."

"And is not that enough?" cried Tarleton. "Heavens! what a black bead-roll of offences; Mrs. Merton would have discarded me for one of them. However thy account has removed my surprise; I heard her praise thee the other day; now, as long as she loved thee, she always abused thee like a pickpocket."

"Ha!—ha!—ha!—and what said she in my favour?"

"Why, that you were certainly very handsome, though you were small; that you were certainly a great genius, though every one would not discover it; and that you certainly had quite the air of high birth, though you were not nearly so well dressed as Beau Tippetly. But *entre nous*, Devereux, I think she hates you, and would play you a trick of spite—revenge is too strong a word—if she could find an opportunity."

"Likely enough, Tarleton; but a coquette's lover is always on his guard; so she will not take me unawares."

"So be it. But tell me, Devereux, who is to be your next mistress, Mrs. Denton, or Lady Clancathcart? the world gives them both to you."

"The world is always as generous with what is worthless as the bishop in the fable was with his blessing. However, I promise thee, Tarleton, that I will not interfere with thy claims, either upon Mrs. Denton or Lady Clancathcart."

"Nay," said Tarleton, "I will own that you are a very Scipio; but it must be confessed, even by you, satirist as you are, that Lady Clancathcart has a beautiful set of features."

"A handsome face, but so vilely made. She would make a splendid picture if, like the goddess Laverna, she could be painted as a head without a body."

"Ha!—ha!—ha!—you have a bitter tongue, Count; but Mrs. Denton, what have you to say against her?"

"Nothing; she has no pretensions for me to contradict. She has a green eye and a sharp voice; a mincing gait and a broad foot. What friend of Mrs. Denton's would not, therefore, counsel her to a prudent obscurity?"

"She never had but one lover in the world," said Tarleton, "who was old, blind, lame, and poor; she accepted him, and became Mrs. Denton."

E 2

"Yes," said I, "she was like the magnet, and received her name from the very first person [1] sensible of her attraction."

"Well, you have a shrewd way of saying sweet things," said Tarleton; "but I must own that you rarely or never direct it towards women individually. What makes you break through your ordinary custom?"

"Because I am angry with women collectively; and must pour my spleen through whatever channel presents itself."

"Astonishing," said Tarleton; "I despise women myself. I always did; but you were their most enthusiastic and chivalrous defender a month or two ago. What makes thee change, my Sir Amadis?"

"Disappointment! they weary, vex, disgust me; selfish, frivolous, mean, heartless—out on them—'tis a disgrace to have their love!"

"*O ciel!* What a sensation the news of thy misogyny will cause; the young, gay, rich, Count Devereux, whose wit, vivacity, splendour of appearance, in equipage and dress, in the course of one season have thrown all the most established beaux and pretty fellows into the shade; to whom dedications, and odes, and billet-doux, are so much waste paper; who has carried off the most general envy and dislike that any man ever was blest with, since St. John turned politician; what! thou all of a sudden to become a railer against the divine sex that made thee what thou art! Fly—fly—unhappy apostate, or expect the fate of Orpheus, at least!"

"None of your railleries, Tarleton, or I shall speak to you of plebeians, and the canaille!"

"*Sacre!* my teeth are on edge already! Oh, the base—base canaille, how I loathe them! Nay, Devereux, joking apart, I love you twice as well for your humour. I despise the sex heartily. Indeed, *sub rosâ* be it spoken, there are few things that breathe which I do not despise. Human nature seems to me a most pitiful bundle of rags and scraps, which the gods threw out of Heaven, as the dust and rubbish there."

"A pleasant view of thy species," said I.

"By my soul it is. Contempt is to me a luxury. I would not lose the privilege of loathing for all the objects which fools ever admired. What does old Persius say on the subject?

'Hoc ridere meum, tam nil, nullâ tibi vendo Iliade.'" [2]

"And yet, Tarleton," said I, "the littlest feeling of all is a delight in contemplating the littleness of other people. Nothing is more contemptible than habitual contempt."

---

[1] Magnes.

[2] "This privilege of mine, to laugh,—such a nothing as it seems—I would not barter to thee for an Iliad."

"Prithee, now," answered the haughty aristocrat, "let us not talk of these matters so subtly—leave me my enjoyment without refining upon it. What is your first pursuit for the morning?"

"Why, I have promised my uncle a picture of that invaluable countenance which Lady Hasselton finds so handsome; and I am going to give Kneller my last sitting."

"So, so, I will accompany you; I like the vain old dog; 'tis a pleasure to hear him admire himself so wittily."

"Come, then!" said I, taking up my hat and sword; and, entering Tarleton's carriage, we drove to the painter's abode.

We found him employed in finishing a portrait of Lady Godolphin.

"He, he!" cried he, when he beheld me approach. "By Got, I am glad to see you, Count Tevereux; dis painting is tamned poor work by oneself, widout any one to make *des grands yeux*, and cry, 'O, Sir Godfrey Kneller, how fine dis is!'"

"Very true, indeed," said I, "no great man can be expected to waste his talents without his proper reward of praise. But, Heavens, Tarleton, did you ever see anything so wonderful?—that hand—that arm—how exquisite! If Apollo turned painter, and borrowed colours from the rainbow, and models from the goddesses, he would not be fit to hold the pallet to Sir Godfrey Kneller."

"By Got, Count Tevereux, you are von grand judge of painting," cried the artist, with sparkling eyes, "and I will paint you as von tamned handsome man!"

"Nay, my Apelles, you might as well preserve some likeness."

"Likeness, by Got! I vill make you like and handsome both. By my shoul you make me von Apelles, I vill make you von Alexander!"

"People in general," said Tarleton, gravely, "believe that Alexander had a wry neck, and was a very plain fellow; but no one can know about Alexander like Sir Godfrey Kneller, who has studied military tactics so accurately, and who, if he had taken up the sword instead of the pencil, would have been at least an Alexander himself."

"By Got, Meester Tarleton, you are as goot a judge of de talents for de war as Count Tevereux of de *génie* for de painting! Meester Tarleton, I vill paint your picture, and I vill make your eyes von goot inch bigger than dey are!"

"Large or small," said I (for Tarleton, who had a haughty custom of contracting his orbs till they were scarce perceptible, was so much offended, that I thought it prudent to cut off his reply), "large or small, Sir Godfrey, Mr. Tarleton's eyes are capable of admiring your genius; why, your painting is like lightning, and one flash of your brush would be sufficient to restore even a blind man to sight."

"It is tamned true," said Sir Godfrey, earnestly; "and it did restore von man to sight once! By my shoul, it did! but sit your-self town, Count Tevereux, and look over your left shoulder—ah, dat is it—and now, praise on, Count Tevereux; de thought of my genius gives you—vat you call it—von animation—von fire, look you—by my shoul, it does!"

And by dint of such moderate panegyric, the worthy Sir Godfrey completed my picture, with equal satisfaction to himself and the original. See what a beautifier is flattery—a few sweet words will send the Count Devereux down to posterity, with at least three times as much beauty as he could justly lay claim to.[1]

CHAPTER IX.

A DEVELOPMENT OF CHARACTER, AND A LONG LETTER—A CHAP-TER, ON THE WHOLE, MORE IMPORTANT THAN IT SEEMS.

THE scenes through which, of late, I have conducted my reader, are by no means episodical; they illustrate far more than mere narration, the career to which I was so honourably devoted. Dissipation—women—wine—Tarle-ton for a friend, Lady Hasselton for a mistress. Let me now throw aside the mask.

[1] This picture represents the Count in an undress. The face is decidedly, though by no means remarkably, handsome; the nose is aquiline—the upper lip short and chiselled—the eyes gray, and the forehead, which is by far the finest feature in the countenance, is peculiarly high, broad, and massive. The mouth has but little beauty; it is severe, caustic, and rather displeasing, from the extreme compression of the lips. The great and prevalent expression of the face is energy. The eye—the brow—the turn of the head—the erect, penetrating aspect—are all strikingly bold, animated, and even daring. And this expression makes a singular contrast to that in another likeness of the Count, which was taken at a much later period of life. The latter portrait represents him in a foreign uniform, decorated with orders. The peculiar sarcasm of the mouth is hidden beneath a very long and thick mustachio, of a much darker colour than the hair (for in both portraits, as in Jervas's picture of Lord Bolingbroke, the hair is left undisguised by the odious fashion of the day). Across one cheek there is a slight scar, as of a sabre cut. The whole character of this portrait is widely different from that in the earlier one. Not a trace of the fire—the animation—which were so striking in the physiognomy of the youth of twenty,—is discoverable in the calm, sedate, stately, yet somewhat stern expression, which seems immovably spread over the paler hue, and the more prominent features of the man of about four or five and thirty. Yet, upon the whole, the face in the latter portrait is handsomer; and, from its air of dignity and reflection, even more impressive than that in the one I have first described.—ED.

To people who have naturally very intense and very acute feelings, nothing is so fretting, so wearing to the heart, as the commonplace affections, which are the properties and offspring of the world. We have seen the birds which, with wings unclipt, children fasten to a stake. The birds seek to fly, and are pulled back before their wings are well spread ; till, at last, they either perpetually strain at the end of their short tether, exciting only ridicule by their anguish, and their impotent impatience ; or, sullen and despondent, they remain on the ground, without an attempt to fly, nor creep, even to the full limit which their fetters would allow. Thus is it with feelings of the keen, wild nature I speak of; they are either striving for ever to pass the little circle of slavery to which they are condemned, and so move laughter by an excess of action, and a want of adequate power ; or they rest motionless and moody, disdaining the petty indulgence they *might* enjoy, till sullenness is construed into resignation, and despair seems the apathy of content. Time, however, cures what it does not kill : and both bird and beast, if they pine not to the death at first, grow tame and acquiescent at last.

What to me was the companionship of Tarleton, or the attachment of Lady Hasselton? I had yielded to the one, and I had half eagerly, half scornfully, sought the other. These, and the avocations they brought with them, consumed my time, and of Time murdered, there is a ghost, which we term *Ennui*. The hauntings of this spectre are the especial curse of the higher orders ; and hence springs a certain consequence to the passions. Persons in those ranks of society, so exposed to Ennui, are either rendered totally incapable of real love, or they love far more intensely than those in a lower station ; for the affections in them are either utterly frittered away on a thousand petty objects (poor shifts to escape the persecuting spectre), or else, early disgusted with the worthlessness of these objects, the heart turns within and languishes for something not found in the daily routine of life. When this is the case, and when the pining of the heart is once satisfied, and the object of love is found, there are two mighty reasons why the love should be most passionately cherished. The first is, the utter indolence in which aristocratic life oozes away, and which allows full food for that meditation which can nurse by sure degrees the weakest desire into the strongest passion ; and the second reason is, that the insipidity and hollowness of all patrician pursuits and pleasures render the excitement of love more delicious and more necessary to the " *ignavi terrarum domini*," than it is to those orders of society more usefully, more constantly, and more engrossingly engaged.

Wearied and sated with the pursuit of what was worthless, my heart, at last, exhausted itself in pining for what was pure. I recurred with a tenderness which I struggled with at first, and which in yielding to, I blushed to acknowledge to the memory of Isora. And in the world, surrounded by all which might be supposed to cause me to forget her, my heart clung to her far more endearingly than it had done in the rural solitudes in which she had first allured it. The truth was this; at the time I first loved her, other passions —passions almost equally powerful—shared her empire. Ambition and pleasure—vast whirlpools of thought—had just opened themselves a channel in my mind, and thither the tides of my desires were hurried and lost. Now those whirlpools had lost their power, and the channels being dammed up, flowed back upon my breast. Pleasure had disgusted me, and the only ambition I had yet courted and pursued had palled upon me still more. I say, the only ambition—for as yet that which is of the loftier and more lasting kind had not afforded me a temptation ; and the hope which had borne the name and rank of ambition had been the hope rather to glitter than to rise.

These passions, not yet experienced when I lost Isora, had afforded me at that period a ready comfort and a sure engrossment. And, in satisfying the hasty jealousies of my temper, in deeming Isora unworthy, and Gerald my rival, I naturally aroused in my pride a dexterous orator as well as a firm ally. Pride not only strengthened my passions, it also persuaded them by its voice ; and it was not till the languid, yet deep, stillness of sated wishes and palled desires fell upon me, that the low accent of a love still surviving at my heart made itself heard in answer.

I now began to take a different view of Isora's conduct. I now began to doubt, where I had formerly believed ; and the doubt, first allied to fear, gradually brightened into hope. Of Gerald's rivalry, at least of his identity with Barnard, and, consequently, of his power over Isora, there was, and there could be, no feeling short of certainty. But of what nature was that power ? Had not Isora assured me that it was not love ? Why should I disbelieve her ? Nay, did she not love myself ? had not her cheek blushed and her hand trembled when I addressed her ? Were these signs the counterfeits of love ? Were they not rather of that heart's dye which no skill *can* counterfeit ? She had declared that she could not, that she could never, be mine ; she had declared so with a fearful earnestness which seemed to annihilate hope ; but had she not also, in the same meeting, confessed that I was dear to her ? Had not her lip given me a sweeter and a more eloquent assurance of that confession than words ?—and could hope perish while love existed ? She had left me—she had bid me farewell for ever ; but.

that was no proof of a want of love, or of her unworthiness. Gerald, or Barnard, evidently possessed an influence over father as well as child. Their departure from * * * * might have been occasioned by him, and she might have deplored, while she could not resist it : or she might *not* even have deplored: nay, she might have desired, she might have advised it, for my sake as well as hers, were she thoroughly convinced that the union of our loves was impossible.

But, then, of what nature could be this mysterious authority which Gerald possessed over her? That which he possessed over the sire, political schemes might account for ; but these, surely, could not have much weight for the daughter. This, indeed, must still remain doubtful and unaccounted for. One presumption, that Gerald was either no favoured lover, or that he was unacquainted with her retreat, might be drawn from his continued residence at Devereux Court. If he loved Isora, and knew her present abode, would he not have sought her? Could he, I thought, live away from that bright face, if once allowed to behold it? unless, indeed, (terrible thought !) there hung over it the dimness of guilty familiarity, and indifference had been the offspring of possession. But was that delicate and virgin face, where changes, with every moment, coursed each other, harmonious to the changes of the mind, as shadows in a valley reflect the clouds of heaven !—was that face, so ingenuous, so girlishly revelant of all,—even of the slightest, the most transitory—emotion, the face of one hardened in deceit and inured to shame? The countenance is, it is true, but a faithless mirror: but what man that has studied women will not own that there is, at least while the down of first youth is not brushed away, in the eye and cheek of a zoned and untainted Innocence, that which survives not even the fruition of a lawful love, and has no (nay, not even a shadowed and imperfect) likeness in the face of guilt? Then, too, had any worldlier or mercenary sentiment entered her breast respecting me, would Isora have flown from the suit of the eldest scion of the rich house of Devereux?—and would she, poor and destitute, the daughter of an alien and an exile, would she have spontaneously relinquished any hope of obtaining that alliance which maidens of the loftiest houses of England had not disdained to desire? Thus confused and incoherent, but thus yearning fondly towards her image and its imagined purity, did my thoughts daily and hourly array themselves ; and, in proportion as I suffered common ties to drop from me one by one, those thoughts clung the more tenderly to that which, though severed from the rich argosy of former love, was still indissolubly attached to the anchor of its hope.

It was during this period of revived affection that I received the following letter from my uncle :—

"I thank thee for thy long letter, my dear boy ; I read it over three times with great delight. Od'sfish, Morton, you are a sad Pickle, I fear, and seem to know all the ways of the town as well as your old uncle did some thirty years ago ! 'Tis a very pretty acquaintance with human nature that your letters display. You put me in mind of little Sid, who was just about your height, and who had just such a pretty, shrewd way of expressing himself in simile and point. Ah, it is easy to see that you have profited by your old uncle's conversation, and that Farquhar and Etherege were not studied for nothing.

"But I have sad news for thee, my child, or rather it is sad for me to tell thee my tidings. It is sad for the old birds to linger in their nest when the young ones take wing and leave them ; but it is merry for the young birds to get away from the dull old tree, and frisk it in the sunshine—merry for them to get mates, and have young themselves. Now, do not think, Morton, that by speaking of mates and young, I am going to tell thee thy brothers are already married : nay, there is time enough for those things, and I am not friendly to early weddings, nor, to speak truly, a marvellous great admirer of that holy ceremony at any age ; for the which there may be private reasons, too long to relate to thee now. Moreover, I fear my young day was a wicked time—a heinous wicked time, and we were wont to laugh at the wedded state, until, body of me, some of us found it no laughing matter.

"But to return, Morton—to return to thy brothers—they have both left me ; and the house seems to me not the good old house it did when ye were all about me ; and, somehow or other, I look now oftener at the church-yard than I was wont to do. You are all gone now—all shot up and become men ; and when your old uncle sees you no more, and recollects that all his own contemporaries are out of the world, he cannot help saying, as William Temple, poor fellow, once prettily enough said, 'Methinks it seems an impertinence in me to be still alive.' You went first, Morton ; and I missed you more than I cared to say : but you were always a kind boy to those you loved, and you wrote the old knight merry letters, that made him laugh, and think he was grown young again —(faith, boy, that was a jolly story of the three Squires at Button's !) —and once a week comes your packet, well filled, as if you did not think it a task to make me happy, which your handwriting always does ; nor a shame to my gray hairs that I take pleasure in the same things that please thee ! So, thou seest, my child, that I

have got through thy absence pretty well, save that I have had no
one to read thy letters to ; for Gerald and thou are still jealous of
each other—a great sin in thee, Morton, which I prithee to reform.
And Aubrey, poor lad, is a little too rigid, considering his years,
and it looks not well in the dear boy to shake his head at the follies
of his uncle. And as to thy mother, Morton, I read her one of
thy letters, and she said thou wert a graceless reprobate to think so
much of this wicked world, and to write so familiarly to thine aged
relative. Now, I am not a young man, Morton ; but the word
aged has a sharp sound with it when it comes from a lady's mouth.

"Well, after thou hadst been gone a month, Aubrey and Gerald,
as I wrote thee word long since, in the last letter I wrote thee with
my own hand, made a tour together for a little while, and that was
a hard stroke on me. But after a week or two Gerald returned ;
and I went out in my chair to see the dear boy shoot—'sdeath,
Morton, he handles the gun well. And then Aubrey returned alone :
but he looked pined, and moping, and shut himself up, and as thou
dost love him so, I did not like to tell thee, till now, when he is
quite well, that he alarmed me much for him ; he is too much
addicted to his devotions, poor child, and seems to forget that the
hope of the next world ought to make us happy in this. Well,
Morton, at last, two months ago, Aubrey left us again, and Gerald
last week set off on a tour through the sister kingdom, as it is called ;
Faith, boy, if Scotland and England are sister kingdoms, 'tis a
thousand pities for Scotland that they are not coheiresses !

"I should have told thee of this news before, but I have had, as
thou knowest, the gout so villainously in my hand, that, till t'other
day, I have not held a pen, and old Nicholls, my amanuensis, is
but a poor scribe ; and I did not love to let the dog write to thee
on all our family affairs—especially as I have a secret to tell thee
which makes me plaguy uneasy. Thou must know, Morton, that
after thy departure Gerald asked me for thy rooms ; and though I
did not like that any one else should have what belonged to thee,
yet I have always had a foolish antipathy to say 'No!' so thy
brother had them, on condition to leave them exactly as they were,
and to yield them to thee whenever thou shouldst return to claim
them. Well, Morton, when Gerald went on his tour with thy
youngest brother, old Nicholls—you know 'tis a garrulous fellow—
told me one night, that his son Hugh—you remember Hugh, a thin
youth, and a tall—lingering by the beach one evening, saw a man,
wrapped in a cloak, come out of the castle cave, unmoor one of the
boats, and push off to the little island opposite. Hugh swears by
more than yea and nay, that the man was Father Montreuil. Now,
Morton, this made me very uneasy, and I saw why thy brother

Gerald wanted thy rooms, which communicate so snugly with the
sea.   So I told Nicholls, slily, to have the great iron gate at the
mouth of the passage carefully locked ; and when it was locked, I
had an iron plate put over the whole lock, that the lean Jesuit might
not creep even through the keyhole.   Thy brother returned, and I
told him a tale of the smugglers, who have really been too daring of
late, and insisted on the door being left as I had ordered ; and I
told him, moreover, though not as if I had suspected his communication with the priest, that I interdicted all further converse with that
limb of the church.   Thy brother heard me with an indifferently
bad grace ; but I was peremptory, and the thing was agreed on.

   " Well, child, the day before Gerald last left us, I went to take
leave of him in his own room—to tell thee the truth, I had forgotten
his travelling expenses—when I was on the stairs of the tower I heard
—by the Lord I did—Montreuil's voice in the outer room, as plainly as
ever I heard it at prayers.   Od'sfish, Morton, I was an angered, and
I made so much haste to the door, that my foot slipped by the way ;
thy brother heard me fall, and came out ; but I looked at him as I
never looked at thee, Morton, and entered the room.   Lo, the priest
was not there ; I searched both chambers in vain ; so I made thy
brother lift up the trap-door, and kindle a lamp, and I searched the
room below, and the passage.   The priest was invisible.   Thou
knowest, Morton, that there is only one egress in the passage, and
that was locked, as I said before, so where the devil—the devil
indeed—could thy tutor have escaped ?   He could not have passed
me on the stairs without my seeing him ; he could not have leaped
the window without breaking his neck ; he could not have got out
of the passage without making himself a current of air—Od'sfish,
Morton, this thing might puzzle a wiser man than thine uncle.
Gerald affected to be mighty indignant at my suspicions ; but, God
forgive him, I saw he was playing a part.   A man does not write
plays, my child, without being keen-sighted in these little intrigues ;
and, moreover, it is impossible I could have mistaken thy tutor's
voice, which, to do it justice, is musical enough, and is the most
singular voice I ever heard—unless little Sid's be excepted.

   " *Apropos*, of little Sid.   I remember that in the Mall, when I
was walking there alone, three weeks after my marriage, De Grammont and Sid joined me.   I was in a melancholic mood ('sdeath,
Morton, marriage tames a man as water tames mice !)—' Aha, Sir
William,' cried Sedley, ' thou hast a cloud on thee—prithee now
brighten it away : see, thy wife shines on thee, from the other end of
the Mall.'   ' Ah, talk not to a dying man of his physic !' said
Grammont [that Grammont was a shocking rogue, Morton !] ' Prithee,
Sir William, what is the chief characteristic of wedlock ? is it a state

of war or of peace?' 'Oh, peace to be sure!' cried Sedley, 'and Sir William and his lady carry with them the emblem.' 'How!' cried I; for I do assure thee, Morton, I was of a different turn of mind. 'How!' said Sid, gravely, 'why the emblem of peace is the *cornucopia*, which your lady and you equitably divide—she carries the *copia*, and you the *cor*—.' Nay, Morton, nay, I cannot finish the jest; for, after all, it was a sorry thing in little Sid, whom I had befriended like a brother, with heart and purse, to wound me so cuttingly; but 'tis the way with your jesters.

"Od'sfish, now how I have got out of my story! Well, I did not go back to my room, Morton, till I had looked to the outside of the iron door, and seen that the plate was as firm as ever: so now you have the whole of the matter. Gerald went the next day, and I fear me much lest he should already be caught in some Jacobite trap. Write me thy advice on the subject. Meanwhile, I have taken the precaution to have the trap-door removed, and the aperture strongly boarded over.

"But 'tis time for me to give over. I have been four days on this letter, for the gout comes now to me oftener than it did, and I do not know when I may again write to thee with my own hand; so I resolved I would e'en empty my whole budget at once. Thy mother is well and blooming; she is, at the present, abstractedly employed in a prodigious piece of tapestry, which old Nicholls informs me is the wonder of all the women.

"Heaven bless thee, my child! Take care of thyself, and drink moderately. It is hurtful, at thy age, to drink above a gallon or so at a sitting. Heaven bless thee again, and when the weather gets warmer, thou must come with thy kind looks, to make me feel at home again. At present the country wears a cheerless face, and everything about us is harsh and frosty, except the blunt, good-for-nothing heart of thine uncle, and that, winter or summer, is always warm to thee.

"WILLIAM DEVEREUX."

"P.S.—I thank thee heartily for the little spaniel of the new breed thou gottest me from the Duchess of Marlborough. It has the prettiest red and white, and the blackest eyes possible. But poor Ponto is as jealous as a wife three years married, and I cannot bear the old hound to be vexed, so I shall transfer the little creature, its rival, to thy mother."

This letter, tolerably characteristic of the blended simplicity, penetration, and overflowing kindness of the writer, occasioned me much anxious thought. There was no doubt in my mind but that

Gerald and Montreuil were engaged in some intrigue for the exiled family. The disguised name which the former assumed, the state reasons which D'Alvarez confessed that Barnard, or rather Gerald, had for concealment, and which proved, at least, that some state plot in which Gerald was engaged was known to the Spaniard, joined to those expressions of Montreuil, which did all but own a design for the restoration of the deposed Line, and the power which I knew he possessed over Gerald, whose mind, at once bold and facile, would love the adventure of the intrigue, and yield to Montreuil's suggestions on its nature ; these combined circumstances left me in no doubt upon a subject deeply interesting to the honour of our house, and the very life of one of its members. Nothing, however, for me to do, calculated to prevent or impede the designs of Montreuil and the danger of Gerald, occurred to me. Eager alike in my hatred and my love, I said, inly, "What matters it whether one whom the ties of blood never softened towards me, with whom, from my childhood upwards, I have wrestled as with an enemy, what matters it whether he win fame or death in the perilous game he has engaged in ? " And turning from this most generous, and most brotherly view of the subject, I began only to think whether the search or the society of Isora also influenced Gerald in his absence from home. After a fruitless and inconclusive meditation on that head, my thoughts took a less selfish turn, and dwelt with all the softness of pity, and the anxiety of love, upon the morbid temperament and ascetic devotions of Aubrey. What, for one already so abstracted from the enjoyments of earth, so darkened by superstitious misconceptions of the true nature of God, and the true objects of his creatures—what could be anticipated but wasted powers and a perverted life ? Alas ! when will men perceive the difference between religion and priestcraft ! When will they perceive that reason, so far from extinguishing religion by a more gaudy light, sheds on it all its lustre ? It is fabled that the first legislator of the Peruvians received from the deity a golden rod, with which in his wanderings he was to strike the earth, until in some destined spot the earth entirely absorbed it, and there—and there alone—was he to erect a temple to the Divinity. What is this fable but the cloak of an inestimable moral ? Our reason is the rod of gold ; the vast world of truth gives the soil, which it is perpetually to sound ; and only where without resistance the soil receives the rod which guided and supported us, will our Altar be sacred and our worship be accepted.

CHAPTER X.

SIR WILLIAM'S letter was still fresh in my mind, when for want of some less noble quarter wherein to bestow my tediousness, I repaired to St. John. As I crossed the hall to his apartment, two men, just dismissed from his presence, passed me rapidly ; one was unknown to me, but there was no mistaking the other—it was Montreuil. I was greatly startled ; the priest not appearing to notice me, and conversing in a whispered, yet seemingly vehement tone, with his companion, hurried on, and vanished through the street door. I entered St. John's room : he was alone, and received me with his usual gaiety.

"Pardon me, Mr. Secretary," said I ; " but if not a question of state, do inform me what you know respecting the taller one of those two gentlemen who have just quitted you ?"

"It *is* a question of state, my dear Devereux, so my answer must be brief ;—very little."

" You know who he is ? "

"Yes, a Jesuit, and a marvellously shrewd one : the Abbé Montreuil."

" He was my tutor."

" Ah, so I have heard."

" And your acquaintance with him is positively and *bonâ fide* of a state nature?"

" Positively and *bonâ fide.*"

"I could tell you something of him ; he is certainly in the service of the Court at St. Germains, and a terrible plotter on this side the channel."

" Possibly ; but I wish to receive no information respecting him."

One great virtue of business did St. John possess, and I have never known any statesman who possessed it so eminently : it was the discreet distinction between friends of the statesman and friends of the man. Much and intimately as I knew St. John, I could never glean from him a single secret of a state nature, until, indeed, at a later period, I leagued myself to a portion of his public schemes. Accordingly I found him, at the present moment, perfectly impregnable to my inquiries ; and it was not till I knew Montreuil's companion was that celebrated intriguant, the Abbé Gaultier, that

I ascertained the exact nature of the priest's business with St. John, and the exact motive of the civilities he had received from Abigail Masham.[1] Being at last forced, despairingly, to give over the attempt on his discretion, I suffered St. John to turn the conversation upon other topics, and as these were not much to the existent humour of my mind, I soon rose to depart.

"Stay, Count," said St. John; "shall you ride to-day?"

"If you will bear me company."

"*Volontiers*—to say the truth, I was about to ask you to canter your bay horse with me first to Spring Gardens,[2] where I have a promise to make to the director; and secondly, on a mission of charity to a poor foreigner of rank and birth, who, in his profound ignorance of this country, thought it right to enter into a plot with some wise heads, and to reveal it to some foolish tongues, who brought it to us with as much clatter as if it were a second gunpowder project. I easily brought him off that scrape, and I am now going to give him a caution for the future. Poor gentleman, I hear that he is grievously distressed in pecuniary matters, and I always had a kindness for exiles. Who knows but that a state of exile may be our own fate! and this alien is sprung from a race as haughty as that of St. John, or of Devereux. The *res angusta domi* must gall him sorely!"

"True," said I, slowly. "What may be the name of the foreigner?"

"Why—complain not hereafter that I do not trust you in state matters—I will divulge—D'Alvarez—Don Diego—an hidalgo of the best blood of Andalusia; and not unworthy of it, I fancy, in the virtues of fighting, though he may be in those of counsel. But— Heavens! Devereux—you seem ill!"

"No, no! Have you ever seen this man?"

"Never."

At this word a thrill of joy shot across me, for I knew St. John's fame for gallantry, and I was suspicious of the motives of his visit.

"St. John, I know this Spaniard—I know him well, and intimately. Could you not commission me to do your errand, and deliver your caution? Relief from me he might accept; from you, as a stranger, pride might forbid it; and you would really confer on

---

[1] *Viz*—That Count Devereux ascertained the priest's communications and overtures from the Chevalier. The precise extent of Bolingbroke's secret negotiations with the exiled Prince is still one of the darkest portions of the history of that time. That negotiations *were* carried on, both by Harley and by St. John, very largely, and very closely, I need not say that there is no doubt.—ED.

[2] Vauxhall.

me a personal and an essential kindness, if you would give me so fair an opportunity to confer kindness upon him."

"Very well, I am delighted to oblige you in any way. Take his direction; you see his abode is in a very pitiful suburb. Tell him from me that he is quite safe at present; but tell him also to avoid, henceforward, all imprudence, all connection with priests, plotters, *et tous ces gens-la*, as he values his personal safety, or at least his continuance in this most hospitable country. It is not from every wood that we make a Mercury, nor from every brain that we can carve a Mercury's genius of intrigue."

"Nobody ought to be better skilled in the materials requisite for such productions than Mr. Secretary St. John!" said I; "and now, adieu."

"Adieu, if you will not ride with me. We meet at Sir William Wyndham's to-morrow."

Masking my agitation till I was alone, I rejoiced when I found myself in the open streets. I summoned a hackney coach, and drove as rapidly as the vehicle would permit, to the petty and obscure suburb to which St. John had directed me. The coach stopped at the door of a very humble, but not absolutely wretched abode. I knocked at the door. A woman opened it, and, in answer to my inquiries, told me that the poor foreign gentleman was very ill—very ill indeed—had suffered a paralytic stroke—not expected to live. His daughter was with him now—would see no one—even Mr. Barnard had been denied admission.

At that name my feelings, shocked and stunned at first by the unexpected intelligence of the poor Spaniard's danger, felt a sudden and fierce revulsion—I combated it. This is no time, I thought, for any jealous, for any selfish, emotion. If I can serve her, if I can relieve her father, let me be contented. "She will see me," I said aloud, and I slipped some money in the woman's hand. "I am an old friend of the family, and I shall not be an unwelcome intruder on the sick room of the sufferer."

"Intruder, sir,—bless you, the poor gentleman is quite speechless and insensible."

At hearing this, I could refrain no longer. Isora's disconsolate, solitary, destitute condition, broke irresistibly upon me, and all scruple of more delicate and formal nature vanished at once. I ascended the stairs, followed by the old woman—she stopped me by the threshold of a room on the second floor, and whispered *"There!"* I paused an instant—collected breath and courage, and entered. The room was partially darkened. The curtains were drawn closely around the bed. By a table, on which stood two or three phials of medicine, I beheld Isora, listening with an eager, a *most* eager and intent face, to a man whose garb betrayed his healing profession, and who, laying a finger on the outstretched palm of his other hand, appeared giving his precise instructions, and uttering that oracular breath which—mere human words to him—was a message of fate itself—a fiat on which hung all that makes life, life, to his trembling and devout listener. Monarchs of earth, ye have not so supreme a power over woe and happiness, as one village leech! As he turned to leave her, she drew from a most slender purse a few petty coins, and I saw that she muttered some words indicative of the shame of poverty, as she tremblingly tended them to the outstretched palm. Twice did that palm close and open on the paltry sum; and the third time the native instinct of the heart overcame the later impulse of the profession. The limb of Galen drew back, and shaking with a gentle oscillation his capitalian honours, he laid the money softly on the table, and buttoning up the pouch of his nether garment, as if to resist temptation, he pressed the poor hand still extended towards him, and bowing over it with a kind respect for which I did long to approach and kiss his most withered and undainty cheek, he turned quickly round, and almost fell against me in the abstracted hurry of his exit.

"Hush!" said I, softly. "What hope of your patient?"

The leech glanced at me meaningly, and I whispered to him to wait for me below. Isora had not yet seen me. It is a notable distinction in the feelings, that all but the solitary one of grief sharpen into exquisite edge the keenness of the senses, but grief blunts them to a most dull obtuseness. I hesitated now to come forward; and so I stood, hat in hand, by the door, and not knowing that the tears streamed down my cheeks as I fixed my gaze upon Isora. She too stood still, just where the leech had left her, with her eyes fixed upon the ground, and her head drooping. The right hand, which the man had pressed, had sunk slowly and heavily by her side, with the small snowy fingers half closed over the palm. There is no describing the despondency which the listless position of that hand spoke, and the left hand lay with a like indolence of sorrow on the table, with one finger outstretched and pointing towards the phials, just as it had, some moments before, seconded the injunctions of the prim physician. Well, for my part, if I were a painter I would come now and then to a sick chamber for a study.

At last Isora, with a very quiet gesture of self-recovery, moved towards the bed, and the next moment I was by her side. If my life depended on it, I could not write one, no, not *one* syllable more of this scene.

CHAPTER XI.

CONTAINING MORE THAN ANY OTHER CHAPTER IN THE SECOND
BOOK OF THIS HISTORY.

MY first proposal was to remove the patient, with all due care and gentleness, to a better lodging, and a district more convenient for the visits of the most eminent physicians. When I expressed this wish to Isora, she looked at me long and wistfully, and then burst into tears. "*You* will not deceive us," said she, "and I accept your kindness at once —from *him* I rejected the same offer."

"Him?—of whom speak you?—this Barnard, or rather—but I know him!" A startling expression passed over Isora's speaking face.

"Know him!" she cried, interrupting me. "You do not—you cannot!"

"Take courage, dearest Isora—if I may so dare to call you— take courage; it is fearful to have a rival in that quarter—but I am prepared for it.—This Barnard, tell me again, do you love him?"

"Love—O God, no!"

"What then: do you still fear him?—fear him, too, protected by the unsleeping eye, and the vigilant hand of a love like mine?"

"Yes!" she said, falteringly, "I fear for *you!*"

"Me!" I cried, laughing scornfully, "me! nay, dearest, there breathes not that man whom you need fear on *my* account.—But, answer me—is not—"

"For Heaven's sake—for mercy's sake!" cried Isora, eagerly, "do not question me—I may not tell you who, or what this man is—I am bound, by a most solemn oath, never to divulge that secret."

"I care not," said I, calmly, "I want no confirmation of my knowledge—this masked rival is my own brother!"

I fixed my eyes full on Isora while I said this, and she quailed beneath my gaze: her cheek—her lips—were utterly without colour, and an expression of sickening and keen anguish was graven upon her face.—She made no answer.

"Yes!" resumed I, bitterly, "it is my brother—be it so—I am prepared—but if you can, Isora, say one word to deny it?"

Isora's tongue seemed literally to cleave to her mouth; at last, with a violent effort, she muttered, "I have told you, Morton, that I am bound by oath not to divulge this secret; nor may I breathe a single syllable calculated to do so—if I deny one name, you may question me on more—and, therefore, to deny one is a breach of my oath. But, beware!" she added, vehemently, "oh! beware how your suspicions—mere vague, baseless suspicions—criminate a brother; and, above all, whomsoever you believe to be the real being under this disguised name, as you value your life, and therefore mine— breathe not to him a syllable of your belief."

I was so struck with the energy with which this was said, that, after a short pause, I rejoined, in an altered tone,—

"I cannot believe that I have aught against life to fear from a brother's hand—but I will promise you to guard against latent danger. But is your oath so peremptory that you cannot deny even one name? —if not, and you *can* deny this, I swear to you that I will never question you upon another."

Again a fierce convulsion wrung the lip and distorted the perfect features of Isora. She remained silent for some moments, and then murmured, "My oath forbids me even that single answer—tempt me no more—now, and for ever, I am mute upon this subject."

Perhaps some slight and momentary anger, or doubt, or suspicion, betrayed itself upon my countenance, for Isora, after looking upon me long and mournfully, said, in a quiet, but melancholy tone, "I see your thoughts, and I do not reproach you for them—it is natural that you should think ill of one whom this mystery surrounds—one too placed under such circumstances of humiliation and distrust. I have lived long in your country—I have seen, for the last few months, much of its inhabitants; I have studied too the works which profess to unfold its national and peculiar character; I know that you have a distrust of the people of other climates; I know that you are cautious and full of suspicious vigilance, even in your commerce with each other; I know, too (and Isora's heart swelled visibly as she spoke), that poverty itself, in the eyes of your com- mercial countrymen, is a crime, and that they rarely feel confidence or place faith in those who are unhappy;—why, Count Devereux, why should I require more of you than of the rest of your nation? Why should you think better of the penniless and friendless girl— the degraded exile—the victim of doubt, which is so often the dis- guise of guilt, than any other—any one even among my own people —would think of one so mercilessly deprived of all the decent and appropriate barriers by which a maiden should be surrounded? No —no—leave me as you found me—leave my poor father where you see him—any place will do for us to die in."

"Isora!" I said, clasping her in my arms, "you do not know me yet; had I found you in prosperity, and in the world's honour— had I wooed you in your father's halls, and girt around with the friends and kinsmen of your race—I might have pressed for more than you will now tell me—I might have indulged suspicion where I perceived mystery, and I might not have loved as I love you now! *Now*, Isora, in misfortune, in destitution, I place without reserve my whole heart—its trust, its zeal, its devotion—in your keeping; come evil or good, storm or sunshine, I am yours, wholly, and for ever. Reject me if you will, I will return to you again; and never—never —save from my own eyes or your own lips—will I receive a single evidence detracting from your purity, or, Isora—mine own, own Isora—may I not add also—from your love?"

. "Too, too generous!" murmured Isora, struggling passionately with her tears, "may Heaven forsake me if ever I am ungrateful to thee; and believe—believe, that if love, more fond, more true, more devoted than woman ever felt before, can repay you, you shall be repaid!"

Why, at that moment, did my heart leap so joyously within me? —why did I say inly—"The treasure I have so long yearned for, is found at last: we have met, and through the waste of years, we will walk together, and never part again?" Why, at that moment of bliss, did I not rather feel a foretaste of the coming woe! Oh, blind and capricious Fate, that gives us a presentiment at one while, and withholds it at another! Knowledge, and Prudence, and calculating Foresight, what are ye?—warnings unto others, not our-selves. Reason is a lamp which sheddeth afar a glorious and general light, but leaveth all that is around it in darkness and in gloom. We foresee and foretell the destiny of others—we march credulous and benighted to our own; and, like Laocoön, from the very altars by, which we stand as the soothsayer and the priest, creep forth, unsuspected and undreamt of, the serpents which are fated to destroy us!

That very day then, Alvarez was removed to a lodging more worthy of his birth, and more calculated to afford hope of his recovery. He bore the removal without any evident sign of fatigue; but his dreadful malady had taken away both speech and sense, and he was already more than half the property of the grave. I sent, however, for the best medical advice which London could afford. They met—prescribed—and left the patient just as they found him. I know not, in the progress of science, what physicians may be to posterity, but in my time they are false witnesses subpœnaed against death, whose testimony always tells less in favour of the plaintiff than the defendant.

Before we left the poor Spaniard's former lodging, and when I was on the point of giving some instructions to the landlady re-specting the place to which the few articles of property belonging to

Don Diego and Isora were to be removed, Isora made me a sign to be silent, which I obeyed. "Pardon me," said she afterwards; "but I confess that I am anxious our next residence should not be known—should not be subject to the intrusion of—of this—"

"Barnard, as you call him. I understand you; be it so!" and accordingly I enjoined the goods to be sent to my own house, whence they were removed to Don Diego's new abode: and I took especial care to leave with the good lady no clue to discover Alvarez and his daughter, otherwise than *through me*. The pleasure afforded me of directing Gerald's attention to myself, I could not resist. "Tell Mr. Barnard, when he calls," said I, "that only through Count Morton Devereux, will he hear of Don Diego D'Alvarez, and the lady his daughter."

"I will, your honour," said the landlady; and then looking at me more attentively, she added: "Bless me! now when you speak, there is a very strong likeness between yourself and Mr. Barnard."

I recoiled as if an adder had stung me, and hurried into the coach to support the patient, who was already placed there.

Now then my daily post was by the bed of disease and suffering; in the chamber of death was my vow of love ratified; and in sadness and in sorrow was it returned. But it is in such scenes that the deepest, the most endearing, and the most holy, species of the passion is engendered. As I heard Isora's low voice tremble with the suspense of one who watches over the hourly severing of the affection of Nature and of early years: as I saw her light step flit by the pillow which she smoothed, and her cheek alternately flush and fade, in watching the wants which she relieved; as I marked her mute, her unwearying tenderness, breaking into a thousand nameless, but mighty, cares, and pervading like an angel's vigilance every—yea, the minutest—course into which it flowed—did I not behold her in that sphere in which woman is most lovely, and in which love itself consecrates its admiration, and purifies its most ardent desires? That was not a time for our hearts to speak audibly to each other; but we felt that they grew closer and closer, and we asked not for the poor eloquence of words. But over this scene let me not linger.

One morning, as I was proceeding on foot to Isora's, I perceived on the opposite side of the way Montreuil and Gerald; they were conversing eagerly: they both saw me. Montreuil made a slight, quiet, and dignified inclination of the head: Gerald coloured, and hesitated. I thought he was about to leave his companion and address me; but, with a haughty and severe air, I passed on, and Gerald, as if stung by my demeanour, bit his lip vehemently, and followed my example. A few minutes afterwards I felt an inclination to regret that I had not afforded him an opportunity of addressing me. "I might," thought I, "have then taunted him with his persecution of Isora, and defied him to execute those threats against me, in which it is evident, from her apprehensions for my safety, that he indulged."

I had not, however, much leisure for these thoughts. When I arrived at the lodgings of Alvarez, I found that a great change had taken place in his condition; he had recovered speech, though imperfectly, and testified a return to sense. I flew upstairs with a light step to congratulate Isora: she met me at the door. "Hush!" she whispered: "my father sleeps!" But she did not speak with the animation I had anticipated.

"What is the matter, dearest?" said I, following her into another apartment: "you seem sad, and your eyes are red with tears, which are not, methinks, entirely the tears of joy at this happy change in your father?"

"I am marked out for suffering," returned Isora, more keenly than she was wont to speak. I pressed her to explain her meaning; she hesitated at first, but at length confessed that her father had always been anxious for her marriage with this *soi-disant* Barnard, and that his first words on his recovery had been to press her to consent to his wishes.

"My poor father," said she, weepingly, "speaks and thinks only for my fancied good; but his senses as yet are only recovered in part, and he cannot even understand me when I speak of you. 'I shall die,' he said, 'I shall die, and you will be left on the wide world?' I in vain endeavoured to explain to him that I should have a protector—he fell asleep muttering those words, and with tears in his eyes."

"Does he know as much of this Barnard as you do?" said I.

"Heavens, no!—or he would never have pressed me to marry one so wicked."

"Does he know even who he is?"

"Yes!" said Isora, after a pause, "but he has not known it long."

Here the physician joined us, and taking me aside, informed me that, as he had foreboded, sleep had been the harbinger of death, and that Don Diego was no more. I broke the news as gently as I could to Isora: but her grief was far more violent than I could have anticipated: and nothing seemed to cut her so deeply to the heart as the thought that his last wish had been one with which she had not complied, and could never comply.

I pass over the first days of mourning—I come to the one after

Don Diego's funeral. I had been with Isora in the morning; I left her for a few hours, and returned at the first dusk of evening with some books and music, which I vainly hoped she might recur to for a momentary abstraction from her grief. I dismissed my carriage, with the intention of walking home, and addressing the woman-servant who admitted me, inquired, as was my wont, after Isora. "She has been very ill," replied the woman, "ever since the strange gentleman left her."

"The strange gentleman?"

Yes, he had forced his way upstairs, despite of the denial the servant had been ordered to give to all strangers. He had entered Isora's room; and the woman, in answer to my urgent inquiries, added that she had heard his voice raised to a loud and harsh key in the apartment; he had stayed there about a quarter of an hour, and had then hurried out, seemingly in great disorder and agitation.

"What description of man was he?" I asked.

The woman answered that he was mantled from head to foot in his cloak, which was richly laced, and his hat was looped with diamonds, but slouched over that part of his face which the collar of his cloak did not hide, so that she could not further describe him than as one of a haughty and abrupt bearing, and evidently belonging to the higher ranks.

Convinced that Gerald had been the intruder, I hastened up the stairs to Isora. She received me with a sickly and faint smile, and endeavoured to conceal the traces of her tears.

"So!" said I, "this insolent persecutor of yours has discovered your abode, and again insulted or intimidated you. He shall do so no more!—I will seek him to-morrow—and no affinity of blood shall prevent—"

"Morton, dear Morton!" cried Isora, in great alarm, and yet with a certain determination stamped upon her features, "hear me! —it is true this man has been here—it is true that, fearful and terrible as he is, he has agitated and alarmed me; but it was only for you, Morton—by the Holy Virgin, it was only for you! 'The moment,' said he, and his voice ran shiveringly through my heart like a dagger, 'the moment Morton Devereux discovers who is his rival, that moment his death-warrant is irrevocably sealed!'"

"Arrogant boaster!" I cried, and my blood burnt with the intense rage which a much slighter cause would have kindled from the natural fierceness of my temper. "Does he think my life is at his bidding, to allow or to withhold? Unhand me, Isora, unhand me! I tell you I will seek him this moment, and dare him to do his worst!"

"Do so," said Isora, calmly, and releasing her hold; "do so;

but hear me first : the moment you breathe to him your suspicions you place an eternal barrier betwixt yourself and me ! Pledge me your faith that you will never, while I live at least, reveal to him— to any one—whom you suspect—your reproach, your defiance, your knowledge—nay, not even your lightest suspicion of his identity with my persecutor—promise me this, Morton Devereux, or I, in my turn, before that crucifix, whose sanctity we both acknowledge and adore—that crucifix which has descended to my race for three unbroken centuries—which, for my departed father, in the solemn vow, and in the death agony, has still been a witness, a consolation, and a pledge, between the soul and its Creator—by that crucifix which my dying mother clasped to her bosom when she committed me, an infant, to the care of that Heaven which hears and records for ever our lightest word—I swear that I will never be yours ! "

"Isora ! " said I, awed and startled, yet struggling against the impression her energy made upon me, "you know not to what you pledge yourself, nor what you require of me. If I do not seek out this man—if I do not expose to him my knowledge of his pursuit and unhallowed persecution of you—if I do not effectually prohibit and prevent their continuance—think well, what security have I for your future peace of mind—nay, even for the safety of your honour or your life ? A man thus bold, daring, and unbaffled in his pursuit, thus vigilant and skilful in his selection of time and occasion—so that, despite my constant and anxious endeavour to meet him in your presence, I have never been able to do so—from a man, I say, thus pertinacious in resolution, thus crafty in disguise, what may you not dread when you leave him utterly fearless by the license of impunity ? Think too, again, Isora, that the mystery dishonours as much as the danger menaces. Is it meet that my betrothed and my future bride should be subjected to these secret and terrible visita-tions—visitations of a man professing himself her lover, and evincing the vehemence of his passion by that of his pursuit ? Isora—Isora —you have weighed not these things—you know not what you demand of me."

"I do ! " answered Isora, "I do know all that I demand of you —I demand of you only to preserve your life."

"How," said I, impatiently, "cannot my hand preserve my life ? and is it for you, the daughter of a line of warriors, to ask your lover and your husband to shrink from a single foe ? "

"No, Morton," answered Isora. "Were you going to battle, I would gird on your sword myself—were, too, this man other than he is, and you were about to meet him in open contest, I would not wrong you, nor degrade your betrothed, by a fear. But I know my persecutor well—fierce, unrelenting—dreadful in his dark and ungovernable passions as he is, he has not the courage to confront you: I fear not the open foe, but the lurking and sure assassin. His very earnestness to avoid you; the precautions he has taken, are alone sufficient to convince you that he dreads personally to oppose your claim, or to vindicate himself."

"Then what have I to fear?"

"Everything! Do you not know that from men, at once fierce, crafty, and shrinking from bold violence, the stuff for assassins is always made? And if I wanted surer proof of his designs than inference, his oath—it rings in my ears now—is sufficient: 'The moment Morton Devereux discovers who is his rival, that moment his death-warrant is irrevocably sealed.' Morton, I demand your promise; or, though my heart break, I will record my own vow."

"Stay—stay," I said, in anger, and in sorrow: "were I to promise this, and for my own safety hazard yours, what could you deem me?"

"Fear not for me, Morton," answered Isora; "you have no cause. I tell you that this man, villain as he is, ever leaves me humbled and abased. Do not think that in all times, and all scenes, I am the foolish and weak creature you behold me now. Remember, that you said rightly I was the daughter of a line of warriors; and I have that within me which will not shame my descent."

"But, dearest, your resolution may avail you for a time; but it cannot for ever baffle the hardened nature of a man. I know my own sex, and I know my own ferocity, were it once aroused."

"But, Morton, you do not know *me*," said Isora, proudly, and her face, as she spoke, was set, and even stern, "I am only the coward when I think of you; a word—a look of mine—can abash this man; or, if it could not, I am never without a weapon to defend myself, or—or——" Isora's voice, before firm and collected, now faltered, and a deep blush flowed over the marble paleness of her face.

"Or what?" said I, anxiously.

"Or thee, Morton?" murmured Isora, tenderly, and withdrawing her eyes from mine.

The tone, the look that accompanied these words, melted me at once. I rose—I clasped Isora to my heart—

"You are a strange compound, my own fairy queen; but these lips—this cheek—those eyes—are not fit features for a heroine."

"Morton, if I had less determination in my heart, I could not love you so well."

"But tell me," I whispered, with a smile, "where is this weapon on which you rely so strongly?"

"Here!" answered Isora, blushingly; and, extricating herself from me, she showed me a small two-edged dagger, which she wore carefully concealed within the folds of her dress. I looked over the bright, keen blade, with surprise, and yet with pleasure, at the latent resolution of a character seemingly so soft. I say, with pleasure, for it suited well with my own fierce and wild temper. I returned the weapon to her, with a smile and a jest.

"Ah!" said Isora, shrinking from my kiss, "I should not have been so bold, if I only feared danger for myself.'

But if, for a moment, we forgot, in the gushings of our affection, the object of our converse and dispute, we soon returned to it again. Isora was the first to recur to it. She reminded me of the promise she required; and she spoke with a seriousness and a solemnity which I found myself scarcely able to resist.

"But," I said, "if he ever molest you hereafter: if again I find that bright cheek blanched, and those dear eyes dimmed with tears, and I know that, in my own house, some one has dared thus to insult its queen, am I to be still torpid and inactive, lest a dastard and craven hand should avenge my assertion of your honour and mine?"

"No, Morton; after our marriage, whenever that be, you will have nothing to apprehend from him on the same ground as before; my fear for you, too, will not be what it is now; your honour will be bound in mine, and nothing shall induce me to hazard it—no, not even your safety. I have every reason to believe that, after that event, he will subject me no longer to his insults—how, indeed, can he, under your perpetual protection? or, for what cause should he attempt it, if he could? I shall be then yours—only and ever yours—what hope could, therefore, then nerve his hardihood or instigate his intrusions? Trust to me at that time, and suffer me to—nay, I repeat, promise me that I may—trust in you now!"

What could I do? I still combated her wish and her request; but her steadiness and rigidity of purpose made me, though reluctantly, yield to them at last. So sincere, and so stern, indeed, appeared her resolution, that I feared, by refusal, that she would take the rash oath that would separate us for ever. Added to this, I felt in her that confidence which, I am apt to believe, is far more akin to the latter stages of real love, than jealousy and mistrust; and I could not believe that either now, or, still less after our nuptials, she would risk aught of honour, or the seeming of honour, from a visionary and superstitious fear. In spite, therefore, of my keen and deep interest in the thorough discovery of this mysterious persecutor; and, still more, in the prevention of all future designs

F

from his audacity, I constrained myself to promise her that I would
on no account seek out the person I suspected, or wilfully betray to
him, by word or deed, my belief of his identity with Barnard.

Though greatly dissatisfied with my self-compulsion, I strove to
reconcile myself to its idea. Indeed, there was much in the peculiar
circumstances of Isora—much in the freshness of her present affliction
—much in the unfriended and utter destitution of her situation—
that, while, on the one hand, it called forth her pride, and made
stubborn that temper which was naturally so gentle and so soft, on the
other hand, made me yield even to wishes that I thought unreasonable,
and consider rather the delicacy and deference due to her condition,
than insist upon the sacrifices which, in more fortunate circumstances, I might have imagined due to myself. Still more indisposed
to resist her wish and expose myself to its penalty was I, when I
considered her desire was the mere excess and caution of her love,
and when I felt that she spoke sincerely when she declared that
it was only for me that she was the coward. Nevertheless, and
despite all these considerations, it was with a secret discontent that
I took my leave of her, and departed homeward.

I had just reached the end of the street where the house was
situated, when I saw there, very imperfectly, for the night was
extremely dark, the figure of a man entirely enveloped in a long
cloak, such as was commonly worn by gallants, in affairs of secrecy
or intrigue ; and, in the pale light of a single lamp near which he
stood, something like the brilliance of gems glittered on the large
Spanish hat which overhung his brow. I immediately recalled the
description the woman had given me of Barnard's dress, and the
thought flashed across me that it was he whom I beheld. "At all
events," thought I, "I may confirm my doubts, if I may not communicate them, and I may watch over her safety if I may not avenge
her injuries?" I therefore took advantage of my knowledge of the
neighbourhood, passed the stranger with a quick step, and then,
running rapidly, returned by a circuitous route to the mouth of a
narrow and dark street, which was exactly opposite to Isora's
house. Here I concealed myself by a projecting porch, and I had
not waited long before I saw the dim form of the stranger walk
slowly by the house. He passed it three or four times, and each
time I thought—though the darkness might well deceive me—that
he looked up to the windows. He made, however, no attempt at
admission, and appeared as if he had no other object than that of
watching by the house. Wearied and impatient at last, I came
from my concealment. "I may *confirm* my suspicions," I repeated,
recurring to my oath, and I walked straight towards the stranger.

"Sir," I said, very calmly, "I am the last person in the world to interfere with the amusements of any other gentleman; but I humbly opine that no man can parade by this house upon so very cold a night, without giving just ground for suspicion to the friends of its inhabitants. I happen to be among that happy number; and I therefore, with all due humility and respect, venture to request you to seek some other spot for your nocturnal perambulations."

I made this speech purposely prolix, in order to have time fully to reconnoitre the person of the one I addressed. The dusk of the night, and the loose garb of the stranger, certainly forbade any decided success to this scrutiny; but methought the figure seemed, despite of my prepossessions, to want the stately height and grand proportions of Gerald Devereux. I must own, however, that the necessary inexactitude of my survey rendered this idea without just foundation, and did not by any means diminish my firm impression that it was Gerald whom I beheld. While I spoke, he retreated with a quick step, but made no answer; I pressed upon him—he backed with a still quicker step: and when I had ended, he fairly turned round, and made at full speed along the dark street in which I had fixed my previous post of watch. .I fled after him, with a step as fleet as his own—his cloak encumbered his flight—I gained upon him sensibly—he turned a sharp corner—threw me out, and entered into a broad thoroughfare. As I sped after him, Bacchanalian voices burst upon my ear, and presently a large band of those young men who, under the name of Mohawks, were wont to scour the town nightly, and, sword in hand, to exercise their love of riot under the disguise of party zeal, became visible in the middle of the street. Through them my fugitive dashed headlong, and, profiting by their surprise, escaped unmolested. 'I attempted to follow with equal speed, but was less successful. "Hallo!" cried the foremost of the group, placing himself in my way.

"No such haste! Art Whig or Tory? Under which king—Bezonian, speak or die?"

"Have a care, sir," said I, fiercely, drawing my sword.

"Treason, treason!" cried the speaker, confronting me with equal readiness. "Have a care, indeed—have *at thee.*"

"Ha!" cried another, "'tis a Tory: 'tis the Secretary's popish friend, Devereux—pike him, pike him."

I had already run my opponent through the sword arm, and was in hopes that this act would intimidate the rest, and allow my escape; but at the sound of my name and political bias, coupled with the drawn blood of their confederate, the patriots rushed upon me with that amiable fury generally characteristic of all true lovers of their country. Two swords passed through my body simultaneously, and I fell bleeding and insensible to the ground. When I recovered I was in my own apartments, whither two of the gentler Mohawks had conveyed me : the surgeons were by my bed-side ; I groaned audibly when I saw them.   If there is a thing in the world I hate, it is in any shape the disciples of Hermes ; they always remind me of that Indian people (the Padæi, I think) mentioned by Herodotus, who sustained themselves by devouring the sick.   "All is well," said one, when my groan was heard.   "He will not die," said another.   "At least not till we have had more fees," said a third, more candid than the rest.   And thereupon they seized me and began torturing my wounds anew, till I fainted away with the pain.   However, the next day I was declared out of immediate danger ;' and the first proof I gave of my convalescence was to make Desmarais discharge four surgeons out of five : the remaining one I thought my youth and constitution might enable me to endure.

That very evening, as I was turning restlessly in my bed, and muttering, with parched lips, the name of "Isora," I saw by my side a figure covered from head to foot in a long veil, and a voice, low, soft, but thrilling through my heart like a new existence, murmured, " She is here ! "

I forgot my wounds, I forgot my pain and my debility—I sprung upwards—the stranger drew aside the veil from her countenance, and I beheld Isora !

" Yes ! " said she, in her own liquid and honied accents, which fell like balm upon my wound, and my spirit, "yes, she whom *you* have hitherto tended is come, in her turn, to render some slight, but woman's services to you. She has come to nurse, and to soothe, and to pray for you, and to be, till you yourself discard her, your handmaid and your slave ! "

I would have answered, but raising her finger to her lips, she arose and vanished ; but from that hour my wound healed, my fever slaked, and whenever I beheld her flitting round my bed, or watching over me, or felt her cool fingers wiping the dew from my brow, or took from her hand my medicine or my food, in those moments, the blood seemed to make a new struggle through my veins, and I felt palpably within me a fresh and delicious life—a life full of youth, and passion, and hope, replace the vaguer and duller being which I had hitherto borne.

There are some extraordinary incongruities in that very mysterious thing *sympathy*. One would imagine that, in a description of things most generally interesting to all men, the most general interest would be found ; nevertheless, I believe few persons would hang breathless over the progressive history of a sick-bed. Yet those gradual stages from danger to recovery, how delightfully interesting they are to all who have crawled from one to the other! and who, at some time or other in his journey through that land of diseases—civilized life—has not taken that gentle excursion? "I would be ill any day for the pleasure of getting well," said Fontenelle to me one morning with his usual *naïveté;* but who would not be ill for the mere pleasure of being ill, if he could be tended by her whom he most loves?

I shall not therefore dwell upon that most delicious period of my life—my sick-bed, and my recovery from it. I pass on to a certain evening in which I heard from Isora's lips the whole of her history, save what related to her knowledge of the real name of one whose persecution constituted the little of romance which had yet mingled with her innocent and pure life. That evening—how well I remember it! we were alone—still weak and reduced, I lay upon the sofa beside the window, which was partially open, and the still air of an evening in the first infancy of spring, came fresh, and fraught, as it were, with a prediction of the glowing woods, and the reviving verdure, to my cheek. The stars, one by one, kindled, as if born of Heaven and Twilight, into their nightly being; and, through the vapour and thick ether of the dense city, streamed their most silent light, holy and pure, and resembling that which the Divine Mercy sheds upon the gross nature of mankind. But, shadowy and calm, their rays fell full upon the face of Isora, as she lay on the ground beside my couch, and with one hand surrendered to my clasp, looked upward till, as she felt my gaze, she turned her cheek blushingly away. There was quiet round and above us; but beneath the window we heard at times the sounds of the common earth, and then insensibly our hands knit into a closer clasp, and we felt them thrill more palpably to our hearts; for those sounds reminded us both of our existence and of our separation from the great herd of our race!

What is love but a division from the world, and a blending of two souls, two immortalities divested of clay and ashes, into one? it is a severing of a thousand ties from whatever is harsh and selfish, in order to knit them into a single and sacred bond! Who loves, hath attained the anchorite's secret; and the hermitage has become dearer than the world. O respite from the toil and the curse of our social and banded state, a little interval art thou, suspended between two eternities—the Past and the Future—a star that hovers between the morning and the night, sending through the vast abyss one solitary ray from heaven, but too far and faint to illumine, while it hallows the earth!

There was nothing in Isora's tale which the reader has not already learnt, or conjectured. She had left her Andalusian home in her early childhood, but she remembered it well, and lingeringly dwelt over it, in description. It was evident that little, in our colder and less genial isle, had attracted her sympathy, or wound itself into her affection. Nevertheless, I conceive that her naturally dreamy and abstracted character had received from her residence and her trials here much of the vigour and the heroism which it now possessed. Brought up alone, music, and books—few, though not ill-chosen, for Shakspeare was one, and the one which had made upon her the most permanent impression, and perhaps had coloured her temperament with its latent, but rich hues of poetry—constituted her amusement and her studies.

But who knows not that a woman's heart finds its fullest occupation within itself? There lies its real study, and within that narrow orbit, the mirror of enchanted thought reflects the whole range of earth. Loneliness and meditation nursed the mood which afterwards, with Isora, became love itself. But I do not wish now so much to describe her character, as to abridge her brief history. The first English stranger, of the male sex, whom her father admitted to her acquaintance, was Barnard. This man was, as I had surmised, connected with him in certain political intrigues, the exact nature of which she did not know. I continue to call him by a name which Isora acknowledged was fictitious. He had not, at first, by actual declaration, betrayed to her his affections: though, accompanied by a sort of fierceness which early revolted her, they soon became visible. On the evening in which I had found her stretched insensible in the garden, and had myself made my first confession of love, I learnt that he had divulged to her his passion and real name; that her rejection had thrown him into a fierce despair—that he had accompanied his disclosure with the most terrible threats against me, for whom he supposed himself rejected, and against the safety of her father, whom he said a word of his could betray; that her knowledge of his power to injure us! *us*—yes, Isora then loved me, and then trembled for my safety!—had terrified and overcome her— and that in the very moment in which my horse's hoofs were heard, and as the alternative of her non-compliance, the rude suitor swore deadly and sore vengeance against Alvarez and myself, she yielded to the oath he prescribed to her — an oath that she would never reveal the secret he had betrayed to her, or suffer me to know who was my real rival.

This was all that I could gather from her guarded confidence! he heard the oath, and vanished, and she felt no more till she was in my arms; then it was that she saw in the love and vengeance of my rival a barrier against our union; and then it was that her generous fear for me conquered her attachment, and she renounced me.

Their departure from the cottage, so shortly afterwards, was at her father's choice and at the instigation of Barnard, for the furtherance of their political projects ; and it was from Barnard that the money came which repaid my loan to Alvarez. The same person, no doubt, poisoned her father against me, for henceforth Alvarez never spoke of me with that partiality he had previously felt. They repaired to London ; her father was often absent, and often engaged with men whom she had never seen before ! he was absorbed and uncommunicative, and she was still ignorant of the nature of his schemes and designs.

At length, after an absence of several weeks, Barnard re-appeared, and his visits became constant; he renewed his suit to her father as well as herself. Then commenced that domestic persecution, so common in this very tyrannical world, which makes us sicken to bear, and which, had Isora been wholly a Spanish girl, she, in all probability, would never have resisted : so much of custom is there in the very air of a climate. But she did resist it, partly because she loved me—and loved me more and more for our separation—and partly because she dreaded and abhorred the ferocious and malignant passions of my rival, far beyond any other misery with which fortune could threaten her. " Your father then shall hang or starve ! " said Barnard, one day in uncontrollable frenzy, and left her. He did not appear again at the house. The Spaniard's resources, fed, probably, alone by Barnard, failed. From house to house they removed, till they were reduced to that humble one in which I had found them. There, Barnard again sought them ; there, backed by the powerful advocate of want, he again pressed his suit, and at that exact moment her father was struck with the numbing curse of his disease. " There and then," said Isora candidly, " I might have yielded at last, for my poor father's sake, if you had not saved me."

Once only (I have before recorded the time), did Barnard visit her in the new abode I had provided for her, and the day after our conversation on that event Isora watched and watched for me, and I did not come. From the woman of the house she at last learned the cause. " I forgot," she said timidly—and in conclusion, " I forgot womanhood, and modesty, and reserve ; I forgot the customs of your country, the decencies of my own ; I forgot everything in this world, but you—you suffering and in danger ; my very sense of existence seemed to pass from me, and to be supplied by a breathless, confused, and overwhelming sense of impatient agony, which ceased not till I was in your chamber, and by your side ! And—and now, Morton, do not despise me for not having considered more, and loved you less."

" Despise you ! " I murmured, and I threw my arms around her,

and drew her to my breast.   I felt her heart beat against my own :
those hearts spoke, though our lips were silent, and in their language
seemed to say : " We are united now, and we will not part."

The starlight, shining with a mellow and deep stillness, was the
only light by which we beheld each other—it shone, the witness and
the sanction of that internal voice, which we owned, but heard not.
Our lips drew closer and closer together, till they met ! and in that
kiss was the type and promise of the after ritual which knit two
spirits into one.   Silence fell around us like a curtain, and the
eternal Night, with her fresh dews and unclouded stars, looked
alone upon the compact of our hearts—an emblem of the eternity,
the freshness, and the unearthly, though awful brightness of the love
which it hallowed and beheld !

BOOK III.

CHAPTER I.

WHEREIN THE HISTORY MAKES GREAT PROGRESS, AND IS MARKED BY ONE IMPORTANT EVENT IN HUMAN LIFE.

SPINOSA is said to have loved, above all other amusements, to put flies into a spider's web ; and the struggles of the imprisoned insects were wont to bear, in the eyes of this grave philosopher, so facetious and hilarious an appearance, that he would stand and laugh thereat until the tears " coursed one another down his innocent nose." Now it so happeneth that Spinosa, despite the general (and, in my most meek opinion, the just) condemnation of his theoretical tenets,[1] was, in character and in nature, according to the voices of all who knew him, an exceedingly kind, humane, and benevolent biped ; and it doth, therefore, seem a little strange unto us grave, sober members of the unphilosophical Many, that the struggles and terrors of these little, winged creatures should strike the good subtleist in a point of view so irresistibly ludicrous and delightful. But, for my part, I believe that that most imaginative and wild speculator beheld in the entangled flies nothing more than a living simile—an animated illustration—of his own beloved vision of Necessity ; and that he is no more to be considered cruel for the complacency with which he gazed upon those agonized types of his system than is Lucan for dwelling, with a poet's pleasure, upon the many ingenious ways with which that Grand Inquisitor of Verse has contrived to vary the simple operation of dying. To the bard, the butchered soldier was only an epic ornament ; to the philosopher, the murdered fly was only a metaphysical illustration. For, without being a Fatalist, or a disciple of Baruch de Spinosa, I must confess that I cannot conceive a greater resemblance to our human and earthly state than the penal predicament of the devoted flies. Suddenly do we find ourselves

---

[1] One ought, however, to be very cautious before one condemns a philosopher. The master's opinions are generally pure—it is the conclusions and corollaries of his disciples that "draw the honey forth that drives men mad." Schlegel seems to have studied Spinosa *de fonte*, and vindicates him very earnestly from the charges brought against him—atheism, &c.—ED.

plunged into that Vast Web—the World ; and even as the insect, when he first undergoeth a similar accident of necessity, standeth amazed and still, and only, by little and little, awakeneth to a full sense of his situation ; so also at the first abashed and confounded, we remain on the mesh we are urged upon, ignorant, as yet, of the toils around us, and the sly, dark, immitigable foe, that lieth in yonder nook, already feasting her imagination upon our destruction. Presently we revive—we stir—we flutter—and Fate, that foe—the old arch-spider, that hath no moderation in her maw—now fixeth one of her many eyes upon us, and·giveth us a partial glimpse of her laidly and grim aspect. We pause in mute terror—we gaze upon the ugly spectre, so imperfectly beheld—the net ceases to tremble, and the wily enemy draws gently back into her nook. Now we begin to breathe again—we sound the strange footing on which we tread—we move tenderly along it, and again the grisly monster advances on us ; again we pause—the foe retires not, but remains still, and surveyeth us ;—we see every step is accompanied with danger—we look round and above in despair—suddenly we feel within us a new impulse and a new power !—we feel a vague sympathy with *that* unknown region which spreads *beyond* this great net ;—*that limitless beyond* hath a mystic affinity with a part of our own frame—we unconsciously extend our wings (for the soul to us is as the wings to the fly !)—we attempt to rise—to soar above this perilous snare, from which we are unable to crawl. The old spider watcheth us in self-hugging quiet, and, looking up to our native air, we think—now shall we escape thee.—Out on it ! We rise not a hair's breadth—we have the *wings*, it is true, but the *feet* are fettered. We strive desperately again—the whole web vibrates with the effort —it will break beneath our strength. Not a jot of it !—we cease— we are more entangled than ever ! wings—feet—frame—the foul slime is over all !—where shall we turn? every line of the web leads to the one den,—we know not—we care not—we grow blind —confused—lost. The eyes of our hideous foe gloat upon us—she whetteth her insatiate maw—she leapeth towards us—she fixeth her fangs upon us—and so endeth my parallel !

But what has this to do with my tale? Ay, Reader, that is thy question ; and I will answer it by one of mine. When thou hearest a man moralize and preach of Fate, art thou not sure that he is going to tell thee of some one of his peculiar misfortunes? Sorrow loves a parable as much as mirth loves a jest. And thus already and from afar, I prepare thee, at the commencement of this, the third of these portions into which the history of my various and wild life will be divided, for that event with which I purpose that the said portion shall be concluded.

It is now three months after my entire recovery from my wounds, and I am married to Isora!—married—yes, but *privately* married, and the ceremony is as yet closely concealed. I will explain.

The moment Isora's anxiety for me led her across the threshold of my house it became necessary for her honour that our wedding should take place immediately on my recovery—so far I was decided on the measure—now for the meſhod. During my illness, I received a long and most affectionate letter from Aubrey, who was then at Devereux Court,—so affectionate was the heart-breathing spirit of that letter—so steeped in all our old household remembrances and boyish feelings, that, coupled as it was with a certain gloom when he spoke of himself and of worldly sins and trials, it brought tears to my eyes whenever I recurred to it;—and many and many a time afterwards, when I .thought his affections seemed estranged from me, I did recur to it to convince myself that I was mistaken. Shortly afterwards I received also a brief epistle from my uncle; it was as kind as usual, and it mentioned Aubrey's return to Devereux Court: "That unhappy boy," said Sir William, "is more than ever devoted to his religious duties; nor do I believe that any priest-ridden poor devil, in the dark ages, ever made such use of the scourge and the penance."

Now, I have before stated that my uncle would, I knew, be averse to my intended marriage; and on hearing that Aubrey was then with him, I resolved, in replying to his letter, to entreat the former to sound Sir William on the subject I had most at heart, and ascertain the exact nature and extent of the opposition I should have to encounter in the step I was resolved to take. By the same post I wrote to the good old knight in as artful a strain as I was able, dwelling at some length upon my passion, upon the high birth, as well as the numerous good qualities of the object, but mentioning not her name; and I added everything that I thought likely to enlist my uncle's kind and warm feelings on my behalf. These letters produced the following ones :—

FROM SIR WILLIAM DEVEREUX.

"'SDEATH! nephew Morton—but I won't scold thee, though thou deservest it. Let me see, thou art now scarce twenty, and thou talkest of marriage, which is the exclusive business of middle age, as familiarly as 'girls of thirteen do of puppy dogs.' Marry!—go hang thyself rather. Marriage, my dear boy, is at the best a treacherous proceeding: and a friend—a true friend will never counsel another to adopt it rashly. Look you—I have had experience in these matters: and, I think, the moment a woman is wedded some terrible revolution happens in her system; all her former good qualities vanish, *hey presto*, like eggs out of a conjurer's box,—'tis true they appear on t'other side of the box, the side turned to other people, but for the poor husband they are gone for ever. Od'sfish, Morton, go to! I tell thee again that I have had experience in these matters, which thou never hast had, clever as thou thinkest thyself. If now it were a good marriage thou wert about to make— if thou wert going to wed power, and money, and places at Court, why, something might be said for thee. As it is, there is no excuse —none. And I am astonished how a boy of thy sense could think of such nonsense. Birth, Morton, what the devil does that signify, so long as it is birth in another country? A foreign damsel, and a Spanish girl, too, above all others! 'Sdeath, man, as if there was not quicksilver enough in the English women for you, you must make a mercurial exportation from Spain, must you! Why, Morton —Morton, the ladies in that country are proverbial. I tremble at the very thought of it. But as for my consent, I never will give it— never; and though I threaten thee not with disinheritance and such like, yet I do ask something in return for the great affection I have always borne thee; and I make no doubt that thou wilt readily oblige me in such a trifle as giving up a mere Spanish donna. So think of her no more. If thou wantest to make love, there are ladies in plenty whom thou needest not to marry. And for my part, I thought that thou wert all in all with the Lady Hasselton—Heaven bless her pretty face! Now don't think I want to scold thee—and don't think thine old uncle harsh—God knows he is not; but my dear, dear boy, this is quite out of the question, and thou must let me hear no more about it. The gout cripples me so that I must leave off. Ever thine old uncle,

"WILLIAM DEVEREUX."

"P.S. Upon consideration, I think, my dear boy, that thou must want money, and thou art ever too sparing. Messrs. Child, or my goldsmiths in Aldersgate, have my orders to pay to thy hand's-writing whatever thou mayst desire; and I do hope that thou wilt now want nothing to make thee merry withal. Why dost thou not write a comedy? is it not the mode still?"

LETTER FROM AUBREY DEVEREUX.

"I HAVE sounded my uncle, dearest Morton, according to your wishes; and I grieve to say that I have found him inexorable. He was very much hurt by your letter to him, and declared he should write to you forthwith upon the subject. I represented to him all that you have said upon the virtues of your intended bride; and I also insisted upon your clear judgment and strong sense upon most points, being a sufficient surety for your prudence upon this. But you know the libertine opinions, and the depreciating judgment of women, entertained by my poor uncle ; and he would, I believe, have been less displeased with the heinous crime of an illicit connection, than the amiable weakness of an imprudent marriage—I might say of any marriage, until it was time to provide heirs to the estate."

Here Aubrey, in the most affectionate and earnest manner, broke off, to point out to me the extreme danger to my interests that it would be to disoblige my uncle ; who, despite his general kindness, would, upon a disagreement on so tender a matter as his sore point, and his most cherished hobby, consider my disobedience as a personal affront. He also recalled to me all that my uncle had felt and done for me ; and insisted, at all events, upon the absolute duty of my delaying, even though I should not break off, the intended measure. Upon these points he enlarged much and eloquently ; and this part of his letter certainly left no cheering or comfortable impression upon my mind.

Now my good uncle knew as much of love, as L. Mummius did of the fine arts,[1] and it was impossible to persuade him that if one wanted to indulge the tender passion, one woman would not do exactly as well as another, provided she were equally pretty. I knew therefore that he was incapable, on the one hand, of understanding my love for Isora, or, on the other, of acknowledging her claims upon me. I had not, of course, mentioned to him the generous imprudence which, on the news of my wound, had brought Isora to my house : for if I had done so, my uncle, with the eye of a courtier of Charles IL, would only have seen the advantage to be derived from the impropriety, not the gratitude due to the devotion ; neither had I mentioned this circumstance to Aubrey,—it seemed to me too delicate for any written communication ; and therefore, in his advice to delay my marriage, he was unaware of the necessity which rendered the advice unavailing. Now then was I in this dilemma, either to marry, and that *instanter*, and so, seemingly, with the most hasty and the most insolent indecorum, incense, wound, and in his interpretation of the act, contemn one whom I loved as I loved my uncle,—or, to delay the marriage, to separate from Isora, and to leave my future wife to the malignant consequences that would necessarily be drawn from a sojourn of weeks in my house. This fact there was no chance of concealing ; servants have more tongues than Argus had eyes, and my youthful extrava-

---

[1] A Roman consul, who, removing the most celebrated remains of Grecian antiquity to Rome, assured the persons charged with conveying them that if they injured any, they should make others to replace them.

gance had filled my whole house with those pests of society. The latter measure was impossible, the former was most painful. Was there no third way?—there was that of a private marriage. This obviated not every evil; but it removed many: it satisfied my impatient love, it placed Isora under a sure protection, it secured and established her honour the moment the ceremony should be declared, and it avoided the seeming ingratitude and indelicacy of disobeying my uncle, without an effort of patience to appease him. I should have time and occasion then, I thought, for soothing and persuading him, and ultimately winning that consent which I firmly trusted I should sooner or later extract from his kindness of heart.

That some objections existed to this mediatory plan, was true enough: those objections related to Isora rather than to myself, and she was the first, on my hinting at the proposal, to overcome its difficulties. The leading feature in Isora's character was generosity; and, in truth, I know not a quality more dangerous, either to man or woman. Herself was invariably the last human being whom she seemed to consider: and no sooner did she ascertain what measure was the most prudent for me to adopt, than it immediately became that upon which she insisted. Would it have been possible for me —man of pleasure and of the world as I was thought to be—no, my good uncle, though it went to my heart to wound thee so secretly— it would *not* have been possible for me, even if I had not coined my whole nature into love: even if Isora had not been to me, what one smile of Isora's really was—it would not have been possible to have sacrificed so noble and so divine a heart, and made myself, in that sacrifice, a wretch for ever. No, my good uncle. I could not have made that surrender to thy reason, much less to thy prejudices. But if I have not done great injustice to the knight's character, I doubt whether even the youngest reader will not forgive him for a want of sympathy with one feeling, when they consider how susceptible that charming old man was to all others.

And herewith I could discourse most excellent wisdom upon that most mysterious passion of love. I could show, by tracing its causes, and its inseparable connection with the imagination, that it is only in certain states of society, as well as in certain periods of life, that love —real, pure, high love can be born. Yea, I could prove, to the nicety of a very problem, that, in the court of Charles II., it would have been as impossible for such a feeling to find root, as it would be for myrtle trees to effloresce from a Duvillier periwig. And we are not to expect a man, however tender and affectionate he may be, to sympathize with that sentiment in another, which, from the accidents of birth and position, nothing short of a miracle could have ever produced in himself.

We were married then in private by a catholic priest. St. John, and one old lady who had been my father's godmother—for I wished for a female assistant in the ceremony, and this old lady could tell no secrets, for, being excessively deaf, nobody ever talked to her, and indeed she scarcely ever went abroad—were the sole witnesses. I took a small house in the immediate neighbourhood of London; it was surrounded on all sides with a high wall which defied alike curiosity and attack. This was, indeed, the sole reason which had induced me to prefer it to many more gaudy or more graceful dwell-ings. But within I had furnished it with every luxury that wealth, the most lavish and unsparing, could procure. Thither, under an assumed name, I brought my bride, and there was the greater part of my time spent. The people I had placed in the house believed I was a rich merchant, and this accounted for my frequent absences— (absences which Prudence rendered necessary) for the wealth which I lavished, and for the precautions of bolt, bar, and wall, which they imagined the result of commercial caution.

Oh the intoxication of that sweet Elysium, that Tadmor in life's desert—the possession of the one whom we have first loved! It is as if poetry, and music, and light, and the fresh breath of flowers, were all blent into one being, and from that being rose our existence! It is content made rapture—nothing to wish for, yet everything to feel! Was that air—the air which I had breathed hitherto? that earth—the earth which I had hitherto beheld? No, my heart dwelt in a new world, and all these motley and restless senses were melted into one sense—deep, silent, fathomless delight!

Well, too much of this species of love is not fit for a worldly tale, and I will turn, for the reader's relief, to worldly affections. From my first re-union with Isora, I had avoided all the former objects and acquaintances in which my time had been so charmingly em-ployed. Tarleton was the first to suffer by my new pursuit; "What has altered you?" said he; "you drink not, neither do you play. The women say you are grown duller than a Norfolk parson, and neither the Puppet-Show, nor the Water-Theatre, the Spring Gardens, nor the Ring, Wills's, nor the Kit-Cat, the Mulberry Garden, nor the New Exchange, witness any longer your homage and devotion.—What has come over you?—speak!"

"Apathy!"

"Ah!—I understand—you are tired of these things; pish, man! —go down into the country, the green fields will revive thee, and send thee back to London a new man! One would indeed find the town intolerably dull, if the country were not, happily, a thousand times duller—go to the country, Count, or I shall drop your friendship."

"Drop it!" said I, yawning, and Tarleton took pet, and did as I desired him. Now had I got rid of my friend as easily as I had found him,—a matter that would not have been so readily accomplished had not Mr. Tarleton owed me certain monies, concerning which, from the moment he had "dropped my friendship," goodbreeding effectually prevented his saying a single syllable to me ever after. There is no knowing the blessings of money until one has learnt to manage it properly.

So much, then, for the friend; now for the mistress. Lady Hasselton had, as Tarleton hinted before, resolved to play me a trick of spite; the reasons of our rupture really were, as I had stated to Tarleton, the mighty effects of little things. She lived in a sea of trifles, and she was desperately angry if her lover was not always sailing a pleasure-boat in the same ocean. Now this was expecting too much from me, and, after twisting our silken strings of attachment into all manner of fantastic forms, we fell fairly out one evening and broke the little ligatures in two. No sooner had I quarrelled with Tarleton, than Lady Hasselton received him in my place, and a week afterwards I was favoured with an anonymous letter, informing me of the violent passion which a certain *dame de la cour* had conceived for me, and requesting me to meet her at an appointed place. I looked twice over the letter, and discovered in one corner of it, two *g's* peculiar to the calligraphy of Lady Hasselton, though the rest of the letter (bad spelling excepted) was pretty decently disguised. Mr. Fielding was with me at the time; "What disturbs you?" said he, adjusting his knee-buckles.

"Read it!" said I, handing him the letter.

"Body of me, you are a lucky dog!" cried the beau. "You will hasten thither on the wings of love."

"Not a whit of it," said I; "I suspect that it comes from a rich old widow, whom I hate mortally."

"A rich old widow!" repeated Mr. Fielding, to whose eyes there was something very piquant in a jointure, and who thought consequently that there were few virginal flowers equal to a widow's weeds. "A rich old widow—you are right, Count, you are right. Don't go, don't think of it. I cannot abide those depraved creatures. Widow, indeed—quite an affront to your gallantry."

"Very true," said I. "Suppose you supply my place?"

"I'd sooner be shot first," said Mr. Fielding, taking his departure, and begging me for the letter to wrap some sugar plums in.

Need I add, that Mr. Fielding repaired to the place of assignation, where he received, in the shape of a hearty drubbing, the kind favours intended for me? The story was now left for me to tell, not for the Lady Hasselton—and that makes all the difference in the manner a story is told—*me* narrante, it is de *te* fabula narratur—*te* narrante and it is de *me* fabula, &c. Poor Lady Hasselton! to be laughed at, and have Tarleton for a lover!

I have gone back somewhat in the progress of my history, in order to make the above honourable mention of my friend and my mistress, thinking it due to their own merits, and thinking it may also be instructive to young gentlemen, who have not yet seen the world, to testify the exact nature and the probable duration of all the loves and friendships they are likely to find in that Great Monmouth Street of glittering and of damaged affections! I now resume the order of narration.

I wrote to Aubrey, thanking him for his intercession, but concealing, till we met, the measure I had adopted. I wrote also to my uncle, assuring him that I would take an early opportunity of hastening to Devereux Court, and conversing with him on the subject of his letter. And after an interval of some weeks, I received the two following answers from my correspondents : the latter arrived several days after the former.

FROM AUBREY DEVEREUX.

"I AM glad to understand from your letter, unexplanatory as it is, that· you have followed my advice. I will shortly write to you more at large; at present I am on the eve of my departure for the North of England, and have merely time to assure you of my affection.

"AUBREY DEVEREUX."

"P.S. Gerald is in London—have you seen him? Oh this world! this world! how it clings to us, despite our education—our wishes, our conscience, our knowledge of the Dread Hereafter!"

LETTER FROM SIR WILLIAM DEVEREUX.

"My Dear Nephew,

"Thank thee for thy letter, and the new plays thou sentest me down, and that droll new paper, the Spectator : it is a pretty shallow thing enough,—though it is not so racy as Rochester or little Sid would have made it ; but I thank thee for it, because it shows thou wast not angry with thine old uncle for opposing thee on thy love whimsies (in which most young men are dreadfully obstinate), since thou didst provide so kindly for his amusement. Well, but, Morton, I hope thou hast got that crotchet clear out of thy mind, and prithee now *don't* talk of it when thou comest down to see me. I hate conversations on marriage more than a boy does flogging—od'sfish, I do. So you must humour me on that point !

"Aubrey has left me again, and I am quite alone—not that I was much better off when he was here, for he was wont, of late, to shun my poor room like a 'lazar house,' and when I spoke to his mother about it, she muttered something about 'example,' and 'corrupting.' S'death, Morton, is your old uncle, who loves all living things, down to poor Ponto the dog, the sort of man whose example corrupts youth? As for thy mother, she grows more solitary every day; and I don't know how it is, but I am not so fond of strange faces as I used to be. 'Tis a new thing for me to be avoided and alone. Why, I remember even little Sid, who had as much venom as most men, once said it was impossible to—Fie now—see if I was not going to preach a sermon from a text in favour of myself! But come, Morton, come, I long for your face again; it is not so soft as Aubrey's, nor so regular as Gerald's, but it is twice as kind as either. Come, before it is too late; I feel myself going; and, to tell thee a secret, the doctors tell me I may not last many months longer. Come, and laugh once more at the old knight's stories. Come, and show him that there is still some one not too good to love him. Come, and I will tell thee a famous thing of old Rowley, which I am too ill and too sad to tell thee now.

"WM. DEVEREUX."

Need I say that, upon receiving this letter, I resolved, without any delay, to set out for Devereux Court? I summoned Desmarais to me; he answered not my call: he was from home—an unfrequent occurrence with the necessitarian valet. I waited his return, which was not for some hours, in order to give him sundry orders for my departure. The exquisite Desmarais hemmed thrice—"Will Monsieur be so very kind as to excuse my accompanying him?" said he, with his usual air and tone of obsequious respect.

"And why?" The valet explained. A relation of his was in England only for a few days—the philosopher was most anxious to enjoy his society—a pleasure which fate might not again allow him.

Though I had grown accustomed to the man's services, and did not like to lose him even for a time, yet I could not refuse his request; and I therefore ordered another of my servants to supply his place. This change, however, determined me to adopt a plan which I had before meditated, viz., the conveying of my own person to Devereux Court on horseback, and sending my servant with my luggage in my post-chaise. The equestrian mode of travelling, is, indeed to this day, the one most pleasing to me; and the reader will find me pursuing it many years afterwards, and to the same spot.

I might as well observe here that I had never entrusted Desmarais, no, nor one of my own servants, with the secret of my marriage with, or my visits to, Isora. I am a very fastidious person on those matters, and of all confidants, even in the most trifling affairs, I do most eschew those by whom we have the miserable honour to be served.

In order, then, to avoid having my horse brought me to Isora's house by any of these menial spies, I took the steed which I had selected for my journey, and rode to Isora's, with the intention of spending the evening there, and thence commencing my excursion with the morning light.

CHAPTER II.

LOVE—PARTING—A DEATH-BED. AFTER ALL HUMAN NATURE IS A BEAUTIFUL FABRIC ; AND EVEN ITS IMPERFECTIONS ARE NOT ODIOUS TO HIM WHO HAS STUDIED THE SCIENCE OF ITS ARCHITECTURE, AND FORMED A REVERENT ESTIMATE OF ITS CREATOR.

IT is a noticeable thing how much fear increases love. I mean—for the aphorism requires explanation—how much we love, in proportion to our fear of losing (or even to our fear of injury done to) the beloved object. 'Tis an instance of the reaction of the feelings—the love produces the fear, and the fear reproduces the love. This is one reason, among many, why women love so much more tenderly and anxiously than we do ; and it is also one reason among many, why frequent absences are, in all stages of love, the most keen exciters of the passion. I never breathed, away from Isora, without trembling for her safety. I trembled lest this Barnard, if so I should still continue to call her persecutor, should again discover and again molest her. Whenever (and that was almost daily) I rode to the quiet and remote dwelling I had procured her, my heart beat so vehemently, and my agitation was so intense, that on arriving at the gate I have frequently been unable, for several minutes, to demand admittance. There was, therefore, in the mysterious danger which ever seemed to hang over Isora, a perpetual irritation to a love otherwise but little inclined to slumber ; and this constant excitement took away from the torpor into which domestic affection too often languishes, and increased my passion even while it diminished my happiness.

On my arrival now at Isora's, I found her already stationed at the window, watching for my coming. How her dark eyes lit into

lustre when they saw me! How the rich blood mantled up under
the soft cheek which feeling had refined of late into a paler hue,
than it was wont, when I first gazed upon it, to wear! Then how
sprang forth her light step to meet me! How trembled her low
voice to welcome me! How spoke, from every gesture of her
graceful form, the anxious, joyful, all-animating gladness of her
heart! It is a melancholy pleasure to the dry, harsh, afterthoughts
of later life, to think one has been thus loved; and one marvels,
when one considers what one is now, how it could have ever been!
That love *of ours* was never made for after years! It could never
have flowed into the common, and cold channel of ordinary affairs!
It could never have been mingled with the petty cares and the low
objects with which the loves of all who live long together in this
sordid and most earthly earth, are sooner or later blended! We
could not have spared to others an atom of the great wealth of our
affection. We were misers of every coin in that boundless treasury.
It would have pierced me to the soul to have seen Isora smile upon
another. I know not even, had we had children, if I should not
have been jealous of my child! Was this selfish love? yes, it was
intensely, wholly selfish; but it was a love made so only by its
excess; nothing selfish on a smaller scale polluted it. There was
not on earth that which the one would not have forfeited at the
lightest desire of the other. So utterly were happiness and Isora
entwined together that I could form no idea of the one with which
the other was not connected. Was this love made for the many
and miry roads through which man must travel? Was it made for
age, or, worse than age, for those cool, ambitious, scheming years
that we call mature, in which all the luxuriance and verdure of
things are pared into tame shapes that mimic life, but a life that
is estranged from nature, in which art is the only beauty, and
regularity the only grace? No, in my heart of hearts, I feel that
our love was not meant for the stages of life through which I have
already passed; it would have made us miserable to see it fritter
itself away, and to remember what it once was. Better as it is!
better to mourn over the green bough than to look upon the sapless
stem. You who now glance over these pages, are you a mother?
if so, answer me one question—Would you not rather that the child
whom you have cherished with your soul's care, whom you have
nurtured at your bosom, whose young joys your eyes have sparkled
to behold, whose lightest grief you have wept to witness, as you
would have wept not for your own; over whose pure and unvexed
sleep you have watched and prayed, and, as it lay before you thus
still and unconscious of your vigil, have shaped out, oh, such bright
hopes for its future lot; would you not rather that, while thus

young and innocent, not a care tasted, not a crime incurred, it went down at once into the dark grave? Would you not rather suffer this grief, bitter though it be, than watch the predestined victim grow and ripen, and wind itself more and more around your heart, and when it is of full and mature age, and you yourself are stricken by years, and can form no new ties to replace the old that are severed, when woes have already bowed the darling of your hope, whom woe never was to touch; when sins have already darkened the bright, seraph, unclouded heart which sin never was to dim; behold it sink day by day altered, diseased, decayed, into the tomb which its childhood had in vain escaped? Answer me: would not the earlier fate be far gentler than the last? And if you *have* known and wept over that early tomb—if you have seen the infant flower fade away from the green soil of your affections—if you have missed the bounding step, and the laughing eye, and the winning mirth which made this sterile world a perpetual holiday—Mother of the Lost, if you have known, and you still pine for these, answer me yet again!—Is it not a comfort, even while you mourn, to think of all that that breast, now so silent, has escaped? The cream, the sparkle, the elixir of life, it had already quaffed; is it not sweet to think it shunned the wormwood and the dregs? Answer me, even though the answer be in tears! Mourner, your child was to you what my early and only love was to me; and could you pierce down, down through a thousand fathom of ebbing thought, to the far depths of my heart, you would there behold a sorrow *and a consolation*, that have something in unison with your own!

When the light of the next morning broke into our room, Isora was still sleeping. Have you ever observed that the young, seen asleep and by the morning light, seem much younger even than they are? partly because the air and the light sleep of dawn bring a fresher bloom to the cheek, and partly, because the careless negligence and the graceful postures exclusively appropriated to youth, are forbidden by custom and formality through the day, and developing themselves unconsciously in sleep, they strike the eye like the ease and freedom of childhood itself. There, as I looked upon Isora's tranquil and most youthful beauty, over which circled and breathed an ineffable innocence—even as the finer and subtler air, which was imagined by those dreamy bards who kindled the soft creations of naiad and of nymph, to float around a goddess—I could not believe that aught evil awaited one for whom infancy itself seemed to linger,—linger as if no elder shape and less delicate hue were meet to be the garment of so much guilelessness and tenderness of heart. I felt, indeed, while I bent over her, and her regular and quiet breath came upon my cheek, that feeling which is exactly the reverse to a presentiment of ill. I felt as if, secure in her own purity, she had nothing to dread, so that even the pang of parting was lost in the confidence which stole over me as I then gazed.

I rose gently, went to the next room and dressed myself—I heard my horse neighing beneath, as the servant walked him lazily to and fro. I re-entered the bed-chamber, in order to take leave of Isora; she was already up. "What!" said I, "it is but three minutes since I left you asleep, and I stole away as gently as time does when with you."

"Ah!" said Isora, smiling and blushing too, "but for my part, I think there is an instinct to know, even if all the senses were shut up, whether the one we love is with us or not. The moment you left me, I felt it at once, even in sleep, and I woke. But you will not, no, you will not leave me yet!"

I think I see Isora now, as she stood by the window which she had opened, with a woman's minute anxiety, to survey even the aspect of the clouds, and beseech caution against the treachery of the skies. I think I see her now, as she stood the moment after I had torn myself from her embrace, and had looked back, as I reached the door, for one parting glance—her eyes all tenderness, her lips parted, and quivering with the attempt to smile—the long, glossy ringlets (throngh whose raven hue the *purpureum lumen* broke like an imprisoned sunbeam) straying in dishevelled beauty over her transparent neck; the throat bent in mute despondency; the head drooping; the arms half extended, and dropping gradually as my steps departed; the sunken, absorbed expression of face, form, and gesture, so steeped in the very bitterness of dejection—all are before me now, sorrowful, and lovely in sorrow, as they were beheld years ago, by the gray, cold, comfortless light of morning!

"God bless you—my own, own love," I said; and as my look lingered, I added, with a full but an assured heart, "and He will!" I tarried no more—I flung myself on my horse, and rode on as if I were speeding *to*, and not *from*, my bride.

The noon was far advanced, as, the day after I left Isora, I found myself entering the park in which Devereux Court is situated. I did not enter by one of the lodges, but through a private gate. My horse was thoroughly jaded; for the distance I had come was great, and I had ridden rapidly; and as I came into the park, I dismounted, and, throwing the rein over my arm, proceeded slowly on foot. I was passing through a thick, long plantation, which belted the park and in which several walks and rides had been cut, when a man crossed the same road which I took, at a little distance before me. He was looking on the ground, and appeared wrapped in such earnest meditation that he neither saw nor heard me. But I had seen enough of him, in that brief space of time, to feel convinced that it was Montreuil whom I beheld. What brought him hither, him, whom I believed in London, immersed with Gerald in political schemes, and for whom these woods were not only interdicted ground, but to whom they must have also been but a tame field of interest, after his audiences with ministers and nobles? I did not, however, pause to consider on his apparition; I rather quickened my pace towards the house, in the expectation of there ascertaining the cause of his visit.

The great gates of the outer court were open as usual: I rode unheedingly through them, and was soon at the door of the hall. The porter, who unfolded to my summons the ponderous door, uttered, when he saw me, an exclamation that seemed to my ear to have in it more of sorrow than welcome.

"How is your master?" I asked.

The man shook his head, but did not hasten to answer: and impressed with a vague alarm, I hurried on without repeating the question. On the staircase I met old Nicholls, my uncle's valet: I stopped and questioned him. My uncle had been seized on the preceding day with gout in the stomach, medical aid had been procured, but it was feared ineffectually, and the physicians had declared, about an hour before I arrived, that he could not, in human probability, outlive the night. Stifling the rising at my heart, I waited to hear no more—I flew up the stairs—I was at the door of my uncle's chamber—I stopped there, and listened; all was still —I opened the door gently—I stole in, and, creeping to the bedside, knelt down and covered my face with my hands; for I required a pause for self-possession, before I had courage to look up. When I raised my eyes, I saw my mother on the opposite side; she sat on a chair with a draught of medicine in one hand, and a watch in the other. She caught my eye, but did not speak; she gave me a sign of recognition, and looked down again upon the watch. My uncle's back was turned to me, and he lay so still that, for some moments, I thought he was asleep; at last, however, he moved restlessly.

"It is past noon!" said he to my mother, "is it not?"

"It is three minutes and six seconds after four," replied my mother, looking closer at the watch.

My uncle sighed. "They have sent an express for the dear boy, madam?" said he.

"Exactly at half-past nine last evening," answered my mother, glancing at me.

"He could scarcely be here by this time," said my uncle, and he moved again in the bed. "Pish—how the pillow frets one."

"Is it too high?" said my mother.

"No," said my uncle, faintly, "no—no—the discomfort is not in the pillow, after all—'tis a fine day—is it not?"

"Very!" said my mother; "I wish you could go out."

My uncle did not answer: there was a pause. "Od'sfish, madam, are those carriage-wheels?"

"No, Sir William—but—"

"There *are* sounds in my ear—my senses grow dim," said my uncle, unheeding her,—"would that I might live another day—I should not like to die without seeing him. 'Sdeath, madam, I do hear something behind!—Sobs, as I live!—Who sobs for the old knight?" and my uncle turned round, and saw me.

"My dear—dear uncle!" I said, and could say no more.

"Ah, Morton," cried the kind old man, putting his hand affectionately upon mine. "Beshrew me, but I think I have conquered the grim enemy now that you are come. But what's this, my boy?—tears—tears,—why little Sid—no, nor Rochester either, would ever have believed this if I had sworn it! Cheer up —cheer up."

But, seeing that I wept and sobbed the more, my uncle, after a pause, continued in the somewhat figurative strain which the reader has observed he sometimes adopted, and which perhaps his dramatic studies had taught him.

"Nay, Morton, what do you grieve for?—that Age should throw off its fardel of aches and pains, and no longer groan along its weary road, meeting cold looks and unwilling welcomes, as both host and comrade grow weary of the same face, and the spendthrift heart has no longer quip or smile wherewith to pay the reckoning? No—no—let the poor pedlar shuffle off his dull pack, and fall asleep. But I am glad you are come: I would sooner have one of your kind looks at your uncle's stale saws or jests than all the long faces about me, saving only the presence of your mother;" and with his characteristic gallantry, my uncle turned courteously to her.

"Dear Sir William!" said she, "it is time you should take your draught; and then would it not be better that you should see the chaplain—he waits without."

"Od'sfish," said my uncle, turning again to me, "'tis the way with them all—when the body is past hope, comes the physician, and when the soul is past mending, comes the priest. No, madam, no, 'tis too late for either.—Thank ye, Morton, thank ye" (as I started up—took the draught from my mother's hand, and besought him to drink it), "'tis of no use; but if it pleases thee, I must,"— and he drank the medicine.

My mother rose, and walked towards the door—it was ajar, and, as my eye followed her figure, I perceived, through the opening, the black garb of the chaplain.

"Not yet," said she, quietly; "wait." And then gliding away, she seated herself by the window in silence, and told her beads.

My uncle continued:—"They have been at me, Morton, as if I had been a pagan; and I believe, in their hearts, they are not a little scandalized that I don't try to win the next world, by trembling like an ague. Faith now, I never could believe that Heaven was so partial to cowards; nor can I think, Morton, that Salvation is like a soldier's muster-roll, and that we may play the devil between hours, so that, at the last moment, we whip in, and answer to our names. Od'sfish, Morton, I could tell thee a tale of that; but 'tis a long one, and we have not time now. Well, well, for my part, I deem reverently and gratefully of God, and do not believe He will be very wrath with our past enjoyment of life, if we have taken care that others should enjoy it too; nor do I think, with thy good mother, and Aubrey, dear child! that an idle word has the same weight in the Almighty's scales as a wicked deed."

"Blessed, blessed are they," I cried through my tears, "on whose souls there is as little stain as there is on yours!"

"Faith, Morton, that's kindly said; and thou knowest not how strangely it sounds, after their exhortations to repentance. I know I have had my faults, and walked on to our common goal in a very irregular line: but I never wronged the living nor slandered the dead, nor ever shut my heart to the poor—'twere a burning sin if I had; and I have loved all men and all things, and I never bore ill-will to a creature. Poor Ponto, Morton, thou wilt take care of poor Ponto, when I'm dead—nay, nay, don't grieve so. Go, my child, go—compose thyself while I see the priest, for 'twill please thy poor mother; and though she thinks harshly of me now, I should not like her to do so *to-morrow!* Go, my dear boy, go."

I went from the room, and waited by the door, till the office of the priest was over. My mother then came out, and said Sir William had composed himself to sleep. While she was yet speaking, Gerald surprised me by his appearance. I learned that he had been in the house for the last three days, and when I heard this, I involuntarily accounted for the appearance of Montreuil. I saluted him distantly, and he returned my greeting with the like pride. He seemed, however, though in a less degree, to share in my emotions; and my heart softened to him for it. Nevertheless we stood apart, and met not as brothers should have met by the death-bed of a mutual benefactor.

"Will you wait without?" said my mother.

"No," answered I, "I will watch over him." So I stole in, with a light step, and seated myself by my uncle's bed-side. He was asleep, and his sleep was as hushed and quiet as an infant's. I looked upon his face, and saw a change had come over it, and was increasing sensibly : but there was neither harshness nor darkness in the change, awful as it was. The soul, so long nurtured on bene-volence, could not, in parting, leave a rude stamp on the kindly clay which had seconded its impulses so well.

The evening had just set in, when my uncle woke ; he turned very gently, and smiled when he saw me.

"It is late," said he, and I observed with a wrung heart, that his voice was fainter.

"No, sir, not very," said I.

"Late enough, my child ; the warm sun has gone down ; and 'tis a good time to close one's eyes, when all without looks gray and chill : methinks it is easier to wish thee farewell, Morton, when I see thy face indistinctly. I am glad I shall not die in the day-time. Give me thy hand, my child, and tell me that thou art not angry with thine old uncle for thwarting thee in that love business. I have heard tales of the girl, too, which make me glad, for thy sake, that it is all off, though I might not tell thee of them before. 'Tis very dark, Morton. I have had a pleasant sleep.—Od'sfish, I do not think a bad man would have slept so well.—The fire burns dim, Morton —it is very cold. Cover me up—double the counterpane over the legs, Morton. I remember once walking in the Mall—little Sid said 'Devereux.'—It is colder and colder, Morton — raise the blankets more over the back. 'Devereux,' said little Sid—faith, Morton, 'tis ice now—where art thou?—is the fire out, that I can't see thee? Remember thine old uncle, Morton—and—and—don't forget poor—Ponto.—Bless thee, my child—bless you all !"

And my uncle died !

CHAPTER III.

A GREAT CHANGE OF PROSPECTS.

 SHUT myself up in the apartments prepared for me (they were not those I had formerly occupied), and refused all participation in my solitude, till, after an in-terval of some days, my mother came to summon me to the opening of the will. She was more moved than I had expected.

" It is a pity," said she, as we descended the stairs, "that Aubrey is not here, and that we should be so unacquainted with the exact place where he is likely to be that I fear the letter I sent him may be long delayed, or, indeed, altogether miscarry."

" Is not the Abbé here ? " said I, listlessly.

" No ! " answered my mother, " to be sure not."

" He has *been* here," said I, greatly surprised. " I certainly saw him on the day of my arrival."

" Impossible !" said my mother, in evident astonishment ; and seeing that, at all events, she was unacquainted with the circumstance, I said no more.

The will was to be read in the little room, where my uncle had been accustomed to sit. I felt it as a sacrilege to his memory to chose that spot for such an office, but I said nothing. Gerald and my mother, the lawyer (a neighbouring attorney, named Oswald), and myself were the only persons present ;—Mr. Oswald hemmed thrice, and broke the seal. After a preliminary, strongly characteristic of the testator, he came to the disposition of the estates. I had never once, since my poor uncle's death, thought upon the chances of his will—indeed, knowing myself so entirely his favourite, I could not, if I had thought upon them, have entertained a doubt as to their result. What then was my astonishment when, couched in terms of the strongest affection, the whole bulk of the property was bequeathed to Gerald ;—to Aubrey the sum of forty, to myself that of twenty, thousand pounds (a capital considerably less than the yearly income of my uncle's princely estates), was allotted. Then followed a list of minor bequests,—to my mother an annuity of three, thousand a year, with the privilege of apartments in the house during her life ; to each of the servants legacies sufficient for independence ; to a few friends, and distant connections of the family, tokens of the testator's remembrance,—even the horses to his carriage, and the dogs that fed from his menials' table, were not forgotten, but were to be set apart from work, and maintained in indolence during their remaining span of life. The will was concluded—I could not believe my senses : not a word was said as a reason for giving Gerald the priority.

I rose calmly enough. " Suffer me, sir," said I to the lawyer, "to satisfy my own eyes." Mr. Oswald bowed, and placed the will in my hands. I glanced at Gerald as I took it : his countenance betrayed, or feigned, an astonishment equal to my own. With a jealous, searching, scrutinizing eye, I examined the words of the bequest ; I examined especially (for I suspected that the names must have been exchanged) the place in which my name and Gerald's occurred. In vain : all was smooth and fair to the eye, not a vestige of possible erasure or alteration was visible.   I looked next at the wording of the will: it was evidently my uncle's—no one could have feigned or imitated the peculiar turn of his expressions ; and, above all, many parts of the will (the affectionate and personal parts) were in his own handwriting.

"The date," said I, "is, I perceive, of very recent period ; the will is signed by two witnesses besides yourself. Who and where are they ? "

" Robert Lister, the first signature, my clerk, he is since dead, sir ! "

" Dead ! " said I ; " and the other witness, George Davis ? "

" Is one of Sir William's tenants, and is below, sir, in waiting."

" Let him come up," and a middle-sized, stout man, with a blunt, bold, open countenance, was admitted.

"Did you witness this will ? " said I.

" I did, your honour ! "

" And this is your handwriting ? " pointing to the scarcely legible scrawl.

" Yees, your honour," said the man, scratching his head, " I think it be, they are my *ees*, and *G*, and *D*, sure enough."

" And do you know the purport of the will you signed ? "

" Anan ! "

" I mean, do you know to whom Sir William—stop, Mr. Oswald—suffer the man to answer me—to whom Sir William left his property ? "

" Noa, to be sure, sir ; the will was a woundy long one, and Maister Oswald there to'd me it was no use to read it over to me, but merely to sign, as a witness to Sir William's handwriting."

" Enough : you may retire ; " and George Davis vanished.

" Mr. Oswald," said I, approaching the attorney, " I may wrong you, and, if so, I am sorry for it, but I suspect there has been foul practice in this deed. I have reason to be convinced that Sir William Devereux could never have made this devise. I give you warning, sir, that I shall bring the business immediately before a court of law, and that if guilty—ay, tremble, sir,—of what I suspect, you will answer for this deed at the foot of the gallows."

I turned to Gerald, who rose while I was yet speaking. Before I could address him, he exclaimed, with evident and extreme agitation :

" You cannot, Morton—you cannot—you dare not insinuate that I, your brother, have been base enough to forge, or to instigate the forgery of, this will ? "

Gerald's agitation made me still less doubtful of his guilt.

" The case, sir," I answered, coldly, " stands thus : my uncle could not have made this will—it is a devise that must seem incredible to all who knew aught of our domestic circumstances. Fraud has been practised, how I know not ! by whom I do know."

"Morton, Morton—this is insufferable—I cannot bear such charges, even from a brother."

"Charges!—your conscience speaks, sir—not I; no one benefits by this fraud but you: pardon me if I draw an inference from a fact."

So saying, I turned on my heel, and abruptly left the apartment. I ascended the stairs which led to my own: there I found my servant preparing the paraphernalia in which that very evening I was to attend my uncle's funeral. I gave him, with a calm and collected voice, the necessary instructions for following me to town immediately after that event, and then I passed on to the room where the deceased lay in state. The room was hung with black— the gorgeous pall, wrought with the proud heraldry of our line, lay over the coffin, and by the lights which made, in that old chamber, a more brilliant, yet more ghastly, day, sat the hired watchers of the dead.

I bade them leave me, and kneeling down beside the coffin, I poured out the last expressions of my grief. I rose, and was retiring once more to my room, when I encountered Gerald.

"Morton," said he, "I own to you, I myself am astounded by my uncle's will. I do not come to make you offers—you would not accept them—I do not come to vindicate myself, it is beneath me; and we have never been as brothers, and we know not their language—but I *do* come to demand you to retract the dark and causeless suspicions you have vented against me, and also to assure you that, if you have doubts of the authenticity of the will, so far from throwing obstacles in your way, I myself will join in the inquiries you institute, and the expenses of the law."

I felt some difficulty in curbing my indignation while Gerald thus spoke. I saw before me the persecutor of Isora—the fraudulent robber of my rights, and I heard this enemy speak to me of aiding in the inquiries which were to convict himself of the basest, if not the blackest, of human crimes; there was something too in the reserved and yet insolent tone of his voice which, reminding me as it did of our long aversion to each other, made my very blood creep with abhorrence. I turned away, that I might not break my oath to Isora, for I felt strongly tempted to do so; and said in as calm an accent as I could command, "The case will, I trust, require no king's evidence; and, at least, I will not be beholden to the man whom my reason condemns for any assistance in bringing upon himself the ultimate condemnation of the law."

Gerald looked at me sternly; "Were you not my brother," said he, in a low tone, "I would, for a charge so dishonouring my fair name, strike you dead at my feet."

"It is a wonderful exertion of fraternal love," I rejoined, with a scornful laugh, but an eye flashing with passions a thousand times more fierce than scorn, "that prevents your adding that last favour to those you have already bestowed on me."

Gerald, with a muttered curse, placed his hand upon his sword; my own rapier was instantly half drawn, when, to save us from the great guilt of mortal contest against each other, steps were heard, and a number of the domestics charged with melancholy duties at the approaching rite, were seen slowly sweeping in black robes along the opposite gallery. Perhaps that interruption restored both of us to our senses, for we said, almost in the same breath, and nearly in the same phrase, "This way of terminating strife is not for us;" and, as Gerald spoke, he turned slowly away, descended the staircase, and disappeared.

The funeral took place at night: a numerous procession of the tenants and peasantry attended. My poor uncle! there was not a dry eye for thee, but those of thine own kindred. Tall, stately, erect in the power and majesty of his unrivalled form, stood Gerald, already assuming the dignity and lordship which, to speak frankly, so well became him; my mother's face was turned from me, but her attitude proclaimed her utterly absorbed in prayer. As for myself, my heart seemed hardened: I could not betray to the gaze of a hundred strangers the emotions which I would have hidden from those whom I loved the most, wrapped in my cloak, with arms folded on my breast, and eyes bent to the ground, I leaned against one of the pillars of the chapel, apart, and apparently unmoved.

But when they were about to lower the body into the vault, a momentary weakness came over me. I made an involuntary step forward, a single but deep groan of anguish broke from me, and then, covering my face with my mantle, I resumed my former attitude, and all was still. The rite was over; in many and broken groups the spectators passed from the chapel: some to speculate on the future lord, some to mourn over the late, and all to return the next morning to their wonted business, and let the glad sun teach them to forget the past, until for themselves the sun should be no more, and the forgetfulness eternal.

The hour was so late that I relinquished my intention of leaving the house that night; I ordered my horse to be in readiness at daybreak, and, before I retired to rest, I went to my mother's apartments: she received me with more feeling than she had ever testified before.

"Believe me, Morton," said she, and she kissed my forehead; "believe me, I can fully enter into the feelings which you must naturally experience on an event so contrary to your expectations. I cannot conceal from you how much I am surprised. Certainly Sir William never gave any of us cause to suppose that he liked either of your brothers—Gerald less than Aubrey—so much as yourself; nor, poor man, was he in other things at all addicted to conceal his opinions."

."It is true, my mother," said I; "it is true. Have you not therefore some suspicions of the authenticity of the will?"

"Suspicions!" cried my mother. "No!—impossible!—suspicions of whom? You could not think Gerald so base, and who else had an interest in deception?—Besides, the signature is undoubtedly Sir William's handwriting, and the will was regularly witnessed; suspicions, Morton—no, impossible! Reflect too, how eccentric and humoursome your uncle always was: suspicions!—no, impossible!"

"Such things have been, my mother, nor are they uncommon: men will hazard their souls, ay, and what to some is more precious still, their lives too—for the vile clay we call money. But enough of this now: the Law—that great arbiter—that eater of the oyster, and divider of its shells—the Law will decide between us, and if against me, as I suppose, and fear the decision will be—why I must be a suitor to fortune, instead of her commander. Give me your blessing, my dearest mother; I cannot stay longer in this house: to-morrow I leave you."

And my mother did bless me, and I fell upon her neck and clung to it. "Ah!" thought I, "this blessing is almost worth my uncle's fortune."

I returned to my room—there I saw on the table the case of the sword sent me by the French king. I had left it with my uncle, on my departure to town, and it had been found among his effects and reclaimed by me. I took out the sword, and drew it from the scabbard.

"Come," said I, and I kindled with a melancholy, yet a deep, enthusiasm, as I looked along the blade, "come, my bright friend, with thee through this labyrinth which we call the world, will I carve my way! Fairest and speediest of earth's levellers, thou makest the path from the low valley to the steep hill, and shapest the soldier's axe into the monarch's sceptre! The laurel and the fasces, and the curule car, and the emperor's purple—what are these but thy playthings, alternately thy scorn and thy reward! Founder of all empires, propagator of all creeds, thou leddest the Gaul and the Goth, and the gods of Rome and Greece crumbled upon their altars! Beneath thee, the fires of the Gheber waved pale, and on thy point the badge of the camel-driver blazed like a sun over the startled East! Eternal arbiter, and unconquerable despot, while the passions of mankind exist! Most solemn of hypocrites—circling blood with glory as with a halo, and consecrating homicide and massacre with a hollow name, which the parched throat of thy votary, in the battle and the agony shouteth out with its last breath! Star of all human destinies! I kneel before thee, and invoke from thy bright astrology an omen and a smile."

CHAPTER IV.

AN EPISODE—THE SON OF THE GREATEST MAN WHO (ONE ONLY EXCEPTED) *EVER ROSE TO A THRONE*, BUT BY NO MEANS OF THE GREATEST MAN (SAVE ONE) *WHO EVER EXISTED*.

BEFORE sunrise the next morning, I had commenced my return to London. I had previously entrusted to the *locum tenens* of the sage Desmarais, the royal gift, and (singular conjunction!) poor Ponto, my uncle's dog. Here let me pause, as I shall have no other opportunity to mention him, to record the fate of the canine bequest. He accompanied me some years afterwards to France, and he died there in extreme age. I shed tears, as I saw the last relic of my poor uncle expire, and I was not consoled even though he was buried in the garden of the gallant Villars, and immortalized by an epitaph from the pen of the courtly Chaulieu.

Leaving my horse to select his own pace, I surrendered myself to reflection upon the strange alteration that had taken place in my fortunes. There did not, in my own mind, rest a doubt but that some villainy had been practised with respect to the will. My uncle's constant and unvarying favour towards me ; the unequivocal expressions he himself from time to time had dropped indicative of his future intentions on my behalf: the easy and natural manner in which he had seemed to consider, as a thing of course, my heritage and succession to his estates ; all, coupled with his own frank and kindly character, so little disposed to raise hopes which he meant to disappoint, might alone have been sufficient to arouse my suspicions at a devise so contrary to all past experience of the testator. But when to these were linked the bold temper, and the daring intellect of my brother, joined to his personal hatred to myself: his close intimacy with Montreuil, whom I believed capable of the darkest designs ; the sudden and evidently concealed appearance of the latter on the day my uncle died ; the agitation and paleness of the attorney; the enormous advantages accruing to Gerald, and to no one else, from the terms of the devise: when these were all united into one focus of evidence, they appeared to me to leave no doubt of the forgery of the testament, and the crime of Gerald. Nor was there anything in my brother's bearing and manner calculated to abate my suspicions. His agitation was real; his surprise might have been feigned; his offer of assistance in investigation was an unmeaning bravado; his conduct to myself testified his continued ill-will towards me—an ill-will which might possibly have instigated him in the fraud, scarcely less than the whispers of interest and cupidity.

But while this was the natural and indelible impression on my mind, I could not disguise from myself the extreme difficulty I should experience in resisting my brother's claim. So far as my utter want of all legal knowledge would allow me to decide, I could perceive nothing in the will itself which would admit of a lawyer's successful cavil: my reasons for suspicion, so conclusive to myself, would seem nugatory to a judge. My uncle was known as a humorist; and prove that a man differs from others in one thing, and the world will believe that he differs from them in a thousand. His favour to me would be, in the popular eye, only an eccentricity, and the unlooked-for disposition of his will only a caprice. Possession, too, gave Gerald a proverbial vantage ground, which my whole life might be wasted in contesting; while his command of an immense wealth might, more than probably, exhaust my spirit by delay, and my fortune by expenses. Precious prerogative of law to reverse the attribute of the Almighty! to fill the *rich* with good things, but to send the poor empty away! *In corruptissimâ republicâ plurimæ leges.* Legislation perplexed is synonymous with crime unpunished. A reflection, by the way, I should never have made, if I had never had a law-suit—sufferers are ever reformers.

Revolving, then, these anxious and unpleasing thoughts, inter-rupted, at times, by regrets of a purer and less selfish nature for the friend I had lost, and wandering, at others, to the brighter antici-pations of rejoining Isora, and drinking from her eyes my comfort for the past, and my hope for the future, I continued and concluded my day's travel.

The next day, on resuming my journey, and on feeling the time approach that would bring me to Isora, something like joy became the most prevalent feeling on my mind. So true it is that misfortunes little affect us so long as we have some ulterior object, which, by arousing hope, steals us from affliction. Alas! the pang of a moment becomes intolerable when we know of nothing *beyond* the moment which it soothes us to anticipate! Happiness lives in the light of

the future : attack the present—she defies you ! Darken the future,
and you destroy her !

It was a beautiful morning: through the vapours, which rolled
slowly away beneath his beams, the sun broke gloriously forth ; and
over wood and hill, and the low plains, which, covered with golden
corn, stretched immediately before me, his smile lay in stillness, but
in joy.   And ever from out the brake and the scattered copse,
which at frequent intervals beset the road, the merry birds sent
a fitful and glad music to mingle with the sweets and freshness of
the air.

I had accomplished the greater part of my journey, and had entered
into a more wooded and garden-like description of country, when I
perceived an old man, in a kind of low chaise, vainly endeavouring
to hold in a little, but spirited horse, which had taken alarm at some
object on the road, and was running away with its driver.   The age
of the gentleman, and the lightness of the chaise, gave me some
alarm for the safety of the driver ; so, tying my own horse to the
gate, lest the sound of his hoofs might only increase the speed and
fear of the fugitive, I ran with a swift and noiseless step along the
other side of the hedge, and, coming out into the road, just before
the pony's head, I succeeded in arresting him, at rather a critical
spot and moment.   The old gentleman very soon recovered his
alarm ; and, returning me many thanks for my interference, requested
me to accompany him to his house, which he said was two or three
miles distant.

Though I had no desire to be delayed in my journey, for the mere
sake of seeing an old gentleman's house, I thought my new acquaint-
auce's safety required me, at least, to offer to act as his charioteer
till we reached his house.   To my secret vexation at that time,
though I afterwards thought the petty inconvenience was amply
repaid by a conference with a very singular and once noted character,
the offer was accepted.   Surrendering my own steed to the care of
a ragged boy, who promised to lead it with equal judgment and
zeal, I entered the little car, and, keeping a firm hand and constant
eye on the reins, brought the offending quadruped into a very
equable and sedate pace.

"Poor Pob," said the old gentleman, apostrophizing his horse ;
"poor Pob, like thy betters, thou knowest the weak hand from the
strong ; and when thou art not held in by power, thou wilt chafe
against love ; so that thou renewest in my mind the remembrance
of its favourite maxim, viz., 'The only preventative to rebellion is
restraint !'"

"Your observation, sir," said I, rather struck by this address,
"makes very little in favour of the more generous feelings by which

we ought to be actuated. It is a base mind which always requires the bit and bridle."

"It is, sir," answered the old gentleman; "I allow it; but, though I have some love for human nature, I have no respect for it; and while I pity its infirmities, I cannot but confess them."

"Methinks, sir," replied I, "that you have uttered in that short speech more sound philosophy than I have heard for months. There is wisdom in not thinking too loftily of human clay, and benevolence in not judging it too harshly, and something, too, of magnanimity in this moderation; for we seldom contemn mankind till they have hurt us, and when they have hurt us, we seldom do anything but detest them for the injury."

"You speak shrewdly, sir, for one so young," returned the old man, looking hard at me; "and I will be sworn you have suffered some cares; for we never begin to think, till we are a little afraid to hope."

I sighed as I answered, "There are some men, I fancy, to whom constitution supplies the office of care; who, naturally melancholy, become easily addicted to reflection, and reflection is a soil which soon repays us for whatever trouble we bestow upon its culture."

"True, sir!" said my companion—and there was a pause. The old gentleman resumed: "We are not far from my home now (or rather my temporary residence, for my proper and general home is at Cheshunt, in Hertfordshire); and, as the day is scarcely half spent, I trust you will not object to partake of a hermit's fare. Nay, nay, no excuse: I assure you that I am not a gossip in general, or a liberal dispenser of invitations; and I think, if you refuse me now, you will hereafter regret it."

My curiosity was rather excited by this threat: and, reflecting that my horse required a short rest, I subdued my impatience to return to town, and accepted the invitation. We came presently to a house of moderate size, and rather antique fashion. This, the old man informed me, was his present abode. A servant, almost as old as his master, came to the door, and, giving his arm to my host, led him, for he was rather lame and otherwise infirm, across a small hall into a long, low apartment. I followed.

A miniature of Oliver Cromwell, placed over the chimney-piece, forcibly arrested my attention.

"It is the only portrait of the Protector I ever saw," said I, "which impresses on me the certainty of a likeness; that resolute, gloomy brow—that stubborn lip—that heavy, yet not stolid, expression—all seem to warrant resemblance to that singular and fortunate man, to whom folly appears to have been as great an instrument of success as wisdom, and who rose to the supreme power, perhaps, no

less from a pitiable fanaticism than an admirable genius. So true
is it that great men often soar to their height, by qualities the least
obvious to the spectator, and (to stoop to a low comparison) resemble
that animal [1] in which the common ligament supplies the place, and
possesses the property, of wings."

The old man smiled very slightly, as I made this remark. "If
this be true," said he, with an impressive tone, "though we may
wonder less at the talents of the Protector, we must be more
indulgent to his character, nor condemn him for insincerity, when
at heart he himself was deceived."

"It is in that light," said I, "that I have always viewed his
conduct. And though myself, by prejudice, a cavalier and a tory,
I own that Cromwell (hypocrite as he is esteemed) appears to me
as much to have exceeded his royal antagonist and victim, in the
virtue of sincerity, as he did in the grandeur of his genius, and the
profound consistency of his ambition."

"Sir," said my host, with a warmth that astonished me, "you
seem to have known that man, so justly do you judge him. Yes,"
said he, after a pause, "yes, perhaps no one ever so varnished to
his own breast his designs—no one, so covetous of glory, was ever
so duped by conscience—no one ever rose to such a height, through
so few acts that seemed to himself worthy of remorse."

At this part of our conversation, the servant, entering, announced
dinner. We adjourned to another room, and partook of a homely
yet not uninviting repast. When men are pleased with each other,
conversation soon gets beyond the ordinary surfaces to talk ; and an
exchange of deeper opinions is speedily effected by what old Barnes [2]
quaintly enough terms, "The Gentleman Usher of all knowledge—
Sermocination !"

It was a pretty, though small room, where we dined ; and I
observed that in this apartment, as in the other into which I had
been at first ushered, there were several books scattered about,
in that confusion and number which show that they have become
to their owner both the choicest luxury and the least dispensable
necessary. So, during dinner time, we talked principally upon
books, and I observed that those which my host seemed to know
the best were of the elegant and poetical order of philosophers, who,
more fascinating than deep, preach up the blessings of a solitude
which is useless, and a content which, deprived of passion, excitement, and energy, would, if it could ever exist, only be a dignified
name for vegetation.

"So," said he, when, the dinner being removed, we were left

[1] The flying squirrel.   [2] In the Gerania.

alone with that substitute for all society—wine! "so you are going to town : in four hours more you will be in that great focus of noise, falsehood, hollow joy, and real sorrow. Do you know that I have become so wedded to the country that I cannot but consider all those who leave it for the turbulent city, in the same light, half wondering, half compassionating, as that in which the ancients regarded the hardy adventurers who left the safe land and their happy homes, voluntarily to expose themselves in a frail vessel to the dangers of an uncertain sea. Here, when I look out on the green fields, and the blue sky, the quiet herds, basking in the sunshine, or scattered over the unpolluted plains, I cannot but exclaim with Pliny, 'This is the true Μουσειον!' this is the source whence flow inspiration to the mind and tranquillity to the heart! And in my love of nature —more confiding and constant than ever is the love we bear to women—I cry with the tender and sweet Tibullus—

'Ego composito securus acervo
Despiciam dites—despiciamque famem.'"1

"These," said I, "are the sentiments we all (perhaps the most restless of us the most passionately) at times experience. But there is in our hearts some secret, but irresistible, principle, that impels us, as a rolling circle, onward, onward, in the great orbit of our destiny ; nor do we find a respite until the wheels on which we move are broken—at the tomb."

"Yet," said my host, "the internal principle you speak of can be arrested before the grave : at least stilled and impeded. You will smile incredulously, perhaps (for I see you do not know who I am), when I tell you that I might once have been a monarch, and that obscurity seemed to me more enviable than empire ; I resigned the occasion : the tide of fortune rolled onward, and left me safe, but solitary and forsaken, upon the dry land. If you wonder at my choice, you will wonder still more when I tell you that I have never repented it."

Greatly surprised, and even startled, I heard my host make this strange avowal. "Forgive me," said I, "but you have powerfully excited my interest ; dare I inquire from whose experience I am now deriving a lesson?"

"Not yet," said my host, smiling, "not till our conversation is over, and you have bid the old anchorite adieu, in all probability, for ever : you will then know that you have conversed with a man, perhaps more universally neglected and contemned than any of his contemporaries. Yes," he continued, "yes, I resigned power, and I got no praise for my moderation, but contempt for my folly ; no

1 Satisfied with my little hoard, I can despise wealth—and fear not hunger.

human being would believe that I could have relinquished that treasure through a disregard for its possession which others would only have relinquished through an incapacity to retain it; and that which, had they seen it recorded in an ancient history, men would have regarded as the height of philosophy, they despised when acted under their eyes, as the extremest abasement of imbecility. Yet I compare my lot with that of the great man whom I was expected to equal in ambition, and to whose grandeur I might have succeeded; and am convinced that in this retreat I am more to be envied than he in the plenitude of his power and the height of his renown; yet is not happiness the aim of wisdom? if my choice is happier than his, is it not wiser?"

"Alas," thought I, "the wisest men seldom have the loftiest genius, and perhaps happiness is granted rather to mediocrity of mind than to mediocrity of circumstance;" but I did not give so uncourteous a reply to my host an audible utterance; on the contrary: "I do not doubt," said I, as I rose to depart, "the wisdom of a choice which has brought you self-gratulation. And it has been said by a man both great and good, a man to whose mind was open the lore of the closet and the experience of courts—that in wisdom or in folly, 'the only difference between one man and another, is whether a man governs his passions or his passions him.' According to this rule, which indeed is a classic and a golden aphorism, Alexander, on the throne of Persia, might have been an idiot to Diogenes in his tub. And now, sir, in wishing you farewell, let me again crave your indulgence to my curiosity."

"Not yet, not yet," answered my host; and he led me once more into the other room. While they were preparing my horse, we renewed our conversation. To the best of my recollection, we talked about Plato; but I had now become so impatient to rejoin Isora that I did not accord to my worthy host the patient attention I had hitherto given him. When I took leave of him he blessed me, and placed a piece of paper in my hand; "Do not open this," said he, "till you are at least two miles hence, your curiosity will then be satisfied. If ever you travel this road again, or if ever you pass by Cheshunt, pause and see if the old philosopher is dead. Adieu!"

And so we parted.

You may be sure that I had not passed the appointed distance of two miles very far, when I opened the paper and read the following words:—

"Perhaps, young stranger, at some future period of a life, which I venture to foretell will be adventurous and eventful, it may afford you a matter for reflection, or a resting-spot for a moral, to remember that you have seen, in old age and obscurity, the son of Him who shook an empire, avenged a people, and obtained a throne, only to be the victim of his own passions and the dupe of his own reason. I repeat now the question I before put to you—was the fate of the great Protector fairer than that of the despised and forgotten

"RICHARD CROMWELL?"

"So," thought I, "it is indeed with the son of the greatest ruler England, or perhaps, in modern times, Europe has ever produced, that I have held this conversation upon content! Yes, perhaps your fate *is* more to be envied than that of your illustrious father; but who *would* envy it more? Strange that while we pretend that happiness is the object of all desire, happiness is the last thing which we covet. Love, and wealth, and pleasure, and honour, —these are the roads which we take, so long that, accustomed to the mere travel, we forget that it was first undertaken, not for the course, but the goal; and, in the common infatuation which pervades all our race, we make the toil the meed, and in following the means forsake the end."

I never saw my host again; very shortly afterwards he died:[1] and Fate, which had marked with so strong a separation the lives of the father and the son, united in that death—as its greatest, so its only universal, blessing—the philosopher and the recluse with the warrior and the chief!

CHAPTER V.

IN WHICH THE HERO SHOWS DECISION ON MORE POINTS THAN ONE—MORE OF ISORA'S CHARACTER IS DEVELOPED.

TO use the fine image in the Arcadia, it was "when the sun, like a noble heart, began to show his greatest countenance in his lowest estate," that I arrived at Isora's door. I had written to her once, to announce my uncle's death, and the day of my return; but I had not mentioned in my letter my reverse of fortunes: I reserved that communication till it could be softened by our meeting. I saw by the countenance of the servant who admitted me that all was well; so I asked no question—I flew

---

[1] Richard Cromwell died in 1712.—ED.

up the stairs—I broke into Isora's chamber, and in an instant she was in my arms.   Ah, Love, Love !   wherefore art thou so transitory a pilgrim on the earth—an evening cloud which hovers on our horizon, drinking the hues of the sun, that grows ominously brighter as it verges to the shadow and the night, and which, the moment that sun is set, wanders on in darkness or descends in tears ?

"And now, my bird of Paradise," said I, as we sat alone in the apartment I had fitted up as the banqueting-room, and on which, though small in its proportions, I had lavished all the love of luxury and of show which made one of my most prevailing weaknesses, "and now, how has time passed with you since we parted ?"

"Need you ask, Morton ?   Ah, have you ever noted a poor dog deserted by its master, or rather not deserted, for that you know is not my case yet," added Isora, playfully, "but left at home while the master went abroad ? have you noted how restless the poor animal is—how it refuses all company and all comfort—how it goes a hundred times a day into the room which its master is wont mostly to inhabit—how it creeps on the sofa or the chair which the same absent idler was accustomed to press—how it selects some article of his very clothing, and curls jealously around it, and hides and watches over it, as I have hid and watched over this glove, Morton ?   Have you ever noted that humble creature whose whole happiness is the smile of one being, when the smile was away ?—then, Morton, you can tell how my time has passed during your absence."

I answered Isora by endearments and by compliments.   She turned away from the latter.

"Never call me those fine names, I implore you," she whispered ; "call me only by those pretty pet words by which I know you will never call any one else.   Bee and bird are my names, and mine only ; but beauty and angel are names you have given, or may give, to a hundred others !   Promise me, then, to address me only in our own language."

"I promise, and lo, the seal to the promise.   But tell me, Isora, do you not love these rare scents that make an Araby of this un-mellowed clime ?   Do you not love the profusion of light which reflects so dazzling a lustre on that soft cheek—and those eyes which the ancient romancer[1] must have dreamt of when he wrote so prettily of "eyes that seemed a temple where love and beauty were married ?" Does not yon fruit take a more tempting hue, bedded as it is in those golden leaves ?   Does not sleep seem to hover with a downier wing over those sofas on which the limbs of a princess have been laid ?   In

---

[1] Sir Philip Sydney, who, if we may judge from the number of quotations from his works scattered in this book, seems to have been an especial favourite with Count Devereux.—ED.

a word, is there not in luxury and in pomp a spell which no gentler or wiser mind would disdain?"

"It may be so!" said Isora, sighing; "but the splendour which surrounds us chills and almost terrifies me. I think that every proof of your wealth and rank puts me farther from you; then, too, I have some remembrance of the green sod, and the silver rill, and the trees upon which the young winds sing and play—and I own that it is with the country, and not the town, that all my ideas of luxury are wed."

"But the numerous attendants, the long row of liveried hirelings, through which you may pass, as through a lane, the caparisoned steeds, the stately equipage, the jewelled tiara, the costly robe which matrons imitate and envy, the music, which lulls you to sleep, the lighted show, the gorgeous stage;—all these, the attributes or gifts of wealth, all these that you have the right to hope you will one day or other command, you will own are what you could very reluctantly forego!"

"Do you think so, Morton? Ah, I wish you were of my humble temper: the more we limit and concentre happiness, the more certain, I think, we are of securing it—they who widen the circle encroach upon the boundaries of danger; and they who freight their wealth upon an hundred vessels are more liable, Morton, are they not, to the peril of the winds and the waves than they who venture it only upon one?"

"Admirably reasoned, my little sophist; but if the one ship sink?"

"Why, I would embark myself in it as well as my wealth, and should sink with it."

"Well, well, Isora, your philosophy will, perhaps, soon be put to the test. I will talk to you to-morrow of business."

"And why not to-night?"

"To-night, when I have just returned! No, to-night I will only talk to you of love!"

As may be supposed, Isora was readily reconciled to my change of circumstances, and indeed that sum which seemed poverty to me, appeared positive wealth to her. But perhaps few men are by nature and inclination more luxurious and costly than myself; always accustomed to a profuse expenditure at my uncle's, I fell insensibly and *con amore* on my *début* in London, into all the extravagancies of the age. Sir William, pleased, rather than discontented with my habits, especially as they were attended with some *éclat*, pressed upon me proofs of his generosity which, since I knew his wealth and considered myself his heir, I did not scruple to accept, and at the time of my return to London after his death, I had not only spent to the full the princely allowance I had received from him, but was above half my whole fortune in debt. However, I had horses and equipages, jewels and plate, and I did not long wrestle with my pride before I obtained the victory, and sent all my valuables to the hammer. They sold pretty well, all things considered, for I had a certain reputation in the world for taste and munificence ; and when I had received the pro- duct and paid my debts, I found that the whole balance in my favour, including, of course, my uncle's legacy, was fifteen thousand pounds.

It was no bad younger brother's portion, perhaps, but I was in no humour to be made a younger brother without a struggle. So I went to the lawyers ; they looked at the will, considered the case, and took their fees. Then the honestest of them, with the coolest air in the world, told me to content myself with my legacy, for the cause was hopeless ; the will was sufficient to exclude a wilderness of elder sons. I need not add that I left this lawyer with a very contemptible opinion of his understanding. I went to another, he told me the same thing, only in a different manner, and I thought him as great a fool as his fellow practitioner. At last I chanced upon a little brisk gentleman, with a quick eye and a sharp voice, who wore a wig that carried conviction in every curl ; had an independent, upright mien, and such a logical, emphatic way of expressing himself, that I was quite charmed with him. This gentleman scarce heard me out before he assured me that I had a famous case of it, that he liked making quick work, and proceeding with vigour, that he hated rogues, and delay which was the sign of a rogue, but not the necessary sign of law, that I was the most fortunate man imaginable in coming to him, and, in short, that I had nothing to do but to commence proceedings, and leave all the rest to him. I was very soon talked into this proposal, and very soon embarked in the luxurious ocean of litigation.

Having settled this business so satisfactorily, I went to receive the condolence and sympathy of St. John. Notwithstanding the arduous occupations both of pleasure and of power, in which he was constantly engaged, he had found time to call upon me very often, and to express by letter great disappointment that I had neither received nor returned his visits. Touched by the phenomenon of so much kindness in a statesman, I paid him in return the only compliment in my power, viz., I asked his advice—with a view of taking it.

"Politics—politics, my dear Count," said he, in answer to that request, "nothing like it ; I will get you a seat in the House by next week,—you are just of age, I think,—Heavens ! a man like you, who has learning enough for a German professor—assurance that would almost abash a Milesian—a very pretty choice of words, and a pointed way of consummating a jest—why, with you by my side, my dear Count, I will soon—"

"St. John," said I, interrupting him, "you forget I am a Catholic!"

"Ah, I did forget that," replied St. John, slowly. "Heaven help me, Count, but I am sorry your ancestors were not converted; it was a pity they should bequeath you their religion without the estate to support it, for papacy has become a terrible tax to its followers."

"I wonder," said I, "whether the earth will ever be governed by Christians, not cavillers; by followers of our Saviour, not by co-operators of the devil; by men who obey the former, and 'love one another,' not by men who walk about with the latter (that roaring lion), 'seeking whom they may devour.' Intolerance makes us acquainted with strange nonsense, and folly is never so ludicrous as when associated with something sacred; it is then like Punch and his wife in Powell's puppet-show, *dancing in the Ark.* For example, to tell those who differ from us that they are in a delusion, and yet to persecute them for that delusion, is to equal the wisdom of our forefathers, who, we are told, in the Dæmonologie of the Scottish Solomon, 'burnt a whole monasterie of nunnes for being misled, not by men, but *dreames!*' "

And being somewhat moved, I ran on for a long time in a very eloquent strain, upon the disadvantages of intolerance; which, I would have it, was a policy as familiar to Protestantism now as it had been to Popery in the dark ages; quite forgetting that it is not the vice of a peculiar sect, but of a ruling party.

St. John, who thought, or affected to think very differently from me on these subjects, shook his head gently, but, with his usual good breeding, deemed it rather too sore a subject for discussion.

"I will tell you a discovery I have made," said I.

"And what is it?"

"Listen: that man is wisest who is happiest—granted. What does happiness consist in? Power, wealth, popularity, and, above all, content! Well, then, no man ever obtains so much power, so much money, so much popularity, and, above all, such thorough self-content as a fool; a fool, therefore (this is no paradox), is the wisest of men. Fools govern the world in purple—the wise laugh at them—but they laugh in rags. Fools thrive at court—fools thrive in state chambers—fools thrive in boudoirs—fools thrive in rich men's legacies. Who is so beloved as a fool? Every man seeks him, laughs at him, and hugs him. Who is so secure in his own opinion—so high in complacency, as a fool? *suâ virtute involvit.* Hark-ye, St. John, let us turn fools—they are the only potentates—the only philosophers of earth. Oh, motley, 'motley's your only wear!' "

"Ha! ha!" laughed St. John; and, rising, he insisted upon carrying me with him to the rehearsal of a new play, in order, as he said, to dispel my spleen, and prepare me for ripe decision upon the plans to be adopted for bettering my fortune.

But, in good truth, nothing calculated to advance so comfortable and praiseworthy an end seemed to present itself. My religion was an effectual bar to any hope of rising in the state. Europe now began to wear an aspect that promised universal peace, and the sword which I had so poetically apostrophized was not likely to be drawn upon any more glorious engagement than a brawl with the Mohawks, any incautious noses appertaining to which fraternity I was fully resolved to slit whenever they came conveniently in my way. To add to the unpromising state of my worldly circumstances, my uncle's death had removed the only legitimate barrier to the acknowledgment of my marriage with Isora, and it became due to her to proclaim and publish that event. Now, if there be any time in the world when a man's friends look upon him most coldly, when they speak of his capacities of rising the most despondingly, when they are most inclined, in short, to set him down as a silly sort of fellow, whom it is no use inconveniencing oneself to assist, it is at that moment when he has made what the said friends are pleased to term an imprudent marriage! It was, therefore, no remarkable instance of good luck that the express time for announcing that I had contracted that species of marriage, was the express time for my wanting the assistance of those kind-hearted friends. Then, too, by the pleasing sympathies in worldly opinion, the neglect of one's friends is always so damnably neighboured by the exultation of one's foes! Never was there a man who, without being very handsome, very rude, or very much in public life, had made unto himself more enemies than it had been my lot to make. How the rascals would all sneer and coin dull jests when they saw me so down in the world! The very old maids, who, so long as they thought me single, would have declared that the will was a fraud, would, directly they heard I was married, ask if Gerald was handsome, and assert, with a wise look, that my uncle knew well what he was about. Then the joy of the Lady Hasselton, and the curled lip of the haughty Tarleton! It is a very odd circumstance, but it is very true, that the people we most despise have the most influence over our actions: a man never ruins himself by giving dinners to his father, or turning his house into a palace in order to feast his bosom friend:—on the contrary, 'tis the poor devil of a friend who fares the worst, and starves on the family joint, while mine host beggars himself to banquet "that disagreeable Mr. A., who is such an insufferable ass," and mine hostess sends her husband to the Fleet by vieing with "that odious Mrs. B., who was always her aversion!"

Just in the same manner, no thought disturbed me, in the step I was about to take, half so sorely as the recollection of Lady Hasselton the coquette, and Mr. Tarleton the gambler. However, I have said somewhere or other that nothing selfish on a small scale polluted my love for Isora—nor did there. I had resolved to render her speedy and full justice; and if I sometimes recurred to the dis-advantages to myself, I always had pleasure in thinking that they were *sacrifices* to her. But to my great surprise, when I first announced to Isora my intention of revealing our marriage, I per-ceived in her countenance, always such a traitor to her emotions, a very different expression from that which I had anticipated. A deadly paleness spread over her whole face, and a shudder seemed to creep through her frame. She attempted, however, to smile away the alarm she had created in me; nor was I able to penetrate the cause of an emotion so unlooked for. But I continued to speak of the public announcement of our union as of a thing decided; and at length she listened to me while I arranged the method of making it, and sympathized in the future projects I chalked out for us to adopt. Still, however, when I proposed a definite time for the re-celebration of our nuptials, she ever drew back, and hinted the wish for a longer delay.

"Not so soon, dear Morton," she would say tearfully, "not so soon; we are happy now, and perhaps when you are with me always, you will not love me so well!"

I reasoned against this notion, and this reluctance, but in vain; and day passed on day, and even week on week, and our marriage was still undeclared. I now lived, however, almost wholly with Isora, for busy tongues could no longer carry my secret to my uncle; and, indeed, since I had lost the fortune which I was expected to inherit, it is astonishing how little people troubled their heads about my movements or myself. I lived then almost wholly with Isora— and did familiarity abate my love? Strange to say, it did not abate even the romance of it. The reader may possibly remember a con-versation with St. John recorded in the Second Book of this history. "The deadliest foe to love," said he, (he who had known all love —that of the senses and that also of the soul!) "is not change, nor misfortune, nor jealousy, nor wrath, nor anything that flows from passion, or emanates from fortune. The deadliest foe to love, is CUSTOM!"

Was St. John right?—I believe that in most instances he was; and perhaps the custom was not continued in my case long enough for me to refute the maxim. But as yet, the very gloss upon the god's wings was fresh as on the first day when I had acknowledged his power. Still was Isora to me the light and the music of exist- ence!—still did my heart thrill and leap within me when her silver and fond voice made the air a blessing. Still would I hang over her, when her beautiful features lay hushed in sleep, and watch the varying hues of her cheek; and fancy, while she slept, that in each low, sweet breath that my lips drew from hers, was a whisper of tenderness and endearment! Still when I was absent from her, my soul seemed to mourn a separation from its better and dearer part, and the joyous senses of existence saddened and shrunk into a single want! Still was her presence to my heart as a breathing atmosphere of poesy which circled and tinted all human things; still was my being filled with that delicious and vague melancholy which the very excess of rapture alone produces—the knowledge we dare not breathe to ourselves that the treasure in which our heart is stored is not above the casualties of fate. The sigh that mingles with the kiss, the tear that glistens in the impassioned and yearning gaze, the deep tide in our spirit, over which the moon and the stars have power; the chain of harmony within the thought, which has a mysterious link with all that is fair, and pure, and bright in Nature, knitting as it were loveliness with love!—all this, all that I cannot express—all that to the young for whom the real world has had few spells, and the world of visions has been a home, who love at last and for the first time,—all that to them are known were still mine.

In truth, Isora was one well calculated to sustain and to rivet romance. The cast of her beauty was so dreamlike, and yet so varying—her temper was so little mingled with the common cha- racteristics of woman; it had so little of caprice, so little of vanity, so utter an absence of all jealous and all angry feeling; it was so made up of tenderness and devotion, and yet so imaginative and fairy-like in its fondness, that it was difficult to bear only the senti- ments of earth, for one who had so little of earth's clay. She was more like the women whom one imagines are the creations of poetry, and yet of whom no poetry, save that of Shakspeare's, reminds us; and to this day, when I go into the world, I never see aught of our own kind which recalls her, or even one of her features, to my memory. But when I am alone with Nature, methinks a sweet sound or a new-born flower, has something of familiar power over those stored and deep impressions which do make her image, and it brings her more vividly before my eyes than any shape or face of her own sex, however beautiful it may be.

There was also another trait in her character which, though arising in her weakness, not her virtues, yet perpetuated the more dream-

like and imaginary qualities of our passion : this was a melancholy
superstition, developing itself in forebodings and omens which
interested, because they were steeped at once in the poetry and in
the deep sincerity of her nature. She was impressed with a strong
and uncontrollable feeling that her fate was predestined to a dark
course and an early end ; and she drew from all things around her
something to feed the pensive character of her thoughts. The
stillness of noon—the holy and eloquent repose of twilight, its rosy
sky, and its soft air, its shadows and its dews, had equally for her
heart a whisper and a spell. The wan stars, where, from the eldest
time, man has shaped out a chart of the undiscoverable future ; the
mysterious moon, to which the great ocean ministers from its
untrodden shrines ; the winds, which traverse the vast air, pilgrims
from an eternal home to an unpenetrated bourne ; the illimitable
Heavens, on which none ever gazed without a vague craving for
something that the earth cannot give, and a vague sense of a former
existence in which that something was enjoyed ; the holy night—
that solemn and circling sleep, which seems, in its repose, to image
our death, and in its living worlds to shadow forth the immortal
realms which only through that death we can survey ;—all had, for
the deep heart of Isora, a language of omen and of doom. Often
would we wander alone, and for hours together, by the quiet and
wild woods and streams that surrounded her retreat, and which we
both loved so well ; and often, when the night closed over us, with
my arm around her, and our lips so near that our atmosphere was
our mutual breath, would she utter, in that voice which "made the
soul plant itself in the ears,"—the predictions which had nursed
themselves at her heart.

I remember one evening, in especial ! The rich twilight had
gathered over us, and we sat by a slender and soft rivulet, over-
shadowed by some stunted yet aged trees. We had both, before
she spoke, been silent for several minutes ; and only when, at rare
intervals, the birds sent from the copse that backed us a solitary and
vesper note of music, was the stillness around us broken. Before
us, on the opposite bank of the stream, lay a valley, in which
shadow and wood concealed all trace of man's dwellings, save at
one far spot, where, from a single hut, rose a curling and thin
vapour,—like a spirit released from earth, and losing gradually its
earthier particles, as it blends itself with the loftier atmosphere of
Heaven.

It was then that Isora, clinging closer to me, whispered her forebodings of death. "You will remember," said she, smiling faintly,
"you will remember me, in the lofty and bright career which yet
awaits you ; and I scarcely know whether I would not sooner have

that memory—free as it will be from all recollection of my failings and faults, and all that I have cost you, than incur the chance of your future coldness or decrease of love."

And when Isora turned, and saw that the tears stood in my eyes, she kissed them away, and said, after a pause,

"It matters not, my own guardian angel, what becomes of me: and now that I am near you, it is wicked to let my folly cost you a single pang. But why should you grieve at my forebodings? there is nothing painful or harsh in them to me, and I interpret them thus: 'If my life passes away before the common date, perhaps it will be a sacrifice to yours.' And it will, Morton—it will. The love I bear to you I can but feebly express now; all of us wish to prove our feelings, and I would give one proof of mine for you. It seems to me that I was made only for one purpose—to love you; and I would fain hope that my death may be some sort of sacrifice to you—some token of the ruling passion and the whole object of my life."

As Isora said this, the light of the moon, which had just risen, shone full upon her cheek, flushed as it was with a deeper tint than it usually wore; and in her eye—her features—her forehead—the lofty nature of her love seemed to have stamped the divine expression of itself.

Have I lingered too long on these passages of life,—they draw near to a close—and a more adventurous and stirring period of manhood will succeed. Ah, little could they, who in after years beheld in me but the careless yet stern soldier—the wily and callous diplomatist—the companion alternately so light and so moodily reserved —little could they tell how soft, and weak, and doting my heart was once!

CHAPTER VI.

AN UNEXPECTED MEETING—CONJECTURE AND ANTICIPATION.

THE day for the public solemnization of our marriage was at length appointed. In fact, the plan for the future that appeared to me most promising was to proffer my services to some foreign Court, and that of Russia held out to me the greatest temptation. I was therefore anxious, as soon as possible, to conclude the rite of a second or public nuptials, and I purposed leaving the country within a week afterwards. My little lawyer assured me that my suit would go on quite as well in my absence, and whenever my presence was necessary he would be sure to inform me of it. I did not doubt him in the least—it is a charming thing to have confidence in one's man of business.

Of Montreuil I now saw nothing; but I accidentally heard that he was on a visit to Gerald, and that the latter had already made the old walls ring with premature hospitality. As for Aubrey, I was in perfect ignorance of his movements; and the unsatisfactory shortness of his last letter, and the wild expressions so breathing of fanaticism in the postscript, had given me much anxiety and alarm on his account. I longed above all to see him,—to talk with him over old times and our future plans, and to learn whether no new bias could be given to a temperament which seemed to lean so strongly towards a self-punishing superstition. It was about a week before the day fixed for my public nuptials, that I received at last from him the following letter :—

"MY DEAREST BROTHER,

"I have been long absent from home—absent on affairs on which we will talk hereafter. I have not forgotten you, though I have been silent, and the news of my poor uncle's death has shocked me greatly. On my arrival here I learnt your disappointment and your recourse to law. I am not so much surprised, though I am as much grieved, as yourself, for I will tell you now, what seemed to me unimportant before. On receiving your letter, requesting consent to your designed marriage, my uncle seemed greatly displeased as well as vexed, and afterwards he heard much that displeased him more; from what quarter came his news I know not, and he only spoke of it in innuendos and angry insinuations. As far as I was able, I endeavoured to learn his meaning, but could not, and to my praises of you I thought latterly he seemed to lend but a cold ear; he told me at last, when I was about to leave him, that you had acted ungratefully to him, and that he should alter his will. I scarcely thought of this speech at the time, or rather I considered it as the threat of a momentary anger. Possibly, however, it was the prelude to that disposition of property which has so wounded you, —I observe too that the will bears date about that period. I mention this fact to you—you can draw from it what inference you will; but I do solemnly believe that Gerald is innocent of any fraud towards you.

"I am all anxiety to hear whether your love continues. I beseech you to write to me instantly and inform me on that head as on all others. We shall meet soon.

"Your ever affectionate Brother,
"AUBREY DEVEREUX."

There was something in this letter that vexed and displeased me : I thought it breathed a tone of unkindness and indifference, which my present circumstances rendered peculiarly inexcusable. So far, therefore, from answering it immediately, I resolved not to reply to it till after the solemnization of my marriage. The anecdote of my uncle startled me a little when I coupled it with the words my uncle had used towards myself on his death-bed ; viz., in hinting that he had heard some things unfavourable to Isora, unnecessary then to repeat ; but still if my uncle had altered his intentions towards me, would he not have mentioned the change and its reasons ? Would he have written to me with such kindness, or received me with such affection ? I could not believe that he would : and my opinions of the fraud and the perpetrator were not a whit changed by Aubrey's epistle. It was clear, however, that he had joined the party against me : and as my love for him was exceedingly great, I was much wounded by the idea.

"All leave me," said I, "upon this reverse,—all but Isora !" and I thought with renewed satisfaction on the step which was about to ensure to her a secure home and an honourable station. My fears lest Isora should again be molested by her persecutor were now pretty well at rest ; having no doubt in my own mind as to that persecutor's identity, I imagined that in his new acquisition of wealth and pomp, a boyish and unreturned love would easily be relinquished ; and that, perhaps, he would scarcely regret my obtaining the prize himself had sought for, when in my altered fortunes it would be followed by such worldly depreciation. In short, I looked upon him as possessing a characteristic common to most bad men, who are never so influenced by love as they are by hatred ; and imagined therefore, that if he had lost the object of the love, he could console himself by exulting over any decline of prosperity in the object of the hate.

As the appointed day drew near, Isora's despondency seemed to vanish, and she listened, with her usual eagerness in whatever interested me, to my continental schemes of enterprise. I resolved that our second wedding, though public, should be modest and unostentatious, suitable rather to our fortunes than our birth. St. John, and a few old friends of the family, constituted all the party I invited, and I requested them to keep my marriage secret until the very day for celebrating it arrived. I did this from a desire of avoiding compliments intended as sarcasms, and visits rather of curiosity than friendship. On flew the days, and it was now the one preceding my wedding. I was dressing to go out upon a matter of business connected with the ceremony, and I then, as I received my hat from Desmarais, for the first time thought it requisite to acquaint that accomplished gentleman with the rite of the morrow. Too well bred was Monsieur Desmarais to testify any other sentiment than pleasure at the news ; and he received my orders and directions for the next day with more than the graceful urbanity which made one always feel quite honoured by his attentions.

"And how goes on the philosophy?" said I,—"faith, since I am about to be married, I shall be likely to require its consolations."

"Indeed, Monsieur," answered Desmarais, with that expression of self-conceit which was so curiously interwoven with the obsequiousness of his address, "indeed, Monsieur, I have been so occupied of late in preparing a little powder very essential to dress, that I have not had time for any graver, though not perhaps more important, avocations."

"Powder—and what is it?"

"Will Monsieur condescend to notice its effect?" answered Desmarais, producing a pair of gloves which were tinted of the most delicate flesh-colour ; the colouring was so nice that, when the gloves were on, it would have been scarcely possible, at any distance, to distinguish them from the naked flesh.

"'Tis a rare invention," said I.

"Monsieur is very good, but I flatter myself it is so," rejoined Desmarais ; and he forthwith ran on far more earnestly on the merits of his powder than I had ever heard him descant on the beauties of Fatalism. I cut him short in the midst of his harangue ; too much eloquence in any line is displeasing in one's dependent.

I had just concluded my business abroad, and was returning homeward with downcast eyes, and in a very abstracted mood, when I was suddenly startled by a loud voice that exclaimed in a tone of surprise : "What !—Count Devereux—how fortunate !"

I looked up, and saw a little dark man, shabbily dressed ; his face did not seem unfamiliar to me, but I could not at first remember where I had seen it,—my look, I suppose, testified my want of memory, for he said, with a low bow,—

"You have forgotten me, Count, and I don't wonder at it ; so please you, I am the person who once brought you a letter from France to Devereux Court."

At this, I recognized the bearer of that epistle which had embroiled me with the Abbé Montreuil. I was too glad of the meeting to show any coolness in my reception of the gentleman, and, to speak candidly, I never saw a gentleman less troubled with *mauvaise honte.*

"Sir !" said he, lowering his voice to a whisper, "it is most fortunate that I should thus have met you ; I only came to town this morning, and for the sole purpose of seeking you out. I am charged with a packet, which I believe will be of the greatest importance to your interests. But," he added, looking round, "the streets are no proper place for my communication ; *parbleu*, there are those about who hear whispers through stone walls—suffer me to call upon you to-morrow."

" To-morrow ! it is a day of great business with me, but I can possibly spare you a few moments, if that will suffice ; or, on the day after, your own pleasure may be the sole limit of our interview."

"*Parbleu*, Monsieur, you are very obliging—very ; but I will tell you in one word who I am, and what is my business. My name is Marie Oswald : I was born in France, and I am the half-brother of that Oswald who drew up your uncle's will."

" Good heavens !" I exclaimed, " is it possible that you know anything of that affair ?"

" Hush—yes, all ! my poor brother is just dead ; and, in a word, I am charged with a packet given me by him on his death-bed. Now, will you see me if I bring it to-morrow ?"

" Certainly ; can I not see you to-night ?"

" To-night ?—No, not well ; *parbleu !* I want a little consideration as to the reward due to me for my eminent services to your lordship. No : let it be to-morrow."

" Well ! at what hour ? I fear it must be in the evening."

" Seven, *s'il vous plait*, Monsieur."

" Enough ! be it so."

And Mr. Marie Oswald, who seemed, during the whole of this short conference, to have been under some great apprehension of being seen or overheard, bowed, and vanished in an instant, leaving my mind in a most motley state of incoherent, unsatisfactory, yet sanguine conjecture.

CHAPTER VII.

THE EVENTS OF A SINGLE NIGHT—MOMENTS MAKE THE HUES IN WHICH YEARS ARE COLOURED.

MEN of the old age ! what wonder that in the fondness of a dim faith, and in the vague guesses which, from the frail ark of reason, we send to hover over a dark and unfathomable abyss,—what wonder that ye should have wasted hope and life in striving to penetrate the future ! What wonder that ye should have given a language to the stars, and to the night a spell, and gleaned from the uncomprehended earth an answer to the enigmas of Fate ! We are like the sleepers who, walking under the influence of a dream, wander by the verge of a precipice, while, in their own deluded vision, they perchance believe themselves surrounded by bowers of roses, and accompanied by those they love. Or, rather like the blind man, who can retrace every step of the path he has *once* trodden, but who can guess not a single inch of that which he has not yet travelled, our Reason can re-guide us over the roads of past experience with a sure and unerring wisdom, even while it recoils, baffled and bewildered, before the blackness of the very moment whose boundaries we are about to enter.

The few friends I had invited to my wedding were still with me, when one of my servants, not Desmarais, informed me that Mr. Oswald waited for me. I went out to him.

"*Parbleu !*" said he, rubbing his hands, "I perceive it is a joyous time with you, and I don't wonder you can only spare me a few moments."

The estates of Devereux were not to be risked for a trifle, but I thought Mr. Marie Oswald exceedingly impertinent. "Sir," said I, very gravely, "pray be seated : and now to business. In the first place may I ask to whom I am beholden for sending you with that letter you gave me at Devereux Court ? and, secondly, what that letter contained ?—for I never read it."

"Sir," answered the man, "the history of the letter is perfectly distinct from that of the will, and the former (to discuss the least important first) is briefly this. You have heard, sir, of the quarrels between Jesuit and Jansenist ? "

"I have."

"Well—but first, Count, let me speak of myself. There were three young men of the same age, born in the same village in France, of obscure birth each, and each desirous of getting on in the world. Two were deuced clever fellows : the third, nothing particular. One of the two at present shall be nameless ; the third, 'who was nothing particular' (in his own opinion, at least, though his friends may think differently), was Marie Oswald. We soon separated : I went to Paris, was employed in different occupations, and at last became secretary, and (why should I disavow it ?) valet to a lady of quality, and a violent politician. She was a furious Jansenist ; of course I adopted her opinions. About this time, there was much talk among the Jesuits of the great genius and deep learning of a young member of the order—Julian Montreuil. Though not residing in the country, he had sent one or two books to France, which had been published and had created a great sensation. Well, sir, my mistress was the greatest intriguante of her party: she was very rich, and tolerably liberal; and, among other packets of which a messenger from England was *carefully* robbed, between Calais and Abbeville, (you understand me, sir, *carefully* robbed: *parbleu!* I wish I were robbed in the same manner every day in my life!) was one from the said Julian Montreuil to a political friend of his. Among other letters in this packet—all of importance—was one descriptive of the English family with whom he resided. It hit them all, I am told, off to a hair; and it described, in particular, one, the supposed inheritor of the estates, a certain Morton, Count Devereux. Since you say you did not read the letter, I spare your blushes, sir, and I don't dwell upon what he said of your talent, energy, ambition, &c. I will only tell you that he dilated far more upon your prospects than your powers; and that he expressly stated what was his object in staying in your family and cultivating your friendship—he expressly stated that £30,000 a year would be particularly serviceable to a certain political cause which he had strongly at heart."

"I understand you," said I; "the Chevalier's?"

"Exactly. ' This sponge,' said Montreuil, I remember the very phrase—'this sponge will be well filled, and I am handling it softly now, in order to squeeze its juices hereafter according to the uses of the party we have so strongly at heart.'"

"It was not a metaphor very flattering to my understanding," said I.

"True, sir. Well, as soon as my mistress learnt this, she remembered that your father, the Marshal, had been one of her *plus chers amis*—in a word, if scandal says true, he had been *the cher ami*. However, she was instantly resolved to open your eyes, and ruin the *maudit Jésuite*: she enclosed the letter in an envelope, and sent me to England with it. I came—I gave it you—and I discovered, in that moment, when the Abbé entered, that this Julian Montreuil was an old acquaintance of my own—was one of the two young men who I told you were such deuced clever fellows. Like many other adventurers, he had changed his name on entering the world, and I had never till now suspected that Julian Montreuil was Bertrand Collinot. Well, when I saw what I had done, I was exceedingly sorry, for I had liked my companion well enough not to wish to hurt him; besides, I was a little afraid of him. I took horse, and went about some other business I had to execute, nor did I visit that part of the country again, till a week ago (now I come to the other business), when I was summoned to the death-bed of my half-brother, the attorney, peace be with him! He suffered much from hypochondria in his dying moments—I believe it is the way with people of his profession—and he gave me a sealed ·packet, with a last injunction to place it in your hands, and your hands only. Scarce was he dead—(do not think I am unfeeling, sir, I had seen very little of him, and he was only my half-brother, my father having married, for a second wife, a foreign lady, who kept an inn, by whom he was blessed with myself)—scarce, I say, was he dead when I hurried up to town ; Providence threw you in my way, and you shall have the document upon two conditions."

" Which are, first to reward you ; secondly, to——"

" To promise you will not open the packet for seven days."

" The devil ! and why ? "

" I will tell you candidly :—one of the papers in the packet, I believe to be my brother's written confession—nay, I know it is—and it will criminate one I have a love for, and who, I am resolved, shall have a chance of escape."

" Who is that one ? Montreuil ? "

" No—I do not refer to him ; but I cannot tell you more. I require the promise, Count—it is indispensable. If you don't give it me, *parbleu*, you shall not have the packet."

There was something so cool, so confident, and so impudent about this man, that I did not well know whether to give way to laughter or to indignation. Neither, however, would have been politic in my situation ; and, as I said before, the estates of Devereux were not to be risked for a trifle.

" Pray," said I, however, with a shrewdness which I think did me credit—" pray, Mr. Marie Oswald, do you expect the reward before the packet is opened ? "

" By no means," answered the gentleman, who in his own opinion was nothing particular ; " by no means ; nor until you and your lawyers are satisfied that the papers enclosed in the packet are sufficient fully to restore you to the heritage of Devereux Court and its demesnes."

There was something fair in this ; and as the only penalty to me, incurred by the stipulated condition, seemed to be the granting escape to the criminals, I did not think it incumbent upon me to lose my cause from the desire of a prosecution. Besides, at that time, I felt too happy to be revengeful ; and so, after a moment's consideration, I conceded to the proposal, and gave my honour as a gentleman, Mr. Oswald obligingly dispensed with an oath—that I would not open the packet till the end of the seventh day. Mr. Oswald then drew forth a piece of paper, on which sundry characters were inscribed, the purport of which was that, if through the papers given me by Marie Oswald, my lawyers were convinced that I could become master of my uncle's property, now enjoyed by Gerald

Devereux, I should bestow on the said Marie £5000 : half on obtaining this legal opinion, half on obtaining possession of the property. I could not resist a smile, when I observed that the word of a gentleman was enough surety for the safety of the man he had a love for, but that Mr. Oswald required a written bond for the safety of his reward. One is ready enough to trust one's friends to the conscience of another, but as long as a law can be had instead, one is rarely so credulous in respect to one's money.

"The reward shall be doubled, if I succeed," said I, signing the paper ; and Oswald then produced a packet, on which was written, in a trembling hand—"For Count Morton Devereux—private—and with haste." As soon as he had given me this precious charge, and reminded me again of my promise, Oswald withdrew. I placed the packet in my bosom, and returned to my guests.

Never had my spirit been so light as it was that evening. Indeed the good people I had assembled thought matrimony never made a man so little serious before. They did not however stay long, and the moment they were gone, I hastened to my own sleeping apartment, to secure the treasure I had acquired. A small escritoire stood in this room, and in it I was accustomed to keep whatever I considered most precious. With many a wistful look and murmur at my promise, I consigned the packet to one of the drawers of this escritoire. As I was locking the drawer, the sweet voice of Desmarais accosted me. Would Monsieur, he asked, suffer him to visit a friend that evening, in order to celebrate so joyful an event in Monsieur's destiny? It was not often that he was addicted to vulgar merriment, but on such an occasion he owned that he was tempted to transgress his customary habits, and he felt that Monsieur, with his usual good taste, would feel offended if his servant, within Monsieur's own house, suffered joy to pass the limits of discretion, and enter the confines of noise and inebriety, especially as Monsieur had so positively interdicted all outward sign of extra hilarity. He implored *mille pardons* for the presumption of his request.

"It is made with your usual discretion—there are five guineas for you : go and get drunk with your friend, and be merry instead of wise. But, tell me, is it not beneath a philosopher to be moved by anything, especially anything that occurs to another,—much less to get drunk upon it ?"

"Pardon me, Monsieur," answered Desmarais, bowing to the ground ; "one ought to get drunk sometimes, because the next morning one is sure to be thoughtful ; and, moreover, the practical philosopher ought to indulge every emotion, in order to judge how that emotion would affect another; at least, this is my opinion."

"Well, go."

"My most grateful thanks be with Monsieur; Monsieur's nightly toilet is entirely prepared."

And away went Desmarais, with the light, yet slow, step with which he was accustomed to combine elegance with dignity.

I now passed into the room I had prepared for Isora's *boudoir*. I found her leaning by the window, and I perceived that she had been in tears. As I paused to contemplate her figure, so touchingly, yet so unconsciously mournful in its beautiful and still posture, a more joyous sensation than was wont to mingle with my tenderness for her swelled at my heart. "Yes," thought I, "you are no longer the solitary exile, or the persecuted daughter of a noble but ruined race; you are not even the bride of a man who must seek in foreign climes, through danger and through hardship, to repair a broken fortune and establish an adventurer's name! At last the clouds have rolled from the bright star of your fate—wealth, and pomp, and all that awaits the haughtiest of England's matrons shall be yours." And at these thoughts, Fortune seemed to me a gift a thousand times more precious than—much as my luxuries prized it —it had ever seemed to me before.

I drew near and laid my hand upon Isora's shoulder, and kissed her cheek. She did not turn round, but strove, by bending over my hand and pressing it to her lips, to conceal that she had been weeping. I thought it kinder to favour the artifice than to complain of it. I remained silent for some moments, and I then gave vent to the sanguine expectations for the future which my new treasure entitled me to form. I had already narrated to her the adventure of the day before—I now repeated the purport of my last interview with Oswald: and, growing more and more elated as I proceeded, I dwelt at last upon the description of my inheritance, as glowingly as if I had already recovered it. I painted to her imagination its rich woods and its glassy lake, and the fitful and wandering brook that, through brake and shade, went bounding on its wild way; I told her of my early roamings, and dilated with a boy's rapture upon my favourite haunts. I brought visibly before her glistening and eager eyes the thick copse where, hour after hour, in vague verse, and still vaguer dreams, I had so often whiled away the day; the old tree which I had climbed to watch the birds in their glad mirth, or to listen unseen to the melancholy sound of the forest deer; the antique gallery and the vast hall which, by the dim twilights, I had paced with a religious awe, and looked upon the pictured forms of my bold fathers, and mused high and ardently upon my destiny to be; the old gray tower which I had consecrated to myself, and the unwitnessed path which led to the yellow beach, and the wide gladness of the solitary sea ; the little arbour which my earliest ambition had reared, that looked out upon the joyous flowers and the merry fountain, and, through the ivy and the jessamine, wooed the voice of the bird, and the murmur of the summer bee ; and, when I had exhausted my description, I turned to Isora, and said in a lower tone, "And I shall visit these once more, and with you."

Isora sighed faintly, and it was not till I had pressed her to speak that she said :

"I wish I could deceive myself, Morton, but, I cannot—I cannot root from my heart an impression that I shall never again quit this dull city, with its gloomy walls and its heavy air. A voice within me seems to say—'Behold from this very window the boundaries of your living wanderings !'"

Isora's words froze all my previous exaltation. "It is in vain," said I, after chiding her for her despondency, "it is in vain to tell me that you have for this gloomy notion no other reason than that of a vague presentiment. It is time now that I should press you to a greater confidence upon all points consistent with your oath to our mutual enemy than you have hitherto given me. Speak, dearest, have you not some yet unrevealed causes for alarm ?"

It was but for a moment that Isora hesitated before she answered with that quick tone which indicates that we force words against the will.

"Yes, Morton, I *will* tell you now, though I would not before the event of this day. On the last day that I saw that fearful man, he said, 'I warn you, Isora D'Alvarez, that my love is far fiercer than hatred ; I warn you that your bridals with Morton Devereux shall be stained with blood. Become his wife, and you perish ! Yea, though I suffer hell's tortures for ever and for ever from that hour, my own hand shall strike you to the heart !' Morton, these words have thrilled through me again and again, as if again they were breathed in my very ear; and I have often started at night and thought the very knife glittered at my breast. So long as our wedding was concealed, and concealed so closely, I was enabled to quiet my fears till they scarcely seemed to exist. But when our nuptials were to be made public, when I knew that they were to reach the ears of that fierce and unaccountable being, I thought I heard my doom pronounced. This, mine own love, must excuse your Isora, if she seemed ungrateful for your generous eagerness to announce our union. And perhaps she would not have acceded to it so easily as she has done were it not that, in the first place, she felt it was beneath your wife to suffer any terror so purely selfish to make her shrink from the proud happiness of being yours in the light of day ; and if she had not felt (here Isora hid her blushing face in my bosom) that she was fated to give birth to another, and that the announcement of our wedded love had become necessary to your honour as to mine ! "

Though I was in reality awed even to terror by learning from Isora's lip so just a cause for her forebodings—though I shuddered with a horror surpassing even my wrath, when I heard a threat so breathing of deadly and determined passions—yet I concealed my emotions, and only thought of cheering and comforting Isora. I represented to her how guarded and vigilant should ever hence-forth be the protection of her husband ; that nothing should again separate him from her side ; that the extreme malice and fierce persecution of this man were sufficient even to absolve her con-science from the oath of concealment she had taken ; that I would procure from the sacred head of our church her own absolution from that vow ; that the moment concealment was over, I could take steps to prevent the execution of my rival's threats ; that, however near to me he might be in blood, no consequences arising from a dispute between us could be so dreadful as the least evil to Isora ; and moreover, to appease her fears, that I would solemnly promise he should never sustain personal assault or harm from my hand ; in short, I said all that my anxiety could dictate, and at last I succeeded in quieting her fears, and she smiled as brightly as the first time I had seen her in the little cottage of her father. She seemed, however, averse to an absolution from her oath, for she was especially scrupulous as to the sanctity of those religious ob-ligations ; but I secretly resolved that her safety absolutely required it, and that at all events I would procure absolution from my own promise to her.

At last Isora, turning from that topic, so darkly interesting, pointed to the heavens, which, with their thousand eyes of light, looked down upon us. "Tell me, love," said she, playfully, as her arm embraced me yet more closely, "if, among yonder stars we could choose a home, which should we select ? "

I pointed to one which lay to the left of the moon, and which, though not larger, seemed to burn with an intenser lustre than the rest. Since that night it has ever been to me a fountain of deep and passionate thought, a well wherein fears and hopes are buried, a mirror in which, in stormy times, I have fancied to read my destiny, and to find some mysterious omen of my intended deeds, a haven which I believe others have reached before me, and a home immortal and unchanging, where, when my wearied and fettered soul is escaped, as a bird, it shall flee away, and have its rest at last.

"What think you of my choice?" said I. Isora looked upward, but did not answer ; and as I gazed upon her (while the pale light of heaven streamed quietly upon her face) with her dark eyes, where the tear yet lingered, though rather to soften than to dim, with her noble, yet tender features, over which hung a melancholy calm, with her lips apart, and her rich locks wreathing over her marble brow, and contrasted by a single white rose (that rose I have now—I would not lose one withered leaf of it for a kingdom !) —her beauty never seemed to me of so rare an order, nor did my soul ever yearn towards her with so deep a love.

It was past midnight. All was hushed in our bridal chamber. The single lamp, which hung above, burnt still and clear ; and through the half-closed curtains of the window, the moonlight looked in upon our couch, quiet, and pure, and holy, as if it were charged with blessings.

"Hush !" said Isora, gently ; "do you not hear a noise below !"

"Not a breath," said I ; "I hear not a breath, save yours."

"It was my fancy, then !" said Isora, "and it has ceased now ; " and she clung closer to my breast and fell asleep. I looked on her peaceful and childish countenance, with that concentrated and full delight with which we clasp all that the universe holds dear to us, and feel as if the universe held nought beside—and thus sleep also crept upon me.

I awoke suddenly ; I felt Isora trembling palpably by my side. Before I could speak to her, I saw standing at a little distance from the bed, a man wrapped in a long dark cloak and masked ; but his eyes shone through the mask, and they glared full upon me. He stood with his arms folded, and perfectly motionless ; but at the other end of the room, before the escritoire in which I had locked the important packet, stood another man, also masked, and wrapped in a disguising cloak of similar hue and fashion. This man, as if alarmed, turned suddenly, and I perceived then that the escritoire was already opened, and that the packet was in his hand. I tore myself from Isora's clasp—I stretched my hand to the table by my bed-side, upon which I had left my sword,—it was gone ! No matter ! I was young, strong, fierce, and the stake at hazard was great. I sprung from the bed, I precipitated myself upon the man who held the packet. With one hand I grasped at the important document, with the other I strove to tear the mask from the robber's face. He endeavoured rather to shake me off than to attack me ; and it was not till I had nearly succeeded in unmasking him that he drew forth a short poniard, and stabbed me in the side. The blow, which seemed purposely aimed to avoid a mortal part, staggered me, but only for an instant. I renewed my gripe at the packet—I tore it from the robber's hand, and collecting my strength, now fast ebbing away, for one effort, I bore my assailant to the ground, and fell struggling with him.

But my blood flowed fast from my wound, and my antagonist, if less sinewy than myself, had greatly the advantage in weight and size. Now for one moment I was uppermost, but in the next his knee was upon my chest, and his blade gleamed on high in the pale light of the lamp and moon. I thought I beheld my death—would to God that I. had! With a piercing cry, Isora sprang from the bed, flung herself before the lifted blade of the robber, and arrested his arm. This man had, in the whole contest, acted with a singular forbearance; he did so now; he paused for a moment and dropped his hand. Hitherto the other man had not stirred from his mute position; he now moved one step towards us, brandishing a poniard like his comrade's. Isora raised her hand supplicatingly towards him, and cried out, "Spare him, spare *him!* Oh, mercy, mercy!" With one stride the murderer was by my side; he muttered some words which passion seemed to render inarticulate; and, half pushing aside his comrade, his raised weapon flashed before my eyes, now dim and reeling. I made a vain effort to rise—the blade descended—Isora, unable to arrest it, threw herself before it— her blood, her heart's blood gushed over me—I saw and felt no more.

When I recovered my senses, my servants were round me; a deep red, wet stain upon the sofa on which I was laid brought the whole scene I had witnessed again before me—terrible and distinct. I sprang to my feet and asked for Isora; a low murmur caught my ear—I turned, and beheld a dark form stretched on the bed, and surrounded, like myself, by gazers and menials; I tottered towards that bed—my bridal bed—with a fierce gesture motioned the crowd away—I heard my name breathed audibly—the next moment I was by Isora's side. All pain, all weakness, all consciousness of my wound, of my very self, were gone—life seemed curdled into a single agonizing and fearful thought. I fixed my eyes upon hers; and though *there* the film was gathering dark and rapidly, I saw yet visible and unconquered, the deep love of that faithful and warm heart which had lavished its life for mine.

I threw my arms around her—I pressed my lips wildly to hers. "Speak—speak!" I cried, and my blood gushed over her with the effort; "in mercy speak!"

Even in death and agony, the gentle being who had been as wax unto my lightest wish, struggled to obey me. "Do not grieve for me," she said, in a tremulous and broken voice; "it *is* dearer to die for you than to live!"

Those were her last words. I felt her breath abruptly cease. The heart, pressed to mine, was still! I started up in dismay—the light shone full upon her face. O God! that I should live to write that Isora was—no more!

BOOK IV.

CHAPTER I.

A RE-ENTRANCE INTO LIFE THROUGH THE EBON GATE— AFFLICTION.

MONTHS passed away before my senses returned to me. I rose from the bed of suffering and of madness, calm, collected, immovable—altered, but tranquil. All the vigilance of justice had been employed to discover the murderers, but in vain. The packet was gone ; and directly I, who alone was able to do so, recovered enough to state the loss of that document, suspicion naturally rested on Gerald, as on one whom that loss essentially benefited. He came publicly forward to anticipate inquiry. He proved that he had not stirred from home during the whole week in which the event had occurred. That seemed likely enough to others ; it is the tools that work, not the instigator— the bravo, not the employer ; but I, who saw in him not only the robber, but that fearful rival who had long threatened Isora that my bridals should be stained with blood, was somewhat staggered by the undeniable proofs of his absence from the scene of that night ; and I was still more bewildered in conjecture by remembering that, so far as their disguises and my own hurried and confused observation could allow me to judge, the person of neither villain, still less that of Isora's murderer, corresponded with the proportions and height of Gerald. Still, however, whether mediately or immediately— whether as the executor or the designer—not a doubt remained on my mind that against his head was justice due. I directed inquiry towards Montreuil—he was abroad at the time of my recovery ; but, immediately on his return, he came forward boldly and at once to meet and even to court the inquiry I had instituted ; he did more— he demanded on what ground, besides my own word, it rested, that this packet had ever been in my possession ; and, to my surprise and perplexity, it was utterly impossible to produce the smallest trace of Mr. Marie Oswald. His half-brother, the attorney, had died, it is true, just before the event of that night ; and it was also true that he had seen Marie on his death-bed ; but no other corroboration of my story could be substantiated, and no other information of the man obtained ; and the partisans of Gerald were not slow in hinting at the great interest I had in forging a tale respecting a will, about the authenticity of which I was at law.

The robbers had entered the house by a back-door, which was found open. No one had perceived their entrance or exit, except Desmarais, who stated that he heard a cry—that he, having spent the greater part of the night abroad, had not been in bed above an hour before he heard it—that he rose and hurried towards my room, whence the cry came—that he met two men masked on the stairs— that he seized one, who struck him in the breast with a poniard, dashed him to the ground, and escaped—that he then immediately alarmed the house, and, the servants accompanying him, he pro- ceeded, despite his wound, to my apartment, where he found Isora and myself bleeding and lifeless, with the escritoire broken open.

The only contradiction to this tale was, that the officers of justice found the escritoire not broken open, but unlocked ; and yet the key which belonged to it was found in a pocket-book in my clothes, where Desmarais said, rightly, I always kept it. How, then, had the escritoire been unlocked? it was supposed by the master-keys peculiar to experienced burglars ; this diverted suspicion into a new channel, and it was suggested that the robbery and the murder had really been committed by common house-breakers. It was then discovered that a large purse of gold, and a diamond cross, which the escritoire contained, were gone. And a few articles of orna- mental *bijouterie*, which I had retained from the wreck of my former profusion in such baubles, and which were kept in a room below- stairs, were also missing. These circumstances immediately con- firmed the opinion of those who threw the guilt upon vulgar and mercenary villains, and a very probable and plausible supposition was built on this hypothesis. Might not this Oswald, at best an adventurer with an indifferent reputation, have forged this story of the packet in order to obtain admission into the house, and recon- noitre, during the confusion of a wedding, in what places the most portable articles of value were stowed? a thousand opportunities, in the opening and shutting of the house-doors, would have allowed an ingenious villain to glide in ; nay, he might have secreted himself in my own room, and seen the place where I had put the packet— certain would he then be that I had selected for the repository of a document I believed so important, that place where all that I most valued was secured ; and hence he would naturally resolve to break open the escritoire, above all other places, which, to an uninformed robber, might have seemed not only less exposed to danger, but equally likely to contain articles of value. The same confusion which enabled him to enter and conceal himself would have also enabled him to withdraw and introduce his accomplice. This notion was rendered probable by his insisting so strongly on my not opening the packet within a certain time; had I opened it immediately, I might have perceived that a deceit had been practised, and not have hoarded it in that place of security which it was the villain's object to discover. Hence, too, in opening the escritoire, he would naturally retake the packet (which other plunderers might not have cared to steal), as well as things of more real price—naturally retake it, in order that his previous imposition might not be detected, and that suspicion might be cast upon those who would appear to have an interest in stealing a packet which I believed to be so inestimably important.

What gave a still greater colour to this supposition was the fact that none of the servants had seen Oswald leave the house, though many had seen him enter. And what put his guilt beyond a doubt in the opinion of many, was his sudden and mysterious disappearance. To my mind, all these circumstances were not conclusive. Both the men seemed taller than Oswald; and I knew that that confusion, which was so much insisted upon, had not—thanks to my singular fastidiousness in those matters—existed. I was also perfectly convinced that Oswald could not have been hid in my room while I locked up the packet; and there was something in the behaviour of the murderer utterly unlike that of a common robber, actuated by common motives.

All these opposing arguments were, however, of a nature to be deemed nugatory by the world, and on the only one of any importance, in their estimation, viz., the height of Oswald being different from that of the robbers, it was certainly very probable that, in a scene so dreadful, so brief, so confused, I should easily be mistaken. Having therefore once flowed into this direction, public opinion soon settled into the full conviction that Oswald was the real criminal, and against Oswald was the whole strength of inquiry ultimately, but still vainly, bent. Some few, it is true, of that kind class, who love family mysteries, and will not easily forego the notion of a brother's guilt, for that of a mere vulgar house-breaker, still shook their heads, and talked of Gerald; but the suspicion was vague and partial, and it was only in the close gossip of private circles that it was audibly vented.

I had formed an opinion by no means favourable to the innocence of Mr. Jean Desmarais; and I took especial care that the Necessitarian, who would only have thought robbery and murder pieces of ill-luck, should undergo a most rigorous examination. I remembered that he had seen me put the packet into the escritoire; and this

II

circumstance was alone sufficient to arouse my suspicion. Desmarais bared his breast gracefully to the magistrate. "Would a man, sir," he said, "a man of my youth, suffer such a scar as that, if he could help it?" The magistrate laughed: frivolity is often a rogue's best policy, if he did but know it. One finds it very difficult to think a coxcomb can commit robbery and murder. Howbeit Desmarais came off triumphantly: and, immediately after this examination, which had been his second one, and instigated solely at my desire, he came to me with a blush of virtuous indignation on his thin cheeks. "He did not presume," he said, with a bow profounder than ever, "to find fault with Monsieur le Comte; it was his fate to be the victim of ungrateful suspicion; but philosophical truths could not always conquer the feelings of the man, and he came to request his dismissal." I gave it him with pleasure.

I must now state my own feelings on the matter: but I shall do so briefly. In my own mind, I repeat, I was fully impressed with the conviction that Gerald was the real, and the head criminal; and thrice did I resolve to repair to Devereux Court, where he still resided, to lie in wait for him, to reproach him with his guilt, and at the sword's point in deadly combat to seek its earthly expiation. I spare the reader a narration of the terrible struggles which nature, conscience, all scruples and prepossessions of education and of blood, held with this resolution, the unholiness of which I endeavoured to clothe with the name of justice to Isora. Suffice it to say that this resolution I forewent at last: and I did so more from a feeling that, despite my own conviction of Gerald's guilt, one rational doubt rested upon the circumstance that the murderer seemed to my eyes of an inferior height to Gerald, and that the person whom I had pursued on the night I had received that wound which brought Isora to my bed-side, and who, it was natural to believe, was my rival, appeared to me not only also slighter and shorter than Gerald, but of a size that seemed to tally with the murderer's.

This solitary circumstance, which contradicted my other impressions, was, I say, more effectual in making me dismiss the thought of personal revenge on Gerald, than the motives which virtue and religion should have dictated. The deep desire of vengeance is the calmest of all the passions, and it is the one which most demands certainty to the reason, before it releases its emotions, and obeys their dictates. The blow which was to do justice to Isora, I had resolved should not be dealt, till I had obtained the most utter certainty that it fell upon the true criminal. And thus, though I cherished through all time, and through all change, the burning wish for retribution, I was doomed to cherish it in secret, and not for years and years to behold a hope of attaining it. Once only I vented my feelings upon Gerald. I could not rest, or sleep, or execute the world's objects till I had done so ; but when they were thus once vented methought I could wait the will of time with a more settled patience, and I re-entered upon the common career of life more externally fitted to fulfil its duties and its aims.

That single indulgence of emotion followed immediately after my resolution of not forcing Gerald into bodily contest. I left my sword, lest I might be tempted to forget my determination. I rode to Devereux Court—I entered Gerald's chamber, while my horse stood unstalled at the gate. I said but few words, but each word was a volume. I told him to enjoy the fortune he had acquired by fraud, and the conscience he had stained with murder. "Enjoy them while you may," I said, "but know that sooner or later shall come a day, when the blood that cries from earth shall be heard in Heaven—and *your* blood shall appease it. Know, if I seem to disobey the voice at my heart, I hear it night and day—and I only live to fulfil at one time its commands."

I left him stunned and horror-stricken. I flung myself on my horse, and cast not a look behind as I rode from the towers and domains of which I had been despoiled. Never from that time would I trust myself to meet or see the despoiler. Once, directly after I had thus braved him in his usurped hall, he wrote to me. I returned the letter unopened. Enough of this ; the reader will now perceive what was the real nature of my feelings of revenge ; and will appreciate the reasons which, throughout this history, will cause me never or rarely to recur to those feelings again, until at least he will perceive a just hope of their consummation.

I went with a quiet air and a set brow into the world. It was a time of great political excitement. Though my creed forbade me the open senate, it could not deprive me of the veiled intrigue. St. John found ample employment for my ambition, and I entered into the toils and objects of my race with a seeming avidity, more eager and engrossing than their own. In what ensues, you will perceive a great change in the character of my memoirs. Hitherto, I chiefly portrayed to you *myself.* I bared open to you my heart and temper — my passions, and the thoughts which belong to our passions. I shall now rather bring before you the natures and the minds of others. The lover and the dreamer are no more ! The satirist and the observer—the derider of human follies, participating while he derides—the worldly and keen actor in the human drama— these are what the district of my history on which you enter will portray me. From whatever pangs to me the change may have been wrought, you will be the gainer by that change. The gaudy dissipation of courts ; the vicissitudes and the vanities of those who haunt them ; the glittering jest, and the light strain ; the passing irony, or the close reflection ; the characters of the great ; the collo- quies of wit ;—these are what delight the temper, and amuse the leisure more than the solemn narrative of fated love. As the monster of the Nile is found beneath the sunniest banks, and in the most freshening wave, the stream may seem to wander on in melody and mirth—the ripple and the beam ; but *who* shall tell what lurks, dark, and fearful, and ever vigilant, below !

CHAPTER II.

AMBITIOUS PROJECTS.

IT is not my intention to write a political history, instead of a private biography. No doubt in the next century, there will be volumes enough written in celebration of that era which my contemporaries are pleased to term the greatest that in modern times has ever existed. Besides, in the private and more concealed intrigues with which I was engaged with St. John, there was something which regard for others would compel me to preserve in silence. I shall therefore briefly state that, in 1712, St. John dignified the peerage by that title which his exile and his genius have rendered so illustrious.

I was with him on the day this honour was publicly announced. I found him walking to and fro his room, with his arms folded, and with a very peculiar compression of his nether lip, which was a custom he had when anything greatly irritated or disturbed him.

"Well," said he, stopping abruptly as he saw me, "well, con- sidering the peacock Harley brought so bright a plume to his own nest, we must admire the generosity which spared this gay dunghill feather to mine !"

"How !" said I, though I knew the cause of his angry metaphor. St. John used metaphors in speech scarcely less than in writing.

"How !" cried the new peer, eagerly, and with one of those flashing looks which made his expression of indignation the most powerful I ever saw. "How ! Was the sacred promise granted to me of my own collateral earldom, to be violated ; and while the weight—the toil—the difficulty—the odium, of affairs, from which Harley, the despotic dullard, shrunk alike in imbecility and fear, had been left exclusively to my share, an insult in the shape of an honour, to be left exclusively to my reward ? You know my disposition is not to over-rate the mere baubles of ambition—you know I care little for titles and for orders in themselves; but the most worthless thing becomes of consequence, if made a symbol of what is of value, or designed as the token of an affront. Listen : a collateral earldom falls vacant—it is partly promised me. Suddenly I am dragged from the House of Commons, where I am all power-ful ; I am given—not this earldom, which, as belonging to my house, would alone have induced me to consent to a removal from a sphere where my enemies allow I had greater influence than any single commoner in the kingdom—I am given, not this, but a miserable compromise of distinction—a new and an inferior rank—given it against my will—thrust into the Upper House, to defend what this pompous driveller, Oxford, is forced to forsake; and not only exposed to all the obloquy of a most infuriate party, opposed to me, but mortified by an intentional affront from the party which, heart and soul, I have supported. You know that my birth is to the full as noble as Harley's—you know that my influence in the Lower House is far greater—you know that my name in the country, nay, throughout Europe, is far more popular—you know that the labour allotted to me has been far more weighty—you know that the late Peace of Utrecht is entirely my framing—that the foes to the measure direct all their venom against me—that the friends of the measure heap upon me all the honour :—when, therefore, this exact time is chosen for breaking a promise formerly made to me—when a pre-tended honour, known to be most unpalatable to me, is thrust upon me—when, at this very time, too, six vacant ribbons of the garter flaunt by me—one resting on the knee of this Harley, who was able to obtain an earldom for himself—the others given to men of far inferior pretensions, though not inferior rank, to my own—myself markedly, glaringly passed by,—how can I avoid feeling that things, despicable in themselves, are become of a vital power, from the evident intention that they should be insults to me ! The insects we despise as they buzz around us become dangerous when they settle on ourselves and we feel their sting ! But," added Bolingbroke, suddenly relapsing into a smile, " I have long wanted a nickname, I have now found one for myself. You know Oxford is called ' The Dragon ; ' well, henceforth call me ' St. George ; ' for, as sure as I live, will I overthrow the Dragon. I say this in jest, but I mean it in earnest. And now that I have discharged my bile, let us talk of this wonderful poem, which, though I have read it a hundred times, I am never wearied of admiring."

" Ah—the Rape of the Lock ! It is indeed beautiful, but I am not fond of poetry now. By the way, how is it that all our modern poets speak to the taste, the mind, the judgment, and never to the *feelings?* Are they right in doing so?"

"My friend, we are now in a polished age. What have feelings to do with civilization?"

"Why, more than you will allow. Perhaps the greater our civilization, the more numerous our feelings. Our animal passions lose in excess, but our mental gain; and it is to the mental that poetry should speak. Our English muse, even in this wonderful poem, seems to me to be growing, like our English beauties, too glitteringly artificial—it wears rouge and a hoop!"

"Ha! ha!—yes, they ornament now, rather than create—cut drapery, rather than marble. Our poems remind me of the ancient statues. Phidias made them, and Bubo and Bombax dressed them in purple. But this does not apply to young Pope, who has shown in this very poem that he can work the quarry as well as choose the gems. But see, the carriage awaits us. I have worlds to do,—first there is Swift to see—next, there is some exquisite Burgundy to taste —then, too there is the new actress; and, by the bye, you must tell me what you think of Bentley's Horace: we will drive first to my bookseller's to see it—Swift shall wait—Heavens! how he would rage if he heard me. I was going to say what a pity it is that that man should have so much littleness of vanity; but I should have uttered a very foolish sentiment if I had!"

"And why?"

"Because, if he had not so much littleness perhaps he would not be so great: what, but vanity, makes a man write and speak, and slave, and become famous? Alas!" and here St. John's countenance changed from gaiety to thought; "'tis a melancholy thing in human nature that so little is good and noble, both in itself and in its source! Our very worst passions will often produce sublimer effects than our best. Phidias (we will apply to him for another illustration) made the wonderful statue of Minerva for his country; but, in order to avenge himself on that country, he eclipsed it in the far more wonderful statue of the Jupiter Olympius. Thus, from a vicious feeling emanated a greater glory than from an exalted principle; and the artist was less celebrated for the monument of his patriotism than for that of his revenge! But *allons, mon cher*, we grow wise and dull. Let us go to choose our Burgundy and our comrades to share it."

However, with his characteristic affectation of bounding ambition, and consequently hope, to no one object in particular, and of mingling affairs of light importance with those of the most weighty, Lord Bolingbroke might pretend not to recur to, or to dwell upon, his causes of resentment—from that time they never ceased to influence him to a great, and for a statesman, an unpardonable, degree. We cannot, however, blame politicians for their hatred, until, without hating any body, we have for a long time been politicians ourselves; strong minds have strong passions, and men of strong passions must hate as well as love.

The next two years passed, on my part, in perpetual intrigues of diplomacy, combined with an unceasing, though secret, endeavour to penetrate the mystery which hung over the events of that dreadful night. All, however, was in vain. I know not what the English police may be hereafter, but, in my time, its officers seem to be chosen, like honest Dogberry's companions, among "the most senseless and fit men." They are, however, to the full, as much knaves as fools; and perhaps a wiser posterity will scarcely believe that, when things of the greatest value are stolen, the owners, on applying to the chief magistrate, will often be told that no redress can be given there, while one of the officers will engage to get back the goods, upon paying the thieves a certain sum in exchange—if this is refused—your effects are gone for ever! A pretty state of internal government.

It was about a year after the murder that my mother informed me of an event which tore from my heart its last private tie, viz., the death of Aubrey. The last letter I had received from him has been placed before the reader; it was written at Devereux Court, just before he left it for ever. Montreuil had been with him during the illness which proved fatal, and which occurred in Ireland. He died of consumption; and when I heard from my mother that Montreuil dwelt most glowingly upon the devotion he had manifested during the last months of his life, I could not help fearing that the morbidity of his superstition had done the work of physical disease. On this fatal news, my mother retired from Devereux Court to a company of ladies of our faith, who resided together, and practised the most ascetic rules of a nunnery, though they gave not to their house that ecclesiastical name. My mother had long meditated this project, and it was now a melancholy pleasure to put it into execution. From that period I rarely heard from her, and by little and little she so shrunk from all worldly objects that my visits, and I believe even those of Gerald, became unwelcome and distasteful.

As to my lawsuit, it went on gloriously, according to the assertions of my brisk little lawyer, who had declared so emphatically that he liked making quick work of a suit. And, at last, what with bribery and feeing, and pushing, a day was fixed for the final adjustment of my claim—it came—the cause was heard and lost. I should have been ruined, but for one circumstance; the old lady, my father's godmother, who had witnessed my first and concealed marriage, left me a pretty estate near Epsom. I turned it into gold, and it was fortunate that I did so soon, as the reader is about to see.

The queen died—and a cloud already began to look menacing
to the eyes of the Viscount Bolingbroke, and therefore to those of
the Count Devereux. "We will weather out the shower," said
Bolingbroke.

"Could not you," said I, "make our friend Oxford the 'Talapat?"[1] and Bolingbroke laughed. All men find wit in the jests
broken on their enemies!

One morning, however, I received a laconic note from him, which,
notwithstanding its shortness and seeming gaiety, I knew well signified that something, not calculated for laughter, had occurred.
I went, and found that his new majesty had deprived him of the
seals and secured his papers. We looked very blank at each other.
At last, Bolingbroke smiled. I must say that, culpable as he was
in some points as a politician—culpable, not from being ambitious
(for I would not give much for the statesman who is otherwise),
but from not having inseparably linked his ambition to the welfare
of his country, rather than to that of a party—for, despite of what
has been said of him, his ambition was never selfish—culpable as
he was when glory allured him, he was most admirable when danger
assailed him![2] and, by the shade of that Tully whom he so idolized,

[1] A thing used by the Siamese for the same purpose as we now use the um-
brella. A work descriptive of Siam, by M. de la Loubere, in which the Talapat
is somewhat minutely described, having been translated into English, and having
excited some curiosity, a few years before Count Devereux now uses the word,
the allusion was probably familiar.—ED.

[2] I know well that it has been said otherwise, and that Bolingbroke has been
accused of timidity for not staying in England, and making Mr. Robert Walpole
a present of his head. The elegant author of "De Vere," has fallen into a very
great, though a very hackneyed error, in lauding Oxford's political character, and
condemning Bolingbroke's, because the former awaited a trial, and the latter
shunned it. A very little reflection might, perhaps, have taught the accomplished
novelist that there could be no comparison between the two cases, because there
was no comparison between the relative *danger* of Oxford and Bolingbroke.
Oxford, as their subsequent impeachment proved, was far more numerously and
powerfully supported than his illustrious enemy; and there is really no earthly
cause for doubting the truth of Bolingbroke's assertion, viz., that "He had received repeated and certain information that a resolution was taken, by those
who had power to execute it, to pursue him to the scaffold." There are certain
situations in which a brave and a good man should willingly surrender life; but I
humbly opine that there may sometimes exist a situation in which he should
preserve it: and if ever man was placed in that latter situation it was Lord
Bolingbroke. To choose *unnecessarily* to put one's head under the axe, without
benefiting any but one's enemies by the act, is, in my eyes, the proof of a fool,
not a hero; and to attack a man for not placing his head in that agreeable and
most useful predicament—for preferring, in short, to live for a world, rather than
to perish by a faction, appears to be a mode of arguing that has a wonderful
resemblance to nonsense. When Lord Bolingbroke was impeached, two men
only out of those numerous retainers in the Lower House who had been wont so
loudly to applaud the secretary of state, in his prosecution of those very measures
for which he was now to be condemned—two men only (General Ross and Mr.
Hungerford), uttered a single syllable in defence of the minister disgraced.—ED.

his philosophy was the most conveniently worn of any person I ever met. When it would have been in the way—at the supper of an actress—in the levées of a court—in the boudoir of a beauty—in the arena of the senate—in the intrigue of the cabinet, you would not have observed a seam of the good old garment. But directly it was wanted—in the hour of pain—in the day of peril—in the suspense of exile—in (worst of all) the torpor of tranquillity, my extraordinary friend unfolded it piece by piece—wrapped himself up in it—sat down—defied the world, and uttered the most beautiful sentiments upon the comfort and luxury of his raiment, that can possibly be imagined. It used to remind me, that same philosophy of his, of the enchanted tent in the Arabian Tale, which one moment lay wrapped in a nut-shell, and the next covered an army.

Bolingbroke smiled, and quoted Cicero, and after an hour's conversation, which on his part was by no means like that of a person whose very head was in no enviable state of safety, he slid at once from a sarcasm upon Steele into a discussion as to the best measures to be adopted. Let me be brief on this point! Throughout the whole of that short session, he behaved in a manner more delicately and profoundly wise than, I think, the whole of his previous administration can equal. He sustained with the most unflagging, the most unwearied, dexterity, the sinking spirits of his associates. Without an act, or the shadow of an act, that could be called time-serving, he laid himself out to conciliate the king, and to propitiate parliament; with a dignified prudence which, while it seemed above petty pique, was well calculated to remove the appearance of that disaffection with which he was charged, and discriminated justly between the king and the new administration, he lent his talents to the assistance of the monarch, by whom his impeachment was already resolved on, and aided in the settlement of the civil list, while he was in full expectation of a criminal accusation.

The new parliament met, and all doubt was over. An impeachment of the late administration was decided upon. I was settling bills with my little lawyer one morning, when Bolingbroke entered my room. He took a chair, nodded to me not to dismiss my assistant, joined our conversation, and when conversation was merged in accounts, he took up a book of songs, and amused himself with it till my business was over and my disciple of Coke retired. He then said, very slowly and with a slight yawn—"You have never been at Paris, I think?"

"Never—you are enchanted with that gay city."

"Yes, but when I was last there, the good people flattered my vanity enough to bribe my taste. I shall be able to form a more unbiassed and impartial judgment in a few days."

"A few days!"

"Ay, my dear count: does it startle you? I wonder whether the pretty *De Tencin* will be as kind to me as she was, and whether *tout le monde* (that most exquisite phrase for five hundred people) will rise now at the Opera on my entrance. Do you think that a banished minister can have any, the smallest, resemblance, to what he was when in power? By gumdragon, as our friend Swift so euphoniously and elegantly says, or swears, by gumdragon, I think not! What altered Satan so after his fall? what gave him horns and a tail? nothing but his disgrace. Oh! years, and disease, plague, pestilence, and famine, never alter a man so much as the loss of power."

"You say wisely; but what am I to gather from your words? is it all over with us in real earnest?"

"Us! with *me* it is indeed all over—*you* may stay here for ever. *I* must fly—a packet-boat to Calais, or a room in the Tower—I must choose between the two. I had some thoughts of remaining —and confronting my trial, but it would be folly—there is a difference between Oxford and me. He has friends, though out of power; I have none. If they impeach him—he will escape; if they impeach me, they will either shut me up like a rat in a cage, for twenty years, till, old and forgotten, I tear my heart out with my confinement, or they will bring me at once to the block. No, no—I must keep myself for another day; and, while they banish me, I will leave the seeds of the true cause to grow up till my return. Wise and exquisite policy of my foes—'Frustra Cassium amovisti, si gliscere et vigere Brutorum emulos passurus es.'[1] But I have no time to lose—farewell, my friend—God bless you—you are saved from these storms; and even intolerance, which prevented the exercise of your genius, preserves you now from the danger of having applied that genius to the welfare of your country: Heaven knows, whatever my faults, I have sacrificed what I loved better than all things—study and pleasure—to her cause. In her wars I served even my enemy Marlborough, in order to serve her; her peace I effected, and I suffer for it. Be it so, I am

'Fidens animi atque in utrumque paratus.'[2]

Once more I embrace you—farewell."

"Nay," said I, "listen to me, you shall not go alone. France is already, in reality, my native country; there did I receive my birth, it is no hardship to return to my *natale solum*—it is an honour

---

[1] Vainly have you banished Cassius, if you shall suffer the rivals of the Brutuses to spread themselves and flourish.

[2] Confident of soul, and prepared for either fortune.

to return in the company of Henry St. John. I will have no refusal; my law case is over, my papers are few, my money I will
manage to transfer. Remember the anecdote you told me, yesterday, of Anaxagoras, who, when asked where his country was,
pointed with his finger to heaven. It is applicable, I hope, as well
to me as to yourself; to me, uncelebrated and obscure, to you, the
senator and the statesman."

In vain Bolingbroke endeavoured to dissuade me from this resolution; he was the only friend fate had left me, and I was resolved
that misfortune should not part us. At last he embraced me
tenderly, and consented to what he could not resist. "But you
cannot," he said, "quit England to-morrow night, as I must."

"Pardon me," I answered, "the briefer the preparation, the
greater the excitement, and what in life is equal to *that?*"

"True," answered Bolingbroke; "to some natures, too restless
to be happy, excitement can compensate for all; compensate for
years wasted, and hopes scattered—compensate for bitter regret at
talents perverted and passions unrestrained. But we will talk
philosophically when we have more leisure. You will dine with
me to-morrow; we will go to the play together—I promised poor
Lucy that I would see her at the theatre, and I cannot break my
word—and an hour afterwards we will commence our excursion to
Paris. And now I will explain to you the plan I have arranged for
our escape."

CHAPTER III..

THE REAL ACTORS SPECTATORS OF THE FALSE ONES.

T was a brilliant night at the theatre. The boxes were
crowded to excess. Every eye was directed towards
Lord Bolingbroke, who, with his usual dignified and
consummate grace of manner, conversed with the various
loiterers with whom, from time to time, his box was filled.

"Look yonder," said a very young man, of singular personal
beauty, "look yonder, my lord, what a panoply of smiles the Duchess
wears to-night, and how triumphantly she directs those eyes, which
they say were once so beautiful, to your box."

"Ah," said Bolingbroke, "her grace does me too much honour;
I must not neglect to acknowledge her courtesy;" and, leaning over
the box, Bolingbroke watched his opportunity till the Duchess of
Marlborough, who sat opposite to him, and who was talking with

great and evidently joyous vivacity to a tall, thin man, beside her, directed her attention, and that of her whole party, in a fixed and concentrated stare, to the emperilled minister. With a dignified smile Lord Bolingbroke then put his hand to his heart, and bowed profoundly ; the Duchess looked a little abashed, but returned the courtesy quickly and slightly, and renewed her conversation.

"Faith, my lord," cried the young gentleman who had before spoken, "you managed that well ! No reproach is like that which we clothe in a smile, and present with a bow."

"I am happy," said Lord Bolingbroke, "that my conduct receives the grave support of a son of my political opponent."

"*Grave* support, my Lord ! you are mistaken—never apply the epithet grave to anything belonging to Philip Wharton. But, in sober earnest, I have sat long enough with you to terrify all my friends, and must now show my worshipful face in another part of the house. Count Devereux, will you come with me to the Duchess's?"

"What ! the Duchess's immediately after Lord Bolingbroke's !—the Whig after the Tory—it would be as trying to one's assurance as a change from the cold bath to the hot to one's constitution."

"Well, and what so delightful as a trial in which one triumphs ? and a change in which one does not lose even one's countenance?"

"Take care, my lord," said Bolingbroke, laughing ; "those are dangerous sentiments for a man like you, to whom the hopes of two great parties are directed, to express so openly, even on a trifle, and in a jest."

"'Tis for that reason I utter them. I like being the object of hope and fear to men, since my miserable fortune made me marry at fourteen, and cease to be aught but a wedded thing to the women. But, sup with me at the Bedford—you, my lord, and the Count."

"And you will ask Walpole, Addison, and Steele,[1] to join us ; eh ?" said Bolingbroke. "No, we have other engagements for to-night ; but we shall meet again soon."

And the eccentric youth nodded his adieu, disappeared, and a minute afterwards was seated by the side of the Duchess of Marlborough.

"There goes a boy," said Bolingbroke, "who, at the age of fifteen, has in him the power to be the greatest man of his day, and in all probability will only be the most singular. An obstinate man is sure of doing well ; a wavering or a whimsical one (which is the same thing) is as uncertain, even in his elevation, as a shuttlecock.

---

[1] All political opponents of Lord Bolingbroke.

But look to the box at the right—do you see the beautiful Lady Mary?"

"Yes," said Mr. Trefusis, who was with us, "she has only just come to town. 'Tis said she and Ned Montague live like doves."

"How!" said Lord Bolingbroke; "that quick, restless eye seems to have very little of the dove in it."

"But how beautiful she is!" said Trefusis, admiringly. "What a pity that those exquisite hands should be so dirty! It reminds me" (Trefusis loved a coarse anecdote) "of her answer to old Madame de Noailles, who made exactly the same remark to her. 'Do you call my hands dirty?' cried Lady Mary, holding them up with the most innocent *naïveté*, 'Ah, Madame, *si vous pouviez voir mes pieds!*'"

"*Fi donc!*" said I, turning away; "but who is that very small, deformed man behind her,—he with the bright black eye?"

"Know you not?" said Bolingbroke; "tell it not in Gath!—'tis a rising sun, whom I have already learned to worship—the young author of the 'Essay on Criticism,' and the 'Rape of the Lock.' Egad the little poet seems to eclipse us with the women as much as with the men. Do you mark how eagerly Lady Mary listens to him, even though the tall gentleman in black, who in vain endeavours to win her attentions, is thought the handsomest gallant in London? Ah, Genius is paid by smiles from all females but Fortune; little, methinks, does that young poet, in his first intoxication of flattery and fame, guess what a lot of contest and strife is in store for him. The very breath which a literary man respires is hot with hatred, and the youthful proselyte enters that career which seems to him so glittering, even as Dame Pliant's brother in the Alchemist entered town—not to be fed with luxury, and diet on pleasure, but 'to learn to quarrel and live by his wits.'"

The play was now nearly over. With great gravity Lord Bolingbroke summoned one of the principal actors to his box, and bespoke a play for the next week: leaning then on my arm, he left the theatre. We hastened to his home, put on our disguises, and, without any adventure worth recounting, effected our escape, and landed safely at Calais.

CHAPTER IV.

PARIS—A FEMALE POLITICIAN, AND AN ECCLESIASTICAL ONE—
SUNDRY OTHER MATTERS.

HE ex-minister was received both at Calais and at Paris with the most gratifying honours—he was then entirely the man to captivate the French. The beauty of his person, the grace of his manner, his consummate taste in all things, the exceeding variety and sparkling vivacity of his conversation, enchanted them. In later life he has grown more reserved and profound, even in habitual intercourse, and attention is now fixed to the solidity of the diamond, as at that time one was too dazzled to think of anything but its brilliancy.

While Bolingbroke was receiving visits of state, I busied myself in inquiring after a certain Madame de Balzac. The reader will remember that the envelope of that letter which Oswald had brought to me at Devereux Court, was signed by the letters C. de B. Now, when Oswald disappeared, after that dreadful night to which even now I can scarcely bring myself to allude, these initials occurred to my remembrance, and Oswald having said they belonged to a lady formerly intimate with my father, I inquired of my mother if she could guess to what French lady such initials would apply. She, with an evident pang of jealousy, mentioned a Madame de Balzac; and to this lady I now resolved to address myself, with the faint hope of learning from her some intelligence respecting Oswald. It was not difficult to find out the abode of one who in her day had played no inconsiderable *rôle* in that Comedy of Errors,—the Great World. She was still living at Paris; what Frenchwoman would, if she could help it, live any where else? "There are a hundred gates," said the witty Madame de Choisi to me, "which lead into Paris, but only two roads out of it,—the convent, or (odious word!) the grave."

I hastened to Madame Balzac's hotel. I was ushered through three magnificent apartments into one, which to my eyes seemed to contain a throne: upon a nearer inspection I discovered it was a bed. Upon a large chair, by a very bad fire—it was in the month of March—sat a tall, handsome woman, excessively painted, and dressed in a manner which to my taste, accustomed to English finery, seemed singularly plain. I had sent in the morning to request permission to wait on her, so that she was prepared for my visit. She rose, offered me her cheek, kissed mine, shed several tears, and in short testified a great deal of kindness towards me. Old ladies, who have flirted with our fathers, always seem to claim a sort of property in the sons!

Before she resumed her seat she held me out at arm's length. "You have a family likeness to your brave father," said she, with a little disappointment; "but—"

"Madame de Balzac would add," interrupted I, filling up the sentence which I saw her *bienveillance* had made her break off, "Madame de Balzac would add that I am not so good-looking. It is true; the likeness is transmitted to me within rather than without; and if I have not my father's privilege to be admired, I have at least his capacities to admire," and I bowed.

Madame de Balzac took three large pinches of snuff. "That is very well said," said she gravely: "very well indeed! not at all like your father, though, who never paid a compliment in his life. Your clothes, by the bye, are in exquisite taste: I had no idea that English people had arrived at such perfection in the fine arts. Your face is a little too long! You admire Racine, of course? How do you like Paris?"

All this was not said gaily or quickly: Madame de Balzac was by no means a gay or a quick person. She belonged to a peculiar school of Frenchwomen, who affected a little languor, a great deal of stiffness, an indifference to forms when forms were to be used by themselves, and an unrelaxing demand of forms when forms were to be observed to them by others. Added to this, they talked plainly upon all matters, without ever entering upon sentiment. This was the school she belonged to; but she possessed the traits of the individual as well as of the species. She was keen, ambitious, worldly, not unaffectionate, nor unkind; very proud, a little of the devotee—because it was the fashion to be so—an enthusiastic admirer of military glory, and a most prying, searching, intriguing, schemer of politics without the slightest talent for the science.

"Like Paris!" said I, answering only the last question, and that not with the most scrupulous regard to truth. "Can Madame de Balzac think of Paris, and not conceive the transport which must inspire a person entering it for the first time? But I had something more endearing than a stranger's interest to attach me to it; I longed to express to my father's friend my gratitude for the interest which I venture to believe she on one occasion manifested towards me."

"Ah! you mean my caution to you against that terrible De Montreuil. Yes, I trust I was of service to you *there.*"

And Madame de Balzac then proceeded to favour me with the whole history of the manner in which she had obtained the letter she had sent me, accompanied by a thousand anathemas against those *atroces Jésuites*, and a thousand eulogies on her own genius and virtues. I brought her from this subject, so interesting to herself, as soon as decorum would allow me : and I then made inquiry if she knew aught of Oswald, or could suggest any mode of obtaining intelligence respecting him. Madame de Balzac hated plain, blunt, blank questions, and she always travelled through a wilderness of parentheses, before she answered them. But at last I did ascertain her answer, and found it utterly unsatisfactory. She had never seen nor heard anything of Oswald since he had left her charged with her commission to me. I then questioned her respecting the character of the man, and found Mr. Marie Oswald had little to plume himself upon in that respect. He seemed, however, from her account of him, to be more a rogue than a villain ; and, from two or three stories of his cowardice, which Madame de Balzac related, he appeared to me utterly incapable of a design so daring and systematic as that of which it pleased all persons who troubled themselves about my affairs, to suspect him.

Finding, at last, that no further information was to be gained on this point, I turned the conversation to Montreuil. I found, from Madame de Balzac's very abuse of him, that he enjoyed a great reputation in the country, and a great favour at court. He had been early befriended by Father la Chaise, and he was now especially trusted and esteemed by the successor of that Jesuit, Le Tellier ;—Le Tellier, that rigid and bigoted servant of Loyola— the sovereign of the king himself—the destroyer of the Port Royal, and the mock and terror of the be-devilled and persecuted Jansenists. Besides this, I learnt what has been before pretty clearly evident—viz., that Montreuil was greatly in the confidence of the Chevalier, and that he was supposed already to have rendered essential service to the Stuart cause. His reputation had increased with every year, and was as great for private sanctity as for political talent.

When this information, given in a very different spirit from that in which I retail it, was over, Madame de Balzac observed— "Doubtless you will obtain a private audience with the king ?"

"Is it possible, in his present age and infirmities ?"

"It ought to be, to the son of the brave Marshal Devereux."

"I shall be happy to receive Madame's instructions how to obtain the honour : her name would, I feel, be a greater passport to the royal presence than that of a deceased soldier ; and Venus's cestus may obtain that grace which would never be accorded to the truncheon of Mars !"

Was there ever so natural and so easy a compliment ? My Venus of fifty smiled.

"You are mistaken, Count," said she; "I have no interest at court: the Jesuits forbid that to a Jansenist: but I will speak this very day to the Bishop of Fréjus: he is related to me, and will obtain so slight a boon for you with ease. He has just left his bishopric: you know how he hated it. Nothing could be pleasanter than his signing himself, in a letter to Cardinal Quiiini—'*Fleuri, évêque de Fréjus par l'indignation divine.*' The king does not like him much; but he is a good man on the whole, though Jesuitical; he shall introduce you."

I expressed my gratitude for the favour, and hinted that possibly the relations of my father's first wife, the haughty and ancient house of La Tremouille, might save the Bishop of Fréjus from the pain of exerting himself on my behalf.

"You are very much mistaken," answered Madame de Balzac: "priests point the road to court, as well as to heaven; and warriors and nobles have as little to do with the former as they have with the latter, the unlucky Duc de Villars only excepted—a man whose ill fortune is enough to destroy all the laurels of France. *Ma foi!* I believe the poor Duke might rival in luck that Italian poet who said, in a fit of despair, that if he had been bred a hatter, men would have been born without heads."

And Madame de Balzac chuckled over this joke till, seeing that no farther news was to be gleaned from her, I made my adieu, and my departure.

Nothing could exceed the kindness manifested towards me by my father's early connections. The circumstance of my accompanying Bolingbroke, joined to my age, and an address which, if not animated nor gay, had not been acquired without some youthful cultivation of the graces, gave me a sort of *éclat* as well as consideration. And Bolingbroke, who was only jealous of superiors in power, and who had no equals in anything else, added greatly to my reputation by his panegyrics.

Everyone sought me—and the attention of society at Paris would, to most, be worth a little trouble to repay. Perhaps, if I had liked it, I might have been the rage; but that vanity was over. I contented myself with being admitted into society as an observer, without a single wish to become the observed. When one has once outlived the ambition of fashion I know not a greater affliction than an over-attention; and the Spectator did just what I should have done in a similar case, when he left his lodgings, "because he was asked every morning how he had slept." In the immediate vicinity of the court, the king's devotion, age, and misfortunes, threw a damp over society; but there were still some sparkling circles, who put the king out of the mode, and declared that the defeats of his generals, made capital subjects for epigrams.   What a delicate and subtle air did hang over those *soirées,* where all that were bright and lovely, and noble and gay, and witty and wise, were assembled in one brilliant cluster ! Imperfect as my rehearsals must be, I think the few pages I shall devote to a description of these glittering conversations must still retain something of that original piquancy which the *soirées* of no other capital could rival or appreciate.

One morning, about a week after my interview with Madame de Balzac, I received a note from her, requesting me to visit her that day, and appointing the hour.

Accordingly I repaired to the house of the fair politician.   I found her with a man in a clerical garb, and of a benevolent and prepossessing countenance.   She introduced him to me as the Bishop of Fréjus, and he received me with an air very uncommon to his countrymen, viz., with an ease that seemed to result from real good nature, rather than artificial grace.

"I shall feel," said he, quietly, and without the least appearance of paying a compliment, "very glad to mention your wish to his Majesty ; and I have not the least doubt but that he will admit to his presence one who has such hereditary claims on his notice. Madame de Maintenon, by the way, has charged me to present you to her, whenever you will give me the opportunity. She knew your admirable mother well, and, for her sake, wishes once to see you. You know, perhaps, Monsieur, that the extreme retirement of her life renders this message from Madame de Maintenon an unusual and rare honour."

I expressed my thanks ; — the bishop received them with a paternal rather than a courtier-like air, and appointed a day for me to attend him to the palace. We then conversed a short time upon indifferent matters, which, I observed, the good bishop took especial pains to preserve clear from French politics. He asked me, however, two or three questions about the state of parties in England—about finance and the national debt—about Ormond and Oxford ; and appeared to give the most close attention to my replies. He smiled once or twice, when his relation, Madame de Balzac, broke out into sarcasms against the Jesuits, which had nothing to do with the subjects in question.

"Ah, *ma chère cousine,*" said he, "you flatter me by showing that you like me not as the politician, but the private relation—not as the Bishop of Fréjus, but as André de Fleuri."

Madame de Balzac smiled, and answered by a compliment.   She was a politician for the kingdom, it is true, but she was also a politician for herself.   She was far from exclaiming, with Pindar, "Thy business, O my city, I prefer willingly to my own." Ah, there is a nice distinction between politics and policy, and Madame de Balzac knew it. The distinction is this : Politics is the art of being wise for others ! Policy is the art of being wise for oneself.

From Madame de Balzac's I went to Bolingbroke. "I have just been offered the place of Secretary of State by the English king on this side of the water," said he ;—"I do not, however, yet like to commit myself so fully. And, indeed, I am not unwilling to have a little relaxation of pleasure, after all these dull and dusty travails of state. What say you to Boulainvilliers to-night—you are asked?"

"Yes ! all the wits are to be there—Anthony Hamilton—and Fontenelle—young Arouet—Chaulieu, that charming old man. Let us go, and polish away the wrinkles of our hearts. What cosmetics are to the face wit is to the temper ; and, after all, there is no wisdom like that which teaches us to forget."

"Come then," said Bolingbroke, rising, "we will lock up these papers, and take a melancholy drive, in order that we may enjoy mirth the better by and bye."

CHAPTER V.

A MEETING OF WITS—CONVERSATION GONE OUT TO SUPPER IN HER DRESS OF VELVET AND JEWELS.

BOULAINVILLIERS ! Comte de St. Saire ! What will our great-grandchildren think of that name ? Fame is indeed a riddle ! At the time I refer to, wit—learning—grace—all things that charm and enlighten—were supposed to centre in one word—*Boulainvilliers!* The good count had many rivals, it is true, but he had that exquisite tact peculiar to his countrymen, of making the very reputations of those rivals contribute to his own. And while he assembled them around him, the lustre of their *bons mots*, though it emanated from themselves, was reflected upon him.

It was a pleasant, though not a costly, apartment, in which we found our host. The room was sufficiently full of people to allow scope and variety to one group of talkers, without being full enough to permit those little knots and coteries which are the destruction of literary society. An old man of about seventy, of a sharp, shrewd, yet polished and courtly expression of countenance, of a great gaiety of manner, which was now and then rather displeasingly contrasted by an abrupt affectation of dignity, that, however, rarely lasted above a minute, and never withstood the shock of a *bon mot*, was the first person who accosted us.   This old man was the wreck of the once celebrated Anthony Count Hamilton!

"Well, my lord," said he to Bolingbroke, "How do you like the weather at Paris?— it is a little better than the merciless air of London—is it not? 'Slife!—even in June one could not go open-breasted in those regions of cold and catarrh—a very great misfortune, let me tell you, my lord, if one's cambric happened to be of a very delicate and brilliant texture, and one wished to penetrate the inward folds of a lady's heart, by developing to the best advantage the exterior folds that covered his own."

"It is the first time," answered Bolingbroke, "that I ever heard so accomplished a courtier as Count Hamilton repine, with sincerity, that he could not bare his bosom to inspection."

"Ah!" cried Boulainvilliers, "but vanity makes a man show much that discretion would conceal."

"*Au diable* with your discretion!" said Hamilton, "'tis a vulgar virtue.   Vanity is a truly aristocratic quality, and every way fitted to a gentleman.   Should I ever have been renowned for my exquisite lace and web-like cambric, if I had not been vain?   Never, *mon cher!*   I should have gone into a convent and worn sackcloth, and from *Count Antoine*, I should have thickened into *Saint Anthony*."

"Nay," cried Lord Bolingbroke, "there is as much scope for vanity in sackcloth as there is in cambric; for vanity is like the Irish ogling master in the Spectator, and if it teaches the play-house to ogle by candle-light, it also teaches the church to ogle by day! But, pardon me, Monsieur Chaulieu, how well you look!   I see that the myrtle sheds its verdure, not only over your poetry, but the poet.   And it is right that, to the modern Anacreon, who has bequeathed to Time a treasure it will never forego, Time itself should be gentle in return."

"Milord," answered Chaulieu, an old man who, though considerably past seventy, was animated, in appearance and manner, with a vivacity and life that would have done honour to a youth— "Milord, it was beautifully said by the Emperor Julian that Justice retained the Graces in her vestibule.   I see, now, that he should have substituted the word *Wisdom* for that of Justice."

"Come," cried Anthony Hamilton, "this will never do.   Compliments are the dullest things imaginable.   For Heaven's sake, let us leave panegyric to blockheads, and say something bitter to one another, or we shall die of *ennui*."

"Right," said Boulainvilliers:—"Let us pick out some poor devil to begin with.   Absent or present?—Decide which."

"Oh, absent," cried Chaulieu; "'tis a thousand times more piquant to slander than to rally!   Let us commence with his

Majesty: Count Devereux, have you seen Madame Maintenon and her devout infant since your arrival?"

"No!—the priests must be petitioned before the miracle is made public."

"What!" cried Chaulieu, "would you insinuate that his Majesty's piety is really nothing less than a miracle?"

"Impossible!" said Boulainvilliers, gravely,—"piety is as natural to kings as flattery to their courtiers: are we not told that they are made in God's own image!"

"If that were true," said Count Hamilton, somewhat profanely—"if that were true, I should no longer deny the impossibility of Atheism!"

"Fie, Count Hamilton," said an old gentleman, in whom I recognized the great Huet, "fie—wit should beware how it uses wings—its province is earth, not heaven."

"Nobody can better tell what wit is not than the learned Abbé Huet!" answered Hamilton with a mock air of respect.

"Psha!" cried Chaulieu, "I thought when we once gave the rein to satire it would carry us *pêle-mêle* against one another. But, in order to sweeten that drop of lemon-juice for you, my dear Huet, let me turn to Milord Bolingbroke, and ask him whether England can produce a scholar equal to Peter Huet, who in twenty years wrote notes to sixty-two volumes of Classics,[1] for the sake of a prince who never read a line in one of them?"

"We have some scholars," answered Bolingbroke; "but we certainly have no Huet. It is strange enough, but learning seems to me like a circle; it grows weaker the more it spreads. We now see many people capable of reading commentaries, but very few indeed capable of writing them."

"True," answered Huet; and in his reply he introduced the celebrated illustration which is at this day mentioned among his most felicitous *bons mots*. "Scholarship, formerly the most difficult and unaided enterprise of Genius, has now been made, by the very toils of the first mariners, but an easy and commonplace voyage of leisure. But who would compare the great men, whose very difficulties not only proved their ardour, but brought them the patience and the courage which alone are the parents of a genuine triumph, to the indolent loiterers of the present day, who, having little of difficulty to conquer, have nothing of glory to attain? For my part, there seems to me the same difference between a scholar of our days and one of the past as there is between Christopher Columbus and the master of a packet-boat from Calais to Dover!"

"But," cried Anthony Hamilton, taking a pinch of snuff with

[1] The Delphin Classics.

the air of a man about to utter a witty thing—"but what have we —we spirits of the world, not imps of the closet,"—and he glanced at Huet—"to do with scholarship? All the waters of Castaly, which we want to pour into our brain, are such as will flow the readiest to our tongue."

"In short, then," said I, "you would assert that all a friend cares for in one's head is the quantity of talk in it?"

"Precisely, my dear Count," said Hamilton seriously; "and to that maxim I will add another, applicable to the opposite sex. All that a mistress cares for in one's heart is the quantity of love in it."

"What! are generosity, courage, honour, to go for nothing with our mistress, then?" cried Chaulieu.

"No; for she will believe, if you are a passionate lover, that you have all those virtues; and if not, she will never believe that you have one."

"Ah! it was a pretty court of love in which the friend and biographer of Count Grammont learned the art!" said Bolingbroke.

"We believed so at the time, my lord; but there are as many changes in the fashion of making love as there are in that of making dresses. Honour me, Count Devereux, by using my snuff-box, and then looking at the lid."

"It is the picture of Charles the Second, which adorns it—is it not?"

"No, Count Devereux, it is the diamonds which adorn it. His Majesty's face I thought very beautiful while he was living; but now, on my conscience, I consider it the ugliest phiz I ever beheld. But I directed your notice to the picture because we were talking of love; and Old Rowley believed that he could make it better than any one else. All his courtiers had the same opinion of themselves; and I dare say the *beaux garçons* of Queen Anne's reign would say that not one of King Charley's gang knew what love was. Oh! 'tis a strange circle of revolutions, that love! Like the earth, it always changes, and yet always has the same materials."

"*L'Amour—l'amour—toujours l'amour*, with Count Anthony Hamilton!" said Boulainvilliers. "He is always on that subject; and *sacre bleu!* when he was younger, I am told he was like Cacus, the son of Vulcan, and breathed nothing but flames."

"You flatter me," said Hamilton. "Solve me now a knotty riddle, my Lord Bolingbroke. Why does a young man think it the greatest compliment to be thought wise, while an old man thinks it the greatest compliment to be told he has been foolish?"

"Is love foolish, then?" said Lord Bolingbroke.

"Can you doubt it?" answered Hamilton; "it makes a man

think more of another than himself! I know not a greater proof of folly!"

"Ah—*mon aimable ami*"—cried Chaulieu; "you are the wickedest witty person I know. I cannot help loving your language, while I hate your sentiments."

"My language is my own—my sentiments are those of all men," answered Hamilton; "but are we not, by the bye, to have young *Arouet* here to-night? What a charming person he is!"

"Yes," said Boulainvilliers. "He said he should be late; and I expect Fontenelle, too, but *he* will not come before supper. I found Fontenelle this morning conversing with my cook on the best manner of dressing asparagus. I asked him, the other day, what writer, ancient or modern, had ever given him the most sensible pleasure? After a little pause, the excellent old man said— 'Daphnus'—'Daphnus!' repeated I, 'who the devil is he?' 'Why,' answered Fontenelle, with tears of gratitude in his benevolent eyes, 'I had some hypochondriacal ideas that suppers were unwholesome; and Daphnus is an ancient physician, who asserts the contrary; and declares,—think, my friend, what a charming theory!—that the moon is a great assistant of the digestion!'"

"Ha! ha! ha!" laughed the *Abbé de Chaulieu*. "How like Fontenelle! what an anomalous creature 'tis! He has the most kindness and the least feeling of any man I ever knew. Let Hamilton find a pithier description for him if he can!"

Whatever reply the friend of the *preux Grammont* might have made was prevented by the entrance of a young man of about twenty-one.

In person he was tall, slight, and very thin. There was a certain affectation of polite address in his manner and mien which did not quite become him; and though he was received by the old wits with great cordiality, and on a footing of perfect equality; yet, the inexpressible air which denotes birth was both pretended to and wanting. This, perhaps, was however owing to the ordinary inexperience of youth: which, if not awkwardly bashful, is generally awkward in its assurance. Whatever its cause, the impression vanished directly he entered into conversation. I do not think I ever encountered a man so brilliantly, yet so easily, witty. He had but little of the studied allusion—the antithetical point—the classic metaphor, which chiefly characterize the wits of my day. On the contrary, it was an exceeding and *naïve* simplicity, which gave such unrivalled charm and piquancy to his conversation. And while I have not scrupled to stamp on my pages some faint imitation of the peculiar dialogue of other eminent characters, I must confess myself utterly unable to convey the smallest idea of his method of making words irresistible. Contenting my efforts, therefore, with describing his personal appearance—interesting, because that of the most striking literary character it has been my lot to meet—I shall omit his share in the remainder of the conversation I am rehearsing, and beg the reader to recall that passage in Tacitus, in which the great historian says, that in the funeral of Junia, "the images of Brutus and Cassius outshone all the rest, from the very circumstance of their being the sole ones excluded from the rite."

The countenance, then, of Marie François Arouet (since so celebrated under the name of Voltaire), was plain in feature, but singularly striking in effect; its vivacity was the very perfection of what Steele once happily called "physiognomical eloquence." His eyes were blue, fiery rather than bright, and so restless that they never dwelt in the same place for a moment;[1] his mouth was at once the worst and the most peculiar feature of his face: it betokened humour, it is true; but it also betrayed malignancy—nor did it ever smile without sarcasm. Though flattering to those present, his words against the absent, uttered by that bitter and curling lip, mingled with your pleasure at their wit a little fear at their causticity. I believe no one, be he as bold, as callous, or as faultless as human nature can be, could be one hour with that man and not feel apprehension. Ridicule, so lavish, yet so true to the mark—so wanton, yet so seemingly just—so bright, that while it wandered round its target, in apparent, though terrible playfulness, it burned into the spot, and engraved there a brand, and a token indelible and perpetual;—this no man could witness, when darted towards another, and feel safe for himself. The very caprice and levity of the jester seemed more perilous, because less to be calculated upon, than a systematic principle of bitterness or satire. Bolingbroke compared him, not unaptly, to a child who has possessed himself of Jupiter's bolts, and who makes use of those bolts in sport, which a god would only have used in wrath.

. Arouet's forehead was not remarkable for height, but it was nobly and grandly formed, and, contradicting that of the mouth, wore a benevolent expression. Though so young, there was already a wrinkle on the surface of the front, and a prominence on the eyebrow, which showed that the wit and the fancy of his conversation were, if not regulated, at least contrasted, by more thoughtful and lofty characteristics of mind. At the time I write, this man has obtained a high throne among the powers of the lettered world.

1 The reader will remember that this is a description of Voltaire as a very young man. I do not know any where a more impressive, almost a more ghastly, contrast, than that which the pictures of Voltaire, grown old, present to Largilliere's picture of him at the age of twenty-four; and he was somewhat younger than twenty-four at the time of which the Count now speaks.—Ed.

What he may yet be, it is in vain to guess : he may be all that is great and good, or—the reverse ; but I cannot but believe that his career is only begun.   Such men are born monarchs of the mind ; they may be benefactors or tyrants : in either case, they are greater than the kings of the physical empire, because they defy armies and laugh at the intrigues of state.   From themselves only come the balance of their power, the laws of their government, and the boundaries of their realm.

We sat down to supper.   "Count Hamilton," said Boulain- villiers, "are we not a merry set for such old fellows ? Why, except- ing Arouet, Milord Bolingbroke, and Count Devereux, there is scarcely one of us under seventy.   Where, but at Paris, would you see *bons vivans* of our age ? *Vivent la joie—la bagatelle !—l'amour !*"

"*Et le vin de Champagne,*" cried Chaulieu, filling his glass ; "but what is there strange in our merriment ?   Philemon,the comic poet, laughed at ninety-seven.   May we all do the same ! "

"You forget," cried Bolingbroke, "that Philemon died of the laughing."

"Yes," said Hamilton ; "but, if I remember right, it was at seeing an ass eat figs.   Let us vow, therefore, never to keep company with asses ! "

"Bravo, Count," said Boulainvilliers, "you have put the true moral on the story.   Let us swear, by the ghost of Philemon, that we will never laugh at an ass's jokes—practical or verbal."

"Then we must always be serious, except when we are with each other," cried Chaulieu.   "Oh, I would sooner take my chance of dying prematurely at ninety-seven than consent to such a vow ! "

"Fontenelle," cried our host, "you are melancholy.   What is the matter ? "

"I mourn for the weakness of human nature," answered Fon- tenelle, with an air of patriarchal philanthropy.   "I told your cook three times about the asparagus ; and now—taste it.   I told him not to put too much sugar, and he has put none.   Thus it is with mankind—ever in extremes, and consequently ever in error !   Thus it was that Luther said, so felicitously and so truly, that the human mind was like a drunken peasant on horseback—prop it on one side, and it falls on the other."

"Ha ! ha ! ha !" cried Chaulieu.   "Who would have thought one could have found so much morality in a plate of asparagus ! Taste this *salsifis.*"

"Pray, Hamilton," said Huet, "what *jeu de mot* was that you made yesterday at Madame D'Epernonville's which gained you such applause?"

"Ah, repeat it, Count," cried Boulainvilliers; "'twas the most classical thing I have heard for a long time."

"Why," said Hamilton, laying down his knife and fork, and preparing himself by a large draught of the champagne—"why, Madame D'Epernonville appeared without her *tour;* you know Lord Bolingbroke, that *tour* is the polite name for false hair. '*Ah, sacre!*' cried her brother, courteously, '*ma sœur, que vous êtes laide aujourd'hui—vous n'avez pas votre tour!*' '*Voilà, pourquoi elle n'est pas si-belle (Cybele),*'" answered I.

"Excellent! famous!" cried we all, except Huet, who seemed to regard the punster with a very disrespectful eye. Hamilton saw it. "You do not think, Monsieur Huet, that there is wit in these *jeux de mots*—perhaps you do not admire wit at all?"

"Yes, I admire wit as I do the wind. When it shakes the trees, it is fine; when it cools the wave it is refreshing; when it steals over flowers, it is enchanting; but when, Monsieur Hamilton, it whistles through the key-hole, it is unpleasant."

"The very worst illustration I ever heard," said Hamilton, coolly. "Keep to your classics, my dear Abbé. When Jupiter edited the work of Peter Huet, he did with wit as Peter Huet did with Lucan, when he edited the classics—he was afraid it might do mischief, and so left it out altogether."

"Let us drink!" cried Chaulieu; "let us drink!" and the conversation was turned again.

"What is that you say of Tacitus, Huet?" said Boulainvilliers.

"That his wisdom arose from his malignancy," answered Huet. "He is a perfect penetrator[1] into human vices; but knows nothing of human virtues. Do you think that a good man would dwell so constantly on what is evil? Believe me—no! A man cannot write much and well upon virtue without being virtuous, nor enter minutely and profoundly into the causes of vice without being vicious himself."

"It is true," said Hamilton: "and your remark, which affects to be so deep, is but a natural corollary from the hackneyed maxim that from experience comes wisdom."

"But, for my part," said Boulainvilliers, "I think Tacitus is not so invariably the analyzer of vice as you would make him. Look at the Agricola and the Germania."

"Ah! the Germany, above all things!" cried Hamilton, dropping a delicious morsel of *sanglier* in its way from hand to mouth, in his hurry to speak. "Of course, the historian, Boulainvilliers, advocates the Germany, from its mention of the origin of the feudal

---

[1] A remark similar to this the reader will probably remember in the Huetiana, and will, I hope, agree with me in thinking it showy and untrue.—ED.

system—that incomparable bundle of excellences, which Le Comte de Boulainvilliers has declared to be *le chef d'œuvre de l'esprit humain;* and which the same gentleman regrets, in the most pathetic terms, no longer exists in order that the seigneur may feed upon *des gros morceaux de bœuf demi-cru,* may hang up half his peasants *pour encourager les autres,* and ravish the daughters of the defunct *pour leur donner quelque consolation."*

"Seriously though," said the old Abbé de Chaulieu, with a twinkling eye, *"the last* mentioned evil, my dear Hamilton, was not without a little alloy of good."

"Yes," said Hamilton, "if it was only the daughters; but perhaps the seigneur was not too scrupulous with regard to the wives."

"Ah! shocking, shocking!" cried Chaulieu, solemnly. "Adultery is, indeed, an atrocious crime. I am sure I would most consciously cry out with the honest preacher—'Adultery, my children, is the blackest of sins. I do declare that I would rather have *ten* virgins in love with me than *one* married woman!'"

We all laughed at this enthusiastic burst of virtue from the chaste Chaulieu. And *Arouet* turned our conversation towards the ecclesiastical dissensions between Jesuits and Jansenists, that then agitated the kingdom. "Those priests," said Bolingbroke, "remind me of the nurses of Jupiter—they make a great clamour, in order to drown the voice of their god."

"Bravissimo!" cried Hamilton. "Is it not a pity, messieurs, that my Lord Bolingbroke was not a Frenchman? He is almost clever enough to be one."

"If he would drink a little more, he would be," cried Chaulieu, who was now setting us all a glorious example.

"What say you, Morton?" exclaimed Bolingbroke; "must we not drink these gentlemen under the table for the honour of our country."

"A challenge! a challenge!" cried Chaulieu. "I march first to the field?"

"Conquest or death!" shouted Bolingbroke. And the rites of Minerva were forsaken for those of Bacchus.

CHAPTER VI.

A COURT, COURTIERS, AND A KING.

 THINK it was the second day after this "feast of
reason" that Lord Bolingbroke deemed it advisable to
retire to Lyons till his plans of conduct were ripened into
decision.   We took an affectionate leave of each other ;
but before we parted, and after he had discussed his own projects of
ambition, we talked a little upon mine.   Although I was a Catholic
and a pupil of Montreuil, although I had fled from England, and
had nothing to expect from the House of Hanover, I was by no
means favourably disposed towards the Chevalier and his cause.   I
wonder if this avowal will seem odd to Englishmen of the next
century.—To Englishmen of the present one, a Roman Catholic,
and a lover of priestcraft and tyranny, are two words for the same
thing ; as if we could not murmur at tithes and taxes—insecurity
of property—or arbitrary legislation, just as sourly as any other
Christian community.   No !   I never loved the cause of the Stuarts
—unfortunate, and therefore interesting, as the Stuarts were ; by a
very stupid, and yet uneffaceable confusion of ideas, I confounded
it with the cause of Montreuil, and I hated the latter enough to
dislike the former : I fancy all party principles are formed much in
the same manner.   I frankly told Bolingbroke my disinclination to
the Chevalier. ·

"Between ourselves be it spoken," said he, "there is but little to
induce a wise man, in *your* circumstances, to join James the Third.
I would advise you rather to take advantage of your father's reputation at the French court, and enter into the same service he did.
Things wear a dark face in England for you, and a bright one
everywhere else."

"I have already," said I, "in my own mind, perceived and
weighed the advantages of entering into the service of Louis.   But
he is old—he cannot live long.   People now pay court to parties—
not to the king.   Which party, think you, is the best—that of
Madame de Maintenon ? "   .

"Nay, I think not ; she is a cold friend, and never asks favours
of Louis for any of her family.   A bold game might be played by
attaching yourself to the Duchesse d'Orléans (the Duke's mother).
She is at daggers-drawn with Maintenon, it is true, and she is a
violent, haughty, and coarse woman ; but she has wit, talent,
strength of mind, and will zealously serve any person of high birth,

who pays her respect. But she can do nothing for you till the
king's death, and then only on the chance of her son's power. But
—let me see—you say Fleuri, the bishop of Fréjus, is to introduce
you to Madame de Maintenon?"

"Yes; and has appointed the day after to-morrow for that
purpose."

"Well, then, make close friends with him—you will not find it
difficult; he has a delightful address, and if you get hold of his
weak points, you may win his confidence. Mark me—Fleuri has
no *faux-brillant*, no genius, indeed, of very prominent order; but
he is one of those soft and smooth minds which, in a crisis like the
present, when parties are contending and princes wrangling, always
slip silently and unobtrusively into one of the best places. Keep in
with Fréjus—you cannot do wrong by it—although you must remember that at present he is in ill odour with the King, and you
need not go with *him twice* to Versailles. But, above all, when
you are introduced to Louis, do not forget that you cannot please
him better than by appearing awestricken."

Such was Bolingbroke's parting advice. The Bishop of *Fréjus*
carried me with him (on the morning we had appointed) to Versailles.
What a magnificent work of royal imagination is that palace! I
know not in any epic a grander idea than terming the avenues which
lead to it the roads "*to Spain, to Holland,*" &c. In London, they
would have been the roads to Chelsea and Pentonville!

As we were driving slowly along in the bishop's carriage, I had
ample time for conversation with that personage, who has since, as
the Cardinal de Fleuri, risen to so high a pitch of power. He
certainly has in him very little of the great man; nor do I know
any where so striking an instance of this truth—that in that game of
honours which is played at courts, we obtain success less by our
talents than our tempers. He laughed, with a graceful turn of badinage, at the political peculiarities of Madame de Balzac: and said
that it was not for the uppermost party to feel resentment at the
chafings of the under one. Sliding from this topic, he then questioned
me as to the gaieties I had witnessed. I gave him a description of
the party at Boulainvilliers'. He seemed much interested in this,
and showed more shrewdness than I should have given him credit
for, in discussing the various characters of the *literati* of the day.
After some general conversation on works of fiction, he artfully
glided into treating on those of statistics and politics, and I then
caught a sudden, but thorough, insight into the depths of his policy.
I saw that, while he affected to be indifferent to the difficulties and
puzzles of state, he lost no opportunity of gaining every particle of
information respecting them; and that he made conversation, in

which he was skilled, a vehicle for acquiring that knowledge which he had not the force of mind to create from his own intellect, or to work out from the *written* labours of others. If this made him a superficial s atesman, it made him a prompt one; and there was never so lucky a minister with so little trouble to himself.[1]

As we approached the end of our destination, we talked of the King. On this subject he was jealously cautious. But I gleaned from him, despite of his sagacity, that it was high time to make all use of one's acquaintance with Madame de Maintenon that one could be enabled to do; and that it was so difficult to guess the exact places in which power would rest after the death of the old king, that supineness and silence made at present the most profound policy.

As we alighted from the carriage, and I first set my foot within the palace, I could not but feel involuntarily, yet powerfully impressed, with the sense of the spirit of the place. I was in the precincts of that mighty court which had gathered into one dazzling focus all the rays of genius which half a century had emitted; the court at which time had passed at once from the morn of civilization into its full noon and glory; the court of Condé and Turenne—of Villars and of Tourville; the court where, over the wit of Grammont, the profusion of Fouquet, the fatal genius of Louvois (fatal to humanity and to France), Love, real Love, had not disdained to shed its pathos and its truth, and to consecrate the hollow pageantries of royal pomp, with the tenderness, the beauty, and the repentance of La Vallière. Still over that scene hung the spells of a genius which, if artificial and cold, was also vast, stately, and magnificent—a genius which had swelled in the rich music of Racine—which had raised the nobler spirit and the freer thought of Pierre Corneille,[2] which had given edge to the polished weapon of Boileau—which had lavished over the bright page of Molière—Molière, more wonderful than all —a knowledge of the humours and the hearts of men, which no dramatist, save Shakspeare, has surpassed. Within those walls still glowed, though now waxing faint and dim, the fame of that monarch who had enjoyed, at least, till his later day, the fortune of Augustus, unsullied by the crimes of Octavius. Nine times, since the sun of that monarch rose, had the Papal Chair received a new occupant! Six sovereigns had reigned over the Ottoman hordes! The fourth emperor, since the birth of the same era, bore sway over Germany!

---

[1] At his death appeared the following punning epigram:

> "*Floruit* sine fructu;
> *Defloruit* sine luctu."

He flowered without fruit, and faded without regret.—ED.

[2] Rigidly speaking, Corneille belongs to a period earlier than that of Louis XIV., though he has been included in the æra formed by that-reign.—ED.

Five czars, from Michael Romanoff to the Great Peter, had held, over their enormous territory, the precarious tenure of their iron power! Six kings had borne the painful cincture of the English crown;[1] two of those kings had been fugitives to that court—to the son of the last it was an asylum at that moment.

What wonderful changes had passed over the face of Europe during that single reign! In England only, what a vast leap in the waste of events, from the reign of the first Charles to that of George the First! I still lingered—I still gazed, as these thoughts, linked to one another in an electric chain, flashed over me! I still paused on the threshold of those stately halls which Nature herself had been conquered to rear! Where, through the whole earth, could I find so meet a symbol for the character and the name which that sovereign would leave to posterity, as this palace itself afforded? A gorgeous monument of regal state raised from a desert—crowded alike with empty pageantries and illustrious names—a prodigy of elaborate artifice, grand in its whole effect, petty in its small details; a solitary oblation to a splendid selfishness, and most remarkable for the revenues which it exhausted, and the poverty by which it is surrounded!

Fleuri, with his usual urbanity—an urbanity that, on a great scale, would have been benevolence—had hitherto indulged me in my emotions; he now laid his hand upon my arm, and recalled me to myself. Before I could apologize for my abstraction, the bishop was accosted by an old man of evident rank, but of a countenance more strikingly demonstrative of the little cares of a mere courtier than any I ever beheld. "What news, Monsieur le Marquis?" said Fleuri, smiling.

"Oh! the greatest imaginable! the king talks of receiving the Danish minister on *Thursday*, which, you know, is his day of *domestic* business! What *can* this portend? Besides," and here the speaker's voice lowered into a whisper, "I am told by the Duc de la Rochefoucault that the king intends, out of all ordinary rule and practice, to take physic to-morrow—I can't believe it—no, I positively can't; but don't let this go farther!"

"Heaven forbid!" answered Fleuri, bowing, and the courtier passed on to whisper his intelligence to others.

"Who's that gentleman?" I asked.

"The Marquis de Dangeau," answered Fleuri; a nobleman of great quality, who keeps a diary of all the king says and does. It will perhaps be a posthumous publication, and will show the world of what importance nothings can be made. I dare say, Count, you

---

[1] Besides Cromwell; v*i*z., Charles I., Charles II., James II., William and Mary, Anne, George I.

have already, in England, seen enough of a court to know that there are some people who are as human echoes, and have no existence except in the noise occasioned by another."

I took care that my answer should not be a witticism, lest Fleuri should think I was attempting to rival him; and so we passed on in an excellent humour with each other.

We mounted the grand staircase, and came to an ante-chamber, which, though costly and rich, was not remarkably conspicuous for splendour. Here the Bishop requested me to wait for a moment. Accordingly, I amused myself with looking over some engravings of different saints. Meanwhile, my companion passed through another door, and I was alone.

After an absence of nearly ten minutes, he returned. "Madame de Maintenon," said he in a whisper, "is but poorly to-day. However, she has eagerly consented to see you—follow me!"

So saying, the ecclesiastical courtier passed on, with myself at his heels. We came to the door of a second chamber, at which Fleuri *scraped* gently. We were admitted, and found therein three ladies, one of whom was reading, a second laughing, and a third yawning, and entered into another chamber, where, alone, and seated by the window, in a large chair, with one foot on a stool, in an attitude that rather reminded me of my mother, and which seems to me a favourite position with all devotees, we found an old woman without rouge, plainly dressed, with spectacles on her nose, and a large book on a little table before her. With a most profound salutation, Fréjus approached, and taking me by the hand, said,—

"Will Madame suffer me to present to her the Count Devereux?"

Madame de Maintenon, with an air of great meekness and humility, bowed a return to the salutation. "The son of Madame la Maréchale de Devereux will always be most welcome to me!" Then, turning towards us, she pointed to two stools, and, while we were seating ourselves, said,—

"And how did you leave my excellent friend?"

"When, Madame, I last saw my mother, which is now nearly a year ago, she was in health, and consoling herself for the advance of years by that tendency to wean the thoughts from this world which (in her own language) is the divinest comfort of old age!"

"Admirable woman!" said Madame de Maintenon, casting down her eyes; "such are, indeed, the sentiments in which I recognize the Maréchale. And how does her beauty wear? Those golden locks, and blue eyes, and that snowy skin, are not yet, I suppose, wholly changed for an adequate compensation of the beauties within!"

"Time, Madame, has been gentle with her; and I have often

thought, though never, perhaps, more strongly than at this moment, that there is in those divine studies, which bring calm and light to the mind, something which preserves and embalms, as it were, the beauty of the body."

A faint blush passed over the face of the devotee. No, no—not even at eighty years of age is a compliment to a woman's beauty misplaced! There was a slight pause. I thought that respect forbade me to break it.

"His Majesty," said the bishop, in the tone of one who is sensible that he encroaches a little, and does it with consequent reverence—"his Majesty, I hope, is well."

"God be thanked, yes, as well as we can expect. It is now nearly the hour in which his Majesty awaits your personal inquiries."

Fleuri bowed as he answered—

"The king, then, will receive us to-day? My young companion is very desirous to see the greatest monarch, and, consequently, the greatest man, of the age."

"The desire is natural," said Madame de Maintenon : and then, turning to me, she asked if I had yet seen King James the Third?

I took care, in my answer, to express that even if I had resolved to make that stay in Paris which allowed me to pay my respects to him at all, I should have deemed that both duty and inclination led me, in the first instance, to offer my homage to one who was both the benefactor of my father, and the monarch whose realms afforded me protection.

"You have not, then," said Madame de Maintenon, "decided on the length of your stay in France?"

"No," said I—and my answer was regulated by my desire to see how far I might rely on the services of one who expressed herself so warm a friend of that excellent woman, Madame la Maréchale—"No, Madame. France is the country of my birth, if England is that of my parentage ; and could I hope for some portion of that royal favour which my father enjoyed, I would rather claim it as the home of my hopes than the refuge of my exile. But "—and I stopped short purposely.

The old lady looked at me very earnestly through her spectacles for one moment, and then, hemming twice with a little embarrassment, again remarked to the bishop, that the time for seeing the king was nearly arrived. Fleuri, whose policy at that period was very like that of the concealed queen, and who was, besides, far from desirous of introducing any new claimants on Madame de Maintenon's official favour, though he might not object to introduce them to her private friend, was not slow in taking the hint. He rose, and I was forced to follow his example.

Madame de Maintenon thought she might safely indulge in a little cordiality when I was just on the point of leaving her, and accordingly blessed me, and gave me her hand, which I kissed very devoutly. An extremely pretty hand it was, too, notwithstanding the good queen's age. We then retired, and, repassing the three ladies, who were now all yawning, repaired to the king's apartments.

" What think you of Madame ? " asked Fleuri.

" What can I think of her," said I, cautiously, " but that greatness seems in her to take its noblest form—that of simplicity ? "

" True," rejoined Fleuri, " never was there so meek a mind joined to so lowly a carriage ! Do you remark any trace of former beauty ? "

" Yes, indeed, there is much that is soft in her countenance, and much that is still regular in her features ; but what struck me most was the pensive and even sad tranquillity that rests upon her face when she is silent."

" The expression betrays the mind," answered Fleuri ; " and the curse of the great is *ennui*."

" Of the great in station," said I, " but not necessarily of the great in mind. I have heard that the Bishop of Fréjus, notwithstanding his rank and celebrity, employs every hour to the advantage of others, and consequently without tedium to himself."

" Aha ! " said Fleuri, smiling gently, and patting my cheek : " see, now, if the air of palaces is not absolutely prolific of pretty speeches." And, before I could answer, we were in the apartments of the king.

Leaving me awhile to cool my heels in a gallery, filled with the butterflies who bask in the royal sunshine, Fréjus then disappeared among the crowd ; he was scarcely gone when I was agreeably surprised by seeing Count Hamilton approach towards me.

" *Mort diable!* " said he, shaking me by the hand, *à l'Anglaise ;* " I am really delighted to see any one here who does not insult my sins with his superior excellence. Eh, now, look round this apartment for a moment ! Whether would you believe yourself at the court of a great king, or the levee of a Roman cardinal ! Whom see you chiefly? Gallant soldiers, with worn brows and glittering weeds ; wise statesmen, with ruin to Austria and defiance to Rome in every wrinkle ; gay nobles in costly robes, and with the bearing that so nicely teaches mirth to be dignified and dignity to be merry? No ! cassock and hat, rosary and gown, decking sly, demure, hypocritical faces, flit, and stalk, and sadden round us. It seems to me," continned the witty Count, in a lower whisper, " as if the old king, having fairly buried his glory at Ramilies and Blenheim, had summoned all these good gentry to sing psalms over it ! But you are waiting for a private audience ? "

" Yes, under the auspices of the bishop of Fréjus."

"You might have chosen a better guide—the king has been too much teased about him," rejoined Hamilton, "and now, that we are talking of him, I will show you a singular instance of what good manners can do at court, in preference to good abilities. You observe yon quiet, modest-looking man, with a sensible countenance, and a clerical garb; you observe how he edges away when any one approaches to accost him; and how, from his extreme dis-esteem of himself, he seems to inspire every one with the same sentiment. Well, that man is a namesake of Fleuri's, the Prior of *Argenteuil;* he has come here, I suppose, for some particular and temporary purpose, since, in reality, he has left the court. Well, that worthy priest—do remark his bow; did you ever see anything so awkward? —is one of the most learned divines that the church can boast of; he is as immeasurably superior to the smooth-faced Bishop of Fréjus as Louis the Fourteenth is to my old friend Charles the Second. He has had equal opportunities with the said bishop; been preceptor to the princes of Conti, and the Count de Vermandois; and yet, I will wager that he lives and dies a tutor—a book-worm—and a prior; while t'other Fleuri, without a particle of merit, but of the most superficial order, governs already kings through their mistresses, kingdoms through the kings, and may, for aught I know, expand into a prime minister, and ripen into a cardinal."

"Nay," said I, smiling, "there is little chance of so exalted a lot for the worthy bishop."

"Pardon me," interrupted Hamilton, "I am an old courtier, and look steadily on the game I no longer play. Suppleness, united with art, may do any thing in a court like this; and the smooth and un-elevated craft of a Fleuri may win even to the same height as the deep wiles of the glittering Mazarin, or the superb genius of the imperious Richelieu."

"Hist!" said I, "the bishop has re-appeared. Who is that old priest, with a fine countenance and an address that will, at least, please you better than that of the Prior of *Argenteuil,* who has just stopped our episcopal courtier?"

"What! do you not know? It is the most celebrated preacher of the day—the great Massillon. It is said that that handsome person goes a great way towards winning converts among the court ladies; it is certain, at least, that when Massillon first entered the profession, he was to the soul something like the spear of Achilles to the body; and though very efficacious in healing the wounds of conscience, was equally ready, in the first instance, to inflict them."

"Ah," said I, "see the malice of wit; and see, above all, how much more ready one is to mention a man's frailties than to enlarge upon his virtues."

"To be sure," answered Hamilton, coolly, and patting his snuff-box—"to be sure, we old people like history better than fiction; and frailty is certain, while virtue is always doubtful."

"Don't judge of all people," said I, "by your experience among the courtiers of Charles the Second."

"Right," said Hamilton. "Providence never assembled so many rascals together before, without hanging them. And he would indeed be a bad judge of human nature who estimated the characters of men in general by the heroes of Newgate and the victims of Tyburn. But your bishop approaches. Adieu!"

"What!" said Fleuri, joining me and saluting Hamilton, who had just turned to depart, "what, Count Antoine! Does anything but whim bring you here to-day?"

"No," answered Hamilton; "I am only here for the same purpose as the poor go to the temples of Caitan—to *inhale the steam of those good things which I see the priests devour.*"

"Ha! ha! ha!" laughed the good-natured bishop, not in the least disconcerted; and Count Hamilton, congratulating himself on his *bon mot*, turned away.

"I have spoken to his Most Christian Majesty," said the bishop: "he is willing, as he before ordained, to admit you to his presence. The Duc de Maine is with the king, as also some other members of the royal family; but you will consider this a private audience."

I expressed my gratitude—we moved on—the doors of an apartment were thrown open—and I saw myself in the presence of Louis XIV.

The room was partially darkened. In the centre of it, on a large sofa, reclined the king; he was dressed (though this, if I may so speak, I rather remembered than noted) in a coat of black velvet, slightly embroidered; his vest was of white satin; he wore no jewels nor orders, for it was only on grand or gala days that he displayed personal pomp. At some little distance from him stood three members of the royal family—them I never regarded—all my attention was bent upon the king. My temperament is not that on which greatness, or indeed any external circumstances, make much impression, but, as following, at a little distance, the Bishop of Fréjus, I approached the royal person, I must confess that Bolingbroke had scarcely need to have cautioned me not to appear too self-possessed. Perhaps, had I seen that great monarch in his *beaux jours*—in the plenitude of his power—his glory—the dazzling and meridian splendour of his person—his court—and his renown, pride might have made me more on my guard against too deep, or at least, too apparent, an impression; but the many reverses of that magnificent sovereign—reverses in which he had shown himself more great than in all his previous triumphs and early successes ; his age—his infirmities—the very clouds round the setting sun—the very howls of joy at the expiring lion—all were calculated, in my mind, to deepen respect into reverence, and tincture reverence itself with awe. I saw before me not only the majesty of Louis-le-Grand, but that of misfortune, of weakness, of infirmity, and of age ; and I forgot at once, in that reflection, what otherwise would have blunted my sentiments of deference, viz. the crimes of his ministers, and the exactions of his reign ! Endeavouring to collect my mind from an embarrassment which surprised myself, I lifted my eyes towards the king, and saw a countenance where the trace of the superb beauty, for which his manhood had been celebrated, still lingered, broken, not destroyed, and borrowing a dignity even more imposing from the marks of encroaching years, and from the evident exhaustion of suffering and disease.

Fleuri said, in a low tone, something which my ear did not catch. There was a pause—only a moment's pause ; and then, in a voice, the music of which I had hitherto deemed exaggerated, the king spoke ; and in that voice there was something so kind and encouraging, that I felt reassured at once. Perhaps its tone was not the less conciliating from the evident effect which the royal presence had produced upon me.

"You have given us, Count Devereux," said the king, "a pleasure which we are glad, in person, to acknowledge to you. And it has seemed to us fitting that the country in which your brave father acquired his fame should also be the asylum of his son."

"Sire," answered I, "Sire, it shall not be my fault if that country is not henceforth my own ; and, in inheriting my father's name, I inherit also his gratitude and his ambition."

"It is well said, sir," said the king ; and I once more raised my eyes, and perceived that his were bent upon me. "It is well said," he repeated, after a short pause ; "and in granting to you this audience, we were not unwilling to hope that you were desirous to attach yourself to our court. The times do not require" (here I thought the old king's voice was not quite so firm as before) "the manifestation of your zeal in the same career as that in which your father gained laurels to France and to himself. But we will not neglect to find employment for your abilities, if not for your sword."

"That sword which was given to me, Sire," said I, "by your Majesty, shall be ever drawn (against all nations but one) at your command ; and, in being your Majesty's petitioner for future favours, I only seek some channel through which to evince my gratitude for the past."

"We do not doubt," said Louis, "that whatever be the number

of the ungrateful we may make by testifying our good pleasure on your behalf, *you* will not be among the number." The king here made a slight, but courteous inclination, and turned round. The observant Bishop of Fréjus, who had retired to a little distance, and who knew that the king never liked talking more than he could help it, gave me a signal. I obeyed, and backed, with all due deference, out of the royal presence.

So closed my interview with Louis XIV. Although his Majesty did not indulge in prolixity, I spoke of him for a long time afterwards as the most eloquent of men. Believe me, there is no orator like a king; one word from a royal mouth stirs the heart more than Demosthenes could have done. There was a deep moral in that custom of the ancients, by which the Goddess of Persuasion was always represented *with a diadem on her head.*

CHAPTER VII.

REFLECTIONS—A SOIRÉE—THE APPEARANCE OF ONE IMPORTANT IN THE HISTORY—A CONVERSATION WITH MADAME DE BALZAC HIGHLY SATISFACTORY AND CHEERING—A REN-CONTRE WITH A CURIOUS OLD SOLDIER—THE EXTINCTION OF A ONCE GREAT LUMINARY.

 HAD now been several weeks at Paris; I had neither eagerly sought, nor sedulously avoided, its gaieties. It is not that one violent sorrow leaves us without power of enjoyment—it only lessens the power, and deadens the enjoyment; it does not take away from us the objects of life— it only forestalls the more indifferent calmness of age. The blood no longer flows in an irregular, but delicious, course of vivid and wild emotion; the step no longer spurns the earth; nor does the ambition wander, insatiable, yet undefined, over the million paths of existence; but we lose not our old capacities—they are quieted, not extinct. The heart can never utterly and long be dormant; trifles may not charm it any more, nor levities delight; but its pulse has not yet ceased to beat. We survey the scene that moves around, with a gaze no longer distracted by every hope that flutters by; and it is therefore that we find ourselves more calculated than before for the graver occupations of our race. The overflowing tem-perament is checked to its proper level, the ambition bounded to its prudent and lawful goal. The earth is no longer so green, nor the heaven so blue, nor the fancy that stirs within us so rich in its creations; but we look more narrowly on the living crowd, and more rationally on the aims of men. The misfortune which has changed us, has only adapted us the better to a climate in which misfortune is a portion of the air. The grief, that has thralled our spirit to a more narrow and dark cell, has also been a chain that has linked us to mankind with a strength of which we dreamt not in the day of a wilder freedom and more luxuriant aspirings. In later life, a new spirit, partaking of that which was our earliest, returns to us. The solitude which delighted us in youth, but which, when the thoughts that make solitude a fairy land are darkened by affliction, becomes a fearful and sombre void, resumes its old spell, as the more morbid and urgent memory of that affliction crumbles away by time. Content is a hermit; but so also is Apathy. Youth loves the solitary couch, which it surrounds with dreams. Age, or Experience (which is the mind's age) loves the same couch for the rest which it affords; but the wide interval between is that of exertion, of labour, and of labour among men. The woe which makes our *hearts* less social, often makes our *habits* more so. The thoughts, which in calm would have shunned the world, are driven upon it by the tempest, even as the birds which forsake the habitable land can, so long as the wind sleeps, and the thunder rests within its cloud, become the constant and solitary brooders over the waste sea; but the moment the storm awakes, and the blast pursues them, they fly, by an overpowering instinct, to some wandering bark, some vestige of human and social life: and exchange, even for danger from the hands of men, the desert of an angry Heaven, and the solitude of a storm.

I heard no more, either of Madame de Maintenon or the king. Meanwhile, my flight and friendship with Lord Bolingbroke had given me a consequence in the eyes of the exiled prince, which I should not otherwise have enjoyed; and I was honoured by very flattering overtures to enter actively into his service. I have before said that I felt no enthusiasm in his cause, and I was far from feeling it for his person. My ambition rather directed its hopes towards a career in the service of France. France was the country of my birth, and the country of my father's fame. There no withering remembrances awaited me—no private regrets were associated with its scenes—and no public penalties with its political institutions. And, although I had not yet received any token of Louis's remembrance, in the ordinary routine of court favours, expectation as yet would have been premature; besides, his royal fidelity to his word was proverbial; and, sooner or later, I indulged the hope to profit by the sort of promise he had insinuated to me. I declined, therefore, with all due respect, the offers of the Chevalier, and continued to live the life of idleness and expectation, until Lord Bolingbroke returned to Paris, and accepted the office of secretary of state in the service of the Chevalier. As he has publicly declared his reasons, in this step, I do not mean to favour the world with his private conversations on the same subject.

A day or two after his return, I went with him to a party given by a member of the royal family. The first person by whom we were accosted—and I rejoiced at it, for we could not have been accosted by a more amusing one—was Count Anthony Hamilton.

"Ah! my Lord Bolingbroke," said he, sauntering up to us; "how are you?—delighted to see you again. Do look at Madame la Duchesse d'Orléans! Saw you ever such a creature? Whither are you moving, my lord? Ah! see him, Count, see him, gliding off to that pretty duchess, of course; well, he has a beautiful bow, it must be owned—why, you are not going too?—what would the world say if Count Anthony Hamilton were seen left to himself? No, no, come and sit down by Madame de Cornuel—she longs to be introduced to you, and is one of the wittiest women in Europe.".

"With all my heart! provided she employs her wit ill-naturedly, and uses it in ridiculing other people, not praising herself."

"Oh! nobody can be more satirical; indeed, what difference is there between wit and satire? Come, Count!"

And Hamilton introduced me forthwith to Madame de Cornuel. She received me very politely; and, turning to two or three people who formed the circle round her, said, with the greatest composure, "Messieurs, oblige me by seeking some other object of attraction; I wish to have a private conference with my new friend."

"I may stay," said Hamilton.

"Ah! certainly; you are never in the way."

"In that respect, *Madame*," said Hamilton, taking snuff, and bowing very low, "in that respect I must strongly remind you of your excellent husband."

"Fie!" cried Madame de Cornuel; then, turning to me, she said, "Ah! Monsieur, if you *could* have come to Paris some years ago, you would have been enchanted with us—we are sadly changed. Imagine the fine old king, thinking it wicked, not to hear plays, but to hear *players* act them, and so making the royal family a company of comedians. *Mon Dieu!* how villainously they perform! but do you know why I wished to be introduced to you?"

"Yes! in order to have a new listener; old listeners must be almost as tedious as old news."

"Very shrewdly said, and not far from the truth. The fact is, that I wanted to talk about all these fine people present, to some one for whose ear my anecdotes would have the charm of novelty.

Let us begin with Louis Armand, Prince of Conti — you see him."

"What, that short-sighted, stout, and rather handsome man, with a cast of countenance somewhat like the pictures of *Henri Quatre*, who is laughing so merrily?"

"*O Ciel!* how droll! No, that handsome man is no less a person than the *Duc d'Orléans*. You see a little ugly thing, like an anatomized ape — there, see — he has just thrown down a chair, and, in stooping to pick it up, has almost fallen over the Dutch ambassadress—that is, Louis Armand, Prince of Conti. Do you know what the Duc d'Orléans said to him the other day? '*Mon bon ami*,' he said, pointing to the prince's limbs—(did you ever see such limbs out of a menagerie, by the bye?)—'*Mon bon ami*, it is a fine thing for you that the Psalmist has assured us "that the Lord delighteth not in any man's legs."' Nay, don't laugh, it is quite true!"

It was now for Count Hamilton to take up the ball of satire; he was not a whit more merciful than the kind Madame de Cornuel. "The Prince," said he, "has so exquisite an awkwardness, that, whenever the king hears a noise, and inquires the cause, the invariable answer is, that 'the Prince of Conti has just tumbled down!' But, tell me, what do you think of Madame d'Aumont? She is in the English head-dress, and looks *triste à la mort.*"

"She is rather pretty, to my taste."

"Yes," cried Madame de Cornuel, interrupting the gentle Antoine —(it did one's heart good to see how strenuously each of them tried to talk more scandal than the other), "yes, she is thought very pretty; but I think her very like a *fricandeau*—white, soft, and insipid. She is always in tears," added the good-natured Cornuel, "after her prayers, both at morning and evening. I asked why; and she answered, pretty simpleton, that she was always forced to pray to be made good, and she feared Heaven would take her at her word! However, she has many worshippers, and they call her the evening star."

"They should rather call her the Hyades!" said Hamilton, "if it be true that she sheds her tears every morning and night, and her rising and setting are thus always attended by rain."

"Bravo, Count Antoine! she shall be so called in future," said Madame de Cornuel. "But now, Monsieur Devereux, turn your eyes to that hideous old woman."

"What! the Duchesse d'Orléans?"

"The same. She is in full dress to-night; but in the day-time you generally see her in a riding habit and a man's wig; she is—"

"Hist!" interrupted Hamilton; "do you not tremble to think

I 2

what she would do if she overheard you? she is such a terrible creature at fighting! You have no conception, Count, what an arm she has. She knows her ugliness, and laughs at it, as all the rest of the world does. The king took her hand one day, and said, smiling, 'What could Nature have meant when she gave this hand to a German princess instead of a Dutch peasant?' 'Sire,' said the Duchesse, very gravely, 'Nature gave this hand to a German princess for the purpose of boxing the ears of her ladies in waiting!'"

"Ha! ha! ha!" said Madame de Cornuel, laughing; "one is never at a loss for jokes upon a woman who eats *salade au lard*, and declares that, whenever she is unhappy, her only consolation is ham and sausages! Her son treats her with the greatest respect, and consults her in all his amours, for which she professes the greatest horror, and which she retails to her correspondents all over the world, in letters as long as her pedigree. But you are looking *at* her son, is he not of a good mien?"

"Yes, pretty well; but does not exhibit to advantage by the side of Lord Bolingbroke, with whom he is now talking. Pray, who is the third personage that has just joined them?"

"Oh, the wretch! it is the Abbé Dubois; a living proof of the folly of the French proverb, which says that Mercuries should *not* be made *du bois*. Never was there a Mercury equal to the Abbé,— but, do look at that old man to the left—he is one of the most remarkable persons of the age."

"What! he with the small features, and comely countenance, considering his years?"

"The same," said Hamilton; "it is the notorious Choisi. You know that he is the modern Tiresias, and has been a woman as well as man."

"How do you mean?"

"Ah, you may well ask!" cried Madame de Cornuel. "Why, he lived for many years in the disguise of a woman, and had all sorts of curious adventures."

"*Mort Diable!*" cried Hamilton; "it was entering your ranks, Madame, as a spy. I hear he makes but a sorry report of what he saw there."

"Come, Count Antoine," cried the lively de Cornuel, "we must not turn our weapons against each other; and when you attack a woman's sex, you attack her individually. But what makes you look so intently, Count Devereux, at that ugly priest?"

The person thus flatteringly designated was Montreuil; he had just caught my eye, among a group of men who were conversing eagerly.

"Hush! Madame," said I, "spare me for a moment;" and I rose, and mingled with the Abbé's companions. "So, you have only arrived to-day," I heard one of them say to him.

"No, I could not dispatch my business before."

"And how are matters in England?"

"Ripe!—if the life of his Majesty (of France) be spared a year longer, we will send the Elector of Hanover back to his principality."

"Hist!" said the companion, and looked towards me. Montreuil ceased abruptly—our eyes met—his fell. I affected to look among the group as if I had expected to find there some one I knew, and then, turning away, I seated myself alone and apart. There, unobserved, I kept my looks on Montreuil. I remarked that, from time to time, his keen dark eye glanced towards me, with a look rather expressive of vigilance than anything else. Soon afterwards his little knot dispersed; I saw him converse for a few moments with Dubois, who received him, I thought distantly; and then he was engaged in a long conference with the Bishop of Fréjus, whom, till then, I had not perceived among the crowd.

As I was loitering on the staircase, where I saw Montreuil depart with the bishop, in the carriage of the latter, Hamilton, accosting me, insisted on my accompanying him to Chaulieu's, where a late supper awaited the sons of wine and wit. However, to the good Count's great astonishment, I preferred solitude and reflection, for that night, to anything else.

Montreuil's visit to the French capital boded me no good. He possessed great influence with Fleuii, and was in high esteem with Madame de Maintenon, and, in effect, very shortly after his return to Paris, the Bishop of Fréjus looked upon me with a most cool sort of benignancy; and Madame de Maintenon told her friend, the Duchesse de St. Simon, that it was a great pity a young nobleman of my birth and prepossessing appearance—(ay! my prepossessing appearance would never have occurred to the devotee, if I had not seemed so sensible of her own)—should not only be addicted to the wildest dissipation, but, worse still, to Jansenistical tenets. After this, there was no hope for me, save in the king's word, which his increasing infirmities naturally engrossing his attention, prevented my hoping too sanguinely, would dwell very acutely on his remembrance. I believe, however, so religiously scrupulous was Louis upon a point of honour, that, had he lived, I should have had nothing to complain of. As it was—but I anticipate!—Montreuil disappeared fiom Paris, almost as suddenly as he had appeared there. And, as drowning men catch at a straw, so, finding my affairs at a very low ebb, I thought I would take advice, even from Madame de Balzac.

I accordingly repaired to her hotel. She was at home, and, fortunately, alone.

"You are welcome, *mon fils*," said she : "suffer me to give you that title—you are welcome—it is some days since I saw you." 1

"I have numbered them I assure you, Madame," said I, "and they have crept with a dull pace ; but you know that business has claims as well as pleasure ! "

"True ! " said Madame de Balzac, pompously : "I myself find the weight of politics a little insupportable, though so used to it ; to your young brain I can readily imagine how irksome it must be ! "

"Would, Madame, that I could obtain your experience by contagion ; as it is I fear that I have profited little by my visit to his Majesty. Madame de Maintenon will not see me, and the Bishop of Fréjus (excellent man !) has been seized with a sudden paralysis of memory, whenever I present myself in his way."

"That party will never do—I thought not," said Madame de Balzac, who was a wonderful imitator of the fly on the wheel ; "*my* celebrity, and the knowledge that *I* loved you for your father's sake, were, I fear, sufficient to destroy your interest with the Jesuits and their tools. Well, well, we must repair the mischief we have occasioned you. What place would suit you best ? "

"Why, anything diplomatic. I would rather travel, at my age, than remain in luxury and indolence even at Paris ! "

"Ah, nothing like diplomacy ! " said Madame de Balzac, with the air of a Richelieu, and emptying her snuff-box at a pinch ; "but have you, my son, the requisite qualities for that science, as well as the tastes ? Are you capable of intrigue ? Can you say one thing and mean another ? Are you aware of the immense consequence of a look or a bow ? Can you live like a spider, in the centre of an inexplicable net—inexplicable as well as dangerous—to all but the weaver ? That, my son, is the art of politics—that is to be a diplomatist ! "

"Perhaps, to one less penetrating than Madame de Balzac," answered I, "I might, upon trial, not appear utterly ignorant of the noble art of state duplicity which she has so eloquently depicted."

"Possibly ! " said the good lady ; "it must indeed be a profound dissimulator to deceive *me*."

"But what would you advise me to do in the present crisis ? What party to adopt—what individual to flatter ? "

Nothing, I already discovered, and have already observed, did the inestimable Madame de Balzac dislike more than a downright question—she never answered it.

" Why, really," said she, preparing herself for a long speech, " I am quite glad you consult me, and I will give you the best advice in my power. *Ecoutez donc*—you have seen the Duc de Maine?"

"Certainly!"

"Hum! ha! it would be wise to follow him; but—you take me —you understand.—Then, you know, my son, there is the Duc d'Orléans—fond of pleasure—full of talent—but you know—there is a little—what do you call it—you understand. As for the Duc de Bourbon, 'tis quite a simpleton—nevertheless we must consider— nothing like consideration—believe me, no diplomatist ever hurries. As for Madame de Maintenon—you know, and I know too, that the Duchesse d'Orléans calls her an old hag—but then—a word to the wise—Eh?—what shall we say to Madame the Duchess herself?— what a fat woman she is—but excessively clever—such a letter writer!—Well—you see, my dear young friend, that it is a very difficult matter to decide upon—but you must already be fully aware what plan I should advise."

"Already, Madame!"

"To be sure! What have I been saying to you all this time?— did you not hear me?—Shall I repeat my advice?"

"Oh, no! I perfectly comprehend you now; you would advise me—in short—to—to—do—as well as I can."

"You have said it, my son. I thought you would understand me on a little reflection."

"To be sure—to be sure," said I.

And three ladies being announced, my conference with Madame de Balzac ended.

I now resolved to wait a little till the tides of power seemed some- what more settled, and I could ascertain in what quarter to point my bark of enterprise. I gave myself rather more eagerly to society, in proportion as my political schemes were suffered to remain torpid. My mind could not remain quiet, without preying on itself; and no evil appeared to me so great as tranquillity. Thus the spring and earlier summer passed on, till, in August, the riots preceding the Rebellion broke out in Scotland. At this time I saw but little of Lord Bolingbroke in private; though, with his characteristic affect- ation, he took care that the load of business, with which he was really oppressed, should not prevent his enjoyment of all gaieties in public. And my indifference to the cause of the Chevalier, in which he was so warmly engaged, threw a natural restraint upon our con- versation, and produced an involuntary coldness in our intercourse— so impossible is it for men to be private friends who differ on a public matter.

One evening I was engaged to meet a large party, at a country-house, about forty miles from Paris. I went, and stayed some days. My horses had accompanied me; and, when I left the château, I resolved to make the journey to Paris on horseback. Accordingly, I ordered my carriage to follow me, and attended by a single groom, commenced my expedition. It was a beautiful still morning—the first day of the first month of autumn. I had proceeded about ten miles, when I fell in with an old French officer. I remember—though I never saw him but that once—I remember his face as if I had encountered it yesterday. It was thin and long, and yellow enough to have served as a caricature, rather than a portrait of Don Quixote. He had a hook nose, and a long sharp chin; and all the lines, wrinkles, curves and furrows, of which the human visage is capable, seemed to have met in his cheeks. Nevertheless, his eye was bright and keen—his look alert—and his whole bearing firm, gallant, and soldier-like. He was attired in a sort of military undress—wore a moustachio, which, though thin and gray, was carefully curled; and at the summit of a very respectable wig was perched a small cocked hat, adorned with a black feather. He rode very upright in his saddle; and his horse, a steady, stalwart quadruped of the Norman breed, with a terribly long tail, and a prodigious breadth of chest, put one stately leg before another in a kind of trot, which, though it seemed, from its height of action, and the proud look of the steed, a pretension to motion more than ordinarily brisk, was, in fact, a little slower than a common walk.

This noble cavalier seemed sufficiently an object of curiosity to my horse to induce the animal to testify his surprise by shying, very jealously and very vehemently, in passing him. This ill-breeding on his part was indignantly returned on the part of the Norman charger, who, uttering a sort of squeak, and shaking his long mane and head, commenced a series of curvets and capers which cost the old Frenchman no little trouble to appease. In the midst of these equine freaks, the horse came so near me as to splash my nether garment, with a liberality as little ornamental as it was pleasurable.

The old Frenchman seeing this, took off his cocked hat very politely, and apologized for the accident. I replied with equal courtesy; and, as our horses slid into quiet, their riders slid into conversation. It was begun and chiefly sustained by my new comrade; for I am little addicted to commence unnecessary socialities myself, though I should think very meanly of my pretensions to the name of a gentleman and a courtier, if I did not return them when offered, even by a beggar.

"It is a fine horse of yours, Monsieur," said the old Frenchman; "but I cannot believe—pardon me for saying so—that your slight

English steeds are so well adapted to the purposes of war as our strong chargers—such as mine for example."

"It is very possible, Monsieur," said I. "Has the horse you now ride done service in the field as well as on the road?"

"Ah! *le pauvre petit mignon*—no!"—(*petit*, indeed—this little darling was seventeen hands high at the very least)—"no, Monsieur; it is but a young creature this—his grandfather served me well!"

"I need not ask you, Monsieur, if you have borne arms—the soldier is stamped upon you!"

"Sir, you flatter me highly!" said the old gentleman, blushing to the very tip of his long lean ears, and bowing as low as if I had called him a *Condé;* "I have followed the profession of arms for more than fifty years."

"Fifty years—'tis a long time!"

"A long time," rejoined my companion, "a long time to look back upon with regret."

"Regret! by Heaven—I should think the remembrance of fifty years' excitement and glory would be a remembrance of triumph."

The old man turned round on his saddle, and looked at me for some moments very wistfully—"You are young, sir," he said, "and at your years I should have thought with you—out —" (then abruptly changing his voice, he continued)—"Triumph, did you say? sir, I have had three sons; they are dead—they died in battle—I did not weep—I did not shed a tear, sir—not a tear! But I will tell you when I did weep. I came back, an old man, to the home I had left as a young one. I saw the country a desert. I saw that the noblesse had become tyrants—the peasants had become slaves—such slaves— savage from despair—even when they were most gay, most fearfully gay, from constitution. Sir, I saw the priest rack and grind, and the seigneur exact and pillage, and the tax-gatherer squeeze out the little the other oppressors had left :—anger, discontent, wretchedness, famine, a terrible separation between one order of people and another—an incredible indifference to the miseries their despotism caused, on the part of the aristocracy—a sullen and vindictive hatred for the perpetration of those miseries on the part of the people—all places sold—even all honours priced, at the court, which was become a public market—a province of peasants—of living men bartered for a few livres, and literally passed from one hand to another—to be squeezed and drained anew by each new possessor— in a word, sir, an abandoned court, an unredeemed noblesse—un-redeemed, sir, by a single benefit which, in other countries, even the most feudal, the vassal obtains from the master—a peasantry famished —a nation loaded with debt, which it sought to pay by tears ;—these are what I saw—these are the consequences of that heartless and miserable vanity, from which arose wars neither useful nor honour-able—these are the real components of that *triumph*, as you term it, which you wonder that I regret."

Now, although it was impossible to live at the court of Louis XIV. in his latter days, and not feel, from the general discontent that prevailed even *there*, what a dark truth the old soldier's speech contained—yet I was somewhat surprised by an enthusiasm so little military in a person whose bearing and air were so conspicuously martial.

"You draw a melancholy picture," said I; "and the wretched state of culture which the lands that we now pass through exhibit, is a witness how little exaggeration there is in your colouring. However, these are but the ordinary evils of war, and, if your country endures them, do not forget that she has also inflicted them. Remember what France did to Holland, and own that it is but a retribution that France should now find that the injury we do to others is (among nations as well as individuals) injury to ourselves."

My old Frenchman curled his moustaches with the finger and thumb of his left hand : this was rather too subtle a distinction for him.

"That may be true enough, Monsieur," said he; "but *morbleu*, those *maudits* Dutchmen deserved what they sustained at our hands. No, sir, no—I am not so base as to forget the glory my country acquired, though I weep for her wounds."

"I do not quite understand you, sir," said I; "did you not just now confess that the wars you had witnessed were neither honourable nor useful? What glory, then, was to be acquired in a war of that character, even though it was so delightfully animated by cutting the throats of 'those *maudits* Dutchmen?'"

"Sir," answered the Frenchman, drawing himself up, "you did *not* understand me. When we punished Holland, we did rightly. *We conquered!*"

"Whether you conquered, or not (for the good folk of Holland are not so sure of the fact)," answered I, "that war was the most unjust in which your king was ever engaged; but pray, tell me, sir, what war it is that you lament?"

The Frenchman frowned—whistled—put out his under lip, in a sort of angry embarrassment—and then, spurring his great horse into a curvet, said,

"That last war with the English!"

"Faith," said I, "that was the justest of all."

"Just!" cried the Frenchman, halting abruptly, and darting at me a glance of fire, "just! no more, sir! no more! I was at Blenheim, and at Ramillies!"

As the old warrior said the last words, his voice faltered; and though I could not help inly smiling at the confusion of ideas, by which wars were just or unjust, according as they were fortunate or not, yet I respected his feelings enough to turn away my face, and remain silent.

"Yes," renewed my comrade, colouring with evident shame, and drawing his cocked hat over his brows, "yes, I received my last wound at Ramillies. *Then* my eyes were opened to the horrors of war; *then* I saw and cursed the evils of ambition; *then* I resolved to retire from the armies of a king who had lost for ever his name, his glory, and his country."

Was there ever a better type of the French nation than this old soldier? As long as fortune smiles on them, it is "*Marchons au diable!*" and "*Vive la gloire!*" Directly they get beat, it is "*Ma pauvre patrie?*" and "*Les calamités affreuses de la guerre!*"

"However," said I, "the old king is drawing near the end of his days, and is said to express his repentance at the evils his ambition has occasioned."

The old soldier shoved back his hat, and offered me his snuff-box. I judged by this that he was a little mollified.

"Ah!" he renewed, after a pause, "Ah! times are sadly changed, since the year 1667; when the young king—he was young then—took the field in Flanders, under the great Turenne. *Sacristie!* What a hero he looked upon his white war-horse! I would have gone—ay, and the meanest and backwardest soldier in the camp would have gone—into the very mouth of the cannon, for a look from that magnificent countenance, or a word from that mouth which knew so well what words were! Sir, there was in the war of '72, when we were at peace with Great Britain, an English gentleman, then in the army, afterwards a marshal of France: I remember, as if it were yesterday, how gallantly he behaved. The king sent to compliment him after some signal proof of courage and conduct, and asked what reward he would have. 'Sire,' answered the Englishman, 'give me the white plume you wore this day.' From that moment the Englishman's fortune was made."

"The flattery went farther than the valour!" said I, smiling, as I recognized in the anecdote the first great step which my father had made in the ascent of fortune.

"*Sacristie!*" cried the Frenchman, "it was no flattery then. We so idolized the king, that mere truth would have seemed disloyalty; and we no more thought that praise, however extravagant, was adulation, when directed to him, than we should have thought there was adulation in the praise we would have given to our first mistress. But it is all changed now! Who now cares for the old priest-ridden monarch?"

And upon this the veteran, having conquered the momentary enthusiasm which the remembrance of the king's earlier glories had excited, transferred all his genius of description to the opposite side of the question, and declaimed, with great energy, upon the royal vices and errors, which were so charming in prosperity, and were now so detestable in adversity.

While we were thus conversing we approached Versailles. We thought the vicinity of the town seemed unusually deserted. We entered the main street—crowds were assembled—a universal murmur was heard—excitement sat on every countenance. Here an old crone was endeavouring to explain something, evidently beyond his comprehension, to a child of three years old ; who with open mouth and fixed eyes, seemed to make up in wonder for the want of intelligence ; there a group of old disbanded soldiers occupied the way, and seemed, from their muttered conversations, to vent a sneer and a jest at a priest, who with downward countenance and melancholy air, was hurrying along.

One young fellow was calling out—"At least, it is a holyday, and I shall go to Paris !"—and, as a contrast to him, an old withered artisan, leaning on a gold-headed cane, with sharp avarice eloquent in every line of his face, muttered out to a fellow-miser—"no business to-day—no money, John—no money !" One knot of women, of all ages, close by which my horse passed, was entirely occupied with a single topic, and that so vehemently, that I heard the leading words of the discussion. "Mourning—becoming—what fashion ?— how long ?—O ciel !" Thus do follies weave themselves round the bier of death !

"What is the news, gentlemen ?" said I.

"News—what, you have not heard it ?—the king is dead !"

"Louis dead—Louis the Great, dead !" cried my companion.

"Louis the Great ?" said a sullen-looking man—"Louis the persecutor !"

"Ah, he's a Huguenot !" cried another with haggard cheeks and hollow eyes, scowling at the last speaker. "Never mind what he says—the king was right when he refused protection to the Heretics—but was he right when he levied such taxes on the Catholics ?"

"Hush !" said a third—"hush—it may be unsafe to speak—there are spies about ; for my part, I think it was all the fault of the Noblesse."

"And the Favourites !" cried a soldier, fiercely.

"And the Harlots !" cried a hag of eighty.

"And the Priests !" muttered the Huguenot.

"And the Tax-gatherers !" added the lean Catholic.

We rode slowly on. My comrade was evidently and poweifully affected.

"So, he is dead!" said he.   "Dead!—well—well—peace be with him. He conquered in Holland—he humbled Genoa—he dictated to Spain—he commanded Condé and Turenne—he—Bah! What is all this" (then, turning abruptly to me, my companion cried)—"I did not speak against the king, did I, sir?"

"Not much."

"I am glad of that—yes, very glad!" And the old man glared fiercely round on a troop of boys, who were audibly abusing the dead lion.

"I would have bit out my tongue, rather than it had joined in the base joy of these yelping curs. Heavens! when I think what shouts I have heard—when the name of that man, then deemed little less than a god, was but breathed!—and now—why do you look at me, sir? My eyes are moist—I know it, sir—I know it. The old battered, broken soldier, who made his first campaigns, when that which is now dust was the idol of France, and the pupil of Turenne—the old soldier's eyes shall not be dry, though there is not another tear shed in the whole of this great empire."

"Your three sons?" said I ; "you did not weep for them?"

"No, sir—I loved them when I was old ; but I loved Louis *when I was young!*"

"Your oppressed and pillaged country?" said I—"think of that."

"No, sir, I will not think of it!" cried the old warrior in a passion. "I will not think of it—to-day, at least."

"You are right, my brave friend ; in the grave let us bury even public wrongs—but let us not bury their remembrance. May the joy we read in every face that we pass—joy at the death of one whom idolatry once almost seemed to deem immortal—be a lesson to future kings!"

My comrade did not immediately answer ; but, after a pause, and we had turned our backs upon the town, he said—

"Joy, sir—you spoke of joy! Yes, we are Frenchmen—we forgive our rulers easily for private vices and petty faults ; but we never forgive them if they commit the greatest of faults, and suffer a stain to rest upon—"

"What?" I asked, as my comrade broke off.

"The national glory, Monsieur!" said he.

"You have hit it," said I, smiling at the turgid sentiment which was so really and deeply felt. "And had you written folios upon the character of your countrymen, you could not have expressed it better."

CHAPTER VIII.

IN WHICH THERE IS REASON TO FEAR THAT PRINCES ARE NOT
INVARIABLY FREE FROM HUMAN PECCADILLOS.

N entering Paris, my veteran fellow-traveller took leave of me, and I proceeded to my hotel. When the first excitement of my thoughts was a little subsided, and after some feelings of a more public nature, I began to consider what influence the king's death was likely to have on my own fortunes : I could not but see, at a glance, that for the cause of the Chevalier, and the destiny of his present exertions in Scotland, it was the most fatal event that could have occurred.

The balance of power, in the contending factions of France, would, I foresaw, lie entirely between the Duke of Orleans and the legitimatized children of the late king ; the latter, closely leagued as they were with Madame de Maintenon, could not be much disposed to consider the welfare of Count Devereux ; and my wishes, therefore, naturally settled on the former. I was not doomed to a long suspense. Every one knows, that the very next day the Duke of Orleans appeared before Parliament, and was proclaimed Regent—that the will of the late king was set aside—and that the Duke of Maine suddenly became as low in power as he had always been despicable in intellect. A little hubbub ensued—people in general laughed at the Regent's finesse—and the more sagacious admired the courage and address of which the finesse was composed. The Regent's mother wrote a letter of sixty-nine pages about it ; and the Duchess of Maine boxed the duke's ears very heartily for not being as clever as herself. All Paris teemed with joyous forebodings ; and the Regent, whom every one, some time ago, had suspected of poisoning his cousins, every one now declared to be the most perfect prince that could possibly be imagined, and the very picture of *Henri Quatre*, in goodness as well as physiognomy. Three days after this event, one happened to myself, with which my public career may be said to commence.

I had spent the evening at a house in a distant part of Paris, and, invited by the beauty of the night, had dismissed my carriage, and was walking home alone, and on foot. Occupied with my reflections, and not very well acquainted with the dangerous and dark streets of Paris, in which it was very rare for those who have carriages to wander on foot, I insensibly strayed from my proper direction. When I first discovered this disagreeable fact, I was in a filthy and obscure lane rather than street, which I did not remember having ever honoured with my presence before. While I was pausing in the vain hope and anxious endeavour to shape out some imaginary chart—some "'map of the mind," by which to direct my bewildered course, I heard a confused noise proceed from another lane at right angles with the one in which I then was. I listened—the sound became more distinct—I recognized human voices in loud and angry alter-cation—a moment more, and there was a scream. Though I did not attach much importance to the circumstance, I thought I might as well approach nearer to the quarter of noise. I walked to the door of the house from which the scream proceeded; it was very small, and mean. Just as I neared it, a window was thrown open, and a voice cried—"Help! help! for God's sake, help!"

"What's the matter?" I asked.

"Whoever you are, save us!" cried the voice, "and that in-stantly, or we shall be murdered:" and, the moment after, the voice ceased abruptly, and was succeeded by the clashing of swords.

I beat loudly at the door—I shouted out—no answer; the scuffle within seemed to increase; I saw a small blind alley to the left; one of the unfortunate women, to whom such places are homes, was standing in it.

"What possibility is there of entering the house?" I asked.

"Oh!" said she, "it does not matter; it is not the first time gentlemen have cut each other's throats *there*."

"What! is it a house of bad repute?"

"Yes; and where there are bullies who wear knives, and take purses—as well as ladies, who—"

"Good heavens!" cried I, interrupting her, "there is no time to be lost. Is there no way of entrance but at this door?"

"Yes, if you are bold enough to enter at another!"

"Where?"

"Down this alley."

Immediately I entered the alley—the woman pointed to a small, dark, narrow flight of stairs—I ascended—the sounds increased in loudness. I mounted to the second flight—a light streamed from a door—the clashing of swords was distinctly audible within—I broke open the door, and found myself a witness and intruder in a scene at once ludicrous and fearful.

A table, covered with bottles and the remnants of a meal, was in the centre of the room; several articles of women's dress were scattered over the floor; two women of unequivocal description were clinging to a man richly dressed, and who having fortunately got behind an immense chair, that had been overthrown, probably in the scuffle, managed to keep off with awkward address a fierce-looking fellow, who had less scope for the ability of his sword arm, from the circumstance of his attempting to pull away the chair with his left hand. Whenever he stooped to effect this object, his antagonist thrust at him very vigorously, and had it not been for the embarrassment his female enemies occasioned him, the latter would, in all probability, have dispatched or disabled his besieger. This fortified gentleman, being backed by the window, I immediately concluded to be the person who had called to me for assistance.

At the other corner of the apartment was another cavalier, who used his sword with singular skill, but who, being hard pressed by two lusty fellows, was forced to employ that skill rather in defence than attack. Altogether, the disordered appearance of the room, the broken bottles, the fumes with which the hot atmosphere teemed,· the evident profligacy of the two women, the half undressed guise of the cavaliers, and the ruffian air and collected ferocity of the assailants, plainly denoted that it was one of those perilous festivals of pleasure in which imprudent gallants were often, in that day, betrayed by treacherous Delilahs into the hands of Philistines, who, not contented with stripping them for the sake of plunder, frequently murdered them for the sake of secrecy.

Having taken a rapid, but satisfactory, survey of the scene, I did not think it necessary to make any preparatory parley. I threw myself upon the nearest bravo with so hearty a good will that I ran him through the body before he had recovered his surprise at my appearance. This somewhat startled the other two ; they drew back and demanded quarter.

"Quarter, indeed !" cried the farther cavalier, releasing himself from his astonished female assailants, and leaping nimbly over his bulwark, into the centre of the room—"quarter, indeed, rascally *ivrognes !* No ; it is our turn now ; and, by Joseph of Arimathea ! you shall sup with Pilate to-night." So saying, he pressed his old assailant so fiercely that, after a short contest, the latter retreated till he had backed himself to the door, he then suddenly turned round, and vanished in a twinkling. The third and remaining ruffian was far from thinking himself a match for three men ; he fell on his knees, and implored mercy. However, the *ci-devant* sus·tainer of the besieged chair was but little disposed to afford him the clemency he demanded, and approached the crestfallen bravo with so grim an air of truculent delight, brandishing his sword, and uttering the most terrible threats, that there would have been small doubt of the final catastrophe of the trembling bully, had not the other gallant thrown himself in the way of his friend.

"Put up thy sword," said he, laughing, and yet with an air of command ; "we must not court crime, and then punish it." Then, turning to the bully, he said, "Rise, Sir Rascal! the devil spares thee a little longer, and this gentleman will not disobey *his*, as well as *thy* master's wishes.—Begone!"

The fellow wanted no second invitation: he sprang to his legs, and to the door. The disappointed cavalier assisted his descent down the stairs with a kick, that would have done the work of the sword to any flesh not accustomed to similar applications. Putting up his rapier, the milder gentleman then turned to *the ladies*, who lay huddled together under shelter of the chair which their intended victim had deserted.

"Ah, Mesdames," said he, gravely, and with a low bow, "I am sorry for your disappointment. As long as you contented yourselves with robbery, it were a shame to have interfered with your innocent amusements; but cold steel becomes serious. Monsieur D'Argenson will favour you with some inquiries to-morrow; at present, I recommend you to empty what remains in the bottle. Adieu! Monsieur, to whom I am so greatly indebted, honour me with your arm down these stairs. You" (turning to his friend) "will follow us, and keep a sharp look behind. *Allons! Vive Henri Quatre!*"

As we descended the dark and rough stairs, my new companion said, "What an excellent antidote to the effects of the vin de champagne is this same fighting. I feel as if I had not tasted a drop these six hours. What fortune brought you hither, Monsieur?" addressing me.

We were now at the foot of the first flight of stairs, a high and small window admitted the moonlight, and we saw each other's faces clearly.

"That fortune," answered I, looking at my acquaintance steadily, but with an expression of profound respect—"that fortune which watches over kingdoms, and which, I trust, may in no place or circumstance be a deserter from your Highness."

"Highness!" said my companion, colouring, and darting a glance, first at his friend and then at me. "Hist—sir, you know me, then—speak low—you know, they for whom you have drawn your sword?"

"Yes, so please your Highness. I have drawn it this night for Philip of Orleans; I trust yet, in another scene, and for another cause, to draw it for the Regent of France!"

CHAPTER IX.

THE Regent remained silent for a moment : he then said, in an altered and grave voice, "*C'est bien, Monsieur!* I thank you for the distinction you have made. It were not amiss," (he added, turning to his comrade,) "that *you* would now and then deign, henceforward, to make the same distinction. But this is neither time nor place for parlance. On, gentlemen ! "

We left the house, passed into the street, and moved on rapidly, and in silence, till the constitutional gaiety of the duke, recovering its ordinary tone, he said, with a laugh—

"Well, now, it is a little hard that a man who has been toiling all day for the public good should feel ashamed of indulging for an hour or two at night in his private amusements ; but so it is. 'Once grave, always grave !' is the maxim of the world—eh, Chatran ? "

The companion bowed. "'Tis a very good saying, please your royal Highness, and is intended to warn us from the sin of *ever* being grave ! "

"Ha-ha ! you have a great turn for morality, my good *Chatran!* " cried the duke, "and would draw a rule for conduct out of the wickedest *bon mot* of Dubois. Monsieur, pardon me, but I have seen you before : you are the Count—"

"Devereux, Monseigneur."

"True, true ! I have heard much of you : you are intimate with Milord Bolingbroke. Would that I had fifty friends like *him*."

"Monseigneur would have little trouble in his regency if his wish were realized," said Chatran.

"*Tant mieux*, so long as I had little odium, as well as little trouble—a happiness which, thanks to you and Dubois, I am not likely to enjoy—But there is the carriage ! "

And the duke pointed to a dark, plain carriage, which we had suddenly come upon.

"Count Devereux," said the merry Regent, "you will enter : my duty requires that, at this seductive hour, I should see a young gentleman of your dangerous age safely lodged at his hotel ! "

We entered, Chatran gave the orders, and we drove off rapidly.

The Regent hummed a tune, and his two companions listened to it in respectful silence.

" Well, well, Messieurs," said he, bursting out at last into open voice, "I will ever believe, in future, that the gods *do* look benignantly on us worshippers of the Alma Venus! Do you know much of Tibullus, Monsieur Devereux? And can you assist my memory with the continuation of the line—

> ' Quisquis amore tenetur, eat—' "
> ————————— " ' tutusque sacerque
> Qualibet, insidias non timuisse decet,' " [1]

answered I.

" *Bon!* " cried the duke. " I love a gentleman, from my very soul, when he can both fight well and read Latin! I hate a man who is merely a wine-bibber and blade drawer. By St. Louis, though it is an excellent thing to fill the stomach, especially with Tokay, yet there is no reason in the world why we should not fill the head too. But here we are. Adieu, Monsieur Devereux—we shall see you at the Palace."

I expressed my thanks briefly at the Regent's condescension, descended from the carriage (which instantly drove off with renewed celerity), and once more entered my hotel.

Two or three days after my adventure with the Regent, I thought it expedient to favour that eccentric prince with a visit. During the early part of his regency, it is well known how successfully he combated with his natural indolence, and how devotedly his moorings were surrendered to the toils of his new office; but when pleasure has grown habit, it requires a stronger mind than that of *Philippe Debonnair* to give it a permanent successor in business. Pleasure is, indeed, like the genius of the fable, the most useful of slaves, while you subdue it: the most intolerable of tyrants the moment your negligence suffers it to subdue you.

The hours in which the prince gave audience to the comrades of his lighter, rather than graver occupations, were those immediately before and after his levee. I thought that this would be the best season for me to present myself. Accordingly, one morning after the levee, I repaired to his palace.

The ante-chamber was already crowded. I sat myself quietly down in one corner of the room, and looked upon the motley groups around. I smiled inly as they reminded me of the scenes my own ante-room, in my younger days of folly and fortune, was wont to exhibit; the same heterogeneous assemblage (only upon a grander scale) of the ministers to the physical appetites and the mental tastes. There was the fretting and impudent mountebank,

[1] Whoever is possessed by Love may go safe and holy whithersoever he likes. It becomes not him to fear snares.

side by side with the gentle and patient scholar—the harlot's envoy and the priest's messenger—the agent of the police, and the licensed breaker of its laws—there ;—but what boots a more prolix description? What is the ante-room of a great man, who has many wants and many tastes, but a panorama of the blended disparities of this compounded world.

While I was moralizing, a gentleman suddenly thrust his head out of a door, and appeared to reconnoitre us. Instantly the crowd swept up to him. I thought I might as well follow the general example, and pushing aside some of my fellow loiterers, I presented myself and my name to the gentleman, with the most ingratiating air I could command.

The gentleman, who was tolerably civil for a great man's great man, promised that my visit should be immediately announced to the prince ; and then, with the politest bow imaginable, slapped the door in my face. After I had waited about seven or eight minutes longer, the gentleman re-appeared, singled me from the crowd, and desired me to follow him ; I passed through another room, and was presently in the Regent's presence.

I was rather startled when I saw, by the morning light, and in déshabille, the person of that royal martyr to dissipation. His countenance was red, but bloated, and a weakness in his eyes added considerably to the jaded and haggard expression of his features. A proportion of stomach rather inclined to corpulency, seemed to betray the taste for the pleasures of the table, which the most radically coarse, and yet (strange to say) the most generally aecomplished and really good-natured of royal profligates, combined with his other qualifications. He was yawning very elaborately over a great heap of papers, when I entered. He finished his yawn (as if it were too brief and too precious a recreation to lose), and then said, "Good morning, Monsieur Devereux ; I am glad that you have found me out *at last.*"

"I was afraid, Monseigneur, of appearing an intruder on your presence, by offering my homage to you before."

"So like my good fortune," said the Regent, turning to a man seated at another table at some distance, whose wily, astute countenance, piercing eye, and licentious expression of lip and brow, indicated at once the ability and vice which composed his character. "So like my good fortune, is it not, Dubois? If ever I meet with a tolerably pleasant fellow, who does not disgrace me by his birth or reputation, he is always so terribly afraid of intruding ! and whenever I pick up a respectable personage without wit, or a wit without respectability, he attaches himself to me like a burr, and can't live a day without inquiring after my health."

Dubois smiled, bowed, but did not answer, and I saw that his look was bent darkly and keenly upon me.

"Well," said the prince, "what think you of our opera, Count Devereux?—It beats your English one—eh?"

"Ah, certainly, Monseigneur; ours is but a reflection of yours."

"So says your friend, milord Bolingbroke, a person who knows about operas almost as much as I do, which, vanity apart, is saying a great deal. I should like very well to visit England—what should I learn best there? In Spain (I shall always love Spain) I learnt to cook."

"Monseigneur, I fear," answered I, smiling, "could obtain but little additional knowledge in that art in our barbarous country. A few rude and imperfect inventions have, indeed, of late years astonished the cultivators of the science; but the night of ignorance rests still upon its main principles and leading truths. Perhaps, what Monseigneur would find best worth studying in England would be—the women."

"Ah, the women all over the world!" cried the Duke, laughing; "but I hear your·*belles Anglaises* are sentimental, and love *à l'Arcadienne*."

"It is true at present: but who shall say how far Monseigneur's example might enlighten them in a train of thought so erroneous?"

"True. Nothing like example, eh, Dubois? What would Philip of Orleans have been but for thee?"

"'L'exemple souvent n'est qu'un miroir trompeur;
Quelquefois l'un se brise où l'autre s'est sauvé,
Et par où l'un périt, un autre est conservé,'[1]

answered Dubois out of *Cinna*.

"Corneille is right," rejoined the Regent. "After all, to do thee justice, *mon petit Abbé*, example has little to do with corrupting us. Nature pleads the cause of pleasure, as Hyperides pleaded that of Phryne. She has no need of eloquence: she unveils the bosom of her client, and the client is acquitted."

"Monseigneur shows at least that he has learnt to profit by my humble instructions in the classics," said Dubois.

The Duke did not answer. I turned my eyes to some drawings on the table—I expressed my admiration of them. "They are mine," said the Regent. "Ah! I should have been much more accomplished as a private gentleman than I fear I ever shall be as a public man of toil and business. Business—bah! But Necessity is the only real sovereign in the world, the only despot for whom there is no law. What! are you going already, Count Devereux?"

---

[1] Example is often but a deceitful mirror; where sometimes one destroys himself, while another comes off safe; and where one perishes, another is preserved.

"Monseigneur's ante-room is crowded with less fortunate persons than myself, whose sins of envy and covetousness I am now answerable for."

"Ah—well! I must hear the poor devils; the only pleasure I have is in seeing how easily I can make them happy. Would to heaven, Dubois, that one could govern a great kingdom only by fair words! Count Devereux, you have seen me to-day as my acquaintance; you see me again as my petitioner. *Bon jour, Monsieur.*"

And I retired, very well pleased with my reception: from that time, indeed, during the rest of my short stay at Paris, the prince honoured me with his especial favour. But I have dwelt too long on my sojourn at the French court. The persons whom I have described, and who alone made that sojourn memorable, must be my apology.

One day I was honoured by a visit from the Abbé Dubois. After a short conversation upon indifferent things, he accosted me thus:—

"You are aware, Count Devereux, of the partiality which the Regent has conceived towards you. Fortunate would it be for that prince" (here Dubois elevated his brows with an ironical and arch expression), "so good by disposition, so injured by example, if his partiality had been more frequently testified towards gentlemen of your merit. A mission of considerable importance, and one demanding great personal address, gives his Royal Highness an opportunity of testifying his esteem for you. He honoured me with a conference on the subject yesterday, and has now commissioned me to explain to you the technical objects of this mission, and to offer to you the honour of undertaking it. Should you accept the proposals, you will wait upon his Highness before his levee to-morrow."

Dubois then proceeded, in the clear rapid manner peculiar to him, to comment on the state of Europe. "For France," said he, in concluding his sketch, "peace is absolutely necessary. A drained treasury, an exhausted country, require it. You see, from what I have said, that Spain and England are the principal quarters from which we are to dread hostilities. Spain we must guard against—England we must propitiate; the latter object is easy in England in any case, whether James or George be uppermost. For whoever is king in England will have quite enough to do at home to make him agree willingly enough to peace abroad. The former requires a less simple and a more enlarged policy. I fear the ambition of the Queen of Spain, and the turbulent genius of her minion Alberoni. We must fortify ourselves by new forms of alliance, at various courts, which shall at once defend *us* and intimidate our enemies. We wish to employ some nobleman of ability and address, on a secret mission to Russia—will you be that person? Your absence from Paris will be but short— you will see a very droll country, and a very droll sovereign; you will return hither, doubly the rage, and with a just claim to more important employment hereafter. What say you to the proposal?"

"I must hear more," said I, "before I decide."

The Abbé renewed. It is needless to repeat all the particulars of the commission that he enumerated. Suffice it that, after a brief consideration, I accepted the honour proposed to me. The Abbé wished me joy, relapsed into his ordinary strain of coarse levity for a few minutes, and then reminding me that I was to attend the Regent on the morrow, departed. It was easy to see that in the mind of that subtle and crafty ecclesiastic, with whose manœuvres private intrigues were always blended with public, this offer of employment veiled a desire to banish me from the imme- diate vicinity of the good-natured Regent, whose favour the aspiring Abbé wished at that exact moment exclusively to monopolize. Mere men of pleasure he knew would not interfere with his aims upon the prince; mere men of business still less; but a man who was thought to combine the capacities of both, and who was moreover distinguished by the Regent, he deemed a more dangerous rival than the inestimable person thus suspected really was.

However, I cared little for the honest man's motives. Adventure to me had always greater charms than dissipation, and it was far more agreeable to the nature of my ambition, to win distinction by any honourable method, than by favouritism at a court, so hollow, so unprincipled, and so grossly licentious as that of the Regent. There to be the most successful courtier was to be the most amusing profligate. Alas, when the heart is away from its objects, and the taste revolts at its excess, Pleasure is worse than palling—it is a torture!—and the devil in Jonson's play did not perhaps greatly belie the truth when he averred "that the pains in his native country were pastimes to the life of a person of Fashion."

The Duke of Orleans received me the next morning with more than his wonted *bonhommie*. What a pity that so good-natured a prince should have been so bad a man! He enlarged more easily and carelessly than his worthy preceptor had done upon the several points to be observed in my mission—then condescendingly told me he was very sorry to lose me from his court, and asked me, at all events, before I left Paris, to be a guest at one of his select suppers. I appreciated this honour at its just value. To these suppers none were asked but the Prince's chums or *roués*,[1] as he was pleased to call them. As, *entre nous*, these chums were for the most part the most good-for-nothing people in the kingdom, I could not but feel highly flattered at being deemed, by so deep a judge of character as the Regent, worthy to join them. I need not say that the invitation was eagerly accepted, nor that I left *Philippe le Débonnaire* impressed with the idea of his being the most admirable person in Europe. What a fool a great man is if he does not study to be affable—weigh a prince's condescension in one scale, and all the cardinal virtues in the other, and the condescension will outweigh them all! The Regent of France ruined his country as much as he well could do, and there was not a dry eye when he died!

A day had now effected a change—a great change in my fate. A new court—a new theatre of action—a new walk of ambition, were suddenly opened to me. Nothing could be more promising than my first employment—nothing could be more pleasing than the anticipation of change. "I must force myself to be agreeable to-night," said I, as I dressed for the Regent's supper. "I must leave behind me the remembrance of a *bon mot*, or I shall be forgotten."

And I was right. In that whirlpool, the capital of France, everything sinks but wit—*that* is always on the surface, and we must cling to it with a firm grasp, if we would not go down to—"the deep oblivion."

CHAPTER X.

ROYAL EXERTIONS FOR THE GOOD OF THE PEOPLE.

WHAT a singular scene was that private supper with the Regent of France and his *roués*! The party consisted of twenty: nine gentlemen of the court besides myself, four men of low rank and character—but admirable buffoons—and six ladies, such ladies as the duke loved best—witty, lively, sarcastic, and good for nothing.

De Chatran accosted me.

"*Je suis ravi, mon cher Monsieur Devereux,*" said he, gravely, "to see you in such excellent company—you must be a little surprised to find yourself here!"

---

[1] The term *Roué*, now so comprehensive, was first given by the Regent to a select number of his friends; according to them, because they would be broken on the wheel for his sake; according to himself, because they deserved to be so broken.—Ed.

"Not at all! every scene is worth one visit. He, my good Monsieur Chatran, who goes to the House of Correction once is a philosopher—he who goes twice is a rogue!"

"Thank you, Count, what am I then—I have been *here* twenty times?"

"Why, I will answer you with a story. The soul of a Jesuit one night, when its body was asleep, wandered down to the lower regions; Satan caught it, and was about to consign it to some appropriate place; the soul tried hard to excuse itself: you know what a cunning thing a Jesuit's soul is! 'Monsieur Satan,' said the spirit; 'no king should punish a traveller as he would a native. Upon my honour, I am merely here *en voyageur.*' 'Go, then,' said Satan, and the soul flew back to its body. But the Jesuit died, and came to the lower regions a second time. He was brought before his Satanic majesty, and made the same excuse. 'No, no,' cried Beelzebub; 'once here is to be only *le diable voyageur*—twice here, and you are *le diable tout de bon.*'"

"Ha! ha! ha!" said Chatran, laughing; "I then am the *diable tout de bon!* 'tis well I *am no worse;* for we reckon the *roués* a devilish deal worse than the very worst of the devils—but see, the Regent approaches us."

And, leaving a very pretty and gay-looking lady, the Regent sauntered towards us. It was in walking, by the bye, that he lost all the grace of his mien. I don't know, however, that one wishes a great man to be graceful, so long as he's familiar.

"Aha, Monsieur Devereux!" said he, "we will give you some lessons in cooking to-night—we shall show you how to provide for yourself in that barbarous country which you are about to visit. *Tout voyageur doit tout savoir!*"

"A very admirable saying; which leads me to understand that *Monseigneur* has been a great traveller," said I.

"Ay, in all things and *all places*—eh, Count!" answered the Regent, smiling; "but," here he lowered his voice a little, "I have never yet learned how *you* came so opportunely to our assistance that night. *Dieu me damne!* but it reminds me of the old story of the two sisters meeting at a gallant's house. 'Oh, sister, how came *you* here?' said one, in virtuous amazement. '*Ciel! ma sœur!*' cries the other; 'what brought *you?*'" [1]

"Monseigneur is pleasant," said I, laughing; "but a man does now and then (though I own it is very seldom) do a good action, without having previously resolved to commit a bad one!"

"I like your parenthesis," cried the Regent, "it reminds me of

[1] The reader will remember a better version of this anecdote in one of the most popular of the English comedies.—ED.

my friend St. Simon, who thinks so ill of mankind, that I asked
him one day, whether it was possible for him to despise any thing
more than men? 'Yes,' said he, with a low bow, 'women!'"

"His experience," said I, glancing at the female part of the
coterie, "was, I must own, likely to lead him to that opinion."

"None of your sarcasms, Monsieur," cried the Regent. "*L'amusement est un des besoins de l'homme*—as I hear young *Arouet* very
pithily said the other day; and we owe gratitude to whomsoever it
may be that supplies that want. Now, you will agree with me that
none supply it like women; therefore we owe them gratitude—
therefore we must not hear them abused. Logically proved, I
think!"

"Yes, indeed," said I, "it is a pleasure to find they have so able
an advocate; and that your Highness can so well apply to yourself
both the assertions in the motto of the great master of fortification,
Vauban—'I destroy, but I defend.'"

"Enough," said the duke gaily, "now to *our fortifications;*"
and he moved away towards the women; I followed the royal
example; and soon found myself seated next to a pretty, and very
small woman. We entered into conversation; and, when once
begun, my fair companion took care that it should not cease, without
a miracle. By the goddess Facundia, what volumes of words issued
from that little mouth! and on all subjects too! church—state—
law—politics — play-houses — lampoons — lace—liveries — kings —
queens — roturiers — beggars — you would have thought, had you
heard her, so vast was her confusion of all things, that chaos had
come again. Our royal host did not escape her. "You never
before supped here *en famille*," said she,—"*Mon Dieu!* it will do
your heart good to see how much the Regent will eat. He has
such an appetite—you know he never eats any dinner, in order to
eat the more at supper. You see that little dark woman he is
talking to?—well, she is *Madame de Parabère*—he calls her his little
black crow—was there ever such a pet name? Can you guess why
he likes her? Nay, never take the trouble of thinking—I will tell
you at once—simply because she eats and drinks so much. *Parole
d'honneur*, 'tis true. The Regent says he likes sympathy in all
things!—is it not droll? What a hideous old man is that *Nocé*—
his face looks as if it had caught the rainbow. That impudent
fellow *Dubois* scolded him for squeezing so many *louis* out of the
good Regent. The yellow creature attempted to deny the fact.
'Nay,' cried Dubois, 'you cannot contradict me; I see their very
ghosts in your face.'"

While my companion was thus amusing herself, *Nocé*, unconscious
of her panegyric on his personal attractions, joined us.

"Ah! my dear *Nocé*," said the lady, most affectionately, "how well you are looking! I am delighted to see you."

"I do not doubt it," said *Nocé*, "for I have to inform you that your petition is granted; your husband will have the place."

"Oh, how eternally grateful I am to you!" cried the lady in an ecstasy; "my poor, dear husband will be so rejoiced. I wish I had wings to fly to him!"

The gallant *Nocé* uttered a compliment—I thought myself *de trop*, and moved away. I again encountered *Chatran*.

"I overheard your conversation with Madame la Marquise," said he, smiling; "she has a bitter tongue—has she not?"

"Very! how she abused the poor rogue *Nocé!*"

"Yes, and yet he is her lover!"

"Her lover!—you astonish me; why, she seemed almost fond of her husband—the tears came in her eyes when she spoke of him."

"She *is* fond of him!" said Chatran, dryly. "She loves the ground he treads on — it is precisely for that reason she favours Nocé; she is never happy but when she is procuring something *pour son cher bon mari*. She goes to spend a week at Nocé's country house, and writes to her husband, with a pen dipped in her blood, saying, 'My *heart* is with thee!'"

"Certainly," said I, "France is the land of enigmas; the sphinx must have been a *Parisienne*. And when Jupiter made man, he made two natures utterly distinct from one another. One was *Human nature*, and the other *French nature!*"

At this moment supper was announced. We all adjourned to another apartment, where, to my great surprise, I observed the cloth laid—the sideboard loaded—the wines ready, but nothing to eat on the table! A Madame de Savori, who was next me, noted my surprise.

"What astonishes you, Monsieur?"

"*Nothing*, Madame!" said I, "that is, the absence of *all* things."

"What! you expected to see supper?"

"I own my delusion—I did."

"It is not cooked yet!"

"Oh! well, I can wait!"

"And officiate too!" said the lady;—"in a word, this is one of the Regent's cooking nights."

Scarcely had I received this explanation, before there was a general adjournment to an inner apartment, where all the necessary articles for cooking were ready to our hand.

"The Regent led the way,
To light us to our prey,"

and, with an irresistible gravity and importance of demeanour,

K

entered upon the duties of *chef.* In a very short time we were all engaged. Nothing could exceed the zest with which every one seemed to enter into the rites of the kitchen. You would have imagined they had been born scullions, they handled the *batterie de cuisine* so naturally. As for me, I sought protection with Madame de **Savori**; and as, fortunately, she was very deeply skilled in the science, she had occasion to employ me in many minor avocations which her experience taught her would not be above my comprehension.

After we had spent a certain time in this dignified occupation, we returned to the *salle à manger.* The attendants placed the dishes on the table, and we all fell to. Whether out of self-love to their own performances, or complaisance to the performances of others, I cannot exactly say, but certain it is that all the guests acquitted themselves *à merveille;* you would not have imagined the Regent the only one who had gone without dinner to eat the more at supper. Even that devoted wife to her *cher bon mari*, who had so severely dwelt upon the good Regent's infirmity, occupied herself with an earnestness that would have seemed almost wolf-like in a famished grenadier.

Very slight indeed was the conversation till the supper was nearly over; then the effects of the wine became more perceptible. The Regent was the first person who evinced that he had eaten sufficiently to be able to talk. Utterly dispensing with the slightest veil of reserve or royalty, he leant over the table, and poured forth a whole tide of jests. The guests then began to think it was indecorous to stuff themselves any more, and, as well as they were able, they followed the host's example. But the most amusing personages were the buffoons: they mimicked, and joked, and lampooned, and lied as if by inspiration. As the bottle circulated, and talk grew louder, the lampooning and the lying were not, however, confined to the buffoons. On the contrary, the best born and best·bred people seemed to excel the most in those polite arts. Every person who boasted a fair name, or a decent reputation at court, was seized, condemned, and mangled in an instant. And how elaborately the good folks slandered! It was no hasty word and flippant·repartee which did the business of the absent — there was a precision, a polish, a labour of malice, which showed that each person had brought so many reputations already cut up. The good-natured convivialists differed from all other backbiters that I have ever met, in the same manner as the toads of Surinam differ from all other toads, viz.: their venomous offspring were not half formed, misshapen tadpoles of slander, but sprung at once into life—well shaped and fully developed.

"*Chantons!*" cried the Regent, whose eyes, winking and rolling, gave token of his approaching that state which equals the beggar to the king, "let us have a song. *Nocé*, lift up thy voice, and let us hear what the tokay has put into thy head!"

Nocé obeyed, and sang as men half drunk generally do sing.

"*O Ciel!*" whispered the malicious Savori, "what a hideous screech—one would think he had *turned his face into a voice!*"

"*Bravissimo!*" cried the duke, when his guest had ceased,— "what happy people we are! Our doors are locked—not a soul can disturb us—we have plenty of wine—we are going to get drunk —and we have all Paris to abuse! what were you saying of Marshal Villars, my little Parabère?"

And pounce went the little Parabère upon the unfortunate marshal. At last, slander had a respite—nonsense began its reign—the full inspiration descended upon the orgies—the good people lost the use of their faculties. Noise—clamour, uproar, broken bottles, falling chairs, and (I grieve to say) their occupants falling too—conclude the scene of the royal supper. Let us drop the curtain.

CHAPTER XI.

AN INTERVIEW.

I WENT a little out of my way, on departing from Paris, to visit Lord Bolingbroke, who at that time was in the country. There are some men whom one never really sees in capitals; one sees their masks, not themselves; Bolingbroke was one. It was in retirement, however brief it might be, that his true nature expanded itself, and, weary of being admired, he allowed one to love, and even in the wildest course of his earlier excesses, to respect him. My visit was limited to a few hours, but it made an indelible impression on me.

"Once more," I said, as we walked to and fro in the garden of his temporary retreat, "once more you are in your element; minister and statesman of a prince, and chief supporter of the great plans which are to restore him to his throne."

A slight shade passed over Bolingbroke's fine brow. "To you, my constant friend," said he, "to you—who of all my friends alone remained true in exile, and unshaken by misfortune—to you I will confide a secret that I would entrust to no other. I repent me already of having espoused this cause. I did so while yet the disgrace of an unmerited attainder tingled in my veins; while I was in the full tide of those violent and warm passions which have so often misled me. Myself attainted—the best beloved of my associates in danger—my party deserted, and seemingly lost but for some bold measure such as then offered ; these were all that I saw. I listened eagerly to representations I now find untrue ; and I accepted that rank and power from one prince which were so rudely and gallingly torn from me by another. I perceive that I have acted imprudently, but what is done, is done ; no private scruples, no private interest, shall make me waver in a cause that I have once pledged myself to serve ; and if I *can* do aught to make a weak cause powerful, and a divided party successful, I will ; but, Devereux, you are wrong, this is *not* my element. Ever in the paths of strife, I have sighed for quiet ; and, while most eager in pursuit of ambition, I have languished the most fondly for content. The littleness of intrigue disgusts me, and while *the branches* of my power soared the highest, and spread with the most luxuriance, it galled me to think of the miry soil in which that power was condemned to strike *the roots*,[1] upon which it stood, and by which it must be nourished.''

I answered Bolingbroke as men are wont to answer statesmen who complain of their calling—half in compliment, half in contradiction, but he replied with unusual seriousness—

'' Do not think I affect to speak thus : you know how eagerly I snatch any respite from state, and how unmovedly I have borne the loss of prosperity and of power. You are now about to enter those perilous paths which I have trod for years. Your passions, like mine, are strong ! Beware, oh, beware, how you indulge them without restraint ! They are the fires which should warm ; let them not be the fires which destroy.'' ·

Bolingbroke paused in evident and great agitation—he resumed : ''I speak strongly, for I speak in bitterness ; I was thrown early into the world ; my whole education had been framed to make me ambitious ; it succeeded in its end. I was ambitious, and of all success—success in pleasure, success in fame. To wean me from the former, my friends persuaded me to marry ; they chose my wife for her connections and her fortune, and I gained those advantages at the expense of what was better than either—happiness ! You know how unfortunate has been that marriage, and how young I was when it was contracted. Can you wonder that it failed in the desired effect ? Every one courted me, every temptation assailed

[1] Occasional Writer.—No. 1. The Editor has, throughout this work, usually, but not invariably, noted the passages in Bolingbroke's writings, in which there occur similes, illustrations, or striking thoughts, correspondent with those in the text.

me ; pleasure even became more alluring abroad, when at home I had no longer the hope of peace : the indulgence of one passion begat the indulgence of another ; and, though my better sense *prompted* all my actions, it never *restrained* them to a proper limit. Thus the commencement of my actions has been generally prudent, and their *continuation* has deviated into rashness, or plunged into excess. Devereux, I have paid the forfeit of my errors with a terrible interest—when my motives have been pure, men have seen a fault in the conduct, and calumniated the motives ; when my conduct has been blameless, men have remembered its former errors, and asserted that its present goodness only arose from some sinister intention—thus I have been termed crafty, when I was in reality rash, and that was called the inconsistency of interest which in reality was the inconstancy of passion.[1] I have reason, therefore, to warn you how you suffer your subjects to become your tyrants ; and believe me no experience is so deep as that of one who has committed faults, and who has discovered their causes."

"Apply, my dear lord, that experience to your future career. You remember what the most sagacious of all pedants,[2] even though he was an emperor, has so happily expressed—'Repentance is a goddess, and the preserver of those who have erred.'"

"May I *find* her so !" answered Bolingbroke ; "but as *Montaigne* or *Charron* would say[3] . . . . 'Every man is at once his own sharper and his own bubble.' We make vast promises to ourselves, and a passion, an example, sweeps even the remembrance of those promises from our minds. One is too apt to believe men hypocrites, if their conduct squares not with their sentiments ; but *perhaps no vice is more rare, for no task is more difficult, than systematic hypocrisy :* and the same susceptibility which exposes men to be easily impressed by the allurements of vice, renders them at heart most struck by the loveliness of virtue. Thus, their language and their hearts worship the divinity of the latter, while their conduct strays

---

[1] This I do believe to be the real (though perhaps it is a new) light in which Lord Bolingbroke's life and character are to be viewed. The same writers who tell us of his ungovernable passions, always prefix to his name the epithets "designing, cunning, crafty," &c. Now I will venture to tell these historians that, if they had studied human nature instead of party pamphlets, they would have discovered that there are certain incompatible qualities which can never be united in one character—that no man can have violent passions *to which he is in the habit of yielding,* and be systematically crafty and designing. No man can be all heat, and at the same time all coolness ; but opposite causes not unoften produce like effects. Passion usually makes men changeable, so sometimes does craft ; hence the mistake of the uninquiring or the shallow ; and hence while * * * writes, and * * * * compiles, will the characters of great men be transmitted to posterity mis-stated and belied — ED.

[2] The Emperor Julian. The original expression is paraphrased in the text.

[3] "Spirit of Patriotism."

the most erringly towards the false shrines over which the former presides. Yes! I have never been blind to the surpassing excellence of GOOD. The still, sweet whispers of virtue have been heard, even when the storm has been loudest, and the bark of Reason been driven the most impetuously over the waves :_ and, at this moment, I am impressed with a foreboding that, sooner or later, the whispers will not only be heard, but their suggestion be obeyed ; and that, far from courts and intrigue, from dissipation and ambition, I shall learn, in retirement, the true principles of wisdom, and the real objects of life."

Thus did Bolingbroke converse, and thus did I listen, till it was time to depart. I left him impressed with a melancholy that was rather soothing than distasteful. Whatever were the faults of that most extraordinary and most dazzling genius, no one was ever more candid [1] in confessing his errors. A systematically bad man either ridicules what is good, or disbelieves in its existence ; but no man can be hardened in vice whose heart is still sensible of the excellence and the glory of virtue.

[1] It is impossible to read the letter to Sir W. Windham, without being remarkably struck with the dignified and yet open candour which it displays. The same candour is equally visible in whatever relates *to himself,* in all Lord Bolingbroke's writings and correspondence, and yet candour is the last attribute usually conceded to him. But never was there a writer whom people have talked of more and read less ; and I do not know a greater proof of this than the ever-repeated assertion (echoed from a most incompetent authority) of the said letter to Sir W. Windham being the finest of all Lord Bolingbroke's writings. It is an article of great value to the history of the times ; but, as to all the higher graces and qualities of composition, it is one of the least striking (and on the other hand it is one of the most verbally incorrect) which he has bequeathed to us (the posthumous works always excepted). I am not sure whether the most brilliant passages— the most noble illustrations—the most profound reflections, and most useful truths —to be found in all his writings, are not to be gathered from the least popular of them—such as that volume entitled "Political Tracts."—ED.

BOOK V.

CHAPTER I.

A PORTRAIT.

MYSTERIOUS impulse at the heart, which never suffers us to be at rest, which urges us onward as by an unseen, yet irresistible, law—human planets in a petty orbit, hurried for ever and for ever, till our course is run and our light is quenched—through the circle of a dark and impenetrable destiny! art thou not some faint forecast and type of our wanderings hereafter? of the unslumbering nature of the soul? of the everlasting progress which we are pre-doomed to make through the countless steps, and realms, and harmonies in the infinite creation? Oh, often in my rovings have I dared to dream so—often have I soared on the wild wings of thought above the "smoke and stir" of this dim earth, and wrought, from the restless visions of my mind, a chart of the glories and the wonders which the released spirit may hereafter visit and behold!

What a glad awakening from self—what a sparkling and fresh draught from a new source of being,—what a wheel within wheel, animating, impelling, arousing all the rest of this animal machine, is the first excitement of Travel! The first free escape from the bonds of the linked and tame life of cities and social vices,—the jaded pleasure and the hollow love, the monotonous round of sordid objects and dull desires,—the eternal chain that binds us to things and beings, mockeries of ourselves,—alike, but oh, how different! the shock that brings us nearer to men only to make us strive against them, and learn, from the harsh contest of veiled deceit and open force, that the more we share the aims of others, the more deeply and basely rooted we grow to the littleness of self.

I passed more lingeringly through France than I did through the other portions of my *route*. I had dwelt long enough in the capital to be anxious to survey the country. It was then that the last scale which the magic of Louis Quatorze and the memory of his gorgeous court had left upon the moral eye, fell off, and I saw the real essence of that monarch's greatness, and the true relics of his reign. I saw the poor, and the degraded, and the racked, and the priest-ridden,

tillers and peoplers of the soil, which made the substance beneath
the glittering and false surface—the body of that vast empire, of
which I had hitherto beheld only the face, and THAT darkly, and
for the most part covered by a mask !

No man can look upon France, beautiful France, her rich soil,
her temperate yet maturing clime, the gallant and bold spirits which
she produces, her boundaries so indicated and protected by nature
itself, her advantages of ocean and land, of commerce and agriculture,
and not wonder that her prosperity should be so bloated, and her
real state so wretched and diseased.

Let England draw the moral, and beware not only of wars which
exhaust, but of governments which impoverish. A waste of the
public wealth is the most lasting of public afflictions ; and "the
treasury which is drained by extravagance must be refilled by
crime." [1]

I remember one beautiful evening an accident to my carriage
occasioned my sojourn for a whole afternoon in a small village.
The *Curé* honoured me with a visit, and we strolled, after a slight
repast, into the hamlet. The priest was complaisant, quiet in
manner, and not ill-informed, for his obscure station and scanty
opportunities of knowledge ; he did not seem, however, to possess
the vivacity of his countrymen, but was rather melancholy and
pensive, not only in his expression of countenance, but his cast of
thought.

"You have a charming scene here ; I almost feel as if it were a
sin to leave it so soon."

We were, indeed, in a pleasant and alluring spot at the time I
addressed this observation to the good Curé. A little rivulet
emerged from a copse to the left, and ran sparkling and dimpling
beneath our feet, to deck with a more living verdure the village
green, which it intersected with a winding, nor unmelodious stream.
We had paused, and I was leaning against an old and solitary
chestnut-tree, which commanded the whole scene. The village was
a little in the rear, and the smoke from its few chimneys rose slowly
to the silent and deep skies, not wholly unlike the human wishes,
which, though they spring from the grossness and the fumes of earth,
purify themselves as they ascend to Heaven. And from the village
(when other sounds, which I shall note presently, were for an instant
still) came the whoop of children, mellowed, by distance, into a
confused, yet thrilling sound, which fell upon the heart like the voice
of our gone childhood itself. Before, in the far expanse, stretched
a chain of hills on which the autumn sun sunk slowly, pouring its
yellow beams over groups of peasantry, which, on the opposite side

[1] Tacitus.

of the rivulet, and at some interval from us, were scattered, partly over the green, and partly gathered beneath the shade of a little grove. The former were of the young, and those to whom youth's sports are dear, and were dancing to the merry music, which (ever and anon blended with the laugh and the tone of a louder jest) floated joyously on our ears. The fathers and matrons of the hamlet were inhaling a more quiet joy beneath the trees, and I involuntarily gave a tenderer interest to their converse by supposing them to sanction to each other the rustic loves which they might survey among their children.

"Will not Monsieur draw nearer to the dancers," said the Curé; "there is a plank thrown over the rivulet a little lower down?"

"No!" said I, "perhaps they are seen to better advantage where we are—what mirth will bear too close an inspection?"

"True, sir," remarked the priest, and he sighed.

"Yet," I resumed, musingly, and I spoke rather to myself than to my companion, "yet, how happy do they seem! what a revival of our Arcadian dreams are the flute and the dance, the glossy trees all glowing in the autumn sunset, the green sod, and the murmuring rill, and the buoyant laugh startling the satyr in his leafy haunts; and the rural loves which will grow sweeter still when the sun has set, and the twilight has made the sigh more tender, and the blush of a mellower hue! Ah, why is it only the revival of a dream? why must it be only an interval of labour and woe—the brief saturnalia of slaves—the green resting spot in a dreary and long road of travail and toil?"

"You are the first stranger I have met," said the Curé, "who seems to pierce beneath the thin veil of our Gallic gaiety; the first to whom the scene we now survey is fraught with other feelings than a belief in the happiness of our peasantry, and an envy at its imagined exuberance. But as it is not the happiest individuals, so I fear it is not the happiest nations, that are the gayest."

I looked at the Curé with some surprise. "Your remark is deeper than the ordinary wisdom of your tribe, my father," said I.

"I have travelled over three parts of the globe," answered the Curé; "I was not always intended for what I am;" and the priest's mild eyes flashed with a sudden light that as suddenly died away. "Yes, I have travelled over the greater part of the known world," he repeated, in a more quiet tone, "and I have noted that where a man has many comforts to guard, and many rights to defend, he necessarily shares the thought and the seriousness of those who feel the value of a treasure which they possess, and whose most earnest meditations are intent upon providing against its loss. I have noted, too, that the joy produced by a momentary suspense of labour is naturally great, in proportion to the toil; hence it is that no

K 2

European mirth is so wild as that of the Indian slave, when a brief holiday releases him from his task. Alas ! that very mirth is the strongest evidence of the weight of the previous chains ; even as, in ourselves, we find the happiest moment we enjoy is that immediately succeeding the cessation of deep sorrow to the mind, or violent torture to the body."[1]

I was struck by this observation of the priest.

" I see now,' said I, "that, as an Englishman, I have no reason to repine at the proverbial gravity of my countrymen, or to envy the lighter spirit of the sons of Italy and France."   .

" No," said the Curé, "the happiest nations are those in whose people you witness the least sensible reverses from gaiety to dejection ; and that *thought*, which is the noblest characteristic of the isolated man, is also that of a people. Freemen are serious, they have objects at their heart worthy to engross attention. It is reserved for slaves to indulge in groans at one moment, and laughter at another."

" At that rate," said I, "the best sign for France will be when the gaiety of her sons is no longer a just proverb, and the laughing lip is succeeded by the thoughtful brow."

We remained silent for several minutes ; our conversation had shed a gloom over the light scene before us, and the voice of the flute no longer sounded musically on my ear. I proposed to the Curé to return to my inn. As we walked slowly in that direction, I surveyed my companion more attentively than I had hitherto done. He was a model of masculine vigour and grace of form ; and, had I not looked earnestly upon his cheek, I should have thought him likely to outlive the very oaks around the hamlet church where he presided. But the cheek was worn and hectic, and seemed to indicate that the keen fire which burns at the deep heart, unseen, but unslaking, would consume the mortal fuel, long before Time should even have commenced his gradual decay.

"You have travelled, then, much, sir," said I, and the tone of my voice was that of curiosity.

The good Curé penetrated into my desire to hear something of his adventures ; and few are the recluses who are not gratified by the interest of others, or who are unwilling to reward it by recalling those portions of life most cherished by themselves. Before we parted that night, he told me his little history. He had been educated for the army ; before he entered the profession he had

---

[1] This reflection, if true, may console us for the loss of those village dances and pleasant holidays for which " merry England " was once celebrated. The loss of them has been ascribed to the gloomy influence of the Puritans, but it has never occurred to the good poets, who have so mourned over that loss, that it is also to be ascribed to the *liberty* which those Puritans *generalized*, if they did not introduce.—ED.

seen the daughter of a neighbour—loved her—and the old story—
she loved him again, and died before the love passed the ordeal of
marriage. He had no longer a desire for glory, but he had for
excitement. He sold his little property and travelled, as he had said,
for nearly fourteen years, equally over the polished lands of Europe,
and the far climates, where Truth seems fable, and Fiction finds her
own legends realized or excelled.

He returned home, poor in pocket, and wearied in spirit. He
became what I beheld him. "My lot is fixed now," said he, in
conclusion; "but I find there is all the difference between quiet and
content; my heart eats itself away here; it is the moth fretting the
garment laid by, more than the storm or the fray would have
worn it."

I said something, commonplace enough, about solitude, and the
blessings of competence, and the country. The Curé shook his
head gently, but made no answer; perhaps he did wisely in thinking
the feelings are ever beyond the reach of a stranger's reasoning.
We parted more affectionately than acquaintances of so short a date
usually do; and when I returned from Russia, I stopped at the
village on purpose to inquire after him. A few months had done
the work: the moth had already fretted away the human garment;
and I walked to his lowly and nameless grave, and felt that it
contained the only quiet in which monotony is not blended with
regret!

CHAPTER II.

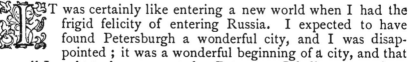

THE ENTRANCE INTO PETERSBURGH—A RENCONTRE WITH AN
INQUISITIVE AND MYSTERIOUS STRANGER—NOTHING LIKE
TRAVEL.

IT was certainly like entering a new world when I had the
frigid felicity of entering Russia. I expected to have
found Petersburgh a wonderful city, and I was disappointed; it was a wonderful beginning of a city, and that
was all I ought to have expected. But never, I believe, was there
a place which there was so much difficulty in arriving at: such
winds—such climate—such police arrangements—arranged, too, by
such fellows! six feet high, with nothing human about them, but
their uncleanness and ferocity! Such vexatious delays, difficulties,
ordeals, through which it was necessary to pass, and to pass, too,
with an air of the most perfect satisfaction and content. By the

Lord! one would have imagined, at all events, it must be an earthly paradise, to be so arduous of access, instead of a Dutch-looking town, with comfortless canals, and the most terrible climate in which a civilized creature was ever frozen to death. "It is just the city a nation of bears would build, if bears ever became architects," said I to myself, as I entered the northern capital, with my teeth chattering, and my limbs in a state of perfect insensibility.

My vehicle stopped, at last, at a hotel to which I had been directed. It was a circumstance, I believe, peculiar to Petersburgh, that, at the time I speak of, none of its streets had a name ; and if one wanted to find out a house, one was forced to do so by oral description. A pleasant thing it was, too, to stop in the middle of a street, to listen to such description at full length, and find oneself rapidly becoming ice as the detail progressed. After I was lodged, thawed, and fed, I fell fast asleep, and slept for eighteen hours, without waking once ; to my mind, it was a miracle that I ever woke again.

I then dressed myself, and, taking my interpreter who was a Livonian, a great rascal, but clever, who washed twice a week, and did not wear a beard above eight inches long, I put myself into my carriage, and went to deliver my letters of introduction. I had one in particular to the Admiral Apraxin ; and it was with him that I was directed to confer, previous to seeking an interview with the Emperor. Accordingly I repaired to his hotel, which was situated on a sort of quay, and was really, for Petersburgh, very magnificent. In this quarter, then, or a little later, lived about thirty other officers of the court, General Jagoyinsky, General Cyernichoff, &c.; and, appropriately enough, the most remarkable public building in the vicinity, is the great slaughter-house—a fine specimen that of practical satire !

On endeavouring to pass through the Admiral's hall, I had the mortification of finding myself rejected by his domestics. As two men in military attire were instantly admitted, I thought this a little hard upon a man who had travelled so far to see his admiralship, and, accordingly, hinted my indignation to Mr. Muscotofsky, my interpreter.

"You are not so richly dressed as those gentlemen," said he.

"That is the reason, is it ?"

"If it so please St. Nicholas, it is ; and, besides, those gentlemen have two men running before them, to cry 'Clear the way !'"

"I had better, then, dress myself better, and take two *avant couriers.*"

"If it so please St. Nicholas."

"Upon this I returned, robed myself in scarlet and gold, took a couple of lacqueys, returned to Admiral Apraxin's, and was admitted in an instant. Who would have thought these savages so like us? Appearances, you see, produce realities all over the world!

The admiral, who was a very great man at court—though he narrowly escaped Siberia, or the knout, some time after—was civil enough to me: but I soon saw that, favourite as he was with the Czar, that great man left but petty moves in the grand chess-board of politics to be played by any but himself: and my proper plan in this court appeared evidently to be unlike that pursued in most others, where it is better to win the favourite than the prince. Accordingly, I lost no time in seeking an interview with the Czar himself, and readily obtained an appointment to that effect.

On the day before the interview took place, I amused myself with walking over the city, gazing upon its growing grandeur, and casting, in especial, a wistful eye upon the fortress or citadel, which is situated in an island, surrounded by the city; and upon the building of which more than one hundred thousand men are supposed to have perished. So great a sacrifice does it require to conquer nature.

While I was thus amusing myself, I observed a man in a small chaise with one horse pass me twice, and look at me very earnestly. Like most of my countrymen, I do not love to be stared at: however, I thought it better in that unknown country to change my intended frown for a good-natured expression of countenance, and turned away. A singular sight now struck my attention, a couple of men with beards that would have hidden a cassowary, were walking slowly along in their curious long garments, and certainly (I say it reverently) disgracing the semblance of humanity, when, just as they came by a gate, two other men of astonishing height, started forth, each armed with a pair of shears. Before a second was over, off went the beards of the first two passengers; and before another second expired, off went the skirts of their garments too—I never saw excrescences so expeditiously lopped. The two operators, who preserved a profound silence during this brief affair, then retired a little, and the mutilated wanderers pursued their way with an air of extreme discomfiture.

"Nothing like travel, certainly!" said I unconsciously aloud.

"True!" said a voice in English behind me. I turned, and saw the man who had noticed me so earnestly in the one horse chaise. He was a tall, robust man, dressed very plainly, and even shabbily, in a green uniform, with a narrow tarnished gold lace; and I judged him to be a foreigner, like myself, though his accent and pronunciation evidently showed that he was not a native of the country in the language of which he accosted me.

"It is very true," said he again ; "there is nothing like travel !"

"And travel," I rejoined, courteously, "in those places where travel seldom extends. I have only been six days at Petersburgh, and till I came hither, I knew nothing of the variety of human nature or the power of human genius. But will you allow me to ask the meaning of the very singular occurrence we have just witnessed?"—

"Oh, nothing," rejoined the man, with a broad strong smile, "nothing but an attempt to make men out of brutes. This custom of shaving is not, thank Heaven, much wanted now—some years ago it was requisite to have several stations for barbers and tailors to perform their duties in. Now this is very seldom necessary : those gentlemen were especially marked out for the operation. By —— (and here the man swore a hearty English and somewhat sea-faring oath, which a little astonished me in the streets of Petersburgh), I wish it were as easy to lop off all old customs ! that it were as easy to clip the *beard of the mind*, sir ! Ha—ha !"

"But the Czar must have found a little difficulty in effecting even this outward amendment, and to say truth, I see so many beards about still that I think the reform has been more partial than universal."

"Ah, those are the beards of the common people, the Czar leaves those for the present. Have you seen the docks yet?"

"No : I am not sufficiently a sailor to take much interest in them."

"Humph ! humph ! you are a soldier, perhaps ?"

"I hope to be so one day or other—I am not yet !"

"Not yet ! humph ! there are opportunities in plenty for those who wish it—what is your profession then, and what do you know best ?"

I was certainly not charmed with the honest inquisitiveness of the stranger. "Sir," said I, "sir, my profession is to answer no questions ; and what I know best is—to hold my tongue !"

The stranger laughed out. "Well, well, that is what all Englishmen know best !" said he ; "but don't be offended—if you will come home with me I will give you a glass of brandy !"

"I am very much obliged for the offer, but business obliges me to decline it—good morning, sir."

"Good morning !" answered the man, slightly moving his hat, in answer to my salutation.

We separated, as I thought, but I was mistaken. As ill-luck would have it, I lost my way in endeavouring to return home. While I was interrogating a French artisan, who seemed in a prodigious hurry, up comes my inquisitive friend in green again. "Ha ! you have lost your way—I can put you into it better than any man in Petersburgh !"

I thought it right to accept the offer ; and we moved on, side by side. I now looked pretty attentively at my gentleman. I have said that he was tall and stout—he was also remarkably well-built, and had a kind of seaman's ease and freedom of gait and manner. His countenance was very peculiar; short, firm, and strongly marked ; a small, but thick moustachio, covered his upper lip—the rest of his face was shaved. His mouth was wide, but closed, when silent, with that expression of iron resolution which no feature *but* the mouth can convey. His eyes were large, well-opened, and rather stern ; and when, which was often in the course of conversation, he pushed back his hat from his forehead, the motion developed two strong deep wrinkles between the eye-brows, which might be in-dicative either of thought or of irascibility—perhaps of both. He spoke quick, and with a little occasional embarrassment of voice, which, however, never communicated itself to his manner. He seemed, indeed, to have a perfect acquaintance with the mazes of the growing city ; and, every now and then, stopped to say when such a house was built—whither such a street was to lead, &c. As each of these details betrayed some great triumph over natural obstacles, and sometimes over national prejudice, I could not help dropping a few enthusiastic expressions in praise of the genius of the Czar. The man's eyes sparkled as he heard them.

"It is easy to see," said I, "that you sympathize with me, and that the admiration of this great man is not confined to Englishmen. How little in comparison seem all other monarchs : they ruin king-doms—the Czar creates one. The whole history of the world does not afford an instance of triumphs so vast—so important—so glorious as his have been. How his subjects should adore him ! "

"No," said the stranger, with an altered and thoughtful manner, "it is not his subjects, but *their posterity*, that will appreciate his motives, and forgive him for wishing Russia to be an empire of MEN. The present generation may sometimes be laughed, sometimes forced, out of their more barbarous habits and brute-like customs, but they cannot be reasoned out of them ; and they don't love the man who attempts to do it. Why, sir, I question whether Ivan IV., who used to butcher the dogs between prayers for an occupation, and between meals for an appetite, I question whether his memory is not to the full as much loved as the living Czar. I know, at least, that when-ever the latter attempts a reform, the good Muscovites shrug up their shoulders, and mutter, 'We did not do these things in the good old days of Ivan IV.' "

"Ah ! the people of all nations are wonderfully attached to their ancient customs ; and it is not unfrequently that the most stubborn enemies to living men are their own ancestors."

"Ha, ha!—true—good!" cried the stranger; and then, after a
short pause, he said in a tone of deep feeling which had not hitherto
seemed at all a part of his character, "We should do that which is
good to the human race, from some principle within, and should not
therefore abate our efforts for the opposition, the rancour, or the
ingratitude that we experience without.   It will be enough reward
for Peter I., if hereafter, when (in that circulation of knowledge
throughout the world which I can compare to nothing better than
the circulation of the blood in the human body) the glory of Russia
shall rest, not upon the extent of her dominions, but that of her
civilization—not upon the number of inhabitants, embruted and
besotted, but the number of enlightened, prosperous, and free men;
it will be enough for him, if he be considered to have laid the first
stone of that great change—if his labours be fairly weighed against
the obstacles which opposed them—if, for his honest and unceasing
endeavour to improve millions, he be not too severely judged for
offences in a more limited circle—and if, in consideration of having
fought the great battle against custom, circumstances, and opposing
nature, he be sometimes forgiven for not having invariably conquered
himself."

As the stranger broke off abruptly, I could not but feel a little
impressed by his words and the energy with which they were spoken.
We were now in sight of my lodging, I asked my guide to enter it;
but the change in our conversation seemed to have unfitted him a
little for my companionship.

"No," said he, "I have business now: we shall meet again;
what's your name?"

"Certainly," thought I, "no man ever scrupled so little to ask
plain questions:" however, I answered him truly and freely.

"Devereux!" said he, as if surprised: "Ha!—well—we shall
meet again.   Good day."

CHAPTER III.

THE CZAR—THE CZARINA—A FEAST AT A RUSSIAN NOBLEMAN'S.

THE next day I dressed myself in my richest attire; and,
according to my appointment, went with as much state as
I could command to the Czar's palace (if an exceedingly
humble abode can deserve so proud an appellation).
Although my mission was private, I was a little surprised by the
extreme simplicity and absence from pomp which the royal residence

presented. I was ushered for a few moments into a paltry ante-chamber, in which were several models of ships, cannon, and houses; two or three indifferent portraits—one of King William III., another of Lord Caermarthen. I was then at once admitted into the royal presence.

There were only two persons in the room—one a female, the other a man; no officers, no courtiers, no attendants, none of the insignia nor the witnesses of majesty. The female was Catherine, the Czarina; the man was the stranger I had met the day before—and Peter the Great. I was a little startled at the identity of the Czar with my inquisitive acquaintance. However, I put on as assured a countenance as I could. Indeed, I had spoken sufficiently well of the royal person to feel very little apprehension at having uncon-sciously paid so slight a respect to the royal dignity.

"Ho—ho!" cried the Czar, as I reverently approached him; "I told you we should meet soon!" and, turning round, he presented me to her majesty. That extraordinary woman received me very graciously; and, though I had been a spectator of the most artificial and magnificent court in Europe, I must confess that I could detect nothing in the Czarina's air calculated to betray her having been the servant of a Lutheran minister and the wife of a Swedish dragoon. Whether it was that greatness was natural to her, or whether (which was more probable) she was an instance of the truth of Suckling's hackneyed thought, in Brennoralt—"Success is a rare paint—hides all the ugliness."

While I was making my salutations, the Czarina rose very quietly, and presently, to my no small astonishment, brought me with her own hand, a tolerably large glass of raw brandy. There is nothing in the world I hate so much as brandy; however, I swallowed the potation as if it had been nectar, and made some fine speech about it, which the good Czarina did not seem perfectly to understand. I then, after a few preliminary observations, entered upon my main business with the Czar. Her Majesty sat at a little distance, but evidently listened very attentively to the conversation. I could not but be struck with the singularly bold and strong sense of my royal host. There was no hope of deluding or misleading him by diplo-matic subterfuge. The only way by which that wonderful man was ever misled was through his passions. His reason conquered all errors but those of temperament. I turned the conversation as artfully as I could upon Sweden and Charles XII. "Hatred to one power," thought I, "may produce love to another; and if it does, the child will spring from a very vigorous parent." While I was on this subject, I observed a most fearful convulsion come over the face of the Czar—one so fearful that I involuntarily looked away. Fortunate was it that I did so. Nothing ever enraged him more than being observed in those constitutional contortions of countenance to which from his youth he had been subjected.

After I had conversed with the Czar as long as I thought decorum permitted, I rose to depart. He dismissed me very complaisantly. I re-entered my fine equipage, and took the best of my way home.

Two or three days afterwards, the Czar ordered me to be invited to a grand dinner at Apraxin's. I went there, and soon found myself in conversation with a droll little man, a Dutch minister, and a great favourite with the Czar. The admiral and his wife, before we sat down to eat, handed round to each of their company a glass of brandy on a plate.

"What an odious custom!" whispered the little Dutch minister, smacking his lips, however, with an air of tolerable content.

"Why," said I, prudently, "all countries have their customs. Some centuries ago, a French traveller thought it horrible in us Englishmen to eat raw oysters. But the English were in the right to eat oysters; and perhaps, by and by, so much does civilization increase, we shall think the Russians in the right to drink brandy. But really (we had now sat down to the entertainment), I am agreeably surprised here. All the guests are dressed like my own countrymen; a great decorum reigns around. If it were a little less cold, I might fancy myself in London or in Paris."

"Wait," quoth the little Dutchman, with his mouth full of jelly broth—"wait till you hear them talk. What think you, now, that lady next me is saying?"

"I cannot guess—but she has the prettiest smile in the world; and there is something at once so kind and so respectful in her manner that I should say she was either asking some great favour, or returning thanks for one."

"Right," cried the little minister, "I will interpret for you. She is saying to that old gentleman—'Sir, I am extremely grateful —(and may St. Nicholas bless you for it)—for your very great kindness in having, the day before yesterday, at your sumptuous entertainment, made me so deliciously—drunk!'"

"You are witty, Monsieur," said I, smiling. "*Se non è vero è ben trovato.*"

"By my soul, it is true," cried the Dutchman; "but, hush!— see, they are going to cut up that great pie."

I turned my eyes to the centre of the table, which was ornamented with a huge pasty. Presently it was cut open, and out—walked a hideous little dwarf.

"Are they going to eat him?" said I.

"Ha—ha!" laughed the Dutchman. "No! this is a fashion of the Czar's, which the admiral thinks it good policy to follow. See, it tickles the hebete Russians. They are quite merry on it."

"To be sure," said I; "practical jokes are the only witticisms savages understand."

"Ay, and if it were not for such jokes now and then, the Czar would be odious beyond measure; but dwarf pies and mock processions make his subjects almost forgive him for having shortened their clothes and clipped their beards."

"The Czar is very fond of those mock processions?"

"Fond!" and the little man sunk his voice into a whisper; "he is the sublimest buffoon that ever existed. I will tell you an instance: (do you like these Hungary wines, by the bye?) On the 9th of last June, the Czar carried me, and half-a-dozen more of the foreign ministers, to his pleasure-house (Peterhoff). Dinner, as usual, all drunk with tokay, and finished by a quart of brandy each, from her Majesty's own hand. Carried off to sleep,—some in the garden—some in the wood.—Woke at four, still in the clouds. Carried back to the pleasure-house, found the Czar there, made us a low bow, and gave us a hatchet apiece, with orders to follow him. Off we trudged, rolling about like ships in the Zuyder Zee, entered a wood, and were immediately set to work at cutting a road through it. Nice work for us of the *corps diplomatique!* And, by my soul, sir, you see that I am by no means a thin man! We had three hours of it—were carried back—made drunk again—sent to bed—roused again in an hour—made drunk a third time; and, because we *could not* be waked again, left in peace till eight the next morning. Invited to court to breakfast—such headaches we had—longed for coffee—found nothing but brandy—forced to drink—sick as dogs—sent to take an airing upon the most damnable little horses —not worth a guilder—no bridles nor saddles—bump—bump—bump we go—up and down before the Czar's window—he and the Czarina looking at us. I do assure you I lost two stone by that ride—two stone, sir!—taken to dinner—drunk again, by the Lord —all bundled on board a *torrenschute*—devil of a storm came on—Czar took the rudder—Czarina on high benches in the cabin, which was full of water—waves beating—winds blowing—certain of being drowned—charming prospect!—tossed about for seven hours—driven into the port of Cronsflot. Czar leaves us, saying, 'Too much of a jest, eh, gentlemen?' All got ashore wet as dog-fishes, made a fire, stripped stark naked, (a Dutch ambassador stark naked —think of it, sir!) crept into some covers of sledges, and rose next morning with the ague—positive fact, sir. Had the ague for two months. Saw the Czar in August—'A charming excursion to my pleasure-house,' said his majesty—'we must make another party there soon.'"

As the Dutchman delivered himself of this little history he was by no means forgetful of the Hungary wines ; and as Bacchus and Venus have old affinity, he now began to grow eloquent on the women.

"What think you of them yourself?" said he, "they have a rolling look, eh?"

"They have so," I answered, "but they all have black teeth— what's the reason?"

"They think it a beauty, and say white teeth are the sign of a blackamoor."

Here the Dutchman was accosted by some one else, and there was a pause.   Dinner at last ceased, the guests did not sit long after dinner, and for a very good reason : the brandy bowl is a great enforcer of a prostrate position!   I had the satisfaction of seeing the company safely under the table.   The Dutchman went first, and, having dexterously manœuvred an escape from utter oblivion for myself, I managed to find my way home, more edified than delighted by the character of a Russian entertainment.

CHAPTER IV.

CONVERSATIONS WITH THE CZAR—IF CROMWELL WAS THE GREAT-
EST MAN (CÆSAR EXCEPTED) WHO EVER *ROSE* TO THE SUPREME
POWER, PETER WAS THE GREATEST MAN EVER *BORN* TO IT.

IT was singular enough that my introduction to the notice of Peter the Great and Philip the Debonnair, should have taken place under circumstances so far similar that both those illustrious personages were playing the part rather of subjects than of princes.   I cannot, however, conceive a greater mark of the contrast between their characters than the different motives and manners of the incognitos severally assumed.

Philip, in a scene of low riot and debauch, hiding the Jupiter under the Silenus—wearing the mask only for the licentiousness it veiled, and foregoing the prerogative of power, solely for indulgence in the grossest immunities of vice.

Peter, on the contrary, parting with the selfishness of state, in order to watch the more keenly over the interests of his people— only omitting to preside in order to examine—and affecting the subject only to learn the better the duties of the prince. Had I leisure, I might here pause to point out a notable contrast, not between the Czar and the Regent, but between Peter the Great and *Louis le Grand*; both creators of a new era,—both associated with a vast change in the condition of two mighty empires. There ceases the likeness, and begins the contrast; the blunt simplicity of Peter, the gorgeous magnificence of Louis; the sternness of a legislator for barbarians, the clemency of an idol of courtiers. One the victorious defender of his country—a victory solid, durable, and just; the other the conquering devastator of a neighbouring people—a victory, glittering, evanescent, and dishonourable. The one, in peace, rejecting parade, pomp, individual honours, and transforming a wilderness into an empire: the other involved in ceremony, and throned on pomp: and exhausting the produce of millions to pamper the bloated vanity of an individual. The one a fire that burns, without enlightening beyond a most narrow circle, and whose lustre is tracked by what it ruins, and fed by what it consumes : the other a luminary, whose light, not so dazzling in its rays, spreads over a world, and is noted, not for what it destroys, but for what it vivifies and creates.

I cannot say that it was much to my credit that, while I thought the Regent's condescension towards me natural enough, I was a little surprised by the favour shown me by the Czar. At Paris, I had *seemed* to be the man of pleasure; that alone was enough to charm Philip of Orleans. But in Russia, what could I seem in any way calculated to charm the Czar? I could neither make ships nor could sail them when they were made; I neither knew, nor what was worse, cared to know, the stern from the rudder. Mechanics were a mystery to me; road-making was an incomprehensible science. Brandy I could not endure—a blunt bearing, and familiar manner, I could not assume. What was it then that made the Czar call upon me, at least twice a week in private, shut himself up with me by the hour together, and endeavour to make me drunk with tokay, in order (as he very incautiously let out one night), "to learn the secrets of my heart?" I thought at first, that the nature of my mission was enough to solve the riddle : but we talked so little about it that, with all my diplomatic vanities fresh about me, I could not help feeling I owed the honour I received less to my qualities as a minister, than to those as an individual.

At last, however, I found that the secret attraction was what the Czar termed the philosophical channel into which our conferences flowed. I never saw a man so partial to moral problems and metaphysical inquiries, especially to those connected with what ought to be the beginning or the end of all moral sciences—politics.

Sometimes we would wander out in disguise, and select some object
from the customs, or things around us, as the theme of reflection
and discussion; nor in these moments would the Czar ever allow
me to yield to his rank what I might not feel disposed to concede
to his arguments.   One day, I remember that he arrested me in
the streets, and made me accompany him to look upon two men
undergoing the fearful punishment of the battaog;[1] one was a
German, the other a Russian; the former shrieked violently—
struggled in the hands of his punishers—and, with the utmost
difficulty, was subjected to his penalty; the latter bore it patiently,
and in silence; he only spoke once, and it was to say, "God bless
the Czar!"

"Can your majesty hear the man," said I, warmly, when the
Czar interpreted these words to me, "and not pardon him?"

Peter frowned, but I was not silenced.   "You don't know the
Russians!" said he, sharply, and turned aside.   The punishment
was now over.   "Ask the German," said the Czar to an officer,
"what was his offence?"   The German, who was writhing and
howling horribly, uttered some violent words against the disgrace
of the punishment, and the pettiness of his fault; what the fault
was I forget.

"Now ask the Russian," said Peter.   "My punishment was
just!" said the Russian, coolly, putting on his clothes as if nothing
had happened; "God and the Czar were angry with me!"

"Come away, Count," said the Czar; "and now solve me a
problem.   I know both those men; and the German, in a battle,
would be the braver of the two.   How comes it that he weeps and
writhes like a girl, while the Russian bears the same pain without a
murmur?"

"Will your majesty forgive me," said I, "but I cannot help
wishing that the Russian had complained more bitterly; insensibility to punishment is the sign of a brute, not a hero.   Do you
not see that the German felt the indignity, the Russian did not;
and do you not see that that very pride, which betrays agony under
the disgrace of the battaog, is exactly the very feeling that would
have produced courage in the glory of the battle.   A sense of
honour makes better soldiers and better men than indifference to
pain."

"But had I ordered the Russian to death, he would have gone
with the same apathy, and the same speech, 'It is just! I have
offended God and the Czar!'"

"Dare I observe, Sire, that the fact would be a strong proof of
the dangerous falsity of the old maxims which extol indifference to

---

[1] A terrible kind of flogging, but less severe than the knout.

death as a virtue. In some individuals it may be a sign of virtue; I allow; but, as a *national* trait, it is the strongest sign of national misery. Look round the great globe. What countries are those where the inhabitants bear death with cheerfulness, or, at least, with apathy? Are they the most civilized—the most free—the most prosperous? Pardon me—no! They are the half-starved, half-clothed, half-human, sons of the forest and the waste; or, when gathered in states, they are slaves without enjoyment or sense beyond the hour: and the reason that they do not recoil from the pangs of death is because they have never known the real pleasures or the true objects of life."

"Yet," said the Czar, musingly, "the contempt of death was the great characteristic of the Spartans."

"And, therefore," said I, "the great token that the Spartans were a miserable horde. Your majesty admires England and the English; you have, beyond doubt, witnessed an execution in that country; you have noted, even where the criminal is consoled by religion, how he trembles, and shrinks—how dejected—how prostrate of heart he is before the doom is completed. Take now the vilest slave, either of the Emperor of Morocco, or the great Czar of Russia. He changes neither tint nor muscle: he requires no consolation: he shrinks from no torture. What is the inference? *That slaves dread death less than the free.* And it should be so. The end of legislation is not to make *death*, but *life*, a blessing."

"You have put the matter in a new light," said the Czar; "but you allow that, in individuals, contempt of death is sometimes a virtue."

"Yes, when it springs from mental reasonings, not physical indifference. But your majesty has already put in action one vast spring of a system, which will ultimately open to your subjects so many paths of existence that they will preserve contempt for its proper objects, and not lavish it solely, as they do now, on the degradation which sullies life, and the axe that ends it. You have already begun the conquest of another and a most vital error in the philosophy of the ancients; that philosophy taught that man should have few wants, and made it a crime to increase, and a virtue to reduce, them. A legislator should teach, on the contrary, that man should have many wants: for wants are not only the sources of enjoyment—they are the sources of improvement; and that nation will be the most enlightened among whose populace they are found the most numerous. You, Sire, by circulating the arts, the graces, create a vast herd of moral wants hitherto unknown, and in those wants will hereafter be found, the prosperity of your people, the fountain of your resources, and the strength of your empire."

In conversation on these topics we often passed hours together, and from such conferences the Czar passed only to those on other topics more immediately useful to him. No man, perhaps, had a larger share of the mere human frailties than Peter the Great; yet I do confess that when I saw the nobleness of mind with which he flung aside his rank as a robe, and repaired from man to man, the humblest or the highest, the artisan or the prince,—the prosperity of his subjects his only object, and the acquisition of knowledge his only means to obtain it,—I do confess that my mental sight refused even to perceive his frailties, and that I could almost have bent the knee in worship to a being whose benevolence was so pervading a spirit, and whose power was so glorious a minister to utility.

Towards the end of January, I completed my mission, and took my leave of the court of Russia.

"Tell the Regent," said Peter, "that I shall visit him in France soon, and shall expect to see his drawings, if I show him my models."

In effect, the next month (February 16), the Czar commenced his second course of travels. He was pleased to testify some regard for me on my departure. "If ever you quit the service of the French court, and your own does not require you, I implore you to come to me; I will give you *carte blanche* as to the nature and appointments of your office."

I need not say that I expressed my gratitude for the royal condescension; nor that, in leaving Russia, I brought, from the example of its sovereign, a greater desire to be useful to mankind than I had known before. Pattern and Teacher of kings, if each country, in each century, had produced one such ruler as you, either all mankind would *now* be contented with despotism, or all mankind would be *free!* Oh! when kings have only to be good, to be kept for ever in our hearts and souls as the gods and benefactors of the earth, by what monstrous fatality have they been so blind to their fame? When we remember the millions, the generations, they can degrade, destroy, elevate or save, we might almost think (even if the other riddles of the present existence did not require a future existence to solve them), we might almost think a hereafter *necessary*, were it but for the sole purpose of requiting the virtues of princes, —or their SINS![1]

---

[1] Upon his death-bed Peter is reported to have said, "God, I dare trust, will look mercifully upon my faults, in consideration of the good I have done my country." These are worthy to be the last words of a king! Rarely has there been a monarch who more required the forgiveness of the Creator ;—yet seldom perhaps has there been a human being who more deserved it.—ED.

CHAPTER V.

RETURN TO PARIS—INTERVIEW WITH BOLINGBROKE—A GALLANT
ADVENTURE—AFFAIR WITH DUBOIS—PUBLIC LIFE IS A DRAMA,
IN WHICH PRIVATE VICES GENERALLY PLAY THE PART OF THE
SCENE-SHIFTERS.

IT is a strange feeling we experience on entering a great
city by night—a strange mixture of social and solitary
impressions. I say by night, because at that time we are
most inclined to feel ; and the mind, less distracted than
in the day by external objects, dwells the more intensely upon its
own hopes and thoughts, remembrances and associations — and
sheds over them, from that one feeling which it cherishes the most,
a blending and a mellowing hue.

It was at night that I re-entered Paris. I did not tarry long at
my hotel, before (though it was near upon midnight) I conveyed
myself to Lord Bolingbroke's lodgings. Knowing his engagements
at St. Germains, where the Chevalier (who had but a very few weeks
before returned to France, after the crude and unfortunate affair of
1715) chiefly resided, I was not very sanguine in my hopes of
finding him at Paris. I was, however, agreeably surprised. His
servant would have ushered me into his study, but I was willing
to introduce myself. I withheld the servant, and entered the room
alone.

The door was ajar, and Bolingbroke neither heard nor saw me.
There was something in his attitude and aspect which made me
pause to survey him, before I made myself known. He was sitting
by a table covered with books. A large folio (it was the Casaubon
edition of Polybius) was lying open before him. I recognized the
work at once—it was a favourite book with Bolingbroke, and we
had often discussed the merits of its author. I smiled as I saw that
that book, which has to statesmen so peculiar an attraction, made
still the study from which the busy, restless, ardent, and exalted
spirit of the statesman before me drew its intellectual food. But at
the moment in which I entered, his eye was absent from the page,
and turned abstractedly in an opposite, though still downcast,
direction. His countenance was extremely pale—his lips were
tightly compressed, and an air of deep thought, mingled, as it
seemed to me, with sadness—made the ruling expression of his
lordly and noble features. "It is the torpor of ambition after one

of its storms," said I, inly—and I approached, and laid my hand on his shoulder.

After our mutual greetings, I said, "Have the dead so strong an attraction that at this hour they detain the courted and courtly Bolingbroke from the admiration and converse of the living?"

The statesman looked at me earnestly—"Have you heard the news of the day?" said he.

"How is it possible? I have but just arrived at Paris."

"You do not know, then, that I have resigned my office under the Chevalier!"

"Resigned your office!"

"Resigned is a wrong word—I received a dismissal. Immediately on his return the Chevalier sent for me—embraced me—desired me to prepare to follow him to Lorraine; and three days afterwards came the Duke of Ormond to me, to ask me to deliver up the seals and papers. I put the latter very carefully in a little letter case, and behold an end to the administration of Lord Bolingbroke! The Jacobites abuse me terribly—their king accuses me of neglect, incapacity, and treachery—and Fortune pulls down the fabric she had built for me, in order to pelt me with the stones!"[1]

"My dear, dear friend, I am indeed grieved for you; but I am more incensed at the infatuation of the Chevalier. Surely, surely he must already have seen his error, and solicited your return."

"Return!" cried Bolingbroke, and his eyes flashed fire—"return! —Hear what I said to the queen mother who came to me to attempt a reconciliation: 'Madam,' said I, in a tone as calm as I could command, 'if ever this hand draws the sword, or employs the pen, in behalf of that prince, may it rot!' Return! not if my head were the price of refusal! Yet, Devereux,"—and here Bolingbroke's voice and manner changed—"Yet it is not at these tricks of fate that a wise man will repine. We do right to cultivate honours; they are sources of gratification to ourselves; they are more—they are incentives to the conduct which works benefit to others; but we do wrong to afflict ourselves at their loss. *Nec querere nec spernere honores oportet*.[2] It is good to enjoy the blessings of fortune: it is better to submit without a pang to their loss. You remember, when you left me, I was preparing myself for this stroke—believe me, I am now prepared."

And in truth Bolingbroke bore the ingratitude of the Chevalier well. Soon afterwards he carried his long cherished wishes for retirement into effect; and Fate, who delights in reversing her disk, leaving in darkness what she had just illuminated, and illumining

---

[1] Letter to Sir W. Windham.—ED.
[2] It becomes us neither to court, nor to despise honours.

what she had hitherto left in obscurity and gloom, for a long interval separated us from each other, no less by his seclusion than by the publicity to which she condemned myself.

Lord Bolingbroke's dismissal was not the only event affecting me that had occurred during my absence from France. Among the most active partisans of the Chevalier, in the expedition of Lord Mar, had been Montreuil. So great, indeed, had been either his services, or the idea entertained of their value, that a reward of extraordinary amount was offered for his head. Hitherto he had escaped, and was supposed to be still in Scotland.

But what affected me more nearly was the condition of Gerald's circumstances. On the breaking out of the rebellion he had been suddenly seized, and detained in prison ; and it was only upon the escape of the Chevalier that he was released ; apparently, how-ever, nothing had been proved against him ; and my absence from the head quarters of intelligence left me in ignorance both of the grounds of his imprisonment, and the circumstances of his release.

I heard, however, from Bolingbroke, who seemed to possess some of that information which the ecclesiastical *intriguants* of the day so curiously transmitted from court to court, and corner to corner, that Gerald had retired to Devereux Court in great disgust at his confinement. However, when I considered his bold character, his close intimacy with Montreuil, and the genius for intrigue which that priest so eminently possessed, I was not much inclined to censure the government for unnecessary precaution in his imprisonment.

There was another circumstance connected with the rebellion which possessed for me an individual and deep interest. A man of the name of Barnard had been executed in England for seditious and treasonable practices. I took especial pains to ascertain every particular respecting him. I learned that he was young, of incon-siderable note, but esteemed clever ; and had, long previously to the death of the queen, been secretly employed by the friends of the Chevalier. This circumstance occasioned me much internal emotion, though there could be no doubt that the Barnard whom I had such cause to execrate, had only borrowed from this minion the disguise of his name.

The Regent received me with all the graciousness and complaisance for which he was so remarkable. To say the truth, my mission had been extremely fortunate in its results ; the only cause in which the Regent was concerned, the interests of which Peter the Great appeared to disregard, was that of the Chevalier ; but I had been fully instructed on that head anterior to my legation.

There appears very often to be a sort of moral fitness between the beginning and the end of certain alliances or acquaintances. This sentiment is not very clearly expressed. I am about to illustrate it by an important event in my political life. During my absence Dubois had made rapid steps towards being a great man. He was daily growing into power, and those courtiers who were neither too haughty nor too honest to bend the knee to so vicious, yet able, a minion, had already singled him out as a fit person to flatter and to rise by. For me, I neither sought nor avoided him ; but he was as civil towards me as his *brusque* temper permitted him to be towards most persons ; and as our careers were not likely to cross one another, I thought I might reckon on his neutrality, if not on his friendship. Chance turned the scale against me.

One day I received an anonymous letter, requesting me to be, at such an hour, at a certain house in the Rue ——. It occurred to me as no improbable supposition, that the appointment might relate to my individual circumstances, whether domestic or political, and I certainly had not at the moment any ideas of gallantry in my brain. At the hour prescribed I appeared at the place of assignation. My mind misgave me when I saw a female conduct me into a little chamber hung with tapestry descriptive of the loves of Mars and Venus. After I had cooled my heels in this apartment for about a quarter of an hour, in sailed a tall woman, of a complexion almost *Moorish.* I bowed—the lady sighed. An *éclaircissement* ensued— and I found that I had the good fortune to be the object of a *caprice*, in the favourite mistress of the Abbé Dubois. Nothing was farther from my wishes ! What a pity it is that one cannot always tell a woman one's mind !

I attempted a flourish about friendship, honour, and the respect due to the *amante* of the most intimate *ami* I had in the world.

" Pooh ! " said the tawny Calypso, a little pettishly—" pooh ! one does not talk of those things here."

" Madame," said I, very energetically, " I implore you to refrain. Do not excite too severe a contest between passion and duty ! I feel that I must fly you—you are already too bewitching."

Just as I rose to depart, in rushes the *femme de chambre*, and announces, not Monsieur, the Abbé, but Monseigneur, the Regent. Of course (the old resort in such cases) I was thrust into a closet ; in marches his royal highness, and is received very cavalierly. It is quite astonishing to me what airs those women give themselves when they have princes to manage ! However, my confinement was not long—the closet had another door—the *femme de chambre* slips round, opens it, and I congratulate myself on my escape.

When a Frenchwoman is piqued, she passes all understanding. The next day I am very quietly employed at breakfast, when my valet ushers in a masked personage, and, behold my gentlewoman again ! Human endurance will not go too far, and this was a case which required one to be in a passion one way or the other; so I feigned anger, and talked with exceeding dignity about the predicament I had been placed in the day before.

"Such must always be the case," said I, "when one is weak enough to form an attachment to a lady who encourages so many others!"

"For your sake," said the tender dame, "for your sake, then, I will discard them all!"

There was something grand in this: it might have elicited a few strokes of pathos, when—never was there anything so strangely provoking—the Abbé Dubois himself was heard in my ante-room. I thought this chance, but it was more; the good Abbé, I afterwards found, had traced cause for suspicion, and had come to pay me a visit of amatory police. I opened my dressing-room door, and thrust in the lady. "There," said I, "are the back-stairs, and at the bottom of the back-stairs is a door."

Would not any one have thought this hint enough? By no means; this very tall lady stooped to the littleness of listening, and, instead of departing, stationed herself by the key-hole.

I never exactly learned whether Dubois suspected the visit his mistress had paid me, or whether he merely surmised, from his spies or her escritoire, that she harboured an inclination towards me; in either case his policy was natural, and like himself. He sat himself down, talked of the Regent, of pleasure, of women, and, at last, of this very tall lady in question.

"*La pauvre diablesse*," said he, contemptuously, "I had once compassion on her; I have repented it ever since. You have no idea what a terrible creature she is—has such a wen in her neck— quite a *goître. Mort diable!*" (and the Abbé spat in his handkerchief). "I would sooner have a *liaison* with the witch of Endor!"

Not content with this, he went on in his usual gross and displeasing manner to enumerate or to forge those various particulars of her personal charms, which he thought most likely to steel me against her attractions. "Thank Heaven, at least," thought I, "that she has gone!"

Scarcely had this pious gratulation flowed from my heart, before the door was burst open, and, pale—trembling—eyes on fire—hands clenched—forth stalked the lady in question. A wonderful proof how much sooner a woman would lose her character than allow it to be called not worth the losing. She entered, and had all the furies of Hades lent her their tongues, she could not have been more eloquent. It would have been a very pleasant scene if one had not been a partner in it. The old *Abbé*, with his keen, astute marked face, struggling between surprise, fear, the sense of the ridiculous, and the certainty of losing his mistress ; the lady, foaming at the mouth, and shaking her clenched hand most menacingly at her traducer—myself endeavouring to pacify, and acting, as one does at such moments, mechanically—though one flatters one-self afterwards that one acted solely from wisdom.

But the Abbé's mistress was by no means content with vindicating herself—she retaliated—and gave so minute a description of the Abbé's own qualities and graces, coupled with so many pleasing illustrations, that in a very little time his coolness forsook him, and he grew in as great a rage as herself. At last she flew out of the room. The Abbé, trembling with passion, shook me most cordially by the hand, grinned from ear to ear, said it was a capital joke, wished me good-bye, as if he loved me better than his eyes, and left the house, my most irreconcilable and bitter foe !

How could it be otherwise? The rivalship the Abbé might have forgiven—such things happened every day to him—but the having been made so egregiously ridiculous, the Abbé could not forgive ; and the Abbé's was a critical age for jesting on these matters, sixty or so. And then such unpalatable sarcasms on his appearance ! "'Tis all over in that quarter," said I to myself, "but we may find another," and I drove out that very day to pay my respects to the Regent.

What a pity it is that one's pride should so often be the bane of one's wisdom ! Ah ! that one could be as good a man of the world in practice as one is in theory ! my master-stroke of policy at that moment would evidently have been this : I should have gone to the Regent and made out a story a little similar to the real one, but with this difference, all the ridicule of the situation should have fallen upon me, and the little Dubois should have been elevated on a pinnacle of respectable appearances ! This, as the Regent told the Abbé everything, would have saved me. I saw the plan ; but was too proud to adopt it ; I followed another course in my game : I threw away the knave, and played with the king, *i.e.* with the Regent. After a little preliminary conversation, I turned the conversation on the Abbé.

"Ah ! the *scélérat !*" said Philip, smiling, "'tis a sad dog, but very clever and *loves me;* he would be incomparable, if he were but decently honest."

"At least," said I, "he is no hypocrite, and that is some praise."

"Hem !" ejaculated the Duke, very slowly, and then, after a pause, he said, "Count, I have a real kindness for you, and I will therefore give you a piece of advice : think as well of Dubois as you can, and address him as if he were all you endeavoured to fancy him."

After this hint, which in the mouth of any prince but Philip of Orleans would have been not a little remarkable for its want of dignity, my prospects did not seem much brighter : however, I was not discouraged.

"The Abbé," said I, respectfully, "is a choleric man : one *may* displease him ; but dare I hope that so long as I preserve inviolate my zeal and my attachment to the interests, and the person of your highness, no—"

The Regent interrupted me. " You mean nobody shall success- fully misrepresent you to me ? No, Count," (and here the Regent spoke with the earnestness and dignity, which, when he did assume, few wore with a nobler grace)—"no, Count, I make a distinction between those who minister to the state, and those who minister to me. I consider your services too valuable to the former to put them at the mercy of the latter. And now that the conversation has turned upon business, I wish to speak to you about this scheme of *Gortz.*"

After a prolonged conference with the Regent upon matters of business, in which his deep penetration into human nature not a little surprised me, I went away, thoroughly satisfied with my visit. I should not have been so had I added to my other accomplishments the gift of prophecy.

Above five days after this interview, I thought it would be but prudent to pay the Abbé Dubois one of those visits of homage which it was already become policy to pay him. "If I go," thought I, "it will seem as if nothing had happened ; if I stay away, it will seem as if I attached importance to a scene I should appear to have forgotten."

It so happened that the Abbé had a very unusual visitor that morning, in the person of the austere but admirable Duc de St. Simon. There was a singular, and almost invariable, distinction in the Regent's mind between one kind of regard and another. His regard for one order of persons always arose either out of his vices or his indolence ; his regard for another, out of his good qualities and his strong sense. The Duc de St. Simon held the same place in the latter species of affection that Dubois did in the former. The Duc was just coming out of the Abbé's closet as I entered the ante- room. He paused to speak to me, while Dubois, who had followed the Duc out, stopped for one moment, and surveyed me with a look like a thunder-cloud. I did not appear to notice it, but St. Simon did.

"That look," said he, as Dubois, beckoning to a gentleman to accompany him to his closet, once more disappeared, "that look bodes you no good, Count."

Pride is an elevation which is a spring-board at one time, and a stumbling-block at another. It was with me more often the stumbling-block than the spring-board. "Monseigneur le Duc," said I, haughtily enough, and rather in too loud a tone considering the chamber was pretty full, "in no court to which Morton Devereux proffers his services shall his fortune depend upon the looks of a low-born insolent, or a profligate priest."

St. Simon smiled sardonically. "Monsieur le Comte," said he, rather civilly, "I honour your sentiments, and I wish you success in the world——and a lower voice."

I was going to say something by way of retort, for I was in a very bad humour, but I checked myself; "I need not," thought I, "make two enemies, if I can help it."

"I shall never," I replied gravely, "I shall never despair, so long as the Duc de St. Simon lives, of winning by the same arts the favour of princes and the esteem of good men."

The Duc was flattered, and replied suitably, but he very soon afterwards went away. I was resolved that I would not go till I had fairly seen what sort of reception the Abbé would give me. I did not wait long—he came out of his closet, and standing in his usual rude manner with his back to the fire-place, received the addresses and compliments of his visitors. I was not in a hurry to present myself, but I did so at last with a familiar, yet rather respectful, air. Dubois looked at me from head to foot, and abruptly turning his back upon me, said with an oath, to a courtier who stood next to him,—"The plagues of Pharaoh are come again—only instead of Egyptian frogs in our chambers, we have the still more troublesome guests—English adventurers!"

Somehow or other my compliments rarely tell; I am lavish enough of them, but they generally have the air of sarcasms; thank Heaven, however, no one can accuse me of ever wanting a rude answer to a rude speech. "Ha! ha! ha!" said I now, in answer to Dubois, with a courteous laugh, "you have an excellent wit, Abbé. Apropos of adventures, I met a Monsieur St. Laurent, Principal of the Institution of St. Michael, the other day. 'Count,' said he, hearing I was going to Paris, 'you can do me an especial favour!' 'What is it?' said I. 'Why, a cast-off valet of mine is living at Paris—he would have gone long since to the galleys, if he had not taken sanctuary in the Church—if ever you meet him, give him a good horse-whipping on my account :—his name is William Dubois.'—'Depend upon it,' answered I to Monsieur St. Laurent, 'that if he is servant to any one not belonging to the royal family, I will fulfil your errand, and horsewhip him soundly; if *in* the service of the royal family, why respect for his masters must oblige me to content myself with putting all persons on their guard against a little rascal, who retains, in all situations, the manners of the apothecary's son, and the roguery of the director's valet.'"

All the time I was relating this charming little anecdote, it would have been amusing to the last degree to note the horrified countenances of the surrounding gentlemen. Dubois was too confounded, too aghast, to interrupt me, and I left the room before a single syllable was uttered. Had Dubois at that time been what he was afterwards, cardinal and prime minister, I should in all probability have had permanent lodgings in the Bastile, in return for my story. Even as it was, the Abbé was not so grateful as he ought to have been, for my taking so much pains to amuse him! In spite of my anger on leaving the favourite, I did not forget my prudence, and accordingly I hastened to the prince. When the Regent admitted me, I flung myself on my knee, and told him, verbatim, all that had happened. The Regent, who seems to have had very little real liking for Dubois, could not help laughing when I ludicrously described to him the universal consternation my anecdote had excited.[1]

"Courage, my dear Count," said he kindly, "you have nothing to fear; return home and count upon an embassy!"

I relied on the royal word, returned to my lodgings, and spent the evening with Chaulieu and Fontenelle. The next day the Duc de St. Simon paid me a visit. After a little preliminary conversation, he unburthened the secret with which he was charged. I was desired to leave Paris in forty-eight hours.

"Believe me," said St. Simon, "that this message was not entrusted to me by the Regent, without great reluctance. He sends you many condescending and kind messages; says he shall always both esteem and like you, and hopes to see you again, some time or other, at the Palais Royal. Moreover, he desires the message to be private, and has entrusted it to me in especial, because hearing that I had a kindness for you, and knowing I had a hatred for Dubois, he thought I should be the least unwelcome messenger of such disagreeable tidings. 'To tell you the truth, St. Simon,' said the Regent, laughing, 'I only consent to have him banished, from a firm conviction, that if I do not, Dubois will take some opportunity of having him beheaded.'"

[1] On the death of Dubois, the Regent wrote to the Count de Nocé, whom he had banished for an indiscreet expression against the favourite, uttered at one of his private suppers : "With the beast dies the venom : I expect you to-night to supper at the Palais Royal."

"'Pray," said I, smiling with a tolerable good grace, "pray give my most grateful and humble thanks to his highness, for his very considerate and kind foresight. I could not have chosen better for myself than his highness has chosen for me : my only regret on quitting France is at leaving a prince so affable as Philip, and a courtier so virtuous as St. Simon."

Though the good Duc went every year to the Abbey de la Trappe, for the purpose of mortifying his sins and preserving his religion, in so impious an atmosphere as the Palais Royal, he was not above flattery ; and he expressed himself towards me with particular kindness after my speech.

At court, one becomes a sort of human ant-bear, and learns to catch one's prey by one's tongue.

After we had eased ourselves a little by abusing Dubois, the Duc took his leave in order to allow me time to prepare for my "journey," as he politely called it. Before he left, he, however, asked me whither my course would be bent ? I told him that I should take my chance with the Czar Peter, and see if his czarship thought the same esteem was due to the disgraced courtier, as to the favoured diplomatist.

That night I received a letter from St. Simon, enclosing one addressed with all due form to the Czar. "You will consider the enclosed," wrote St. Simon, "a fresh proof of the Regent's kindness to you ; it is a most flattering testimonial in your favour, and cannot fail to make the Czar anxious to secure your services."

I was not a little touched by a kindness, so unusual in princes to their discarded courtiers, and this entirely reconciled me to a change of scene which, indeed, under any other circumstances, my somewhat morbid love for action and variety would have induced me rather to relish than dislike.

Within thirty-six hours from the time of dismissal, I had turned my back upon the French capital.

CHAPTER VI.

A LONG INTERVAL OF YEARS—A CHANGE OF MIND AND ITS CAUSES.

THE last accounts received of the Czar reported him to be at Dantzic. He had, however, quitted that place when I arrived there. I lost no time in following him, and presented myself to his Majesty one day after his dinner, when he was sitting with one leg in the Czarina's lap, and a bottle of the best *eau de vie* before him. I had chosen my time well ; he received me most graciously, read my letter from the Regent—about which, remembering the fate of Bellerophon, I had had certain apprehensions, but which proved to be, in the highest degree, complimentary—and then declared himself extremely happy to see me again. However parsimonious Peter generally was towards foreigners, I never had ground for personal complaint on that score. The very next day I was appointed to a post of honour and profit about the royal person ; from this I was transferred to a military station, in which I rose with great rapidity ; and I was only occasionally called from my warlike duties, to be entrusted with diplomatic missions of the highest confidence and importance.

It is this portion of my life—a portion of nine years, to the time of the Czar's death—that I shall, in this history, the most concentrate and condense. In truth, were I to dwell upon it at length, I should make little more than a mere record of political events— differing, in some respects, it is true, from the received histories of the time, but containing nothing to compensate in utility for the want of interest. That this was the exact age for adventurers, Alberoni and Dubois are sufficient proofs. Never was there a more stirring, active, restless period—never one in which the genius of intrigue was so pervadingly at work. I was not less fortunate than my brethren. Although scarcely four and twenty when I entered the Czar's service, my habits of intimacy with men much older—my customary gravity, reserve, and thought—my freedom, since Isora's death, from youthful levity or excess—my early entrance into the world—and a countenance prematurely marked with the lines of reflection, and sobered by its hue—made me appear considerably older than I was. I kept my own counsel, and affected to be so ; youth is a great enemy to one's success ; and more esteem is often bestowed upon a wrinkled brow than a plodding brain.

All the private intelligence which, during this space of time, I had received from England was far from voluminous. My mother still enjoyed the quiet of her religious retreat. A fire, arising from the negligence of a servant, had consumed nearly the whole of Devereux Court (the fine old house ! till *that* went, I thought even England held one friend). Upon this accident, Gerald had gone to London ; and, though there was now no doubt of his having been concerned in the Rebellion of 1715, he had been favourably received at court, and was already renowned throughout London, for his pleasures, his excesses, and his munificent profusion.

Montreuil, whose lot seemed to be always to lose, by intrigue, what he gained by the real solidity of his genius, had embarked very largely in the rash but gigantic schemes of Gortz and Alberoni ; schemes which, had they succeeded, would not only have placed a new king upon the English throne, but wrought an utter change over the whole face of Europe. With Alberoni and with Gortz fell Montreuil. He was banished France and Spain ; the penalty of death awaited him in Britain ; and he was supposed to have thrown himself into some convent in Italy, where his name and his character were unknown. In this brief intelligence was condensed all my information of the actors in my first scenes of life. I return to that scene on which I had now entered.

At the age of thirty-three, I had acquired a reputation sufficient to content my ambition—my fortune was larger than my wants—I was a favourite in courts—I had been successful in camps—I had already obtained all that would have rewarded the whole lives of many men superior to myself in merit—more ardent than myself in desires. I was still young—my appearance, though greatly altered, manhood had rather improved than impaired. I had not forestalled my constitution by excesses, nor worn dry the sources of pleasure by too large a demand upon their capacities ; why was it then, at that golden age—in the very prime and glory of manhood—in the very zenith and summer of success—that a deep, dark, pervading melancholy fell upon me ? A melancholy so gloomy that it seemed to me as a thick and impenetrable curtain drawn gradually between myself and the blessed light of human enjoyment. A torpor crept upon me—an indolent, heavy, clinging languor, gathered over my whole frame— the physical and the mental : I sat for hours without book, paper, object, thought, gazing on vacancy—stirring not—feeling not—yes, feeling, but feeling only one sensation, a sick, sad, drooping despond- ency—a sinking in of the heart—a sort of gnawing within, as if something living were twisted round my vitals, and, finding no other food, preyed, though with a sickly and dull maw, upon *them*. This disease came upon me slowly : it was not till the beginning of a second year, from its obvious and palpable commencement, that it grew to the height that I have described. It began with a distaste to all that I had been accustomed to enjoy or to pursue. Music, which I had always passionately loved, though from some defect in the organs of hearing, I was incapable of attaining the smallest knowledge of the science, music lost all its diviner spells, all its properties of creating a new existence, a life of dreaming and vague luxuries, within the mind—it became only a monotonous sound, less grateful to the languor of my faculties than an utter and dead stillness. I had never been what is generally termed a boon companion, but I had had the social vanities, if not the social tastes : I had insensibly loved the board which echoed with applause at my sallies, and the comrades who, while they deprecated my satire, had been complaisant enough to hail it as wit. One of my weaknesses is a love of show, and I had gratified a feeling not the less cherished because it arose from a petty source, in obtaining for my equipages, my mansion, my banquets, the celebrity which is given no less to magnificence than to fame ; now I grew indifferent alike to the signs of pomp, and to the baubles of taste—praise fell upon a listless ear, and (rare pitch of satiety !) the pleasures that are the offspring of our foibles delighted me no more. I had early learned from Bolingbroke a love for the converse of men, eminent, whether for wisdom or for wit ; the graceful badinage, or the keen critique—the sparkling flight of the winged words which circled and rebounded from lip to lip, or the deep speculation upon the mysterious and unravelled wonders of man, of nature, and the world—the light maxim upon manners, or the sage inquiry into the mines of learning ; all and each had possessed a link to bind my temper and my tastes to the graces and fascination of social life. Now a new spirit entered within me : the smile faded from my lip, and the jest departed from my tongue ; memory seemed no less treacherous than fancy, and deserted me the instant I attempted to enter into those contests of knowledge in which I had been not undistinguished before. I grew confused and embarrassed in speech —my words expressed a sense utterly different to that which I had intended to convey, and at last, as my apathy increased, I sat at my own board, silent and lifeless, freezing into ice the very powers and streams of converse which I had once been the foremost to circulate and to warm.

At the time I refer to, I was minister at one of the small continental courts, where life is a round of unmeaning etiquette and wearisome ceremonials, a daily labour of trifles—a ceaseless pageantry of nothings —I had been sent there upon one important event, the business resulting from it had soon ceased, and all the duties that remained for me to discharge were of a negative and passive nature. Nothing that could arouse—nothing that could occupy faculties that had for years been so perpetually wound up to a restless excitement was left for me in this terrible reservoir of *ennui*. I had come thither at once from the skirmishing and wild warfare of a Tartar foe ; a war in which, though the glory was obscure, the action was perpetual and exciting. I had come thither, and the change was as if I had passed from a mountain stream to a stagnant pool.

Society at this court reminded me of a state funeral, everything was pompous and lugubrious, even to the drapery—even to the feathers—which, in other scenes, would have been consecrated to associations of levity or of grace ; the hourly pageant swept on slow, tedious, mournful, and the object of the attendants was only to entomb the Pleasure which they affected to celebrate. What a change for the wild, the strange, the novel, the intriguing, the varying life, which, whether in courts or camps, I had hitherto led. The internal change that came over myself is scarcely to be wondered at ; the winds stood still, and the straw they had blown from quarter to quarter, whether in anger or in sport, began to moulder upon the spot where they had left it.

From this cessation of the aims, hopes, and thoughts of life, I was awakened by the spreading, as it were, of another disease—the dead, dull, aching pain at my heart, was succeeded by one acute and intense ; the absence of thought gave way to one thought more terrible—more dark—more despairing than any which had haunted me since the first year of Isora's death ; and from a numbness and pause, as it were, of existence, existence became too keen and intolerable a sense. I will enter into an explanation.

At the Court of ——, there was an Italian, not uncelebrated for his wisdom, nor unbeloved for an innocence and integrity of life, rarely indeed to be met with among his countrymen. The acquaintance of this man, who was about fifty years of age, and who was devoted, almost exclusively, to the pursuit of philosophical science, I had sedulously cultivated. His conversation pleased me ; his wisdom improved ; and his benevolence, which reminded me of the traits of La Fontaine, it was so infantine, made me incline to love him. Upon the growth of the fearful malady of mind which seized me, I had discontinued my visits and my invitations to the Italian ; and Bezoni (so was he called) felt a little offended by my neglect. As soon, however, as he discovered my state of mind, the good man's resentment left him. He forced himself upon my solitude, and would sit by me whole evenings—sometimes without exchanging a word—sometimes with vain attempts to interest, to arouse, or to amuse me.

At last, one evening, it was the era of a fearful suffering to me, our conversation turned upon those subjects which are at once the most important, and the most rarely discussed. We spoke of *religion*. We first talked upon the theology of revealed religion. As Bezoni warmed into candour, I perceived that his doctrines differed from my own, and that he inly disbelieved that divine creed which Christians profess to adore. From a dispute on the ground of faith, we came to one upon the more debateable ground of reason. We turned from the subject of revealed, to that of natural, religion ; and we entered long and earnestly into that grandest of all earthly speculations—the metaphysical proofs of the immortality of the soul. Again the sentiments of Bezoni were opposed to mine. He was a believer in the dark doctrine which teaches that man is dust, and that all things are forgotten in the grave. He expressed his opinions with a clearness and precision the more impressive because totally devoid of cavil and of rhetoric. I listened in silence, but with a deep and most chilling dismay. Even now I think I see the man as he sat before me, the light of the lamp falling on his high forehead and dark features ; even now I think I hear his calm, low voice—the silver voice of his country—stealing to my heart, and withering the only pure and unsullied hope which I yet cherished there.

Bezoni left me, unconscious of the anguish he bequeathed me, to think over all he had said. I did not sleep, nor even retire to bed. I laid my head upon my hands, and surrendered myself to turbulent, yet intense reflection. Every man who has lived much in the world, and conversed with its various tribes, has, I fear, met with many who, on this momentous subject, profess the same tenets as Bezoni. But he was the first person I had met of that sect who had evidently thought long and deeply upon the creed he had embraced. He was not a voluptuary, nor a boaster, nor a wit. He had not been misled by the delusions either of vanity or of the senses. He was a man, pure, innocent, modest, full of all tender charities, and meek dispositions towards mankind ; it was evidently his interest to believe in a future state : he could have had nothing to fear from it. Not a single passion did he cherish which the laws of another world would have condemned. Add to this, what I have observed before, that he was not a man fond of the display of intellect, nor one that brought to the discussions of wisdom the artillery of wit. He was grave, humble, and self-diffident, beyond all beings. I would have given a kingdom to have found something in the advocate by which I could have condemned the cause ; I could not, and I was wretched.

I spent the whole of the next week among my books. I ransacked whatever in my scanty library the theologians had written, or the philosophers had bequeathed upon the mighty secret. I arranged their arguments in my mind. I armed myself with their weapons. I

felt my heart spring joyously within me as I felt the strength I had
acquired, and I sent to the philosopher to visit me, that I might
conquer and confute him. He came : but he spoke with pain and
reluctance. He saw that I had taken the matter far more deeply to
heart than he could have supposed it possible in a courtier, and a
man of fortune and the world. Little did he know of me or my
secret soul. I broke down his reserve at last. I unrolled my
arguments. I answered his, and we spent the whole night in
controversy. He left me, and I was more bewildered than ever.

To speak truth, he had devoted years to the subject : I had
devoted only a week. He had come to his conclusions step by
step ; he had reached the great ultimatum with slowness, with care,
and, he confessed, with anguish and with reluctance. What a match
was I, who brought a hasty temper, and a limited reflection, on that
subject, to a reasoner like this ? His candour staggered and chilled
me even more than his logic. Arguments that occurred not to me,
upon my side of the question, *he* stated at length, and with force ; I
heard, and, till he replied to them, I deemed they were unanswerable—the reply came, and I had no counter-word. A meeting of
this nature was often repeated ; and when he left me, tears crept
into my wild eyes, my heart melted within me, and I wept.

I must now enter more precisely than I have yet done into my
state of mind upon religious matters at the time this dispute with
the Italian occurred. To speak candidly, I had been far less
shocked with his opposition to me upon matters of doctrinal faith,
than with that upon matters of abstract reasoning. Bred a Roman
Catholic, though pride, consistency, custom, made me externally
adhere to the Papal Church, I inly perceived its errors, and smiled
at its superstitions. And in the busy world, where so little but
present objects, or *human* anticipations of the future, engross the
attention, I had never given the subject that consideration which
would have enabled me (as it has since) to separate the dogmas of
the priest from the precepts of the Saviour, and thus confirmed my
belief as the Christian, by the very means which would have loosened
it as the Sectarian. So, that at the time Bezoni knew me, a certain
indifference to—perhaps arising from an ignorance of—doctrinal
points, rendered me little hurt by arguments against opinions which
I embraced indeed, but with a lukewarm and imperfect affection.
But it was far otherwise upon abstract points of reasoning, far otherwise, when the hope of surviving this frail and most unhallowed
being was to be destroyed. I might have been indifferent to cavil
upon *what* was the word of God, but never to question of the justice
of God himself. In the whole world, there was not a more ardent
believer in our imperishable nature, nor one more deeply interested

in the belief. Do not let it be supposed that because I have not often recurred to Isora's death (or because I have continued my history in a jesting and light tone), that that event ever passed from the memory which it had turned to bitterness and gall. Never, in the mazes of intrigue, in the festivals of pleasure, in the tumults of ambition, in the blaze of a licentious court, or by the rude tents of a barbarous host,—never, my buried love, had I forgotten thee! That remembrance, had no other cause existed, would have led me to God. Every night, in whatever toils or objects, whatever failures or triumphs, the day had been consumed—every night before I laid my head upon my widowed and lonely pillow, I had knelt down, and lifted my heart to Heaven, blending the hopes of that heaven with the memory and the vision of Isora. Prayer had seemed to me a commune not only with the living God, but with the dead by whom His dwelling is surrounded. Pleasant and soft was it to turn to one thought, to which all the holiest portions of my nature clung, between the wearying acts of this hard and harsh drama of existence. Even the bitterness of Isora's early and unavenged death passed away, when I thought of the heaven to which she was gone, and in which, though I journeyed now through sin and travail, and recked little if the paths of others differed from my own, I yet trusted, with a solemn trust, that I should meet her at last. There was I to merit her with a love as undying, and at length as pure, as her own. It was this that at the stated hour in which, after my prayer for our reunion, I surrendered my spirit to the bright and wild visions of her far, but *not impassable* home,—it was this which for that single hour made all around me a paradise of delighted thoughts! It was not the little earth, nor the cold sky, nor the changing wave, nor the perishable turf—no, nor the dead wall, and the narrow chamber which were round me then! No dreamer ever was so far from the localities of flesh and life as I was in that enchanted hour: a light seemed to settle upon all things around me; her voice murmured on my ear, her kisses melted on my brow; I shut my eyes, and I fancied that I beheld her!

Wherefore was this comfort?—whence came the spell which admitted me to this fairy land? What was the source of the hope, and the rapture, and the delusion? Was it not the deep certainty that *Isora yet existed*—that her spirit, her nature, her love were preserved, were inviolate, were the same? That they watched over me yet, that she knew that in that hour I was with her—that she felt my prayer— that even then she anticipated the moment when my soul should burst the human prison-house, and be once more blended with her own?

What! and was this to be no more? Were those mystic and sweet revealings to be mute to me for ever?. Were my thoughts of

L 2

Isora to be henceforth bounded to the charnel-house and the worm? Was she indeed *no more? No more*—O, intolerable despair!— Why, there was not a thing I had once known, not a dog that I had caressed, not a book that I had read, which I could know that I should see *no more*, and, knowing, not feel something of regret. No more! were we, indeed, parted for ever and for ever? Had she gone in her young years, with her warm affections, her new hopes, all green and unwithered at her heart, at once into dust, stillness, ice? And had I known her only for one year, one little year, to see her torn from me by a violent and bloody death, and to be left a mourner in this vast and eternal charnel, without a solitary consolation, or a gleam of hope? Was the earth to be henceforth a mere mass conjured from the bones and fattened by the clay of our dead sires?—were the stars and the moon to be mere atoms and specks of a chill light, no longer worlds, which the ardent spirit might hereafter reach, and be fitted to enjoy? Was the heaven—the tender, blue, loving heaven, in whose far regions I had dreamt was Isora's home, and had, therefore, grown better and happier when I gazed upon it, to be nothing but cloud and air? and had the love, which had seemed so immortal, and so springing from that which had not blent itself with mortality, been but a gross lamp fed only by the properties of a brute nature, and placed in a dark cell of clay, to glimmer, to burn, and to expire with the frail walls which it had illumined? Dust, death, worms, —were these the heritage of love and hope, of thought, of passion, of all that breathed, and kindled, and exalted, and *created* within?

Could I contemplate this idea, could I believe it possible? *I could not.* But against the abstract, the logical arguments for that idea—had I a reply? I shudder as I write that at *that* time I had not! I endeavoured to fix my whole thoughts to the study of those subtle reasonings which I had hitherto so imperfectly conned; but my mind was jarring, irresolute, bewildered, confused; my stake seemed too vast to allow me coolness for the game.

Whoever has had cause for some refined and deep study in the midst of the noisy and loud world, may perhaps readily comprehend that feeling which now possessed me; a feeling that it was utterly impossible to abstract and concentrate one's thoughts, while at the mercy of every intruder, and fevered and fretful by every disturbance. Men, early and long accustomed to mingle such reflections with the avocations of courts and cities, have grown callous to these interruptions, and it has been in the very heart of the multitude that the profoundest speculations have been cherished and produced; but I was not of this mould. The world, which before had been dis-tasteful, now grew insufferable; I longed for some seclusion, some utter solitude, some quiet and unpenetrated nook, that I might give my undivided mind to the knowledge of these things, and build the tower of divine reasonings by which I might ascend to heaven. It was at this time, and in the midst of my fiercest internal conflict, that the great Czar died, and I was suddenly recalled to Russia.

"Now," I said, when I heard of my release, "now shall my wishes be fulfilled."

I sent to Bezoni. He came, but he refused, as indeed he had for some time done, to speak to me further upon the question which so wildly engrossed me. "I forgive you," said I, when we parted, "I forgive you for all that you have cost me; I feel that the moment is now at hand when my faith shall frame a weapon wherewith to triumph over yours!"

Father in Heaven! thanks be to Thee that my doubts were at last removed, and the cloud rolled away from my soul.

Bezoni embraced me, and wept over me. "All good men," said he, "have a mighty interest in your success; for me there is nothing dark, even in the mute grave, if it covers the ashes of one who has loved and served his brethren, and done, with a wilful heart, no living creature wrong."

Soon afterwards the Italian lost his life in attending the victims of a fearful and contagious disease, whom even the regular practitioners of the healing art hesitated to visit.

At this moment I am, in the strictest acceptation of the words, a believer and a Christian. I have neither anxiety nor doubt upon the noblest and the most comforting of all creeds, and I am grateful, among the other blessings which faith has brought me—I am grateful that it has brought me CHARITY! Dark to all human beings was Bezoni's doctrine—dark, above all, to those who have mourned on earth—so withering to all the hopes which cling the most enduringly to the heart, was his unhappy creed—that he who knows how inseparably, though insensibly, our moral legislation is woven with our supposed self-interest, will scarcely marvel at, even while he condemns, the unwise and unholy persecution which that creed universally sustains! Many a most wretched hour, many a pang of agony and despair, did those doctrines inflict upon myself; but I know that the intention of Bezoni was benevolence, and that the practice of his life was virtue: and while my reason tells me that God will not punish the reluctant and involuntary error of one to whom all God's creatures were so dear, my religion bids me hope that I shall meet Him in that world where no error *is*, and where the Great Spirit to whom all human passions are unknown, avenges the momentary doubt of His justice by a proof of the infinity of His mercy.

BOOK VI.

CHAPTER I.

THE RETREAT.

ARRIVED at St. Petersburgh, and found the Czarina, whose conjugal perfidy was more than suspected, tolerably resigned to the extinction of that dazzling life, whose incalculable and godlike utility it is reserved for posterity to appreciate! I have observed, by the way, that, in general, men are the less mourned by their families in proportion as they are the more mourned by the community. The great are seldom amiable; and those who are the least lenient to our errors are invariably our relations!

Many circumstances at that time conspired to make my request to quit the imperial service appear natural and appropriate. The death of the Czar, joined to a growing jealousy and suspicion between the English monarch and Russia, which, though long existing, was now become more evident and notorious than heretofore, gave me full opportunity to observe that my pardon had been obtained from King George three years since, and that private as well as national ties rendered my return to England a measure not only of expediency but necessity. The imperial Catherine granted me my dismissal in the most flattering terms, and added the high distinction of the order founded in honour of the memorable feat by which she had saved her royal consort and the Russian army, to the order of St. Andrew, which I had already received.

I transferred my wealth, now immense, to England, and, with the pomp which became the rank and reputation Fortune had bestowed upon me, I commenced the long land journey I had chalked out to myself. Although I had alleged my wish to revisit England as the main reason of my retirement from Russia, I had also expressed an intention of visiting Italy previous to my return to England. The physicians, indeed, had recommended to me that delicious climate as an antidote to the ills my constitution had sustained in the freezing skies of the north; and in my own heart I had secretly appointed some more solitary part of the Divine Land for the scene of my purposed hermitage and seclusion. It is indeed astonishing how those who have lived much in cold climates yearn for lands of mellow light and summer luxuriance ; and I felt for a southern sky the same resistless longing which sailors, in the midst of the vast ocean, have felt for the green fields and various landscape of the shore.

I traversed, then, the immense tracts of Russia—passed through Hungary—entered Turkey, which I had wished to visit, where I remained a short time ; and, crossing the 'Adriatic, hailed, for the first time, the Ausonian shore. It was the month of May—that month, of whose lustrous beauty none in a northern clime can dream—that I entered Italy. It may serve as an instance of the power with which a thought, that however important, is generally deemed of too abstract and metaphysical a nature deeply to engross the mind, possessed me then, that I—no cold nor unenthusiastic votary of the classic Muse—made no pilgrimage to city or ruin, but, after a brief sojourn at Ravenna, where I dismissed all my train, set out alone to find the solitary cell for which I now sickened with a hermit's love.

It was at a small village at the foot of the Apennines that I found the object of my search. Strangely enough, there blended with my philosophical ardour a deep mixture of my old romance. Nature, to whose voice the dweller in cities, and struggler with mankind, had been so long obtuse, now pleaded audibly at my heart, and called me to her embraces, as a mother calls unto her wearied child. My eye, as with a new vision, became open to the mute yet eloquent loveliness of this most fairy earth ; and hill and valley—the mirror of silent waters—the sunny stillness of woods, and the old haunts of satyr and nymph—revived in me the fountains of past poetry, and became the receptacles of a thousand spells, mightier than the charms of any enchanter save Love—which was departed--Youth, which was nearly gone—and Nature, which (more vividly than ever) existed for me still.

I chose, then, my retreat. As I was fastidious in its choice, I cannot refrain from the luxury of describing it. Ah, little did I dream that I had come thither, not only to find a divine comfort, but the sources of a human and most passionate woe ! Mightiest of the Roman bards ! in whom tenderness and reason were so entwined, and who didst sanctify even thine unholy errors with so beautiful and rare a genius ! what an invariable truth one line of thine has expressed : "Even in the fairest fountain of delight there is a secret and evil spring eternally bubbling up and scattering its bitter waters over the very flowers which surround its margin !"

In the midst of a lovely and tranquil vale was a small cottage ; that was my home. The good people there performed for me all the hospitable offices I required. At a neighbouring monastery I had taken the precaution to make myself known to the superior. Not

all Italians—no, nor all monks—belong to either of the two great
tribes into which they are generally divided—knaves or fools.
The Abbot Anselmo was a man of rather a liberal and enlarged
mind ; he not only kept my secret, which was necessary to my
peace, but he took my part, which was, perhaps, necessary to my
safety.   A philosopher, who desires only to convince himself, and
upon one subject, does not require many books.   Truth lies in a
small compass ; and for my part, in considering any speculative
subject, I would sooner have with me one book of Euclid, as a
model, than all the library of the Vatican, as authorities.   But then
I am not fond of drawing upon any resources but those of reason
for reasonings ; wiser men than I am are not so strict.   The few
books that I did require were, however, of a nature very illicit in
Italy ; the good father passed them to me from Ravenna, under his
own protection.   "I was a holy man," he said, "who wished to
render the Catholic church a great service, by writing a vast book·
against certain atrocious opinions ; and the works I read were, for
the most part, works that I was about to confute."   This report
gained me protection and respect ; and, after I had ordered my
agent at Ravenna to forward to the excellent abbot a piece of plate,
and a huge cargo of a rare Hungary wine, it was not the abbot's
fault if I was not the most popular person in the neighbourhood.

But to my description :—my home was a cottage—the valley in
which it lay was divided by a mountain stream, which came from
the forest Apennine, a sparkling and wild stranger, and softened
into quiet and calm as it proceeded through its green margin in the
vale.   And that margin, how dazzling green it was ! At the distance
of about a mile from my hut, the stream was broken into a slight
waterfall, whose sound was heard distinct and deep in that still
place : and often I paused, from my midnight thoughts, to listen to
its enchanted and wild melody.   The fall was unseen by the ordinary wanderer, for, there, the stream passed through a thick
copse ; and even when you pierced the grove, and gained the
water-side, dark trees hung over the turbulent wave, and the silver
spray was thrown upward through the leaves, and fell in diamonds
upon the deep green sod.

This was a most favoured haunt with me ; the sun glancing
through the idle leaves—the music of the water—the solemn absence
of all other sounds, except the songs of birds, to which the ear
grew accustomed, and, at last, in the abstraction of thought, scarcely
distinguished from the silence—the fragrant herbs—and the un-
numbered and nameless flowers which formed my couch—were all
calculated to make me pursue uninterruptedly the thread of contemplation which I had, in the less voluptuous and harsher solitude

of the closet, first woven from the web of austerest thought. I say pursue, for it was too luxurious and sensual a retirement for the conception of a rigid and severe train of reflection ; at least it would have been so to me. But, when the thought *is once born*, such scenes seem to me the most fit to cradle and to rear it. The torpor of the physical, appears to leave to the mental, frame a full scope and power ; the absence of human cares, sounds, and intrusions, becomes the best nurse to contemplation ; and even that delicious and vague sense of enjoyment which would seem, at first, more genial to the fancy than the mind, preserves the thought undisturbed, because contented ; so that all but the scheming mind becomes lapped in sleep, and the mind itself lives distinct and active as a dream ;—a dream, not vague, nor confused, nor unsatisfying, but endowed with more than the clearness, the precision, the vigour, of waking life.

A little way from this waterfall was a fountain, a remnant of a classic and golden age. Never did Naiad gaze on a more glassy mirror, or dwell in a more divine retreat. Through a crevice in an overhanging mound of the emerald earth, the father stream of the fountain crept out, born, like Love, among flowers, and in the most sunny smiles ; it then fell, broadening and glowing, into a marble basin, at whose bottom, in the shining noon, you might see a soil which mocked the very hues of gold, and the water insects, in their quaint shapes, and unknown sports, grouping or gliding in the midmost wave. A small temple, of the lightest architecture, stood before the fountain ; and, in a niche therein, a mutilated statue—possibly of the Spirit of the Place. By this fountain, my evening walk would linger till the short twilight melted away, and the silver wave trembled in the light of the western star. Oh ! then, what feelings gathered over me as I turned slowly homeward ; the air still, breathless, shining—the stars, gleaming over the woods of the far Apennine—the hills, growing huger in the shade—the small insects humming on the wing—and, ever and anon, the swift bat, wheeling round and amidst them—the music of the waterfall deepening on the ear ; and the light and hour lending even a mysterious charm to the cry of the weird owl, flitting after its prey,— all this had a harmony in my thoughts, and a food for the meditations in which my days and nights were consumed. The World moulders away the fabric of our early nature, and Solitude rebuilds it on a firmer base.

CHAPTER II.

THE VICTORY.

EARTH ! Reservoir of life, over whose deep bosom brood the wings of the Universal Spirit, shaking upon thee a blessing and a power—a blessing and a power to produce and reproduce the living from the dead, so that our flesh is woven from the same atoms which were once the atoms of our sires, and the inexhaustible nutriment of Existence is Decay ! O eldest and most solemn Earth, blending even thy loveliness and joy with a terror and an awe ! thy sunshine is girt with clouds, and circled with storm and tempest : thy day cometh from the womb of darkness, and returneth unto darkness, as man returns unto thy bosom. The green herb that laughs in the valley, the water that sings merrily along the wood ; the many-winged and all-searching air, which garners life as a harvest, and scatters it as a seed ; all are pregnant with corruption and carry the cradled death within them, as an oak banquetetli the destroying worm. But who that looks upon thee, and loves thee, and inhales thy blessings, will ever mingle too deep a moral with his joy ? Let us not ask whence come the garlands that we wreathe around our altars, or shower upon our feasts : will they not bloom as brightly, and breathe with as rich a fragrance, whether they be plucked from the garden or the grave ? O Earth, my Mother Earth ! dark Sepulchre that closes upon all which the Flesh bears, but Vestibule of the vast regions which the Soul shall pass, how leapt my heart within me when I first fathomed thy real spell !

Yes! never shall I forget the rapture with which I hailed the light that dawned upon me at last ! Never shall I forget the suffo-eating—the full—the ecstatic joy, with which I saw the mightiest of all human hopes accomplished ; and felt, as if an angel spoke, that there is a life beyond the grave ! Tell me not of the pride of ambition—tell me not of the triumphs of science : never had am-bitiou so lofty an end as the search after immortality ! never had science so sublime a triumph as the conviction that immortality will be gained ! I had been at my task the whole night,—pale alche-mist, seeking from meaner truths to extract the greatest of all ! At the first hour of day, lo ! the gold was there : the labour, for which I would have relinquished life, was accomplished ; the dove de-scended upon the waters of my soul. I fled from the house. I was possessed as with a spirit. I ascended a hill, which looked for leagues over the sleeping valley. A gray mist hung around me like a veil; I paused, and the great Sun broke slowly forth; I gazed upon its majesty, and my heart swelled. "So rises the soul," I said, "from the vapours of this dull being; but the soul waneth not, neither setteth it, nor knoweth it any night, save that from which it dawneth!"—The mists rolled gradually away, the sunshine deepened, and the face of nature lay in smiles, yet silently, before me. It lay before me, a scene that I had often witnessed, and hailed, and worshipped; *but it was not the same:* a glory had passed over it; it was steeped in a beauty and a holiness, in which neither youth, nor poetry, nor even love, had ever robed it before! The change which the earth had undergone was like that of some being we have loved—when death is passed, and from a mortal it becomes an angel!

I uttered a cry of joy, and was then as silent as all around me. I felt as if henceforth there was a new compact between nature and myself. I felt as if every tree, and blade of grass, were henceforth to be eloquent with a voice, and instinct with a spell. I felt as if a religion had entered into the earth, and made oracles of all that the earth bears; the old fables of Dodona were to become realized, and *the very leaves* to be hallowed by a sanctity, and to murmur with a truth. I was no longer only a part of that which withers and decays: I was no longer a machine of clay, moved by a spring, and to be trodden into the mire which I had trod; I was no longer tied to humanity by links which could never be broken, and which, if broken, would avail me not. I was become, as by a miracle, a part of a vast, though unseen, spirit. It was not to the matter, but to the essences, of things that I bore kindred and alliance; the stars and the heavens resumed over me their ancient influence; and, as I looked along the far hills and the silent landscape, a voice seemed to swell from the stillness, and to say, "I am the life of these things, a spirit distinct from the things themselves. It is to me that you belong for ever and for ever; separate, but equally indissoluble; apart, but equally eternal!"

I spent the day upon the hills. It was evening when I returned. I lingered by the old fountain, and saw the stars rise, and tremble, one by one, upon the wave. The hour was that which Isora had loved the best, and that which the love of her had consecrated the most to me. And never, oh, never, did it sink into my heart with a deeper sweetness, or a more soothing balm. I had once more knit my soul to Isora's: I could once more look from the toiling and the dim earth, and forget that Isora had left me, in dreaming of our reunion. Blame me not, you who indulge in a religious hope more severe and more sublime—you who miss no footsteps from the earth, nor pine for a voice that your human wanderings can hear no more—blame me not, you whose pulses beat not for the wild love of the created, but whose spirit languishes only for a nearer commune with the Creator—blame me not too harshly for my mortal wishes, nor think that my faith was the less sincere because it was tinted in the most unchanging dyes of the human heart, and indissolubly woven with the memory of the dead! Often from our weaknesses our strongest principles of conduct are born ; and from the acorn, which a breeze has wafted, springs the oak which defies the storm.

The first intoxication and rapture consequent upon the reward of my labour passed away ; but, unlike other excitement, it was followed not by languor, or a sated and torpid calm ; a soothing and delicious sensation possessed me—my turbulent senses slept ; and Memory, recalling the world, rejoiced at the retreat which Hope had acquired.

I now surrendered myself to a nobler philosophy than in crowds and cities I had hitherto known. I no longer satirized—I inquired ; I no longer derided—I examined. I looked from the natural proofs of immortality to the written promise of our Father—I sought not to baffle men, but to worship Truth—I applied myself more to the knowledge of good and evil—I bowed my soul before the loveliness of Virtue ; and though scenes of wrath and passion yet lowered in the future, and I was again speedily called forth—to act—to madden —to contend—perchance to sin — the Image is still unbroken, and the Votary has still an offering for its Altar !

CHAPTER III.

THE HERMIT OF THE WELL.

THE thorough and deep investigation of those principles from which we learn the immortality of the soul, and the nature of its proper ends, leads the mind through such a course of reflection and of study—it is attended with so many exalting, purifying, and, if I may so say, etherealizing thoughts, that I do believe no man has ever pursued it, and not gone back to the world a better and a nobler man than he was before. Nay, so deeply must these elevating and refining studies be conned, so largely and sensibly must they enter the intellectual system, that I firmly think that even a sensualist who has only considered the subject with a view to convince himself that he is clay, and has therefore an excuse to the curious conscience for his grosser desires ;

nay, should he come to his wished for, yet desolate, conclusion, from which the abhorrent nature shrinks and recoils, I do nevertheless firmly think, should the study have been long and deep, that he would wonder to find his desires had lost their poignancy, and his objects their charm. He would descend from the Alp he had climbed to the low level on which he formerly deemed it a bliss to dwell, with the feeling of one who, having long drawn in high places an empyreal air, has become unable to inhale the smoke and the thick vapour he inhaled of yore. His soul once aroused would stir within him, though he felt it not, and though he grew not a believer, he would cease to be only the voluptuary.

I meant at one time to have here stated the arguments which had perplexed me on one side, and those which afterwards convinced me on the other. I do not do so for many reasons, one of which will suffice, viz., the evident and palpable circumstance that a dissertation of that nature would, in a biography like the present, be utterly out of place and season. Perhaps, however, at a later period of life, I may collect my own opinions on the subject into a separate work, and bequeath that work to future generations, upon the same conditions as the present memoir.

One day I was favoured by a visit from one of the monks at the neighbouring abbey. After some general conversation he asked me if I had yet encountered the Hermit of the Well? "No," said I, and I was going to add, that I had not even heard of him, "but I now remember that the good people of the house have more than once spoken to me of him as a rigid and self-mortifying recluse."

"Yes," said the holy friar; "Heaven forbid that I should say aught against the practice of the saints and pious men to deny unto themselves the lusts of the flesh, but such penances may be carried too far. However, it is an excellent custom, and the Hermit of the Well is an excellent creature. *Santa Maria!* what delicious stuff is that Hungary wine your scholarship was pleased to bestow upon our father Abbot. He suffered me to taste it the eve before last. I had been suffering with a pain in the reins, and the wine acted powerfully upon me as an efficacious and inestimable medicine. Do you find, my son, that it bore the journey to your lodging here, as well as to the convent cellars?"

"Why, really, my father, I have none of it here; but the people of the house have a few flasks of a better wine than ordinary, if you will deign to taste it in lieu of the Hungary wine."

"Oh — oh!" said the monk, groaning, "my reins trouble me much—perhaps the wine may comfort me!" and the wine was brought.

"It is not of so rare a flavour as that which you sent to our reverend father," said the monk, wiping his mouth with his long sleeve. "Hungary must be a charming place—is it far from hence? —It joins the heretical—I pray your pardon—it joins the continent of England, I believe?"

"Not exactly, father; but whatever its topography, it is a rare country—for those who like it! But tell me of this Hermit of the Well. How long has he lived here—and how came he by his appellation? Of what country is he—and of what birth?"

"You ask me too many questions at once, my son. The country of the holy man is a mystery to us all. He speaks the Tuscan dialect well, but with a foreign accent. Nevertheless, though the wine is not of Hungary, it has a pleasant flavour. I wonder how the rogues kept it so snugly from the knowledge and comfort of their pious brethren of the monastery."

"And how long has the hermit lived in your vicinity?"

"Nearly eight years, my son. It was one winter's evening that he came to our convent in the dress of a worldly traveller, to seek our hospitality, and a shelter for the night, which was inclement and stormy. He stayed with us a few days, and held some conversation with our father Abbot; and one morning, after roaming in the neighbourhood to look at the old stones and ruins, which is the custom of travellers, he returned, put into our box some certain alms, and two days afterwards he appeared in the place he now inhabits, and in the dress he assumes."

"And of what nature, my father, is the place, and of what fashion the dress?"

"Holy St. Francis!" exclaimed the father, with a surprise so great that I thought at first it related to the wine, "Holy St. Francis—have you not seen the well yet?"

"No, father, unless you speak of the fountain about a mile and a quarter distant."

"Tush—tush!" said the good man, "what ignoramuses you travellers are; you affect to know what kind of slippers Prester John wears and to have been admitted to the bed-chamber of *the Pagoda of China;* and yet, when one comes to sound you, you are as ignorant of everything a man of real learning knows as an Englishman is of his missal. Why, I thought that every fool in every country had heard of the Holy Well of St. Francis, situated exactly two miles from our famous convent, and that every fool in the neighbourhood had seen it."

"What the fools, my father, whether in this neighbourhood or any other, may have heard or seen, I, who profess not ostensibly to belong to so goodly an order, cannot pretend to know; but be assured that the Holy Well of St. Francis is as unfamiliar to me as the Pagoda of China—Heaven bless *him*—is to you."

Upon this the learned monk, after expressing due astonishment, offered to show it to me; and as I thought I might by acquiescence get rid of him the sooner, and as, moreover, I wished to see the abbot, to whom some books for me had been lately sent, I agreed to the offer.

The well, said the monk, lay not above a mile out of the customary way to the monastery; and after *we* had finished the flask of wine, we sallied out on our excursion,—the monk upon a stately and strong ass—myself on foot.

The abbot, on granting me his friendship and protection, had observed that I was not the only stranger and recluse on whom his favour was bestowed. He had then mentioned the Hermit of the Well, as an eccentric and strange being, who lived an existence of rigid penance, harmless to others, painful only to himself. This story had been confirmed in the few conversations I had ever interchanged with my host and hostess, who seemed to take a peculiar pleasure in talking of the Solitary; and from them I had heard also many anecdotes of his charity towards the poor, and his attention to the sick. All these circumstances came into my mind as the good monk indulged his loquacity upon the subject, and my curiosity became, at last, somewhat excited respecting my fellow recluse.

I now learned from the monk that the post of Hermit of the Well was an office of which the present anchorite was by no means the first tenant. The well was one of those springs frequent in Catholic countries, to which a legend and a sanctity are attached; and twice a year, once in the spring, once in the autumn, the neighbouring peasants flocked thither, on a stated day, to drink, and lose their diseases. As the spring most probably did possess some medicinal qualities, a few extraordinary cures had occurred; especially among those pious persons who took not biennial, but constant draughts;—and to doubt its holiness was downright heresy.

Now, hard by this well was a cavern, which, whether first formed by nature or art, was now, upon the whole, constructed into a very commodious abode; and here, for years beyond the memory of man, some solitary person had fixed his abode to dispense and to bless the water, to be exceedingly well fed by the surrounding peasants, to wear a long gown of serge or sackcloth, and to be called the Hermit of the Well. So fast as each succeeding anchorite died there were enough candidates eager to supply his place; for it was no bad *métier* to some penniless impostor to become the quack and patentee of a holy specific. The choice of these candidates always rested with the superior of the neighbouring monastery ; and it is not impossible that he made an indifferently good per-centage upon the annual advantages of his protection and choice.

At the time the traveller appeared, the former hermit had just departed this life, and it was, therefore, to the vacancy thus occasioned, that he had procured himself to be elected. The incumbent appeared quite of a different mould from the former occupants of the hermitage. He accepted, it is true, the gifts laid at regular periods upon a huge stone between the hermitage and the well, but he distributed among the donors alms far more profitable than their gifts. He entered no village, borne upon an ass laden with twin sacks, for the purpose of sanctimoniously robbing the inhabitants ; no profane songs were ever heard resounding from his dwelling by the peasant incautiously lingering at a late hour too near its vicinity ; my guide, the monk, complained bitterly of his unsociability, and no scandalous legend of nymph-like comforters and damsel visitants haunting the sacred dwelling, escaped from the garrulous friar's well-loaded budget.

"Does he study much?" said I, with the interest of a student.

"I fear me not," quoth the monk. "I have had occasion often to enter his abode, and I have examined all things with a close eye —for, praised be the Lord, I have faculties more than ordinarily clear and observant—but I have seen no books therein, excepting a missal, and a Latin or Greek Testament, I know not well which ;— nay, so incurious or unlearned is the holy man that he rejected even a loan of the 'Life of St. Francis,' notwithstanding it has many and rare pictures, to say nothing of its most interesting and amazing tales."

More might the monk have said, had we not now suddenly entered a thick and sombre wood. A path cut through it was narrow, and only capable of admitting a traveller on foot or horseback ; and the boughs overhead were so darkly interlaced that the light scarcely, and only in broken and erratic glimmerings, pierced the canopy.

"It is the wood," said the monk, crossing himself, "wherein the wonderful adventure happened to St. Francis, which I will one day narrate at length to you."

"And we are near the well, I suppose?" said I.

"It is close at hand," answered the monk.

In effect we had not proceeded above fifty yards before the path brought us into a circular space of green sod, in the midst of which was a small square stone building, of plain, but not inelegant, shape, and evidently of great antiquity. At one side of this building was an iron handle, for the purpose of raising water, that cast itself into a stone basin, to which was affixed by a strong chain, an iron cup. An inscription, in monkish Latin, was engraved over the basin, requesting the traveller to pause and drink, and importing that what that water was to the body, faith was to the soul; near the cistern was a rude seat, formed by the trunk of a tree. The door of the well-house was of iron, and secured by a chain and lock; perhaps the pump was so contrived that only a certain quantum of the sanctified beverage could be drawn up at a time, without application to some mechanism within: and wayfarers were thereby prevented from helping themselves *ad libitum*, and thus depriving the anchorite of the profit and the necessity of his office.

. It was certainly a strange, lonely, and wild place; and the green sward, round as a fairy ring, in the midst of trees, which, black, close, and huge, circled it like a wall: and the solitary gray building in the centre, gaunt and cold, and startling the eye with the abruptness of its appearance, and the strong contrast made by its wan hues to the dark verdure and forest gloom around it !

I took a draught of the water, which was very cold and tasteless, and reminded the monk of his disorder in the reins, to which a similar potation might possibly be efficacious. To this suggestion the monk answered that he would certainly try the water some other time; but that at present the wine he had drunk might pollute its divine properties. So saying, he turned off the conversation by inviting me to follow him to the hermitage.

In our way thither he pointed out a large fragment of stone, and observed that the water would do me evil instead of good if I forgot to remunerate its guardian. I took the hint, and laid a piece of silver on the fragment.

A short journey through the wood brought us to the foot of a hill covered with trees, and having at its base a strong stone door, the entrance to the excavated home of the anchorite. The monk gently tapped thrice at this door, but no answer came. "The holy man is from home," said he, "let us return."

We did so; and the monk, keeping behind me, managed as he thought, unseen, to leave the stone as naked as we had found it ! We now struck through another path in the wood, and were soon at the convent. I did not lose the opportunity to question the abbot respecting his tenant: I learnt from him little more than the particulars I have already narrated, save that in concluding his details, he said:

"I can scarcely doubt but that the hermit is, like yourself, a person of rank; his bearing and his mien appear to denote it. He has given, and gives yearly, large sums to the uses of the convent: and, though he takes the customary gifts of the pious villagers, it

is only by my advice, and for the purpose of avoiding suspicion.
Should he be considered rich, it might attract cupidity ; and there
are enough bold hands and sharp knives in the country to place the
wealthy and the unguarded in some peril. Whoever he may be—
for he has not confided his secret to me—I do not doubt but that
he is doing penance for some great crime ; and, whatever be the
crime, I suspect that its earthly punishment is nearly over. The
hermit is naturally of a delicate and weak frame, and year after year
I have marked him sensibly wearing away ; so that when I last
saw him, three days since, I was shocked at the visible ravages
which disease or penance had engraven upon him. If ever Death
wrote legibly, its characters are in that brow and cheek."

"Poor man ! Know you not even whom to apprise of his decease
when he is no more ? "

"I do not yet ; but the last time I saw him he told me that he
found himself drawing near his end, and that he should not quit
life without troubling me with one request."

After this the abbot spoke of other matters, and my visit
expired.

Interested in the recluse more deeply than I acknowledged to
myself, I found my steps insensibly leading me homeward by the
more circuitous road which wound first by the holy well. I did not
resist the impulse, but walked musingly onward by the waning
twilight, for the day was now over, until I came to the well. As
I emerged from the wood, I started involuntarily and drew back.
A figure, robed from head to foot in a long sable robe, sate upon
the rude seat beside the well ; sate so still, so motionless, that
coming upon it abruptly in that strange place, the heart beat irre-
gularly at an apparition so dark in hue, and so death-like in its
repose. The hat, large, broad, and overhanging, which suited the
costume, was lying on the ground ; and the face, which inclined
upward, seemed to woo the gentle air of the quiet and soft skies.
I approached a few steps, and saw the profile of the countenance
more distinctly than I had done before. It was of a marble whiteness ; the features, though sharpened and attenuated by disease,
were of surpassing beauty ; the hair was exceedingly, almost effem-
inately, long, and hung in waves of perfect jet on either side ; the
mouth was closed firmly, and deep lines, or rather furrows, were
traced from its corners to either nostril. The stranger's beard, of
a hue equally black as the hair, was dishevelled and neglected, but
not very long ; and one hand, which lay on the sable robe, was
so thin and wan you might have deemed the very starlight could
have shone through it. I did not doubt that it was the recluse.
whom I saw ; I drew near and accosted him.

"Your blessing, holy father, and your permission to taste the healing of your well."

Sudden as was my appearance, and abrupt my voice, the hermit evinced by no startled gesture a token of surprise. He turned very slowly round, cast upon me an indifferent glance, and said, in a sweet and very low tone,

"You have my blessing, stranger; there is water in the cistern—drink, and be healed."

I dipped the bowl in the basin, and took sparingly of the water. In the accent and tone of the stranger, my ear accustomed to the dialects of many nations, recognized something English; I resolved, therefore, to address him in my native tongue, rather than the indifferent Italian in which I had first accosted him.

"The water is fresh and cooling; would, holy father, that it could penetrate to a deeper malady than the ills of flesh : that it could assuage the fever of the heart, or lave from the wearied mind the dust which it gathers from the mire and travail of the world."

Now the hermit testified surprise; but it was slight and momentary. He gazed upon me more attentively than he had done before, and said, after a pause,

"My countryman! and in this spot! It is not often that the English penetrate into places where no ostentatious celebrity dwells to sate curiosity and flatter pride. My countryman!—it is well, and perhaps fortunate. Yes," he said, after a second pause, "yes; it were indeed a boon, had the earth a fountain for the wounds which fester, and the disease which consumes the heart."

"The earth has oblivion, father, if not a cure."

"It is false!" cried the hermit, passionately, and starting wildly from his seat; "the earth has *no* oblivion. The grave—is *that* forgetfulness? No, no—*there is no grave for the soul!* The deeds pass—the flesh corrupts—but the memory passes not, and withers not. From age to age, from world to world, through eternity, throughout creation, it is perpetuated—an immortality—a curse—*a hell!*"

Surprised by the vehemence of the hermit, I was still more startled by the agonizing and ghastly expression of his face.

"My father," said I, "pardon me, if I have pressed upon a sore. I also have that within, which, did a stranger touch it, would thrill my whole frame with torture, and I would fain ask from your holy soothing, and pious comfort, something of alleviation or of fortitude."

The hermit drew near to me; he laid his thin hand upon my arm, and looked long and wistfully in my face. It was then that a suspicion crept through me which after observation proved to be true, that the wandering of those dark eyes and the meaning of that blanched brow were tinctured with insanity.

"Brother, and fellow man," said he, mournfully, "hast thou in truth suffered? and dost thou still smart at the remembrance? We are friends then. If thou hast suffered as much as I have, I will fall down and do homage to thee as a superior; for pain has its ranks, and I think at times, that none ever climbed the height that I have done. Yet you look not like one who has had nights of delirium, and days in which the heart lay in the breast, as a corpse endowed with consciousness might lie in the grave, feeling the worm gnaw it, and the decay corrupt, and yet incapable of resistance or of motion. Your cheek is thin, but firm; your eye is haughty and bright; you have the air of one who has lived with men, and struggled and not been vanquished in the struggle. Suffered! No, man, no—*you* have not suffered!"

"My father, it is not in the countenance that Fate graves her records. I have, it is true, contended with my fellows; and if wealth and honour be the premium, not in vain: but I have not contended against Sorrow with a like success; and I stand before you, a being who, if passion be a tormentor, and the death of the loved a loss, has borne that which the most wretched will not envy."

Again a fearful change came over the face of the recluse—he grasped my arm more vehemently, "You speak my own sorrows—you utter my own curse—I will see you again—you may do my last will better than yon monks. Can I trust you? If you have in truth known misfortune, I will!—I will—yea, even to the outpouring ——Merciful, merciful God, what would I say—what would I reveal!"

Suddenly changing his voice, he released me, and said, touching his forehead with a meaning gesture, and a quiet smile, "You say you are my rival in pain? Have you ever known the rage and despair of the heart mount *here?* It is a wonderful thing to be calm as I am now, when that rising makes itself felt in fire and torture!"

"If there be aught, father, which a man who cares not what country he visit, or what deed—so it be not of guilt or shame—he commit, can do towards the quiet of your soul, say it, and I will attempt your will."

"You are kind, my son," said the hermit, resuming his first melancholy and dignified composure of mien and bearing, "and there is something in your voice, which seems to me like a tone that I have heard in youth. Do you live near at hand?"

"In the valley, about four miles hence; I am, like yourself, a fugitive from the world."

"Come to me then to-morrow at eve; to-morrow!—No, that is a holy eve, and I must keep it with scourge and prayer. The next at sunset. I shall be collected then, and I would fain know more of you than I do. Bless you, my son—adieu."

"Yet stay, father, may I not conduct you home?"

"No—my limbs are weak, but I trust they can carry me to that home, till I be borne thence to my last. Farewell! the night grows, and man fills even these shades with peril. The eve after next, at sunset, we meet again."

So saying, the hermit waved his hand, and I stood apart, watching his receding figure, until the trees cloaked the last glimpse from my view. I then turned homeward, and reached my cottage in safety, despite of the hermit's caution. But I did not retire to rest: a powerful foreboding, rather than suspicion, that, in the worn and wasted form which I had beheld, there was identity with one whom I had not met for years, and whom I had believed to be no more, thrillingly possessed me.

"Can—can it be?" thought I. "Can grief have a desolation, or remembrance an agony, sufficient to create so awful a change? And of all human beings, for that one to be singled out; that one in whom passion and sin were, if they existed, nipped in their earliest germ, and seemingly rendered barren of all fruit! If too, almost against the evidence of sight and sense, an innate feeling has marked in that most altered form the traces of a dread recognition, would not his memory have been yet more vigilant than mine? Am I so changed that he should have looked me in the face so wistfully, and found there nought save the lineaments of a stranger?" And, actuated by this thought, I placed the light by the small mirror which graced my chamber. I recalled, as I gazed, my features as they had been in earliest youth. "No," I said, with a sigh, "there is nothing here that he should recognize."

And I said aright: my features, originally small and delicate, had grown enlarged and prominent. The long locks of my youth (for only upon state occasions did my early vanity consent to the fashion of the day) were succeeded by curls, short and crisped; the hues, alternately pale and hectic, that the dreams of romance had once spread over my cheek, had settled into the unchanging bronze of manhood; the smooth lip, and unshaven chin, were clothed with a thick hair; the once unfurrowed brow was habitually knit in thought; and the ardent, restless expression that boyhood wore had yielded to the quiet unmoved countenance of one, in whom long custom has subdued all outward sign of emotion, and many and various events left no prevalent token of the mind, save that of an habitual, but latent resolution. My frame, too, once scarcely less slight than a woman's, was become knit and muscular, and nothing was left by which, in the foreign air, the quiet brow, and the athletic form, my very mother could have recognized the slender figure and changeful face of the boy she had last beheld. The very·sarcasm of the eye was gone: and I had learnt the world's easy lesson—the dissimulation of composure.

I have noted one thing in others, and it was particularly noticeable in me, viz., that few who mix very largely with men, and with the courtier's or the citizen's design, ever retain the key and tone of their original voice. The voice of a young man is as yet modulated by nature, and expresses the passion of the moment ; that of the matured pupil of art expresses rather the customary occupation of his life : whether he aims at persuading, convincing, or commanding others, his voice irrevocably settles into the key he ordinarily employs ; and, as persuasion is the means men chiefly employ in their commerce with each other, especially in the regions of a court, so a tone of artificial blandness and subdued insinuation is chiefly that in which the accents of worldly men are clothed ; the artificial intonation, long continued, grows into nature, and the very pith and basis of the original sound fritter themselves away. The change was great in me, for at that time, which I brought in comparison with the present, my age was one in which the voice is yet confused and undecided, struggling between the accents of youth and boyhood ; so that even this most powerful and unchanging of all claims upon the memory was in a great measure absent in me ; and nothing but an occasional and rare tone could have produced even that faint and unconscious recognition which the hermit had confessed.

I must be pardoned these egotisms, which the nature of my story renders necessary.

With what eager impatience did I watch the hours to the appointed interview with the hermit languish themselves away ! However, before that time arrived, and towards the evening of the next day, I was surprised by the rare honour of a visit from Anselmo himself. He came attended by two of the mendicant friars of his order, and they carried between them a basket of tolerable size, which, as mine hostess afterwards informed me, with many a tear, went back somewhat heavier than it came, from the load of certain *receptacula* of that rarer wine which she had had, the evening before, the indiscreet hospitality to produce.

The abbot came to inform me that the hermit had been with him that morning, making many inquiries respecting me. "I told him," said he, "that I was acquainted with your name and birth, but that I was under a solemn promise not to reveal them, without your consent ; and I am now here, my son, to learn from you whether that consent may be obtained ?"

"Assuredly not, holy father!" said I, hastily ; nor was I contented until I had obtained a renewal of his promise to that effect. This seemed to give the abbot some little chagrin : perhaps the hermit had offered a reward for my discovery. However, I knew that Anselmo, though a griping, was a trustworthy, man, and I felt safe in his renewed promise. I saw him depart with great satisfaction, and .gave myself once more to conjectures respecting the strange recluse.

As, the next evening, I prepared to depart towards the hermitage, I took peculiar pains to give my person a foreign and disguised appearance. A loose dress, of rude and simple material, and a high cap of fur, were pretty successful in accomplishing this purpo-e. And, as I gave the last look at the glass before I left the house, I said, inly, "If there be any truth in my wild and improbable conjecture respecting the identity of the anchorite, I think time and this dress are sufficient wizards to secure me from a chance of discovery. I will keep a guard upon my words and tones, until, if my thought be verified, a moment fit for unmasking myself arrives. But would to God that the thought be groundless ! In such circumstances, and after such an absence, to meet *him !* No ; and yet ——Well, this meeting will decide."

CHAPTER IV.

THE SOLUTION OF MANY MYSTERIES—A DARK VIEW OF THE LIFE AND NATURE OF MAN.

POWERFUL, though not clearly developed in my own mind, was the motive which made me so strongly desire to preserve the incognito during my interview with the hermit. I have before said that I could not resist a vague, but intense, belief that he was a person whom I had long believed in the grave ; and I had more than once struggled against a dark, but passing suspicion, that that person was in some measure —mediately, though not directly—connected with the mysteries of my former life. If both these conjectures were true, I thought it possible that the communication the hermit wished to make, might be made yet more willingly to me as a stranger than if he knew who was in reality his confidant. And, at all events, if I could curb the impetuous gushings of my own heart, which yearned for immediate disclosure, I might, by hint and prelude, ascertain the advantages and disadvantages of revealing myself.

I arrived at the well: the hermit was already at the place of rendezvous, seated in the same posture in which I had before seen him. I made my reverence, and accosted him.

"I have not failed you, father."

"That is rarely a true boast with men," said the hermit, smiling mournfully, but without sarcasm; "and were the promise of greater avail, it might not have been so rigidly kept."

"The promise, father, seemed to me of greater weight than you would intimate," answered I.

"How mean you?" said the hermit, hastily.

"Why, that we may perhaps serve each other by our meeting: you, father, may comfort me by your counsels; I you by my readiness to obey your request."

The hermit looked at me for some moments, and, as well as I could, I turned away my face from his gaze. I might have spared myself the effort. He seemed to recognize nothing familiar in my countenance; perhaps his mental malady assisted my own alteration.

"I have inquired respecting you," he said, after a pause, "and I hear that you are a learned and wise man, who have seen much of the world, and played the part both of soldier and of scholar, in its various theatres: is my information true?"

"Not true with respect to the learning, father, but true with regard to the experience. I have been a pilgrim in many countries of Europe."

"Indeed!" said the hermit, eagerly. "Come with me to my home, and tell me of the wonders you have seen."

I assisted the hermit to rise, and he walked slowly towards the cavern, leaning upon my arm. Oh, how that light touch thrilled through my frame! How I longed to cry, "Are you not the one whom I have loved, and mourned, and believed buried in the tomb?" But I checked myself. We moved on in silence. The hermit's hand was on the door of the cavern, when he said, in a calm tone, but with evident effort, and turning his face from me while he spoke:

"And did your wanderings ever carry you into the farther regions of the north? Did the fame of the great Czar ever lead you to the city he has founded?"

"I am right—I am right!" thought I, as I answered, "In truth, holy father, I spent not a long time at Petersburgh; but I am not a stranger either to its wonders, or its inhabitants."

"Possibly, then, you may have met with the English favourite of the Czar of whom I hear in my retreat that men have lately spoken somewhat largely?" The hermit paused again. We were now in a long, low passage, almost in darkness. I scarcely saw him, yet I heard a convulsed movement in his throat, before he uttered the remainder of the sentence. "He is called the Count Devereux."

"Father," said I, calmly, "I have both seen and known the man."

"Ha!" said the hermit, and he leant for a moment against the wall; "known him—and—how—how—I mean, where is he at this present time?"

"That, father, is a difficult question, respecting one who has led so active a life. He was ambassador at the court of ——, just before I left it."

We had now passed the passage, and gained a room of tolerable size; an iron lamp burnt within, and afforded a sufficient, but some-what dim light. The hermit, as I concluded my reply, sunk down on a long stone bench, beside a table of the same substance, and leaning his face on his hand, so that the long, large sleeve he wore, perfectly concealed his features, said, "Pardon me, my breath is short, and my frame weak—I am quite exhausted—but will speak to you more, anon."

I uttered a short answer, and drew a small wooden stool within a few feet of the hermit's seat. After a brief silence he rose, placed wine, bread, and preserved fruits before me, and bade me eat. I seemed to comply with his request, and the apparent diversion of my attention from himself somewhat relieved the embarrassment under which he evidently laboured.

"May I hope," he said, "that were my commission to this—to the Count Devereux—you would execute it faithfully and with speed? Yet stay—you have a high mien, as of one above fortune, but your garb is rude and poor; and if aught of gold could compensate your trouble, the hermit has other treasuries beside this cell."

"I will do your bidding, father, without robbing the poor. You wish then that I should seek Morton Devereux—you wish that I should summon him hither—you wish to see, and to confer with him?"

"God of mercy forbid!" cried the hermit, and with such vehe-mence that I was startled from the design of revealing myself, which I was on the point of executing. "I would rather that these walls would crush me into dust, or that this solid stone would crumble beneath my feet—ay, even into a bottomless pit, than meet the glance of Morton Devereux!"

"Is it even so?" said I, stooping over the wine cup; "ye have been foes then, I suspect.—Well, it matters not—tell me your errand, and it shall be done."

"Done!" cried the hermit, and a new, and certainly a most natural suspicion darted within him, "done! and—fool that I am!

—who, or what are you, that I should believe you take so keen an interest in the wishes of a man utterly unknown to you? I tell you that my wish is that you should cross seas and traverse lands until you find the man I have named to you. Will a stranger do this, and without hire—no—no—I was a fool, and will trust the monks, and give gold, and then my errand will be sped."

"Father, or rather, brother," said I, with a slow and firm voice, "for you are of mine own age, and you have the passion and the infirmity which make brethren of all mankind, I am one to whom all places are alike : it matters not whether I visit a northern or a southern clime—I have wealth, which is sufficient to smooth toil—I have leisure, which makes occupation an enjoyment. More than this, I am one, who in his gayest and wildest moments has ever loved mankind, and would have renounced at any time his own pleasure for the advantage of another. But at this time, above all others, I am most disposed to forget myself, and there is a passion in your words which leads me to hope that it may be a great benefit which I can confer upon you."

"You speak well," said the hermit, musingly, "and I may trust you ; I will consider yet a little longer, and to-morrow at this hour, you shall have my final answer. If you execute the charge I entrust to you, may the blessing of a dying and most wretched man cleave to you for ever !—But hush—the clock strikes—it is my hour of prayer."

And, pointing to a huge black clock that hung opposite the door, and indicated the hour of nine (according to our English mode of numbering the hours), the hermit fell on his knees, and, clasping his hands tightly, bent his face over them in the attitude of humiliation and devotion. I followed his example. After a few minutes he rose —"Once in every three hours," said he, with a ghastly expression, "for the last twelve years have I bowed my soul in anguish before God, and risen to feel that it was in vain—I am cursed without and within !"

"My father, my father, is this your faith in the mercies of the Redeemer who died for Man ?"

"Talk not to me of faith !" cried the hermit, wildly. "Ye laymen and worldlings know nothing of its mysteries and its powers. But begone ! the dread hour is upon me, when my tongue is loosed, and my brain darkened, and I know not my words, and shudder at my own thoughts. Begone ! no human being shall witness those moments—they are only for Heaven and my own soul."

So saying, this unhappy and strange being seized me by the arm and dragged me towards the passage we had entered. I was in doubt whether to yield to, or contend with, him ; but there was a glare in his eye, and a flush upon his brow, which, while it betrayed the dreadful disease of his mind, made me fear that resistance to his wishes might operate dangerously upon a frame so feeble and reduced. I therefore mechanically obeyed him. He opened again the entrance to his rugged home, and the moonlight streamed wanly over his dark robes and spectral figure.

"Go," said he, more mildly than before—"go and forgive the vehemence of one whose mind and heart alike are broken within him. Go, but return to-morrow at sunset. Your air disposes me to trust you."

So saying, he closed the door upon me, and I stood without the cavern alone.

But did I return home? Did I hasten to press my couch in sleep and sweet forgetfulness, while he was in that gloomy sepulture of the living, a prey to anguish, and torn by the fangs of madness and a fierce disease? No—on the damp grass, beneath the silent skies, I passed a night, which could scarcely have been less wretched than his own. My conjecture was now, and in full, confirmed. Heavens! how I loved that man—how, from my youngest years, had my soul's fondest affections interlaced themselves with him!— with what anguish had I wept his imagined death? and now to know that he lay within those walls, smitten from brain to heart with so fearful and mysterious a curse—to know, too, that he dreaded the sight of me—of me who would have laid down my life for his!—the grave, which I imagined his home, had been a mercy to a doom like this.

"He fears," I murmured, and I wept as I said it, "to look on one who would watch over, and soothe, and bear with him, with more than a woman's love! By what awful fate has this calamity fallen on one so holy and so pure? or by what pre-ordered destiny did I come to these solitudes, to find at the same time a new charm for the earth, and a spell to change it again into a desert and a place of woe?"

All night I kept vigil by the cave, and listened if I could catch moan or sound; but everything was silent: the thick walls of the rock kept even the voice of despair from my ear. The day dawned, and I retired among the trees, lest the hermit might come out unawares and see me. At sun-rise I saw him appear for a few moments, and again retire, and I then hastened home, exhausted and wearied by the internal conflicts of the night, to gather coolness and composure for the ensuing interview, which I contemplated at once with eagerness and dread.

At the appointed hour I repaired to the cavern: the door was partially closed; I opened it, hearing no answer to my knock, and walked gently along the passage; but I now heard shrieks, and

M

groans, and wild laughter as I neared the rude chamber. I paused
for a moment, and then in terror and dismay entered the apartment.
It was empty, but I saw near the clock a small door; from within
which the sounds that alarmed me proceeded. I had no scruple in
opening it, and found myself in the hermit's sleeping chamber; a
small dark room, where, upon a straw pallet, lay the wretched
occupant in a state of frantic delirium. I stood mute and horror-
struck, while his exclamations of frenzy burst upon my ear.

"'There—there!" he cried, "I have struck thee to the heart,
and now I will kneel, and kiss those white lips, and bathe my hands
in that blood. Ha!—do I hate thee?—hate—ay—hate, abhor,
detest! Have you the beads there?—let me tell them. Yes, I will
go to the confessional—confess? No, no—all the priests in the
world could not lift up a soul so heavy with guilt. Help—help—
help! I am falling—falling—there is the pit, and the fire, and the
devils! Do you hear them laugh?—I can laugh too!—ha—ha—
ha! Hush, I have written it all out, in a fair hand—he shall read
it—and then, O God! what curses he will heap upon my head!
Blessed St. Francis, hear me! Lazarus, Lazarus, speak for me!"

Thus did the hermit rave, while my flesh crept to hear him. I
stood by his bed-side, and called on him, but he neither heard nor
saw me. Upon the ground, by the bed's head, as if it had dropped
from under the pillow, was a packet sealed and directed to myself:
I knew the hand-writing at a glance, even though the letters were
blotted and irregular, and possibly traced in the first moment that
his present curse fell upon the writer. I placed the packet in my
bosom: the hermit saw not the motion, he lay back on the bed,
seemingly in utter exhaustion. I turned away, and hastened to the
monastery for assistance. As I hurried through the passage, the
hermit's shrieks again broke upon me, with a fiercer vehemence than
before. I flew from them, as if they were sounds from the abyss of
Hades. I flew till, breathless, and half-senseless myself, I fell down
exhausted by the gate of the monastery.

The two most skilled in physic of the brethren were immediately
summoned, and they lost not a moment in accompanying me to the
cavern. All that evening, until midnight, the frenzy of the maniac
seemed rather to increase than abate. But at that hour exactly,
indeed, as the clock struck twelve, he fell all at once into a deep
sleep.

Then for the first time, but not till the weary brethren had, at
this favourable symptom, permitted themselves to return for a brief
interval to the monastery, to seek refreshment for themselves, and
to bring down new medicines for the patient—then, for the first
time, I rose from the hermit's couch by which I had hitherto kept

watch, and repairing to the outer chamber, took forth the packet superscribed with my name. There, alone in that gray vault, and by the sepulchral light of the single lamp, I read what follows :

THE HERMIT'S MANUSCRIPT.

"Morton Devereux, if ever this reach you, read it, shudder, and, whatever your afflictions, bless God that you are not as I am. Do you remember my prevailing characteristic as a boy? No, you do not. You will say 'devotion!' It was not! 'Gentleness.' It was not—it was JEALOUSY! Now does the truth flash on you? Yes, that was the disease that was in my blood, and in my heart, and through whose ghastly medium every living object was beheld. Did I love you? Yes, I loved you—ay, almost with a love equal to your own. I loved my mother—I loved Gerald—I loved Montreuil. It was a part of my nature to love, and I did not resist the impulse. You I loved better than all ; but I was jealous of each. If my mother caressed you or Gerald—if *you* opened your heart to either, it stung me to the quick. I it was who said to my mother, 'Caress him not, or I shall think you love him better than me.' I it was who widened, from my veriest childhood, the breach between Gerald and yourself. I it was who gave to the childish reproach a venom, and to the childish quarrel a barb. Was this love? Yes, it *was* love ; but I could not endure that ye should love one another as ye loved me. It delighted me when one confided to my ear a complaint against the other, and said, 'Aubrey, this blow could not have come from thee !'

"Montreuil early perceived my bias of temper : he might have corrected it, and with ease. I was not evil in disposition ; I was insensible of my own vice. Had its malignity been revealed to me, I should have recoiled in horror. Montreuil had a vast power over me ; he could mould me at his will. Montreuil, I repeat, might have saved me, and thyself, and a third being, better and purer than either of us was, even in our cradles. Montreuil did not : he had an object to serve, and he sacrificed our whole house to it. He found me one day weeping over a dog that I had killed. 'Why did you destroy it?' he said ; and I answered, 'Because it loved Morton better than me !' And the priest said, 'Thou didst right, Aubrey !' Yes, from that time he took advantage of my infirmity, and could rouse or calm all my passions in proportion as he irritated or soothed it.

"You know this man's object during the latter period of his residence with us : it was the restoration of the House of Stuart. He was alternately the spy and the agitator in that cause. Among more comprehensive plans for effecting this object was that of securing the heirs to the great wealth and popular name of Sir William Devereux. This was only a minor mesh in the intricate web of his schemes : but it is the character of the man to take exactly the same pains, and pursue the same laborious intrigues, for a small object as for a great one. His first impression, on entering our house, was in favour of Gerald ; and I believe he really likes him to this day better than either of us. Partly your sarcasms, partly Gerald's disputes with you, partly my representations—for I was jealous even of the love of Montreuil—prepossessed him against you. He thought too, that Gerald had more talent to serve his purposes than yourself, and more facility in being moulded to them ; and he believed our uncle's partiality to you far from being unalienable. I have said that, at the latter period of his residence with us, he was an agent of the exiled cause. At the time I *now* speak of, he had not entered into the great political scheme which engrossed him afterwards. He was merely a restless and aspiring priest, whose whole hope, object, ambition, was the advancement of his order. He knew that whoever inherited, or whoever shared, my uncle's wealth, could, under legitimate regulation, promote *any* end which the heads of that order might select ; and he wished therefore to gain the mastery over us all. Intrigue was essentially woven with his genius, and by intrigue only did he ever seek to arrive at any end he had in view.[1] He soon obtained a mysterious and pervading power over Gerald and myself. Your temper at once irritated him, and made him despair of obtaining an ascendant over one who, though he testified in childhood none of the talents for which he has since been noted, testified, nevertheless, a shrewd, penetrating and sarcastic power of observation and detection. You, therefore, he resolved to leave to the irregularities of your own nature, confident that they would yield him the opportunity of detaching your uncle from you, and ultimately securing to Gerald his estates.

" The trial at school first altered his intentions. He imagined that he then saw in you powers which might be rendered availing to him : he conquered his pride—a great feature in his character—and he resolved to seek your affection. Your subsequent regularity of habits, and success in study, confirmed him in his resolution ; and when he learnt, from my uncle's own lips, that the Devereux estates would devolve on you, he thought that it would be easier to secure your affection to him than to divert that affection which my uncle had conceived for you. At this time I repeat, he had no particular object in view ; none, at least, beyond that of obtaining, for the

---

[1] It will be observed that Aubrey frequently repeats former assertions : this is one of the most customary traits of insanity.—Ed.

interest of his order, the direction of great wealth and some political influence. . Some time after—I know not exactly when, but before we returned to take our permanent abode at Devereux Court—a share in the grand political intrigue which was then in so many branches carried on throughout England, and even Europe, was confided to Montreuil.

"In this I believe he was the servant of his order, rather than immediately of the exiled house ; and I have since heard that even at that day he had acquired a great reputation among the professors of the former. You, Morton, he decoyed not into this scheme before he left England : he had not acquired a sufficient influence over you to trust you with the disclosure. To Gerald and myself he was more confidential. Gerald eagerly embraced his projects through a spirit of enterprise—I through a spirit of awe and of religion. RELIGION ! Yes,—then,—long after,—now,—when my heart was and is the home of all withering and evil passions, Religion reigned—reigns, over me a despot and a tyrant. Its terrors haunt me at this hour—they people the earth and the air with shapes of ghastly menace ! They—Heaven pardon me ! what would my madness utter ? Madness ?—madness ? Ay *that* is the real scourge, the real fire, the real torture, the real hell, of this fair earth !

"Montreuil, then, by different pleas, won over Gerald and myself. He left us, but engaged us in constant correspondence. 'Aubrey,' he said, before he departed, and when he saw that I was wounded by his apparent cordiality towards you and Gerald—'Aubrey,' he said, soothing me on this point, 'think not that I trust Gerald or the arrogant Morton as I trust you. *You* have my real heart and my real trust. It is necessary to the execution of this project, so important to the interests of religion, and so agreeable to the will of Heaven, that we should secure all co-operators ; but they, your brothers, Aubrey, are the tools of that mighty design—you are its friend.' Thus it was that, at all times when he irritated too sorely the vice of my nature, he flattered it into seconding his views ; and thus, instead of conquering my evil passions, he conquered by them. Curses——No, no, no !—I *will* be calm.

"We returned to Devereux Court, and we grew from boyhood into youth. I loved you then, Morton. Ah ! what would I not give now for one pure feeling, such as I felt in your love ? Do you remember the day on which you had extorted from my uncle his consent to your leaving us for the pleasures and pomps of London ? Do you remember the evening of that day, when I came to seek you, and we sat down on a little mound, and talked over your projects, and you spoke then to me of my devotion, and my purer and colder feelings ? Morton, at that very moment my veins burnt with passion !—at that very moment my heart was feeding the vulture fated to live and prey within it for ever! Thrice did I resolve to confide in you, as we then sat together, and thrice did my evil genius forbid it. You seemed, even in your affection to me, so wholly engrossed with your own hopes—you seemed so little to regret leaving me—you stung, so often and so deeply, in our short conference, that feeling which made me desire to monopolize all things in those I loved, that I said inly—' Why should I bare my heart to one who can so little understand it?' And so we turned home, and you dreamt not of that which was then within me, and which was destined to be your curse and mine.

"Not many weeks previous to that night, I had seen one whom to see was to love! Love!—I tell you, Morton, that *that* word is expressive of soft and fond emotions, and there should be another expressive of all that is fierce, and dark, and unrelenting in the human heart !—all that seems most like the deadliest and the blackest hate, and yet is not hate! I saw this being, and from that moment my real nature, which had slept hitherto, awoke! I remember well, it was one evening in the beginning of summer that I first saw her. She sat alone in the little garden beside the cottage door, and I paused, and, unseen, looked over the slight fence that separated us, and fed my eyes with a loveliness that I thought till then, only twilight or the stars could wear! From that evening I came, night after night, to watch her from the same spot ; and every time I beheld her, the poison entered deeper and deeper into my system. At length I had an opportunity of being known to her—of speaking to her—of hearing her speak—of touching the ground she had hallowed—of entering the home where she dwelt!

"I must explain : I said that both Gerald and myself corresponded privately with Montreuil—we were both bound over to secrecy with regard to you—and this, my temper, and Gerald's coolness with you, rendered an easy obligation to both ;—I say my temper—for I loved to think I had a secret not known to another ; and I carried this reserve even to the degree of concealing from Gerald himself the greater part of the correspondence between me and the Abbé. In his correspondence with each of us, Montreuil acted with his usual skill ; to Gerald, as the elder in years, the more prone to enterprise, and the manlier in aspect and in character, was allotted whatever object was of real trust or importance. Gerald it was who, under pretence of pursuing his accustomed sports, conferred with the various agents of intrigue who from time to time visited our coast ; and to me the Abbé gave words of endearment, and affected the language of more entire trust. ' Whatever,' he would say, ' in our present half-mellowed projects, is exposed to danger, but does not

promise reward, I entrust to Gerald; hereafter, far higher employment, under far safer and surer auspices, will be yours. We are
the heads—be ours the nobler occupation to plan—and let us leave
to inferior natures the vain and perilous triumph to execute what we
design.'

"All this I readily assented to; for, despite my acquiescence
in Montreuil's wishes, I loved not enterprise, or rather I hated
whatever roused me from the dreamy and abstracted indolence
which was most dear to my temperament. Sometimes, however,
with a great show of confidence, Montreuil would request me to
execute some quiet and unimportant commission; and of this nature
was one I received while I was thus, unknown even to the object,
steeping my soul in the first intoxication of love. The plots then
carried on by certain ecclesiastics, I need not say extended, in one
linked chain, over the greater part of the continent. Spain, in
especial, was the theatre of these intrigues; and among the tools
employed in executing them were some, who, though banished from
that country, still, by the rank they had held in it, carried a certain
importance in their very names. Foremost of these was the father
of the woman I loved—and foremost, in whatever promised occupation to a restless mind, he was always certain to be.

" Montreuil now commissioned me to seek out a certain Barnard
(an underling in those secret practices or services, for which he
afterwards suffered, and who was then in that part of the country),
and to communicate to him some messages, of which he was to be
the bearer to this Spaniard. A thought flashed upon me—Mon
treuil's letter mentioned, accidentally, that the Spaniard had never
hitherto seen Barnard :—could I not personate the latter—deliver
the messages myself, and thus win that introduction to the daughter
which I so burningly desired, and which, from the close reserve of
the father's habits, I might not otherwise effect? The plan was
open to two objections : one, that I was known personally in the
town in the environs of which the Spaniard lived, and he might
therefore very soon discover who I really was; the other, that I was
not in possession of all the information which Barnard might possess,
and which the Spaniard might wish to learn; but these objections
had not much weight with me. To the first, I said inly, 'I will
oppose the most constant caution; I will go always on foot, and
alone—I will never be seen in the town itself—and even should the
Spaniard, who seems rarely to stir abroad, and who, possibly, does
not speak our language—even should he learn, by accident, that
Barnard is only another name for Aubrey Devereux, it will not be
before I have gained my object; nor, perhaps, before the time when
I myself may wish to acknowledge my identity.' To the second

objection I saw a yet more ready answer. 'I will acquaint Mon-treuil at once,' I said, 'with my intention ; I will claim his conniv-ance as a proof of his confidence, and as an essay of my own genius of intrigue.' I did so ; the priest, perhaps delighted to involve me so deeply, and to find me so ardent in his project, consented. For-tunately, as I before said, Barnard was an underling—young—unknown—and obscure. My youth, therefore, was not so great a foe to my assumed disguise as it might otherwise have been. Mon-treuil supplied all requisite information. I tried (for the first time, with a beating heart and a tremulous voice) the imposition! it succeeded—I continued it. Yes, Morton, yes !—pour forth upon me your bitterest execration—in me—in your brother—in the brother so dear to you—in the brother whom you imagined so passionless—so pure—so sinless—behold that Barnard—the lover—the idolatrous lover—the foe—the deadly foe—of Isora Alvarez !"

Here the manuscript was defaced for some pages, by incoherent and meaningless ravings. It seemed as if one of his dark fits of frenzy had at that time come over the writer. At length, in a more firm and clear character than that immediately preceding it, the manuscript continued as follows :

"I loved her, but even then it was with a fierce and ominous love—(ominous of what it became). Often in the still evenings, when we stood together watching the sun set—when my tongue trembled but did not dare to speak—when all soft and sweet thoughts filled the heart and glistened in the eye of that most sensitive and fairy being—when my own brow, perhaps, seemed to reflect the same emotions—feelings, which I even shuddered to conceive, raged within me. Had we stood together, in those moments, upon the brink of a precipice, I could have wound my arms around her, and leaped with her into the abyss. Every thing but one nursed my passion ; nature—solitude—early dreams—all kindled and fed that fire : Religion only combated it ; I knew it was a crime to love any of earth's creatures as I loved. I used the scourge and the fast [1]—I wept hot—burning tears—I prayed, and the intensity of my prayer appalled even myself, as it rose from my maddened heart, in the depth and stillness of the lone night : but the flame burnt higher and more scorchingly from the opposition ; nay, it was the very knowledge that my love was criminal that made it assume so fearful and dark a shape. 'Thou art the cause of my downfall from

[1] I need not point out to the Novel-reader how completely the character of Aubrey has been stolen in a certain celebrated French Romance—But the writer I allude to is not so unmerciful as M. de Balzac, who has pillaged scenes in the Disowned, with a most gratifying politeness.

Heaven !' I muttered, when I looked upon Isora's calm face—thou feelest it not, and I could destroy thee and myself—myself—the criminal—thee the cause of the crime !'

"It must have been that my eyes betrayed my feelings that Isora loved me not—that she shrunk from me even at the first—why else should I not have called forth the same sentiments which she gave to you? Was not my form cast in a mould as fair as yours?—did not my voice whisper in as sweet a tone?—did I not love her with as wild a love? Why should she not have loved me? I was the first whom she beheld—she would—ay, perhaps she would have loved me, if you had not come and marred all. Curse yourself, then, that you were my rival !—curse yourself that you made my heart as a furnace, and smote my brain with frenzy—curse—O, sweet Virgin, forgive me !—I know not—I know not what my tongue utters or my hand traces !

"You came, then, Morton, you came—you knew her—you loved her—she loved you. I learned that you had gained admittance to the cottage, and the moment I learned it, I looked on Isora, and felt my fate, as by intuition : I saw at once that she was prepared to love you—I saw the very moment when that love kindled from conception into form—I saw—and at that moment my eyes reeled and my ears rung as with the sound of a rushing sea, and I thought I felt a cord snap within my brain, which has never been united again.

"Once only, after your introduction to the cottage, did I think of confiding to you my love and rivalship ; you remember one night when we met by the castle cave, and when your kindness touched and softened me, despite of myself. The day after that night I sought you, with the intention of communicating to you all ; and while I was yet struggling with my embarrassment, and the suffocating tide of my emotions, you premeditated me, by giving me *your* confidence. Engrossed with your own feelings, you were not observant of mine ; and as you dwelt and dilated upon your love for Isora, all emotions, save those of agony and of fury, vanished from my breast. I did not answer you then at any length, for I was too agitated to trust to prolix speech ; but by the next day I had recovered myself, and I resolved, as far as I was able, to play the hypocrite. 'He cannot love her as I do !' I said ; 'perhaps I may, without disclosure of my rivalship, and without sin in the attempt, detach her from my reason.' Fraught with this idea, I collected myself—sought you—remonstrated with you—represented the worldly folly of your love, and uttered all that prudence preaches —in vain, when it preaches against passion !

"Let me be brief. I saw that I made no impression on you—I

M 2

stifled my wrath—I continued to visit and watch Isora. I timed my opportunities well—my constant knowledge of your motions allowed me to do that ; besides, I represented to the Spaniard the. necessity, through political motives, of concealing myself from you ; hence, we never encountered each other. One evening, Alvarez had gone out to meet one of his countrymen and confederates. I found Isora alone, in the most sequestered part of the garden,—her loveliness, and her exceeding gentleness of manner, melted me. For the first time audibly, my heart spoke out, and I told her of my idolatry. Idolatry ! ay, *that* is the only word, since it signifies both worship and guilt ! She heard me timidly, gently, coldly. She spoke—and I found confirmed, from her own lips, what my reason had before told me—that there was no hope for me. The iron that entered, also roused, my heart. 'Enough !' I cried fiercely, 'you love this Morton Devereux, and for him I am scorned.' Isora blushed and trembled, and all my senses fled from me. I scarcely know in what words my rage and my despair clothed themselves ; but I know that I divulged myself to her—I know that I told her I was the brother—the rival—the enemy of the man she loved,—I know that I uttered the fiercest and the wildest menaces and execrations—I know that my vehemence so overpowered and terrified her that her mind was scarcely less clouded—less lost, rather, than my own. At that moment, the sound of your horse's hoofs was heard ; Isora's eyes brightened, and her mien grew firm. 'He comes,' she said, 'and he will protect me !'—'Hark !' I said, sinking my voice, and, as my drawn sword flashed in one hand, the other grasped her arm with a savage force—'hark, woman !' I said—and an oath of the blackest fury accompanied my threats—'swear that you will never divulge to Morton Devereux who is his real rival—that you will never declare to him nor to any one else, that the false Barnard and the true Aubrey Devereux are the same—swear this, or I swear (and I repeated, with a solemn vehemence, that dread oath), that I will stay here—that I will confront my rival—that, the moment he beholds me, I will plunge this sword into his bosom—and that, before I perish myself, I will hasten to the town, and will utter there a secret which will send your father to the gallows—now, your choice ?'

"Morton, you have often praised, my uncle has often jested at, the womanish softness of my face. There have been moments when I have seen that face in the glass, and known it not, but started in wild affright, and fancied that I beheld a demon ; perhaps in that moment this change was over it. Slowly Isora gazed upon me— slowly blanched into the hues of death grew her cheek and lip— slowly that lip uttered the oath I enjoined. I released my gripe,

and she fell to the earth, sudden and stunned as if struck by lightning. I stayed not to look on what I had done—I heard your step
advance—I fled by a path that led from the garden to the beach—
and I reached my home without retaining a single recollection of
the space I had traversed to attain it.

"Despite the night I passed—a night which I will leave you to
imagine—I rose the next morning with a burning interest to learn
from you what had passed after my flight, and with a power, peculiar
to the stormiest passions, of an outward composure while I listened
to the recital. I saw that I was safe, and I heard, with a joy so
rapturous, that I question whether even Isora's assent to *my* love
would have given me an equal transport, that, she had rejected you.
I uttered some advice to you commonplace enough—it displeased
you, and we separated.

"That evening, to my surprise, I was privately visited by Montreuil. He had some designs in hand which brought him from
France into the neighbourhood, but which made him desirous of
concealment. He soon drew from me my secret; it is marvellous,
indeed, what power he had of penetrating, ruling, moulding my
feelings and my thoughts. He wished, at that time, a communication to be made and a letter to be given, to Alvarez. I could not
execute this commission personally, for you had informed me of
your intention of watching if you could not discover or meet with
Barnard, and I knew you were absent from home on that very
purpose. Nor was Montreuil himself desirous of incurring the risk
of being seen by you—you over whom, sooner or later, he then
trusted to obtain a power equal to that which he held over your
brothers. Gerald then was chosen to execute the commission. He
did so—he met Alvarez for the first and the only time on the beach,
by the town of ——. You saw him, and imagined you beheld the
real Barnard.

"But I anticipate—for you did not inform me of that occurrence,
nor the inference you drew from it, till afterwards. You returned,
however, after witnessing that meeting, and for two days your
passions (passions which, intense and fierce as mine, show that,
under similar circumstances, you might have been equally guilty)
terminated in fever. You were confined to your bed for three or
four days; meanwhile I took advantage of the event.—Montreuil
suggested a plan which I readily embraced. I sought the Spaniard,
and told him in confidence that you were a suitor—but a suitor
upon the most dishonourable terms—to his daughter. I told him,
moreover, that you had detected his schemes, and in order to
deprive Isora of protection, and abate any obstacles resulting from
her pride, to betray him to the government. I told him that his

best and most prudent, nay, his only chance of safety for Isora and himself was to leave his present home, and take refuge in the vast mazes of the metropolis. I told him not to betray to you his knowledge of your criminal intentions, lest it might needlessly exasperate you. I furnished him wherewithal to repay you the sum which you had lent him, and by which you had commenced his acquaintance: and I dictated to him the very terms of the note in which the sum was to be enclosed. After this I felt happy. You were separated from Isora—she might forget you—you might forget her. I was possessed of the secret of her father's present retreat—I might seek it at my pleasure, and ultimately—so hope whispered—prosper in my love.

"Some time afterwards you mentioned your suspicions of Gerald; I did not corroborate, but I did not seek to destroy, them. 'They already hate each other,' I said: 'can the hate be greater? meanwhile, let it divert suspicion from me!' Gerald knew of the agency of the real Barnard, though he did not know that I had assumed the name of that person. When you taxed him with his knowledge of the man, he was naturally confused. You interpreted that confusion into the fact of being your rival, while in truth it arose from his belief that you had possessed yourself of his political schemes. Montreuil, who had lurked chiefly in the islet opposite 'the Castle Cave,' had returned to France on the same day that Alvarez repaired to London. Previous to this, we had held some conferences together upon my love. At first he had opposed and reasoned with it, but, startled and astonished by the intensity with which it possessed me, he gave way to my vehemence at last. I have said that I had adopted his advice in one instance. The fact of having received his advice—the advice of one so pious—so free from human passion—so devoted to one object, which appeared to him, the cause of Religion—advice, too, in a love so fiery and overwhelming;—that fact made me think myself less criminal than I had done before. He advised me yet further. 'Do not seek Isora,' he said, 'till some time has elapsed—till her new-born love for your brother has died away—till the impression of fear you have caused in her is somewhat effaced—till time and absence too have done their work in the mind of Morton, and you will no longer have for your rival, one who is not only a brother, but a man of a fierce, resolute, and unrelenting temper.'

"I yielded to this advice—partly because it promised so fair; partly because I was not systematically vicious, and I wished, if possible, to do away with our rivalship; and principally because I knew, in the meanwhile, that if I was deprived of her presence, so also were you; and jealousy with me was a far more intolerable and engrossing passion than the very love from which it sprung. So time passed on—you affected to have conquered your attachment ; you affected to take pleasure in levity, and the idlest pursuits of worldly men. I saw deeper into your heart. For the moment I entertained the passion of love in my own breast, my eyes became gifted with a second vision to penetrate the most mysterious and hoarded secrets in the love of others.

"Two circumstances of importance happened before you left Devereux Court for London ; the one was the introduction to your service of Jean Desmarais, the second was your breach with Montreuil. I speak now of the first. A very early friend did the priest possess, born in the same village as himself, and in the same rank of life ; he had received a good education, and possessed natural genius. At a time when, from some fraud in a situation of trust which he had held in a French nobleman's family, he was in destitute and desperate circumstances, it occurred to Montreuil to provide for him by placing him in our family. Some accidental and frivolous remark of yours, which I had repeated in my corre-spondence with Montreuil, as illustrative of your manner, and your affected pursuits at that time, presented an opportunity to a plan before conceived. Desmarais came to England in a smuggler's vessel, presented himself to you as a servant, and was accepted. In this plan Montreuil had two views — first, that of securing Desmarais a place in England, tolerably profitable to himself, and convenient for any plot or scheme which Montreuil might require of him in this country ; secondly, that of setting a perpetual and most adroit spy upon all your motions.

" As to the second occurrence to which I have referred, viz. your breach with Montreuil——"

Here Aubrey, with the same terrible distinctness which had characterized his previous details, and which shed a double horror over the contrast of the darker and more frantic passages in the manuscript, related what the reader will remember Oswald had narrated before, respecting the letter he had brought from Madame de Balzac. It seems that Montreuil's abrupt appearance in the hall had been caused by Desmarais, who had recognized Oswald, on his dismounting at the gate, and had previously known that he was in the employment of the Jansenistical *intriguante*, Madame de Balzac.

Aubrey proceeded then to say that Montreuil, invested with far more direct authority and power than he had been hitherto, in the projects of that wise order whose doctrines he had so darkly per-verted, repaired to London ; and that, soon after my departure for the same place, Gerald and Aubrey left Devereux Court in company with each other ; but Gerald, whom very trifling things diverted from any project, however important, returned to Devereux Court, to accomplish the prosecution of some rustic *amour*, without even reaching London. Aubrey, on the contrary, had proceeded to the metropolis, sought the suburb in which Alvarez lived, procured, in order to avoid any probable chance of meeting me, a lodging in the same obscure quarter, and had renewed his suit to Isora. The reader is already in possession of the ill success which attended it. Aubrey had at last confessed his real name to the father. The Spaniard was dazzled by the prospect of so honourable an alliance for his daughter. From both came Isora's persecution, but in both was it resisted. Passing over passages in the manuscript of the most stormy incoherence and the most gloomy passion, I come to what follows—

"I learned then from Desmarais, that you had taken away her and the dying father; that you had placed them in a safe and honourable home. That man, so implicitly the creature of Montreuil, or rather of his own interest, with which Montreuil was identified, was easily induced to betray you also to me—me whom he imagined, moreover, utterly the tool of the priest, and of whose torturing interest, in this peculiar disclosure, he was not at that time aware. I visited Isora in her new abode, and again and again she trembled beneath my rage. Then, for the second time, I attempted force. Ha! ha! Morton! I think I see you now!—I think I hear your muttered curse! Curse on! When you read this I shall be beyond your vengeance—beyond human power. And yet I think if I were mere clay—if I were the mere senseless heap of ashes that the grave covers—if I were not the thing that must live for ever and for ever, far away in unimagined worlds, where nought that has earth's life can come—I should tremble beneath the sod as your foot pressed, and your execration rung over it. A second time I attempted force—a second time I was repulsed by the same means —by a woman's hand and a woman's dagger. But I knew that I had one hold over Isora from which, while she loved you, I could never be driven: I knew that by threatening your *life*, I could command her will, and terrify her into compliance with my own. I made her reiterate her vow of concealment; and I discovered, by some words dropping from her fear, that she believed you already suspected me, and had been withheld, by her entreaties, from seeking me out. I questioned her more, and soon perceived that it was (as indeed I knew before) Gerald whom you suspected, not me; but I did not tell this to Isora. I suffered her to cherish a mistake profitable to my disguise; but I saw at once that it might betray me, if you ever met and conferred at length with Gerald upon this point ; and I exacted from Isora a pledge that she would effectually and for ever bind you not to breathe a single suspicion to him. When I had left the room, I returned once more to warn her against uniting herself with you. Wretch, selfish, accursed wretch that you were, why did you suffer her to transgress that warning?

" I fled from the house, as a fiend flies from a being whom he has possessed. I returned at night to look up at the window, and linger by the door, and keep watch beside the home which held Isora. Such, in her former abode, had been my nightly wont. I had no evil thought nor foul intent in this customary vigil—no, not one! Strangely enough, with the tempestuous and overwhelming emotions which constituted the greater part of my love, was mingled, — though subdued and latent—a stream of the softest, yea, I might add, almost of the holiest tenderness. Often after one of those outpourings of rage, and menace, and despair, I would fly to some quiet spot, and weep, till all the hardness of my heart was wept away. And often in those nightly vigils I would pause by the door and murmur, ' This shelter, denied not to the beggar and the beggar's child, this would you deny to me, if you could dream that I was so near you. And yet, had you loved me, instead of lavishing upon me all your hatred and your contempt—had you loved me, I would have served and worshipped you as man knows not worship or service. You shudder at my vehemence now—I could not then have breathed a whisper to wound you. You tremble now at the fierceness of my breast—you would then rather have marvelled at its softness.'

" I was already at my old watch when you encountered me—you addressed me, I answered not—you approached me, and I fled. Fled—there—there was the shame, and the sting of my sentiments towards you. I am not naturally afraid of danger, though my nerves are sometimes weak, and have sometimes shrunk from it. I have known something of peril in late years, when my frame has been bowed and broken—peril by storms at sea, and the knives of robbers upon land—and I have looked upon it with a quiet eye. But you, Morton Devereux, you I always feared. I had seen from your childhood others, whose nature was far stronger than mine, yield and recoil at yours—I had seen the giant and bold strength of Gerald quail before your bent brow—I had seen even the hardy pride of Montreuil baffled by your curled lip, and the stern sarcasm of your glance—I had seen you, too, in your wild moments of ungoverned rage, and I knew that if earth held one whose passions were fiercer than my own, it was you. But your passions were sustained even in their fiercest excess—your passions were the mere weapons of your mind—my passions were the tortures and the

tyrants of mine. Your passions seconded your will—mine blinded
and overwhelmed it. From my infancy, even while I loved you
most, you awed me ; and years, in deepening the impression, had
made it indelible. I could not confront the thought of your knowing
all, and of meeting you after that knowledge. And this fear, while
it unnerved me at some moments, at others only maddened my
ferocity the more by the stings of shame and self-contempt.

"I fled from you—you pursued—you gained upon me—you remember now how I was preserved. I dashed through the inebriated
revellers who obstructed your path, and reached my own lodging,
which was close at hand ; for the same day on which I learned Isora's
change of residence I changed my own in order to be near it. Did
I feel joy for my escape ? No—I could have gnawed the very flesh
from my bones in the agony of my shame. 'I could brave,' I said,
'I could threat—I could offer violence to the woman who rejected
me, and yet I could not face the rival for whom I am scorned !' At
that moment a resolution flashed across my mind, exactly as if a
train of living fire had been driven before it. Morton, I resolved
to murder you, and in that very hour ! A pistol lay on my table—
I took it, concealed it about my person, and repaired to the shelter
of a large portico, beside which I knew that you must pass to your
own home in the same street. Scarcely three minutes had elapsed
between the reaching my house and the leaving it on this errand. I
knew, for I had heard swords clash, that you would be detained
some time in the street by the rioters—I thought it probable also that
you might still continue the search for me ; and I knew even that,
had you hastened at once to your home, you could scarcely have
reached it before I reached my shelter. I hurried on—I arrived at
the spot—I screened myself and awaited your coming. You came,
borne in the arms of two men—others followed in the rear—I saw
your face destitute of the hue and aspect of life, and your clothes
streaming with blood. I was horror-stricken. I joined the crowd—
I learnt that you had been stabbed, and it was feared mortally.

"I did not return home—no, I went into the fields, and lay out
all night, and lifted up my heart to God, and wept aloud, and peace
fell upon me—at least, what was peace compared to the tempestuous
darkness which had before reigned in my breast. The sight of you,
bleeding and insensible—you, against whom I had harboured a
fratricide's purpose—had stricken, as it were, the weapon from my
hand, and the madness from my mind. I shuddered at what I had
escaped—I blessed God for my deliverance—and with the gratitude
and the awe came repentance—and repentance brought a resolution
to fly, since I could not wrestle with my mighty and dread temptation :—the moment that resolution was formed, it was as if an incubus

were taken from my breast. Even the next morning I did not return home—my anxiety for you was such that I forgot all caution—I went to your house myself—I saw one of your servants to whom I was personally unknown. I inquired respecting you, and learned that your wound had not been mortal, and that the servant had over-heard one of the medical attendants say you were not even in danger.

"At this news I felt the serpent stir again within me, but I resolved to crush it at the first—I would not even expose myself to the tempta-tion of passing by Isora's house—I went straight in search of my horse—I mounted, and fled resolutely from the scene of my soul's peril. 'I will go,' I said, 'to the home of our childhood—I will surround myself by the mute tokens of the early love which my brother bore me—I will think—while penance and prayer cleanse my soul from its black guilt—I will think that I am also making a sacrifice to that brother.'

"I returned then to Devereux Court, and I resolved to forego all hope—all persecution—of Isora! My brother—my brother, my heart yearns to you at this moment, even though years and distance, and above all, my own crimes, place a gulf between us which I may never pass—it yearns to you when I think of those quiet shades, and the scenes where, pure and unsullied, we wandered together, when life was all verdure and freshness, and we dreamt not of what was to come! If even now my heart yearns to you, Morton, when I think of that home and those days, believe that it had some softness and some mercy for you then. Yes, I repeat, I resolved to subdue my own emotions, and interpose no longer between Isora and yourself. Full of this determination, and utterly melted towards you, I wrote you a long letter; such as we would have written to each other in our first youth. Two days after that letter all my new purposes were swept away, and the whole soil of evil thoughts which they had covered, not destroyed, rose again as the tide flowed from it, black and rugged as before.

"The very night on which I had written that letter, came Montreuil secretly to my chamber. He had been accustomed to visit Gerald by stealth, and at sudden moments; and there was something almost supernatural in the manner in which he seemed to pass from place to place, unmolested and unseen. He had now conceived a villainous project; and he had visited Devereux Court in order to ascertain the likelihood of its success; he there found that it was necessary to involve me in his scheme. My uncle's physician had said privately that Sir William could not live many months longer. Either from Gerald, or my mother, Montreuil learned this fact; and he was resolved, if possible, that the family estates should not glide from all

chance of his influence over them into your possession. Montreuil
was literally as poor as the rigid law of his order enjoins its disciples
to be ; all his schemes required the disposal of large sums, and in no
private source could he hope for such pecuniary power as he was
likely to find in the coffers of any member of our family—yourself
only excepted. It was this man's boast to want, and yet to command,
all things ; and he was now determined that if any craft, resolution,
or guilt, could occasion the transfer of my uncle's wealth from you to
Gerald, or to myself, it should not be wanting.

  " Now, then, he found the advantage of the dissensions with each
other, which he had either sown or mellowed in our breasts. He
came to turn those wrathful thoughts which, when he last saw me, I
had expressed towards you, to the favour and success of his design.
He found my mind strangely altered, but he affected to applaud the
change. He questioned me respecting my uncle's health, and I told
him what had really occurred, viz. that my uncle had, on the preceding day, read over to me some part of a will which he had just
made, and in which the vast bulk of his property was bequeathed
to you. At this news Montreuil must have perceived at once the
necessity of winning my consent to his project ; for, since I had seen
the actual testament, no fraudulent transfer of the property therein
bequeathed could take place without my knowledge that some fraud
had been recurred to. Montreuil knew me well—he knew that
avarice, that pleasure, that ambition, were powerless words with
me, producing no effect and affording no temptation ; but he knew
that passion, jealousy, spiritual terrors, were the springs that moved
every part and nerve of my moral being. The two former then he
now put into action—the last he held back in reserve. He spoke to
me no further upon the subject he had then at heart ; not a word
further on the disposition of the estates—he spoke to me only of
Isora and of you ; he aroused, by hint and insinuation, the new sleep
into which all those emotions—the furies of the heart—had been for
a moment lulled. He told me he had lately seen Isora—he dwelt
glowingly on her beauty—he commended my heroism in resigning
her to a brother whose love for her was little in comparison to mine
—who had, in reality, never loved *me*—whose jests and irony had
been levelled no less at myself than at others. He painted your
person and your mind, in contrast to my own, in colours so covertly
depreciating as to irritate more and more, that vanity with which
jealousy is so woven, and from which, perhaps (a Titan son of so
feeble a parent), it is born. He hung lingeringly over all the
treasure that you would enjoy, and that I—I, the first discoverer,
had so nobly, and so generously relinquished.

  " ' Relinquished ! ' I cried, ' no, I was driven from it, I left it not while a hope of possessing it remained.' The priest affected astonishment. 'How! was I sure of that? I had, it is true, wooed Isora; but would she, even if she had felt no preference for Morton, would she have surrendered the heir to a princely wealth for the humble love of the younger son? I did not know women; with them all love was either wantonness, custom, or pride—it was the last principle that swayed Isora. Had I sought to enlist it on my side? Not at all. Again, I had only striven to detach Isora from Morton; had I ever attempted the much easier task of detaching Morton from Isora? No, never;' and Montreuil repeated his panegyric on my generous surrender of my rights. I interrupted him; 'I had not surrendered—I never would surrender while a hope remained. But, where was that hope, and how was it to be realized?' After much artful prelude, the priest explained. He proposed to use every means to array against your union with Isora, all motives of ambition, interest and aggrandizement. 'I know Morton's character,' said he, 'to its very depths. His chief virtue is honour—his chief principle is ambition. He will not attempt to win this girl otherwise than by marriage, for the very reasons that would induce most men to attempt it, viz. her unfriended state, her poverty, her confidence in him, and her love, or that semblance of love, which he believes to be the passion itself. This virtue—I call it so, though it is none, for there is no virtue out of religion—this virtue, then, will place before him only two plans of conduct, either to marry her or to forsake her. Now, then, if we can bring his ambition, that great lever of his conduct, in opposition to the first alternative, only the last remains; I say that we *can* employ that engine in your behalf—leave it to me, and I will do so. Then, Aubrey, in the moment of her pique, her resentment, her outraged vanity, at being thus left, you shall appear; not as you have hitherto done, in menace and terror, but soft, subdued, with looks all love—with vows all penitence—vindicating all your past vehemence, by the excess of your passion, and promising all future tenderness by the influence of the same motive, the motive which to a woman pardons every error, and hallows every crime. Then will she contrast your love with your brother's—then will the scale fall from her eyes—then will she see what hitherto she has been blinded to, that your brother, to yourself, is a satyr to Hyperion—then will she blush and falter, and hide her cheek in your bosom.'—'Hold, hold!' I cried; 'do with me what you will, counsel, and I will act!'"

Here again the manuscript was defaced by a sudden burst of execration upon Montreuil, followed by ravings that gradually blackened into the most gloomy and incoherent outpourings of madness; at length, the history proceeded.

"You wrote to ask me to sound our uncle on the subject of your intended marriage. Montreuil drew up my answer, and I constrained myself, despite my revived hatred to you, to transcribe its expressions of affection. My uncle wrote to you also; and we strengthened his dislike to the step you had proposed, by hints from myself disrespectful to Isora, and an anonymous communication dated from London, and to the same purport. All this while I knew not that Isora had been in your house; your answer to my letter seemed to imply that you would not disobey my uncle. Montreuil, who was still lurking in the neighbourhood, and who at night privately met or sought me, affected exultation at the incipient success of his advice. He pretended to receive perpetual intelligence of your motions and conduct, and he informed me now that Isora had come to your house on hearing of your wound; that you had not (agreeably, Montreuil added to his view of your character) taken advantage of her indiscretion; that immediately on receiving your uncle's and my own letters, you had separated yourself from her; and that, though you still visited her, it was apparently with a view of breaking off all connection by gradual and gentle steps; at all events, you had taken no measures towards marriage. 'Now, then,' said Montreuil, 'for one finishing stroke, and the prize is yours. Your uncle cannot, you find, live long: could he but be persuaded to leave his property to Gerald or to you, with only a trifling legacy (comparatively speaking) to Morton, that worldly-minded and enterprising person would be utterly prevented from marrying a penniless and unknown foreigner. Nothing but his own high prospects, so utterly above the necessity of foitune in a wife, can excuse such a measure now, even to his own mind; if, therefore, we can effect this transfer of property, and in the meanwhile prevent Morton from marrying, your rival is gone for ever, and with his brilliant advantages of wealth will also vanish his merits in the eyes of Isora. Do not be startled at this thought; there is no crime in it; I, your confessor, your tutor, the servant of the Church, am the last person to counsel, to hint, even, at what is criminal; but the end sanctifies all means. By transferring this vast property, you do not only ensure your object, but you advance the great cause of Kings, the Church, and of the Religion which presides over both. Wealth, in Morton's possession, will be useless to this cause, perhaps pernicious: in your hands, or in Gerald's, it will be of inestimable service. Wealth produced fiom the public should be applied to the uses of the public, yea, even though a petty injury to one individual be the price.'

"Thus, and in this manner, did Montreuil prepare my mind for the step he meditated; but I was not yet ripe for it. So inconsistent is guilt, that I could commit murder—wrong—almost all villainy that passion dictated, but I was struck aghast by the thought of fraud. Montreuil perceived that I was not yet wholly his, and his next plan was to remove me from a spot where I might check his measures. He persuaded me to travel for a few weeks. 'On your return,' said he, 'consider Isora yours ; meanwhile, let change of scene beguile suspense.' I was passive in his hands, and I went whither he directed.

"Let me be brief here on the black fraud that ensued. Among the other arts of Jean Desmarais, was that of copying exactly any hand-writing. He was then in London, in your service : Montreuil sent for him to come to the neighbourhood of Devereux Court. Meanwhile, the priest had procured from the notary who had drawn up, and who now possessed, the will of my unsuspecting uncle, that document. The notary had been long known to, and sometimes politically employed by, Montreuil, for he was half-brother to that Oswald, whom I have before mentioned as the early comrade of the priest and Desmarais. This circumstance, it is probable, first induced Montreuil to contemplate the plan of a substituted will. Before Desmarais arrived, in order to copy those parts of the will which my uncle's humour had led him to write in his own hand, you, alarmed by a letter from my uncle, came to the Court, and on the same day Sir William (taken ill the preceding evening) died. Between that day and the one on which the funeral occurred, the will was copied by Desmarais ; only Gerald's name was substituted for yours, and the forty thousand pounds left to him—a sum equal to that bestowed on myself—was cut down into a legacy of twenty thousand pounds to you. Less than this Montreuil dared not insert as the bequest to you ; and it is possible that the same regard to probabilities prevented all mention of himself in the substituted will. This was all the alteration made. My uncle's writing was copied exactly ; and, save the departure from his apparent intentions in your favour, I believe not a particle in the effected fraud was calculated to excite suspicion. Immediately on the reading of the will, Montreuil repaired to me, and confessed what had taken place.

"'Aubrey,' he said, 'I have done this for your sake partly ; but I have had a much higher end in view than even your happiness, or my affectionate wishes to promote it. I live solely for one object—the aggrandizement of that holy order to which I belong ; the schemes of that order are devoted only to the interests of Heaven, and by serving them, I serve Heaven itself. Aubrey, child of my adoption and of my earthly hopes, those schemes require carnal instruments, and work, even through Mammon, unto the goal of righteousness. What I have done, is just before God and man. I have wrested a weapon from the hand of an enemy, and placed it in the hand of an ally. I have not touched one atom of this wealth, though, with the same ease with which I have transferred it from Morton to Gerald, I might have made my own private fortune. I have not touched one atom of it ; nor for you, whom I love more than any living being, have I done what my heart dictated. I might have caused the inheritance to pass to you. I have not done so. Why? Because, then, I should have consulted a selfish desire at the expense of the interests of mankind. Gerald is fitter to be the tool those interests require than you are. Gerald I have made that tool. You, too, I have spared the pangs which your conscience, so peculiarly, so morbidly acute, might suffer at being selected as the instrument of a seeming wrong to Morton. All required of you is silence. If your wants ever ask more than your legacy, you have, as I have, a claim to that wealth which your pleasure allows Gerald to possess. Meanwhile, let us secure to you that treasure dearer to you than gold.'

" If Montreuil did not quite blind me by speeches of this nature, my engrossing, absorbing passion required little to make it cling to any hope of its fruition. I assented, therefore, though not without many previous struggles, to Montreuil's project, or rather to its concealment ; nay, I wrote some time after, at his desire, and his dictation, a letter to you, stating feigned reasons for my uncle's alteration of former intentions, and exonerating Gerald from all connivance in that alteration, or abetment in the fraud you professed that it was your open belief had been committed. This was due to Gerald ; for at that time, and for aught I know, at the present, he was perfectly unconscious by what means he had attained his fortune ; he believed that your love for Isora had given my uncle offence, and hence your disinheritance ; and Montreuil took effectual care to exasperate him against you, by dwelling on the malice which your suspicions and your proceedings against him so glaringly testi-fied. Whether Montreuil really thought you would give over all intention of marrying Isora upon your reverse of fortune, which is likely enough, from his estimate of your character, or whether he only wished by any means, to obtain my acquiescence in a measure important to his views, I know not, but he never left me, nor ever ceased to sustain my fevered and unhallowed hopes, from the hour in which he first communicated to me the fraudulent substitution of the will, till we repaired together to London. This we did not do so long as he could detain me in the country, by assurances that I should ruin all by appearing before Isora until you had entirely deserted her.

" Morton, hitherto I háve written as if my veins were filled with
water, instead of the raging fire that flows through them until it
reaches my brain, and there it stops, and eats away all things—even
memory, that once seemed eternal! Now I feel as I approach the
consummation of—Ha—of what—ay, of what? Brother, did you
ever, when you thought yourself quite alone—at night—not a breath
stirring—did you ever raise your eyes, and see exactly opposite to
you, a devil;—a dread thing, that moves not, speaks not, but glares
upon you with a fixed, dead, unrelenting eye?—that thing is before
me now, and·witnesses every word I write. But it deters me not!
no, nor terrifies me. I have said that I would fulfil this task, and
I have nearly done it; though at times the gray cavern yawned, and
I saw its rugged walls stretch—stretch away, on either side, until
they reached hell; and there I beheld—but I will not tell you, till
we meet there! Now I am calm again—read on.

" We could not discover Isora, nor her home; perhaps the priest
took care that it should be so; for, at that time, what with his
devilish whispers and my own heart, I often scarcely knew what
I was, or what I desired; and I sat for hours and gazed upon the
air, and it seemed so soft and still that I longed to make an opening
in my forehead that it might enter there, and so cool and quiet the
dull, throbbing, scorching anguish that lay like molten lead in my
brain; at length we found the house. 'To-morrow,' said the Abbé,
and he shed tears over me—for there were times when that hard
man did feel;—'to-morrow, my child, thou shalt see her—but be
soft and calm.' To-morrow came; but Montreuil was pale, paler
than I had ever seen him, and he gazed upon me and said, 'Not
to-day, son, not to-day; she has gone out, and will not return till
nightfall.' My brother, the evening came, and with it came Desmarais; he came in terror and alarm. 'The villain Oswald,' he
said, 'has betrayed all;' he drew me aside and told me so.
'Harkye, Jean,' he whispered, 'harkye—your master has my
brother's written confession, and the real will; but I have provided
for your safety, and if he pleases it, for Montreuil's. The packet
is not to be opened till the seventh day—fly before then.' 'But I
know,' added Desmarais,'where the packet is placed;' and he took
Montreuil aside, and for awhile I heard not what they said; but I
did overhear Desmarais at last, and I learnt that it was your *bridal
night*.

" What felt I then? The same tempestuous fury—the same
whirlwind and storm of heart that I had felt before, at the mere
anticipation of such an event? No; I felt a bright ray of joy flash
through me. Yes, joy; but it was that joy which a conqueror feels
when he knows his mortal foe is in his power, and when he dooms

that enemy to death. 'They shall perish—and on this night,' I said inly. 'I have sworn it—I swore to Isora that the bridal couch should be stained with blood, and I will keep the oath! I approached the pair—they were discussing the means for obtaining the packet. Montreuil urged Desmarais to purloin it from the place where you had deposited it, and then to abscond; but to this plan Desmarais was vehemently opposed. He insisted that there would be no possible chance of his escape from a search so scrutinizing as that which would necessarily ensue, and he was evidently resolved not *alone* to incur the danger of the *theft*. 'The Count,' said he, 'saw that I was present when he put away the packet. Suspicion will fall solely on me. Whither should I fly? No—I will serve you with my talents, but not with my life.' 'Wretch,' said Montreuil, 'if that packet is opened, thy life is already gone.'—'Yes,' said Desmarais; 'but we may yet purloin the papers, and throw the guilt upon some other quarter. What if I admit you when the Count is abroad? What if you steal the packet, and carry away other articles of more seeming value? What, too, if you wound *me* in the arm or the breast, and I coin some terrible tale of robbers, and of my resistance, could we not manage then to throw suspicion upon common housebreakers—nay, could we not throw it upon Oswald himself? Let us silence that traitor by death, and who shall contradict our tale? No danger shall attend this plan. I will give you the key of the escritoire—the theft will not be the work of a moment.' Montreuil at first demurred to this proposal, but Desmarais was, I repeat, resolved not to incur the danger of the theft alone; the stake was great, and it was not Montreuil's nature to shrink from peril, when once it became necessary to confront it. 'Be it so,' he said, at last, 'though the scheme is full of difficulty and of danger: be it so. We have not a day to lose. To-morrow the Count will place the document in some place of greater safety, and unknown to us—the deed shall be done to-night. Procure the key of the escritoire—admit me this night—I will steal disguised into the chamber—I will commit the act from which you, who alone could commit it with safety, shrink. Instruct me exactly as to the place where the articles you speak of are placed: I will abstract them also. See, that if the Count wake, he has no weapon at hand. Wound yourself, as you say, in some place not dangerous to life, and to-morrow, or within an hour after my escape, tell what tale you will. I will go, meanwhile, at once to Oswald; I will either bribe his silence—ay, and his immediate absence from England —or he shall die. A death that secures our own self-preservation is excusable in the reading of all law, divine or human!'

"I heard, but they deemed me insensible: they had already

begun to grow unheeding of my presence. Montreuil saw me, and his countenance grew soft. 'I know all,' I said, as I caught his eye which looked on me in pity, 'I know all—they are married. Enough !—with my hope ceases my love : care not for me.'

" Montreuil embraced and spoke to me in kindness and in praise. He assured me that you had kept your wedding so close a secret that he knew it not, nor did even Desmarais, till the evening before —till after he had proposed that I should visit Isora that very day. I know not, I care not, whether he was sincere in this. In whatever way one line in the dread scroll of his conduct be read, the scroll was written in guile, and in blood was it sealed. I appeared not to notice Montreuil or his accomplice any more. The latter left the house first. Montreuil stole forth, as he thought, unobserved ; he was masked, and in complete disguise. I, too, went forth. I hastened to a shop where such things were procured ; I purchased a mask and cloak similar to the priest's. I had heard Montreuil agree with Desmarais that the door of the house should be left ajar, in order to give greater facility to the escape of the former ; I re-paired to the house in time to see Montreuil enter it. A strange, sharp sort of cunning, which I had never known before, ran through the dark confusion of my mind. I waited for a minute, till it was likely that Montreuil had gained your chamber ; I then pushed open the door, and ascended the stairs. I met no one—the moon-light fell around me, and its rays seemed to me like ghosts, pale and shrouded, and gazing upon me with wan and lustreless eyes. I know not how I found your chamber, but it was the only one I entered. I stood in the same room with Isora and yourself—ye lay in sleep—Isora's face——. O, God ! I know no more—no more of that night of horror—save that I fled from the house reeking with blood—a murderer—and the murderer of Isora !

" Then came a long, long dream. I was in a sea of blood— blood-red was the sky, and one still, solitary star that gleamed far away with a sickly and wan light, was the only spot, above and around, which was not of the same intolerable dye. And I thought my eyelids were cut off, as those of the Roman consul are said to have been, and I had nothing to shield my eyes from that crimson light, and the rolling waters of that unnatural sea. And the red air burnt through my eyes into my brain, and then that also, methought, became blood ; and all memory—all images of memory—all idea— wore a material shape, and a material colour, and were blood, too. Everything was unutterably silent, except when my own shrieks rang over the shoreless ocean, as I drifted on. At last I fixed my eyes—the eyes which I might never close—upon that pale and single star ; and after I had gazed a little while, the star seemed

to change slowly—slowly—until it grew like the pale face of that
murdered girl, and then it vanished utterly, and *all* was blood!

"This vision was sometimes broken—sometimes varied by others
—but it always returned; and when at last I completely woke from
it, I was in Italy, in a convent. Montreuil had lost no time in
removing me from England. But once, shortly after my recovery,
for I was mad for many months, he visited me, and he saw what
a wreck I had become. He pitied me; and when I told him I
longed above all things for liberty—for the green earth and the fresh
air, and a removal from that gloomy abode, he opened the convent
gates, and blessed me, and bade me go forth. 'All I require of
you,' said he, 'is a promise. If it be understood that you live, you
will be persecuted by inquiries and questions, which will terminate
in a conviction of your crime: let it therefore be reported in England
that you are dead. Consent to the report, and promise never to
quit Italy, nor to see Morton Devereux.

"I promised—and that promise I have kept; but I promised not
that I would never reveal to you, in writing, the black tale which I
have now recorded. May it reach you. There is one in this vicinity
who has undertaken to bear it to you; he says he has known
misery—and when he said so, his voice sounded in my ear like
yours; and I looked upon him, and thought his features were cast
somewhat in the same mould as your own—so I have trusted him.
I have now told all. I have wrenched the secret from my heart
in agony and with fear. I have told all—though things which I
believe are fiends, have started forth from the grim walls around
to forbid it—though dark wings have swept by me, and talons, as
of a bird, have attempted to tear away the paper on which I write
—though eyes, whose light was never drunk from earth, have glared
on me—and mocking voices and horrible laughter have made my
flesh creep, and thrilled through the marrow of my bones—I have
told all—I have finished my last labour in this world, and I will
now lie down and die.

                                        "AUBREY DEVEREUX."

The paper dropped from my hands. Whatever I had felt in
reading it, I had not flinched once from the task. From the first
word even to the last, I had gone through the dreadful tale, nor
uttered a syllable, nor moved a limb. And now as I rose, though
I had found the being who to me had withered this world into one
impassable desert—though I had found the unrelenting foe and the
escaped murderer of Isora—the object of the execration and vin-
dictiveness of years—not one single throb of wrath—not one single
sentiment of vengeance, was in my breast. I passed at once to the

bedside of my brother; he was awake, but still and calm—the calm and stillness of exhausted nature. I knelt down quietly beside him. I took his hand, and I shrank not from the touch, though by that hand the only woman I ever loved had perished.

"Look up, Aubrey!" said I, struggling with tears which, despite of my most earnest effort, came over me; "look up, all is forgiven. Who on earth shall withhold pardon from a crime which on earth has been so awfully punished? Look up, Aubrey; I am your brother, and I forgive you. You are right—my childhood *was* harsh and fierce; and had you feared me less you might have confided in me, and you would not have sinned and suffered as you have done now. Fear me no longer. Look up, Aubrey, it is Morton who calls you. Why do you not speak? My brother, my brother—a word, a single word, I implore you."

For one moment did Aubrey raise his eyes—one moment did he meet mine. His lips quivered wildly—I heard the death rattle—he sunk back, and his hand dropped from my clasp. My words had snapped asunder the last chord of life. Merciful Heaven! I thank thee that those words were the words of pardon!

CHAPTER V.

IN WHICH THE HISTORY MAKES A GREAT STRIDE TOWARDS THE FINAL CATASTROPHE—THE RETURN TO ENGLAND, AND THE VISIT TO A DEVOTEE.

T night, and in the thrilling forms of the Catholic ritual, was Aubrey Devereux consigned to earth. After that ceremony I could linger no longer in the vicinity of the hermitage. I took leave of the abbot and richly endowed his convent in return for the protection it had afforded to the anchorite and the masses which had been said for his soul. Before I left Anselmo, I questioned him if any friend to the hermit had ever, during his seclusion, held any communication with the abbot respecting him. Anselmo, after a little hesitation, confessed that a man, a Frenchman, seemingly of no high rank, had several times visited the convent, as if to scrutinize the habits and life of the anchorite, he had declared himself commissioned by the hermit's relations to make inquiry of him from time to time; but he had given the abbot no clue to discover himself, though Anselmo had especially hinted at the expediency of being acquainted with some quarter to which he could direct any information of change in the hermit's habits or health. This man had been last at the convent about two months before the present date; but one of the brothers declared that he had seen him in the vicinity of the well on the very day on which the hermit died. The description of this stranger was essentially different from that which would have been given of Montreuil, but I imagined that if not the Abbé himself, the stranger was one in his confidence or his employ.

I now repaired to Rome, where I made the most extensive, though guarded, inquiries after Montreuil, and at length I learned that he was lying concealed, or rather unnoticed, in England, under a disguised name; having, by friends or by money, obtained therein a tacit connivance, though not an open pardon. No sooner did I learn this intelligence, than I resolved forthwith to depart to that country. I crossed the Alps—traversed France—and took ship at Calais for Dover.

Behold me then upon the swift seas bent upon a double purpose —reconciliation with a brother whom I had wronged, and vengeance —no, not vengeance, but *justice* against the criminal I had discovered! No! it was not revenge—it was no infuriate, no unholy desire of inflicting punishment upon a personal foe, which possessed me—it was a steady, calm, unwavering resolution, to obtain justice against the profound and systematized guilt of a villain who had been the bane of all who had come within his contact, that nerved my arm and engrossed my heart. Bear witness, Heaven, I am not a vindictive man! I have, it is true, been extreme in hatred as in love; but I have ever had the power to control myself from yielding to its impulse. When the full persuasion of Gerald's crime reigned within me, I had thralled my emotion, I had curbed it within the circle of my own heart, though there, thus pent and self-consuming, it was an agony and a torture; I had resisted the voice of that blood which cried from the earth against a murderer, and which had consigned the solemn charge of justice to my hands. Year after year I had nursed an unappeased desire; nor ever when it stung the most, suffered it to become an actual revenge. I had knelt in tears and in softness by Aubrey's bed—I had poured forth my pardon over him—I had felt, while I did so,—no, not so much sternness as would have slain a worm. By his hand had the murtherous stroke been dealt—on his soul was the crimson stain of that blood which had flowed through the veins of the gentlest and the most innocent of God's creatures—and yet the blow was unavenged, and the crime forgiven. For him there was a palliative, or even a gloomy but an unanswerable excuse. In the confession which had so terribly solved the mystery of my life, the seeds of that curse, which had grown at last into MADNESS, might be discovered even in the first dawn of Aubrey's existence. The latent poison might be detected in the morbid fever of his young devotion—in his jealous cravings of affection—in the first flush of his ill-omened love, even before rivalship and wrath began. Then, too, his guilt had not been regularly organized into one cold and deliberate system—it broke forth in impetuous starts, in frantic paroxysms—it was often wrestled with, though by a feeble mind—it was often conquered by a tender, though a fitful temper—it might not have rushed into the last and most awful crime, but for the damning instigation and the atrocious craft of one, who (Aubrey rightly said) could wield and mould the unhappy victim at his will. Might not, did I say? Nay, but for Montreuil's accursed influence, had I not Aubrey's own word that that crime never *would have* been committed? He had resolved to stifle his love—his heart had already melted to Isora and to me—he had already tasted the sweets of a virtuous resolution, and conquered the first bitterness of opposition to his passion. Why should not the resolution thus auspiciously begun have been mellowed into effect? Why should not the grateful and awful remembrance of the crime he had escaped continue to preserve him from meditating crime anew?- And (O, thought, which, while I now write, steals over me and brings with it an unutterable horde of emotions!) but for that all-tainting, all-withering, influence, Aubrey's soul might at this moment have been pure from murder, and Isora, —the living Isora,—by my side!

What wonder, as these thoughts came over me, that sense, feeling, reason, gradually shrunk and hardened into one stern resolve? I looked as from a height over the whole conduct of Montreuil : I saw him in our early infancy with no definite motive, (beyond the general policy of intrigue,) no fixed design, which might somewhat have lessened the callousness of the crime, not only fomenting dissensions in the hearts of brothers—not only turning the season of warm affections and yet of unopened passion, into strife and rancour—but seizing upon the inherent and reigning vice of our bosoms, which he should have seized to crush—in order only by that master-vice to weave our characters, and sway our conduct to his will, whenever a cool-blooded and merciless policy required us to be of that will the minions and the tools. Thus had he taken hold of the diseased jealousy of Aubrey, and by that handle, joined to the latent spring of superstition, guided him on his wretched course of misery and guilt. Thus, by a moral irresolution in Gerald had he bowed him also to his purposes, and by an infantine animosity between that brother and myself, held us both in a state of mutual hatred which I shuddered to recall. Readily could I now perceive that my charges or my suspicions against Gerald, which, in ordinary circumstances, he might have dispassionately come forward to disprove, had been represented to him by Montreuil in the light of groundless and wilful insults; and thus he had been led to scorn that full and cool explanation which, if it had not elucidated the mystery of my afflictions, would have removed the false suspicion of guilt from himself, and the real guilt of wrath and animosity from me.

The crime of the forged will, and the outrage to the dead and to myself, was a link in his woven guilt which I regarded the least. I looked rather to the black and the consummate craft by which Aubrey had been implicated in that sin; and my indignation became mixed with horror when I saw Montreuil working to that end of fraud by the instigation not only of a guilty and unlawful passion, but of the yet more unnatural and terrific engine of *frenzy;*—of a maniac's despair. Over the peace—the happiness—the honour—the virtue of a whole family, through fraud and through blood, this priest had marched onward to the goal of his icy and heartless ambition, unrelenting and unrepenting: "but not," I said, as I clenched my hand till the nails met in the flesh, "not for ever unchecked and unrequited!"

But in what manner was justice to be obtained? A public court of law? What! drag forward the deep dishonour of my house—the gloomy and convulsive history of my departed brother — his crime and his insanity? What! bring that history, connected as it was with the fate of Isora, before the curious and the insolent gaze of the babbling world? Bare that awful record to the jests, to the scrutiny, the marvel and the pity, of that most coarse of all tribunals —an English court of law? and that most torturing of all exposures —the vulgar comments of an English public? Could I do this? Yea, in the sternness of my soul, I felt that I could submit even to that humiliation, if no other way presented itself by which I could arrive at justice. *Was* there no other way?—at that question conjecture paused—I formed no scheme, or rather, I formed a hundred and rejected them all; my mind settled, at last, into an indistinct, unquestioned, but prophetic, resolution, that, whenever my path crossed Montreuil's, it should be to his destruction. I asked not how, nor when, the blow was to be dealt; I felt only a solemn and exultant certainty that, whether it borrowed the sword of the law, or the weapon of private justice, *mine* should be the hand which brought retribution to the ashes of the dead and the agony of the survivor.

So soon as my mind had subsided into this determination, I suffered my thoughts to dwell upon subjects less sternly agitating.

Fondly did I look forward to a meeting with Gerald, and a reconciliation of all our early and most frivolous disputes. As an atonement for the injustice my suspicions had done him, I resolved not to reclaim my inheritance. My fortune was already ample, and all that I cared to possess of the hereditary estates were the ruins of the old house and the copses of the surrounding park ; these Gerald would in all likelihood easily yield to me : and with the natural sanguineness of my temperament, I already planned the reconstruction of the ancient building, and the method of that solitary life in which I resolved that the remainder of my years should be spent.

Turning from this train of thought, I recurred to the mysterious and sudden disappearance of Oswald : *that* I was now easily able to account for. There could be no doubt but that Montreuil had (immediately after the murder), as he declared he would, induced Oswald to quit England, and preserve silence, either by bribery or by threats. And when I recalled the impression which the man had made upon me—an impression certainly not favourable to the elevation or the rigid honesty of his mind—I could not but imagine that one or the other of these means Montreuil found far from difficult of success. The delirious fever into which the wounds and the scene of that night had thrown me, and the long interval that consequently elapsed before inquiry was directed to Oswald, gave him every opportunity and indulgence in absenting himself from the country, and it was not improbable that he had accompanied Aubrey to Italy.

Here I paused, in deep acknowledgment of the truth of Aubrey's assertion, that "under similar circumstances, I might perhaps have been equally guilty." My passions had indeed been "intense and fierce as his own ;" and there was a dread coincidence in the state of mind into which each of us had been thrown by the event of that night, which made the epoch of a desolated existence to both of us ; if mine had been but a passing delirium, and his a confirmed and lasting disease of the intellect, the causes of our malady had been widely different. He had been the criminal—*I* only the sufferer.

Thus as I leant over the deck, and the waves bore me homeward, after so many years and vicissitudes, did the shadows of thought and memory flit across me. How seemingly apart, yet how closely linked, had been the great events in my wandering and wild life. My early acquaintance with Bolingbroke, whom for more than nine years I had not seen, and who, at a superficial glance, would seem to have exercised influence over my public, rather than my private, life—how secretly, yet how powerfully had that circumstance led even to the very thoughts which now possessed me, and to the very object on which I was now bound. But for that circumstance, I might not have learnt of the retreat of Don Diego D'Alvarez in his last illness ; I might never have renewed my love to Isora ; and whatever had been her fate, destitution and poverty would have been a less misfortune than her union with me. But for my friendship for Bolingbroke, I might not have visited France, nor gained the favour of the Regent, nor the ill offices of Dubois, nor the protection and kindness of the Czar. I might never have been ambassador at the Court of ——, nor met with Bezoni, nor sought an asylum for a spirit sated with pomp and thirsting for truth, at the foot of the Apennines, nor read that history (which, indeed, might then never have occurred), that now rankled at my heart, urging my movements and colouring my desires. Thus, by the finest, but the strongest, meshes, had the thread of my political honours been woven with that of my private afflictions. And thus, even at the licentious festivals of the Regent of France, or the lifeless parade of the Court of ——, the dark stream of events had flowed onward beneath my feet, bearing me insensibly to that very spot of time, from which I now surveyed the past and looked upon the mist and shadows of the future.

Adverse winds made the little voyage across the Channel a business of four days. On the evening of the last we landed at Dover. Within thirty miles of that town was my mother's retreat ; and I resolved, before I sought a reconciliation with Gerald, or justice against Montreuil, to visit her seclusion. Accordingly, the next day, I repaired to her abode.

What a contrast is there between the lives of human beings ! Considering the beginning and the end of all mortal careers are the same, how wonderfully is the interval varied ! Some, the weeds of the world, dashed from shore to shore—all vicissitude—enterprise—strife—disquiet ; others, the world's lichen—rooted to some peaceful rock—growing—flourishing—withering on the same spot,—scarce a feeling expressed—scarce a sentiment called forth—scarce a tithe of the properties of their very nature expanded into action.

There was an air of quiet and stillness in the red quadrangular building, as my carriage stopped at its porch, which struck upon me, like a breathing reproach to those who sought the abode of peace with feelings opposed to the spirit of the place. A small projecting porch was covered with ivy, and thence issued an aged portress in answer to my summons.

"The Countess Devereux," said she, "is now the superior of society," (convent they called it not,) "and rarely admits any st .ger."

1 gave in my claim to admission, and was ushered into a small

parlour : all there, too, was still—the brown oak wainscoting—the huge chairs—the few antique portraits—the *uninhabited* aspect of the chamber—all were silently eloquent of quietude—but a quietude comfortless and sombre. At length, my mother appeared, I sprung forward—my childhood was before me—years—care—change were forgotten—I was a boy again—I sprung forward, and was in my mother's embrace ! It was long before, recovering myself, I noted how lifeless and chill was that embrace, but I did so at last, and my enthusiasm withered at once.

We sate down together, and conversed long and uninterruptedly, but our conversation was like that of acquaintances, not the fondest and closest of all relations—(for I need scarcely add that I told her not of my meeting with Aubrey, nor undeceived her with respect to the date of his death). Every monastic recluse that I had hitherto seen, even in the most seeming content with retirement, had loved to converse of the exterior world, and had betrayed an interest in its events—for my mother only, worldly objects and interests seemed utterly dead. She expressed little surprise to see me—little surprise at my alteration ; she only said that my mien was improved, and that I reminded her of my father ; she testified no anxiety to hear of my travels or my adventures—she testified even no willingness to speak of herself—she described to me the life of one day, and then said that the history of ten years was told. A close cap confined all the locks for whose rich luxuriance and golden hue she had once been noted—for here they were not the victim of a vow, as in a nunnery they would have been—and her dress was plain, simple and un-adorned : save these alterations of attire, none were visible in her exterior—the torpor of her life seemed to have paralyzed even time —the bloom yet dwelt in her unwrinkled cheek—the mouth had not fallen—the faultless features were faultless still. But there was a deeper stillness than ever breathing through this frame : it was as if the soul had been lulled to sleep—her mien was lifeless—her voice was lifeless—her gesture was lifeless—the impression she produced was like that of entering some chamber which has not been entered before for a century. She consented to my request to stay with her all the day—a bed was prepared for me, and at sunrise the next morning I was folded once more in the chilling mechanism of her embrace, and dismissed on my journey to the metropolis.

N

CHAPTER VI.

THE RETREAT OF A CELEBRATED MAN, AND A VISIT TO A GREAT POET.

 ARRIVED in town, and drove at once to Gerald's house: it was not difficult to find it, for in my young day it had been the residence of the Duke of —— ; and wealthy as I knew was the owner of the Devereux lands, I was somewhat startled at the extent and the magnificence of his palace. To my inexpressible disappointment, I found that Gerald had left London a day or two before my arrival on a visit to a nobleman nearly connected with our family, and residing in the same county as that in which Devereux Court was situated. Since the fire, which had destroyed all of the old house but the one tower, which I had considered as peculiarly my own, Gerald, I heard, had always, in visiting his estates, taken up his abode at the mansion of one or other of his neighbours; and to Lord ——'s house I now resolved to repair. My journey was delayed for a day or two, by accidentally seeing at the door of the hotel, to which I drove from Gerald's house, the favourite servant of Lord Bolingbroke. This circumstance revived in me, at once, all my attachment to that personage, and hearing he was at his country house, within a few miles from town, I resolved the next morning to visit him. It was not only that I contemplated with an eager, yet a melancholy interest, an interview with one whose blazing career I had long watched, and whose letters (for during the years we had been parted he wrote to me often) seemed to testify the same satiety of the triumphs and gauds of ambition which had brought something of wisdom to myself; it was not only that I wished to commune with that Bolingbroke in retirement whom I had known the oracle of statesmen, and the pride of courts; nor even that I loved the man, and was eager once more to embrace him; a fiercer and more active motive urged me to visit one whose knowledge of all men, and application of their various utilities, were so remarkable, and who, even in his present peace and retirement, would, not improbably, be acquainted with the abode of that unquiet and plotting ecclesiastic whom I now panted to discover, and whom Bolingbroke had of old often guided or employed.

When my carriage stopped at the statesman's door, I was informed that Lord Bolingbroke was at his farm. Farm! how oddly did that word sound in my ear, coupled as it was with the name of one so brilliant and so restless.

I asked the servant to direct me where I should find him, and, following the directions, I proceeded to the search alone. It was a day towards the close of autumn, bright, soft, clear, and calm as the decline of a vigorous and genial age. I walked slowly through a field robbed of its golden grain, and as I entered another, I saw the object of my search. He had seemingly just given orders to a person in a labourer's dress, who was quitting him, and with downcast eyes he was approaching towards me. I noted how slow and even was the pace which, once stately, yet rapid and irregular, had betrayed the haughty, but wild, character of his mind. He paused often, as if in thought, and I observed that once he stopped longer · than usual, and seemed to gaze wistfully on the ground. Afterwards (when I had joined him) we passed that spot, and I remarked, with a secret smile, that it contained one of those little mounds in which that busy and herded tribe of the insect race, which have been held out to man's social state at once as a mockery and a model, held their populous home. There seemed a latent moral in the pause and watch of the disappointed statesman by that mound, which afforded a clue to the nature of his reflections.

He did not see me till I was close before him, and had called him by his name, nor did he at first recognize me, for my garb was foreign, and my upper lip unshaven ; and, as I said before, years had strangely altered me : but when he did, he testified all the cordiality I had anticipated. I linked my arm in his, and we walked to and fro for hours, talking of all that had passed since and before our parting, and feeling our hearts warm to each other as we talked.

"The last time I saw you," said he, "how widely did our hopes and objects differ ; yours from my own—you seemingly had the vantage-ground, but it was an artificial eminence, and my level state, though it appeared less tempting, was more secure. I had just been disgraced by a misguided and ungrateful prince. I had already gone into a retirement, where my only honours were proportioned to my fortitude in bearing condemnation—and my only flatterer was the hope of finding a companion and a Mentor in myself. You, my friend, parted with life before you ; and you only relinquished the pursuit of Fortune at one court, to meet her advances at another. Nearly ten years have flown since that time—my situation is but little changed—I am returned, it is true, to my native soil, but not to a soil more indulgent to ambition and exertion than the scene of my exile. My sphere of action is still shut from me—

my mind is still banished.[1] You return young in years, but full of
successes. Have they brought you happiness, Devereux? or have
you yet a temper to envy my content?"

"Alas!" said I, "who can bear too close a search beneath the
mask and robe? Talk not of me now. It is ungracious for the
fortunate to repine—and I reserve whatever may disquiet me within,
for your future consolation and advice. At present speak to me of
yourself—you are happy, then?'

"I am!" said Bolingbroke, emphatically.—"Life seems to me
to possess two treasures—one glittering and precarious, the other of
less rich a show, but of a more solid value. The one is Power, the
other Virtue; and there is this main difference between the two—
Power is entrusted to us as a loan ever required again, and with a
terrible arrear of interest—Virtue obtained by us as a *boon* which we
can only lose through our own folly, when once it is acquired. In
my youth I was caught by the former—hence my errors and my
misfortunes! In my declining years I have sought the latter; hence
my palliatives and my consolation. But you have not seen my home,
and *all* its attractions," added Bolingbroke, with a smile, which
reminded me of his former self. "I will show them to you." And
we turned our steps to the house.

As we walked thither I wondered to find how little melancholy
was the change Bolingbroke had undergone. Ten years, which
bring man from his prime to his decay, had indeed left their trace
upon his stately form, and the still unrivalled beauty of his noble
features; but the manner gained all that the form had lost. In his
days of more noisy greatness, there had been something artificial and
unquiet in the sparkling alternations he had loved to adopt. He
had been too fond of changing wisdom by a quick turn into wit—
too fond of the affectation of bordering the serious with the gay—
business with pleasure. If this had not taken from the polish of his
manner, it had diminished its dignity and given it the air of being
assumed and insincere. Now all was quiet, earnest, and impressive;
there was tenderness even in what was melancholy: and if there
yet lingered the affectation of blending the classic character with his
own, the character was more noble, and the affectation more unseen.
But this manner was only the faint mirror of a mind which, retaining
much of its former mould, had been embellished and exalted by
adversity, and which, if it banished not its former frailties, had
acquired a thousand new virtues to redeem them.

"You see," said my companion, pointing to the walls of the hall,
which we had now entered, "the subject which at present occupies

1 I need scarcely remind the reader that Lord Bolingbroke, though he had re-
ce.ved a full pardon, was forbidden to resume his seat in the House of Lords.—ED.

the greater part of my attention. I am meditating how to make the hall most illustrative of its owner's pursuits. You see the desire of improving, of creating, and of associating the improvement and the creation with ourselves, follows us banished men even to our seclusion. I think of having those walls painted with the implements of husbandry, and through pictures of spades and ploughshares, to express my employments, and testify my content in them."

"Cincinnatus is a better model than Aristippus, confess it," said I, smiling. "But if the senators come hither to summon you to power, will you resemble the Roman, not only in being found at your plough, but in your reluctance to leave it, and your eagerness to return?"

"What shall I say to you?" replied Bolingbroke. "Will you play the cynic if I answer *no?* We *should not* boast of despising power, when of use to others, but of being contented to live without it. This is the end of my philosophy! But let me present you to one whom I value more now than I valued power at any time."

As he said this, Bolingbroke threw open the door of an apartment, and introduced me to a lady with whom he had found that domestic happiness denied him in his first marriage.—The niece of Madame de Maintenon, this most charming woman, possessed all her aunt's wit, and far more than all her aunt's beauty.[1] She was in weak health; but her vivacity was extreme, and her conversation just what should be the conversation of a woman who shines without striving for it.

The business on which I was bound only allowed me to stay two days with Bolingbroke, and this I stated at first, lest he should have dragged me over his farm.

"Well," said my host, after vainly endeavouring to induce me to promise a longer stay, "if you *can* only give us two days, I must write and excuse myself to a great man with whom I was to dine to-day: yet, if it were not so inhospitable, I should like much to carry you with me to his house; for I own that I wish you to see my companions, and to learn that if I still consult the oracles, they are less for the predictions of fortune than as the inspirations of the god."

"Ah!" said Lady Bolingbroke, who spoke in French, "I know whom you allude to. Give him my homage, and assure him, when he next visits us, we will appoint six *dames du palais* to receive and pet him."

---

[1] "I am not ashamed to say to you that I admire her more every hour of my life."—*Letter from Lord Bolingbroke to Swift.*

Bolingbroke loved her to the last; and perhaps it is just to a man so celebrated for his gallantries, to add that this beautiful and accomplished woman seems to have admired and *esteemed* as much as she loved him.—ED.

Upon this I insisted upon accompanying Bolingbroke to the house of so fortunate a being, and he consented to my wish with feigned reluctance, but evident pleasure.

"And who," said I to Lady Bolingbroke, "is the happy object of so much respect?"

Lady Bolingbroke answered laughing, that nothing was so pleasant as suspense, and that it would be cruel in her to deprive me of it; and we conversed with so much zest, that it was not till Bolingbroke had left the room for some moments, that I observed he was not present. I took the opportunity to remark that I was rejoiced to find him so happy, and with such just cause for happiness.

"He *is* happy, though, at times, he is restless. How, chained to this oar, can he be otherwise?" answered Lady Bolingbroke, with a sigh: "but his friends," she added, "who most enjoy his retirement, must yet lament it. His genius is not wasted here, it is true: where *could* it be wasted? But who does not feel that it is employed in too confined a sphere? And yet—" and I saw a tear start to her eye—"I, at least, ought not to repine. I should lose the best part of my happiness if there was nothing I could console him for."

"Believe me," said I, "I have known Bolingbroke in the zenith of his success; but never knew him so worthy of congratulation as *now!*"

"Is that flattery to him or to me?" said Lady Bolingbroke, smiling archly, for her smiles were quick successors to her tears.

"*Detur digniori!*" answered I; "but you must allow that, though it is a fine thing to have all that the world can give, it is still better to gain something that the world cannot take away?"

"Sèe you also a Philosopher?" cried Lady Bolingbroke, gaily. "Ah, poor me! In my youth, my poition was the cloister;[1] in my later years I am banished to *the porch!* You have no conception, Monsieur Devereux, what wise faces and profound maxims we have here; especially as all who come to visit my lord think it necessary to quote Tully, and talk of solitude as if it were a heaven! *Les pauvres bons gens!* they seem a little surprised when Henry receives them smilingly—begs them to construe the Latin—gives them good wine, and sends them back to London with faces half the length they were on their arrival. *Mais voici Monsieur le fermier philosophe!*"

And Bolingbroke entering, I took my leave of this lively and interesting lady, and entered his carriage.

As soon as we were seated, he pressed me for my reasons for refusing to prolong my visit. As I thought they would be more opportune after the excursion of the day was over, and as, in truth, I was not eager to relate them, I begged to defer the narration till

---

[1] She was brought up at St. Cyr.—ED.

our return to his house at night, and then I directed the conversation into a new channel.

"My chief companion," said Bolingbroke, after describing to me his course of life, "is the man you are about to visit : he has his frailties and infirmities—and in saying that, I only imply that he is human—but he is wise, reflective, generous, and affectionate ; add these qualities to a dazzling wit, and a genius deep, if not sublime, and what wonder that we forget something of vanity and something of fretfulness—effects rather of the frame than of the mind ; the wonder only is that, with a body the victim to every disease, crippled and imbecile from the cradle, his frailties should not be more numerous, and his care, his thoughts, and attentions not wholly limited to his own complaints—for the sickly are almost of necessity selfish—and that mind must have a vast share of benevolence which can always retain the softness of charity and love for others, when pain and disease constitute the morbid links that perpetually bind it to self. If this great character is my chief companion, my chief correspondent is not less distinguished ; in a word, no longer to keep you in suspense, Pope is my companion, and Swift my correspondent."

"You are fortunate—but so also are they. Your letter informed me of Swift's honourable exile in Ireland—how does he bear it ?"

"Too feelingly—his disappointments turn his blood to acid. He said, characteristically enough, in one of his letters, that in fishing once when he was a little boy, he felt a great fish at the end of his line, which he drew up almost to the ground, but it dropped in, and the disappointment, he adds, vexes him to this day, and he believes it to be the type of all his future disappointments : [1] it is wonderful how reluctantly a very active mind sinks into rest."

[1] In this letter Swift adds, "I should be ashamed to say this if you (Lord Bolingbroke) had not a spirit fitter to bear your own misfortunes than I have to think of them ; " and this is true. Nothing can be more striking, or more honourable to Lord Bolingbroke, than the contrast between Swift's letters and that nobleman's upon the subject of their mutual disappointments. I especially note the contrast, because it has been so grievously the cant of Lord Bolingbroke's decriers to represent his affection for retirement as hollow, and his resignation in adversity as a boast rather than a fact. Now I will challenge any one *thoroughly* and dispassionately to examine what is left to us of the life of this great man, and after having done so, to select from all modern history an example of one who, in the prime of life and height of ambition, ever passed from a very active and exciting career into retirement and disgrace, and bore the change—long, bitter, and permanent as it was—with a greater and more thoroughly sustained magnanimity than did Lord Bolingbroke. He has been reproached for taking part in political contests in the midst of his praises and "affected enjoyment" of retirement ; and this, made matter of reproach, is exactly the subject on which he seems to me the *most* worthy of praise. For, putting aside all motives for action, on the purity of which men are generally incredulous, as a hatred to ill government (an antipathy

"Yet why should retirement be rest? Do you recollect in the first conversation we ever had together, we talked of Cowley? Do you recollect how justly, and even sublimely, he has said, ' Cogitation is that which distinguishes the solitude of a God from that of a wild beast?'"

"It is finely said," answered Bolingbroke, "but Swift was born not for cogitation, but action—for turbulent times, not for calm. He ceases to be great directly he is still; and his bitterness at every vexation is so great that I have often thought, in listening to him, of the Abbé de Cyran, who, attempting to throw nutshells out of the bars of his window, and constantly failing in the attempt, exclaimed in a paroxysm of rage, ' Thus does Providence delight in frustrating my designs!'"

"But you are fallen from a far greater height of hope than Swift could ever have attained—you bear this change well, but not, *I hope*, without a struggle."

"You are right—*not* without a struggle; while corruption thrives I will not be silent; while bad men govern, I will not be still."

In conversation of this sort passed the time, till we arrived at Pope's villa.

We found the poet in his study—indued as some of his pictures represent him, in a long gown and a velvet cap. He received Bolingbroke with great tenderness, and being, as he said, in robuster health than he had enjoyed for months, he insisted on carrying us to his grotto. I know nothing more common to poets than a pride in what belongs to their houses; and perhaps to a man not ill-natured, there are few things more pleasant than indulging the little weaknesses of those we admire. We sat down in a small temple made entirely of shells; and whether it was that the Creative Genius gave an undue charm to the place, I know not: but as the murmur

wonderfully strong in wise men, and wonderfully weak in fools), the honest impulse of the citizen, and the better and higher sentiment, to which Bolingbroke appeared peculiarly alive, of affection to mankind—putting these utterly aside—it must be owned that resignation is the more noble in proportion as it is the less passive—that retirement is only a morbid selfishness if it prohibit exertions for others; that it is only really dignified and noble when it is the shade whence issue the oracles that are to instruct mankind; and that retirement of this nature is the sole seclusion which a good and wise man will covet or commend. The very philosophy which makes such a man seek the *quiet*, makes him eschew the *inutility* of the hermitage. Very little praiseworthy to me would have seemed Lord Bolingbroke among his haymakers and ploughmen, if among haymakers and ploughmen he had looked with an indifferent eye upon a profligate minister and a venal parliament; very little interest in my eyes would have attached itself to his beans and vetches, had beans and vetches caused him to forget that if he was happier in a farm, he could be more useful in a senate, and made him forego, in the sphere of a bailiff, all care for re-entering that of a legislator.—Ed.

of a rill, glassy as the Blandusian fountain, was caught, and re-given from side to side by a perpetual echo, and through an arcade of trees, whose leaves, ever and anon, fell startingly to the ground beneath the light touch of the autumn air, you saw the sails on the river pass and vanish, like the cares which breathe over the smooth glass of wisdom, but may not linger to dim it, it was not difficult to invest the place, humble as it was, with a classic interest, or to recall the loved retreats of the Roman bards, without smiling too fastidiously at the contrast.

> " Sweet Echo, sweetest nymph, that liv'st unseen,
> Within thy airy shell,
> By slow Meander's margin green,
> Or by the violet embroidered vale
> Where the lovelorn nightingale
> Nightly to thee her sad song mourneth well ;
> Sweet Echo, dost thou shun those haunts of yore,
> And in the dim caves of a northern shore
> Delight to dwell ! "

"Let the compliment to you, Pope," said Bolingbroke, "atone for the profanation of weaving three wretched lines of mine with those most musical notes of Milton."

"Ah !" said Pope, "would that you could give me a fitting inscription for my fount and grotto? The only one I can remember is hackneyed, and yet it has spoilt me, I fear, for all others.

> " Hujus Nympha loci, sacri custodia fontis
> Dormio dum blandæ sentio murmur aquæ ;
> Parce meum, quisquis tanges cava marmora, somnum
> Rumpere ; sive bibas, sive lavêre, tace." [1]

" We cannot hope to match it," said Bolingbroke, "though you know I value myself on these things. But tell me your news of Gay —is he growing wiser ?"

"Not a whit ; he is for ever a dupe to the *spes credula ;* always talking of buying an annuity, that he may be independent, and always spending as fast as he earns, that he may appear munificent."

"Poor Gay ! but he is a common example of the improvidence of his tribe, while you are an exception. Yet mark, Devereux, the

---

[1] Thus very inadequately translated by Pope. (See his Letter to Edward Blount, Esq., descriptive of his grotto.)

> " Nymph of the grot, these sacred springs I keep,
> And to the murmur of these waters sleep :
> Ah, spare my slumbers ; gently tread the cave,
> And drink in silence, or in silence lave."

It is, however, quite impossible to convey to an unlearned reader the exquisite and spirit-like beauty of the Latin verses.—ED.

N 2

inconsistency of Pope's thrift and carefulness : he sends a parcel of fruit to some ladies with this note, 'Take care of the papers that wrap the apples, and return them safely ; they are the only copies I have of one part of the Iliad.' Thus, you see, our economist saves his paper, and hazards his epic ! "

Pope, who is always flattered by an allusion to his negligence of fame, smiled slightly and answered, " What man, alas, ever profits by the lessons of his friends ? How many exact rules has our good Dean of St. Patrick laid down for both of us—how angrily still does he chide us for our want of prudence and our love of good living. I intend, in answer to his charges on the latter score, though I vouch, as I well may, for our temperance, to give him the reply of the sage to the foolish courtier——"

" What was that ? " asked Bolingbroke.

" Why the courtier saw the sage picking out the best dishes at table. 'How,' said he with a sneer, 'are sages such epicures ? '— ' Do you think, sir,' replied the wise man, reaching over the table to help himself, 'do you think, sir, that the Creator made the good things of this world only for fools ? '"

" How the Dean will pish and pull his wig, when he reads your illustration," said Bolingbroke, laughing. " We shall never agree in our reasonings on that part of philosophy. Swift loves to go out of his way to find privation or distress, and has no notion of Epicurean wisdom ; for my part, I think the use of knowledge is to make us happier. I would compare the mind to the beautiful statue of Love by Praxiteles—when its eyes were bandaged, the countenance seemed grave and sad, but the moment you removed the bandage, the most serene and enchanting smile diffused itself over the whole face."

So passed the morning, till the hour of dinner, and this repast was served with an elegance and luxury which the sons of Apollo seldom command.[1] As the evening closed, our conversation fell upon friendship, and the increasing disposition towards it, which comes with increasing years. "Whilst my mind," said Bolingbroke, "shrinks more and more from the world, and feels in its independence less yearning to external objects, the ideas of friendship return oftener, they busy me, they warm me more. Is it that we grow more tender as the moment of our great separation approaches? or is it that they who are to live together in another state (for friendship exists not but for the good) begin to feel more strongly that divine sympathy which is to be the great bond of their future society ? "[2]

[1] Pope seems to have been rather capricious in this respect ; but in general he must be considered open to the sarcasm of displaying the bounteous host to those who did not want a dinner, and the niggard to those who did.—ED.

[2] This beautiful sentiment is to be found, with very slight alteration, in a letter from Bolingbroke to Swift.—ED.

While Bolingbroke was thus speaking, and Pope listened with all the love and reverence which he evidently bore to his friend stamped upon his worn but expressive countenance, I inly said, " Surely, the love between minds like these should live and last without the changes that ordinary affections feel ! Who would not mourn for the strength of all human ties, if hereafter these are broken and asperity succeed to friendship, or aversion to esteem ? *I*, a wanderer, without heir to my memory and wealth, shall pass away, and my hasty and un-mellowed fame will moulder with my clay ; but will the names of those whom I now behold ever fall languidly on the ears of a future race, and will there not for ever be some sympathy with their friend-ship, softer and warmer than admiration for their fame ? "

We left our celebrated host about two hours before midnight, and returned to Dawley.

On our road thither I questioned Bolingbroke respecting Montreuil, and I found that, as I had surmised, he was able to give me some information of that arch-schemer. Gerald's money and hereditary influence had procured tacit connivance at the Jesuit's residence in England, and Montreuil had for some years led a quiet and unoffend-ing life, in close retirement. " Lately, however," said Bolingbroke, "I have learnt that the old spirit has revived, and I accidentally heard, three days ago, when conversing with one well informed on state matters, that this most pure administration have discovered some plot or plots with which Montreuil is connected ; I believe he will be apprehended in a few days."

" And where lurks he ? "

" He was, I heard, last seen in the neighbourhood of your brother's property at Devereux Court, and I imagine it probable that he is still in that neighbourhood."

This intelligence made me resolve to leave Dawley even earlier than I had intended, and I signified to Lord Bolingbroke my in-tention of quitting him by sunrise the next morning. He endeavoured in vain to combat my resolution. I was too fearful lest Montreuil, hearing of his danger from the state, might baffle my vengeance by seeking some impenetrable asylum, to wish to subject my meet-ing with him, and with Gerald, whose co-operation I desired, to any unnecessary delay. I took leave of my host therefore that night, and ordered my carriage to be in readiness by the first dawn of morning.

CHAPTER VII.

THE PLOT APPROACHES ITS DÉNOUEMENT.

ALTHOUGH the details of my last chapter have somewhat retarded the progress of that *dénouement* with which this volume is destined to close, yet I do not think the destined reader will regret lingering over a scene in which, after years of restless enterprise and exile, he beholds the asylum which fortune had prepared for the most extraordinary character with which I have adorned these pages.

It was before daybreak that I commenced my journey. The shutters of the house were as yet closed; the gray mists rising slowly from the earth, and the cattle couched beneath the trees, the cold, but breezeless freshness of the morning, the silence of the un-awakened birds, all gave an inexpressible stillness and quiet to the scene. The horses slowly ascended a little eminence, and I looked from the window of the carriage, on the peaceful retreat I had left. I sighed as I did so, and a sick sensation, coupled with the thought of Isora, came chill upon my heart. No man happily placed in this social world, can guess the feelings of envy with which a wanderer like me, without tie or home, and for whom the roving eagerness of youth is over, surveys those sheltered spots in which the breast garners up all domestic bonds, its household and holiest delights; the companioned hearth, the smile of infancy, and dearer than all, the eye that glasses our purest, our tenderest, our most secret thoughts; these,—oh, none who enjoy them know how they for whom they are not have pined and mourned for them!

I had not travelled many hours, when, upon the loneliest part of the road, my carriage, which had borne me without an accident from Rome to London, broke down. The postillions said there was a small inn about a mile from the spot; thither I repaired: a blacksmith was sent for, and I found the accident to the carriage would require several hours to repair. No solitary chaise did the inn afford; but the landlord, who was a freeholder and a huntsman, boasted one valuable and swift horse, which he declared was fit for an emperor or a highwayman. I was too impatient of delay not to grasp at this intelligence. I gave mine host whatever he demanded for the loan of his steed, transferred my pistols to an immense pair of holsters, which adorned a high demi-pique saddle, wherewith he obliged me, and, within an hour from the date of the accident, recommenced my journey.

The evening closed, as I became aware of the presence of a fellow traveller. He was, like myself, on horseback. He wore a short, dark gray cloak, a long wig of a raven hue, and a large hat, which, flapping over his face, conspired, with the increasing darkness, to allow me a very imperfect survey of his features. Twice or thrice he had passed me, and always with some salutation, indicative of a desire for further acquaintance ; but my mood is not naturally too much inclined to miscellaneous society, and I was at that time peculiarly covetous of my own companionship. I had, therefore, given but a brief answer to the horseman's courtesy, and had ridden away from him with a very unceremonious abruptness. At length, when he had come up to me for the fourth time, and for the fourth time had accosted me, my ear caught something in the tones of his voice which did not seem to me wholly unfamiliar. I regarded him with more attention than I had as yet done, and replied to him more civilly and at length. Apparently encouraged by this relaxation from my reserve, the man speedily resumed.

"Your horse, sir," said he, "is a fine animal, but he seems jaded :—you have ridden far to-day, I'll venture to guess."

"I have, sir ; but the town where I shall pass the night is not above four miles distant, I believe."

"Hum—ha l—you sleep at D——, then?" said the horseman inquisitively.

A suspicion came across me—we were then entering a very lonely road, and one notoriously infested with highwaymen. My fellow equestrian's company might have some sinister meaning in it. I looked to my holsters, and leisurely taking out one of my pistols, saw to its priming, and returned it to its depositary. The horseman noted the motion, and he moved his horse rather uneasily, and I thought timidly, to the other side of the road.

"You travel well armed, sir," said he, after a pause.

"It is a necessary precaution, sir," answered I, composedly, "in a road one is not familiar with, and with companions one has never had the happiness to meet before."

"Ahem !—ahem !—*Parbleu, Monsieur le Comte,* you allude to me ; but I warrant this is not the first time *we* have met."

"Ha !" said I, riding closer to my fellow traveller, "you know me then—and we *have* met before. I thought I recognized your voice, but I cannot remember when or where I last heard it."

"Oh, Count, I believe it was only by accident that we commenced acquaintanceship, and only by accident, you see, do we now resume it. But I perceive that I intrude on your solitude. Farewell, Count, and a pleasant night at your inn."

"Not so fast, sir," said I, laying firm hand on my companion's shoulder, "I know you now, and I thank Providence that I have found you. Marie Oswald, it is not lightly that I will part with you!"

"With all my heart, sir, with all my heart. But *morbleu, Monsieur le Comte*, do take your hand from my shoulder—I am a nervous man, and your pistols are loaded—and perhaps you are choleric and hasty. I assure you I am far from wishing to part with you abruptly, for I have watched you for the last two days, in order to enjoy the honour of this interview."

"Indeed! your wish will save both of us a world of trouble. I believe you may serve me effectually—if so, you will find me more desirous and more able than ever to show my gratitude."

"Sir, you are too good," quoth Mr. Oswald, with an air far more respectful than he had yet shown me. "Let us make to your inn, and there I shall be most happy to receive your commands." So saying, Marie pushed on his horse, and I urged my own to the same expedition.

"But tell me," said I, as we rode on, "why you have wished to meet me?—me whom you so cruelly deserted and forsook?"

"Oh, *parbleu*—spare me there! it was not I who deserted you —I was compelled to fly—death—murder—on one side;—safety, money, and a snug place in Italy, as a lay-brother of the Institute, on the other! What could I do?—You were ill in bed—not likely to recover—not able to protect me from my present peril—in a state that in all probability never would require my services for the future. Oh, Monsieur le Comte, it was not desertion—that is a cruel word—it was self-preservation, and common prudence."

"Well," said I, complaisantly, "you apply words better than I applied them. And how long have you been returned to England?"

"Some few weeks, Count, not more. I was in London when you arrived—I heard of that event—I immediately repaired to your hotel—you were gone to my Lord Bolingbroke's—I followed you thither—you had left Dawley when I arrived there—I learnt your route and followed you. *Parbleu* and *morbleu*, I find you, and you take me for a highwayman!"

"Pardon my mistake: the clearest sighted men are subject to commit such errors, and the most innocent to suffer by them. So Montreuil *persuaded* you to leave England—did he also persuade you to return?"

"No—I was charged by the Institute with messages to him and others. But we are near the town, Count, let us defer our conversation till then."

We entered D——, put up our horses, called for an apartment—

to which summons Oswald added another for wine—and then the virtuous *Marie* commenced his explanations. I was deeply anxious to ascertain whether Gerald had ever been made acquainted with the fraud by which he had obtained possession of the estates of Devereux ; and I found that, from Desmarais, Oswald had learned all that had occurred to Gerald since Marie had left England. From Oswald's prolix communication, I ascertained that Gerald was, during the whole of the interval between my uncle's death and my departure from England, utterly unacquainted with the fraud of the will. He readily believed that my uncle had found good reason for altering his intentions with respect to me ; and my law proceedings, and violent conduct towards himself, only excited his indignation, not aroused his suspicions. During this time, he lived entirely in the country, indulging the rural hospitality and the rustic sports which he especially affected, and secretly, but deeply, involved with Montreuil in political intrigues. All this time the Abbé made no farther use of him than to borrow whatever sums he required for his purposes. Isora's death, and the confused story of the document given me by Oswald, Montreuil had interpreted to Gerald according to the interpretation of the world ; viz., he had thrown the suspicion upon Oswald, as a common villain, who had taken advantage of my credulity about the will—introduced himself into the house on that pretence—attempted the robbery of the most valuable articles therein—which, indeed, he had succeeded in abstracting—and who, on my awaking and contesting with him and his accomplice, had, in self-defence, inflicted the wounds which had ended in my delirium, and Isora's death. This part of my tale Montreuil never contradicted, and Gerald believed it to the present day. The affair of 1715 occurred ; the government, aware of Gerald's practices, had anticipated his design of joining the rebels—he was imprisoned—no act of overt guilt on his part was proved, or at least brought forward —and the government not being willing, perhaps, to proceed to violent measures against a very young man, and the head of a very powerful house, connected with more than thirty branches of the English hereditary nobility, he received his acquittal just before Sir William Wyndham, and some other suspected Tories, received their own.

Prior to the breaking out of that rebellion, and on the eve of Montreuil's departure for Scotland, the priest summoned Desmarais, whom, it will be remembered, I had previously dismissed, and whom Montreuil had since employed in various errands, and informed him that he had obtained, for his services, the same post under Gerald which the Fatalist had filled under me. Soon after the failure of the rebellion, Devereux Court was destroyed by accidental fire; and Montreuil, who had come over in disguise, in order to renew his attacks on my brother's coffers (attacks to which Gerald yielded very sullenly, and with many assurances that he would no more incur the danger of political and seditious projects); now advised Gerald to go up to London, and, in order to avoid the suspicion of the government, to mix freely in the gaieties of the court. Gerald readily consented; for, though internally convinced that the charms of the metropolis were not equal to those of the country, yet he liked change, and Devereux Court being destroyed, he shuddered a little at the idea of rebuilding so enormous a pile. Before Gerald left the old tower (*my tower*) which was alone spared by the flames, and at which he had resided, though without his household, rather than quit a place where there was such "excellent shooting," Montreuil said to Desmarais, "This ungrateful *seigneur de village* already shows himself the niggard; he must know what *we* know—that is our only sure hold of him—but he must not know it yet,"—and he proceeded to observe that it was for the hot-beds of courtly luxury to mellow and hasten an opportunity for the disclosure. He instructed Desmarais to see that Gerald (whom even a valet, at least one so artful as Desmarais, might easily influence) partook to excess of every pleasure,—at least of every pleasure which a gentleman might, without derogation to his dignity, enjoy. Gerald went to town, and very soon became all that Montreuil desired.

Montreuil came again to England; his great project, Alberoni's project, had failed. Banished France and Spain, and excluded Italy, he was desirous of obtaining an asylum in England, until he could negotiate a return to Paris. For the first of these purposes (the asylum) interest was requisite; for the latter (the negotiation) money was desirable. He came to seek both these necessaries in Gerald Devereux. Gerald had already arrived at that prosperous state when money is not lightly given away. A dispute arose; and Montreuil raised the veil, and showed the heir on what terms his estates were held.

Rightly Montreuil had read the human heart. So long as Gerald lived in the country, and tasted not the full enjoyments of his great wealth, it would have been highly perilous to have made this disclosure; for, though Gerald had no great love for me, and was bold enough to run any danger, yet he was neither a Desmarais nor a Montreuil. He was that most capricious thing, a man of honour; and at that day, he would instantly have given up the estates to me, and Montreuil and the philosopher to the hangman. But, after two or three years of every luxury that wealth could purchase—after living in those circles, too, where wealth is the highest possible merit, and public opinion, therefore, only honours the rich, fortune became far more valuable, and the conscience far less nice. Living at Devereux Court, Gerald had only 30,000*l.* a year; living in London, he had all that 30,000*l.* a year can purchase; a very great difference this indeed! Honour is a fine bulwark against a small force; but, unbacked by other principle, it is seldom well manned enough to resist a large one. When, therefore, Montreuil showed Gerald that he could lose his estate in an instant—that the world would never give him credit for innocence, when guilt would have conferred on him such advantages—that he would therefore part with all those *et cætera* which, now in the very prime of life, made his whole idea of human enjoyments—that he would no longer be the rich, the powerful, the honoured, the magnificent, the envied, the idolized lord of thousands, but would sink at once into a younger brother, dependent on the man he most hated for his very subsistence —since his debts would greatly exceed his portion—and an object through life of contemptuous pity, or of covert suspicion—that all this change could happen at a word of Montreuil's, what wonder that he should be staggered,—should hesitate, and yield? Montreuil obtained then, whatever sums he required; and, through Gerald's influence, pecuniary and political, procured from the minister a tacit permission for him to remain in England, under an assumed name, and in close retirement. Since then, Montreuil (though secretly involved in treasonable practices) had appeared to busy himself solely in negotiating a pardon at Paris. Gerald had lived the life of a man who, if he has parted with peace of conscience, will make the best of the bargain, by procuring every kind of pleasure in exchange; and *le petit* Jean Desmarais, useful to both priest and spendthrift, had passed his time very agreeably—laughing at his employers, studying philosophy, and filling his pockets; for I need scarcely add that Gerald forgave him without much difficulty for his share in the forgery. A man, as Oswald shrewdly observed, is seldom inexorable to those crimes by which he has profited. "And where lurks Montreuil now?" I asked; "in the neighbourhood of Devereux Court?"

Oswald looked at me with some surprise. "How learned you that, sir? It is true. He lives quietly and privately in that vicinity. The woods around the house, the caves in the beach, and the little isle opposite the castle, afford him in turn an asylum; and the convenience with which correspondence with France can be there carried on makes the scene of his retirement peculiarly adapted to his purposes."

I now began to question Oswald respecting himself; for I was not warmly inclined to place implicit trust in the services of a man who had before shown himself at once mercenary and timid. There

was little cant or disguise about that gentleman; he made few
pretences to virtues which he did not possess; and he seemed
now, both by wine and familiarity, peculiarly disposed to be frank.
It was he who in Italy (among various other and less private com-
missions) had been appointed by Montreuil to watch over Aubrey;
on my brother's death, he had hastened to England, not only to
apprise Montreuil of that event, but charged with some especial
orders to him from certain members of the Institute.   He had
found Montreuil, busy, restless, intriguing, even in seclusion, and
cheered by a recent promise, from Fleuri himself, that he should
speedily obtain pardon and recal.   It was, at this part of Oswald's
story, easy to perceive the causes of his renewed confidence in me.
Montreuil, engaged in new plans and schemes, at once complicated
and vast, paid but a slight attention to the wrecks of his past
projects.   Aubrey dead—myself abroad—Gerald at his command—
he perceived, in our House, no cause for caution or alarm.   This,
apparently, rendered him less careful of retaining the venal services
of Oswald, than his knowledge of character should have made him;
and when that gentleman, then in London, accidentally heard of
my sudden arrival in this country, he at once perceived how much
more to his interest it would be to serve me than to maintain an
ill-remunerated fidelity to Montreuil.   In fact, as I have since
learned, the priest's discretion was less to blame than I then
imagined; for Oswald was of a remarkably impudent, profligate,
and spendthrift turn; and his demands for money were considerably
greater than the value of his services; or perhaps, as Montreuil
thought, when Aubrey no longer lived, than the consequence of his
silence.   When, therefore, I spoke seriously to my new ally of my
desire of wreaking ultimate justice on the crimes of Montreuil, I
found that his zeal was far from being chilled by my determination
—nay, the very cowardice of the man made him ferocious; and the
moment he resolved to betray Montreuil, his fears of the priest's
vengeance made him eager to destroy where he betrayed.   I am
not addicted to unnecessary procrastination.   Of the unexpected
evidence I had found I was most eager to avail myself.   I saw at
once how considerably Oswald's testimony would lessen any difficulty
I might have in an explanation with Gerald, as well as in bringing
Montreuil to justice: and the former measure seemed to me necessary to ensure, or at least to expedite the latter.   I proposed,
therefore, to Oswald, that he should immediately accompany me to
the house in which Gerald was then a visitor; the honest Marie,
conditioning only for another bottle, which he termed a travelling
comforter, readily acceded to my wish.   I immediately procured a
chaise and horses; and in less than two hours from the time we

entered the inn, we were on the road to Gerald. What an impulse to the wheel of destiny had the event of that one day given !

At another time, I might have gleaned amusement from the shrewd roguery of my companion, but he found me then but a dull listener. I served him, in truth, as men of his stamp are ordinarily served : so soon as I had extracted from him whatever was meet for present use, I favoured him with little farther attention. He had exhausted all the communications it was necessary for me to know ; so, in the midst of a long story about Italy, Jesuits, and the wisdom of Marie Oswald, I affected to fall asleep; my companion soon followed my example in earnest, and left me to meditate, undisturbed, over all that I had heard, and over the schemes now the most promising of success. I soon taught myself to look with a lenient eye on Gerald's after-connivance in Montreuil's forgery ; and I felt that I owed to my surviving brother so large an arrear of affection for the long injustice I had rendered him, that I was almost pleased to find something set upon the opposite score. All men, perhaps, would rather forgive than be forgiven. I resolved, therefore, to affect ignorance of Gerald's knowledge of the forgery ; and even should he confess it, to exert all my art to steal from the confession its shame. From this train of reflection my mind soon directed itself to one far fiercer and more intense ; and I felt my heart pause, as if congealing into marble, when I thought of Montreuil and anticipated justice.

It was nearly noon on the following day when we arrived at Lord ——'s house. We found that Gerald had left it the day before, for the enjoyment of the field-sports at Devereux Court, and thither we instantly proceeded.

It has often seemed to me that if there be, as certain ancient philosophers fabled, one certain figure pervading all nature, human and universal, it is *the circle*. Round, in one vast monotony, one eternal gyration, roll the orbs of space. Thus moves the spirit of creative life, kindling, progressing, maturing, decaying, perishing, reviving and rolling again, and so onward for ever through the same course ; and thus even would seem to revolve the mysterious mechanism of human events and actions. Age, ere it returns to " the second childishness, the mere oblivion " from which it passes to the grave, returns also to the memories and the thoughts of youth ; its buried loves arise—its past friendships rekindle. The wheels of the tired machine are past the meridian, and the arch through which they now decline, has a correspondent likeness to the opposing segment through which they had borne upward in eagerness and triumph. Thus it is, too, that we bear within us an irresistible attraction to our earliest home. Thus it is that we say, "it matters not where our mid-course is run, but we will *die* in the place where we were born—in the point of space whence *began* the circle, there also shall *it end!*" This is the grand orbit through which Mortality passes only once; but the same figure may pervade all through which it moves on its journey to the grave. Thus, one peculiar day of the round year has been to some an era, always colouring life with an event. Thus, to others, some peculiar place has been the theatre of strange action, influencing all existence, whenever, in the recurrence of destiny, that place has been revisited. Thus was it said by an arch-sorcerer of old, whose labours yet exist, though perhaps, at the moment I write, there are not three living beings who know of their existence—that there breathes not that man who would not find, did he minutely investigate the events of life, that, in some fixed and distinct spot, or hour, or person, there lived, though shrouded and obscure, the pervading demon of his fate; and whenever, in their several paths, the two circles of being touched, that moment made the unnoticed epoch of coming prosperity or evil. I remember well that this bewildering, yet not unsolemn reflection, or rather fancy, was in my mind, as, after the absence of many years, I saw myself hastening to the home of my boyhood, and cherishing the fiery hope of there avenging the doom of that love which I had there conceived. Deeply, and in silence, did I brood over the dark shapes which my thoughts engendered; and I woke not from my reverie till, as the gray of the evening closed around us, we entered the domains of Devereux Court. The road was rough and stony, and the horses moved slowly on. How familiar was everything before me! the old pollards which lay scattered in dense groups on either side, and which had lived on from heir to heir, secure in the little temptation they afforded to cupidity, seemed to greet me with a silent, but intelligible welcome. Their leaves fell around us in the autumn air, and the branches, as they waved towards me, seemed to say, "Thou art returned, and thy change is like our own: the green leaves of *thy* heart have fallen from thee one by one—like us thou survivest, but thou art desolate!" The hoarse cry of the rooks gathering to their rest, came fraught with the music of young associations on my ear. Many a time in the laughing spring had I lain in these groves, watching, in the young brood of those citizens of air, a mark for my childish skill and careless disregard of life. We acquire mercy as we acquire thought—I would not *now* have harmed one of those sable creatures for a king's ransom!

As we cleared the more wooded belt of the park, and entered the smooth space, on which the trees stood alone and at rarer intervals, while the red clouds, still tinged with the hues of the departed sun, hovered on the far and upland landscape—like Hope flushing over Futurity—a mellowed, yet rapid murmur, distinct from the more distant dashing of the sea, broke abruptly upon my ear. It was the voice of that brook whose banks had been the dearest haunt of my childhood; and now, as it burst thus suddenly upon me, I longed to be alone, that I might have bowed down my head and wept as if it had been the welcome of a living thing! At once, and as by a word, the hardened lava, the congealed stream of the soul's Etna, was uplifted from my memory, and the bowers and palaces of old, the world of a gone day, lay before me! With how wild an en-thusiasm had I apostrophized that stream on the day in which I first resolved to leave its tranquil regions and fragrant margin for the tempest and tumult of the world. On that same eve, too, had Aubrey and I taken sweet counsel together—on that same eve had we sworn to protect, to love, and to cherish one another!—AND NOW!—I saw the very mound on which we had sat—a solitary deer made it his couch, and, as the carriage approached, the deer rose, and I then saw that he had been wounded, perhaps in some contest with his tribe, and that he could scarcely stir from the spot. I turned my face away, and the remains of my ancestral house rose gradually in view. That house was indeed changed; a wide and black heap of ruins spread around; the vast hall, with its oaken rafters and huge hearth, was no more—I missed *that*, and I cared not for the rest. The long galleries, the superb chambers, the scenes of revelry or of pomp, were like the court companions who amuse, yet attach us not; but the hall—the old hall—the old, hospitable hall—had been as a friend in all seasons, and to all comers, and its mirth had been as open to all as the heart of its last owner! My eyes wandered from the place where it had been, and the tall, lone, gray tower, consecrated to my ill-fated namesake, and in which my own apartments had been situated, rose, like the last of a warrior band, stern, gaunt, and solitary, over the ruins around.

The carriage now passed more rapidly over the neglected road, and wound where the ruins, cleared on either side, permitted access to the tower. In two minutes more I was in the same chamber with my only surviving brother. Oh, why—why can I not dwell upon that scene—that embrace, that reconciliation?—alas! the wound is not yet scarred over.

I found Gerald, at first, haughty and sullen; he expected my. reproaches and defiance—against them he was hardened; he was not prepared for my prayers for our future friendship, and my grief for our past enmity, and he melted at once!

But let me hasten over this. I had well-nigh forgot that, at the

close of my history, I should find one remembrance so endearing,
and one pang so keen. Rapidly I sketched to Gerald the ill fate of
Aubrey ; but lingeringly did I dwell upon Montreuil's organized,
and most baneful, influence over him, and over us all ; and I
endeavoured to arouse in Gerald some sympathy with my own deep
indignation against that villain. I succeeded so far as to make him
declare that he was scarcely less desirous of justice than myself ; but
there was an embarrassment in his tone of which I was at no loss to
perceive the cause. To accuse Montreuil publicly of his forgery
might ultimately bring to light Gerald's latter knowledge of the
fraud. I hastened to say that there was now no necessity to submit
to a court of justice a scrutiny into our private, gloomy, and eventful
records. No, from Oswald's communications I had learned enough
to prove that Bolingbroke had been truly informed, and that Montreuil had still, and within the few last weeks, been deeply involved
in schemes of treason—full proof of which could be adduced, far
more than sufficient to ensure his death by the public executioner.
Upon this charge I proposed at the nearest town (the memorable
seaport of * * * *) to accuse him, and to obtain a warrant for
his immediate apprehension—upon this charge I proposed alone to
proceed against him, and by it alone to take justice upon his more
domestic crimes.

My brother yielded at last his consent to my suggestions. " I
understand," said I, " that Montreuil lurks in the neighbourhood of
these ruins, or in the opposite islet. Know you if he has made his
asylum in either at this present time ? "

" No, my brother," answered Gerald, " but I have reason to
believe that he is in our immediate vicinity, for I received a letter
from him three days ago, when at Lord ——'s, urging a request that
I would give him a meeting here, at my earliest leisure, previous to
his leaving England."

" Has he really then obtained permission to return to France ? "

" Yes," replied Gerald, " he informed me in this letter that he
had just received intelligence of his pardon."

" May it fit him the better," said I, with a stern smile, " for a
more lasting condemnation. But if this be true we have not a
moment to lose : a man so habitually vigilant and astute will speedily
learn my visit hither, and forfeit even his appointment with you,
should he, which is likely enough, entertain any suspicion of our
reconciliation with each other—moreover, he may hear that the
government have discovered his designs, and may instantly secure the
means of flight. Let me, therefore, immediately repair to * * * * ,
and obtain a warrant against him, as well as officers to assist our
search. In the meanwhile you shall remain here, and detain him,

should he visit you;—but where is the accomplice?—let us seize *him* instantly, for I conclude he is with you!"

"What, Desmarais?" rejoined Gerald. "Yes, he is the only servant, beside the old portress, which these poor ruins will allow me to entertain in the same dwelling with myself: the rest of my suite are left behind at Lord ——'s. But Desmarais is not now within; he went out about two hours ago."

"Ha!" said I, "in all likelihood to meet the priest—shall we wait his return, and extort some information of Montreuil's lurking-hole?"

Before Gerald could answer, we heard a noise without, and presently I distinguished the bland tones of the hypocritical Fatalist, in soft expostulation with the triumphant voice of Mr. Marie Oswald. I hastened out, and discovered that the lay-brother, whom I had left in the chaise, having caught a glimpse of the valet gliding among the ruins, had recognized, seized, and by the help of the postillions,. dragged him to the door of the tower. The moment Desmarais saw me, he ceased to struggle: he met my eye with a steady, but not disrespectful firmness; he changed not even the habitual hue of his countenance—he remained perfectly still in the hands of his arresters; and if there was any vestige of his mind discoverable in his sallow features and glittering eye, it was not the sign of fear, or confusion, or even surprise; but a ready promptness to meet danger, coupled, perhaps, with a little doubt whether to defy or to seek first to diminish it.

Long did I gaze upon him—struggling with internal rage and loathing—the mingled contempt and desire of destruction with which we gaze upon the erect aspect of some small, but venomous and courageous reptile—long did I gaze upon him before I calmed and collected my voice to speak—

"So I have *thee* at last! First comes the base tool, and that will I first break, before I lop off the guiding hand."

"So please Monsieur my Lord the Count," answered Desmarais, bowing to the ground; "the tool is a file, and it would be useless to bite against it."

"We will see that," said I, drawing my sword: "prepare to die!" and I pointed the blade to his throat with so sudden and menacing a gesture that his eyes closed involuntarily, and the blood left his thin cheek as white as ashes: but he shrank not.

"If Monsieur," said he, with a sort of smile, "*will* kill his poor old, faithful servant, let him strike. Fate is not to be resisted; and prayers are useless!"

"Oswald," said I, "release your prisoner; wait here, and keep strict watch. Jean Desmarais, follow me!"

I ascended the stairs, and Desmarais followed. "Now," I said, when he was alone with Gerald and myself, "your days are numbered: you will fall; not by my hand, but by that of the executioner. Not only your forgery, but your robbery, your abetment of murder, are known to me; your present lord, with an indignation equal to my own, surrenders you to justice. Have you aught to urge, not in defence—for to that I will not listen—but in atonement? *Can* you now commit any act which will cause me to forego justice on those which you *have* committed?" Desmarais hesitated. "Speak," said I. He raised his eyes to mine with an inquisitive and wistful look.

"Monsieur," said the wretch, with his obsequious smile, "Monsieur has travelled—has shone—has succeeded—Monsieur must have made enemies: let him name them, and his poor old *faithful* servant will do his best to become the humble instrument of their *fate!*"

Gerald drew himself aside, and shuddered. Perhaps till then he had not been fully aware how slyly murder, as well as fraud, can lurk beneath urbane tones and laced ruffles.

"I have no enemy," said I, "but one; and the hangman will do my office upon him; but point out to me the exact spot where at this moment he is concealed, and you shall have full leave to quit this country for ever. That enemy is Julian Montreuil!"

"Ah, ah!" said Desmarais, musingly, and in a tone very different from that in which he usually spoke; "must it be so, indeed? For twenty years of youth and manhood, I have clung to that man, and woven my destiny with his, because I believed him born under the star which shines on statesmen and on pontiffs. Does dread Necessity now impel me to betray him?—Him, the only man I ever loved. So—so—so! Count Devereux, strike me to the core—I will *not* betray Bertrand Collinot!"

"Mysterious heart of man," I exclaimed inly, as I gazed upon the low brow, the malignant eye, the crafty lip of this wretch, who still retained one generous and noble sentiment at the bottom of so base a breast. But if it sprung there, it only sprung to wither!

"As thou wilt," said I; "remember, death is the alternative. By thy birth-star, Jean Desmarais, I should question whether perfidy be not *better luck* than hanging—but time speeds—farewell; I shall meet thee on thy day of trial."

I turned to the door to summon Oswald to his prisoner. Desmarais roused himself from the reverie in which he appeared to have sunk.

"Why do I doubt?" said he, slowly. "Were the alternative his, would he not hang me as he would hang his dog if it went mad and menaced danger? My very noble and merciful master," continued the Fatalist, turning to me, and relapsing into his customary manner, "it is enough! I can refuse nothing to a gentleman who has such insinuating manners. Montreuil *may be* in your power this night; but that rests solely with me. If I speak not, a few hours will place him irrevocably beyond your reach. If I betray him to you, will Monsieur swear that I shall have my pardon for past *errors?*"

"On condition of leaving England," I answered, for slight was my comparative desire of justice against Desmarais; and since I had agreed with Gerald not to bring our domestic records to the glare of day, justice against Desmarais was not easy of attainment; while, on the other hand, so precarious seemed the chance of discovering Montreuil before he left England, without certain intelligence of his movements, that I was willing to forego any less ardent feeling, for the speedy gratification of that which made the sole surviving passion of my existence.

"Be it so," rejoined Desmarais; "there is better wine in France! And Monsieur, my present master—Monsieur Gerald, will you too pardon your poor Desmarais for his proof of the great attachment he always bore to you?"

"Away, wretch!" cried Gerald, shrinking back; "your villainy taints the very air!"

Desmarais lifted his eyes to Heaven, with a look of appealing innocence; but I was wearied with this odious farce.

"The condition is made," said I: "remember, it only holds good if Montreuil's person is placed in our power. Now explain."

"This night, then," answered Desmarais, "Montreuil proposes to leave England by means of a French privateer, or pirate, if that word please you better. Exactly at the hour of twelve, he will meet some of the sailors upon the sea-shore, by the Castle Cave; thence they proceed in boats to the islet, off which the pirate's vessel awaits them. If you would seize Montreuil, you must provide a force adequate to conquer the companions he will meet. The rest is with you; my part is fulfilled."

"Remember! I repeat if this be one of thy inventions, thou wilt hang.".

"I have said what is true," said Desmarais, bitterly; "and were not life so very pleasant to me, I would sooner have met the rack."

I made no reply; but summoning Oswald, surrendered Desmarais to his charge. I then held a hasty consultation with Gerald, whose mind, however, obscured by feelings of gloomy humiliation, and stunned perhaps by the sudden and close following order of events, gave me but little assistance in my projects. I observed his feelings with great pain; but that was no moment for wrestling with them.

I saw that I could not depend upon his vigorous co-operation; and that even if Montreuil sought him, he might want the presence of mind and the energy to detain my enemy. I changed therefore the arrangement we had first proposed.

"I will remain here," said I, "and I will instruct the old portress to admit to me any one who seeks audience with you. Meanwhile, Oswald and yourself, if you will forgive, and grant my request to that purport, will repair to * * * * , and informing the magistrate of our intelligence, procure such armed assistance as may give battle to the pirates, should that be necessary, and succeed in securing Montreuil; this assistance may be indispensable; at all events, it will be prudent to secure it : perhaps for Oswald alone, the magistrates would not use that zeal and expedition, which a word *of yours* can command."

"Of mine," said Gerald, "say rather of yours; you are the lord of these broad lands!"

"Never, my dearest brother, shall they pass to me from their present owner; but let us hasten now to execute justice, we will talk afterwards of friendship."

I then sought Oswald, who, if a physical coward, was morally a ready, bustling and prompt man; and I felt that I could rely more upon him than I could at that moment upon Gerald: I released him therefore of his charge, and made Desmarais a close prisoner, in the inner apartment of the tower; I then gave Oswald the most earnest injunctions to procure the assistance we might require, and to return with it as expeditiously as possible : and cheered by the warmth and decision of his answer, I saw him depart with Gerald, and felt my heart beat high with the anticipation of midnight and retribution.

CHAPTER VIII.

THE CATASTROPHE.

IT happened unfortunately, that the mission to * * * * was indispensable. The slender accommodation of the tower forbade Gerald the use of his customary attendants, and the neighbouring villagers were too few in number, and too ill provided with weapons, to encounter men cradled in the very lap of danger; moreover, it was requisite, above all things, that no rumour or suspicion of our intended project should obtain wind, and, by reaching Montreuil's ears, give him some safer opportunity of escape. I had no doubt of the sincerity of the Fatalist's communication, and if I had, the subsequent conversation I held with him, when Gerald and Oswald were gone, would have been sufficient to remove it. He was evidently deeply stung by the reflection of his own treachery, and singularly enough, with Montreuil seemed to perish all his worldly hopes and aspirations. Desmarais, I found, was a man of much higher ambition than I had imagined, and he had linked himself closely to Montreuil, because, from the genius and the resolution of the priest, he had drawn the most sanguine auguries of his future power. As the night advanced, he grew visibly anxious, and, having fully satisfied myself that I might count indisputably upon his intelligence, I once more left him to his meditations, and, alone in the outer chamber, I collected myself for the coming event. I had fully hoped that Montreuil would have repaired to the tower in search of Gerald, and this was the strongest reason which had induced me to remain behind : but time waned, he came not, and at length it grew so late that I began to tremble lest the assistance from * * * * should not arrive in time.

It struck the first quarter after eleven : in less than an hour my enemy would be either in my power, or beyond its reach ; still Gerald and our allies came not—my suspense grew intolerable, my pulse raged with fever ; I could not stay for two seconds in the same spot ; a hundred times had I drawn my sword, and looked eagerly along its bright blade. "Once," thought I, as I looked, "thou didst cross the blade of my mortal foe, and to my danger, rather than victory ; years have brought skill to the hand which then guided thee, and in the red path of battle thou hast never waved in vain. Be stained but once more with human blood, and I will prize every drop of that blood beyond all the triumphs thou hast brought me !" Yes, it had been with a fiery and intense delight that I had learned that Montreuil would have companions to his flight in lawless and hardened men, who would never yield him a prisoner without striking for his rescue ; and I knew enough of the courageous and proud temper of my purposed victim to feel assured that, priest as he was, he would not hesitate to avail himself of the weapons of his confederates, or to aid them with his own. Then would it be lawful to oppose violence to his resistance, and with my own hand to deal the death-blow of retribution. Still as these thoughts flashed over me, my heart grew harder, and my blood rolled more burningly through my veins. "They come not, Gerald returns not," I said, as my eye dwelt on the clock, and saw the minutes creep one after the other—"it matters not—HE at least shall not escape!—were he girt by a million, I would single him from the herd; one stroke of this right hand is all that I ask of life, then let them avenge him if they will." Thus resolved, and despairing at last of the return of Gerald, I left the tower, locked the outer door, as a still further security against my prisoner's escape, and repaired with silent, but swift, strides to the beach by the Castle Cave. It wanted about half an hour to midnight; the night was still and breathless, a dim mist spread from sea to sky, through which the stars gleamed forth heavily, and at distant intervals. The moon was abroad, but the vapours that surrounded her gave a watery and sicklied dulness to her light, and wherever in the niches and hollows of the cliff, the shadows fell, all was utterly dark, and unbroken by the smallest ray: only along the near waves of the sea and the whiter parts of the level sand were objects easily discernible. I strode to and fro for a few minutes before the Castle Cave; I saw no one, and I seated myself in stern vigilance upon a stone, in a worn recess of the rock, and close by the mouth of the Castle Cave. The spot where I sat was wrapped in total darkness, and I felt assured that I might wait my own time for disclosing myself. I had not been many minutes at my place of watch before I saw the figure of a man approach from the left; he moved with rapid steps, and once when he passed along a place where the wan light of the skies was less obscured I saw enough of his form and air to recognize Montreuil. He neared the cave—he paused—he was within a few paces of me—I was about to rise, when another figure suddenly glided from the mouth of the cave itself.

"Ha!" cried the latter, "it is Bertrand Collinot—Fate be lauded!"

Had a voice from the grave struck my ear, it would have scarcely amazed me more than that which I now heard. Could I believe my senses? the voice was that of Desmarais, whom I had left locked within the inner chamber of the tower. "Fly," he resumed, "fly instantly; you have not a moment to lose—already the stern Morton waits thee—already the hounds of justice are on thy track, tarry not for the pirates, but begone at once."

"You rave, man! What mean you? the boats will be here immediately. While you yet speak methinks I can descry them on the sea. Something of this I dreaded when, some hours ago, I caught a glimpse of Gerald on the road to * * * * . I saw not the face of his companion, but I would not trust myself in the tower —yet I must await the boats—flight is indeed requisite, but *they* make the only means by which flight is safe!"

"Pray, then, thou who believest, pray that they may come soon, or thou diest—and I with thee! Morton is returned—is reconciled to his weak brother. Gerald and Oswald are away to * * * *, for men to seize and drag thee to a public death. I was arrested—threatened; but one way to avoid prison and cord was shown me. Curse me, Bertrand, for I embraced it. I told them thou wouldst fly to-night, and with whom. They locked me in the inner chamber of the tower—Morton kept guard without. At length I heard him leave the room—I heard him descend the stairs, and lock the gate of the tower. Ha! ha! little dreamt he of the wit of Jean Desmarais. *Thy* friend must scorn bolt and bar, Bertrand Collinot. They had not searched me—I used my instruments—thou knowest that with those instruments I could glide through stone walls!—I opened the door—I was in the outer room—I lifted the trap-door which old Sir William had had boarded over, and which thou hadst so artfully and imperceptibly replaced, when thou wantedst secret intercourse with thy pupils—I sped along the passage—came to the iron door—touched the spring thou hadst inserted in the plate which the old knight had placed over the key-hole—and have come to repair my coward treachery—to save and to fly with thee. But, while I speak, we tread on a precipice. Morton has left the house, and is even now, perhaps, in search of thee."

"Ha! I care not if he be," said Montreuil, in a low, but haughty tone. "Priest though I am, I have not assumed the garb, without assuming also the weapon, of the layman. Even now I have my hand upon the same sword which shone under the banners of Mar; and which once, but for my foolish mercy, would have rid me for ever of this private foe."

"Unsheath it now, Julian Montreuil!" said I, coming from my retreat, and confronting the pair.

Montreuil recoiled several paces. At that instant a shot boomed along the waters.

"Haste, haste," cried Desmarais, hurrying to the waves, as a boat, now winding the cliff, became darkly visible; "haste, Bertrand, here are Bonjean and his men—but they are pursued!"

Once did Montreuil turn, as if to fly; but my sword was at his breast, and, stamping fiercely on the ground, he drew his rapier, and parried and returned my assault; but he retreated rapidly towards the water while he struck; and wild and loud came the voices from the boat, which now touched the shore.

"Come—come—come—the officers are upon us; we can wait not a moment!" and Montreuil, as he heard the cries, mingled with oaths and curses, yet quickened his pace towards the quarter whence they came. His steps were tracked by his blood—twice had my sword passed through his flesh; but twice had it failed my

vengeance, and avoided a mortal part. A second boat, filled also
with the pirates, followed the first ; but then another and a larger
vessel bore black and fast over the water—the rush and cry of men
were heard on land—again and nearer a shot broke over the heavy
air—another and another—a continued fire. The strand was now
crowded with the officers of justice. The vessel beyond forbade
escape to the opposite islet. There was no hope for the pirates
but in contest, or in dispersion among the cliffs or woods on the
shore. They formed their resolution at once, and stood prepared
and firm, partly on their boats—partly on the beach around them.
Though the officers were far more numerous, the strife—fierce,
desperate, and hand to hand—seemed equally sustained. Montreuil,
as he retreated before me, bore back into the general *mêlée*, and, as
the press thickened, we were for some moments separated. It was
at this time that I caught a glimpse of Gerald ; *he* seemed also then
to espy me, and made eagerly towards me. Suddenly he was
snatched from my view. The fray relaxed ; the officers, evidently
worsted, retreated towards the land, and the pirates appeared once
more to entertain the hope of making their escape by water. Probably
they thought that the darkness of the night might enable them to
baffle the pursuit of the adverse vessel, which now lay expectant
and passive on the wave. However this be, they made simultaneously to their boats, and, among their numbers, I descried
Montreuil. I set my teeth with a calm and prophetic wrath. But
three strokes did my good blade make through that throng before I
was by his side ; he had at that instant his hold upon the boat's
edge, and he stood knee-deep in the dashing waters. I laid my
grasp upon his shoulder, and my cheek touched his own as I hissed
in his ear, " I am with thee yet ! " He turned fiercely—he strove,
but he strove in vain, to shake off my grasp. The boat pushed
away, and his last hope of escape was over. At this moment the
moon broke away from the mist, and we saw each other plainly,
and face to face. There was a ghastly, but set despair in Montreuil's
lofty and proud countenance, which changed gradually to a fiercer
aspect, as he met my gaze. Once more, foot to foot, and hand to
hand, we engaged ; the increased light of the skies rendered the
contest more that of skill than it had hitherto been, and Montreuil
seemed to collect all his energies, and to fight with a steadier and a
cooler determination. Nevertheless the combat was short. Once,
my antagonist had the imprudence to raise his arm, and expose his
body to my thrust : his sword grazed my cheek—I shall bear the
scar to my grave—mine passed twice through his breast, and he fell,
bathed in his blood, at my feet.

" Lift him ! " I said, to the men who now crowded round. They did so, and he unclosed his eyes, and glared upon me as the death-pang convulsed his features, and gathered in foam to his lips. But his thoughts were not upon his destroyer, nor upon the wrongs he had committed, nor upon any solitary being in the linked society which he had injured.

"Order of Jesus," he muttered, "had I but lived three months longer, I—"

So died Julian Montreuil.

Conclusion.

MONTREUIL was not the only victim in the brief combat of that night; several of the pirates and their pursuers perished, and among the bodies we found Gerald. He had been pierced, by a shot, through the brain, and was perfectly lifeless when his body was discovered. By a sort of retribution, it seems that my unhappy brother received his death-wound from a shot, fired [probably at random] by Desmarais; and thus the instrument of the fraud he had tacitly subscribed to became the minister of his death. Nay, the retribution seemed even to extend to the very method by which Desmarais had escaped; and, as the reader has perceived, the subterranean communication which had been secretly reopened to deceive my uncle, made the path which had guided Gerald's murderer to the scene which afterwards ensued. The delay of the officers had been owing to private intelligence, previously received by the magistrate to whom Gerald had applied, of the number and force of the pirates, and his waiting in consequence for a military reinforcement to the party to be despatched against them. Those of the pirates who escaped the conflict escaped also the pursuit of the hostile vessel; they reached the islet, and gained their captain's ship. A few shots between the two vessels were idly exchanged, and the illicit adventurers reached the French shore in safety; with them escaped Desmarais, and of him, from that hour to this, I have heard nothing—so capriciously plays Time with villains!

Marie Oswald has lately taken unto himself a noted inn on the North Road, a place eminently calculated for the display of his various talents; he has also taken unto himself a WIFE, of whose tongue and temper he has been known already to complain with no Socratic meekness; and we may therefore opine that his misdeeds have not altogether escaped their fitting share of condemnation.

Succeeding at once, by the death of my poor brother, to the DEVEREUX estates, I am still employed in rebuilding, on a yet more costly scale, my ancestral mansion. So eager and impatient is my desire for the completion of my undertaking, that I allow rest neither

by night or day, and half the work will be done by torch-light.
With the success of this project terminates my last scheme of
Ambition.

Here, then, at the age of thirty-four, I conclude the history of
my life.   Whether in the star which, as I now write, shines in upon
me, and which a romance, still unsubdued, has often dreamed to be
the bright prophet of my fate, something of future adventure, suffering, or excitement, is yet predestined to me; or whether life will
muse itself away in the solitudes which surround the home of my
past childhood, and the scene of my present retreat, creates within
me but slight food for anticipation or conjecture.   I have exhausted
the sources of those feelings which flow, whether through the channels
of anxiety or of hope, towards the future; and the restlessness of
my manhood, having attained its last object, has done the labour of
time, and bequeathed to me the indifference of age.

If love exists for me no longer, I know well that the memory of
that which has been is to me far more than a living love is to others;
and perhaps there is no passion so full of tender, of soft, and of
hallowing associations, as the love which is stamped by death.   If
I have borne much, and my spirit has worked out its earthly end
in travail and in tears, yet I would not forego the lessons which my
life has bequeathed me, even though they be deeply blended with
sadness and regret.   No! were I asked what best dignifies the
present, and consecrates the past; what enables us alone to draw a
just moral from the tale of life; what sheds the purest light upon
our reason; what gives the firmest strength to our religion; and,
whether our remaining years pass in seclusion or in action, is best
fitted to soften the heart of man, and to elevate the soul to God, I
would answer, with Lassus, it is "EXPERIENCE!"

THE END.

Richard Clay and Sons, London and Bungay.